Fatal Majesty

Fatal Majesty

A NOVEL OF MARY, QUEEN OF SCOTS

Reay Tannahill

ST. MARTIN'S PRESS ❧ NEW YORK

ISBN 0-312-19881-7

First published in Great Britain by Orion Books Ltd

This book is dedicated, with appreciation, to
Susan Lamb,
whose idea it was.

Contents

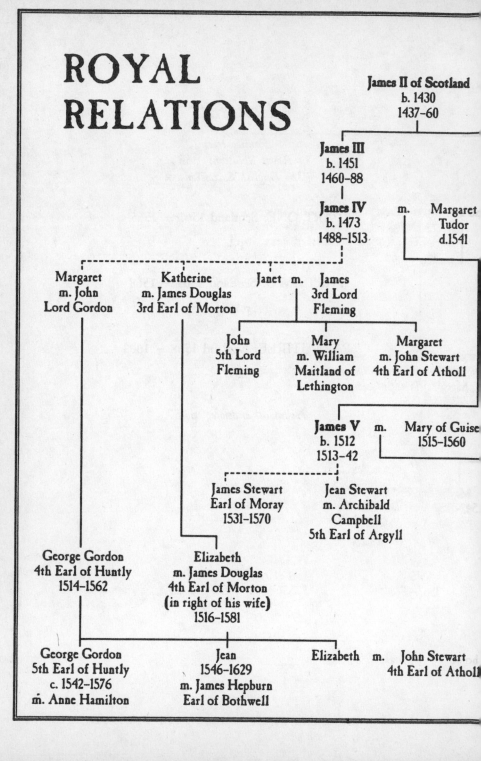

ROYAL RELATIONS

James II of Scotland
b. 1430
1437–60

James III
b. 1451
1460–88

James IV   m.   Margaret
b. 1473   Tudor
1488–1513   d.1541

Margaret   Katherine   Janet m. James
m. John   m. James Douglas   3rd Lord
Lord Gordon   3rd Earl of Morton   Fleming

John   Mary   Margaret
5th Lord   m. William   m. John Stewart
Fleming   Maitland of   4th Earl of Atholl
                  Lethington

James V   m.   Mary of Guise
b. 1512   1515–1560
1513–42

James Stewart   Jean Stewart
Earl of Moray   m. Archibald
1531–1570   Campbell
                      5th Earl of Argyll

George Gordon   Elizabeth
4th Earl of Huntly   m. James Douglas
1514–1562   4th Earl of Morton
                      (in right of his wife)
                      1516–1581

George Gordon   Jean   Elizabeth m. John Stewart
5th Earl of Huntly   1546–1629   4th Earl of Atholl
c. 1542–1576   m. James Hepburn
m. Anne Hamilton   Earl of Bothwell

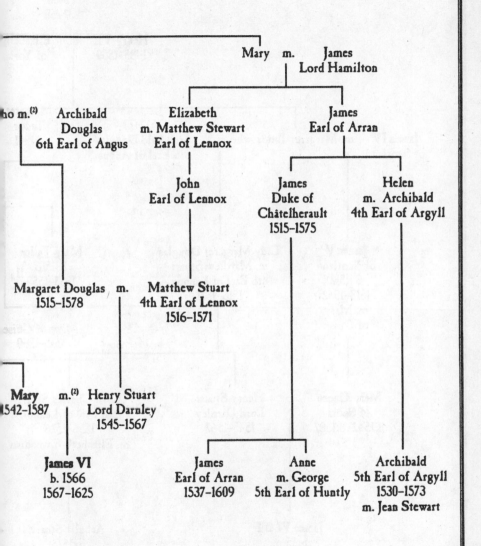

Mary m. James
Lord Hamilton

...ho m.(2) Archibald
Douglas
6th Earl of Angus

Elizabeth
m. Matthew Stewart
Earl of Lennox

James
Earl of Arran

John
Earl of Lennox

James
Duke of
Châtelherault
1515-1575

Helen
m. Archibald
4th Earl of Argyll

Margaret Douglas m.
1515-1578

Matthew Stuart
4th Earl of Lennox
1516-1571

Mary m.(2) Henry Stuart
1542-1587 Lord Darnley
1545-1567

James VI
b. 1566
1567-1625

James
Earl of Arran
1537-1609

Anne
m. George
5th Earl of Huntly

Archibald
5th Earl of Argyll
1530-1573
m. Jean Stewart

...ho m.(2) Margaret Fleming

THE ENGLISH

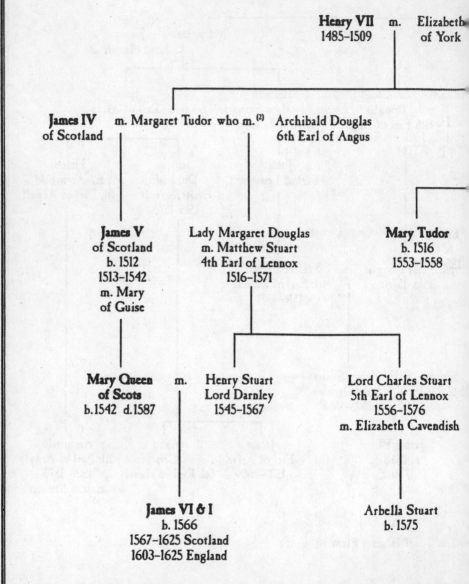

Henry VII m. **Elizabeth**
1485–1509 of York

James IV m. Margaret Tudor who m. (2) Archibald Douglas
of Scotland 6th Earl of Angus

James V Lady Margaret Douglas **Mary Tudor**
of Scotland m. Matthew Stuart b. 1516
b. 1512 4th Earl of Lennox 1553–1558
1513–1542 1516–1571
m. Mary
of Guise

Mary Queen m. Henry Stuart Lord Charles Stuart
of Scots Lord Darnley 5th Earl of Lennox
b.1542 d.1587 1545–1567 1556–1576
m. Elizabeth Cavendish

James VI & I Arbella Stuart
b. 1566 b. 1575
1567–1625 Scotland
1603–1625 England

SUCCESSION

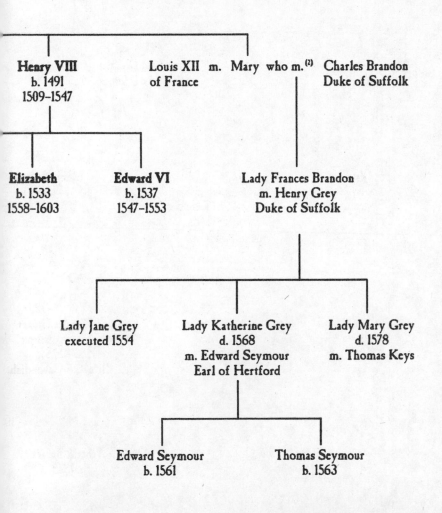

Henry VIII
b. 1491
1509-1547

Louis XII m. Mary who m.[2] Charles Brandon
of France   Duke of Suffolk

Elizabeth
b. 1533
1558-1603

Edward VI
b. 1537
1547-1553

Lady Frances Brandon
m. Henry Grey
Duke of Suffolk

Lady Jane Grey
executed 1554

Lady Katherine Grey
d. 1568
m. Edward Seymour
Earl of Hertford

Lady Mary Grey
d. 1578
m. Thomas Keys

Edward Seymour
b. 1561

Thomas Seymour
b. 1563

PART ONE

SCOTLAND 1561 – 1565

Chapter One

AUGUST 1561

1

Although it was high summer, there was a thick white sea mist shrouding the Firth of Forth on the day when Mary Queen of Scots sailed home from France to take up her throne.

She should have been welcomed by lords and ladies in velvet and jewels; heralds in scarlet and gold; loyal addresses, fanfares of trumpets, cheering throngs. But there were only a few open-mouthed bystanders.

Her subjects had not expected to see her so soon. In truth, many of them would have preferred not to see her at all.

2

Because of the mist, the first warning anyone had was the rhythmic chant of an invisible leadsman. In the port of Leith, where square-rigged merchant ships came and went almost daily throughout the sailing season, such a sound was familiar enough, but on this particular morning there were other sounds that were less familiar. The men working on the jetties stopped to listen, heads cocked, but only a handful of them, one a fisherman who had spent five terrible years as a galley slave in the Mediterranean, knew enough to interpret the meaning of the shrilling whistles and the whisper of many oars pulling as one.

The fleetest of the fisherman's sons, sent running for the provost, found him at the desk in his counting house, tranquilly sharpening a pen.

'Mercy me!' exclaimed the provost, when the boy had gasped out his message. 'Great galleys, ye say?'

'Aye, and my father says they're awful well drilled. He thinks they must be cerry ... uh ... ceremonial ones. Royal ones.'

The provost, who had been assured on the best authority that there was

3

no truth in the rumour that Mary Stewart was about to abandon her life of lotus-eating luxury in France for one of porridge-eating austerity in Scotland, wasted no time on reviewing possible alternatives. 'Mercy on us!' he exclaimed. 'It'll be the queen! Where's my clerk? I'll need messengers. I'll need my steward. I'll need my chain of office. The queen! Mercy me!'

Hurrying down to the shore ten minutes later, he found a gathering crowd of Leith's population there ahead of him and a long, beautiful galley, its sails furled, its cannon firing the salute, gliding in over the grey satin waters towards the harbour entrance. From sails to oars – twenty-five a side, and each of them as long as the galley was wide – everything that was not carved and gilded was of a pure and spotless white, forming the most dramatic of backdrops for the dark-clad group of people assembled in the prow.

At their head stood a tall, graceful, black-gowned figure with a coquettish little black velvet cap perched on her red-gold head. There could be no mistaking Mary Stewart – queen of Scots since six days after she was born; educated in France to become the bride of its future king; queen of the French as well as the Scots for a few brief months; then, suddenly, a widow. And still only eighteen years old.

A voice shouted commands, the silvery whistles shrilled, the oars leapt from the water, and the galley flowed on under its own diminishing momentum to the smoothest of berthings inside the harbour wall. The people of Leith were not easily impressed, especially by French seamanship, but a ripple of approval passed through the crowd and, within minutes, the queen was stepping ashore from a gilded ramp that had appeared seemingly from nowhere.

By that time, Provost Lamb and four of his fellow merchants were ready to greet her, drawn up in a sturdy, bearded line, models of bourgeois respectability in their short cloaks, plain dark doublets and hose, narrow white ruffs, and neat small caps with corded trims. The provost's chain of office was the only indication of the wealth Leith's merchants were able to command but were much too wise to advertise – especially to royalty, which was always short of money.

Bending low, they swept off their caps with the aplomb of years of practice. They had done a good deal of bowing and scraping to the queen's late mother who, until just over a year before, had ruled and come near to ruining Scotland in her daughter's name.

His gaze resting deferentially on the cobbles at his feet, Provost Lamb said, '*Bonjour, votre majesté. Bienvenue en Écosse. Bienvenue chez vous.*'

4

After which, raising his head in expectation of, at best, a nod of gracious condescension, at worst a flurry of French from some court functionary, he was astounded to meet, instead, a pair of large amber eyes sparkling with youthful and very feminine mischief.

'I thank ye, gude maister,' replied her majesty demurely. 'Whit a lichtsome walcome hame on sic a dreich day!' Then, tempted by his expression into something very near a giggle, 'I am still mindful, you see, of my native tongue.'

The provost, entranced, beamed back at her, forgetting the problems of protocol that beset him, forgetting the political and religious troubles her arrival foreshadowed, forgetting even the battered stones of Leith, the towerless kirk, the ruinous preceptory and the hundreds of cannonball scars that still remained as witness to the recent civil war and the siege its citizens had withstood on a diet of boiled horse and roasted rat.

He thought only, 'What a bonnie lassie!'

3

He had sent messengers off to Edinburgh, he told her – bowing again, just to be on the safe side – but if they found none of her great lords in residence, they might have to ride on to Niddry or Aberdour or Kinneil. It could take hours for an official welcoming party to turn up, so, in the meantime, would her majesty deign to honour his house with her presence?

Her majesty said that nothing would give her greater pleasure, on the understanding that it neither jibbed nor heeled nor plunged, but stood firmly on solid ground.

It was an education, as they walked along the jetty and up the slight incline to his house, to see how the people responded to her. Most were there out of vulgar curiosity rather than loyalty to a crown which they had little reason to love, but in no time at all she had beguiled them into something very near worship. It was only partly a matter of her looks and grace; far more, it was the enchantment of her smile and the readiness with which she paused to speak to anyone and everyone, wide-eyed children and blushing boys, stout washerwomen and floury bakers, weedy clerks and weatherbeaten sailors. The provost, in intervals of fretting over how he was entertain her until the lords arrived, supposed she must have inherited her magic from her father, who'd had a genius for charming folk, though not for much else.

5

When they reached his house at last, he heard himself saying, with a trace of desperation, 'Here we are, your grace. Ye'll be tired after your journey. Would ye maybe like a wee lie down on my best bed for an hour or two?'

There was an understanding twinkle in her eye as she replied, 'What an excellent idea.'

It freed him to threaten his steward with instant death if there wasn't a midday dinner fit for a queen on the table in two hours; to set his grooms scouring the town for some means of transporting the vast number of roped packs and banded chests being unloaded both from the white galley and another that had emerged from the mist, this one resplendent in scarlet and gold; and to distribute the lesser members of the queen's entourage among his fellow citizens. It was not a large entourage by royal standards, only about sixty in all, but its members ranged from a courteous handful of great noblemen by way of a dratted nuisance of a poet down to a pair of touchy professional embroiderers and three seasick upholsterers.

It was a slightly nervous Andrew Lamb who at midday sat himself down, by royal command, to dine with the queen, her three distinguished uncles, the four lovely young ladies-in-waiting known as the Four Maries, and two diminutive lapdogs, but it turned into one of the pleasantest meals he could remember. The Marquis d'Elboeuf admired the new French drawleaf table that was the provost's pride and joy, the Duc d'Aumale commended the silver plate on the sideboard, the queen said the barley pottage was the best she had ever tasted, and the Maries teased him into trying to guess what all the banded chests contained. They were still merrily at table when they heard the clatter of a large troop of horse approaching over the cobbles of the Kirkgait.

'That'll be your majesty's lords come to welcome you,' the provost said with honest regret. 'Your brother Lord James is maybe with them. I'd heard tell he was in Edinburgh.'

Before his eyes, all the queen's lightness of spirit vanished, although the smile remained. In the merest fraction of a second, Mary Stewart ceased to be a frivolous girl and became, graciously, a queen.

4

Without haste, Mary rose to her feet, held out her ringless white hands to be rinsed with rosewater, thanked the page who dried them, spoke a few appreciative words to the steward, smiled at the table servants, and finally strolled out through the friendly doorway of the provost's friendly house into the far from friendly world that awaited her.

She had known what she was coming home to, and had no one to blame but herself.

The leaders of the riding party were already dismounted, one of them half-turned away giving orders to the train of men and led horses behind. Of the three well set up figures striding towards her, one was indeed her brother, the Lord James Stewart.

Or, more accurately, her eldest half-brother. Their father, King James V, had exercised his royal prerogative to such effect that Mary, his sole legitimate child, was possessed of no fewer than nine illegitimate brothers and sisters, each of them acknowledged by the king and, in the case of the seven sons, endowed by the Vatican – on a *quid pro quo* basis – with church benefices that guaranteed them a comfortable existence for life at no cost to the Crown. Lord James, as a small boy, had been created commendator of St Andrews, but although he had subsequently renounced the Catholic faith, he showed no sign of renouncing the benefices that went with it.

He was now thirty, tall and muscular, dressed with expensive restraint in the black of fashion rather than of mourning, with twinned gold buttons on his doublet, gold embroidery edging the fine white linen of his ruff and shirt cuffs, a double gold chain round his neck and a plume in his flat velvet cap. His features were more striking than handsome, with strong bones, a wide forehead, brown eyes that gave little away, a sharp chin, and the long Stewart nose carried to ridiculous extremes.

It was an excellent nose for looking down but, with deliberation, Mary denied him the opportunity by extending her hand for him to kiss, so that he was forced, instead of embracing her, to bend the knee to her in full view of the crowds that had been flocking into Leith in the hours since she had landed. She had read somewhere that the Ottoman Turks had a law requiring whoever gained power to execute all his brothers in order to eliminate any possibility of a war of succession. It had not previously occurred to her what a sensible idea it was. Because there was no doubt in her mind that James envied her the throne. Nor any doubt that, during the years of her absence, he had taken every opportunity to show people what a good king he would have made.

And yet, and yet ... He had visited her twice in France, and she thought he was mildly fond of her, as she was of him. Certainly, she would make little progress in Scotland without his advice and experience.

7

So, having made her point, she smiled into his harassed face, and raised him up, and drew him forward to embrace him. The crowd cheered.

Lord James was not a man to whom smiling came naturally, but he did his best. 'Welcome home, sister. I'm blithe to see you.' He waved a hand towards his companions. 'Ye'll remember Argyll and Erskine?'

She smiled warmly at Lord Erskine, the elder of the two, deducing from the faint ripple of movement in his immensely long and fatly spiralling beard that he must be smiling back. But the Earl of Argyll was another matter. He was about James's age, a big man with deepset eyes and a Roman nose, whose marriage to Mary's and James's half-sister Jean was so famously incompatible as to be a subject of gossip even in France. His gaze was unresponsive as he bent the knee to her and said, with a soft Highland sibilance that came oddly from such a hard-looking man, 'It iss an unexpected honour to haff your machesty home at last.'

'Thank you,' she replied. He was one of the most powerful of her lords and one who clearly stood in need of being charmed.

James rubbed his hands. 'Well, we'd better get started back. We left them cleaning up Holyroodhouse for you. Lighting the fires and sweeping out the spiders and cobwebs. That kind of thing.'

Since he was obviously trying to be humorous – or she hoped he was – she smiled again, cooperatively, and turned her eyes towards the train of broken-down nags that appeared to pass for horses. There was not a palfrey or jennet among them, and not a side saddle to be seen.

James, correctly interpreting the faint lift of her brows, said, 'Ladies in Scotland always ride pillion. Ye'll come with me, of course.' He gestured towards his big Flemish mare, so long in the back that he could have taken not only his sister but all four of her Maries up behind.

She stared at him. He could not, surely, believe that she would be prepared to make her first appearance before her subjects in the rôle of her brother's passenger, sitting perched on his mare's rump, holding on with her arms round his waist …

No. She would ride alone, on a horse gilded and tasselled, saddled, bridled and plumed as befitted a queen.

'I think not,' she said, and sensed rather than saw Fleming, the most beloved and easily the quickest-witted of her Four Maries, raise a daintily gloved hand towards two servants lurking in the shadows. Suppressing the bubble of amusement rising in her throat, she went on, 'Although the ship carrying my stable seems to have been delayed on the voyage, my side saddle and trappings came with us in the galley.'

The servants stepped forward, carrying between them the banded chest with the royal cipher surmounting the figure 63, and, as Fleming produced the key from its hiding place in her gauntlet, Mary gestured towards a bay gelding that might, just possibly, have had a hint of Arab in his very mixed ancestry. 'He will do.'

Was James disappointed? Mary could not tell.

But she turned towards him, and smiled at him again, and said with the optimism that so often overrode her intelligence and was, in the end, to be the ruin of her, 'My dear James. The die is cast, the suspense over. I am here – and I depend on you to tell me what I must do.'

5

The three-mile ride to the royal palace of Holyroodhouse, on the fringes of Edinburgh, was a triumph. The sun was struggling to come out but Mary did not see it. Neither did she see the buildings or the landscape of the Scotland she had left as a small child thirteen years before. All she saw was the people running from the fields and houses to the roadside as she passed.

She might have come, as her uncle, the Duc de Guise, had advised, with a troop of French halberdiers and arquebusiers to protect her, but instead she had brought only a small retinue of friends and servants. It had been a gamble, but elatedly she knew that it had succeeded.

There was no dour or sullen face to be seen, nothing but animation as, rumour scampering ahead, the crowds thickened into throngs, waving and cheering, smiling, bowing, curtseying, ready and willing to be enchanted by the laughing, vivacious young woman who, as far as looks and charm went, was just the kind of queen they would have chosen if anyone had asked them. A stranger she might be, and an idolatrous Catholic in a dourly Protestant land, but she was tall and regal, graceful and beautiful, and Lord James would put her right.

And if he didn't, John Knox would.

6

By the evening, Mary might reasonably have welcomed a wee lie down on Provost Lamb's best bed if it had not been for the excitement that had possessed her since dawn and grown ever more intense as the hours passed. Now, with the iron drawbridge of Holyroodhouse threatening to collapse under the weight of the lords and lairds hastening over it to pay their respects, she had decided to change out of her widow's black, well though it became her, into something different. Long ago she had learned – with delight, since she loved clothes and jewels – that a display of splendour was an essential adjunct of royal power. Tonight seemed the perfect opportunity for putting the principle into practice.

To Fleming, she said, 'The pearl-embroidered white satin, I think,' and Fleming's eyes danced responsively.

The Maries were skilled at reading her mind. All four of them had sailed with her to France thirteen years before, five-year-old ladies-in-waiting to a five-year-old queen, confusing everyone – including themselves – by all having the same Christian name but stubbornly resistant to being addressed by their surnames. They had whiled away hour after hour of the voyage squabbling over an acceptable allocation of diminutives, with Beaton finally becoming 'Mhairi', Livingston 'Marion', Seton 'Maria', and Fleming 'Mallie'. For some reason, the only one to whom her new name had clung had been Fleming.

Despite being separated from their mistress during much of their growing up, they had remained her dearest and most loyal friends, closer to her than sisters, and their bond with her had, she knew, forged another private bond among themselves so that, different though they were in personality, they very rarely disagreed.

Beaton, dark-haired, dark-eyed and languid, was the most classically beautiful of the four and perhaps a little too conscious of it, while Livingston was the opposite, energetic, carefree and with a heart overflowingly kind. Seton was the quiet one, meek and patient and sometimes oppressively devout, but still worldly enough to be vain of her ability to dress the queen's hair as none of the others could. And finally there was Fleming who, through her mother, an illegitimate daughter of James IV, was first cousin to Mary herself.

Although she was of an age with the others, she had always seemed younger. Partly it was because she was delicate in build and feature, with wide blue eyes and soft fair hair that gave her a look of waiflike innocence. But it went deeper than that. Whereas the others had grown naturally into adult selves that had been predictable almost from childhood, Fleming had suffered a more difficult transition. Even now, despite her surface composure and her undoubted intelligence, she did not seem to be quite sure who she was. Mary, wondering about it once or twice, had begun to suspect that it might have something to do with her seductive and wayward mother, who had not only conceived a child by King Henri

II of France but boasted of it, thus incurring the enmity of both Catherine de' Medici, Henri's queen, and Diane de Poitiers, his official mistress. For Lady Fleming's sensitive small daughter, it must have been an extraordinarily embarrassing time and that, perhaps, was why she had retreated into herself. But some day, when she overcame her private shyness – and when her figure matured a little – she was going to be ravishing.

Now, shaking out the luxuriant white skirts from their wrappings in one of the sea chests, she sniffed at them, said, 'Pff! Damp!' and sprinkled them vigorously with musk.

Mary chuckled. 'No one will notice.'

James had not, after all, been joking about the spiders and the cobwebs. It was a long time since the royal apartments in the big corner tower of the palace had been occupied and, every fire, candle and lamp in the place having been lit, the atmosphere reeked of steam and dust.

With the bedchamber full of servants and chests, of feather beds being unrolled, bolsters unpacked and bed curtains hung, Mary and her ladies had been driven into the adjoining dressing room, which was no more than twelve feet square, with thick walls and a single small, deeply embrasured window through which the traces of a watery sunset were just visible. After Mary Livingston, long-limbed and gawky, had stubbed her toe or cracked her elbow four times in five minutes, Fleming had suggested that she might care to dig herself in somewhere, so that the rest of them could use her as a rallying point.

Hooks, hooks, hooks. Beaton unhooking the black cloth travelling gown, and the figured black silk bodice and skirt. Livingston hooking up the white silk underskirt over the stiffened farthingale; then the white tulle underbodice with its gathered yoke and ruff; the separate satin sleeves; and the sleeveless overgown of pearl-embroidered white satin with its low square neck, pointed waist, and quilted puffs round the armholes. Seton twining the diadem into Mary's pinned-up red-gold hair. Fleming searching out the pearl *jazerines* – the chains for draping over the bodice – and a *carcanet* necklace to sit round the base of the ruff.

'The ruby and diamond one,' Mary said, hooking her favourite pearl drops into her ears.

Rings, bracelets, brooches ...

'Enough!'

All her life she had been a queen, but a queen required only to look like one and behave herself as one – never, independently, to act as one. Always she had been surrounded and guided by advisers, men great and powerful in their own right, many of them, like her Guise uncles, related to her so that she instinctively did as they told her. When she had been in doubt about anything – even when she had not – they had been there for her to turn to.

Now, she was on her own except for a brother she scarcely knew and did not altogether trust, and one other man who was almost a stranger to her and whom she trusted even less.

She raised her chin and straightened her shoulders. There had been great turning points in her life before; first when she had married François, her beloved childhood companion; then when he had been crowned king of France and she had become its queen. But that was in the past, a past from which she had chosen to turn away. Of all the days in her life, *this* was the one that mattered, because on this day she was truly a queen at last and her destiny was in her own hands. And in God's.

With a trace of uncertainty, she said, 'Will I do?'

The Four Maries exclaimed in unison, 'You look superb.'

7

Holyrood's royal audience chamber – which was low-ceilinged, not very large by the French standards to which she was accustomed, and which had been hung earlier that day with Flemish tapestries that had been languishing mustily in a cellar for years – was full to bursting with men of all shapes and sizes, clad in dark wools or satins and smelling of haste and horse sweat. In Scotland, personal acquaintance with the sovereign mattered more than title, land or riches, which meant that every man of consequence within thirty miles had been in such a hurry to greet the queen that every wife and daughter of consequence within thirty miles had been told, 'No, ye're not coming. Ye'd slow me down, and I want to get there before Melville ... or Lindsay ... or Spens ... or Crawford ...'

It did not mean that they were loyal to the queen, or prepared to let her dictate to them. It meant only that they wanted her to think they were.

Like sensible men, Lord James Stewart and William Maitland of Lethington were keeping out of the way, backs against the wall, observing everything but saying little. They had argued out the political and religious implications of the queen's return so exhaustively in the past that there was nothing left to argue about, even if there might be a good deal once they had the opportunity of sitting round a table with her.

'Tch!' muttered Lord James after a while, his eyes on the pallid, red-bearded, middle-aged man bending the knee before his sister. 'Would ye look at Morton? Why can he never manage to look clean?'

Lethington, who was the cleverest man in Scotland, held his peace. The Greeks had believed that there was symmetry in all things, moral, material and metaphysical; that body and spirit were each a reflection of the other. In Lethington's view, the food stains on Morton's doublet and the piggy, distrustful eyes perfectly reflected the soul within, but he could hardly say so. The Earl of Morton was head of the Douglases and a very important man, and criticising him – unless you happened to be the queen's brother – was one of the riskier forms of self-indulgence.

Happily, at that moment a diversion arrived in the person of the English ambassador, Thomas Randolph, a small dark man, half-Welsh by blood and wholly Welsh by temperament. For someone well versed in the ways of courts, he was looking curiously ill at ease.

Lord James greeted him with no more than an abstracted nod, but Lethington's 'Randolph!' was so extravagantly affable that the ambassador's brows drew together into a thick, black, suspicious frown.

'Well?' Lethington said.

In no doubt about his meaning, Randolph hesitated. What *did* he think of her, now that he could see her, this young woman whose personal charms and political importance he had always thought to be vastly overrated?

Over the years, there had been repeated rumours from across the Channel that Mary was incurably ill and her little husband impotent. It had made them seem a harmless enough pair even when the king of France, Mary's father-in-law, had taken a hand in the game of power by contesting Elizabeth's right to succeed to the throne of England, to which Mary had a legitimate claim. Elizabeth had been furious, although in Randolph's view her sovereignty had never really been in danger. But François's death and Mary's return home had changed things.

If Randolph had been a disinterested observer, he would have admitted frankly that Mary was everything a queen ought to be, if rather too tall for his taste. But he was not a disinterested observer, and the living reality of a young and beautiful Catholic sovereign in Scotland with her eyes set on the Protestant throne of England threatened to add a whole new dimension to his own diplomatic problems. And just when everything had been going so nicely, too.

Gloomily, he remembered the reassuring terms in which he had written to Sir William Cecil, Elizabeth's principal secretary, only ten days before. Mary would be coming, he had said – if she came at all – to a country in which she would find no welcome, a country which believed that she intended its ruin. Lord James Stewart, the Earl of Morton and Secretary Lethington would be glad if she never returned home. Furthermore, the voyage from France would be a dangerous venture for a sick, crazed woman ...

It would have been politically convenient to England for Mary to be sick and crazed. Dead would have been better.

Now, his eyes swivelling from the dazzlingly sane and healthy figure seated under her canopy of state to the sycophantic crowd that filled the audience chamber, he returned them at last to meet the quizzical grey gaze of Maitland of Lethington.

He frowned again and inwardly cursed. It was almost as if Lethington knew what he was thinking; Lethington, whose position of secretary of state gave him almost unlimited powers. Was it possible – *was* it possible – that he had been monitoring Randolph's correspondence with Cecil?

'I will write immediately to my queen,' Randolph said with unnatural formality, 'to tell her that your queen has arrived home safely in Scotland, and to the warmest of welcomes from her nobles. My queen will be delighted.'

'Excellent! And when *your* queen writes to express her delight to *my* queen, I have no doubt that I will be instructed to write back to say how delighted *my* queen is at *your* queen's delight.'

Randolph, breathing heavily through his nose, was saved from the need to reply by Lord James, whose attention was elsewhere. 'Would you look at that!' he muttered. 'The duke. He *crossed* himself.'

'It's the third Tuesday in the month,' Lethington said.

Even Lord James was betrayed into a slightly sour smile. The religious – and therefore political – affiliations of Scotland's leading nobleman did indeed change almost as often as the phases of the moon. It was not perhaps surprising that, after two miraculously consistent years of Protestantism, he should have suffered a relapse at the sight of his beautiful young Catholic sovereign.

Especially since it was his greatest ambition to marry her off to his son, the Earl of Arran.

8

The Earls of Morton, Glencairn, Ochiltree, and Atholl had come and gone, Mary being equally charming to them all. She would have liked to

14

show extra favour to Atholl, who was the only Catholic among them, but it would have been politically unwise when religion was such a sensitive issue.

Now, extending a queenly hand to the only duke in Scotland – who was no less a Scot for having a French dukedom – she was aware of being scrutinised by the little group consisting of her taciturn brother, her lean and elegant secretary of state, and the small dark shrewd-looking person who was the English ambassador. They were, she supposed, appraising her performance, but that was something to which queens grew accustomed very early in their lives. On the crest of her own private wave of exaltation, she was tempted to laugh at them outright.

Everything was going beautifully, although perhaps a little too informally. James should have offered to be by her side to make everyone known to her. As it was, she had to rely on the whispered promptings of the four well-connected Maries, prettily bestowed around her chair of state, to identify the various lords as they approached her. Perhaps it was for the best. Not having to introduce themselves was making an excellent impression on them.

But the Duc de Châtelherault needed no introduction. She said, '*Monsieur le duc*. My dear cousin.'

She remembered him from her childhood as a slender, goodlooking, rather affected man, but now he was thickset and ageing, with a lingering air of sophistication, pouched eyes, and wine-laden breath. Unfortunately, although he might be something of a nonentity in person, in position he was not, because he was both head of the powerful family of Hamilton and – although his royal Stewart blood was little more than a trickle in his veins – the heir presumptive to her throne. It occurred to her suddenly that, for most of the eighteen years of her life, he must have been waiting and hoping that she would die. Poor man.

She said, 'What a joy it is to see you again!' and smiled on him brilliantly.

He didn't notice at first, because he was too busy staring at her necklace. 'That's nice,' he said. 'They're good rubies, those. I like a good ruby.'

'*Cousin!*'

'Sorry, my dear. Well now, it's fine to see you home and we've a lot to talk about. But there's no rush. There's just one thing that I promised my son Arran I'd raise with you straight off.'

She could guess what it was going to be.

'You'll need to be marrying again, and he'd be the ideal husband for

15

you. Well, you know him, don't you? He's twenty-four, a goodlooking boy with a good soldierly background, and he's never been wed. He's devoted to you. All this time he's been waiting for you. Oh, it would be a fine match.'

A fine match it would certainly be from Châtelherault's point of view. To be father of the king would be almost as good as being king himself.

He was still holding her hand and he squeezed it coaxingly. 'What do you say?'

There were many things she could have said, among them – maliciously – that she was perfectly well aware that the Earl of Arran, however devoted to herself, had recently offered for the hand of Elizabeth of England and been turned down because Elizabeth was passionately in love with her Master of the Horse, whose wife had just died in the *most* suspicious circumstances.

Instead, retrieving her hand, she said, 'Alas, cousin, queens are not their own mistresses in matters of the heart. My marriage is something we must all take time to discuss seriously, in full council. But you can be assured that the Earl of Arran's name will figure prominently in our discussions.' Right at the bottom of the list, if she had any say in the matter. 'And now, if you will forgive me, I see my Lord Seton approaching.'

9

Randolph, who as a diplomat was expert at observing, if not always correctly interpreting, the expressions on the faces of his betters, murmured, 'Now, what was that about? Why's the duke looking so pleased with himself?'

But when he turned to Lethington, he found that gentleman's eyes as limpid as a child's. It was no wonder, he thought irritably, that even his closest associates never knew what to make of Lethington. In Randolph's view, there wasn't a soul in either Scotland or England equipped to deal with him, except perhaps England's Secretary Cecil. And even he was a doubtful quantity, being the driest of dry sticks and utterly devoid of humour.

So he said roundly, 'Yes. All right. She's managing to enchant every single one of them, whether they like it or not. But that's today, and it won't last. What about tomorrow, when the glow wears off? What about when she orders you all back to the church of Rome?'

It was Lord James who answered. 'She won't,' he said. 'I've told her. She knows how the country feels. She knows we'd oppose it to the death.'

'Yes, that's all very well. You've had things all your own way for the last year or so, with her in France and no representative of the Crown here since her mother died, but now she's back you can't force your anointed queen to observe laws you've passed without her assent.'

Austerely, James said, 'The laws were passed in the name of the people, and the people's assent matters more to God than the assent of queens.'

'Tchoof!' Randolph muttered. 'I hope it's not sedition you're talking. If it is, you'll get no support from England. Elizabeth's not been long enough on her own throne to sanction that kind of thing.'

'Och, don't worry. I've told my sister the laws against idolatry don't apply to her. She can hear her own Mass in private, and no objections raised, as long as she keeps quiet about it. It's called compromise.'

'No objections raised? I should have thought you'd have John Knox objecting at the top of his lungs?'

Lord James had a knack, when cornered, of dismissing inconvenient truths with the loftiness of Jehovah at the Last Judgement. 'No,' he said. And that was that.

Lethington made a faint sound that might have been a laugh or a cough, and Lord James glowered at him, but the secretary merely flapped a long-fingered hand and murmured, 'The dust from the tapestries.'

10

The day over, Mary was at last able to retire to her still disorderly bedchamber, the room with the plaster frieze of flowers and fruit, and the high wooden ceiling with its diamond-shaped panels bearing the arms and initials of her long-dead father, King James V, and her recently dead mother, Mary of Guise.

She was already in her bedgown, reminding Fleming, who had just brought her a cup of hippocras and some almond wafers, to send one of her enamel-mounted cameo portraits to Provost Lamb of Leith, in thanks for his kindness, when the air was ripped apart by a blast of sound so bizarre that, at first, it was impossible to identify the source.

'Mother of God!' exclaimed Fleming, and ran to one of the windows.

It was a moment before she turned and, with a gasp, said, 'Madame. It's your subjects. In the courtyard. They've come to serenade you. *Hundreds* of them!'

Mary removed her hands from her ears. 'How kind.' Her voice quavered slightly.

There were, indeed, hundreds of them, with fiddles and stringed rebecs, and they were singing, lugubriously, what one of the Scots servants, hurriedly summoned, said were psalms of joy and thanksgiving.

Music was Mary's greatest pleasure, but she disciplined herself to stand at one of the windows, listening and smiling, for the better part of an hour. The execution might be imperfect, she told Fleming severely, but the sentiments were impeccable. Her heart was truly touched.

The only emotional false note was struck right at the end. As the musicians turned away, one man remained, staring up at her window, a tall, bearded figure in a long dark gown and flat cap.

Mary said, 'Oh, dear. I wonder who that is? *He* doesn't look very joyful.'

It was Seton, the most devout of the Maries, who answered. 'I think it's the Protestant preacher, John Knox, Madame.'

Chapter Two

1542-1561

1

After such a day, it was not surprising that Mary's body should have been too tired and her mind too restless for sleep, that her night should have been filled with dreams that were not dreams at all but memories stripped bare by the isolation of the dark.

Every minute of the hours gone by, every word and look, every unspoken thought of the people who had surrounded her had been saturated with the past, with the rumours and prejudices of yesterday, and the day before, and the day before that. She knew that she, as a real and living person, must have come as a surprise to some of her lords. She had herself been surprised by the faces and personalities of men whose lives had touched on hers in one way or another but whom she had, until now, known only by reputation.

Reputations were rarely the product of immaculate truth. She always felt more comfortable when she could see people's eyes, even though she knew that they, too, could lie.

As she slipped in and out of her light, uneasy sleep during the course of that long night, it was the clear grey gaze of Maitland of Lethington that haunted her – disturbingly, although there was nothing at all disturbing about it except its humour and charm. She believed the charm to be genuine and uncontrived, but charm was not what she had wanted to see. She had wanted to see penitence.

She had been told, before she left France, that there were only two men in Scotland without whom she would find herself adrift, the two men who had been ruling the country, theoretically on their queen's behalf – though the theory had been theirs, not hers – since her mother's death the year before. One was her brother James, the other Lethington, who had been her mother's highly effective secretary of state and on whom her mother had relied without reservation. She had also liked him greatly.

19

When he had failed her in the end, throwing in his lot with the Protestant rebels, her feeling of betrayal had been so intense that she had been able to write no more to her daughter than, 'I cannot speak of it.'

Mary herself, preparing for her return to Scotland, had written to him in the most unambiguous terms. She knew of his ability, she had said; she knew of his influence; she was prepared to accept his service and his loyalty – but only if that loyalty was undivided. Without reference to her, he had been conducting negotiations with England. If he wished to be assured of Mary's favour, he must instantly sever the English connection. Then, and only then, would she be prepared to place a guarded trust in him. 'I will not, however, conceal from you,' she had concluded, 'that if anything goes wrong *after* I have trusted you, you are the one I will first blame.'

She had received no reply. And tonight there had been humour and charm in the cool grey eyes, but nothing else. No deference. No apologies.

Restlessly, she leaned over to pull back one of the suffocating bed hangings and Fleming stirred on her makeshift pallet, murmuring sleepily, 'Madame?'

Mary might have said, 'Light more candles. Talk to me. Play for me.' Instead, she replied, 'It's nothing,' and lay down again, and pretended to go to sleep. But her mind would not rest.

2

Lethington – and England ...

Scotland's oldest and most dedicated enemy. There had been no need for others. Thanks to England, peril had hung about Mary's head since the days of her infancy, as it had hung round the heads of all the Stewart kings. Four of her five predecessors had died during wars with England; all five of them had succeeded to the throne as children. Until they had been of an age to rule, they had been pawns in the hands of their nobles.

And so had she. She had been six months old when it all began. The man who was now the Duc de Châtelherault, ruling as governor in her name, had made a treaty with Henry VIII of England, promising Mary as bride to Henry's son and Scotland itself as her dowry. Three months later he had changed his mind and, abandoning both Protestantism and England, had returned to the Catholic fold and the traditional alliance with France.

Scotland had paid the price in four years of renewed war with England, during which the Border country had been ravaged, Edinburgh burned, Holyrood sacked, and the Scots army put to rout. In the end, desperate for more active support from the French, Châtelherault had signed another contract, bartering away Mary's future for a second time. In exchange for arms, money and soldiers, Mary was to become bride to the small son of Henri II of France.

Henri, delighted to be offered a military base from which to threaten England, had rewarded the governor with his dukedom.

3

Mary's only recollection of an infancy during which she had been bundled, in perpetual flight from the invading English, from one cold and draughty castle to another, was her mother's love and warmth. Her first clear memory was of being taken from her mother at the age of five and shipped to safety in France, of the splendour of the French royal fleet, the excitement of roaring winds and raging seas, the juvenile satisfaction of being the only one of her retinue not to be seasick.

She had been welcomed at court as the most adorable child, although her mother's mother, the Duchesse Antoinette, had thrown up her hands in horror at her clothes. Did Scotland know nothing of fashion? Rapidly, Mary had acquired a new wardrobe blissfully full of bright taffetas and gold and silver damasks, of furred trimmings and coloured shoes, of deerskin gloves and crystal mirrors; chests full of pearls and rings and jewelled buttons.

It was some compensation for being separated from her retinue, even from her four little Maries; for being forbidden to speak anything but French and relegated to the French royal nursery. Fortunately, she was resilient by nature, so that she had fallen easily into the habit of loving the littler ones and mothering them and ordering them about – especially François, who was a year younger than she and was to be her husband one day.

François.

Her husband. Her child. They had taken to each other at once, to the cooing delight of the court. She, sociable as a puppy and bouncing with health, had cared for him devotedly, while he, pale and sickly, timid and uncertain with everyone except herself, had worshipped her, trailing around at her heels like one of the army of pets that accompanied the royal nursery wherever it went.

And it had gone everywhere, passing its sun-filled days, months and years in a noisy and chaotic progress from one palace to another – palaces huge, marbled and magnificent, from Meudon to Blois, from Chambord to Anet to St Germain – sometimes attached to the court and sometimes not, but always with its own vast train of chamberlains, *maîtres d'hôtel*, doctors, pages, masters of the wardrobe; its scores of *valets de chambre* and ladies to care for the increasing number of royal babies; its laundresses, apothecaries, barbers, pantry aides, masters of the roast, soup cooks and sauce cooks, salt powderers, wafer makers ...

4

After an eighteen-year lifetime of strange rooms, unfamiliar beds, and the night sounds of unaccustomed places, it was not the strangeness of Holyrood that now kept her wakeful. When she was sure from their breathing that Fleming and Seton were asleep, she sat up and, hands clasped round her knees, gave herself over to reflecting on the years that had brought her back, in the end, to the country of her birth. The past was not something she had ever tried to analyse before; young people didn't, because it was the future that beckoned.

But in the last hours it had been driven home to her that she could no longer afford to see Scotland, as she had always seen it until now, through French eyes.

No, Secretary Lethington. Nothing to do with you.

She had been too young at first to understand that the austerities of the Scotland she had left were not solely those of war and climate, or that she had moved from one extreme to another, from the most impoverished to the most sophisticated court in Europe, from a country where the ruler was first among equals to one where kings were kings – and queens, queens – by divine right and behaved accordingly. Susceptible by age and temperament, she had absorbed the French court's view of royalty as readily as she had absorbed everything else.

She was entering her twelfth year when it was first revealed to her that life was not always to be carefree and golden. Now sufficiently mature to be severed from the royal nursery, she had been granted her own household and, in celebration, had invited her two adored uncles, the eldest of her mother's six brothers, François, Duc de Guise, and Charles de Guise, Cardinal de Lorraine to dine with her. Throughout her time in

22

France, they had been to her like two fathers, replacing the one she had lost when she was six days old. They were very grand, very important, and she was in awe of them even while she worshipped them.

Duc François, who was France's most famous soldier – tall, hawk-faced, scarred, with a short dark beard and large, almond-shaped eyes not unlike Mary's own – had tasted his wine, nodded approvingly, and said, 'Your childhood is over. Now you must learn to be a queen.'

Slightly above herself with the excitement of it all, she had tilted her chin with an hauteur that was not wholly mischievous. 'I already know. I *am* a queen, so I *must* know.'

'Of course.'

She had waited, but he had said no more. It was his way, his very effective way, of forcing her to think further. The Duc de Guise rarely argued with people; he left them to argue with themselves.

After a little, she had asked doubtfully, 'Is it not enough to be born a queen?'

Her other uncle, the cardinal, a soft-skinned version of his brother, smoother and subtler, had waved the servants away. He spoke, as he always did, rather as if he were delivering a sermon, precisely phrased and perfectly ordered. 'You are already queen of the Scots. In three or four years, you will be wife to the dauphin and, when God wills it, queen of France. You are also a beloved child of the family of Guise. You thus have three sets of duties and three sets of loyalties. To Scotland, to France, and to the Guises. They will not conflict if you are an apt pupil. The interests of France and Guise are the same, while the power of France will enable you to protect Scotland against its enemies and bring it the comfort of French governance.'

Divided loyalties were not something she had thought about but, listening to her uncle's analysis, she realised that there were, indeed, things she must learn if she were to rule well. When François became king, he would, unless he changed a great deal, continue to defer to her judgement, so that as queen of France she would be more than a mere consort. François had been unwell that morning and it came to her now that she must never allow him to be as burdened with affairs of state as his father who, even on the most festive occasions, even when he was truly enjoying himself, always looked exhausted enough to break down and weep.

She had not, then, known that Guise ambitions and the determination of the Montmorencys to frustrate them would have been enough to make any but a man of stone break down and weep. Nor had she even begun to suspect that the cardinal, as well as being one of the best informed and most intricately minded politicians in Europe, was also one of the most manipulative, so that his concern with her future was not altogether disinterested.

He said, 'Do you understand what I am saying?'

'Yes, uncle.'

'Good. Then I myself will instruct you, or arrange to have you instructed in all that you must know.'

It had been dismaying to discover how much that meant. She was already learning Latin, Italian, Spanish and Greek. She could draw adequately, embroider beautifully, sing prettily and play the lute charmingly. She was sufficiently cultured to admire architecture by de l'Orme, ceilings by Primaticcio, gardens by Mercoliano, portraits by Clouet; to appreciate poems by Ronsard and motets by Maillard; and to acquit herself as gracefully at balls, banquets and *mascarades* as at archery and the chase.

Now, in addition, she was to be launched into the unfamiliar seas of statecraft; to be taught about justice, administration and finance; about the shifting alliances of Europe and the whys and wherefores of them; about the truth underlying the words and promises of emperors, kings and popes. Since she was, by nature, more responsive to instincts than ideas, to emotions than abstractions, she found it hard work. But nothing would have induced her to admit it.

5

When her uncle the cardinal felt that she had grasped the fundamentals, he had suggested that she might put her knowledge to account in Scots affairs. She had not then seen that, for him, Scotland was no more than a place to be practised on.

She gave a silent chuckle, remembering how she had laboured over the careful opinions set out in letters to her mother, letters in which the phrase '*mon oncle Charles dit que ...*' had appeared with a good deal more frequency than '*moi, je crois que ...*' Her mother must have been amused, but she had always written back to congratulate her daughter on the progress she was making and to clarify certain things about which Mary, far away in France, was not perhaps fully informed. The name of the preacher John Knox had begun to crop up, and the spread of Protestantism, and the increasing rebelliousness of the Protestant lords.

Even so, in the context of the syllabus her uncle had designed for her, it was hard for Mary to give as much attention as she might have done to the affairs of the country whose queen she was. From France, as from everywhere else, Scotland appeared as little more than a barbarian wilderness pinned to the furthest margins of the map. The papal nuncio – rather impolitely, Mary thought – had been heard to refer to it as the arse of the world. In European terms, it was no more than an impoverished tract of mountainous and rainswept country of interest only to the allies and enemies of strategically important England, which presided over the north-south trade routes round Europe.

The Scots were said to be proud of their independence but, although they fought the English often, their wars always ended in stalemate, not because the Scots won any of the battles but because the English were apt to lose interest after a while and decide to go home.

6

On Sunday 24th April 1558, when Mary was just over fifteen and François fourteen, had come their wedding day, the culmination of the last ten years of Mary's life. The cathedral of Notre Dame had been transformed with arches, canopies, gold carpets and *fleur-de-lys*, and there was a vast stage in front where the first part of the ceremony took place.

Rarely, if ever, had Paris seen such pageantry, a procession of such splendour. Fittingly, it had been arranged and was led by Mary's uncle and France's hero, the Duc de Guise, who had just reconquered a Calais that for more than two hundred years had been occupied by the English. With his victory, France had become whole again, and the crowds greeted him with a roar of acclamation that seemed to shake the foundations of Notre Dame itself. The Swiss Guards had stalked before him, tall and splendid, and behind had followed musicians clothed in yellow and red, playing clarions and hautboys, viols and citterns.

His dark, hard-featured face had shown little sign of pleasure in the homage paid him – this was, after all, not his but his niece's day of glory – but Mary knew that his heart must be swelling with triumph. She grudged him none of it, and was herself exalted by it.

After the duke had come the princes of the blood and of the church, cloaked in rich velvets and rare furs, glittering with gold and gems. And, after them, François, small and immature, wearing a shoulder cape of ermine over robes of embroidered blue, his eyes fixed and his mouth twitching a little under the golden coronet. His fair hair was curled and pomaded, and the red patches on his skin hidden by a white cosmetic paste, so that he looked his very best and, although he was not physically robust, contrived to walk, head high, royally, as befitted the future king of France. Mary had been proud of him.

She had been prouder still when François's father had led her into the people's view and their pleasure in her had echoed like thunder – a bride who had chosen to defy tradition by wearing, not cloth of gold, but the white that so perfectly became her. In France, white was associated with mourning but there was no hint of anything other than rapture at her appearance, at her long train, her height and gracefulness, the dazzling diamond collar round her slender neck, and the jewelled crown on her red-gold hair. She had intended to look like a goddess – and she did. For once, none of the expensive royal ladies following her had been able to compete. It had been *very* satisfying.

The details of the day had passed her by, lost in the ceremonial and the need to do and say what it had been decreed that she should do and say. But there was one moment whose warmth would never leave her, the moment when the Cardinal de Bourbon slipped one of the king's own rings first on the third finger of François's hand, and then on the third finger of hers, joining them in marriage.

After the Mass, there had been a banquet during which Mary's crown had weighed so heavily that it had been necessary to take it off and give it to a lord-in-waiting to hold. And after that there had been a grand ball, when Mary danced with the king and François with his mother. And when that ended in the late afternoon, they had all gone in procession to the palace of the *parlement*, where there had been a supper of surpassing magnificence and another ball, with *mascarades* and mummers and golden mechanical horses and silver-sailed ships on wheels, so exquisitely made that they might have been real. Some of the younger princes rode the horses and piloted the ships, and some of the ladies – including Queen Catherine de' Medici and Mary herself – were sufficiently trusting to embark as passengers on their voyages around the ballroom.

When the long day was over, Mary's new mother-in-law, with whom she had nothing in common except love of François, had insisted that the traditionally exuberant ceremony of bedding the bride be curtailed, not for decency's sake but because François was exhausted. And when everyone had been cleared out of the bridal chamber, she had said, 'Come, *mio bambino*. I will take you to your own bed. You must rest now or you will be ill.'

'*No!*'

Although he was so drained that his eyes could barely stay open and his lips were almost bloodless, François had succeeded in drawing himself up and saying in a voice that he tried to make manly, although it was still a boy's, 'Marie is my wife now. I will not leave her.'

Mary had hugged him, with passionate tears in her eyes.

That had been the only passion on their wedding night, or on most of the nights that followed. Left to themselves at last, the bride and groom had collapsed into their petal-strewn feather bed and from there, holding hands childishly, straight into sleep.

7

The fragrance of the petals had lingered for almost six months after their marriage, while the rejoicings went on and on, and everyone and everything conspired to make the life of Mary and her husband – no longer simply dauphin of France but also king of Scotland – as happy and carefree as it could ever be, and would never be again.

Mary had always been admired and pampered; now she was flattered outrageously. Everyone, including foreign ambassadors, ecstatically acknowledged her as the loveliest princess in Europe. Songs were dedicated to her smiling eyes and her soft, sweet voice. Ronsard wrote poems to her long slender hands and alabaster brow. Ladies sought to match her flawless complexion with bleaches of mercury water and ceruse; used rhubarb and white wine to lighten their hair to something approaching reddish-gold; copied not only her gowns but her style. It had made her giggle, privately, to see short, stout ladies adopting her own graceful inclination of the head, which had become natural to her as she had grown tall but made dumpy women seem to be peering into their companions' bosoms rather than their faces.

But she had one great talent which they did not even try to emulate because they did not understand it. She didn't understand it herself. All she knew was that she seemed to have the ability to charm everyone she met – except her mother-in-law, plain-looking and devious, whom she had robbed of her firstborn son.

27

Although marriage and a nominal maturity had entitled François and Mary to be kept informed about matters of state, they were not expected to air their opinions, and certainly not to have those opinions attended to.

It meant that Mary had no say at all in something that was to be of the first importance to her – the tactical moves that followed the death of her namesake, Queen Mary I of England who, most devout of Catholics, was succeeded by Elizabeth, daughter of Henry VIII by his second wife, Anne Boleyn. Since Holy Church had never recognised Henry's divorce from his first wife, Elizabeth was in Catholic eyes illegitimate. She was also suspected of being a Protestant, which was worse.

When rulers died, all the pieces on the chessboard of Europe shifted and Mary discovered, with her first adult awareness of it and the first faint stirrings of resentment, that she was as much a pawn as she had ever been. Because if Elizabeth were to be eliminated from the English succession, it was Mary who, by virtue of descent from Henry VII, had the strongest claim to the throne.

And so, out of what might have been duty to his daughter-in-law or simple political opportunism – which was just as likely, although she had not seen it at the time – King Henri II had promptly proclaimed her queen of England, Ireland and Scotland and ordered the royal arms of England to be quartered with those of France and Scotland on flags, banners, surcoats and gold plate for the table.

She had had to pretend to be pleased.

Next day, as she and François cantered home after flying a favourite peregrine, François – who had still to learn that royal pronouncements were not inevitably transformed, as by divine sleight of hand, into deeds accomplished – had said, 'I shall like to be king of England. It is excellent that we can bring England into France's sphere without war.'

'Yes. I mean, it *would* be, but do you think the Lady Elizabeth will give up the throne so easily?'

By any normal standards, it was an absurd question, but Mary, knowing how François seethed with uncertainties under his adolescent veneer of self-consequence, always did her best to help him. On this occasion, since he had been present at a consultation between his father and her uncle the cardinal, he was able to respond with a promptness that pleased her as much as it did him.

'It would depend on a number of things,' he said, pursing his small mouth judiciously, and went on to talk of sacraments and coronations and discussions with the English privy council. 'It is *you* who should be queen of England,' he concluded stoutly, holding out a hand to her. 'And if they will not see sense, so that we have to invade England in pursuit of your claim, then we *will* invade England. I will not have you fretting about it. All will be well, you'll see.'

His affection warmed her, as it always did, but his words were the merest bravado. France's coffers, she knew from her uncles, were empty. She said, 'It would cost too much.'

'My father the king can afford *anything* that touches on the honour of France.' Then, with one of his wild bursts of energy, he set spurs to his mare and went dashing off ahead, his voice floating back to her. 'Never fear, my Marie!'

Accepting the challenge, she raced after him. On horseback, nothing frightened her. It was only later that, snatching a brief hour of the solitude so rarely granted to princes, she looked to the future and discovered that she *was* afraid.

Reprovingly, she told herself that, by God's will and God's justice, it was her destiny to become queen consort of France and queen regnant of England as well as Scotland, and it was not for her to concede any fraction of what God had ordained for her. But it made no difference. The invasion of England would be a huge and terrifying enterprise, and for it to be embarked upon in her name would lay an awesome responsibility on her. And if it weren't embarked upon, everyone would look foolish, including herself. She didn't *want* to be queen of England. Really, her father-in-law – much though she loved and admired him – had gone too far.

9

Her eyelids beginning to droop with weariness, she thought, was that really how I felt at the time? Or am I seeing everything, already, from a different perspective?

Aware that the dawn must be near, she lay down, murmuring again to the cool grey eyes that had watched her from across her audience chamber a few hours before, *No, don't flatter yourself, Secretary Lethington. Nothing to do with you.*

And then she fell straight into sleep and the nightmares that, awake, she could not face, that had begun with the agonising end of her father-

29

in-law, who had taken a splintered lance through the eye and spent ten days dying, with his wife and Mary at his bedside throughout.

A little over two months later, on a wet and windy day at Reims, a frightened and apathetic François had been crowned king in his place, while in Scotland civil war had broken out and Elizabeth of England, crowned despite everything and in a rage over Mary's pretensions to her throne, had revenged herself by sending money to the Protestant lords who were in revolt against Mary's mother, the regent. Mary could imagine Lethington's cool grey *reasonable* gaze as he and Elizabeth had negotiated her betrayal.

And after that, when Mary had been queen of France for nine anxious months, her grandmother, the Duchesse Antoinette, had come to her and curtsied, and said, '*Majesté...*' and then, '*Ma petite*, you must be strong ...' They had known for days that her mother was dead, but had been unable to bring themselves to tell her.

In the passion of weeping to which she had succumbed and the nervous collapse that had followed, she had suffered not only loss but guilt, a guilt of the spirit. She had loved her mother deeply, but it had been a love without intimacy. She had not sensed how ill and tired her mother was. She had not sensed that she was dead.

10

'Madame! Madame!' It was Fleming, her voice full of anxiety. 'Seton, help me! I can't wake her.'

But Mary shuddered and turned away. She did not want to be woken until she had seen the horrors through. Until she had sat by François's bedside while he, too, died. Six months after her mother. From an inflammation of the brain.

Her husband. Her child.

He had not been dead a week before everyone in Europe was talking about whom she should marry next. She had felt, not like a pawn but a fly trapped helplessly in the web of European alliances. There was a long, long list of spiders waiting to swallow her up – from Don Carlos of Spain, to the kings of Denmark and Sweden, to Châtelherault's son, Arran, and the young Lord Darnley, who had Tudor blood in him and a claim of his own to the throne of England.

England ...

She did not want another husband. She wanted François – who had loved her for herself, not for her throne.

Spiders, spiders ...

The eyes hovering over hers when she dragged herself awake were not clear and grey and considering, but vividly blue and filled with concern.

'Madame, you were weeping as if your heart would break,' Fleming said. 'I had to wake you.'

And then, with the exasperation of relief, 'Seton, will you stop standing there telling your beads in that unhelpful way, and go and find a soothing draught for her majesty. A fresh pillow, too. This one is soaked with tears.'

Chapter Three

AUGUST 1561

1

With some difficulty, Mallie Fleming succeeded in insinuating herself into the queen's retiring room, a small room currently full of large and noisy Guise uncles, one of them complaining about the weather, another about the surliness of the people, and a third about the fiddles and rebecs of the night before.

As she stood waiting to be noticed, the voice of the youngest of them, the Marquis d'Elboeuf, who was only three or four years older than the queen herself, rose above the others. '*Pfui! L'Écosse! Ma pauvre Marie!* I will wager anything that, before the month is out, you will be yearning for the orchards and vineyards of Touraine, and the sun and soft winds of Poitou.'

The queen tilted her chin within its crisp little white ruff and said, 'Nonsense, René!' but Fleming remembered how she had wept as Calais receded in the wake of her great galleys; had wept for the Loire, and her life there, and for France itself. Her misery had lasted for most of the voyage. Softly, endlessly, she had sighed, *Adieu, France! Adieu, ma chère France ...*

'I cannot understand,' the queen went on, 'why you are all so determined to depress me. In fact, I wish you would go away, because I have a great deal to do. Yes, Fleming?'

As the uncles departed, shrugging and laughing, Fleming murmured, 'Lord James Stewart and your secretary of state are waiting to see you, Madame.'

'Yes. No ...' The queen thought for a moment, a finger to her lips, then said, 'I can spare Lord James five minutes, but please tell Secretary Lethington that I shall be occupied for most of the week. I will summon him if I need him.'

'Madame!'

Mary shook her head. 'No, Lethington has had too much freedom in the past. My mother placed her trust in him and he failed her. I do not intend to make the same mistake. So I will start as I mean to go on. I value his abilities but he is, after all, no more than one of my officials. It will do him no harm to be reminded that *my* wishes are paramount. Give him my message, please.'

Mallie Fleming, who would have been desperately in love with the handsome and heart-stoppingly charming Lethington if he had not been so old – he was thirty, at least – said weakly, 'Yes, Madame,' and thought, 'How dreadful! I wonder if I can get Seton to do it?'

Half a dozen words and the hint of a smile was all it had taken.

'However,' the queen went on, 'I will see my brother now. I must ask him to tell the people of Edinburgh how much pleasure their recital gave me yesterday evening ...'

Fleming's eyebrows rose and Mary's air of regal condescension dissolved into a giggle. 'Don't!' she said. 'It was kindly meant, after all. Now, we must, really *must* do something about making this room habitable. If we have a table, chairs, a daybed and some of the smaller tapestries, it will do very well for cosy little suppers and gossipy evenings. Will you see to it, please?'

'Yes, Madame.'

2

With exhilaration and an increasing lightness of heart, Mary spent the following days finding her way about, learning the landscape of her future, of her new life, her new adventure. Even the weather behaved itself – more or less.

The palace of Holyroodhouse, once the guest house of the abbey of Holyrood, had been improved by her father and grandfather into a royal residence, with private apartments for the sovereign accommodated in the four-storeyed corner tower. The English had burned down most of the rest of the palace in 1544, so there had been a good deal of rebuilding since then, not all of it as ambitious as the new frontage with its turreted bays and splendid Great Hall and chapel. Behind it, in lesser ranges of buildings arranged round two courtyards, were guest apartments, servants' lodgings, stables, armouries, kitchens, bakehouses, brewhouses and all the other necessary appurtenances of a sixteenth-century royal residence. The immediate precincts included formal arbours and knot gardens, orchards and vegetable plots, and there was also an extensive wild park.

All this, however, was something to be inspected at leisure. Mary's immediate concern was to reinforce the favourable impression she had made on her people the previous day.

She asked James, therefore, to take her on a tour round Edinburgh, and it was a handsome cavalcade that set out an hour before midday, headed by the queen, the gold-studded skirts of her black velvet riding dress falling elegantly from her side saddle and a matching beret set on her flaming hair. Tall and slender, she always looked well in the saddle, even when her mount was mouse-coloured and no more than thirteen hands high. She hoped it would not be long before her Master of the Horse extricated her own stable from Tynemouth, in the north of England, where it had been landed by mistake and was being held by the warden because the horses had no passports.

Beside the queen rode Lord James and behind her, two by two, the Maries, whose looks always caused heads to turn. The Guise uncles came after, tall and dark, with the soldierly Sieur de Brantôme, the mercurial poet Châtelard, and the other French gentlemen of her suite.

The crowds in the Highgait fell back at their approach, unaccustomed, after twenty colourless years, to a ruling sovereign coming among them. The older ones, watching the queen smiling and chatting to her subjects, remembered the unforced charm of James V and thought, 'Just like her father!'

To French-trained eyes, Edinburgh was an unexpectedly handsome city, its broad, stone-paved main street built on a mile-long hog's-back ridge running east to west, with crooked, cluttered wynds or alleys branching off at either side to end abruptly where the land fell away. Overall, it was barely half as broad as it was long.

There seemed to be no large, stately houses; instead, the hewn stone buildings stood shoulder to shoulder, narrow and tall, with outside staircases leading to the different floors, which were inhabited by different families. James, who was showing a worrying tendency to explain everything that could be explained, said, 'The ground floors have stone-vaulted roofs and the builders pack sand down over the vaults to give a solid base for the floor above. We don't have ...' His voice came to a bitten-off halt as he saw that he had lost his sister's attention.

Her brows were drawn together in concentration and she was looking right through him. Then her forehead lightened and, pleasedly, she exclaimed, 'Coal!'

Setting foot on the waterfront at Leith the morning before, she had felt no real sense of coming home, had waited in vain for some spark to rekindle her sense of belonging. And now it had happened, though it had taken her a little time to identify the source. Like towns and cities the world over, Edinburgh smelled of sewage and horses and too many people and animals living in too constricted a space. But whereas householders in France burned wood or charcoal in their hearths and braziers, those of Scotland burned smoky, malodorous sea-coal. The smell of Edinburgh's coal was the smell of Scotland as she remembered it. How queer, she thought, that something so ordinary should have such an effect on her.

James repeated, 'Coal?' but she laughed and said, 'Never mind. Show me what they sell in all those booths lining the house fronts.'

A little to her surprise, they sold expensive things like sugar and spices, olives, honey and green ginger, dates and almonds and raisins of Corinth. They sold threads and jerkin points, too, ribbons and purses, needles and combs. And there were knives and sword belts and long daggers which James said were known as whingers or stabbing swords.

Mary, who had a distaste for violence, turned away to smile back at the people smiling and waving to her with such gratifying enthusiasm. It was an enthusiasm they also extended to James and the Maries, but not to the French gentlemen riding behind.

At the highest and farthest point from the palace was the castle, strong and impregnable, growing dramatically out of the rock on which it stood, a rock which fell sheer away on all sides except to the east, from which they were approaching. Today, however, Mary wanted to see her subjects, not her fortifications, so they stopped short of it and picked their way downhill by the West Bow to the southern base of the castle rock. It was pleasantly sheltered from the winds that had whipped around them on the higher ground. 'There's a big market here on Fridays,' James said, 'but ye won't want to see that.'

'Won't I? Why not?'

'For one thing, it's coarse. And for another thing, it's so crowded ye can't move. Smiths, bakers, butchers, skinners, soutars, fletchers, surgeons, money changers, weavers and candle makers as well as most of the folk who live in the town. There's about eight thousand of them. The burgesses get served first, then everybody else.'

'It sounds lovely. I *do* want to see it!'

'Not when ye're under *my* protection,' her brother told her austerely. 'Ye can take whatever risks you like when I'm not here, of course.'

She twinkled at him. 'How kind!' But he was impervious to irony, so with an inward sigh she gestured towards the road they were entering, one whose houses spoke, for the first time, of riches.

'Nobody's rich in Scotland,' he said. 'All the country's money's been going straight into the pockets of the priests for years.'

It was Mary's impression that, for the last two or three years at least, the main occupation of her Protestant lords had been taking the country's money right back out of the pockets of the priests again, but she forbore to say so.

Nor did James pursue it. 'It's called the Cowgait,' he said. 'It used to be a country lane, but it's where most of the lords stay when they have to be in Edinburgh for the parliament and suchlike. I can't afford anything of the sort myself, so Argyll usually gives me a lodging.'

The link between poverty and moral authority had long been a cliché of the godly, and Mary knew that her brother habitually made use of it. When he had visited her in France earlier in the year – to discuss her possible return to Scotland and her intentions as to its governing – references to the thinness of his purse had cropped up almost as often as references to John Knox. He had even tried to persuade her to bestow on him the vacant earldom of Moray and the very substantial estates and income that went with it. He had wanted the earldom, he said, to give him the formal status that, as the illegitimate son of a king, he had always been denied; he hadn't mentioned money. She might, she thought, have been more sympathetic if it had not been for the size and lavishness of the retinue he had brought with him.

Whatever he said, he *could* not be poor. He had been commendator of the wealthy Augustinian priory of St Andrews since he was a child, which gave him free use of its lands and revenues. And even in France she had heard rumours – which she would have liked to, but could not quite, disbelieve – that when he and the Earl of Argyll had marched on St Andrews in 1559 to 'convert' the town to Protestantism, James had made a handsome profit from the vandalising of the cathedral that had followed. All its valuables had disappeared and the tombs of the prosperous dead had been broken open and robbed of their grave goods. Mary could not, admittedly, visualise James, in person, walking off with the armbone of the apostle in one hand and the crucifix of St Margaret in the other, but even such a stern moralist as he need not have disdained to accept gifts of melted-down gold or unattributable jewels from benefactors who admired the work he was doing for the Protestant cause.

On one score, at least, she could disarm him. 'My *dear* James,' she said, 'it is quite unsuitable for you to have to lodge with Argyll, or anywhere other than at Holyroodhouse.' She turned her head. 'Fleming, please see that a set of apartments is prepared for Lord James. Immediately.'

Through pearly, if slightly gritted teeth, Mallie Fleming said, 'Yes, Madame.'

She loved and was deeply loyal to the queen, and had learned to submit willingly to the many discomforts and inconveniences entailed in being a royal lady-in-waiting. But she supposed that she must have too much Stewart blood in her for submissiveness to come naturally, because there was one thing – one very small thing – to which she thought she would never become resigned. She had no idea what the penalties for *lèse-majesté* were but was beginning to feel that, if she had to say, 'Yes, Madame,' or 'No, Madame,' just once more, she was going to find out.

Especially if it entailed easing the path of Lord James Stewart who was, like the queen, her first cousin and whom she had detested since as far back as she could remember.

3

Everything had gone so beautifully for the first four days after Mary's arrival that when, on the fifth day, everything ceased to go beautifully, the shock was severe.

It was Sunday and, since Lord James had said that no one would object to her hearing Mass – though not every day, and on the understanding that she made no public display of it – she duly led her cheerful, gossiping uncles, ladies and household through the Great Hall that occupied most of the first floor of the west range of the palace and into the chapel at the far end.

It was a handsome chapel, with carved ceiling, painted friezes, a royal pew pillared in gold and scarlet, and a panelled chancellory wall behind the altar. It did not trouble her that it was by no means as splendid as the royal chapels she was accustomed to in France. The familiar peace of the spirit entered her, as it always did, with the first notes of the *Kyrie*, a peace that grew and warmed her as the *a cappella* voices took up the *Gloria*. Her choice of setting limited by the size of her makeshift little choir – which consisted of two of her young pages and two tenor and two bass valets who did not sing as well as they served – she had decided on the lovely old Josquin version of *L'homme armé*, and her pleasure in it was intense after the days of music-less worship in the private oratory attached to her audience chamber.

> ... *Adoramus te, glorificamus te.*
> *Gratias agimus tibi*
> *Propter magnam gloriam tuam.*
> *Domine Deus, Rex coelistis,*
> *Deus ...*

Only slowly did the voices from the forecourt begin to intrude. Scots voices, raucous voices, not voices conversing but voices shouting, threatening, rising to a clamour. Everyone in the chapel jumped as a handful of pebbles struck against the latticed and barred window.

Mary, rigid in her seat, gave no sign of having noticed. The members of her choir, momentarily losing the counterpoint, faltered their way towards it again.

> ... *Qui tollis peccata mundi,*
> *Miserere nobis.*
> *Qui tollis peccata mundi,*
> *Suscipe deprecationem ...*

A voice shouted, 'Death to the idolatrous priest!' and the cry was taken up at once by other voices. It was a clumsy phrase better suited to pen and paper than to speech, but that made it no less alarming. There were feet scuffling and kicking against the iron-bound door downstairs. In France, there would have been a company of armed guards to stop such a demonstration before it even began, but Holyrood had no more than a lackadaisical handful. Who had probably hesitated to annoy their fellow citizens by barring their path.

'Death to the idolatrous priest!'

It was repeated again and again, went on and on, becoming almost a chant, and Mallie Fleming, seeing poor Father Domville's hands shaking as he raised the chalice, at last turned her head and resignedly met her mistress's eyes. It was clear that someone must find out what was happening, and equally clear that it was less provocative for a young Scotswoman to do so than for any of the French members of the queen's retinue. Hoping that the practice would live up to the theory, Fleming crossed herself, curtsied, and slipped out.

38

At the head of the stone turnpike stair she stopped, swallowing nervously. The noise here was much louder than inside the chapel and it sounded as if there was a mob just beyond the great wooden door at the foot. Hands were hammering against it and Fleming wondered how long it would be before it occurred to someone to find a battering ram. If they broke in, she could do nothing. Although the stairs were only wide enough to take three or four men at a time, she did not think they would stop to debate with her whether the queen had, or had not, the right to celebrate Mass if she wanted to.

How had it all begun? How had they found out? She supposed some of the palace servants must have seen the preparations, or smelled the incense, and gone hurrying up to Edinburgh to spread the word. And where was Lord James, the brother whose promises the queen had trusted? The brother with the wide, thin-lipped mouth, the jutting chin, the air of consequence, the humourless morality.

Catching sight of two servants bovinely brushing down the tapestries in the Great Hall, she snapped, 'Go and find Lord James Stewart. *This minute!*'

They went, although she had no great hope of their succeeding. Or even of trying very hard.

Bracing herself, the beginnings of the *Credo* flowing out of the chapel above her and the sounds of violence exploding from the foot of the stairs below, she adjusted the folds of her skirt to hide her rosary and began to descend. She could not – dared not – open the door, but it occurred to her that she might make her way through the ground-floor service rooms to emerge into the forecourt by the entrance at the corner of the tower.

When she did, it was to discover that there were fewer rioters than she had thought and that their leader, the man shouting loudest against the idolatrous priest, was someone who, after only four days back in Scotland, she already knew both by sight and by reputation – one of the most rabid of the Protestant lords, a man who saw force as the solution to everything, a man with no graces whatsoever, the man known as Patrick Lindsay of the Byres.

Who happened to be married to Euphemia, Lord James's sister on his mother's side.

Innocently strolling towards the protesters over the rain-wet cobbles, Mallie exclaimed, 'My goodness! What *is* going on?'

They were too busy to hear her.

It was not easy, at a fair and slender eighteen, to impose one's personality on a bunch of sturdy ruffians animated – she suspected – as much by fondness for a fight as by religious conviction. Approaching as closely as she dared, however, and remembering what she knew of the reformed religion, she raised her voice and, with piercing clarity, said, 'I thought it was a sin to make an affray on the Sabbath?'

Thirty pairs of fists were stilled. Thirty pairs of eyes turned towards her. Patrick Lindsay of the Byres said, 'What?'

Then, and only then, did Lord James put in an appearance, rounding the corner from the far end of the building with a measured stride and no appearance of haste at all. 'What's this?' he said in surprise. 'What are you doing here, Patrick?'

Lindsay said, 'It's that sister of yours, setting up idols in the realm. We're supposed tae have got rid of all that.'

'Oh, is that what it is?' Lord James sounded bluff and hearty and quite unconcerned. 'Well, I know how ye feel, but this kind of thing won't do. Papistry or no papistry, I can't have you broiling and brangling outside the queen's door. Anyway, ye've no need to worry. Once her friends go back to France we'll have no more bother with priests. So why don't ye all go home? I'll stay here and make sure there's no danger of anyone else sneaking in to listen to all that hocus-pocus.'

So saying, and with a belated nod to his simmering cousin, he planted his broad shoulders against the staircase door and waited.

An order was an order and, after a moment, the rioters, scratching their chins and looking disappointed, began reluctantly to depart.

Mallie Fleming hesitated. It was not for a lady-in-waiting to say anything, but something undoubtedly needed to be said. Just as something needed to be done, and soon.

After a moment of trying to persuade herself that her suspicions stemmed only from her dislike of James, she raised her bright blue eyes to his expressionless brown ones and said, 'If you will forgive me, cousin, I believe that her majesty needs better protection than she has had this morning. What use are guards who are no more than gatekeepers? And not very effective gatekeepers, either. It won't do.'

She was only a cousin, and twelve years younger than he, and a mere female, which enabled him to say patronisingly, 'This is Scotland, not France. The queen doesn't need armed men between herself and her subjects. Now, away back to your chapel, lassie. There'll be no more trouble now I'm here. That's the end of it.'

She went, since there was nothing else she could do.

It was not quite the end. That evening several hundred citizens of Edinburgh returned to Holyroodhouse, not this time with fiddles and stringed rebecs but with surly voices and surlier faces. There was no demonstration, no violence. Lord James had forbidden it. They did not even force their way into the palace forecourt, but stood beyond the gatehouse, relatively quiet but unmistakably there. Once or twice a few voices embarked on one of the more melancholy psalms, but soon faded away.

> 'And though I were even at death's door,
> Yet would I fear none ill,
> For why thy rod and shepherd's crook ...'

Up in her apartments, the queen said after a while, 'Livingston, close the shutters, get out the dice, set up the board, and let us amuse ourselves with a lovely, noisy game of backgammon.'

5

'I will not have it,' she declared next morning, her smile no less imperious than her words.

It was her first day of business and she, Lord James and Secretary Lethington were seated round the table in her bedchamber, which also served as a private office, with Fleming and Seton doing their best to look invisible in a corner and, in the audience chamber outside in case they were needed, two of the other officers of state – clerk-register MacGill, and justice clerk Bellenden.

'Aye, well,' Lord James replied without a flicker. 'News has a habit of getting out and ye won't find many Scots prepared to countenance the reintroduction of idolatry. Their Protestant principles are too important to them.'

There was an edge to the queen's softly modulated young voice. 'Indeed? Yet, as I recall, you assured me – you guaranteed to me – that there would be no objection to my worshipping as I chose in my own palace.'

Her brother did not hesitate. 'I offered ye a promise, in good faith and on my own account, of freedom to worship, but I am not the keeper of other folks' consciences. If they fear that ye mean to try and bring them back to the pope of Rome, it is their right to resist.'

'Their *right* to resist? To resist their queen? And with violence?'

'No, no. A bit of noise, maybe, but no violence. The reformed church abhors violence.'

She stared at him. 'Which, of course, is why the reformed church last year decreed the death penalty for any of my subjects found guilty of saying or hearing Mass.'

6

Lethington watched and listened with the deepest interest. Mary Stewart had always been an elusive figure, a Hydra with one youthful head of her own and innumerable weaving and shifting others belonging to the Guise and Valois advisers who counselled her as to what she should do. Neither his rare, brief meetings with her in France nor the flood of letters that poured from her secretaries' pens – a batch of no fewer than three hundred had been entrusted to him for distribution earlier in the year – had served to cast any light on her own personality or ideas. If she had any.

Now, he looked forward to discovering how many of the things done, the statements made in her name, were a true reflection of her own views. Not too many, he hoped, remembering in particular a letter from her eleven-year-old brother-in-law, the new king of France, to the members of her council in Scotland, stating that his dearest sister was prepared to grant them her sincere love, despite their sins, and instructing them to behave themselves, 'so that they may not make her regret having been so benign'.

This had very nearly resolved all problems by causing the council to succumb to communal apoplexy but, its blood pressure back to normal, it had replied that Mary was queen of the Scots, and that they were her dutiful and loyal subjects. As they always had been and always would be.

They had said it, and they had meant it. And not for the first time. With mild intellectual discomfort, Lethington recalled an occasion during the civil war when he had found himself explaining to England's Secretary Cecil – a man who in diplomacy, if not in religion, valued reason far above faith – that the mere fact of the Protestant lords having taken up arms against the French regent, their queen's mother and deputy, did not mean that they were any less loyal to the queen herself. Their purpose, indeed, was to assist her majesty by saving her realm from the tyranny of foreign rule.

The first few years of her mother's regency had made it clear that Mary of Guise's object was to reduce Scotland, fully and finally, to a Catholic dependency of the Catholic France of which her daughter was destined to be queen. By the time John Knox returned to Scotland in 1559 and began sweeping all hesitancy away with the passion of his beliefs and the extraordinary power of his rhetoric, her relationship with the lords was already rank with distrust. It was the last straw when two thousand well-trained and well-armed French troops arrived to supplement the two thousand already there.

Lethington, who had been appointed secretary of state in 1558 after four years as assistant, had always prided himself on being ruled by his brain, not his emotions, but four thousand French troops in addition to the continuing influx of high-level French administrators had sufficed to convince him that, widely travelled though he was in both body and mind, he was unequivocally a Scotsman at heart. It was time that Scotland ceased to be a plaything of others and reached out towards its own fulfilment.

He had stayed with the regent until the last possible moment, in case – somehow – he could stave off the inevitable, but in the end he had gone.

By abandoning the regent for the Protestant lords, he had forfeited the trust of the regent's daughter Mary Queen of Scots. By leaving it so late, he had also come close to forfeiting the trust of the lords. But he had succeeded in regaining their good opinion – if with reservations, since, as he well knew, they thought him too clever for comfort – and he now had to gain the queen's.

7

The lords had been quick to form their own opinion of Mary in the week since her arrival. Several of them had gone so far as to tell Lethington outright, 'She's soft. Not like her mother. You and Lord James should be able to keep her in order, no bother.'

Perhaps, or perhaps not. If he and James were to displace the Guises and the Valois who had guided her for so long, they had agreed that she would have to be handled with tact and delicacy.

James, whose notion of tact and delicacy was all his own, was saying, 'The death penalty's only for the third offence. Anyway, the church of

Rome can hardly complain about that kind of thing. What about all those heretics it's sent to the stake in its time? Take George Wishart ...'

Once James was launched on the subject of Wishart there would be no stopping him. Gently, Lethington cleared his throat.

The queen's eyes turned towards him. 'You wish to speak, Secretary?'

'With respect, we have a good deal to discuss. Perhaps we might compromise in the matter of your Mass by agreeing to learn the lesson of yesterday and to bear it in mind when we consider tomorrow?'

Her eyebrows rose. 'You are implying that I should not reprimand my people, but should accept having been reprimanded by them?'

He had not expected her to be so quick. With no inclination to enter into a discussion of principles, he shrugged lightly. '*Vox populi, vox dei.*'

The queen considered him for a moment. 'If you believe that, I fear we shall not deal well together.'

James also took him seriously. 'The voice of the people is the voice of God? No. Not even John Knox would go as far as that.'

Lethington knew that John Knox would go as far as that, and a damned sight further if he felt like it. The Lord might have given ten commandments to Moses, but He had given any number of supplementaries to Knox. Resignedly, Lethington said, 'An ill-timed pleasantry. I apologise.' Then, glancing at James, he laid their cards on the table.

'Lord James,' he said, 'has spoken of your subjects' uneasiness in the matter of your religion and their fears for their own. We both believe that it would be wise for you to issue an immediate proclamation to reassure them.' He paused. 'If, of course, your majesty wishes to reassure them?'

It was the first, the key issue of the new reign, the issue that, unsatisfactorily resolved, would cast every other issue into the shade and might well bring about another civil war.

Rising to her feet, the queen walked towards the window. She was an unusually tall and graceful girl, her complexion fine and pure, her nose unquestionably Stewart but not yet inelegantly so, her coiled pearl-banded hair as silken as the veiling that fell from the back of her neat black cap, her mouth small and shapely. Her eyes alone would have been enough to make a beauty of her – well spaced, almond-shaped, and of a clear light amber in colour. Time would tell how much truth there was in the smile that, in general, seemed to inhabit them.

After a moment, her gaze on the outdoors, she said, 'I will speak frankly to you. A year ago, you and the lords dared to summon a parliament and enact laws designed to destroy Holy Church in Scotland. You rejected the authority of the pope. You decreed the death penalty for celebrating Mass. All without my assent. Your enactments, therefore, like your parliament, were illicit according to the law of nations.'

It had not, of course, been as simple as that, and Mary herself – or her French advisers – had not been blameless, but it did not seem the moment to argue.

She allowed a pause to develop. Lethington and Lord James waited. And waited. Lethington sensed, suddenly, that she had rehearsed it all.

Her voice began again, 'However ...'

James, behind her back, gave Lethington a brisk nod of satisfaction. It was going to be all right.

'However, I am prepared – for the time being – to disregard all that. My immediate concern is to remind my subjects that I am their anointed queen and that we must trust one another. I will not hide from you that I would like to bring them back to the true church, but I will not do so through constraint.'

She turned to face them again. 'Lord James, Secretary Lethington. I am prepared to accept your advice until I am in a position to judge for myself whether it is sound. If you tell me that I should issue a decree of tolerance, I will do so. But tolerance cannot be one-sided. If I am prepared to tolerate the Protestantism of my people, they must be prepared to tolerate my adherence to the church of Rome. I will not give up my private Mass.'

Knox wasn't going to be pleased. 'One Mass is more fearful to me than an army of ten thousand enemies ...' He had said it before, and Lethington had no doubt that he would say it again, many times. Starting, probably, in the pulpit of St Giles next Sunday.

James said, 'Well, that's all right, then. We drafted something, just in case. Read it out, Lethington.'

The draft was short and to the point. Until her majesty had the opportunity to consult with her parliament, the religious *status quo* remained, though with the proviso that no one was to molest any of her domestic servants in the practice of their religion.

Mary said, 'Yes. It will do. You may issue it at once. Now, what is the next item ...'

8

Outside, in her audience chamber, there was someone making a great deal of noise. For a brittle moment, Mary failed to recognise that, although the shouting was no less contumacious than on the previous day, it was not threatening – merely loud, hectoring, and confused about the rôle of the letter 'f' in the alphabet.

'Fitye mean, the queen's in council? Fitye mean she's no' receiving? Fitye mean ye canny tell her I'm here? It's me, man – *me*! Fitye mean, who's "me"?'

Mary glanced at her brother and then at her secretary of state. James's expression was verging on the baleful, but Lethington looked as if he were trying not to laugh. Eyeing the quill in his long fingers, he murmured helpfully, 'The Earl of Huntly.'

It was all very well for Lethington to find it amusing, Mary thought irritably – and then realised that he had justification, because her Master of the Household was French and probably wasn't understanding a word of it.

Without waiting to be asked, Mallie Fleming said, 'Yes, Madame,' and vanished from the room.

In the audience chamber she found not only the Earl of Huntly, but a goodly part of his family – wife, three daughters, and four of his nine sons – who had ridden down from Aberdeen to greet their sovereign.

Big, hulking, long-haired and bellicose, Huntly was about fifty years old and the greatest of the Scots Catholic nobles, ruling, as the queen's lieutenant of the north, a vast area on her semi-official behalf and to his own considerable profit. No doubt he expected to be more important than ever now, Fleming guessed, because – the French soldiery having been sent home incontinent – the queen had no army of her own. If she needed one, she would have to call on the lords to raise their tenants, kinsmen and bondsmen on her behalf. And if she needed an army to subdue the Protestants, it would be the Catholic lords she would have to turn to.

Superficially, Huntly might be forthright to excess, but his character was notoriously changeable, not to say shifty. No one trusted him an inch. Mallie Fleming knew a good deal about him, since he was yet another cousin of hers on the wrong side of the royal blanket.

The sons and daughters ranged in age from the early twenties down to about ten, and one of the daughters was saying collectedly, 'Papa, you mustn't get excited. It's not good for you.'

'*Excited?* Fitye talking about, lassie? I'm not getting excited.' His complexion was an interesting shade of crimson and a rebellious tuft of brown hair was standing upright on the top of his head.

The daughter was about fifteen or sixteen, which meant she must be Jean – the Lady Jean Gordon. Mallie smiled at her mischievously, receiving a pensive stare in return, and then said, 'Cousin Huntly, what a delightful surprise. Her majesty has been awaiting your arrival with the greatest impatience.'

With the exception of Jean Gordon, whose large eyes grew even larger, the family accepted this unlikely statement at its face value.

The countess, a small, redoubtable, grey-haired woman with protruberant eyes and a fortune in gold chains round her neck, silenced her husband with an, 'Och, man, behave yerself, will ye!' and then said, 'Mary Fleming, is it? How's your ma? We only heard about her majesty's arrival late last Thursday, and we set out first thing Friday. We've been on horseback ever since. Where is she, then? Where's the queen?'

It was clear that any postponement of their royal audience would be ill received and, since the queen could not afford to alienate Huntly, Mallie unhesitatingly sacrificed the convenience of Lord James and Secretary Lethington on the altar of necessity.

Smilingly, she said, 'Thank you, cousin, my mother is well. I will go and tell her majesty you are here, while Monsieur de Bussot arranges some refreshment for you. You must be tired after your journey.'

9

Resignedly, Lethington and Lord James gathered their papers together and removed themselves from the royal presence, Lord James sour-faced on principle – to be dismissed for the sake of Huntly, of all people! – but Lethington relieved to be given the opportunity of having the decree of tolerance copied and distributed before the queen changed her mind. One could never be sure.

He nodded cheerfully to Huntly as they passed in the doorway and was rewarded by the slight rearrangement of the big, triangular face which was Huntly's idea of a smile. Huntly, he had always found, was no more difficult to handle than any of the other lords. His motives were unfailingly transparent, and his famous instability arose largely from the fact that he was so easy to provoke; the challenge lay in keeping up with who was currently engaged on provoking him.

James made a hobby of it.

Lethington had found himself involved in one of their more spectacular confrontations two or three months before when the Estates had decreed that all places and monuments of idolatry should be destroyed. Since someone had to do it, the Earls of Arran, Argyll and Glencairn had been sent off to the west and Lord James and Lethington to the north.

It had not been a task Lethington particularly relished but it had turned out to be surprisingly pleasurable. James's men-at-arms had wielded the levers and battering rams while their two leaders had enjoyed the fresh air and the scenery, chased the occasional deer, been entertained in the strong stone keeps of the local lairds, dealt with the messengers from Edinburgh who pursued them around the countryside and, in between times, cantered through a summer landscape smelling of swiftly growing barley and blossom from the bean fields, and talked over problems of state.

'I don't see what ye expect to gain from all this looking ahead,' James had said with mind-numbing frequency. 'With everything changing from day to day, ye *can't* look ahead. The only thing to do is deal with each situation as it arises, and hope for the best.'

'What a pity you don't read Greek. Demosthenes made a very good case for it. If you don't look where you're going, you're unlikely to arrive anywhere except at the end of a blind alley.'

They were sitting their horses outside a chapel near Huntly's keep of Aboyne while James's men-at-arms, whose early enthusiasm had after five weeks given way to boredom, half-heartedly hacked at the pulpit, put their shoulders to the font, and kicked in a window or two preparatory to loading the candlesticks, plate, ornaments and vestments onto one of the packhorses.

James was saying, 'But ye know as well as I do that ...' when they became aware of the thunder of hooves and turned to see a party of about twenty horsemen spurring over the rise above them. Their leader, a great bear of a man, was wearing a full suit of expensive-looking white and gilt armour and brandishing a huge sword as if he had every intention of using it.

Disgustedly pulling his own short arming sword from its scabbard, James jerked his mount's head round, saying, 'Huntly! Wouldn't ye know? That man'll have a seizure one of these days, carrying a hundredweight of armourplate around on his back. And if he doesn't, his horse will.'

Then, raising his voice, he bellowed, 'Don't be a fool, Huntly!'

Lethington, who like James was wearing no more armour than a padded jack, sighed and set a hand to the hilt of his rapier. His travels in Europe had taught him that rapier and dagger were a more effective defence than sword alone, but he knew himself to be sadly out of practice. Nor did he regard the shedding of blood as a useful occupation.

James's sixty men-at-arms, with a ragged cheer, leapt on their horses and formed a square three deep around Lord James and Lethington.

James, sword still loosely in hand, folded his arms comfortably and glowered through the serried ranks of pikes at their attackers. It was the kind of situation he relished.

It looked as if there were going to be an almighty crash but, at the last moment, as Huntly's men swerved off to either side of the square, the earl himself hauled on his reins with such force that his mount came to a furiously tossing halt with the bunched muscles of its hindquarters almost skidding along the ground.

Tipping up his visor, he roared, 'Fitye think ye're doing? Fitye mean by destroying my property? Fitye mean' – it came as something of an afterthought – 'by laying impious hands on the sacred vessels of the Lord?'

'We're carrying out the decree of the Estates, as ye know damn' well.'

'Destruction of all places and monuments of idolatry. Oh, aye!' Huntly rode round the wall of pikes and failed to find an entrance. Returning, he resumed, 'And fit are ye going to do wi' the altar plate, tell me that? Melt it down for to pay for a new plume for your bonnet?'

Gently, Lethington tapped his rapier back into its scabbard.

Lord James said patronisingly, 'It will go into safe keeping.'

'Aye, but whose?'

It was a fair question.

'That will be for the Estates to decide,' James said, and then added unwisely, 'Don't worry, we're not thieves.'

With quiet enjoyment, Lethington waited for the howl of glee from Huntly that inevitably followed.

'Are ye not? Then fit about the vestments and plate from St Giles, eh? That bluidy Edinburgh town council took them into what they called "safe keeping" but fit did they do wi' them? They sold them off just a month back – and what for? For to pay John Knox's wages, that's what for!'

It was perfectly true.

Beady eyes glinting from under his visor, Huntly sheathed his sword and waggled a mailed hand at the packhorses with their loads of ecclesiastical ornaments collected not just from this chapel, but from all the others that had been despoiled during the preceding weeks. Huntly might often act like a fool, but he was perfectly capable of marshalling a sensible argument when his own interests were at stake.

'I don't give a docken for your "safe keeping" or your "honesty"! The law's on *my* side, fitever ye say. Destruction of places and monuments means buildings, not their contents. And the church of Rome is who the contents belong to. Ye canny just confiscate them.' There was a metallic squeaking from enamelled bevor and gilded gorget as he shook his head

49

reprovingly. 'And as for putting them in safe keeping – well, even if ye're not thinking of thieving this lot to pay John Knox his next quarter's wages, it would be a terrible burden on your Protestant principles to have to guard the sacred vessels of idolatry. So I'll make a suggestion.' He smiled sunnily.

Since James appeared to have been deprived of speech, Lethington spoke for the first time. 'Yes?'

'I'll do ye a favour. I'll take them off your hands.'

'Ye-e-s?'

'Och, not for myself! No, no. I've already got the plate and ornaments from St Machar's tucked away in one of my dungeons, and this stuff can go with them until it's needed again.'

'And when is that likely to be?'

'Och, man! Ye know as well as I do. When the queen comes back and restores Scotland to the church of Rome, of course.'

10

James had tried to haggle, but no one could remember which chapel had been the source of which ornaments, and since many of the chapels had been either on Huntly's vast estates or those of the vacant earldom of Moray, which he had been administering and profiting from for the last dozen years, it was Huntly who won in the end. He was too important, too powerful to alienate.

James had controlled his temper well. He prided himself on never raising his voice in anger. Coldly, he had conceded Huntly's point. Coldly, he had watched Huntly and his men ride away with their booty.

Coldly, afterwards, he had said, 'He will be sorry that he crossed me.'

11

Now, in the gardens of Holyroodhouse, the queen had found a stretch of rough grass tucked away beyond some trellises. 'Good!' she said. 'We shall have our archery butts here. Seton, please find Lord James and Secretary Lethington and tell them that Lord Huntly has gone and that I am now free to continue our discussions. Bring them here. I am tired of being indoors.'

'Yes, Madame.' Seton curtsied and went.

Mallie Fleming watched pleasedly. She had a wager with Livingston as to how many times each of the Maries said, 'Yes, Madame,' in the course of a day, and Seton had just won her a point.

'Perhaps we might also have a lawn for pall mall, Madame?' suggested Beaton. It was a game to which she was much attached, admirably setting off the grace of a shapely shoulder and finely turned wrist without involving too much expenditure of energy.

The queen said, 'Of *course*,' and went on wickedly, 'But we must also find somewhere to lay out a few holes of golf, and Lord James tells me there are deer in the park for the chase, and space enough for flying the hawks. And you know, I have been looking at that great hill there – Arthur's Seat, is it called? – and wondering whether we might not take up mountaineering. Did you say something, Fleming? That *cannot* have been a groan?'

'No, Madame.'

It was true. Her sharp intake of breath had been caused by something entirely different and she was grateful that the queen had misinterpreted it.

Lord James and Secretary Lethington were striding towards them along one of the trellised walks, two men of much the same age, much alike in height, dressed much the same in dark, elegant doublets and hose that would have been equally at home at the royal courts of England or France, with silken blackwork embroidery on their fine white linen collars and cuffs, and black velvet court bonnets rakishly angled on well-barbered heads over smooth-skinned, weather-tanned faces.

But they could not have been more different. It was not simply that James's hair was foxy red and Lethington's raven black; that James's eyes were round and of that pure dark glossy brown that always looked either startled or censorious, whereas Lethington's were clear, humorous, and translucently grey. It was not even that James's mouth appeared always to be under lock and key, whereas Lethington's was friendly and flexible; that James's nose was long and bony where Lethington's was classically aquiline; that James would some day be stout, but Lethington never.

James had no charm at all. Lethington ...

Mallie Fleming lowered her eyes in case they should give her away. Even as her heart ran wild, there was a voice inside her head reminding her fiercely of pride and self-discipline and the stupidity of unrequited loving. Such a man could have no possible interest in the queen's four frivolous ladies. He probably couldn't even tell them apart yet.

51

When the queen glanced up from the knot bed, it seemed to Lethington that her manner was slightly less chill than it had been earlier, although perhaps it was no more than pleasure in the gardens and the reappearance of the sun after so many grey days. Knox was already making capital out of those. The very face of heaven had reflected the sorrow, dolour, darkness and impiety the queen had brought with her to Scotland. The sun had not been seen to shine two days before her arrival, nor two days after ...

It had certainly been a most unseasonable August.

'Let us resume our business,' the queen said.

'Yes. Your majesty will wish to consider the composition of your privy council,' Lethington said. 'It need not be appointed immediately, of course ...'

A scent that was pungent but not unattractive gusted into the air as the queen brushed her hand over a shrub with many-fingered leaves and bright yellow flowers and raised a questioning eyebrow at him. He shook his head. Horticulture was a closed book to him.

With genuine amusement, she said, 'I thought not. It is rue, the herb of grace. I would not expect you to know about that. Where the other meaning of the word is concerned – well, we will come to that in due course.' Straightening up, she turned and began to stroll along the grassy walk. 'Let us, in the meantime, talk of governments and privy councils.'

Lord James, considerately though unnecessarily giving Lethington time to recover from this unheralded attack, fell into step beside her and began laying down the law. 'Yes. Ye'll need to keep a balance. Ye'll need to ...'

She stopped him with a raised hand, traces of amusement still in her face. 'I'll need to? My dear James, be careful. Don't tell me what I *need* to do.'

'Oh, all right, then,' he said huffily. 'You tell *us*.'

Flattery and soft words, in James's view, too often served to obscure God's truth and on that basis he had always refused to cultivate the social graces. His bluntness contributed powerfully to the impression of moral virtue that was his most striking characteristic. People trusted him because they considered that a plainspoken man, a man who said what he thought, must be an honest man. It did not occur to them that a man who said what he thought did not necessarily say *all* that he thought.

Mary was so unaccustomed to being treated with anything other than the deference due to a queen that she found James's tone more peculiar than offensive. Her eyes widening, she said, 'The duty of my privy council is to assist me in governing my realm by giving me advice that I may choose to take, or to ignore. It should therefore include men of differing opinions, men from different parts of the country, and representatives of both the Catholic and the reformed churches. Am I correct?'

'Yes, well that's a fair summary, I suppose, though I hope ye *won't* ignore the advice of men who know a lot more than you do. Ye'll want ...' He trotted out all the expected names. His own, of course. Then eleven lords – including Châtelherault, Argyll, Glencairn, Atholl, Huntly, Bothwell and Morton – and the four officers of state headed by Secretary Lethington.

Mary said lightly, 'What? No John Knox?' Then, 'I will consider your suggestions and give you my decision in due course. Now, secretary ...'

13

'I instructed you, I believe, to sever your connection with the English court. Have you done so?'

He had known that the question must arise. If she had been older, she might have approached it differently, but she was young and inexperienced, and it was natural that she should feel the need to assert her authority.

'No, your majesty.'

'You are very cool about it for a servant who has deliberately chosen to disobey his sovereign.' Her anger over his disobedience was real enough, though it was tempered by the recognition that Lethington must know as well as she did that she needed some connection with the English court. What she wanted was to feel that the situation was under her direction and control, not his.

'There were reasons for maintaining the connection which I believed your majesty would approve.'

'Then why did you not tell me what they were?'

'Confidentiality. They had to do with your claim to the throne of England and I was reluctant to commit them to writing.'

It was not what she had expected, but the pause lasted no longer than a heartbeat before she said, 'There are such things as ciphers.'

'The orthodox ciphers are easy to break, and I understood that your French secretaries were not yet familiar with the principles laid out in the *Steganographia* of Trithemius.'

Nothing in the world would have induced her ask who Trithemius was. 'Then perhaps you might care to tell me now.' She gestured dismissal to the Maries, who regretfully dropped back a few paces.

'Yes?' the queen said.

14

Lethington had long been aware that Scotland's one hope for the future lay in union with the old enemy, England – not a union born of weakness, bringing Scotland under an English, rather than a French yoke, but a voluntary union that would give full acknowledgement to Scotland's value in the scheme of things. He had not been able to see how to achieve it until, while he was negotiating on the lords' behalf for English arms and money to bring the civil war at home to an end, he had made the acquaintance of England's new queen, Elizabeth. She was clever and witty, and Lethington had taken a liking to her although she had not dazzled him, as she did so many other men.

It had not taken him long to discover that, although she was clever at tactics, she had no talent for strategy. After the ups and downs of her early life, it was scarcely surprising that her sole concern should be to survive from one day to the next, but she appeared to have no dynastic ambition, not to care who followed after her. When demands for her to marry and produce heirs had been raised in parliament, she had dismissed them with some sentimental rhetoric about being married to the kingdom of England.

She had been playing political games, of course – even while making a spectacle of herself with her Master of the Horse – but in truth there were few eligible husbands on the market. Marriage for queens, even more than kings, was a bargaining counter in the endless game of foreign alliances, and after the disaster of her sister Mary Tudor's alliance with Philip of Spain, Elizabeth could not afford to enter into any but a Protestant match. It was a pity that she had refused the Scots lords' opportunist offer of Châtelherault's son, the Protestant Earl of Arran, since any child of theirs could – if Mary died childless – have inherited both thrones. Châtelherault had simmered irritably for months over her dismissal of Arran as 'too poor and not personally agreeable'.

Secretary Cecil was determined that Elizabeth should marry, but Lethington could not imagine her conceding even a token share of power to a husband. And if she did not marry, it seemed to him that Scotland need not, after all, be the disregarded junior partner in any union with England. Not if a Stewart were to ascend the English throne.

15

'Yes?' Mary said again.

Unhurriedly, Lethington replied, 'There has been much talk of your contesting Elizabeth's right to the throne of England which, however justifiable it may be, has led to a certain tension between ourselves and your majesty's cousin, Queen Elizabeth. I am sure you appreciate that, as things stand, your claim could only be enforced by war. Since Scotland does not have the strength – or, to be truthful, the inclination – to go to war, such enforcement would fall to France. You know better than we whether France, now that you are no longer its queen, has the will to pursue your claim. Especially in view of her own problems at the present time.'

'Go on,' Mary said, oblivious to the salty breeze that, finding its way into the garden, was catching the gauzy white veil that fell from the back of her cap and sending it billowing in the air. One of her ladies darted forward helpfully, but the queen waved her away.

'Go on,' she repeated.

'Lord James and I have discussed this at length, and in our view any attempt to unseat Elizabeth would be doomed from the start.'

There was no reason, Mary thought, for him to know that she had long ago come to the same conclusion. He and James were probably terrified that she was going to begin talking about invading England.

'So?'

'As I am sure you are aware, Elizabeth declares that she has no intention of marrying. And even if she were to marry, she might die without issue. She is also nine years older than your majesty, and life is uncertain.' Lethington paused. 'What I am saying is that, if she could be persuaded to acknowledge you as her heir presumptive, you might – without war and perhaps, even, in the not too distant future – find yourself able to take up your rightful position on the throne of England.'

There was a long silence. Then she said, 'Or if not I, my son. For I must marry again.'

'Yes.'

In terms of practical politics, Lethington knew that what he had in mind was full of imponderables, but if ever a game were worth the

55

candle ... He was offering Mary something that would satisfy both her royal dignity and her sense of justice – which might, he thought, be all that *she* wanted – while at the same time opening the way to the union of the crowns that was becoming his own obsession.

Mary said, 'It offends me to hear you say, "if she could be persuaded". My right to the throne is infinitely superior to hers. However, I understand your argument.' There was a faraway look in her amber eyes, and a hint of excitement. 'Perhaps you will tell me how your persuasions are progressing?'

Her secretary of state, accustomed to tailoring his words to suit his hearer, said calmly, 'I have had a favourable response from Secretary Cecil. A little evasive, perhaps, though that is to be expected, and he does not say whether he has discussed the matter with Elizabeth herself.'

Mary had been well trained. 'And what would be the *quid pro quo*?'

There was one, of course, but although it marched more closely with Scotland's desires than with Mary's own, Lethington did not conceal it. 'It would be impossible for Elizabeth to acknowledge you if there appeared to be any danger of your attempting, as Mary Tudor did, to reimpose Catholicism on England.'

Mary said, 'I have already made it clear that my policy will be one of religious tolerance. I even recall saying as much to Sir Nicholas Throckmorton, Elizabeth's ambassador in France. Is that not enough?'

'You must prove it in Scotland first.'

It had been the deciding factor. Lord James had been dismissive of Mary's claim to the throne of England until Lethington had suggested that it could be a means of controlling her if she returned to Scotland determined on bringing the country back to France and Rome – which she had the power to do, even though she was only eighteen years old and a green girl. Monarchs always had such power, because there were other monarchs to come to their aid if a rebellious people tried to contest it.

'But that will take some time.' Mary did not seem to be offended.

Lord James, having left everything to Lethington because he had a way with words, decided that enough was enough. 'Well, that's all right then,' he said. 'If you're agreed on the principle, we can get on with the practice. Ye're right about negotiations taking a while, but negotiations always do.' Privately, he thought that the longer such negotiations took, the better, because once Mary was assured of the English succession – if she ever was – any hold he and Lethington had over her would disappear.

'I'll tell you what,' he went on bracingly. 'If you leave it all to us, and follow our advice in the meantime about how ye should govern Scotland, we'll make sure that Elizabeth declares you her successor. That's a promise. What d'ye say?'

Unlike his sister, he failed to observe the slightly pained look on Lethington's face, and was taken aback when she giggled. 'What a decisive man you are, James dear,' she said, 'but I have the feeling that, although it is you who make the promises, it is Secretary Lethington who will have to do all the work.'

It was satisfying to see the responsive glint in Lethington's eyes. She wondered whether she ought to remind him that he would have to work very hard indeed to overcome her distrust of him, but decided to hold her peace.

Instead, she embraced both of them in an enchanting smile. 'And I think he should start immediately. I would like him to leave for Elizabeth's court at the earliest possible moment. Tomorrow would not be too soon.'

Chapter Four

SEPTEMBER 1561

1

Jean Gordon said, 'Papa, you mustn't get excited. It's not good for you.' She seemed to say it almost as often as she said her *Aves*, and she didn't know why she bothered. He never paid the slightest attention. But for once, he didn't yelp, 'Fitye talking aboot? I'm not getting excited!' For once, he yelped, 'Fit else d'ye expect?'

Edinburgh was giving the queen a ceremonial welcome, during which she was to be presented with the keys to the city. Various theatrical spectacles had been arranged to mark the stages of her ride back down the royal mile from the castle to Holyroodhouse, and now Huntly had discovered that one of the spectacles was not on the official programme but had been mounted in a spirit of regrettably private enterprise.

'D'ye know what they're bluidy well going to do? Burn a bluidy effigy of a priest right under her nose! It's that bluidy Protestant town council! Of course I'm getting excited! Oot of my way, lassie. I'll soon settle them!'

Settling them turned out to involve an intricate and not altogether satisfactory series of compromises, so that when her majesty's cavalcade reached the Salt Tron it was confronted by a bonfire with not one but three human effigies crackling in the flames, though at least none of them was a priest.

With the provost muttering an unconvincing, 'Tut-tut!' on her right, Mary turned to find Huntly pushing towards her from the left.

'Cousin!' Her greeting was noticeably less dulcet than usual.

'It's Korah, Dathan and Abiram,' he explained.

Mary was not fluent in the Book of Numbers. 'Indeed?'

Unaware that for her majesty it was almost the last straw, Jean Gordon intervened helpfully, 'They're meant to represent the evil of false sacrifices.'

'How interesting.'

For a terrible moment, Jean saw the reflected flames take on a life of their own in the queen's golden eyes.

So, prosaically – since people losing their tempers was something she was well accustomed to – she added, 'It's more fun down the road. They're slaughtering a dragon in the meat market at the Nether Bow.'

The flames flickered, and then the queen laughed. 'I look forward to it. Lady Jean, you must come to court. I approve of you!'

2

Resplendent in cloth of gold and her most magnificent rubies, Mary had dined with the provost and burgesses in the Great Hall of the castle and it had been a conscientiously polite but dreary affair. Then she had been handed into a throne-like litter – which showed an alarming tendency to wobble, the six sturdy lairds shouldering the poles not being all of the same height – to be carried back down a Highgait lined with her rejoicing subjects to Holyroodhouse.

The tone of the spectacles designed to enliven her progress had been set at the Butter Tron weighhouse, where, from a high scaffolding draped with the sun, moon and stars of a vividly painted cloth sky, a small, worried-looking angel had descended, dangling on the end of a wire, awkwardly bearing the keys of the city and two large books bound in purple velvet. Mary had been genuinely amused until she leaned over to receive the books and discovered that one of them was the Bible of the reformed church and the other the Protestant Service Book. Next, at the Tolbooth, there had been four gauzily clad, blushing maidens gabbling extracts from a famous – or infamous – satire on Catholicism and kings, and after that a further succession of spectacles whose superficial gaiety had failed to mask their doctrinaire intent. As for Korah, Dathan and Abiram ...

By the time Mary reached Holyrood again she was convinced that John Knox had been behind it all. So, with James's grudging assent, she summoned him to an audience two mornings later.

'I wish Lethington was here,' James said fretfully, but Lethington had left for England three days before and it fell to James to try and explain Knox to his sister before the preacher was ushered in.

'He's a good man,' he said. 'He's a great man, in fact, but maybe a wee bit intransigent.'

Which was one way of putting it. James knew all too well that Knox

59

couldn't be relied on to make the smallest concession to anyone, not even Mary, queen though she was. In his view, since he had God on his side he didn't need anyone else; his own admonitions and God's will would suffice to bring about the unchallenged and unchallengeable supremacy of the Protestant faith. Lethington said – though not in public – that he was the kind of man who started holy wars and it was a pity he couldn't be brought to accept that God and John Knox would lose nothing by listening to some intelligent political advice from the more worldly-wise among His congregation.

'Knox is so convinced he's right,' James went on, 'and of course he *is* right, that he doesn't care who he offends. He won't compromise. There's only one thing that matters to him, the actual, revealed Word of God.'

'He sounds captivating.'

'I don't like this meeting,' James said. 'I'm not easy about it. I know ye're good at charming people, but ...' He broke off, shaking his head. 'Aye, well. We'll see. Ye'll just need to take care not to upset him.'

She turned an astounded gaze on him, and then, since he appeared not to understand, said succinctly, 'It is he who should not upset me.'

3

He was not a very tall man, neither was he a young man. His beard, long and waving, was thickly streaked with grey, and he was wearing the formal dress of the European scholar, a black, shawl-collared overgown and a shallow, brimmed biretta over a caul. But however ordinary he at first appeared, his immense self-assurance and the size and brilliance of his eyes gave him a presence that was far from ordinary. Mary, who had thought of him – for no very good reason – as loud, coarse, a huckster of fraudulent truths, swiftly revised her assessment.

'Master Knox,' she greeted him, smiling into the extraordinary eyes.

There was no softening in them, no flicker of response. He merely stared at her as if she were a piece of furniture.

She was not accustomed to having her charm rejected, but she had no intention of going to war. Despite what she had said to James, she knew very well that it was foolish to provoke someone whose word carried so much weight. A gentle skirmish, she had thought, to teach the man that she was not to be trifled with.

At least he was sufficiently house-trained to address her as your majesty, even to give her a qualified welcome back to Scotland.

Momentarily disconcerted to discover that, Scot though he was, he had an English accent, she swiftly recovered herself and expressed sympathy with him over the death of his wife the previous year, whereupon he commiserated with her – if rather brusquely – over the death of her husband. She said how much pleasure the citizens of Edinburgh had given her on the night of her arrival, with their fiddles and rebecs, and how delighted she had been by the masques and spectacles of two days before. He said the money would have been better spent on something useful, like feeding the poor.

Which effectively put an end to the courtesies.

She said, 'Yes, let us talk frankly, Master Knox, for I must take issue with you on certain matters where I believe you not to be acting in the best interests of the country.'

It was clear that he had been waiting for something of the sort. Before her startled gaze, he seemed to grow a foot in stature and his eyes blazed out at her, whether with godly passion or ungodly loathing she could not at first be sure. But, staring into the long face, with its prominent, narrow-boned nose, its unexpectedly full-lipped and sensual mouth, Mary abruptly became aware that he was not only a strikingly handsome man in the dark, harsh mould of her Guise uncles, but also a man possessed of an overpowering animal magnetism.

For the first time she had an inkling of how he had succeeded in taking over the hearts and minds of half her realm. She had known that he was a dangerous man but not, until now, just how dangerous.

4

He said, 'If to preach the truth of God, to expose the deceit, pride and tyranny of the Roman Antichrist, is to act against the best interests of the country, then I cannot be acquitted.'

It was not the perfect start for a cool and rational discussion of the religious and political situation.

Mary said, 'I see. But let us for the moment put our religious differences aside. In your book, *The first blast of the trumpet against the monstrous regiment of women*, you say, "To promote a woman to bear rule, superiority, dominion or empire above any realm, nation or city, is repugnant to nature, contumelious to God, a thing most contrary to his revealed will and approved ordinance". How dare you deny my very right to rule?'

61

'The book was written not against your majesty but against Mary Tudor, that wicked Jezebel of England.'

'Possibly, but it argues against all women.'

She barely listened to his reply – which was long, intricate, and liberally besprinkled with references to Plato, St Paul, the Emperor Nero, Christ Jesus and Beelzebub – because her mind was running ahead.

On the Sunday after she had issued her decree of tolerance, he had preached a violent sermon against her in St Giles. 'Idolatry is the cause why God destroyeth the posterity of princes ... one Mass is more fearful to me than an army of ten thousand enemies ...' He was a fanatic and he had to be stopped. James said that the Word of God was, for Knox, the first, last and only word. If she could defeat him there ...

When he had finished, she said, 'Very well. You believe you have Biblical authority for dismissing a woman's right to rule. But explain to me, please ...'

Her heart was pounding as she met the domineering eyes, felt the power of the man. It was not, after all, a skirmish. It was war, and not a war of the intellect, of religious disputation. For no good reason, it was intense and personal.

She began again. 'The Bible also says that the order of society laid down by God is designed to prevent the world relapsing into chaos, and that God commands subjects to obey their princes. That means whether or not the prince is a woman. And it means in everything, including religion.'

He did not wave his arms, nor beat his breast, nor indulge in any of the dramatic gestures to which preachers habitually resorted. He stood rigidly erect, hands clasped before him, and pointed out that, if subjects took their faith from their rulers rather than from God, the children of Abraham would have followed the religion of the Pharaohs and the Apostles would have clung to the gods of Rome. Where, then, would have been the religion of Christ Jesus?

She could not deny it, but neither could she afford to leave it there. 'They did not, however, raise their swords against their princes.'

'God had not given them the means.'

The implication horrified her. She exclaimed, 'You are saying that it is acceptable for subjects, if they *do* have the means, to resist their princes *by violence?*'

'If a father in a frenzy is about to slay his own children, is it wrong for the children to disarm him and lock him up until the frenzy has left him?

It is the same with princes and their subjects. This, Madam, is not disobedience to princes but obedience to God.'

He was a terrible man, a dreadful man, a demagogue without human feeling, a man who knew everything of God's wrath and nothing of God's love. He was saying almost outright that, if it suited him, he would summon every Protestant in the land to declare war on her. Real war, not a war of words.

She had not realised what a nervous strain the last ten days had been until she found the uncontrollable tears of anger and frustration leaping to her eyes. She gasped, 'I see that my people should obey you and not me; should do what they wish, not what I command. I see that I am to be subject to them, not they to me.'

'God forbid that I should tell anyone to obey me! Subjection to God is the greatest dignity that flesh can get upon the face of the earth, for it shall carry them to everlasting glory.'

Her voice soaring, she almost screamed at him, 'How dare you speak to me like that! How dare you speak as if God is yours alone! How dare you speak as if my passion for God, my love of God, my faith in God, are inferior to yours? As if at the judgement seat you will be raised up and I cast down!'

Knox said nothing and, hearing the echoes of her own anger and anguish, she knew that she had given him a weapon against her. With an immense effort of will, she brought her voice back to cool and rational normal. 'We both worship the Lord truly, but in different ways. To me, the church of Rome is the true church. It is not so for you. Can we not try to meet on the ground that is common to us both?'

They continued to talk, but the purpose had gone. Whatever Mary's own religious beliefs, she was primarily concerned with political practicalities; whatever Knox's political aims, he could see them only in terms of the gospels.

In the end, Beaton came to say that it was noon, and her majesty was called to dinner.

5

Knox went away satisfied in his victory but disturbed in his mind. He had expected an arrogant, Frenchified young woman, well taught but not intelligent, charming but false, and – since that was what he had expected – that was what he had found. What he had not expected was a young woman who evoked a human response in him; a young woman who had been as aware of him as he was of her; a Mary who was also Eve the temptress, a very personal instrument of the devil.

It violently reinforced his need to destroy her. 'If there be not in her,' he declared later that day, 'a proud mind, a crafty wit and a heart obdurate against God and his truth, I am more wrong than I have been in all my life before.'

6

'I knew it was a mistake,' James said, and his sister replied tartly, 'Then perhaps it would have been more useful if you had participated in our discussion instead of just standing looking on.'

'Well, it was difficult with you on the one side and Knox on the other.'

The rain, which had been threatening all morning, began beating against the window and Mary shivered from a cold more imagined than real. In a few weeks, when her new cooks and valets and chamber women arrived from France to help turn Holyrood into something more like a royal palace, she would begin dining in state. In the meantime, it was pleasant to be cosy and informal in her retiring room.

Pushing away her trencher of fish stew, so heavily sauced with cinnamon that she had no idea what kind of fish it was, she said, 'Really? But I fear you will have to choose between myself and Master Knox, decide where your loyalties lie. They cannot be divided. That man believes that it is lawful for subjects to resist an "ungodly" prince. Do you agree with him?'

After a moment, to her unqualified astonishment, he leaned over and gave her a badly aimed peck on the cheek. 'You're not an ungodly prince,' he said. 'You're my wee sister.'

With something between a sob and a laugh, she said, 'Oh, *James*!'

But she had noted the evasion.

The pigeon was no improvement on the fish. Rejecting it with a sigh, she raised her goblet of Gascon wine and sipped thoughtfully.

'Enough of Master Knox,' she said. 'I have been thinking. It is time I showed myself in other parts of my realm. This seems a good opportunity. Where should I go? Linlithgow, Stirling, Perth, St Andrews … ?'

Queen Elizabeth of England had set off on her summer travels weeks before – the royal progress that offered not only a change of scene, but took the court out of London during the plague season, emptied Whitehall and Greenwich palaces so that they could be cleaned, and enabled her subjects in the countryside to see and admire a queen who would otherwise have been a stranger to them.

Elizabeth had made one change from her father's day. Henry VIII had in general stayed at his own lesser residences, of which he maintained about fifty scattered strategically around the south-east of England, but Elizabeth – who was of a more parsimonious disposition – preferred to quarter herself on those of her nobles to whom she wished to show favour. Or, said some, disfavour. Entertaining the queen for a few days was one of the fastest known routes to bankruptcy, since few houses and even fewer incomes were equipped to accommodate, feed and amuse not only the queen, but throngs of courtiers and state officials, the entire company of the Yeomen of the Guard, an escort of Gentlemen Pensioners, and all twenty household departments, including cellar, spicery, buttery and laundry. The royal baggage train of horse-drawn carts numbered close on three hundred.

Ten days after leaving Edinburgh, Lethington located the court at the moated manor of Shepburgh, near Notwich. Since his rôle as envoy of the queen of Scots required him to stand on his dignity, he had to insist on the harassed Gentleman Usher ejecting a trio of Elizabeth's lesser lords from one of the lodging parlours in order to provide him with an appropriately distinguished bed for the night. His men-at-arms would have to fend for themselves, which they were used to, but Lethington had to invite his three clerks to share his lodging, because he needed them close at hand.

The inconvenience did not trouble him. He was no stranger to it. He had been fifteen when he graduated from St Andrews and twenty-five when he had taken up his post with Mary of Guise, and most of the years between had been spent studying, and occasionally tutoring for derisory fees, at the universities of Paris and Montpellier, Bologna, Leiden and Cracow. There had been a particularly tight period in Prague, when the delectable young woman called Anna who had been his mistress at the time had annoyed him greatly by selling an armful of his books so that the pair of them could eat. Even today, he was still apt to think of food as no more than fuel, and was immune to the offers of sinecures and bribes that frequently came his way, simply because titles and possessions didn't interest him.

It didn't mean that he was immune to the colour, vitality and extravagance of the court of Elizabeth. As he set off to arrange an audience with the queen, his spirits soared. At the court of Scotland in the days of Mary of Guise, there had always been a sense of carefulness, and since her overthrow there had been no court at all. Lethington placed no particular value on the light-hearted and light-headed company he now saw around him, but at least they didn't all look like mourners trying to find a funeral.

Shouldering his way politely through the crowds in the hall, he received friendly nods from a few gentlemen of his acquaintance and sparkling smiles from a number of ladies, all of them brilliant in satins and diamonds although it was not yet midday. He had been told that Secretary Cecil might be in the gallery, so, suiting his pace and manner to the company, he strolled up the wide stone staircase and – lean, sardonic and as unruffled as if he had just ridden four miles rather than four hundred – entered the gallery to find himself face to face with the queen of England.

He dropped instantly to one knee which, after ten relentless days in the saddle, was not as easy as he succeeded in making it look, and she, giving him her hand, greeted him with flattering enthusiasm. She was dressed extravagantly as always, in a cream satin gown embroidered all over in coral and gold, and among the pearls and beads round her neck was a long gold chain with enough weight of bullion in its swinging tassel to black the eye of any kneeling envoy who failed to keep his wits about him.

'Get up, man,' she said. 'Get up. We have missed you these last months. We are starved for Latin tags. Robert, here, has no education. Come, walk beside me. You may take Robert's place. Go away, Robert!'

Lord Robert Dudley – whose cream satin doublet and trunkhose, slashed with coral, mirrored the colours of Elizabeth's gown too closely for it to be accidental – was the queen's Master of the Horse and, according to popular belief, her lover. Raising a satanic eyebrow at Lethington, whom he knew well, he fell back a step or two among the crowd of courtiers who, like the queen, took their daily exercise in the form of a half-hour's stroll up and down any available gallery. It was what the doctors recommended.

Elizabeth beamed at Lethington, and said, 'Well?' He knew that she liked him but – as someone else's envoy – did not trust him an inch. The feeling was mutual. He beamed back at her.

66

Because the two queens' personalities were so different, he had forgotten that there was a physical resemblance between them, though it did not go far beyond their pale skins and reddish hair. Elizabeth was five or six inches shorter than Mary, but had none of her cousin's air of delicacy, and whereas Mary – in Lethington's as yet limited experience – appeared soft, warm and graceful even when displeased, Elizabeth was bright, brittle and controlled except when, for her own good reasons, she chose to lose her temper. The essential difference, perhaps, was that Mary had always known herself to be a queen and had the easy assurance that went with it, whereas Elizabeth, for the first twenty-five years of her life, had never known whether she was destined for the throne or the scaffold.

Mary's charm made her appealing as well as lovely; Elizabeth, though handsome enough, seemed to Lethington to lack sexual attractiveness. She was, however, clever, formidable and wilfully unpredictable. Depending on her mood, or her political judgement – it could be hard to tell which – she was capable of keeping ambassadors, emissaries and supplicants waiting about for days, or else hurrying them through their business so fast that they found themselves leaving before they had properly arrived.

Since Lethington had not formally presented his credentials or been formally received, they should, as they walked, have spoken inconsequentially of the weather or the portraits on the walls. Instead, before they had taken three steps, Elizabeth ruined his elegantly structured plan of campaign by saying, 'Let us not trouble about the formalities. Tom Randolph writes that my cousin, your queen, has come home.'

Lethington gave a mock groan, as he knew would be expected of him. 'Alas, he has forestalled me. I was here to make intimation of it.'

'Yes, it is a sad thing. *"Nihil est dictum, quod non est dictum prius".*'

There is nothing one can say that has not been said before.

He smiled. 'To which I can only reply as Donatus did, *"Pereant, inquit, qui ante nos nostra dixerunt".*'

'Bravo! "Confound those who have uttered our words before us." Robert, did you hear that? However, you may tell my cousin that, although it comes late, I take her message kindly.'

'Thank you. I am also required to convey to you her majesty's desire to increase the amity between your two realms.'

Elizabeth had little time for empty rhetoric except when she herself was its source. 'Well, that's easily done,' she declared robustly. 'All it requires is her ratification of the Treaty of Edinburgh. Have you brought it?'

Lethington, whose outlook could best have been described as

67

philosophical pragmatism, was not above being irritated by people whose main object in life was to make other people's lives difficult. It was one of Elizabeth's most conspicuous talents.

The Treaty of Edinburgh, which had ended the civil war fourteen months earlier, had been a three-way affair involving Scotland, England and France, and had been signed by representatives of Mary and François pending ratification by the royal couple themselves. This had never been given, although most of the military terms had since been fulfilled. Lethington knew very well that there was only one unfulfilled clause in the treaty in which Elizabeth was even remotely interested – the one requiring Mary and François to cease quartering their arms with those of England 'hereafter'. Which implied that Mary should give up her claim to the English throne for all time to come.

And that, of course, was now entirely contrary to Mary's, James's and Lethington's own political purposes.

Coolly, he said, 'Since the treaty placed certain duties jointly on her majesty and her husband, and since her majesty has since become a widow, there is some doubt as to the continuing validity of some of the clauses. When I left Edinburgh there had not been time to summon the Estates to discuss the matter, and my queen had not expected you, Madame, to look for an answer so soon.'

'God's death! Don't play lawyers' tricks with me, Lethington. It's your queen's claim to my crown and that word "hereafter" that worry you, is it not? Well, if you are unhappy, that is your misfortune. Because I will not – I *will* not – have her continue to aim at *my* throne!'

Abruptly, she stopped and glared at him, her eyebrows, plucked almost to invisibility, raised over large, round eyes that were as brown and shining as chestnuts. 'You have the impertinence to smile, Lord Secretary?'

He did not withdraw the smile. 'An apposite quotation slipped into my mind, and I cannot decide whether you are more likely to be amused by it, or to send me to the Tower.'

'You will have to try me, then, will you not?'

'If you command, Madame. It was, *"Hoc volo, sic iubeo, sit pro ratione voluntas"*.' He waited, invisibly holding his breath, while anger, concentration and finally satisfaction chased one other across her face.

'Ha! I have it,' she exclaimed. 'That jaundiced old reprobate, Juvenal! "It is my will, so let it be! Let my wishes stand substitute for reason".'

Then, the wrath gone as if it had never been, she said admiringly,

'What a risk taker you are, my friend! I know of no one else who would dare to put *me* in my place!'

'Would I attempt such a thing, your majesty? It was the merest coincidence that the quotation came to my mind.'

'No, no. Do not undo your good work. Let us by all means follow the dictates of reason. Secretary Cecil will arrange for you to attend me in my presence chamber. But not now, since we are called to dine.' She turned her head. 'Robert! You will give up your place at the high table to Lethington.'

Lethington could not imagine Mary treating her lover like a lapdog, but one could never tell.

8

No one mentioned Scotland or the Scots for the next twenty-four hours. After dinner there was dancing, and after that a travelling company of players performed *The Union of the Two Noble and Illustre Families of Lancaster and York* in the hall while bored young courtiers played cards or backgammon in the gallery. Then there was supper, followed by a masque in which Robert Dudley appeared as Orpheus and was much applauded by the queen, and then more dancing. Next morning came a deer hunt during which Elizabeth, on her palfrey, lurked behind a screened butt and took occasional aim with her arbalest at the deer which, brought in for the purpose, were being driven back and forth in a netted enclosure before her.

Not until the hour before dinner was Lethington summoned to appear before the queen who, this time, was standing in front of her scarlet chair of state in the ground floor parlour that had been commandeered as her presence chamber. Secretary Cecil, Lord Robert Dudley, and three of her ladies were in attendance.

This time, the discussion was ruthlessly to the point.

Without preliminary, Elizabeth said, 'I am aware from Lord James Stewart's letters to me that you and he hope to discourage my cousin from adopting a pro-French, pro-Catholic policy by offering her the succession to the throne of England.'

Privately cursing James for his ill-placed frankness, Lethington smiled and said, 'That is an oversimplification.'

'Perhaps, but I see no reason to wrap things up. What would she offer in exchange?'

It was one of Elizabeth's peculiarities that she spoke two different versions of the English language. In public, her style could be so convoluted as to be barely comprehensible even to the liveliest intelligence, while in private her bluntness was little short of brutal. There was nothing in between, and the only thing one could be sure of was that, if she was being obscure, it was because she meant to be.

Lethington, thinking rapidly, said, 'My queen would surrender all present claims to your throne and ratify a suitably revised version of the treaty. I cannot urge too strongly on your majesty that the perpetual amity between Scotland and England which so many of us desire can only be assured if my queen is a party to it.'

'But I, also, must be a party to it, and princes do not always have a liking for their successors.'

It was an unexpectedly honest admission. Lethington glanced at Cecil, a small, thin, inscrutable black figure outlined against the flowered wall hangings, then at Rob Dudley, a handsome man tastefully got up, today, in scarlet and grey to complement Elizabeth's scarlet-embroidered pink. Dudley grinned cheerfully back at him because, Lethington guessed, he regarded the whole question of Mary's succession as academic. When he achieved his ambition of marrying Elizabeth and fathering the next king of England, Mary's claim would become irrelevant.

'Such likes and dislikes are surely unworthy of your majesty,' Lethington said.

Elizabeth's lips twisted and her eyes went dark. 'Your perception is at fault, my friend. I was not speaking from emotion or pique. I know my people, you see. If they were out of sympathy with me, they would go to my heir, would choose the rising in preference to the falling star. Think how dangerous it could be if that heir were a powerful princess and a near neighbour. You cannot expect me to love my own winding sheet.'

After a considering moment, he said, 'True. But if, in default of the English succession, my queen were to force Scotland back to Catholicism – as with French help she might – the danger would be even greater. Because you have many Catholics still in your realm, perhaps more than you know, and my queen and country could therefore become – though God preserve us from it – the focus for a Catholic uprising against your power and authority.' He paused. 'Especially since, in the eyes of Rome, my queen is of legitimate birth and you are not.'

She did not fly out at him, but said sombrely, 'Then it is six of one and half a dozen of the other, is it not? Whether I acknowledge her, or whether I don't, she will always be a focus for rebellion. So quote no more Juvenal at me, my friend, when I say again, I *will* not have it.'

9

Late that same afternoon, when Lethington, having had a final, private half hour with Secretary Cecil, was already a dozen miles away on his journey home, Elizabeth summoned Cecil to her chamber and demanded, 'Well? Is he in love with her?'

With his scholar's cap and the black velvet gown discreetly adorned with gold filigree buttons, with his long face, pronged beard and curling eyebrows, Cecil was an unfailingly stately man, shrewd, ambitious and dedicated, who looked very much older – and had never looked younger – than his forty-one years.

His mistress's question was by no means as womanish as it might have sounded to someone who knew her less well than Cecil. His tones measured as always, he replied, 'I believe he may to some degree have fallen victim to her charm and beauty ...'

'God's death! I am becoming very tired of hearing about her charm and beauty!'

'... but in general I do not doubt his good faith. I believe that, having now discovered that the queen of Scots has an agreeable personality, he hopes to use her to unite the dissident factions among the lords and give some stability to the country. He and Lord James, I would imagine, have raised the question of the succession simply as a means of keeping her – ummm – temporarily contented. They cannot possibly view it as a factor in any future union between our two countries, since it will be invalidated when you yourself marry and give birth to heirs of your body.'

Elizabeth, who had become so inured to such hints that she no longer even heard them, said thoughtfully, 'I wonder. I think we may sometimes underestimate the quality of his mind. But it does not matter, because whether I acknowledge Mary as my heir presumptive, or whether I do not, for as long as she lives she will be a danger to me and to my throne, the focus – as Lethington so helpfully pointed out – for any league of the Catholic powers against Protestant England. Something must be done about her.'

'Yes,' Cecil said. 'She must be neutralised.'

He would have said destroyed, except that he had a great deal of work

71

to do and had neither the time nor the inclination to stand and listen to his mistress doing her best to sound shocked.

10

Lethington reached Edinburgh again twenty-three days after he had left it, to discover that the queen was at her hunting seat of Falkland, the nearest thing Scotland had to a palace in the French style. With a faint sigh, he mounted a fresh horse and set off for Fife. He knew Falkland well. Mary's father had settled it on Mary of Guise for life, and it had been her favourite residence during the years of her widowhood and regency.

It was mid-morning when he arrived to find that the queen had swept her retinue off to the tennis court, leaving Lord James – who claimed to have more useful things to do with his hands than pat wee balls about – in one of the window alcoves of the great Lyon chamber, busily scribbling letters too confidential to be dictated.

'She's having the time of her life,' James said, 'playing the country maiden in the parks and woods. Last week, ye wouldn't have thought she'd be up to it. How did ye get on with Elizabeth?'

Lethington sank into a chair. 'Let's have your news first. I had your despatch about your sister's meeting with Knox. A disaster, I gathered?'

'Aye. He drove her to tears and she impressed him more than he wanted to be impressed. In a word, they didn't get on. Then she decided on a progress, so we've had a day or two each at Linlithgow, Stirling, Perth, Dundee and St Andrews.'

'How did it go?'

'Well enough. The ordinary folk think she's wonderful, and there's no doubt she's got a knack of charming them, but she won't give up her Mass, so we had a bit of trouble on both Sundays. Argyll had to give one of the priests a bloody nose at Stirling, and I came to blows with Huntly at St Andrews.'

'I suppose that *was* necessary?'

'It was. There's only one way of dinning sense into folks' heads, and that's by thumping them together. What else was there? Yes. I'll tell ye a worrying thing. Ye know the rumours we've always heard about her health? Well, she fainted clean away in Perth. In public. On her horse, in the street!'

'Probably her menses. It takes some women like that.'

72

'Does it?'

Not for the first time, Lethington found himself wondering whether James could possibly still be a virgin. It seemed unlikely, considering that he had been sixteen or seventeen before he was converted to Protestantism and learned that fornication was one of the seven deadly sins, but he had never, during all the years of Lethington's friendship with him, shown any inclination to go whoring. And Lethington doubted that it was, as in his own case, a matter of fastidiousness.

James said, 'Maybe that explains it. Lethington, are ye all right? What's the matter?'

Lethington, his eyes closing, said, 'I have ridden eight hundred miles in a hurry, with only a two-day break. I ache all over and I could do with a year's sleep. Does that answer your question?'

11

Something over two hours later, by which time Lethington had not only snatched a brief rest but told Lord James all he needed to know about his discussions with Elizabeth, an outburst of chattering and laughter heralded the return of Mary and her court. Sweeping in – tall, graceful, and glowing – she greeted Lethington with mild surprise and even milder pleasure. Only her ladies, who had suffered her spurts of frustration for three long weeks, detected the undertone of 'what has taken you so long?' She even said airily, 'Let us dine first, and then we will talk.'

While they dined, however, she plied him with questions about the English court and especially about Elizabeth's gowns and jewels and how she wore her hair. And was it true that she had a dull, sallow complexion? A year before, the English ambassador in Paris had promised Mary a portrait of her, but it had not arrived and she had no real idea of what her cousin looked like. Lord James, when asked, had been hopelessly vague, but Lethington kept them all in a ripple of laughter on everything from the swinging gold tassel that could have felled a kneeling envoy at twenty paces, to Lord Robert Dudley playing Orpheus in a tunic that left little to the imagination.

Mary said, 'Has she no sense of royalty, that she should be in love with such a commoner? Her Master of the Horse!'

'He's a very good Master of the Horse.' And then, as the laughter died down, 'He is, really. And although his grandfather was no more than a squire, he himself has known Elizabeth for more than a dozen years – he was a schoolfellow of her brother's – and rescued her from difficulty more than once during Mary Tudor's reign, when he could ill afford it. He's an engaging fellow and one of the few courtiers whose motives she doesn't distrust, so she is able to relax with him.'

Mary said, 'And?'

'Now what else can your majesty *possibly* wish to know?' Lethington meditated, but before he could go on, James intervened.

Both Elizabeth and Cecil had been very much impressed when they had first met James – upright, sober-minded, a model of well-publicised rectitude – and he, basking in their approval, had returned, and continued to return the compliment by holding them in the highest esteem, even to the extent of forgiving the spendthrift luxury of Elizabeth's court and, without a quiver, accepting Dudley in abbreviated dress and knitted silk tights, with a garland in his hair.

'Ye'd like Dudley,' he told his sister. 'He's a fine figure of a man, and godly, too, though ye mightn't think it.'

'That makes *all* the difference!' Then she turned back to Lethington. 'You were about to say?'

'I was about to say that I suspect your cousin's love for Dudley to be less consuming than it formerly was, though I should add that it is not a subject on which I would count myself an expert.'

Mallie Fleming, unwarily glancing up, discovered herself catching his eye and had to force her gaze to move airily on until it was brought to an incontinent halt in a corner of the ceiling. It was a handsome ceiling, ablaze with azure and vermilion and rose of Paris, with touches of white and verdigris and gold. Had he meant it? Did he really know little of love, or was it just the kind of thing men said? He had been married, she knew, for six or seven years, and according to Seton, who was some kind of cousin of his, his wife was sweet and pretty but very frail, which was why she had never been seen at court even in the early days of their marriage.

Lethington, momentarily diverted by the mystery of how on earth the voluptuous Jenny Fleming had produced such a shy and nervous daughter, resumed what he had been saying. 'The essential question, of course, is will Elizabeth marry him. I think it highly unlikely. A sovereign's matchmaking is too delicate a subject, politically, to be decided by personal desire. She will make a royal match, or none.'

Reflectively, the queen of Scots said, 'How sad that one of us is not a man. Then we could have married each other and all our problems would be solved.'

They walked afterwards in the courtyard, vast, lawned and pleasant, but scarcely had Lethington embarked on his report than James said, 'Ye don't need me. I've heard it already and I've got a builder coming over from St Andrews with some drawings for the extension to my house there. The Lady Agnes has given me strict instructions about it and I have to see they're obeyed.'

'Can it be ...' said Mary, addressing the empty air behind Lord James's vanishing form, 'that my brother is *excited* about his forthcoming nuptials?'

Lethington laughed. 'I would not care to express an opinion. However, I think he and Lady Agnes will suit very well.'

'Oh, dear. Do you? Well, I shall give him a splendid wedding when the day comes. Which reminds me ...' She stopped and pointed up at one of the stone carvings on the wall. 'You have been here before and perhaps you know. I have been told that this medallion represents Medea, but Mary Beaton says that the sculptures were done in the 1530s and everyone knows it to be a portrait of one of my father's mistresses – James's mother. Is it? She looks a dragon.'

'The Lady Margaret Douglas. Yes.'

'Yes, she is the model for the sculpture, or yes, she is a dragon?'

'Both.'

'Oh. Well, never mind, let us go back to Elizabeth. You say that, in private, she does not deny my claim, but that she fears my intentions. Why should she do so?'

'First and foremost, she is of a suspicious turn of mind – partly by nature, but mainly from experience. For all the twenty-five years before she came to the throne, she was at the mercy of others, betrayed by promises and betrayed also by people. There are few whom she trusts.'

Mary said, 'Yes, I can understand that. Until two years ago, I myself led such a happy and sheltered life that my natural inclination is the reverse. I prefer to trust people rather than mistrust them. With the exception of yourself, of course ...' She said it smilingly. 'But I have enough imagination to see that in my cousin's case, it would be otherwise.'

'You also made the tactical error,' Lethington went on drily, 'of favourably impressing Nicholas Throckmorton, her ambassador in France, whom she knows to be a very shrewd gentleman.'

'But surely that should have helped to convince her of my virtue?'

'The opposite. It meant you were even cleverer and more dangerous than she thought.'

The queen's eyes danced, like a small child aware of having been naughty but sure of being forgiven. 'Ooooh, dear!'

Lethington was thirty-three years old and not unfamiliar with feminine wiles, but Mary did it very well and without losing any of her dignity. He grinned at her, and said, 'Just so!'

At the end of a further half hour, she threw her hands in the air, exclaiming, 'And that is the beginning and the end of it? But how can I prove my good faith, how can I prove that there is not the most distant likelihood of my leading a crusade against her, if she refuses to believe *anything*?'

Many thoughts had occurred to him during his long ride home, among them one that he was virtually certain would appeal to her. 'I believe that if you and Elizabeth were to meet, you might prove to be more persuasive than I.'

Her eyes lit up. 'But that is *exactly* what I would like! Could it be arranged? I am sure that, once we come face to face, all our difficulties will be at an end.'

Her certainty was really quite touching. He said, 'Shall I see what can be done?'

13

They parted, Lethington to mount yet again to return to Edinburgh, where he knew there to be a large budget of despatches and papers awaiting his attention, and Mary to think carefully over what had been said and then to write privately to her uncle the cardinal about it. It was only his opinion she wanted, she told herself, not his advice.

Her brief and wary relationship with her secretary of state had changed amazingly in only a few hours. At dinner she had seen him for the first time in an informal mood and he had been delightful. Their subsequent discussion in the garden, with no James to drain the vitality from it, had shown her something of his calibre, and although he was certainly far too well acquainted with Elizabeth and Cecil, there had been nothing to make her doubt his loyalty to herself. But to like him personally was not the same as to trust him politically, and she knew she must be careful. She must not risk forgetting how he had betrayed her mother, who had also liked him very much – and had paid for it.

Lethington, for his part, had discovered that Mary was more receptive to rational argument than he had dared to hope. There was still no sign of the religious bigotry that might have been expected of a pupil of France and the Guises, and where Elizabeth, her mind already made up, was accustomed to say flatly, 'I will not', Mary's attitude appeared to be, 'I might, if you can give me good reason'.

Even so, it would be a mistake to place too high a value on her good sense. He had proposed the meeting with Elizabeth as one step in a campaign that would certainly entail much time and trouble, but she did not appear to see it so. It was the only sign of immaturity he had so far detected in her, this belief that her charm was her greatest weapon and perhaps the only weapon she needed. It might prove to be her greatest weakness. The political realities might sometimes be influenced by personal relationships, but seldom extensively and never conclusively.

Where he himself was concerned, he was resigned to the knowledge that she would expect personal loyalty from him – and would not understand any other kind. Would not understand that, however much he might find himself liking her, his loyalty was not and could not be to her as Mary Stewart, his charming royal mistress. It could only be to her as Mary Stewart, queen of the people of Scotland.

To others it might be a fine distinction. To Lethington it was as wide as the ocean.

14

That night, Mary dreamed for the first time of Elizabeth, a dream of such startling vividness that when she sat up in bed and opened her eyes the dream was still there, the figure still standing by her bedside – a woman of middling height and middling good looks, dark-eyed, sallow-skinned even in the faint light of the vigil candle, grossly overdressed and in a spitting bad temper.

'... dare you use the arms of England!' the mannish voice was shouting. 'How dare you!'

Mary was not accustomed to being shouted at. And although she did not want Elizabeth to be annoyed with her, she could not permit her to take that tone.

Sweetly reasonable, she replied, 'But you yourself use the arms of France as well as England. And France is not yours.'

'God's death!' Seeing Mary wince, Elizabeth repeated it with apparent relish. 'God's death! England has held territory in France for two hundred years. I am entitled.'

Mary thought, I should really point out that England lost its last foothold in France before you came to the throne, but perhaps it would not be tactful. England was very sensitive about Calais. So she said, 'It was my late, beloved father-in-law who ordered me to quarter England's arms with my own. But I've stopped. I have, truly.'

The other woman pursed her lips. 'You swear?'

'Oh, yes. After my husband died. And I would so much like to thank you for the kind message of condolence you sent me then. It touched me very deeply.'

Elizabeth sniffed. 'We're cousins, after all.'

'Do you think we might also be friends?'

'We'll have to see about that!'

Mary smiled her most charming, her most regal smile, the one that always brought results. 'We must meet,' she said. 'That is the first thing.'

The domineering eyes considered her. 'Perhaps. But I won't have you raising my Catholic subjects against me!'

'I would *never* do such a thing.'

'Mmm. Well, we'll see.'

Mary said, 'Perhaps we could ...' but the figure by her bedside had gone.

The smile still on her face, Mary thought, 'Oh, well,' then lay down and went peacefully back to sleep. Charm and soft words always worked wonders.

15

At the end of the month, Mary and her small court – sadly depleted by the departure of her adoring poet Châtelard, the Sieur de Brantôme and her two elder Guise uncles – returned to Edinburgh.

To Edinburgh, and John Knox, and a town council which had celebrated its re-election by making proclamation of the standard municipal statutes, one of which, unfortunately, ordered 'priests, nuns, adulterers, fornicators and all such filthy persons' to depart the city on pain of branding and banishment.

Mary's forbearance suffered a sharp setback.

'How dare they class my palace priests with adulterers and fornicators!

And to threaten them with branding! It is directly contrary to the decree of tolerance I issued in August. I will not have it!'

She sounded remarkably like Elizabeth, who would have concluded by snapping, 'Send them to the Tower!'

Mary snapped the next best thing. 'Send them to the Tolbooth!'

Lethington found himself struggling with an insane desire to laugh.

'I mean it,' Mary said.

'Yes, your majesty.'

The provost and bailies objected loudly to being sent to the Tolbooth, and John Knox objected even more loudly on their behalf. Lord James read John Knox a lecture about moderating his language in the interests of law and order, and John Knox told him he was a son of Belial, a Judas, a Pharisee, an Asmodeus, a Moloch, a parasite, a lickspittle, a freethinker, an earwig ...

Lord James didn't have the vocabulary to compete.

It took Lethington some considerable time to resolve the problem to everyone's satisfaction, and in the process Knox took a strong dislike to him as well as to James. Not that they had ever been twin souls. Knox had no sense of proportion at all, and had always seen Lethington as a *politique*, one whose tolerance and prudence marked him out as a man of little faith.

But the queen was happy. For the first time, she had put her foot down, and her brother and secretary of state had done as she told them. It was her first true victory.

Chapter Five

1561 - 1562

1

Holyrood at the end of October was cold, damp, dreary and depressing. Mary Seton, languidly stitching at a cushion cover, drew blood from her finger. Mary Livingston, tinkling quietly on the virginals, struck three wrong notes in a row. Mary Beaton, copying out motet parts from Attaignant, resignedly scraped out an error. Mary Fleming, reading aloud from Ronsard, broke off halfway through one of his less felicitous couplets.

'Madame,' she said.

'Yes, I know.' The queen lowered her embroidery to her lap. 'We cannot go on like this. I am beginning to feel like Penelope at her loom, weaving by day and unravelling by night, leading the virtuous life and never seeing an end to it.'

'And it isn't impressing Master Knox and his friends at all,' Livingston pointed out. 'I know they hate to think of people enjoying themselves, but couldn't we have just *one* little ball to save us expiring from boredom?'

'Or even one of the new puppet plays?' suggested Seton, who didn't care much for dancing.

The other Maries frowned at her.

Thoughtfully, Fleming said, 'The ambassador from Savoy will be here soon. Surely even Master Knox wouldn't expect us to greet him with long faces and Lenten fare? It should be a matter of pride for your majesty's court to be seen to be just as civilised and gorgeous as the other courts of Europe.'

The queen laughed. 'I wouldn't vouch for Master Knox, but you are perfectly right. And if you can think of any way of making Lord Morton or Lord Lindsay of the Byres even ordinarily polite and tidy, let alone civilised and gorgeous, please tell me.'

They spent some time discussing which of Mary's subjects might be invited to bring some style and vitality to the court, and it was a discussion that brought home to Mary, with unexpected clarity, how different was her position in Scots society from what it had been in France. There, she had belonged to both royal and ducal circles, had been able to choose her intimates from among her social equals. She had no such choice in Scotland. Not only did she lack lawful kindred whose status matched her own, but she was inhibited by political considerations from forming friendships with the earls who were the highest-ranking of her nobles. She could not be at ease with them, in case they dared to presume.

Fortunately, there were three of her illegitimate siblings to whom she had become attached, all of them, according to the censorious James, shockingly irresponsible. The eldest was Lord Robert, who was ripe for any escapade; then Lord John, whose youth and high spirits masked a surprisingly cultivated mind; and finally the captivating and frivolous Jean, Countess of Argyll, whose husband had been threatening to divorce her almost since the day they were married. It would have taken iron fetters to keep the countess at home when she scented diversion elsewhere.

With the enthusiastic cooperation of the Maries, the queen soon had Ogilvies, Erskines, Sempills and Gordons on her list. Then she said, 'And I think we might have Lord Bothwell.'

There was a silence, which Seton broke with an exclamation of 'Madame!'

'What? You mean he's not very respectable? I know that, but at least he is young and lively and well travelled.'

Mallie Fleming giggled. 'Lively' was certainly one way of describing Bothwell's overpowering animal vigour, while many of his travels had originated in the need to escape from the enraged fathers of his discarded mistresses. Fleming knew a good deal about him, since he was yet another cousin of hers through – neatest of ironies – another discarded mistress. Her own grandmother, after bearing an illegitimate daughter – Jenny Stewart, now Lady Fleming – to James IV, had gone on to the respectability of a marriage from which Bothwell was descended. Fleming didn't dislike him personally, but politically she knew him to be a shocking nuisance.

Seton said perseveringly, 'But, Madame, he is on bad terms with almost everybody. The Earl of Arran, for example, and your brother, Lord James, and ...'

Mary did not have to ask why. She knew that Bothwell's family, the Hepburns, were traditional enemies of Arran's family, the Hamiltons, but both Arran's and James's present antagonism to him stemmed from an occasion during the civil war when the Protestant lords had been waiting anxiously for funds to arrive from England and Bothwell had waylaid the messenger and relieved him of the money. Although a Protestant himself, he was a dedicated enemy of all things English and had been unswervingly loyal to Mary of Guise. Unpaid, the rebel army had begun to melt away, which explained the lords' enmity but was an exploit for which Mary of Guise's daughter, of all people, could not condemn him.

Certainly, she would trust Bothwell very much more than she trusted Arran, whose wild talk and uncontrolled behaviour were increasingly becoming a matter for concern. His anxiety to marry her was public knowledge, and now there were rumours than he planned to abduct her. James and Lethington were talking of doubling the size of her new bodyguard of twelve halberdiers.

Gaily, she said, 'On bad terms? Oh, dear, how dreadful. But if that is so, they will have to come to court, to kiss and make up on pain of my displeasure. I will have no stupid feuds among *my* nobles.'

The Maries exchanged uneasy glances, aware, as the queen was not, that every noble in the land had a bitter and long-running feud with some other noble. It did not seem the best time to say so and, tactfully, Fleming changed the subject.

'I've just thought, Madame. By the time the ambassador from Savoy arrives, your brother will have set off on his law-enforcing expedition to the Borders. He will miss all the fun.'

'Oh, *dear*,' said the queen again. 'How dreadful!'

2

Lord James enjoyed himself on the Borders, which were notoriously lawless, a perpetual battle ground where warring families bounded and rebounded from Scotland to England and back again, killing, burning, stealing cattle, and killing and burning again in the name of vengeance. Enforcing the law, here, was one of the few areas of political life where there was no need to negotiate or manipulate, where there were no ifs and buts and no sensibilities to be pandered to.

Where, if you were lucky enough to be an officer of the Crown and if you didn't approve of someone, you didn't waste time arguing. You simply hanged him.

James hanged twenty malefactors, bullied a few dozen more and, when he set out for Edinburgh again, much refreshed, haled fifty of the more vociferous of the remainder back with him to explain themselves to the privy council.

3

Meanwhile, the ambassador from Savoy, having arrived in doubt, departed in delight. Nothing could have been more enjoyable than his stay at the court of the liveliest and loveliest princess in Europe, even if her realm was so bitingly cold and windy that he was beginning to feel like a freeze-dried Scandinavian stockfish. He regretted that his stay was so short, but he was on his way to England and Elizabeth.

Not until he had been gone several days did he discover that he had lost the best bass singer he had ever employed.

In pursuit of her plan to liven up the court, Mary had said, 'We must do something about my singers. Certainly, we need a new bass who knows how to sustain a note better than poor Planson, and it would be lovely to have an *haute-contre*. Beaton shall be in charge of that. If we cannot find the people we need in Scotland, then we must send to France and Italy.'

And so Mary Beaton, taking shameless advantage of the ambassadorial habit of trailing musicians around with them on their journeyings, had set about bribing David Riccio to remain in Edinburgh. He was an ugly little Italian in his early thirties who not only had a magnificent voice but was amusing, well educated and had a gift for languages, all useful accomplishments when singing at court was no more than a part-time occupation and musicians were expected to fulfil some other function as well. Most of the members of Mary's choir did duty as *valets de chambre*, but it seemed to Beaton that Davie might be a useful addition to the small secretariat which dealt with the queen's foreign correspondence.

The queen and the other Maries took to him at once, not only because everything from *gaudes* in chapel to *vaudevilles* in the royal apartments improved beyond recognition, but because little Davie had a mischievous eye, a wicked tongue, and was up to date with all the European court gossip of which they were beginning to feel starved.

The candlemakers of Edinburgh had rubbed their hands with glee when the queen began entertaining, not only because the palace was blazing from end to end, but because it was blazing with candles made from beeswax, which sold at thirty times the price of tallow. Royalty did not like tallow's sooty sparks and greasy smells.

Royalty, in the person of Mary, did not much like the smells of her nobles, either. Reared under the Italianate influence of Catherine de' Medici, she herself was accustomed to bath at least once a week, but her subjects preferred perfume to water and most of their filigreed buttons and beads were stuffed with scent balls reeking of ambergris, musk, rosemary or cinnamon. There were times when the combined impact of perfume, stale sweat, damp wool, spilled wine, flea-repelling southern-wood and the smoke from the fires became hard to bear.

But Mary learned to resign herself. It was a small price to pay for bringing her court to life, not only for others' sakes but for her own. She had always enjoyed balls and masques and music, colour and movement, but she had not foreseen how necessary they would become as a counterbalance to the short, grey, wet days of the Scots winter, days that dulled her spirits, made her brain leaden. It was a delight not only to command her subjects to court but to tell them what they must wear. At one ball, it was jewel colours for everyone; at another, nothing but black and white; at a third, only silver and gold. Fleming, her large blue eyes seraphic, had said that Madame really ought to invite Master Knox, but Mary had resisted the temptation.

On an evening in early December, when the court was throwing itself with more vigour than decorum into dancing the *volte*, Mary became aware of Lord James materialising at her side, looking thoroughly sour-faced at the sight of Mary Livingston and Lord Bothwell twirling like dervishes. There was something about dancing that brought out the worst in the righteous.

Livingston loved dancing, whatever form it took, but Mary had been watching Bothwell with curiosity and deciding that, for him, it was no more than a way of burning off energy. He was not a tall man – shorter by several inches than she was herself – but his powerful, muscular physique amply compensated for his lack of height. She could see nothing of the graceful courtier in him and no subtlety at all. Not that there was anything surprising about that; she already knew that Lethington's was the only subtle mind in the whole of Scotland.

Bothwell had a loud voice, a broken nose, swarthy skin, and dark brown hair and eyes. There was a hint of fleshiness about his jaw and over his brows. But he was not a man to be ignored. She had heard from her mother that he was a bonny fighter, and he looked as if he would enjoy it.

Her mother had also told her that he was an honest man, and as stubborn as a mule where his principles were concerned. In a word, he was unique among the Scots lords. Mary had seen little of him since her return; it would do no harm, she thought, to see more.

Now, summoning up a smile of sisterly pleasure, she welcomed James home, and asked whether his expedition to the Borders had been successful.

He told her.

At the end, in a low voice, she said, 'You hanged – how many people? – *in my name!*'

'Yes. Well, everything I do is in your name. You're the queen.'

The *volte* was over, and Lord Bothwell stood before them, flushed and breathless, begging to take his leave of the queen.

A few moments later, Mary's and James's half-brother, Lord John Stewart, also begged to be excused.

And after that it was René d'Elboeuf, lingering survivor of the Guise uncles who had escorted her home from France.

Lord James glowered at all three of them, but Mary, who would in other circumstances have wondered why they were leaving long before the ball was over, dismissed them with a perfunctory smile.

She said, 'James, I know that law and order must be enforced, but I *cannot* be associated with this kind of rough justice. It is quite improper to execute people without a trial. What if they were innocent?'

James snorted. 'Innocent? On the Borders? There's not a soul in the East or West March that wasn't born steeped in sin.'

She said, 'We were all born in sin. Most of us make up for it by virtuous living.'

Nodding his head towards her departing courtiers, James replied, 'Not those three.'

5

To Mary's annoyance, he was right.

Next morning, she received a furious petition from the assembly of the reformed kirk.

The Earl of Bothwell, Lord John Stewart, and René, Marquis d'Elboeuf, had, it seemed, gone straight from Holyroodhouse to the home of a young woman named Alison Craik, whom they believed to be the Earl of Arran's whore, and had attempted to force their way in with the object of bedding her. This would have been the deadliest of insults to Arran, if he had not been a devoted member of the reformed kirk and spotlessly innocent of any improper association. And the woman concerned was the impeccably virtuous stepdaughter of an upstanding Edinburgh merchant.

It was an outrage against decency, an impiety both heinous and horrible, and the complainants demanded that the queen's majesty take immediate action against the perpetrators.

The queen's majesty, installed in her chair of state, surveyed the culprits before her and said severely, 'I hope you are ashamed of yourselves.'

Her uncle René, who after four months in Scotland had a perfectly adequate grasp of the language, opened his eyes wide and succeeded in looking as if he did not understand a word that had been spoken. Bothwell, clad in his Borderer's buff leather doublet and pale hose, merely looked bored, his lips almost imperceptibly puckered as if he were whistling under his breath. It was Lord John who, smothering a grin, said, 'Well, it wasn't as bad as all that. You know what Arran's like! He's crazy. He's a pain in the ... I mean, he's a pain. High principles, rigid morality, loves your majesty with a pure and holy love, but keeps us all worried stiff by threatening to abduct you. We decided it was time to teach him a lesson. He has this wench in St Mary's Wynd and we thought we'd show him up for the hypocrite he is by catching him in the act. That's all there was to it.'

Mary was very fond of both John and René, not only for family reasons but because they were likeable in themselves. She knew that their bad behaviour had arisen from no more than youthful high spirits.

About Bothwell, she was not so sure, because he had already packed too much experience into his twenty-five years to be able to plead that kind of excuse. He ranked as one of her leading nobles, was a privy councillor, hereditary Lord High Admiral of Scotland, and a warden of the Border Marches. She was told that he was also an adventurer, a womaniser, and a braggart, but she had seen no direct evidence of it, although she recognised that, in her presence, he would be on his best behaviour.

She had no doubt that he was the ringleader.

She said, 'Lord Bothwell?'

'I have nothing to add, your majesty, though I'm dolefu' that you have been troubled in the matter.'

'That, I suppose, is something. The complainants say you were intending forcibly to – er – bed the girl yourselves ...'

Bothwell gave a snort of laughter. 'Not I. I've never had to force a woman in my life. I just wait and they come running.'

The queen's lips curled in distaste. 'Indeed,' she said flatly. Then she scanned the culprits' faces once more and went on, 'I will not have my court discredited by such behaviour. I intend to tell the assembly that I have given all three of you a stern rebuke and since, in view of Lord Bothwell's feud with Lord Arran, I believe him to have been largely at fault, I do not wish to see him again at court until I give him leave.'

James, who had been standing by saying nothing, opened his mouth. 'He'd be better cooling his ardour in prison.'

But Mary shook her head.

She thought, afterwards, that she had made a mistake, because Bothwell, when she dismissed him, was not at all downcast but, on the contrary, went swaggering out of her audience chamber with a ferocious sideways glare at James, as if he were throwing him a challenge.

6

Late that same afternoon, after a few hours in Ainslie's tavern, Bothwell and Lord John Stewart let it be known that they proposed to mount a second assault on the virtue of Alison Craik, and dared anyone to stop them.

The news spread rapidly, as they had intended, and very soon partisans of the Earl of Arran began to collect at the Mercat Cross, wearing leather jacks, carrying pikes, and declaring themselves ready to guard the lady's honour with their lives. Bothwell, joyfully, had already gathered together a body of his own supporters and was preparing to march up the Highgait towards them.

Bloodshed seemed inevitable, and the tenants of the luckenbooths began feverishly packing away their goods. Nervous bystanders disappeared into the darkness of the wynds. The overhanging galleries of the houses filled up with hopeful spectators.

The provost having had the town bell rung to summon the help of Edinburgh's citizens in putting down the threatened affray, the Highgait was soon milling with people. The difficulty was that, in a town where every man carried arms and had no hesitation in using them, and where men were emerging simultaneously from every point of the compass in a darkness lit only by the torches of the booths, it was not immediately apparent who was friend, and who enemy. Which was an open invitation to settle, with every appearance of good citizenship, old scores which had nothing whatsoever to do with Bothwell, Arran or, indeed, Mistress Alison Craik.

In the confusion, it was not altogether surprising that it took some time for the palace to respond to news of the impending battle. For most of the court, the sound of the town bell had been muffled by music and laughter, while the more serious-minded, like Lord James, were deeply engrossed elsewhere in hammering out a compromise over the redistribution of Catholic church property which they hoped to impose on Knox and the kirk assembly.

James, hearing the bell, did no more than send a servant to enquire why it was being rung. But when the man eventually returned, the news he brought was enough to set James, Argyll and Huntly, in unholy alliance, shouting for their armour and their men-at-arms. Leaping to the saddle, they fought their way up the Canongait, forcing their horses into the crowd and laying about them with the flat of their swords. Huntly speeded their progress considerably by brandishing a German wheel-lock pistol before which everyone scattered, since such weapons were commonly believed to blow up of their own accord. If James had had breath to spare, he would have reminded him in no uncertain terms that he was banned by law from carrying such a thing in proximity to the court.

It was not difficult to identify the heart of the disturbance, with one mob yelling, 'A Hamilton! A Hamilton!' and the other, 'A Hepburn! A Hepburn!' Nor was it difficult to break up the affray. There was nothing like a small troop of horse for putting foot warriors to rout.

At the end, sitting his mare at the Mercat Cross and addressing the populace at large, James delivered himself of a coldly pious lecture that put a disappointing period to what had looked like developing into a enjoyable evening's entertainment.

7

Mary said, 'I do *not* understand these feuds. Why can people not make an effort to tolerate one another? It is not so very difficult.'

Lethington, who had been visiting his wife at Haddington and missed the fun, said, 'Unfortunately, it is. It's not simply a question of individuals disliking each other. It's a question of families hating each other through the generations.'

'But why?'

He shrugged. 'Someone, at some time, probably appropriated a piece of land, or a woman, or a title. No one forgets, and every slight, real or imagined, that follows, fuels the quarrel.'

'But it's not *civilised*!'

'No.' He hesitated for a moment. 'I think perhaps I should warn you that your lords have been unnaturally well behaved since your return – and the strain is beginning to tell.'

Lord James said, 'Ye need to take a firm stand. If ye won't put Bothwell in jail, ye'll have to ban him from Edinburgh.'

'Then I should ban Arran, too.'

'No. He was the one who was provoked.'

'That didn't entitle him to start an affray.' She looked questioningly at Lethington.

It was a matter of checks and balances. Bothwell was a troublemaker and would never be anything else, whereas Arran was no more than a nuisance who could be controlled. Lethington nodded. 'I think Lord James may be right.'

'Oh, very well.' Brightening, she changed the subject. 'Now, Secretary Lethington, what does my cousin Elizabeth say about a meeting between us?'

Through Secretary Cecil, my cousin Elizabeth had said that she suspected Mary of duplicity and hypocrisy; that nothing would induce her to believe a single word that Mary uttered, especially if it had anything to do with the church of Rome; and that she was beginning to fear that Lord James and Lethington had allowed themselves to become Mary's dupes. Cecil had added that he himself wanted nothing to do with Mary or the proposed meeting. In his view, the Scots lords would be well advised to depose Mary and give the throne to Châtelherault.

Lethington smiled peaceably. 'I have had no direct reply from your cousin, only from her secretary. We must continue to be patient.'

8

James said, 'Well, ye needn't think I'm going. If ye're paying him the honour of staying at his castle, ye might as well not have banished the fellow at all!'

'Really, James! It's only for one night and honour has nothing whatever to do with it. I am going to Crichton – and you are coming with me – because our brother happens to be marrying Bothwell's sister. I wouldn't dream of insulting John by refusing to attend, especially when he is my favourite among all my brothers.'

'Is that so? Ye don't want to insult him but ye don't mind insulting me?'

'Ah, but I don't think of you first as my brother. I think of you as my leading minister.'

He liked that, as she had known he would.

It was almost true. The government of the country was not in Mary's hands, nor in those of the parliament that rarely met, nor even of the privy council. With the implicit consent of all interested parties, it was Lord James and Secretary Lethington who were the *de facto* government, James concerning himself largely with affairs at home and Lethington with affairs abroad. Publicly, it was James, the model of probity, who was the dominant figure, but Mary had learned that Lethington was behind almost everything. James was not a thinker; Lethington was.

It did not disturb her, since she did not intend the two men's joint régime to last. When she knew more about the affairs of her realm, she would take its governing firmly into her own hands. In the meantime, she sat under her cloth of state at privy council meetings, stitching away at her embroidery – a habit that irritated all her councillors intensely – while she listened and learned. It was only when the talk was of merks and feus and customs dues that her attention was apt to wander.

'Do come, James,' she said. 'John will be dreadfully disappointed if you don't, and it will do you no harm to be civil to Bothwell for once.'

Crichton castle was little more than eight miles from Edinburgh and the most domesticated of Bothwell's three strongholds. Although it was built round a courtyard and presented a grim outer face to the world, its halls were large and its rooms handsome, with the luxury of tiled floors and huge and welcoming fireplaces. In January, the undulating lands around it might be patched with snow, but it was easy to imagine the high, well-masoned walls glowing golden in the August sun, with green bracken, yellow ragwort and purple thistles blazing around them.

Bothwell said, 'The fireflies dance here on summer nights. They're bonny. Your majesty should come and see them some time.'

'I should like that.'

Nothing in Mary's limited experience of Bothwell had prepared her for

90

the man he could be, as distinct from the man he normally was; for the discipline and courtesy of his manner, his occasional sardonic humour, or the excellence of his entertainment. The marriage ceremony was held according to the lugubrious Protestant rite but the banquet that followed was as extravagant as even a queen's heart could desire. Not until years later did she discover that Bothwell had been forced to sell some of his lands to pay for the occasion, or that his Borderers had been largely responsible for the lavishness of the table. There were does and roe deer in hundreds, partridge and plover, moorhens, wild geese and wild duck. There were also, for herself and the bridal party, a variety of the daintier and lighter dishes to which her French palate was accustomed.

She hadn't known that Bothwell had passed much of his adolescence in France, some of it with his erratic father, the Fair Earl, and some as a student in Paris. He showed her his library and she was fascinated to discover in it not only modern studies of science and geometry but French translations of Latin works on military history and theory. And although his Scots accent was broad, it was not slovenly, while his spoken French was excellent.

When they left next morning, after the banquet and the sports and the dancing, her uncle René d'Elboeuf said he had never seen such a splendid bridal even in France. He was overstating it, as out of courtesy he was bound to do, but it had been, at the very least, instructive.

9

There was another wedding a month later, that of Lord James to the Lady Agnes Keith, which, thanks to Mary's intervention, was celebrated with the greatest splendour. The prophets of the Old Testament would not have approved, and neither did their successor, John Knox. Neither, indeed, did James – or not in principle. But his sense of self-worth revelled in it.

Weddings brought out the best in Mary, her warmheartedness and her generosity. Although her privy council might, with reason, have found cause for complaint in their sovereign dissociating herself from affairs of state in order to occupy herself with cloth of silver for the bridal dress and pearls and jewels for the bridal billiments, there was no denying that business went both more swiftly and more surely when they did not have to think about royal prerogatives and royal preferences every time they opened their mouths.

On the day before the wedding, in a very private ceremony, Mary conferred on her brother the earldoms of Mar and of Moray.

As he knelt before her chair of state, she said regally, 'On the strength of your character, your personality, your probity, you have made a place for yourself in the life and in the heart of my realm, and you have done this without holding any formal position beyond membership of my privy council, without even the authority that goes with a title of nobility. You have been no more than the half-brother of a queen who' – she twinkled at him – 'has six other half-brothers as well. But I value you above all. In these last months I have learned to rely on your knowledge and judgement. It will make me happy, and I know it will make my subjects happy, if I acknowledge your services by investing you, now, with the ancient and distinguished titles of the earldoms of Mar and Moray. And Huntly will have a fit when he finds out.'

After this slightly unorthodox speech, she tapped him again briskly on either shoulder with the sword and said, 'Oh, for goodness' sake, get up, James. That was what you wanted, wasn't it?'

She hadn't meant that James wanted Huntly to have a fit, but Lethington, standing by in the rôle of witness, reflected that he would certainly see it as a bonus. Huntly had come to regard the earldom of Moray as part of his own patrimony and was going to be very angry indeed at losing it. But since, in political terms, he was as much an *enfant terrible* as either Arran or Bothwell, any reduction of his lands and power was to be welcomed.

James, in his most businesslike way, said, 'Thank you, sister. Now, it's settled – is it not? – that my earldom of Mar is to be announced as your wedding gift to me, but we'll keep quiet about Moray until a bit later. We'll need to catch Huntly off guard, because I won't be able to take possession without some show of force.'

Mary exclaimed, 'I hope not! You seem to me to be making a great fuss about nothing. If I create you Earl of Moray, that surely is the end of it?'

She still did not understand her lords at all.

10

Next day, John Knox preached the marriage sermon in St Giles' cathedral to a congregation whose members wore a decent sobriety on their faces and enough indecent riches on their backs to have fed the nation's poor for years to come. He didn't hesitate to mention it.

The queen attended as a spectator, dripping with her favourite rubies and pearls and clothed in a relatively subdued crimson velvet, so as not to outshine the bride. In any case, on a cold February day velvet was much cosier than precious tissues. The bride, Lady Agnes Keith, was nineteen years old, with a trim figure, a long heart-shaped face – slightly marred by a very small, prim mouth – and sufficient strength of character to ignore the vulgar ostentation of her silver gown. Which, as she pointed out to her cousin Jean Gordon, she would *never* have worn from choice.

Jean, tempted, nodded her neat little head. 'Yes. Something more refined, like cloth of gold, would have suited you better.' Sometimes she despaired of Agnes; she had no sense of adventure at all.

After the ceremony, along a route lined with citizens who hadn't seen so much excitement for years, the congregation proceeded sedately to the palace of Holyrood for three days of feasting, balls, masques, pageants, and an occasional venture outdoors for hawking, archery, quintain and pall mall.

The former Lord James Stewart, clad in tasteful dark blue satin, looked more benign than anyone had ever seen him as he accepted congratulations on his marriage and his elevation to Earl of Mar. Only his maternal uncle, Lord Erskine, who himself had a good legal claim to the title, was not entirely happy.

During the course of the festivities, the queen drank the health of her cousin Elizabeth from a gold cup which she then presented to Tom Randolph. He, having been instructed by Cecil to observe Mary closely, reported back that, if the queen of Scots' frequently voiced friendship towards Elizabeth was insincere, she must be the best actress the world had ever seen.

William Maitland of Lethington, dancing a dutiful *branle* with Mary Fleming, exerted himself to charm her out of her nervousness. Mysteriously, his efforts had quite the opposite effect. He could not understand why she seemed to find him so frightening. No one else did.

David Riccio, the new Italian bass who had joined the queen's chamber singers was much admired for the quality of his voice, though not for his looks. Even in the singers' elegant livery of blue and gold, he bore a marked resemblance to a monkey.

Jean Gordon, in the course of a *galliard*, lost her heart irrevocably to young Alexander Ogilvie of Boyne. She would have preferred not to, because one of her brothers was murderously at feud with his family, but even sixteen years of being neat and controlled were not proof against a pair of Highland blue eyes and the certainty that she had found the other half of her own self.

Huntly was present, despite having subjected the queen to a thoroughly insubordinate diatribe on her failure to do anything about bringing Scotland back to the church of Rome, but the Earl of Bothwell was absent, having been banned from Edinburgh, as was the Earl of Arran, who might swear undying devotion to Mary but refused to attend her court until she gave up her Mass. His father, the Duc de Châtelherault, however, never missed such an affair if he could help it.

Eyeing Mary's magnificent ruby collar of knots and double crescent moons, he said, 'I haven't seen that one before. Beautifully matched stones. Was it dear?'

She smothered a choke of laughter. 'I don't know. It was a gift from my husband.'

'Uh-huh.' He raised his pouched gaze and Mary's laughter died. Now that she knew him better, she neither liked nor trusted him, and although she made light of his son's eccentricities, she was becoming wary of the ambitions of the entire Hamilton family. The duke went on, 'I just came over to say, will you look at your brother? Have you ever seen him so jocose? That's what love does, my dear. I've told you before, but it bears repeating. It's high time you were thinking of marrying again.'

It was true, and she was indeed thinking about it. But not for love.

11

For women of rank, marriage was a business arrangement, a matter of alliances between families, of land and dowries and titles. It was the same for queens, but on a grander scale. Love did not enter into it, or only as a secondary consideration.

When François died, Mary had become the most eligible royal bride in Europe, more so than Elizabeth, who was older, less beautiful, a Protestant, and tarnished by intimacy with her Master of the Horse. But a second marriage was not something to be rushed. The marriage of queens had even greater implications than the marriage of kings. Whereas a king's wife was no more than a consort, the husband of a queen normally became king, and entitled at the very least to share his wife's right to rule.

Night after night, she and the Maries had discussed suitable candidates over games of dice or cards in the privacy of her little retiring room, with one of her musicians playing the lute quietly in the background. David Riccio had a particularly delicate touch.

Don Carlos, heir to the throne of Spain; the king of Denmark; the Archduke Charles of Austria ...

Mary said, 'Now, *he* is said to be handsome, but he's no more than a third son, and I believe he is at present negotiating for the hand of my cousin Elizabeth.'

'And we don't want to annoy *her*!' exclaimed Fleming.

'But we don't want him to marry her, either,' Livingston objected. 'If she bore him children, Madame would never become queen of England.'

Rattling the dice in her hand, Fleming said thoughtfully, 'If only there were someone your majesty could marry for love as well as from policy. But I don't believe there is a king or prince in the whole of Europe to make a woman's heart beat faster! Or none that I have seen or heard of.' She began collecting the dice boxes together. 'In any case, think how heartbreaking it would be to marry someone for love, and then find that you could rarely be together because he had to rule his own country while you continued to rule yours.'

The queen giggled. 'Whereas if I married from policy and found my husband unlovable, it would be a positive blessing!'

Mary Beaton said, 'We haven't mentioned Erik of Sweden.'

The lute in the background gave a sudden discordant twang and they all turned to see the lutenist bent over it, convulsed with laughter.

Mary said, 'Davie?'

'Ees just a story I know about him, Madame. Ees nothing.'

'No, tell us!'

'He ees having his portrait painted, *si*? And he is a long, tall man and ver' proud of hees legs, so he show them off by wearing ver' short breeches stuffed out ver' wide. And a lovely lady come to admire, and he bow to her, and one of the quillons of his sword catches in a fold of his breeches and makes a tear ...'

'Stop laughing, Davie. Go on.'

'*Si*, Madame. It ees then he discovers that, for the stuffing, hees tailor has used not flock or horsehair, but bran. And so – shoosh! – right there before the lady's eyes, all the bran come pouring out on to the floor around him, and he ees left standing in a leetle mountain of husks with breeches that droop like empty pudding bags. With such a grand, serious man, ees funny, no?'

It was so much the kind of silly gossip that had nourished the court of France that, for a moment, Mary felt quite homesick.

95

Smiling, she said, 'There is your answer, Beaton. I think we should continue *not* to mention Erik of Sweden!'

On another evening, picking up her cards, she had sighed and said, 'Despite all the difficulties of marrying into a foreign royal house, I can't – I really can't – marry a commoner.'

'Would one of the great English nobles be a possibility?' Beaton ventured. 'It might encourage Elizabeth to recognise you.'

'The Duke of Norfolk!' exclaimed Fleming, who was trying to take an educated interest in affairs of state. 'He has a great deal of influence.'

'He already has a wife,' Beaton pointed out.

'No, he hasn't. She died in childbirth.'

'Yes, but he's just married again.'

'Oh. Well, perhaps there's someone else. Madame certainly can't marry one of our own lords. All the others would instantly unite to tear him limb from limb.' She laid down her cards. 'I have a prime.'

The queen laid down her own. 'But I have a flush.'

12

'*Have* you heard ...' murmured Jean Gordon, her large eyes almost popping with excitement.

It was clear to Alexander Ogilvie that she was teasing him. She was such a darling, and the whole thing was impossible. 'Yes?' he said, a reluctant smile touching his handsome mouth.

'... that Master Knox has spoken to ...'

'Yes?'

'... Lord Bothwell ...'

'Yes?'

'... and to the Earl of Arran ...'

'Yes?

'And he lectured them about ...' She dropped her voice to a lower register and rounded her vowels out beautifully. ' "God's fear, and the profit of you both, and the tranquillity of this realm".'

He grinned. 'Yes?'

'And they've agreed to forget their quarrel and be *friends!*'

'Never!'

'It's true. Bothwell went to Master Knox to say he'd had enough of the feud. He's always short of money and it was costing too much to keep a large bodyguard with him all the time. And Master Knox, who claims that his great-grandfather, grandfather and father all served under previous earls of Bothwell, said he would see what he could do. So he spoke to Arran – who worships him only slightly less than God – and Arran agreed.'

She stopped, because Alexander Ogilvie's Highland-blue eyes were turning her knees to water, and gasped, 'Oh, Alexander,' then looked around guiltily at the group applauding those who were playing quintain in the gardens of Holyrood. But no one seemed to have noticed.

He said mechanically, 'How do you know?'

She collected herself. 'I was walking down the Highgait and I saw them going into a tavern *arm in arm*. And then I happened to meet Lord John Stewart, and I asked him about it. I thought he was going to laugh himself into fits. He's probably on his way here now to spread the news.'

But the tall, dashing figure that appeared just then from the direction of the archery butts was another John – Sir John Gordon, her own third brother, who had recently and in the most scandalous circumstances stolen both an inheritance and a wife from members of Alexander's family.

Alexander's face stiffened, but he was a well-bred young man who knew better than to make a scene within the confines of a royal palace. Instead, he turned back to Jean and she found, despairingly, that he was bowing to her and saying, 'You will forgive me for leaving you, Lady Jean, but I find that I do not care for some of the company here.'

13

Arran and Bothwell remained friends for precisely four days, after which Arran rushed into the house on the corner of the Nether Bow and the small, covered first-floor gallery that served as John Knox's study, crying, 'I am betrayed. Judas, Judas! Treason!'

Knox, who was busy, sighed and, pinching the bridge of his nose between his fingers, said, 'Yes, my lord. Tell me,' then listened patiently to the tale the young man poured out, a young man whose hold on reality, he saw, had finally snapped, a young man who was deranged, drowning in dreams, his head full of fantasies.

When at last he came to an end, Knox clapped him on the shoulder and said with more kindliness than was his wont, 'Aye, sir, it is a weighty matter, but not one that should be told to all and sundry without certainty of the truth. I judge that there may have been some new failure of understanding between yourself and Lord Bothwell. Ye should go to your father's house and take some rest, and then pray to the Lord for guidance, who will illuminate the eyes of your mind and make ye see all things clearly again.'

'Do you think so?'

'The Lord our God will not suffer ye to persist in error.'

'No, He won't, will he? I'll do that.'

And he was off. From his window, Knox watched him go, running as if in panic to where he had stabled his horse. His mind had never been well balanced, and in the last few months ...

Shaking his head, the preacher muttered, 'Tch, tch!' and, abandoning the problem to the Lord, went back to preparing his sermon for Sunday.

14

Mary was at Falkland, next day, when a messenger arrived bearing a letter from Arran, an extraordinary effusion that was almost incomprehensible because of its wild scrawl and its random mixture of Scots and French.

Exclaiming, 'Jesu, the man has run mad!' she handed it to her brother. 'See what you can make of that, if anything.'

Her brother's expression was noncommittal when he looked up again. 'He's saying Bothwell has a plan for the pair of them to murder me and Lethington, then to abduct you and imprison you and take over the government of the country themselves. One of them would marry you, but he doesn't say which. I'd put my money on Bothwell.'

'Yes, but can you decipher the bit about why he has decided to reveal the plot?'

'He says he thinks Bothwell's real purpose is to ruin him and the entire house of Hamilton.'

'Which means that he has enough sense left to recognise that the plot would be likely to fail. James, do you believe *any* of it?'

'I would put nothing past Bothwell.'

'Even being so stupid as to trust Arran?'

'It might seem worth the gamble. The fact that Arran's second in line to your throne could impress some folk into supporting them.'

'Only if they don't know Arran! James, this is horrible. I wish you wouldn't treat it quite so matter-of-factly.'

'Well, I'll burst into tears, if you'd prefer.'

She thought she had misheard. She couldn't remember him ever having made a joke before.

He said, 'Don't worry. I'll deal with it.'

15

A few days later, Arran and Bothwell were brought before the queen and her privy council, Arran pallid, fair, and so skeletal that he looked as if his bones ought to be jangling, Bothwell loud, swarthy and contemptuous.

Mary thought for a moment that she would faint as Arran turned towards her, threw his arms open, and raved in a voice as high-pitched as an hysterical boy's about what a joy it had been to take her to wife and lie with her in the marriage bed. He would have gone on except that James nodded at one of the pikemen guarding him, and the pikeman struck him a buffet over the mouth that silenced him, though only for a moment.

All it did was change the material of his ravings. 'Kill me! That's what you want. That's what you all want.' He flung an arm towards Bothwell. 'That's what *he* wants. That was why he proposed treason to me.' Bothwell made a movement and Arran cowered back, mad and pitiful, shrieking, 'Don't let him touch me! High treason! I accuse him of high treason!'

To Lethington, standing beside her chair of state, Mary murmured, 'This is sickening. He is possessed by demons. We cannot let it go on.'

But Lethington replied, 'We must.'

Bothwell raised his voice. 'Why do you listen to a lunatic? This plot is nothing but the invention of an ailing mind and I deny it, on my life. But if the lords here present believe there is a case to answer, I'll save them from pretending to try and judge honestly between us by challenging the poor fool to trial by combat.'

Fists clenched on his hips, a sneer curling his mouth, he scanned the faces of the councillors and saw what he expected to see.

Mary sighed. Since the wedding at Crichton, she had come to recognise that he was one of those people who reacted instinctively to the company he was in. He was reacting now to the hostility of almost everyone on the council. How was it possible for him to have made so many enemies in so few years? What devil drove him on to insult them and provoke them?

Lord James said, 'Combat would be inappropriate, in view of Lord Arran's condition of mind.'

Bothwell laughed, raspingly. 'You call it a mind, do you? Very well, let us settle matters not here in this stronghold of prejudice, but in a proper court of law.'

Lord James said, 'We will consider it.' Then, 'Take them both away.'

16

'I don't believe there really was a conspiracy,' Mary said afterwards in the privacy of her retiring room.

Lethington was silent, but James said irritatingly, 'There's no smoke without fire.'

'Nonsense. *If* anyone were to ask me,' the queen said, nibbling on a Pisan biscuit, 'I would banish Arran to his father's care, and tell Bothwell to go away and not draw attention to himself for the next six months. But I suppose the case must go to court.'

Lethington shook his head. 'There's too much gossip for us to dismiss the matter, but as for bringing the case to court ... You may not be aware that in Scots law the penalty for bearing false witness is death. If we held a trial and Arran's accusations against Bothwell were disproved, Arran would have to be executed.'

James helped himself to a biscuit. 'These are good, aren't they? Lethington's right. And it's not politically wise to execute heirs to the throne. We'll just have to keep him locked up out of harm's way.'

'Where?'

'There's some dungeons under the Great Hall at the castle. That's where we usually put folk like him.'

'Usually? Do we have so many dangerous, blue-blooded fools? No, don't answer. How depressing it all is! What about Bothwell?'

'He's probably innocent, and that's not a word I ever thought I'd hear myself using of him. On the other hand, he's been negotiating with the English and I don't like it.'

'I don't recall you objecting to Secretary Lethington negotiating with the English?'

'Oh, very humorous.' Lord James swirled the wine in his cup. 'Bothwell's always short of money and he's taking bribes from some of the lords in the north of England to undermine my attempts to bring law and order to the Borders.'

'I wouldn't have thought it of him,' Mary said disconsolately, 'but he can't be allowed to break the law. If you're sure ... ?'

'I'm sure,' her brother said, 'and it'll do him no harm to cool *his* heels in the castle dungeons, too.'

17

'That went very well,' James said with satisfaction as he and Lethington strolled up the Canongait after an excellent dinner. The queen's new Master of the Roast was truly a master, and she had recently brought a superlative new sauce cook over from France.

Lethington nodded. Even after more than six months of Mary proving amenable to their guidance, James had decided it would still be wise to do some weeding out of the competition.

'Three birds with one stone. Not bad, eh?' James said.

'Three?'

'Well, there's Bothwell ...'

'How long were you thinking of holding him?'

'Forever, if I can get away with it.'

Lethington said, 'James, I know you want to – we both want to – nullify him politically, but you can't keep him locked up without trial forever, certainly not on the word of a madman. The bribery tale was a fiction, I take it?'

'The end justifies the means. You know that as well as I do.'

'Possibly.'

James waved to John Knox, who was standing at the window of his study looking uplifted. 'And the second wee bird,' he said, 'is Arran, of course. And the third's his father.'

'Ah.' It was true. Châtelherault had been so shamed by the affair that he and the Hamiltons would certainly lie low for a while at least.

'So,' James said, 'when are ye off to England again?'

'Soon, but not quite yet. I've just heard that Elizabeth has decided she is prepared to have a meeting with your sister after all, which means that we have a good deal to discuss before I set out.'

He said no more, because he did not want his diplomacy undermined again by James writing to Elizabeth to tell her all about it.

Neither did he enquire whether James had any more wee birds on his list. He could already guess the answer. The next one was certainly going to be Huntly, and for him James was going to need not a stone but a sizeable rock.

'Ledington, *mi amigo!*'

'Your grace.' Lethington bent his head, successfully ignoring the amethyst ring extended towards him as if expecting to be kissed. Alvaro de Quadra, Bishop of Aquilia, was Philip of Spain's ambassador in England and it was not always clear which rôle he considered himself to be fulfilling at any given moment. His use of Spanish rather than Latin suggested that, today, he was being ambassadorial.

He was. 'Let us walk,' he said. 'I have received a most encouraging message from my sovereign. You will be pleased.'

They had met, by pre-arranged accident, in the soaring, marvellously arched nave of St Paul's cathedral. It was a place of public resort and one that appealed to Lethington's ironical cast of mind, especially since the bishop didn't turn a hair at the crooks, confidence men, cutpurses and pickpockets who frequented it; at the usurers in the south transept, the horse dealers in the central aisle, the sellers of benefits, ballads and broadsheets in the north; the knights, the gulls, the upstarts, the scholars, the doctors and the beggars everywhere. St Paul's was where the gallant came to show himself off and to be measured by his tailor while he stared out of the west door at the criminals hanging from the gallows.

De Quadra said, 'As you know, I have always been a warm partisan of the idea of a match between your lovely queen and Don Carlos, the excellent son of my sovereign. The family of Guise has spoken to my sovereign on this matter, and I have this very day received a message to say that he is not averse to embarking on negotiations to bring such a marriage about.'

'How splendid,' Lethington said. He could have done without Guise interference in Scots affairs, and he could certainly do without negotiations for a Spanish marriage, which had no place in his current plans.

'The good Don Carlos, of course, is young. But consider the grandeur that lies before him.'

'One's eyes are blinded,' Lethington said.

De Quadra looked at him, but could detect nothing in his face other than a suitable respect. 'It would be a match of unequalled splendour for your exquisite queen.'

'How true,' responded Lethington.

'Let us communicate further,' de Quadra said. 'But privately. My master does not wish the matter to be bruited abroad at such an early stage.'

'How wise. In any case, I must first consult the queen my mistress.'

The flourish of Lethington's parting bow could not have been surpassed. Watching him go — a tall, lean, competent and clever man with his hand on the dagger at his belt — de Quadra thought, 'What a very sophisticated man, for a Scot.'

19

Elizabeth had just changed her mind for something like the dozenth time. She would not meet Mary after all.

'With Catholics and Huguenots now at war in France, my councillors are unanimously opposed to my meeting the queen your mistress, who is Catholic and half-French and far too closely associated with the family of Guise, whose ambition appears to be to exterminate every Protestant in the country. My answer is therefore no, and it is final.'

Lethington said, 'I am no more enamoured of the Guise family than you are, your majesty. And although the queen my mistress is indeed of their blood she is of a more temperate disposition. That her uncles bear a measure of responsibility for the discord in France distresses her deeply.'

'Oh, hey, nonny, nonny!' said Elizabeth sarcastically. 'In that case, she will already have written to them begging them to desist from their atrocities against the Huguenots?'

'No. She believes a country's internal affairs are a matter for that country alone, and would no more offer advice to the French on French affairs than she would accept advice from the French on the affairs of Scotland.'

'Very neat. It is always a pleasure to deal with a man who has his wits about him.' They were in the cloistered bowling alley at Greenwich palace and, bending, she sent her wooden bowl skimming along the concave clay bed and watched, with satisfaction, as five of the skittles fell. There was much cooing and clapping from the throng of ladies and courtiers crowded along the leaning boards, although Dudley took the trick by walking over to brush some imaginary grit from the surface, saying, 'Your majesty would have had all nine, if it had not been for that.'

Lethington wished, sometimes, that royalty was not so averse to sitting round a table in a civilised fashion. It was hard to conduct even a rational discussion, far less a confidential one, in a bowling alley.

Bending, he sent his own bowl down the alley; five pins went down, as he had intended, though a sixth teetered dangerously. He said, 'In any case, we know a truce to be imminent. That should dispose of your councillors' objections.'

'It will not last.'

A few days earlier, she had thought it would. She had even written to Mary saying how much she was looking forward to their meeting. Her Master of the Revels had been instructed to devise masques to entertain the two queens on the great occasion. Her treasurer, adding up the likely costs of a court expedition to a meeting place in the north of England, had turned pale and added them up all over again.

Drily, Lethington had told Cecil, 'There is really no need for another Field of Cloth of Gold.'

Cecil, who still disapproved of the whole idea, did not mince words. 'If you are prepared to believe that my queen will go to meet your queen – who is nine years younger than she and said to be more beautiful, more graceful and more charming – in anything less than the grandest style, you are more of a fool than I take you for. Women! I despair of them!'

Lethington had smiled a little absently, familiar by now with Cecil's complaints about Elizabeth being unmanageable, while Elizabeth in turn complained that Cecil did far too much managing behind her back. They had the technique so beautifully orchestrated that it was sometimes difficult to know which of them had originated an idea, and which of them had the greater influence over the other. He wondered occasionally how much time they spent practising.

One thing Lethington did know, however, was that Cecil's influence over Elizabeth in the matter of Mary would always be inimical. It did not make his own task impossible, but it did complicate it.

Now, she snapped. 'And I wish to hear no more of the subject at present. If a truce is agreed, I will then decide whether my meeting with your mistress should go forward. But if there is continued or renewed war across the Channel, there will be no question of it. Let us continue with our game, if you please.'

20

For another four weeks he waited while Elizabeth wavered. If he had not been vaguely uneasy as to what everyone – and specifically James – was getting up to in his absence, he would have enjoyed the court of England as much as always, its extravagance, its bustle, its riches. Even the competitiveness, the backbiting, the feuds – as bitter as those of Scotland, though better disguised – at least had the merit of unfamiliarity. The weather, unfortunately, was terrible.

In one of the budgets of despatches that came to him by courtesy of Randolph and Cecil – taking only four days by the diplomatic standing post, even in this torrential summer – were two letters from Lord James, from which he learned of the latest episode in one Scots feud that would certainly have repercussions. Or, in James's hands, could be made to. Because the villain of the piece was Huntly's third son, Sir John Gordon, who had wounded Lord Ogilvie in a street brawl in Edinburgh.

It was the last and unforgivable sin in an unusually disreputable affair involving wives, stepsons, rape, disinheritance and desertion. According to James's first letter, Sir John Gordon was deservedly languishing in prison, but his second letter reported that the young man had escaped and was believed to be making for Huntly's domains in the north.

There was nothing Lethington could do but shrug his shoulders and continue to wait for Elizabeth to make up her mind.

21

She did, at last, ten days after the truce had been agreed in France, ratifying York as a suitable meeting place and suggesting a date in the early autumn.

Cecil prepared a safe conduct for Mary to enter on English soil and Elizabeth, as Lethington prepared to depart, gave him a portrait of herself to take back to her cousin.

'She will be delighted beyond measure,' he said truthfully. 'She has been wearing me down for months with demands to know what "my cousin Elizabeth" looks like.'

'And what have you replied?'

He grinned. 'That I am a mere man and that it is beyond me to describe Gloriana in terms that the queen my mistress would not take as the ravings of a besotted lover.'

She tapped him with her fan. 'You are a shocking flirt, sir.'

Despite the four hundred miles that lay ahead of him, despite the bad inns, the worse post horses and the endless, squelching mud, he set off for home on 11th July in the highest of high spirits.

Mary was ecstatic. In the hours after his return she made him repeat to her, not once but again and again, everything Elizabeth had said and how she had looked when she said it. Her eyes went constantly to the portrait. 'Is it really like her? Does it do her justice?'

She was like a green girl demanding news of her sweetheart.

After that it was how large a train would Elizabeth bring to York? Because it was essential that Mary's should match or surpass it. And the Scots court's liveries, trappings and tents, must be of unequalled splendour. Mary knew that her own jewels would outshine Elizabeth's, but she must give the most careful thought to her gowns.

'Should we take the hawks and the hounds? And is there time for my Master of the Horse to send abroad for some barbs or Spanish jennets? Because I *will* not have my lords appear at such an occasion mounted on those dreadful commoners of theirs. And ...'

Closing the door after she had at last released him, he overheard her exclaim to Mary Livingston, 'What a truly *blessed* relief that the truce was signed! If everything had fallen through I could not have borne it!'

23

The news that everything had fallen through arrived the next day.

It was Lethington, of course, who had to break it to Mary. His own exasperation well concealed, he said, 'It seems that the truce was broken almost before the ink dried on it. Catholics and Protestants are at one another's throats again and I am afraid it means that Elizabeth will feel compelled to cancel your meeting.'

He was left floundering by her reaction. He had recognised that she would be disappointed but, believing her a sensible young woman, was wholly unprepared for the storm of tears that overtook her. For perhaps the first time in his life, he was at a loss for words.

Mallie Fleming almost pushed him out of the room. 'Will you *please* go away! Really, could you not have broken the news to her more gently? Yesterday, you raised her to the heights and now, without even trying to soften the blow, you come straight out with news which you must have known would plunge her into the depths.'

The girl's blue eyes were furious, and there was no trace of the constraint that had become familiar to him in the months of their acquaintance. It had been a slender acquaintance, certainly, but he was experienced at reading people and, once he had summed her up as a pretty, rather shy young woman who might, or might not, grow out of her shyness, he had given her no more thought than he gave to the other Maries. It came as something of a surprise to find her in the rôle of tiger defending her young.

He said, 'But ...'

'She will be prostrated for the whole day! She's a very emotional person, you know, and she has been on tenterhooks for months. She has built so much on this meeting!'

'So have we all.' Lethington frowned, but his eyes were abstracted.

In the small corner of her mind that was not occupied by her anger for the queen, Mallie recognised that the frown was not for her. She didn't interest him enough.

Lethington went on, 'But she knows – surely she knows? – that there is always the possibility of things going wrong? When they do, one can only sigh, and shuffle the cards again, and begin the game again. That is how the world works.'

'Perhaps it seems so to you. But the queen is *human*. Unlike you, she has a heart as well as a mind.'

Lethington had been called many things in his time, but never inhuman. He stared for a moment into Fleming's flashing eyes, then turned on his heel and left.

With a dismal sniff, Mallie thought, 'After that, he will probably never speak to me again.' Then she raised her voice. 'Yes, Madame. I'm coming,' and went back to the queen.

24

Two days later, a messenger arrived from Elizabeth to say that her meeting with Mary was now out of the question, but that the idea might usefully be revived in the following summer. It took Mary some time to convince herself that it was indeed circumstances rather than preference that had brought about the postponement and, even then, the faintest of shadows remained. For weeks Elizabeth had been saying first one thing and then another, and when she had at last come out with an unequivocal, 'Yes', it had turned out not to be unequivocal after all.

It drove home to Mary that she herself was negotiating from a position of weakness and it did not please her to be Elizabeth's supplicant.

England's relations with the predominantly Catholic countries of Europe were, at best, uneasy; Mary's own, though personal rather than political, were excellent. It was time to make clear to Elizabeth that she had powerful friends.

She sent for her little bass singer, Davie Riccio.

'Can I rely on your discretion?'

'To the death, Madame,' he replied promptly.

She hesitated for only a moment. 'I already keep my personal secretary, Monsieur Raullet, very busy with letters abroad, but I wish to write more. I wish to write very privately, in particular, to friends who will be prepared to make clear to the queen of England that they *are* my friends. Do you understand?'

He beamed. '*Si, certo*, Madame! It ees – how do you say? – a sad waste to hide your light under a bush!'

She laughed. 'You mean "under a bushel", but the principle is the same. We will begin tomorrow. I wish to see, first, how well you can take dictation. When I am satisfied, we will see how you manage when I tell you what I wish to say and then leave the saying of it to you.'

He almost danced out of her presence and she heard him burst into song on the staircase beyond her audience chamber. He was an amusing little man.

25

James said, 'Well, if we're not going south to meet Elizabeth, why don't we go north? It's time ye visited the Highlands. Let the folk see their queen. It's a fine landscape, and there's good hunting. It would make a change for you, give you a holiday.'

'What a lovely idea!'

After a reflective moment, James went on, 'We could do something about Huntly when we're up that way. It's his duty to enforce the law in his territories, but he's harbouring an escaped criminal. It makes no difference that it's his son. He should have handed young Gordon back to us when he broke out of prison. As things stand, and with Huntly being Catholic, it doesn't reflect well on you.'

'No, and I am becoming very tired of him bullying me for being so tolerant to the reformed church.'

Inspired, James said, 'We could make a proper expedition of it, if ye like. In fact, we could kill three birds with one stone.' He glowered at

Lethington, who was having trouble keeping his countenance. 'We could bring Huntly to heel. We could lay hands on John Gordon again ...'

Lethington said, 'Just out of interest ... By law, Gordon should have paid the surgeon who attended to Lord Ogilvie's injuries. Did he?'

'No. That's a good point. And last ...'

It was Mary who interrupted this time, her eyes limpid with innocence. 'And last, but by no means least, we could install you in your earldom of Moray.'

James looked from his sister to his friend, and back again. 'I'm glad ye're enjoying yourselves. What's funny about that?'

Lethington said, 'Nothing at all. We were simply admiring your ability to think of so many irrefutable arguments on the spur of the moment. It promises to be a most interesting expedition.'

Chapter Six

1562 – 1563

1

Mary knew nothing of the Highlands, had no more than the vaguest childhood memories of gazing out northwards from the royal castle at Stirling – which, like Edinburgh to the east, was perched high on a crag – and having the tantalising sense of being poised between two worlds, with the green lowlands stretching away behind her and the mountains rising ahead, layer upon layer of them in every imaginable shade of purple. There had been no question of venturing into the heart of them when she was five years old, and there was no question now. Her entourage of courtiers, ladies, soldiers and packhorses was not one for the hills.

There was excitement enough even so, and as they followed the low-lying eastern coastline she found herself constantly drawing her companions' attention to the colour and the light. 'Green and purple and amethyst and amber! And see how they change, minute by minute, as the sun and the clouds cast changing shadows. It's like magic. Don't you find it so, Master Randolph? Look how the sun is lighting up that waterfall!'

Thomas Randolph was there only because he knew his duty. Nothing else would have induced him to accompany the court on its long and lumbering progress through an empty landscape, bordered by threatening grey seas on the right, threatening purple mountains on the left, and nothing but sodden yellow barley fields in between. He bowed. 'Your majesty's words are, as always, apt to the moment.'

Although his eyes were expressionless under the thick dark brows, she said suspiciously, 'I think I need Secretary Lethington to interpret that for me.'

Lethington, laughing, glanced behind them. 'I believe that "waterfall" may have been the word the ambassador had in mind.'

With perfect timing, the inky clouds that had been chasing them from

110

the south-east opened to send the rain down in sheets that, in a matter of seconds, turned to blankets, and then to torrents bouncing off the land. A sudden wild wind came driving in off the North Sea.

'Urrrr-rrr-rr,' shuddered Randolph, drawing his sheepskin cloak more closely around him and wondering whether he could bribe one of the royal huntsmen to let him have a deerskin that didn't hold its own weight of water for days afterwards.

The queen, wrapped in her own deerskin riding cloak and a cloth hood expensively waterproofed with beeswax, raised her voice again. 'Isn't it exhilarating! Oh, what an adventure!'

2

It took them just over two interminable weeks to reach Aberdeen, with a select few of the company being allocated guest chambers at the castles which the queen honoured with her presence, and everyone else having to bed down where they could. There was one night when Randolph was reduced to sharing the stables with the packhorses. It was a salutary reminder that for many of Mary's lords the English were not friends but enemies.

Aberdeen was Huntly's town, but there was no sign of the earl. The countess was there, however – small, redoubtable, and gold-garlanded as always – with her daughter Jean and an impressive train of attendants. Her grey head bobbing, she said, 'Aye, well. He's away. He didn't know you were coming. Are you in health? You're looking well.' The protruberant eyes shifted. 'Oh, and there's James, too. How's my niece Agnes? You're looking after her all right, are you?'

James's smile barely approached lukewarm. 'Yes.'

Mary said, 'Cousin ...'

'Aye, well. I wanted to talk to you about my son. My poor laddie, John. I know he's offended you, but I have to speak as a mother. He's young, that's all. There's not an ounce of wickedness in him. Jean here'll tell you.'

Dutifully, Jean said, 'He's just a bit high-spirited.'

'He's playing ducks and drakes with the law,' James replied bluntly. 'If he returns himself voluntarily to prison, her majesty might be prepared to consider a pardon. Not otherwise.'

Mary, who had agreed that this was James's expedition, to be handled as he thought best, nodded in agreement. It seemed a reasonable

111

compromise although she thought he might have used a friendlier tone of voice.

3

In Edinburgh, the Earl of Bothwell had grown tired of staring out of his prison window at the rain that had been falling steadily during his four months behind bars. At the end of August, he decided it was time to leave.

With some hard-muscled assistance from two of his fellow prisoners, he succeeded in breaking one of the bars and, in the darkness of the night, squeezing himself through the gap and hanging by his hands for a few moments while he surveyed what he could see of the descent. The curtain wall of the castle merged directly into the crag on which it stood, and Bothwell was a man of the hills, not a mountaineer, but, whistling under his breath and searching with a patience honed by years of lying in wait in Border ambushes, he found the footholds and handholds he needed to carry him crabwise down the vertiginous face of the castle rock.

Afterwards, taking his time about it, he went to visit his mother, then on to Crichton, and finally to his Border keep of Hermitage, where he waited to discover what would happen next. Prudently, he began sounding out the possibilities of a hurried and unpublicised voyage to France.

4

To James's surprise, Sir John Gordon obeyed the command to surrender himself. Unfortunately, he then changed his mind, escaped once more, and reappeared with close on a thousand horsemen, harrying Mary's train as it set out for Inverness.

'*What* is he doing?' she demanded furiously. 'Is he just showing off, or is he seriously thinking of attacking us?'

James said, 'There's a rumour that he's planning to murder Lethington and me, then carry you off and force you to marry him.'

She went off in a peal of laughter. 'Now, where have I heard that before?' Turning to Randolph, she demanded, 'Are my cousin Elizabeth's nobles equally obsessed by the idea of kidnapping their queen and murdering her advisers?'

Randolph sneezed vigorously. 'Beg pardon, your majesty. I don't think so.' He sneezed again.

James said, 'Well, let's push on. We'll be at Darnaway soon.'

Darnaway, the traditional seat of the earls of Moray, was a decaying, forest-ringed stronghold a few miles from the sea, and there, in the presence of as many local lairds, bondsmen and tacksmen as could be brought together at short notice, Mary formally announced that she had invested the Lord James Stewart with the earldom of Moray and that every man's duty was henceforth to him.

There was a stolid lack of expression on the assembled faces, and the Earl of Atholl, himself a northerner, murmured in Lethington's ear, 'Huntly is not much to their liking but they are used to him and he is, after all, a man of these parts. James is as much a foreigner as if he was an Englishman. He will not be having an easy time.'

'He'll manage,' Lethington said automatically, although privately he was by no means sure. It was easy to forget that the civilised little south-eastern segment of Scotland bounded by St Andrews, Stirling, Edinburgh and the road to England – the Scotland he and James knew best – was an artificial entity; that the lives of most Scots were controlled not by royal commandment but by the sterner majesty of ocean and mountain.

He remembered how he himself, only two years before, had discovered a new perspective on the land that had borne him when, a man of the sheltered lowlands, he had stood alone one evening outside the Earl Marischal's stronghold of Dunnottar, unassailably perched on the end of a great coastal cliff and virtually cut off from the land by a deep, drawbridge-spanned chasm. Then, for the first time in his life, he had found himself responding to the power and the magic of the sea. He had stood for the better part of two hours and, by the time a servant came in search of him, had reached the stage of thinking that, if the intellectual excitement of trying to shape a new future for his country had not taken such possession of his soul, he could live here contentedly forever, severed from the world, alone with his books.

Now, for no particular reason, he found his eyes coming to rest on Mallie Fleming, blue-eyed, delicate and damp, who appeared to have been far less ruffled by these last testing weeks than she had been by his own brief failure to understand that her mistress was not only a queen but an over-emotional girl. He had learned a good deal from that encounter, and some of it had been disturbing.

Mallie Fleming, aware of his gaze, guessed it to be as politely detached as always and took care not to meet it. She had taught herself, now, to behave almost normally when she encountered him in the course of her everyday duties, but a direct exchange of looks was beyond her. With discouraging certainty, she knew that if she tried to acknowledge his glance with a suitably slight and distant smile, it would turn out to be at best artificial, at worst tremulous.

When his installation was over, James said with every evidence of satisfaction, 'That ought to set the cat among the pigeons. If the good Lord Almighty didn't frown on gambling, I'd be taking wagers on how long it will be before Huntly hears about it.'

That he had heard about it by the time the royal procession reached Inverness two days later was clear from the fact that the keeper of the castle – one of Huntly's sons – barred its doors against the queen. It was high treason. When, in the end, the gates were opened, James had the young man seized and peremptorily hanged from the battlements.

5

'What? Must we leave my lovely Highlanders so soon?' Mary said a few days later. She had fallen swiftly under the enchantment of the landscape, the mountains, the air, the sense of freedom, and above all of the clansmen who came down from their glens to have a look at the ruler to whom they paid lip-service but not much else – strange, wild-looking men wearing plaids over long-sleeved tunics in muted stripes and checks, and legs bare save for tight-fitting trews that did no more than cover the thigh.

'How wonderful to be one of them! How wonderful to be any man at all – to lie by night in the fields and stride about by day in jack and steel helmet, a Glasgow buckler on one's arm and a broadsword at one's hip.'

James said prosaically, 'Ye'd change your tune after the first snowfall. And yes, we have to go. We have to get back to Aberdeen and settle Huntly. It might take time.'

It was to take five weeks, during which Huntly first tried to temporise and then disappeared, while his son, the dashing Sir John, reappeared and annoyed James very much by taking almost half his arquebusiers prisoner. There could be no doubt that the Gordons were now in open rebellion, and those members of the privy council who had been assigned to trail round the countryside with a sovereign who was enjoying herself very much more than they were, finally said enough was enough and declared both men outlawed.

The court was still installed at Aberdeen, waiting with increasing impatience for some resolution of the affair, when Lethington received a budget of urgent despatches from Edinburgh which sent him hurrying to the royal presence. Finding Mary surrounded by teachers and students from the university, he hesitated only for a moment before wending his seemingly unconcerned way towards the two Maries who were in attendance.

'Mallie,' he murmured to the fairer of the two. 'I need to talk to her majesty at once and privately. Can you arrange it?'

For a moment, the world stood on its head. Not 'demoiselle', not 'Fleming', not 'Mary', but 'Mallie'. It was an intimacy without any foundation that she knew of. Her eyes leaping to his face, she saw that he was not even conscious of what he had said because, although he appeared to be his usual cool and urbane self, his mind was racing. With a faint gasp, she replied, 'I'll try.'

Soon he was closeted with the queen, who said, 'What can be so urgent?'

'I have had no formal communication from London, but what I do have is more than rumour. My first despatch reports that, about ten days ago, your majesty's cousin Elizabeth fell ill with smallpox. According to the second, dated the sixteenth, she was thought to be dying.'

The silence was almost tangible.

'More than a week ago,' Mary said.

'Yes.'

'How distressing.' But it was mechanical, meaningless. 'Does Master Randolph have more recent news?'

'There were despatches for him from Cecil, but they made no mention of the queen's illness.'

'In case we should hear of it?'

'Perhaps.'

Mallie Fleming, in unobtrusive attendance, thought what a pair of *politiques* they were. They gave no sign of human concern at all. It was understandable, of course, because if Elizabeth were to die, or was already dead …

Lethington said, 'I have sent one of my clerks to Edinburgh to ensure that any further despatches are brought to me with all possible speed.'

The queen said, 'Then we can only wait. But the sooner we dispose of our present concerns, the better. I might have to set out for London at once. How frustrating not to *know*!'

If it had been left to Huntly, he would have taken to the heather until James decided to give up and go home. Unfortunately, his countess, guided by her advisers among the local witches and ignoring her daughter Jean's, 'No, really, mother!', chose to bully him into standing up for his rights.

At the head of a thousand ill-trained and undisciplined men, therefore, he marched to confront the very much smaller royal army at Corrichie, twelve miles to the west of Aberdeen.

The result was predictable to everyone except Huntly himself, because the royal army was officered by experienced soldiers such as Kirkcaldy of Grange and led by James, who enjoyed a fight, and Lethington, who didn't, but had a genius for inspiring others to give of their best. The queen watched the battle from a vantage point from which the combatants looked like jointed dolls and she could not see the blood as the Gordons were coldly massacred.

At the end of the day, Huntly and two of his sons – Sir John and seventeen-year-old Adam – were haled as captives before James and Lethington, and it was then that, face to face with the new Earl of Moray, Huntly got excited for the last time. Inside the mud-spattered but still spectacular white and gilt armour, his heart swelled and burst. The cords standing out on his temples and the eyes staring in death, his great figure slipped sideways from the saddle and crashed to the ground.

'A pity,' James remarked after a moment. 'There was a word or two I wanted to say to him.'

It was for the best. The same rule applied as in the Arran case of a few months before. Executing peers of the realm was a politically chancy business, even when the peer happened to be Huntly and John Knox would have been delighted.

Young Sir John Gordon, however, could not be allowed to escape the punishment he deserved.

Neither could the queen.

7

James said, 'Ye'll have to be there, ye know.'

'Never! James, I couldn't!'

'Everyone knows he was plotting to kidnap you and marry you. For love, he said. If ye don't attend, there'll be folk who say it was because ye encouraged him.'

He failed, deliberately, to warn his sister that it would not be the simple beheading that was the usual fate of the well-bred criminal. Executions for treason were not like that. They began, but did not end, with the scaffold and the rope.

Before the noose was placed round the young man's neck, he turned towards the queen and, his head flung proudly back, declared, 'I need no ministers of God to salve my soul. My only crime has been to love my queen, and your majesty's presence is all the solace I require.'

The delicate colour draining from her face, Mary sat in her chair of state, her lips clenched against the tears, and forced herself to watch while justice was done; while the once dashing young man was hauled up in the air, his eyes starting from their sockets, his body twirling, his legs and arms capering like those of some grotesque, ill-managed puppet.

She was a queen, and it was necessary to be strong. But to be hard was beyond her. She knew her own eyes to be staring and her face rigid as she fought the almost overmastering desire to turn away. Without moving, she whispered to James, 'How long must I go on watching? How long before it is over?'

'They'll cut him down in a minute or two. Then they'll disembowel him and quarter him.'

'They'll *what*?' Sharply, shudderingly, she turned to him. 'No! I won't – I can't – stay and watch that!' Her voice was almost pleading. 'It is enough, surely it is enough that I should have seen the death sentence carried out?'

James didn't answer.

The young man's legs had stilled by the time they cut the rope and his body subsided onto the scaffold floor. Then the executioner raised his knife and plunged it into him in a deep, sweeping cut from waist to groin.

The body screamed.

It was the most terrible, shocking sound Mary had ever heard.

Wildly, she clutched at James's arm, her eyes full of horror. *'Dear God! He isn't dead! He isn't dead!'*

'He isn't meant to be. I told you. There'd be no point drawing and quartering him if he was dead already.'

She did not faint although, more than anything, she wanted to. She gave way instead, and in full view of everyone, to a fit of extravagant and uncontrollable weeping. In the end she had to be almost carried to her chamber.

117

James's judgement had miscarried badly, for the public spectacle of Mary's tears did far more damage to her reputation than her absence would have done. It was not softness of heart, said fast-spreading rumour, that had brought the tears on. It was guilt.

8

Jean Gordon did not weep, but stood neatly with her sisters and wondered what would happen next. Her father was dead and the family would be dispossessed of title, estates and lands. Two of her brothers had died barbarously. Her eldest brother was in prison and might be spared but would have nothing to inherit. Adam, the youngest, was in prison too.

Her mother had said she would be too busy seeing to the embalming of her husband's body to attend the execution of her son. 'It's been a sore business,' she had gone on, 'but it cannot be laid at Mary's door. She was just doing what bluidy James Stewart and Secretary Lethington told her. And I know which of those two had the most to gain.'

9

Back in the haven of Holyrood a few days later, Mary – recovered from one misery only to be afflicted by another – sat at the side of the fire in her bedchamber, with Lethington opposite. Both were wrapped in layer upon layer of clothing.

Mary moaned, 'I feel terrible. Do you feel terrible?'

'Yes, Madame.' Lethington dabbed at his perspiring brow. 'And I'm cold.'

'I ache all over.'

The queen's French apothecary had said they were suffering from the English Sweat, a new disease that was becoming quite fashionable. It would cure itself in a few days, but in the meantime perhaps her majesty would wish him to apply leeches? Mary had shivered, sneezed, and said, 'No. Go away.'

'Tell me about Elizabeth,' she said.

Lethington's normally pleasant voice emerged as a strangled croak. 'According to my latest information, she has recovered well. I have most of the details now. What seems to have happened was that she made the mistake of taking a bath because she was feeling feverish ...'

Mary looked at him.

'Usually, she has a bath once a month whether she needs it or not, but there was an outbreak of smallpox so she took an extra one as a prophylactic. Then she went outdoors, and afterwards developed a temperature.'

He threw off three of his cloaks. 'Lord, but I'm hot. Anyway, her German doctor diagnosed smallpox, and she refused to believe him. But he was right and five days later Cecil was summoned to be told the queen was dying.'

'I know how she must have felt.'

'She said that, if she died, Robert Dudley was to be appointed protector of the realm and given an annual income of £20,000.'

'Jesu!'

At that moment, the door opened to admit Lord James, revoltingly healthy. 'I hear you're not well,' he said.

His sister, regarding him with loathing, turned back to Lethington, who was putting two of his cloaks back on again. 'The privy council,' he resumed, 'met to discuss her successor. Cecil writes that your majesty's name was not mentioned.'

'Whose was?'

'The Countess of Lennox. The Earl of Huntingdon. Lady Katherine Grey.'

'Their claims are all inferior to mine.' She coughed painfully.

James said, in the tone of a man who didn't know what all the fuss was about, 'But Elizabeth's recovered, hasn't she?' And then, with the best of intentions and the poorest of perceptions, added bracingly, 'Don't fash yourself, Mary. It wouldn't be the end of the world if you didn't get the English succession, now would it?'

Lethington, closing his eyes for an anguished moment, opened his mouth to speak but groaned instead.

It had been a good year for James. By a series of happy accidents, he had been enabled to defeat most of the potential opposition to his own power and influence by neutralising Châtelherault and the Hamiltons, wiping out both the Gordons and the Gordon influence in the north, and issuing such dire threats against the escaped Bothwell as to leave that gentleman with little alternative but to flee the country. On a personal level, he had gained the earldom of Moray with its revenues of 1,000 merks a year, the sheriffdoms of Elgin, Forres and Inverness, and was in the process of furnishing Darnaway from the rich spoils of Huntly's castle of Strathbogie.

What next? Fleetingly – and perhaps because his headache was making him feel uncharitable – Lethington reconsidered the phrase 'happy accidents'. But James was too moral for them to have been anything else.

Even so, with the earldom of Moray he had gained something of more value than title, estates and revenues. He had gained the makings of a private army. It had long been the custom in Scotland for landowners to accept 'bonds of manrent' from lesser men in their territory, bonds by which those lesser men promised their personal service and that of their dependants in return for maintenance and protection; there was always an undertaking to 'ride and go' if required. It was a system that operated at all levels of traditional society and one that gave those at the top, notably the earls, the sense of power and independence that was such a trial to a Crown with no army of its own. And now James, too, was in a position to call on the service of scores of lords and lairds, each capable of bringing in from forty to two hundred men. No longer did his influence rest only on his royal blood and strength of personality.

Lethington himself, as one of the small but growing body of professional men who owned little land and neither offered nor accepted bonds of manrent, existed outside the system – a dangerously exposed place to be unless one took care, as Lethington did, to remain on good terms with all the opposing factions within it. There was a price to be paid. Some people called him 'the chameleon', others 'the Scots Machiavelli'.

The queen sneezed wretchedly and James said, 'Why don't ye just go to your bed for a few days, my dear, and forget about everything until ye're better? Worrying never did anyone any good.'

His sister surveyed him through red-rimmed eyes, but her voice had lost none of its habit of command when she said, 'If that's the best you can do, James, I don't want to hear it. Go away.'

10

Lethington's family home was an ancient, L-shaped tower house a few miles east of Edinburgh. It was forbidding from the outside as, built for defence, such houses were apt to be, and inside, too, it had a spartan simplicity. It was the simplicity not only of necessity but of choice, however, because its owner, Sir Richard Maitland of Lethington, was a man who would have been much at home among the Athenians of Classical times, a philosopher, a poet, a lawyer with a satiric cast of mind. He was sixty-seven years old, and newly blind, and the only person in the world whom his son revered.

On a frosty morning in early February, Lethington dismounted outside the tower house and turned to see his father in the doorway, one hand resting on the arm of his daughter Marie, and the other on that of Lethington's wife, Janet. The tranquil, silvery head was tilted, as he assessed the meaning of what he heard, tried to count the horses and riders and men-at-arms, put a number to the baggage ponies.

As Lethington strode forward to embrace him, he said, 'And where are you off to now, my son?'

'London, and then France.'

His wife gasped, 'Oh, William! It will be months!'

Turning to kiss her, he felt her trembling and saw the sudden tears in her hazel eyes. 'We see little enough of you even when you are at Holyrood, but France ...'

Her voice trailed away.

It was true. The queen hated to be deprived, even for a few hours, of those upon whom she relied. In summer, the situation was manageable, but in winter, when there was no moon, permission to spend a night away was no permission at all.

Lethington had long given up trying to persuade Janet to join him in Edinburgh. Theirs had been an arranged marriage, but although she was pretty, and sweet, and he was fond of her, she had always been timid and had become no less so as the years passed. Her health was becoming a matter of concern to him, because increasingly – sometimes, he thought, exclusively – she had become possessed by guilt over her failure to bear him the sons without whom she did not believe he could be happy. During the ten years of their marriage, she had suffered four miscarriages and two stillbirths but still she would not give up. Or permit him to give up.

He said, teasingly, the only thing he could say. 'Since I will be away for so long, I think I might risk snatching the next two days and nights with you before I set out on my long, cold journey. But you must promise not to tell the queen!'

She gave a watery laugh and gripped his hand convulsively. 'Oh,

William, as if I would!'

Over dinner, his father, who had been a Lord of Session for years and had recently been appointed Lord Privy Seal, said, 'So, what is the purpose of your mission?'

Into his voice, Lethington put the smile his father could no longer see. 'The queen has become stubbornly attached to the idea of a match with Don Carlos. After marriage to the king of France, she is not prepared to look lower than she must for a new husband, and the heir to the throne of Spain is the most promising candidate on offer. I am going to London to discuss it with the Spanish ambassador, de Quadra.'

'Indeed! And what does Lord James have to say about that?'

'He doesn't know. Her majesty and I mounted a most elaborate charade to deceive him into believing that my purpose is to offer Scotland's mediation in the renewed war between England and France.'

'But why?'

'Because I am not prepared to have him ruin my diplomacy by writing to Elizabeth to tell her what I am up to. He has done it before.'

His father, who still courteously held to the old faith, knew his son well enough to say, drily, 'I would not have expected you to be so little disturbed by the possibility of a foreign king for Scotland, especially one who is an ardent upholder of Holy Church.'

Lethington hesitated. The truth was that he was proposing to make a virtue of necessity by using carefully sown rumours of such a match as a means of inducing Elizabeth to grant Mary the succession. And since he was virtually sure that Mary had more interest in her future throne than in her future husband, he thought that, if the former could be made contingent on the latter, everything might work out very well.

But the daring diplomacy which he so much enjoyed was not, he knew, of a kind to recommend itself to his father, so he said merely, 'I am a servant of the Crown.'

Sir Richard nodded. It was an acceptable answer. But Marie, the only one of Lethington's four sisters still unmarried, raised a quizzical eyebrow at him, and changed the subject. 'You won't forget,' she said, 'to bring back any poems you find on your travels? Traditional ones for father's collection, modern ones for mine.'

'Of course. Now, tell me, what of brother John? Has he completed his studies in France? Shall I see him there, or is he already on his way home?'

12

He was to regret, afterwards, that he had left Scotland when he did, because it meant that James was left on his own to handle a scandal that might otherwise have been suppressed.

He had left the court at Rossend, when it was on its way to St Andrews, and it was on the very first night at St Andrews that the crisis blew up.

It was late when Mary began preparing for bed, tired after a day spent smiling and waving and talking to the crowds in the city, which had a population almost twice the size of Edinburgh's. Nor had smiling and talking been enough. She had had to submit, with all the charm expected of her, to being shown the archery butts at Smalmonth, where she might like to practise, and the West Sands where she might choose to ride. And all the time there had been a sleety, biting wind coming in off the North Sea.

She might have felt better if the house she was occupying had been warm and welcoming. But she was proposing an extended stay and James had hired a merchant's house for her in South Street. He himself, as commendator of the Augustinian priory, occupied the Prior's House and also had a lodging at the Hospitium Novum, but neither, he said, was equipped to accommodate even his sister's slimmed-down court. Agnes, moreover, was in an interesting condition and he didn't think she should be incommoded.

But although thirty packhorses laden with tapestries, bed hangings, linen, clothes, chairs, cups, trenchers, platters, even scented rushes for the floors, had been sent ahead, and although every fire in the place was blazing, there was no sense of comfort. Mary was overcome by an urgent desire to be pampered, to be tucked into her cosy feather bed by loving hands, cocooned from the world.

Only Fleming and Beaton were on duty. Fleming, with the queen's discarded riding dress in her arms, had gone off in search of a mislaid clothes chest, while Beaton had vanished to the kitchens to prepare the queen's ritual cup of warm hippocras. Mary was in her chemise with one of the chamber women standing by, holding her discarded ribbon garters and waiting for the queen to finish rolling down her knitted and embroidered silk stockings, when without warning the door crashed open.

It was one of the gentlemen of her court, the poet Châtelard, who had been among her retinue when she sailed from France for Scotland, had left again with her Guise uncles, but had returned in the previous autumn to rejoin the court at Aberdeen. He amused her, a wild, romantic young man who swore that he would die if she rejected him.

And how could she possibly reject him, she had laughed. 'Who else could dance with me so elegantly, or flatter me so outrageously, or compose and recite such sweet lyrics to my *beaux yeux*?'

Beaton, who had been in attendance, had giggled. 'None of your lords, certainly. Can you imagine the Earl of Argyll reciting poetry to you!'

'Jesu! The only thing he would recite would be an anathema.'

And now the poet was scarlet in the face, and far from sober, and he had all the strength of drunkenness as he lunged across the room at his queen, his goddess, his inspiration, his mistress, his cruel princess.

'Châtelard! How dare you!' Mary snapped, crossing her arms over her breasts and leaping to her feet so that the shift fell and covered her long, beautiful legs. But he was impervious to the authority in her voice, impervious to the chamber women, impervious to everything except the object of his desire. His arms were around her and his open mouth was seeking hers and the smell of wine was overpowering. Even as she struggled to push him away, his hand was at the frilled neck of her shift and his body was thrusting hard against hers. There was a sharp, ripping sound and the shift tore from neck to waist.

Twisting her head away, Mary screamed at the pitch of her lungs. And would have screamed again, and again, except that the predatory hand came up to clamp itself over her mouth while the breathless voice gasped over and over, '*Non, non! Ma reine, mon amour! Je t'adore.*'

The reek of wine was nauseating and, although she tried to bite at his hand and tear at his face with her nails, none of it made any impression. He was past all feeling except for the one desire that possessed him.

Somehow she succeeded in tearing her mouth free, gasping air into her lungs to scream again – but no one came. One of the chamber women was wailing uselessly, while the other was dragging at him from behind. But he flung her away with a single sweep of his arm, and all the time he was pushing, pushing, pushing towards the high curtained bed.

Never in her life before had anyone dared to lay violent hands upon Mary and all her strength suddenly deserted her. She knew she was on the verge of fainting, her consciousness coming and going like clouds over the sun.

And then she saw that Fleming was there, snatching the long-handled warming pan from the bed and bringing it down with elemental violence on the poet's head. And the grooms of the chamber were erupting through the door, with Mary's bodyguard and her brother James, sword drawn, on their heels.

'Use it,' she shrieked. 'Use it! Kill him, kill him!' and as they tore the half-stunned Châtelard away from her, collapsed weeping on the floor.

13

From the first opening crash of the door until James's appearance, no more than two or three minutes had passed, although it had seemed like an eternity. Her grooms had been downstairs, and James about to leave for the Prior's House. But because the house was unfamiliar to them, with two sets of winding stone stairs that distorted the direction of sound, they had not at first been able to identify where the screams were coming from. Châtelard himself had found her almost by chance, by running up the first set of stairs he saw and looking in every room.

She was too distraught to face up to decision, too distraught to do anything other than leave things to James.

If Lethington had been there, he would have said, 'Ship the silly fellow back to France. Or kill him if you must. But do it quietly.'

James, however, was a firm believer in the due process of law, and so Châtelard was brought to trial on a charge of *lèse-majesté* and, having been found guilty, was publicly executed at the Mercat Cross, although Mary this time was not present.

From the scaffold, the young man read out some lines from a poem by Ronsard and then, in ringing tones, cried out his own farewell to 'the most beautiful and the most cruel princess in the world'.

There wasn't a soul in Scotland, England, France or Spain who didn't hear all about it in a matter of days.

14

It was the third and by far the most direct insult to Mary's virtue in less than a year, and each of them had left damaging echoes behind. Arran, and Sir John Gordon, and now Châtelard had all claimed that their crimes had been committed for love of her.

125

John Knox had the time of his life on the subject of queens who impiously enticed men to their doom.

When she had somewhat recovered, Mary wrote to Lethington in London, 'It was a Huguenot plot. I know it. I should have remembered that he was an adherent of the Montmorencys, who have always hated the family of Guise. I should have guessed that he was a Huguenot. By discrediting me, he must have hoped to discredit not only Catholicism and the Guises in France, but me, myself, in the eyes of King Philip of Spain. Pray explain all this to my cousin Elizabeth. She is a woman; she will understand.'

Lethington, receiving this tear-stained missive, tried and failed to imagine any man daring to make an attempt on Elizabeth's virtue. Woman she might be, but he could not think that she would understand and did not in the least fancy trying to explain it to her.

There were other tear-stained effusions in the weeks that followed.

First, the Duc de Guise died at the hands of a Huguenot assassin – the man who had been a father to Mary in her early girlhood; who had given her his strength, love and support all through her life. He had been the one person she had felt she could always turn to, even if only in her thoughts, even when far away. She did not know how she could go on without him.

And after him, it was his younger brother, the Marquis d'Aumale, who was dead of wounds received at Dreux.

And then it was her favourite half-brother – the lively and lovable Lord John Stewart, who had wed Bothwell's sister in splendour only a year before.

Which reminded her ... 'Be so good as to enquire into the charge on which my cousin Elizabeth has imprisoned Lord Bothwell in the Tower of London. I take it as unfriendly of her so to treat a man who is not a subject of hers, but of mine. You have my authorisation to negotiate for his release.'

Bothwell, choosing exile in preference to recapture, had sailed some weeks before in a merchant ship for France, a ship that had unfortunately been driven into an English port to seek haven from a storm. The English at Berwick, who liked Bothwell as little as he did them, had succeeded in capturing him and, after some delay, despatching him to London. As far as Lethington could discover, Elizabeth had no real justification for holding him; on the other hand, the Tower seemed as good a place as any for him to cool his heels until Mary's privy council decided what to do about him.

Carelessly, Lethington said to Cecil, 'My queen is annoyed that your queen should be holding Lord Bothwell instead of returning him to justice in Edinburgh.'

'Is she?' Cecil said. 'You must let me have an official note about it.'

15

The death of the Duc de Guise complicated Lethington's mission because France promptly settled her internal differences and turned her united attention to expelling the English garrison from Le Havre. This, while lending weight to the Scots' seemingly disinterested offer of mediation, had an effect on Elizabeth's temper which was far from beneficial.

It was a temper already frayed by renewed parliamentary demands that she marry and supply England with a successor about whom there would be no dispute. 'And I know who is behind *that* campaign,' she said caustically, 'because the man who started the agitation happens to be a friend of someone who would very much like to be our husband, and father of our heir.'

She glared at Robert Dudley, her Master of the Horse, who was mounted on a goodlooking barb and, in his spectacular white and green state livery, perhaps a trifle overdressed for a mild trot round the park at Whitehall at the end of winter. She herself was on one of her palfreys, while Lethington had a courser from the royal stables which was showing all the signs of being under-exercised.

Dudley smiled innocently and, when the queen's baleful eyes had left him, winked at Lethington.

'Marriage and heirs!' Elizabeth went on. 'What else is a woman for?' Then, with one of her abrupt changes of subject, she said, 'Secretary Cecil tells me you have been in London for more than three weeks. Why have you not presented yourself before now?'

His reasons had been of the best, although she would not have thought them so. He had, in fact, and according to plan, been engaged in long, very private and very intricate discussions with de Quadra about the Spanish marriage – discussions so intricate that, however much he enjoyed the fencing that helped to lend them conviction, had ultimately begun to pall. His primary purpose, after all, was to ensure that they were less private than de Quadra wanted them to be.

Just as de Quadra spied on de Foix, the French ambassador in London, so de Foix spied on de Quadra, both of them then going straight to Cecil to tell him whatever each regarded as improper about the dealings of the other. In general, Cecil – who spied on both of them – already knew. It was however an admirable means, for someone like Lethington, of having information conveyed to Cecil without appearing to be directly involved at all, the kind of information that would remind Cecil and Elizabeth of the ever-present possibility of a Catholic league against England, but the kind of information that he could, if necessary, convincingly deny.

He said, 'I have been lodging with a friend. I had some private business to attend to and did not feel justified in imposing on your hospitality while I did so.'

Elizabeth snorted. 'That makes a pleasant change. There are times when I think my court exists only to provide people with free board and lodging. I have just learned that the royal kitchens last year cooked 1240 oxen, 8200 sheep, 2330 deer, 760 calves, and ... How many pigs, Robert?'

'Almost two thousand,' Dudley replied as smoothly as if he really knew.

'God's death! Can you not remember even one figure with exactitude?' She turned back to Lethington. 'I begin to think I must charge guests for their lodging. I shall be bankrupt if we go on like this. So what is this I hear about marriage plans for your queen, my cousin?'

He was politely mystified. 'I cannot guess what you have heard, your majesty. All my queen's subjects certainly wish her to marry safely and happily, as yours do you, but she is in no haste. It is not a subject on which I have dared to speak to her ...'

'Hah!'

'... but there are certain considerations that limit her choice. As with you, she will never, for example, marry basely. As queen of Scots and queen dowager of France, she may look for the most distinguished of matches.'

A sudden, disquieting glitter leapt to the round brown eyes under their plucked brows.

Lethington thought at first that he must be suffering from some affliction of the hearing, or indeed of the brain, when the imperious voice responded, 'I know who she needs. She needs Lord Robert, here. Nature has implanted in him so many graces that, if I myself were thinking of marrying, I would prefer him above all the princes in the world.'

Lethington's courser, sensitive to his rider's hands, executed a few brisk sidesteps.

Glancing across at Lord Robert, Lethington saw that he was equally dumbstruck – the commoner whose father had been executed for treason, the man whose intimacy with Elizabeth had been the talk of Europe for years, the man whose wife had died in highly suspicious circumstances; the man who, for good and sufficient reasons of his own, was the driving force behind the current parliamentary demand that the queen should marry.

And the man who, by so doing, had angered his queen and needed to be taught a lesson. Lethington, for a moment, had thought she was serious.

Successfully keeping his countenance, he said, 'My mistress will be overcome that you should consider giving up to her someone whom you prize so dearly. There could be no more extraordinary expression of your majesty's love for her. But I cannot think that she would consent to deprive you, whom she loves equally, of the joy and solace of Lord Robert's company.'

Lord Robert opened his mouth but was ignored as Elizabeth, her temper improving with every word, exclaimed, 'Ah! If only Lord Robert's brother shared his looks and charm! Then my cousin and I could have a Dudley each.'

Lethington – sternly subduing an inclination to say 'Errr ...' – waited, and after a moment, cocking her curled and jewelled head, she went on, 'It had not previously occurred to me, but if your mistress is to marry happily and safely as you desire, and if our English parliament is to view her claim to the succession more favourably than it does now, then she must obviously marry an English gentleman.'

She was enjoying herself, which was more than could be said for Lethington or Dudley. The malice was unmistakable as, expansively, she went on, 'And since no one is better able to judge an English gentleman than his queen, I shall choose for her. Yes. She shall have Robert Dudley.'

She almost sounded as if she meant it. But she didn't, of course. She couldn't.

Lethington's smile was beginning to feel as fixed as a fly in amber, but he was not prepared to continue being a target for her mockery. 'It would be too great a sacrifice to ask of you, your majesty, but I think – I *think* – I may have a solution. Why do you not marry Lord Robert yourself? Then you could bequeath to my mistress both your throne *and* your husband.'

Acknowledging the hit, the full, painted royal mouth twisted into a sweet-sour grimace. 'What an admirable idea, my friend. What would we do without you? As to the other business you supposedly wished to broach, the mediation between ourselves and France, you may speak to Secretary Cecil. And now I will race you round the park and back to the King Street gate. That horse of yours' – she smiled again – 'clearly needs to have the fidgets galloped out him.'

16

In May – by which time Lethington was in France carelessly mentioning
to Catherine de' Medici the possibility of a Spanish match for Mary, just
as he had equally carelessly mentioned the possibility of a French match
to de Quadra – Mary herself was deeply exasperated to receive a
messenger from her uncle the cardinal.

He, having decided that it would not after all be in France's interest for
Mary to make a Spanish match, had been having discussions with the
Hapsburg emperor and had settled with him that she was to marry the
youngest imperial son, the Archduke Charles of Austria. The cardinal
knew that his niece would recognise the wisdom of such a course.

If Mary had been the kind of person who relieved her feelings by
throwing things, some expensive pieces of Murano glass might have met
their doom. As it was, she said thoughtfully to Fleming, 'How very
embarrassing, when we know the Archduke Charles to be a long-standing
and favoured suitor of my cousin Elizabeth.'

Fleming said, 'Yes. I suppose that, for her, his good looks must make
up for his being a younger son.'

The queen meditated for a moment. 'You know, I really think it is my
duty to send the messenger on to Elizabeth. I mean, she is entitled to
know. It is the least I can do.'

Mallie Fleming, a picture of innocence, said, 'Yes, Madame.'

Although the queen was frequently mischievous, she had never before
known her to be spiteful. It made a refreshing change.

17

With the crown, sword and sceptre borne before her, with banners flying
and trumpets sounding, the queen of Scots, blinding in orange damask
embroidered in silver, led the procession of lords temporal, lords spiritual
and burgesses up the long hill from Holyroodhouse to the newly-built
Tolbooth next to St Giles cathedral for the first full, law-giving
parliament of her reign.

Once everyone had settled down, which took some time, the new lord
chancellor – the Earl of Morton – rose to make the opening speech.

Morton was a very different man from his predecessor, the late Earl of Huntly, a man who had been born plain James Douglas and had acquired his earldom by the simple expedient of marrying the woman in whose right it was. There were many of her lords whom Mary disliked – Lindsay of the Byres, loud and violent; Ruthven, weird and disturbing; Argyll, sour and critical – but Morton was the most distasteful of all. She disliked the full, round, red beard that stretched from cheekbone to cheekbone, every hair of it seeming to crinkle independently. She disliked the pouched brown eyes and the small mouth so submerged in his whiskers that it was visible only when open. She disliked the coarse voice that emerged from it, with the artificial English accent he had acquired during a period of exile in England and had never quite lost. She disliked the fleshy-knuckled hands and the bitten nails. He was one of her privy councillors, her lord chancellor, the head of the Douglases, one of her leading noblemen, but he was a peasant at heart, slovenly, self-seeking, and narrow-minded.

The sentiments expressed in his opening speech, however, could scarcely have been more high-flown. The Three Estates were adjured to lay aside all personal interests and bend their minds to the service of their God and their country; to think of themselves not as three estates but as one, united in friendship and purpose.

It sounded unimpeachable, but the call for unity passed straight over the heads of John Knox and the Earl of Moray, because Knox boiled over when he discovered that the Lords of the Articles who were responsible for drafting legislation were not proposing to introduce laws to establish the reformed church as the only church of the realm.

James, discussing it all beforehand with his sister while they were out hawking in the park at Holyrood, had said it wasn't the right time.

'But when I arrived back in Scotland, I issued a decree maintaining the religious *status quo* until I had an opportunity to consult with my Three Estates. This, surely, is my opportunity.'

'No, well ...' James had said. 'Lethington's got enough problems with his English and French negotiations without us making an issue of our own religious differences. We don't want to cramp his style. Everything's been going along quite nicely here, and I think we should let things stay as they are for the time being.'

'But I made a promise, and I would like to keep it. I cannot imagine that Master Knox has forgotten it.'

'He doesn't always get his own way. Ye could forestall him by making a few minor concessions before parliament opens.'

Mary, frowning, blew her silver whistle three times to summon the peregrine falcon back from the freedom of the heavens to the prison of swivel and hood on her gauntleted wrist. She was a beautiful bird with marigold eyes, a back like silken slate and breast feathers cross-barred below a throat as smoothly creamy as new butter. 'Well, I suppose you know best.'

In the event, it gave her a certain satisfaction that, where John Knox was concerned, her doubts proved to be justified, and even more satisfaction that it was James he turned on first – James who, said Knox, was more interested in his own aggrandisement than in the state of the kirk; James who had become a temporiser, a court puppet; James who, by sacrificing faith to expediency, had put himself beyond redemption. He was as bad as Lethington.

James objected to being shouted at. Although it would not have been true to say that he felt guilty, his conscience was not as snow-white as he would have liked. The result was that he, who never lost his temper, promptly lost it and shouted back.

Knox refused to apologise.

James said, 'Well, if you're going to behave like that about it ...'

Knox said, 'I am', though not so succinctly. Whereas, on the occasion of an earlier confrontation with James, he had called him little worse than an earwig, this time he covered the entire Biblical alphabet of sinners, from Abihu, Ahab and Ananias by way of Jabin and Jehoiakim to Uzziah and Zelophehad.

James, who had never heard of most of them, did not try to argue. He merely yelled, 'Man, ye've got no sense!' and stamped off.

But Mary did not escape. Undismayed – indeed, stimulated – Knox went on to preach one of his most impassioned tirades in St Giles, in which the queen and the rumours of a Spanish marriage for her figured large.

Mary, almost as angry with James for persuading her to go back on her word as she was with Knox for his thunderings, summoned the preacher for a reprimand and was not at all mollified by his arrival in the company of Lord Stewart of Ochiltree, a man of little consequence save for his royal name and much-diluted royal blood, whose sixteen-year-old daughter the fifty-year-old preacher had recently begun courting. Mary detested the thought of Knox being allied, however distantly, to the house of Stewart and suspected Knox of having embarked on the affair solely to infuriate her.

But today her concern was with his attitude to herself.

'How dare you?' she stormed at him. 'I do not believe that any prince has ever been so treated! Despite all your scoldings, I have been as tolerant towards you as any man could possibly expect. I have even invited you to come to me when you have a complaint against me. But it seems I cannot be quit of you or your endless accusations against me!'

To Knox, the tears born of her frustration reflected only the weakness, the godlessness, of an idolatrous woman.

'It is my duty,' he said, 'to speak plain.'

'To speak plain? About my marriage? What have you to do with my marriage? What *are* you within this realm?'

'A subject born in it, Madam.'

John Erskine of Dun was there, an elderly man, a reformer but a meek and kindly one. 'Yer majesty,' he said, 'don't be upset. Your subjects have a natural interest in who you choose to wed and they know there is not a prince in Europe but admires your beauty and excellence, and longs for your favours.'

She liked him and she trusted him. Dabbing at her eyes, sniffing, she began to recover herself. 'Is that true?'

'Would I say it otherwise?'

And then Knox, true to form, ruined it all by saying, 'Give up your weeping, Madam. I cannot abide tears. I am wounded even by the tears of children justly chastised.'

'*You* are wounded?' she shrieked. 'I cannot bear any more. Go, go, go!' She should have known better than to summon him. No one in the world had such a capacity for reducing her to tears of rage.

On his way out, Knox cast his burning gaze over Mary Fleming and Mary Beaton, perfectly coiffed, perfectly gowned, perfectly groomed as always, and, shaking his head, said, 'Aye, aye, you silly lassies. But remember that your gay gear will avail you nothing when death approaches.'

Closing the door after him, Mary Beaton said reflectively, 'He really has a most splendid beard. I wonder if he uses curling papers on it at night?'

18

Lethington, arriving back in London early in June after several fruitless but enjoyable weeks among the French, whom he liked in their own country, if not in his, was summoned to Greenwich seven days later. It was roughly what he would have expected. Two days for Elizabeth to hear that he was back, three days to try and discover what he was up to, and a further two days to disabuse him of any idea that his comings and goings were of the slightest interest to her.

This time she received him with formality, forcing him to run the gauntlet of the tapestry-hung Great Hall, the bodyguards in the watching chamber, and an hour's wait in the presence chamber, full of noblemen, knights, gentlemen and malicious gossip. For anyone new to the ways of courts, it would have been an intimidating experience, and was of course designed to be so.

There were bird cages in the windows of her privy chamber, tapestries on the walls and, on the floor, the coarse rush matting which encouraged kneeling envoys to keep their business brief and to the point.

She wasted no time on preliminaries. 'I now know of your negotiations with Spain over a possible marriage for your queen, and she herself has sent to tell me of negotiations with Austria over an alternative match with the Archduke Charles. I therefore say to you formally that, if your queen accepts either suitor, or any other member of the house of Hapsburg, I will be compelled to regard her as my enemy. If, on the other hand, she agrees to marry to my satisfaction, I will be her friend and sister, and favour her succession to my throne after my death.'

Lethington allowed no trace of jubilation to show in face or voice, although it was exactly what he had been hoping for. He had not expected Elizabeth to commit herself so openly or so soon. He said, 'My mistress will be delighted by your interest in her affairs. May I ask ...'

'No, you may not. Am I a marriage broker to find a husband for her? You may go with Secretary Cecil who has some despatches for you to take back to Scotland. And now, good morrow to you.'

19

Following Cecil through a maze of halls and galleries to the lodging that accommodated the secretary's office, bedchamber and confidential clerks, Lethington silently congratulated himself. Elizabeth's brusqueness had been the clearest indication that the thought of Mary marrying a powerful Catholic prince had been giving both Elizabeth and Cecil sleepless nights.

It was what he had intended. The next step was to try and discover from Cecil whom Elizabeth would regard as an acceptable husband for her cousin. Not Robert Dudley, presumably.

Waving a couple of stray clerks out of his office, Cecil tried to straighten up, clutched at his back and groaned. His black robes disguised the slightness of his figure, but nothing could disguise the unhealthy floridness of his complexion.

Lethington said sympathetically, 'Oh, dear. No better?'

'Six months of meadowsweet infusions inside and chickweed poultices outside, and they have made no difference at all. I find it hard to put my mind to anything.' Gingerly, Cecil lowered himself onto an oak settle and extracted half a dozen papers from among those littering the fringed green cloth on his table.

'I have letters here for Lord James and Master Knox. And this is one from my queen to yours concerning Lord Lennox.'

Lennox?

Matthew Stuart, Earl of Lennox, was a Scot who had been exiled since the 1540s for the crime of allying himself with Henry VIII against Scotland's then governor Châtelherault, a crime that had had its genesis in the age-old feud between the Lennox Stuart and the Hamilton families. Lennox had subsequently married Henry's niece, and the marriage had produced two sons who had the distinction of being related to the ruling houses of both England and Scotland. The elder, Henry Stuart, Lord Darnley, was a pretty boy of seventeen.

And now, Lethington discovered, scanning the paper in his hand, Elizabeth was asking Mary to permit the Earl of Lennox to return to Scotland for the first time in almost twenty years to see to his estates there. Why? Lennox was a Catholic and no great favourite of Elizabeth's. There were some, however – notably the Countess of Lennox – who saw young Darnley as an eligible husband for Mary.

Putting the paper together with the others, as if it were neither particularly interesting nor particularly relevant, he said, 'Might we go back to the matter of whom the queen your mistress would see as a suitable husband for *my* queen ...'

Cecil's grey eyebrows, with their tilde-like curves, drew together impatiently. 'Allow me to disabuse you of any idea that my queen is interested in who your queen chooses to marry, as long as he is not likely to prove a danger to England. In any case, I have no doubt that my queen will marry in due course and bear children to succeed her. It means that there is no purpose in discussing either your queen's husband, or her rights in the succession. Also, the subject is becoming tedious.'

As answers went, it was at best disingenuous. Lethington said, 'I wonder if you know the tale of the Chinese philosopher who, for the emperor's pleasure and his own reward, undertook to teach a mule to speak within a given time – safe in the knowledge that either the mule, the philosopher or the emperor would be dead before the time had run out. The future being full of uncertainties, do you not think it wiser to base one's policy on the situation as it stands? *"Vita summa brevis spem nos vetat incohare longam"*.'

Life is too short for long-distance hopes.

Since Cecil and his mistress lived almost entirely on a hand-to-mouth basis – and Elizabeth's refusal to make up her mind about the succession, or indeed anything else, was a classic example of it – Cecil should have conceded the point. Instead, he said drily, 'It is possible to admire Horace's poetry without agreeing with his views.'

Lethington shrugged. 'I accept that the situation may change in the years to come. In the meantime, however, a promise of the succession if the queen your mistress should choose not to marry would effectively discourage the queen *my* mistress from looking abroad for a husband. Which would suit both of us.' He was in no position to be quite so categorical about it, but he needed some kind of answer.

Cecil was disinclined to give him one. 'Successions, promises, husbands! I have more important things to think about.' He groaned. 'Why this backache should affect my bowels I do not know. Your pardon, but I must go to the garderobe.'

20

Lethington waited for someone to come in on some pretext, to make sure that he was not reading papers he was not supposed to be reading. No one did. Meditatively, he waited a little longer, then rose to his feet and strolled towards the window. Cecil's work table happened to be in the way.

Most of the papers strewn on it seemed to be accounts and despatches, but among them was a scribbled list in Cecil's own hand, laid out in columns as if Cecil had been trying to clarify something in his mind. Lethington's eyes had already passed over it before he realised what it was – a comparison of the merits of two of the leading candidates for the position of husband to the queen of England.

Or the queen of Scotland?

He knew Cecil's hand well and could read the thin, spiky characters as easily as if they were those of a professional clerk.

Under the heading 'Birth', he read of the Archduke Charles of Austria, 'Nephew of the present emperor and brother to his heir'. And of Robert Dudley, 'Born of a knight, his grandfather but a squire'.

Under the heading 'Wealth', the archducal entry said, '3,000 ducats a year'. Dudley's entry said, 'Dependent on the queen. And in debt'.

But it was the heading 'Fertility' that set Lethington's brain whirling. The marriage of the archduke's father had been blessed with 'multitudes of children', which held out hope for the archduke himself. But by Dudley's name was the laconic comment, '*Nuptiae sterile*. Brother also'.

Silently, Lethington returned to his chair.

Dudley had been married for ten years, his brother for even longer, but there had been no children of either marriage and 'sterile' suggested that neither had there been miscarriages or stillbirths.

Lethington knew more than he would have chosen about miscarriages and stillbirths. He had been worrying off and on for two or three weeks over a letter Janet had sent him in France, saying that she had conceived again, and that this time she would carry the child to term, and that this time it would live. He had not wanted to go to her bed on that February night at his father's house, but to have refused her would have been a cruelty that was beyond him.

He forced his mind back to Dudley. The sterility of his marriage need not be conclusive, but Lethington, who had heard gossip of mistresses, had never heard gossip of bastards. And, in view of the purpose of the list, Cecil would certainly have noted their existence if there had been any.

It was a fascinating thought that, if Dudley was indeed infertile, he could have been bedding Elizabeth for years without risk. If he was infertile, it was also the best of arguments against Elizabeth marrying him. And if he was infertile, was that why she had so generously offered him to Mary?

If Mary failed to bear children, it would weaken not only her claim to the English succession but to the support of foreign powers. A lack of direct heirs was apt to diminish the authority of a ruling house.

He glanced up innocently from his note block as Cecil re-entered the room, looking less testy and saying, 'That's better. Where were we?'

Withstanding the temptation to reply, 'We were wondering why you left me with an open invitation to read what was on your desk,' Lethington said blandly, 'You were going to suggest a match for *my* queen that would please *your* queen.'

Cecil actually smiled. 'No, I wasn't. Find your own king. Personally, I do not care if your queen never marries.'

137

What a devious man he was. He had always disliked Dudley – enough, it now seemed, to try and forestall not only any possibility of that gentleman's being elevated to the throne of England but even to the throne of that cold, wet, despised wilderness to the north of England's borders.

21

Lethington was closeted with Mary for a full five days after he reached home again, because there was much that, during his absence, he had chosen not to commit to writing, not even in cipher.

Where the Spanish marriage was concerned, he reported that Catherine de' Medici would certainly try to influence Philip II against it while at the same time denying any possibility of a match between Mary and her thirteen-year-old brother-in-law, Charles IX of France.

Mary said, 'But I'm not thinking of marrying Charles.'

'No. That was my contribution. Philip will not believe Catherine's denial, which will cancel out her interference in the matter of Don Carlos.'

And so it went on.

The queen was oddly lethargic about it all, and although Elizabeth's promise of the succession if Mary married someone of whom she approved brought a brief sparkle to her eyes, it was a sparkle that vanished almost at once to be replaced by resentment at Elizabeth's presumption.

Lethington, after being away from court for almost five months, could only guess at the toll those months had taken of Mary's spirits, with the Châtelard affair, and the deaths of her two Guise uncles and her beloved brother John. But she was still the queen and, however depressed and discouraged she might be, could not be excused from attending to affairs of state. 'I cannot emphasise too strongly,' he resumed, 'that a marriage with Don Carlos would end any possibility of amity with England, whereas …'

Mary listened with a dull inner anger. Why should she *care* what her cousin Elizabeth thought?

She had known that her life in Scotland was not going to be easy, that she would have to offer not only smiles and waves to her people, but congenial words. She had known that she was going to have to make many concessions that she would have preferred not to make. She had known that in the early days, at least, she would need James's guidance, and Secretary Lethington's. And so she had faithfully followed James's advice about her conduct of affairs, even when her own instincts were against it, and things had consistently gone wrong. Failing to consult parliament about the religious question had been only the most recent example. Every time it had been she, not he, who took the blame. She was no longer sure that she could trust him.

And now here was Lethington, who knew perfectly well that her mind was set on the Spanish match, pointing out all the arguments against it. His words were well chosen, his grey eyes as clear as always, and his voice familiarly pleasant and unexcited, but he seemed to be sympathising with everyone's point of view except her own.

She said, 'I wish to hear no more of Elizabeth's views on my marriage. My right to succeed to the throne of England is unarguable, and it is insulting on my cousin's part to try to qualify it by linking it to my choice of husband.'

Since she was obviously not in the mood to be amused by Elizabeth's playful offer of Robert Dudley, Lethington did not mention it.

22

Royalty on its high horse had been one of the recurring hazards of Lethington's life for nine years, so he was not unduly undisturbed. But, despite his natural resilience, he was feeling the after-effects of his lengthy negotiations and his two thousand miles in the saddle, and it was a little wearily that he went off to make his peace with James, who was being offended in a high-nosed way over being kept in the dark about his doings.

He was just entertaining him, in confidence, with the Dudley nonsense – and Dudley's deficiencies as a potential husband – when one of his clerks came to tell him that a messenger had arrived urgently from his father.

There was no letter. There had not been time. Sir Richard's messenger, an old man, wrinkled as a walnut, whom Lethington had known all his life, stood cap in hand, scarlet with haste and sorrow, and stammered out that the lady of Lethington had miscarried of her child. She was near to death. Would Maister William come before it was too late to give her comfort?

Lethington sprang to his feet, but found that his legs would not support him. Then James's hand was on his shoulder, and his voice was saying with unusual solicitude, 'Are ye all right? Ye'd better go. I'll explain to Mary.'

Mutely, Lethington nodded. He could not bring himself to speak, could not say that, for the first time in all his thirty-five years, he had in a single moment learned the terrible, heart-wrenching truth of ordinary human guilt and sorrow.

Chapter Seven

1563 – 1565

1

'Two virgin queens in one isle!' Mary Livingston exclaimed. 'What a frightening thought! Forty-eight, forty-nine, fifty. Pass me another pin, someone.' She found it a serious responsibility being in charge of the queen's jewels but an enjoyable one, except when, as now, she was reduced to sitting on the floor with a silk cloth spread out before her, counting second-size pearls on to fine silver pins for the embroiderers. 'Who gave you that idea, Beaton?'

'Master Randolph.' Beaton preened just a little and the others smiled, knowing that she held the English ambassador's middle-aged heart in her elegant palm. 'After he had told her majesty, yet again, that the queen his mistress would cease to be her friend unless she married to suit Elizabeth, I pointed out to him that, great as was Madame's desire to please Elizabeth, it was difficult for her to do so when Elizabeth persisted in telling her, not who it *would* please her for Madame to marry, but only who would *not* please her. And I said that Elizabeth must surely have someone in mind, and such an important man as Master Randolph *must* know who ...'

Livingston chuckled. 'What an immoral girl you are, Beaton!'

'... and in the end he told me that, in his opinion, she didn't really want Madame to marry anyone at all.'

'Well, if that's true, it is very silly of her,' Mallie Fleming said. 'Because Madame certainly must marry somebody. She's not one of those rare people born to be alone. In my own view, one of the reasons why her health is suffering is that she has so much love to give and no one to receive it.'

'There's us,' Livingston said cheerfully.

'Yes, and we matter too much to her. Have you caught the look on her face when she sees you and John Sempill gazing into each other's eyes?'

141

Livingston had the grace to blush.

Mallie went on, 'She's terrified of losing us – even one of us. She needs a husband, and it scarcely matters who he is, as long as he can give her children. Then she would be happy.'

Livingston surveyed her thoughtfully. Fleming had always been more complex than the other Maries, pretty and capable on the surface yet unsure of herself underneath, especially with people she didn't know well. But in these last months, Livingston suddenly realised, she had changed. Without the rest of them noticing, she had grown up. 'You've become very perceptive,' she said.

Mallie said, 'Have I? I don't know. But I do know that, with some women, all their love goes to their husband. With others, their children come first. Anyway, Madame's marriage is none of Elizabeth's business. It's outrageous that she should try and dictate to her!'

'That,' Beaton commented, 'is just what Secretary Lethington said. He arrived back this morning to find a stiff letter from Cecil telling him we must all behave ourselves and do what Elizabeth says. Master Randolph went quite red in the face when the secretary said, with that sardonic smile of his, that we Scots were becoming more than a little tired of the English habit of trying to dictate to us.'

'Good for him!' Livingston exclaimed.

Mallie Fleming said nothing, because the queen came in just then, followed by Davie Riccio, bright, funny and monkeylike, with a handful of papers in his hand for her majesty to sign.

The queen, reading swiftly through her letters for France and scrawling her customary *Marie R* at the foot, said, 'Get out the dice, Fleming, and we can have a nice, cheerful game when I have finished these.'

Davie stood by, beaming. 'Ah-ha! They are good dice, *si*?'

Livingston said, 'Good dice? Are there bad ones?'

'*Mamma mia!*' He began counting on his fingers. 'There are *quattordici* – fourteen, *si, esatto* – bad kinds that I know of. Some have faces longer than others, so that they fall most often on one side. Others are loaded with lead or *mercurio* – quicksilver. Some are on one side *concavo* – concave? – and others *convesso*. Not so that you are able to see, *ovviamente!*'

Innocently, Livingston asked, 'Do you have any such dice?'

His smile was like that of a smoke-blackened gargoyle over the blinding purple and gold satin doublet. 'Is possible. But bad dice are not all. There are also tricks.'

'Teach us.'

The queen said, 'I can see that my after-supper card and dice parties will not in future be complete without Davie to show us all the underworld gaming tricks that queens and courtiers are not supposed to know about!'

2

Mallie had not seen Lethington for eight long months; not since he had left court on the eve of the Châtelard affair. When he had returned from his English and French mission, she herself had been enjoying a few days' much needed respite at her brother's home, and by the time she resumed her duties he had been called away to his dying wife. The queen had given him a further four weeks to attend to his family affairs while the court went on a progress to the west and south-west.

On the cold February days after he had first gone, Mallie had found herself waking in the morning with a heart empty at the knowledge that she would not see him that day, or the next, or the next, not even at a distance, not even in passing. But as the weeks had gone by and as the queen – assailed by one personal tragedy after another – had leaned on her and the other Maries more and more, she had taught herself to put away her personal concerns and the dreams that could never be fulfilled.

She could not give her life to wishing for the impossible. If she had not been the person she was, she would have reminded herself of her own royal blood and of his status as no more than the son of a laird, without even the lowliest title of his own. But the gulf between them had nothing to do with that. The truth was that she was as fit to be loved by the sophisticated, ascetic, clever Lethington as she was to be pope.

Her resolve to face things as they were, not as she would have liked them to be, had had a salutary effect. She had become more at ease with herself and less cool with others. She had even begun, tentatively, to flirt with some of the more attractive courtiers, with the startling result that three of the younger lords, in succession, had thrown themselves at her feet and declared an undying passion for her. Beaton, the acknowledged beauty, hadn't liked that at first, but seemed to have grown accustomed.

And now Lethington was back, and Mallie prayed that she would be able to sustain her strength, that she would no longer find conversation with him one of the more refined forms of torture.

She was able to put it to the test the next day when the queen decreed an archery contest and Mallie found herself shooting against Lethington.

The first moments were difficult. They were never anything else when one had to commiserate with a man over the death of his wife.

Lethington said, 'Thank you. She was a very sweet person, and it is a source of regret to me that my duties so often kept us apart. Her health had not been good for some years.' He glanced at the queen, who was shooting against James. 'This seems an opportune moment to ask you about her majesty. She does not look well.'

'She isn't. She has always suffered from *crises des nerfs* that take the physical form of stomach pains and fevers. Usually, they come days or weeks after whatever caused them, as if she allows her defences to relax when the challenge has faded. This is a little different, but she has had a year full of stresses and strains and frustrations and she is on the very edge of breaking down.'

'Certainly, the deaths of her Guise uncles, and the Châtelard affair ...'

She turned on him sharply. 'You don't understand, do you! It's not only that. You yourself – *when* you are here! – are far from guiltless, because you and James and Master Knox and Lord Morton are all manipulating her in one way or another. You give her nothing to do but sign documents, and smile, and be charming; to show herself as a beautiful, graceful figurehead. You deprive her of her reason for existing. If you go on as you are doing, you may find her taking everything into her own hands, simply to save her sanity. She is, after all, the queen. She has a divine right to rule.'

She knew enough about Lethington to guess that, for him, divine right would not figure high on the list of royal qualifications but he said only, 'Is it as bad as that?'

'Yes. And there's something else. She is not only a queen whose power is fettered, but a woman with no outlet for her warmth of heart. This bargaining over husbands does not make things better.'

Lethington found himself wondering whether his memory was at fault. The last time Mallie Fleming had censured him for upsetting the queen she had seemed both young and excitable, but in what she was saying now, manner and content alike were those of someone very much more mature. He noticed also, as she unburdened herself of her bow, her half-empty quiver and thick leather glove, that she had lost her waiflike fragility and was prettily rounded in all the right places.

She exclaimed, 'Jesu, but I *detest* archery! Oh, well done, my Lord Secretary. Not that I would have expected anything else.'

His arrow had flown true, as his arrows always did, straight to the centre of the target, the painted belly of a painted parrot. He said, 'I do the best I can. Should I apologise?'

He was being deliberately provocative, but although the temptation was great she did not succumb.

She realised elatedly that it was all right. She could face him, she could even scold him on her majesty's behalf without her heart leaping to her eyes or doing mad whirligigs somewhere down in her boned bosom. She didn't yet know whether she could meet him on other terms; whether she could talk to him without the lifeline of the queen to cling to. Certainly, she didn't know what she would do if ever there were a clash between her loyalty to the queen and her love for him.

In the meantime, brightly, she waved. 'There's Jean Gordon. She will tell you, as I have been trying to do, that there are few things more dangerous for a man than to assume that speaking kindly to a woman and making concessions to her feminine frailty are a substitute for allowing her a say in her own destiny.'

Lethington said, 'But how can we afford to do anything else, when the queen's destiny is ours and Scotland's, too?'

4

The crisis in the queen's health came in December, not long after her birthday, when she was struck by a crippling pain in her side and had to be carried from her library to her bed, where her physician Arnault, diagnosing too much dancing on her birthday or, alternatively, too much praying in an icy chapel, bandaged her as tightly as a swaddled babe, and gave her an emetic, and seemed to be doing his best to kill her.

It was days before the pain faded, leaving her weak and drained, but early on the 21st Seton went running to the other Maries for help, not because the queen had had a relapse but because she was insisting on getting up.

The queen refused to listen to sense. 'For more than two years, John Knox has been condemning me from the pulpit as an evil woman, a vile idolater, a plague to this realm. And now I have him at last. Today, he is being tried for treason and *nothing* will keep me away! I shall wear the scarlet velvet.'

She entered the chamber in procession, pausing before her chair of state to survey Master Knox seated, bareheaded as a supplicant, at the end of the council table. Then she laughed and, half turning to the Maries, said all too audibly, 'That man has made me weep. Now we shall see if I can make *him* weep.'

Lethington, who had no great hope of winning the case against Knox but believed that he needed to be taught a lesson, sensed the rustle of disapproval from the assembled nobles and privy councillors. The queen's remarks had had the effect of reducing the trial, before it had even begun, from a legitimate enquiry to the level of a personal squabble.

And it was indeed a perfectly legitimate enquiry. Some over-zealous Protestants had forced their way, during the queen's absence on her western progress, into the chapel at Holyrood and, one thing having led to another, two of them had been arrested for disturbing the peace. Predictably, John Knox had interfered by sending out notices summoning all the Protestants in Scotland to appear in Edinburgh on the day of their trial to demonstrate support for their brethren.

It was a practice known as 'convocating the queen's lieges', one of long standing that had originated in days when courts were less than impartial and easily overawed by a show of force, and it was technically treasonable although normally no action was taken against the offenders. Mary, however, who for so long had been raging uselessly against Knox, had joyfully seen an opportunity of getting the better of him.

The formalities over, Mary enquired, her eyes glowing, 'Well, Master Knox, do you acknowledge the crime of convocating my lieges without my authority?'

No one, except presumably his late wife, had ever seen Knox without his scholar's cap and cowl, but the fact that his luxuriant iron-grey beard turned out to be partnered by an incongruously bald pate diminished his dignity not at all. It was the blazing passion of his beliefs that held the attention.

With no suggestion of irony, he began, 'May it please your majesty to hear my simple answer ...'

Twenty minutes later, he came to the end of an oration during which he proved to his own satisfaction that, the Mass being an abomination, the two men who had been charged with the crime of disrupting it had done no more wrong to the queen's majesty than if they had taken from her a cup of poison when she was about to drink it. Knowing, however, that the fury and rage of an idolatrous prince would blind her to the truth of the affair, most certain it was that he, the said John, had summoned the legions of the godly to demonstrate the justice of their brethren's case.

Lethington replied equably, 'Well, these are heads on which we are unlikely to agree. But it is not the queen's Mass that is the issue. It is that, by convocating the queen's lieges, you acted contrary to the law of the land.'

'My Lord, I have said ...'

It took a good deal of concentration, when one was being swept along on the tide of Knox's rhetoric, to identify the many flaws in his logic and Lethington was still one metaphorical step behind when, quite without warning, Knox abandoned 'the reprobate and the elect, the fire unstaunchable and the endless torment' to point out, in innocently aggrieved tones and plain and simple language, that virtually every one of the lords seated round the table had themselves been guilty of convocating the queen's lieges, without her permission, just four years before.

It was perfectly true. And from that illegal deed had followed the civil war and the victory of the Protestant cause.

Although the case went wordily on for a further two hours, everyone knew that Knox had won. He was unanimously acquitted, his influence not weakened but strengthened, and there seemed to be nothing that could be done about him.

5

Mary's disappointment was intense and Lethington found himself taking a good deal of the blame. Philosophically, he reflected that he deserved it. In encouraging her to pursue the case, he had miscalculated badly.

Mallie Fleming, despatched by the queen on some private errand, overtook him in the audience hall on his way out. She had already passed him with a smile when she stopped and turned. 'I think perhaps Madame was a little unfair to you. It was she who was so determined to bring the case. I'm sorry.'

He was taken aback. Less fluently than usual, he said, 'Thank you,' and then, his long mouth curling at the corners, 'Perhaps allowing the queen her head was not such a good idea after all?'

'*Please* don't give up!' Her eyes were wide and blue and mocking. 'It's early days and you have had very little practice.'

And then she was gone.

147

The queen's spirits were still low when the year ended. 'I need to be amused,' she exclaimed. 'I *must* be amused. Let us have the most spectacular Twelfth Night celebration anyone has ever seen. Let us make preparing for it an entertainment in itself.'

Spectacular, in the queen's vocabulary, was synonymous with extravagant, and Treasurer Richardson, entering the Great Hall with Secretary Lethington, paled perceptibly and said, 'Pray God her majesty means to pay for it herself.'

Although Twelfth Night was known as the bean king's festival, on this occasion it was not a king who had been chosen to 'find' the bean in the Twelfth Night cakes. It was a queen who was the central figure in the masques, the leading dancer in the ballet, and the ruler – for one night only – of all she surveyed.

Mallie Fleming in the freshly unfolded flower of her beauty.

She wore no stiffened farthingale, no boning, no ruff, no formal cap on tightly bound hair. Instead, she appeared as a young Greek goddess in graceful, flowing cloth of silver, her neck, shoulders and arms ablaze with jewels, her golden hair long, silken and waving, held back loosely in a circlet of diamonds.

There was not a man present who did not find himself rethinking his dreams. Tom Randolph, standing next to Lethington, groaned. 'Venus incarnate! What a woman!' Young Alexander Ogilvie, who normally preferred his beauties neat and brown-haired, murmured, 'I have never seen anyone so lovely.' Even the scholar George Buchanan, a Classical dictionary in unprepossessing human shape, meditated a Latin verse on her perfections. Lethington said nothing, because it would not have been wise.

Fleming herself, free for a night from the queen's shadow, revelled in it all, though the only man whose opinion she valued gave no sign of what he thought.

7

At the end of March, Tom Randolph, who had never been so embarrassed in his life, formally conveyed to the queen of Scots and her privy council that her majesty the queen of England wished her cousin to marry one of her own most loyal subjects, the Lord Robert Dudley.

With the greatest joviality and as if unaware that Elizabeth had made the same playful suggestion, for good and sufficient reasons of her own, several months before, James Stewart, Earl of Moray, declared, 'That's a good notion!'

The Earl of Morton, who had heard rumours of it, muttered through the wild red thicket of his beard, 'Och, well, he'd be better than that Spanish lunatic.'

Argyll, who had also heard rumours, nodded. 'Aye, it iss a possibility. He iss a ferry stout Protestant.'

Glencairn, Rothes, Boyd and Kirkcaldy of Grange, who cared not at all whom the queen married as long as he was not a Catholic and a foreigner, said, 'It's worth thinking about.'

It was the first Mary had heard of it. With her most charming smile, she said, 'My cousin's Master of the Horse? What an amusing conceit! Now, if we might be serious, Master Randolph ...'

8

That night, the figure appeared at her bedside again to disturb her restless sleep, a figure with familiar features now that she had seen a portrait, although it was one of those portraits painted by the dozen to be sent to prospective suitors for their delectation, or favoured subjects for their galleries, or cousin-queens for their information. A high, polished forehead; round, brown, wide-open eyes under heavy lids and plucked and pencilled brows; a thick-boned, hooked nose; a small, full, bright mouth, which meant nothing, because portrait painters never painted any other kind of mouth; unnaturally red hair tucked away under a jewelled coif; a short neck within the ruff and high-collared overgown.

An arrogant face, with no warmth or softness in it.

Even in her dreams, Mary was in a quandary. James and Lethington said she must stay on good terms with Elizabeth, and she recognised that it would be the best way to assure the succession. But Elizabeth was going too far.

'Well?' the figure demanded. 'What's your answer?'

Mary said reproachfully, 'Cousin, you must not demean me by offering me such a husband.'

The figure snorted. 'Demean you? You will take whom I offer and be grateful for him.'

'No.' She was determinedly reasonable. 'I will take a royal and Catholic husband, and if you continue to insult me I will turn you off your throne. With Spanish or French support, I can be queen of England tomorrow.'

'You don't mean that. You would not dare.'

She had no idea whether she meant it or not; whether she would dare or not. She said, 'It is preferable to marrying your cast-off lover in the hope of succeeding to your throne when I am too old to be interested. You must see that.'

The figure plumped itself down in a chair and swore. 'God's death, I can stop you any time I choose. I know everything you get up to.'

'You mean that my brother James writes and tells you? I'm aware of that. But I take care that he *doesn't* know everything I get up to.'

'No?'

Mary giggled. 'Oh, no.' Davie Riccio had turned out to be an excellent amanuensis and now wrote all the letters abroad that she preferred no one else to know about – to His Holiness, and the Duke of Savoy, and the new Hapsburg emperor – seeking their moral support. When good relations were decisively established, she would be able to ask for their financial and even military support, too, if she needed it. She was, after all, the queen. She was – at least in dreams – perfectly entitled to do what she wanted to do.

She said, 'I have powerful friends and, unlike you, no enemies.'

'If you play games with me, it will bring you nothing but grief.'

Mary lay down, pulling her coverlet cosily about her against the March chill, and murmured, 'We shall see.'

9

James, Lethington and Randolph didn't get to bed at all.

Somewhere in the darkest hours of the night, Randolph said for the dozenth time, 'If Mary accepts Dudley, Elizabeth will heap wealth and honours on him, and just think what that'll do for amity between our countries. It'll strengthen the royal authority in Scotland. It'll ensure peace. It'll enrich the whole nation.'

Lethington said, 'Do you honestly believe all that?'

Randolph, scarlet from the wine he had drunk, glared at him and said, 'Yes, of course.'

Lethington, who was famous for never losing his temper, said, 'Dudley would need more than fine phrases for his dowry. The only thing that might – and only might – make him acceptable to Mary would be an armourplated guarantee of the succession.'

James rose and stretched, loosening the ties at the neck of his shirt. It was his sole concession to the lateness of the hour and the informality of the occasion. Scratching his fingernails thoughtfully through his short, crisp beard, he said, 'I can't see what your difficulty is, Lethington. We want Mary married. And to a Protestant. And not to a foreigner. Elizabeth's offering us a solution and we should jump at it. I like Dudley, he's a sensible man. Knox likes him, too. So what's your objection?'

Randolph, turning to Lethington, saw that the clear grey eyes were like ice water. Lethington said, at last, 'It is insulting, not just to Mary herself but to Scotland.'

James was dismissive. 'Och, come on, man! We've enough problems without standing on our dignity. Mary'll come round to the idea. She'll have to.'

Randolph thought it a very sensible view for James to take. He hiccupped. 'He's right, Lethington, you know.'

Lethington did not mention Dudley's probable sterility, but studied James thoughtfully, the doubts about him that had first stirred after the Huntly expedition reawakening. If Mary were to remain childless, James might be seen as having a claim to her crown. It was something to be borne in mind.

James yawned. 'Why don't we hold some formal discussions.'

Happily, Randolph agreed. He hadn't expected to overcome the first hurdle so easily.

10

It did not occur to James that he was becoming overconfident, that his sister might resent his assumption that she would unfailingly follow his advice, even in something that offended against all her instincts.

It was not, however, easy for her to override him when he had so much support from her largely Protestant privy council. Guided by him and Lethington, she had in the years since her return neglected the Catholic lords who were her natural allies, but now she was beginning to think it had been a mistake.

The Earl of Atholl was the greatest of them since Huntly's death. He was also a brave man and an honest one, and married to Jean Gordon's sister Elizabeth. One day in May, he came to discuss with her a deer hunt he was arranging for her at his castle of Blair. 'Your majesty will never have been seeing anything like it,' he assured her. 'Two thousand beasts being driven in, and the bucks with their antlers up so that they are looking like a forest thundering towards you. Och, it is a great sight, and great sport. You will be having the time of your life.'

Afterwards, it turned out that he had something else to say. 'I was hearing the other day from my cousin Lennox. He was wondering if your majesty has been able to consider the letter from Queen Elizabeth asking you to permit him to be returning to Scotland.'

It was almost a year since she had received the letter. At the time, James had said, 'Ignore it. We don't want the man here. Châtelherault's taken possession of some of his lands and Argyll has others. They'd make a·terrible fuss if he tried to get them back. And Lennox is ambitious, which means ye can't rely on him.'

Now, to Atholl, Mary said smilingly, 'Would it please you if I permitted him to come back?'

'Very much.'

'Then I shall do so.'

It was satisfying to be able to please Atholl, make a concession to Elizabeth, and annoy James, all at the same time.

11

More and more she was in need of allies, because it was not only James who had become overconfident. Since the débâcle of his trial, John Knox had gone completely out of control.

With no power in the formal sense, he had an extraordinary and continuing power over men's minds. Outrageous as were his attacks on the queen, his hearers found it easier to accept what he said than to question it. It finally reached the stage where a number of Mary's more open-minded lords felt compelled to meet him and try to persuade him to tone down his language.

It was Lethington who inevitably bore the brunt of it, and everything at first went as he had known it would. When he charged Knox with deliberately turning her subjects' hearts against their queen, Knox replied by quoting extracts from his prayers and sermons. 'O Lord, purge her heart from the venom of idolatry ... deliver her from her bondage to Satan ... let this poor realm escape that plague and vengeance which inevitably follows idolatry.'

What, he asked, was wrong with that?

On and on it went, until Knox dared to go further than he had ever dared before.

Somehow or other, they had arrived at the question of which was to be obeyed – God's law or the law of princes. It was an awkward question since, as Mary herself had pointed out to Knox during their first encounter, one of God's laws was that people should obey the law of princes, but Knox had become adept at negotiating this particular obstacle in his didactic path and was in the course of doing so when Lethington interrupted him.

He said, smiling, 'If the queen were to command me to slay John Knox because she is offended at him, I would not obey her. Which is to say, I would follow God's law rather than the law of princes. But if she commanded others to do it, or condemned him under some pretext of justice, I do not know whether I am bound to go actively to his aid.'

With one of his sharp flashes of humour, Knox replied, 'I ask no favours for myself. But the Word of God says that, if you believe me innocent but suffer me to die when you have the power to save me, you would be guilty of my blood.'

It was a new concept to most of those present. To stand aside while a crime was being committed had never been seen as, in itself, criminal. Lethington said, 'Prove it.'

It was, of course, possible to prove almost anything from the Bible if, like Knox, you knew it by heart and could select the Words of God that suited your argument and ignore those that did not. In the course of his reply, Knox proved that God required idolatry to be suppressed. That an ungodly ruler had no more right to be exempt from God's law in this matter than any ordinary subject. That God required idolaters to die the death. And that godly subjects had the right to exercise God's law, on His behalf, against ungodly rulers.

It was an incitement to murder, revolution, and regicide, but most of his hearers were swept on, enthralled and unthinking, past these new and jagged rocks in the torrent of his rhetoric. Only Lethington, James, the Master of Maxwell, and a handful of others heard what he was really saying.

Afterwards, the Master of Maxwell shook his head admiringly. 'He's amazing. Where does he get the energy from? I'm worn out just listening to him, but there he is, fifty-one years old and newly married to Ochiltree's girl, and it hasn't slowed him down at all.'

James, who regarded such remarks as in very poor taste, looked worried. 'He's going too far. He's justifying *any* action anyone feels like taking against Mary. And yet, ye know, except for Calvin, he does know more about God's word than anyone else in the world ...'

With a touch of asperity, Lethington said, 'He should. That's who he thinks he is.'

12

What with Knox, and the Dudley affair, and the certainty that Mary was up to something, Lethington should have been less than his usual urbane self. But for the first time in his adult life, politics and diplomacy were not the first thing he thought of when he woke in the morning, or the last thing when he fell asleep at night.

To his own astonishment and disbelief, he was in love.

It must have been growing, he supposed, deep inside him for months before the Twelfth Night revelation, perhaps since the time, almost two years before, when a very young-seeming Mallie Fleming had pushed him from the queen's presence for failing to handle Mary with the kid gloves he had not known he needed. Even then, there had been a spark that had interested him. The other Maries were bright and pleasant girls, but in Mallie Fleming he had sensed something more.

And then he had been away for months, and afterwards Janet had died, Janet to whom he owed his loyalty. And in the meantime Mallie Fleming had ceased to be a nervous girl and become a self-possessed young woman, and a very beautiful one.

He had been increasingly, but not compellingly aware of her until Twelfth Night, when his hour had struck and his life had been changed. Aesthetic perfection and sexual attraction had had something to do with it. There had been liking, too, and a sense of personal mystery, of depths of which she herself was perhaps not yet aware. And what else?

Suddenly, amusedly, he recognised that he was trying to apply his analytical mind to something that defied analysis, something that was not a sum of parts but the illogical, indefinable, glorious, totally absorbing whole that went by the name of love.

It was a love he could never have imagined, as far from the friendly warmth he had felt for Janet as the heavens from the earth. It was a thing of silver and stars, of bright eyes and bright wit, of a surpassingly vivid and intense desire. He had said nothing to her. He tried to behave as if nothing had changed between himself and Mallie Fleming. But she possessed every moment of his private thoughts.

13

It distracted him a little from his proper concerns, so that, when Elizabeth wrote to him and also to James, saying that she no longer wished the Earl of Lennox to return to Scotland and that Mary should therefore rescind her permission, he responded, as did James, with an unequivocal and sarcastic negative.

It made the pair of them even less popular with the queen of England than they already were with the queen of Scotland.

As a result, when Mary decided to send an envoy to London to discuss arrangements for a meeting about the Dudley marriage, she said, as if they were two erring small boys, 'Well, I can hardly send either of *you*. I cannot imagine that my cousin would even receive you. But I must do something to restore her to humour, or all our negotiations over the succession will have been wasted. I will send Sir James Melville.'

Privately, she was no more favourable to the idea of the Dudley marriage than she had been at the start. Privately, she still wanted a Spanish alliance. But Davie Riccio had come to her a few days before, bursting with gossip.

'Ees news from my friend who ees with the king's singers in Spain, Madame! Ees about Don Carlos. My friend say he ees ill in the head!'

Mary had always been aware that the future king of Spain was an unstable youth, but mere instability, however regrettable, was a minor factor in relation to his rank. She said, 'He is an emotional young man, no more. He will grow out of it.'

Davie looked at her doubtfully. 'But Madame, everyone know that he order his valet to eat his shoes and then throw the unhappy man out of the window!'

'Jesu!' It had stopped her only momentarily. 'Perhaps he has a hot temper. I am sure he will recover in time.'

Time was what she needed, and she had decided to play for it by consenting to talks about talks about the Dudley marriage suggestion. It was also why she was sending the less experienced Melville to London in place of Lethington.

155

'Melville?' James said. 'That's a good idea. He's smooth. He's a new face. Yes, Elizabeth'll like him. Why not?'

14

Mallie Fleming said uneasily, 'I'll have to ask Secretary Lethington,' and then looked reproachfully at Jean Gordon, who was laughing at her.

Although Lethington seemed blithely unaware of it, the whole court was gossiping about his thirty-six-year-old passion for a girl of twenty-two, as if there were something improper about it. The other Maries said it was jealousy, which was generous of them, and Mallie thought perhaps they were right, though not in the way they meant. It seemed to her that he had for so long been the one calm, clever, incorruptible figure on Scotland's public scene that both friends and enemies were deriving pleasure from the discovery that he was human, after all.

She herself had seen no sign of his being moonstruck. She didn't understand how the gossip had started. She didn't believe it.

She said, 'Silly rumours!'

'But, my dear, the man's walking on air,' Jean told her. 'And, clever though he is, even he isn't clever enough to conceal the expression in his eyes when you walk into a room.'

'Well, he hasn't said anything to me.'

'No doubt he has his reasons.'

'Such as?'

Jean cocked her neat brown head. 'I don't know.'

'Exactly.'

Since it was not at all easy to have a private and confidential conversation at court, Mallie steeled herself to go to his office.

He leapt to his feet and, for the briefest of brief moments, she saw the expression Jean had spoken of. Or thought she saw it. She didn't know. She couldn't afford to be distracted by it.

In her dreams, the dreams that would not go away, she called him William when she wasn't addressing him by one of the innumerable variants on 'my heart's love', but in the flesh she didn't dare.

'Lord Secretary,' she said crisply, 'I have a favour to ask of you.'

He didn't reply with, 'Your wish is my command,' but just with, 'Yes, demoiselle?'

She was grateful for the formality. 'Lord Bothwell, as you may know, is a cousin of mine. When Queen Elizabeth released him from the Tower last summer, it was only on parole. So he has been forced to remain in England, as the reluctant guest of a variety of reluctant hosts.'

'I am aware of it.'

'And now he wants to go to France. He writes to me that it would be helpful if you, among others, would be so kind as to reinforce his request to Elizabeth.'

'And what, if one may ask, is the attraction of France?'

'All his troubles have left him financially straitened and he believes he might be appointed to the captaincy of the Scottish Archers there.'

'Ah.'

She waited, and waited, torn between the wish that she hadn't come – she was not so *very* fond of her cousin Bothwell, after all – and the desire to stay for ever. In the end she said, a little tartly, 'Is there some difficulty?'

His eyes were clear and grey as ice water but his mouth was amused. 'I can think of very much better reasons for speeding Lord Bothwell on his way to France. My informants tell me that he has been threatening to murder me ...'

'*No*! But why?'

'I am not at all sure, except that it is the general custom to attribute to me a deviousness that I am not aware of possessing. He probably holds me responsible for his imprisonment following the Arran affair and, of course, when he was exiled, her majesty gave to me the abbey lands of Haddington which were formerly in his possession.'

He thought for a few moments more. 'I must tell you frankly that I think your cousin was born to trouble as the sparks fly upward.' He saw the admission in her eyes and his own eyes gleamed. 'That being so, the further away from Scotland he is, the happier we will be. I will write to Elizabeth, with all the enthusiasm at my command, urging her to permit Lord Bothwell to take himself off to France, where he can earn an honest living and disturb us no more.'

Beaton had said to her, 'Flutter your eyelashes at him. It works wonders,' but she was glad she hadn't. As she said, 'Thank you,' and took her leave, her nerve ends were tingling with recognition of his intense awareness of her. If she had resorted to flirtatious tricks, she knew she would have killed whatever there was.

Whatever there was ...

She would not beckon, because she sensed that, if she beckoned, he would not come.

Sir James Melville was a sleek, elegant and slightly effeminate gentleman, still under thirty and well acquainted with the courts of Europe where he had until recently been engaged in cultivating his diplomatic skills, his charm and – Elizabeth maliciously guessed – his *mignons*.

The temptation was too much for her. Although there had been sufficient traffic between her court and Mary's for her to be perfectly well informed about her cousin's appearance and talents, there was a certain piquancy in putting teasing questions about her to a man who was not interested in women.

'Which of us is the fairer?' she demanded.

Lethington had warned him that Elizabeth could be skittish. With barely a moment's hesitation, Melville replied, 'Your majesty is beyond question the fairest queen in England, and ours the fairest queen in Scotland.'

She smiled opulently. 'Good. And which of us is the taller?'

'I believe my queen has the advantage of height.'

'Since I am neither too high nor too low, she is over tall. Music, now. Does your queen play well?'

'I believe so,' Melville replied.

'Does she dance well?'

'With much grace.'

It took only a day or two for him to form a very poor opinion of Elizabeth's sincerity and to see that there was more of fear than friendship in her attitude towards Mary. He was a diplomat, however, and soon learned what kind of flattery she appreciated. When he said that he believed she would never marry, because then she would be but queen of England, where now she was king and queen both, it was very well received indeed.

Which made it all the more interesting that the highlight of his visit turned out to be an investiture which he was commanded to attend – an investiture at which Robert Dudley, Master of the Horse, was elevated from being a commoner unworthy of a queen, to the high distinction of the earldom of Leicester and barony of Denbigh.

As Dudley, unnaturally grave and subdued, knelt before Elizabeth and bowed his head, the impeccably barbered and scented nape of his neck became visible above his ruff – which tempted the queen, with a frolicsome smile, to lean forward and tickle it. Dudley did no more than jerk slightly, but a tide of crimson flowed into his skin and receded as all the nobles present – who included not only Melville but the ambassadors of France and Spain – drew in a faint, concerted breath.

Afterwards, regal once more, the queen returned the sword of state to her ceremonial swordbearer for restoration to its red and gold scabbard, and commanded her trusty and well-beloved – and now very eligible – Earl of Leicester, splendid in coronet and scarlet mantle, to rise to his feet.

'Well, Sir James,' Elizabeth said, 'what do you think of my new creation?'

'To be trusty and well-beloved by your majesty should suffice for any man. His earldom can be no more than the gilt on the gingerbread even for one whom my own queen holds in as high regard as she does my Lord Leicester.' And if Elizabeth could penetrate the logic of that particular pronouncement, he thought, it was more than he could.

'Oh, very good,' she said. Then, her eyes following his, she laughed. 'But you fancy that lad more!'

Her ceremonial swordbearer. He was an extraordinarily beautiful young man, tall, golden-fair, slender and long-legged.

Melville, aware of having been caught out, suavely resumed his diplomat's smile. 'There can be no comparison, I think. No woman of spirit could prefer a beardless and lady-faced youth.'

He had been abroad too long. Not until some little time later did he discover that the beautiful young man was Henry Stuart, Lord Darnley, in whose veins ran the royal blood of both Tudors and Stewarts. Whose father, the Earl of Lennox, had just returned to Scotland to be restored to his estates.

16

After Melville, back in Edinburgh, had made his report and left, James said, 'What did she mean about Darnley? I don't like it. Was it supposed to be some kind of hint? I don't understand it after all the fuss she made about whether his father should or shouldn't be allowed back.'

Lethington, who had his own views on Melville and also knew Elizabeth very much better than James did, said, 'I don't think we should read too much into it. Although, according to him, when she said, "But you fancy that lad more", she meant "you Scots", I think she may just as easily have meant Melville personally. I would guess that she was being playful. Half her effectiveness as queen rests on her ability to keep people

159

on the *qui vive*. Anyway, she has agreed to the conference about Dudley, which is something.'

Letherington himself was in a difficult position. Knowing that Dudley might well prove to be only half a husband, he did not like the match. But everyone else did, and it meant that, as so often, he had to temporise. With no title, no estates, no right of birth, no family alliances, no army of adherents, his only strength was strength of personality. It did not allow him the luxury of taking an independent stand. To oppose the lords openly would be to abandon all hope of influencing not only them but his whole vision of the future.

In his view, the only merit of the marriage project, which had been in the air for seven long months, had been the implied promise, sometimes more than implied, that Dudley and the succession went together.

But when the conference took place at the end of November, the Earl of Moray and Secretary Lethington were blandly informed that Mary was expected to marry the new Earl of Leicester for his own sake. Then, afterwards, her majesty Queen Elizabeth of England might – conceivably, perhaps, possibly – deign to consider the question of the succession.

Even James was annoyed.

Thoughtfully, Lethington said, 'When I was last in London, I heard a preacher – who had much in common with our friend Master Knox – describe women in general as "wanton flippergibs". The occasional good one, he said, was like an eel put in a bag amid five hundred snakes, so that even if a man was lucky enough to grope out the one eel from among all the snakes, yet he had at best but a wet eel by the tail. I thought at the time that he must have had Elizabeth in mind.'

They were riding back from Berwick to Edinburgh and Tom Randolph, sitting his horse like a sack of meal, burst out, 'You're not being reasonable. You talk as if you can't trust the queen my mistress. You talk as if you can't trust her promises about the Earl of Leicester. Well, you can trust them a damned sight more than *we* can trust what the queen *your* mistress would do with the promise of the succession if it was granted to her.'

Lethington's cool grey eyes surveyed him. 'Are you saying that Elizabeth fears a Catholic uprising in my mistress's name?'

Flustered, Randolph replied, 'No, of course not.'

'Well, what are you saying?'

'It's not like that.'

'What *is* it like?'

Patiently, Lethington waited, sure now that Elizabeth was deliberately

160

wasting everyone's time. If she couldn't prevent Mary from marrying, she hoped to postpone it for as long as possible; and if the worst came to the worst, she wanted Mary in the safe hands of a husband whose first loyalty was to Elizabeth and England. Which was why Dudley had been offered. The situation was, of course, complicated by the facts that Elizabeth did not want to part with him and that Dudley did not in the least wish to be married to the queen of Scots. He had written to James to say so.

Randolph was a long way from a fool, and he knew better than to waste his energy trying to defeat Lethington. He said, 'You *know* what it's like. It's time I retired. I'm getting too old for this. Dear Lord, but the queen your mistress is going to be annoyed, isn't she?'

17

The worrying thing was that she wasn't annoyed.

She smiled. 'It doesn't surprise me. My Lord Secretary and my Lord Ambassador will simply have to go on negotiating, won't they? They have my authority to do so without troubling me in the matter. And now, if you will forgive me, I have letters to write.'

It was the letters that worried Lethington. In the last few months, Mary's messengers had been flying back and forward by land and sea. Packets of despatches came and went, of which Lethington and James knew only as much as she chose to tell them. Davie Riccio had been made responsible for most of her personal correspondence with the Guises and other friends in France, and Davie Riccio was generally suspected of being a papal agent. Lethington didn't know whether he was or not, just as he didn't know whether there was any truth in the rumours of a secret league of Catholic sovereigns in Europe, to which Mary was believed to belong. What he did know was that Mary was becoming far too close to her private household, many of whom were Catholics and foreigners, taking too much advice from men who, from Riccio down, knew nothing about Scots affairs and whose self-serving instinct was to pander to her every whim.

He said something of this to James, who replied gloomily, 'Ye know what she's doing. She's lost a lot of Catholic goodwill in the last three years, thanks to us, and now she's trying to set things right. She's probably asking for advice and assistance from that damned cardinal uncle of hers. Maybe even a subsidy from the pope of Rome. I don't like it.'

It might, Lethington suspected, be no more than a means of venting her frustration, but the risk of a Catholic king for Scotland remained very real. Even a minor princeling would, in the queen's eyes, be a more acceptable match than a man of Dudley's background. Everything was on a knife edge. Unless the English marriage, with all its attendant disadvantages, were settled now, it never would be.

Three years before, James and Lethington – for the sake of present and future peace for Scotland – had promised Mary that, if she followed their advice, they would guarantee her the English succession. She had, on the whole, kept her part of the bargain. If they failed her, neither of them doubted the consequences. It would be an end of their influence and the opening of an era fraught, once more, with danger. She would choose other advisers, pursue her own course, and the result could be another civil war.

They wrote, therefore, to Cecil in terms for which they had no authority and which Mary might justifiably construe as treasonable if she ever found out. If Elizabeth, they said, could be persuaded to make a satisfactory offer on the succession, they and the Scots lords would enforce the marriage on Mary.

Cecil wrote back, explaining the problems and saying that the decision was not Elizabeth's alone.

James and Lethington wrote again, tearing his arguments apart.

Cecil wrote back, saying it wasn't his fault.

Lethington wrote again, saying that the possibility of union between Scotland and England was of too great importance to both present and future generations for this opportunity to be allowed to slip for want of a little more strength of mind and purpose.

But letters, whether sober or impassioned, concealed as much as they revealed. Cecil, convinced, as Lethington was not, that there *was* a secret Catholic league in Europe planning some great counter-coup against the reformed church, could see Mary only as its vehicle. If she – who had been shaped and nurtured by the Guises – were granted the English succession, she would not wait for Elizabeth to die. She would cast not only Scotland but England back into the arms of the Antichrist. It would make no difference whom she married.

So deeply ingrained was this suspicion in the minds of both Cecil and Elizabeth that nothing Lethington could say had any effect. They respected Lethington greatly, liked him despite his duplicity over the 'secret' Spanish marriage negotiations, recognised the quality of his mind, recognised that he knew far more about Mary's personality and motives than they did, accepted that he believed she would never launch a

Catholic crusade against England, and that, if she tried, he and the Earl of Moray could control her.

Measured against their own obsession, however, it all went for nothing. They thought themselves realists, and Lethington a deluded optimist.

18

Before Lethington's final letter reached Cecil, Cecil had sent off a despatch to Randolph which reduced that gentleman to tears.

After six years of declaring herself a devoted friend of the Protestant party in Scotland, Elizabeth had now granted permission for a certain young Catholic nobleman – Henry Stuart, Lord Darnley, pale-blue blooded, highly marriageable, and heir to more family feuds than one would care to shake a stick at – to cross the Border and pay court to the equally marriageable young queen of Scots.

Randolph didn't know how he was going to explain it away to James and Lethington, who had spent so many weary months steering their queen in the direction of Dudley.

PART TWO

SCOTLAND 1565 – 1568

Chapter Eight

FEBRUARY-APRIL 1565

1

T he tall and exquisite newcomer was the nearest thing to a Greek god ever to appear at Mary's court, where – merry, lively and colourful though it had become over the last three years – most of the gentlemen were of no more than average height, average physique, average cleanliness, and less than average gallantry.

The young Lord Darnley put them all to shame, his figure slender and shapely, his hair fair and curly, his hazel eyes lucent, his nose short and straight, his complexion soft and smooth, his mouth little short of rosebud. As he straightened up from kissing the queen's hand, he took the opportunity to demonstrate that he not only knew something about the art of flattery but had also had the benefit of a Classical education.

'*Nunc scio quid sit amor!*' he breathed, gazing into her smiling eyes.

The Earl of Morton, standing next to Lethington, muttered, 'What was that?'

'A quotation from the poet Virgil. "Now I know what love is!"'

A frivolous royal court was not Morton's natural habitat and one thing he disliked about holding the office of lord chancellor was that he was forever having to chase around after the queen on her progresses or, as now, when she went hunting in the Fife countryside. He said grumpily, 'Why could he not just say it in honest Scots? It's not what ye'd call an original thought, and it doesnae rhyme either.'

Lethington laughed aloud, as much at Morton himself – whose views on 'prancing ninnies' were all too well known – as at what he had said. But it was going to be instructive, he reflected, to discover whether this godlike youth was truly well educated or had come equipped with a dictionary of short, easy-to-memorise Latin phrases suitable for all occasions. He was said to have at least a nodding acquaintance with culture but, if not, the queen would soon find him out.

And then he became aware of a pair of gentian blue eyes surveying him with amused reproach. It did not greatly worry him that his passion for Mallie Fleming seemed to have become public knowledge. He had taken pains not to yearn after her like some half-fledged schoolboy, not to gaze too deeply into her eyes when they spoke or danced, not to attach himself to her own personal court of admirers, all of them younger and more eligible than he. But when she summoned him, he went, and once or twice the unexpected sight of her might, he supposed, have sparked some revealing change in his expression. It would have been enough for the watchers and the gossips who made it their business to know everything there was to know about anyone who had influence at the court of the queen of Scots.

He abandoned Morton and went across. She said, 'That was shocking. Lord Darnley thought you were laughing at *him!*' And Jean Gordon, beside her, added with the wide-eyed innocence that, he had learned, was a sign of mischief, 'He really did. He won't like you, if you're not careful.'

Mallie said pointedly, 'And the queen is very taken with him.'

'How can you tell?'

'Believe me, she is.'

Jean Gordon said, 'Well, he's taller than she is. It must be lovely for her to feel small and sheltered for a change.'

Lethington laughed again, this time soundlessly. Even though he knew that political storm clouds were close to breaking, he had never felt more cheerful in his life. Both brain and body told him that the simple fact of being in love should not be enough for him. But it was. There was a purity about it that bewitched him.

The queen summoned him and, when he had gone, Jean said, 'If my heart wasn't otherwise engaged, I'd fight you for him.'

'Yes.' Mallie sighed. 'What about Master Ogilvie?'

'What about him? Mallie, I can't do *anything* with things as they are. My brother's still in ward, and unless the queen relents and restores the Huntly title and estates to him, I won't even have a dowry worth mentioning.' Her neat mouth drooped. 'Even if I had, I think the family feud's too strong. I wish I was a man, not a female piece of property, then I could do what I wanted and the devil take everybody else.'

Mallie envied her. Jean Gordon would always know what she wanted, even if she didn't achieve it. Mallie's own problems were more complex.

If only he would say something.

Lord Darnley was a welcome addition to the royal household, an elegant young man accomplished in riding, hunting, dancing, playing the lute, even in writing poetry, and sufficiently cosmopolitan to be accepted into Mary's inner circle, the small group of attendants and friends who shared her informal musical evenings, supper parties, and card parties. He was courteous and deferential, and a willing participant in one of her favourite escapades, when she and the Maries disguised themselves as men and went sauntering around the streets of Edinburgh pretending to be ordinary mortals. He even dined with James and accompanied him to one of Master Knox's sermons, which suggested that, Catholic though he was, he had some grasp of the political realities.

Mary liked him particularly for his social ease, something that few of her Scots courtiers had succeeded in mastering. She had almost forgotten the pleasure of flirting. In France, where flirtation had been elevated to a fine art, there had been no need for her to curb her vivacity for fear of its being misunderstood, but she had discovered all too soon that, in Scotland, it was different. In Scotland, the lightest coquetry was taken to be full of meaning. Darnley knew better. He made her feel light-hearted again.

She had met him twice before, once when, aged fourteen, he had attended François's coronation, and again when, just after his sixteenth birthday, he had come to France to offer his condolences on François's death. On both occasions, he had been sent by his mother, who had so obviously rehearsed him in what he was to do and say that their conversations had been extraordinarily stilted. And now he was nineteen, and although his ambitious mother was no doubt still instructing him in what to do, he had become a more believable person.

He had always been spoken of as a possible husband for Mary, but very low on the list. His maternal grandmother had been sister to Henry VIII of England, and on his father's side he was descended from a sister of James III of Scotland. In comparison with Don Carlos of Spain, Charles IX of France, or even the Archduke Charles of Austria, his rank was inferior. But in comparison with Elizabeth's recently ennobled commoner of a lover ...

Mary sighed, and wondered whether perhaps Don Carlos might have been cured of the illness in his head.

Tom Randolph had had a hard time in the weeks before Darnley's arrival, when everyone had been demanding to know what Elizabeth thought she was about, permitting the boy to come north. No one other than the Catholic earls had a kind word to say for him. But when the young man duly appeared, the furore began to die down a little. The lords, observing his pretty face and pretty manners, dismissed him as a harmless lightweight. His father might be a good Catholic and his mother a crusading one, but he clearly wasn't. On a personal level, at least, he didn't appear to be dangerous. Gradually – with the voluble exception of his family's longstanding enemies, Châtelherault and the Hamiltons – they stopped worrying about the likelihood of having Lennox's son for a king.

Even so, the Earl of Moray didn't like the situation at all and Randolph found himself, night after night, having to listen to his complaints over the lack of response from either Cecil or Elizabeth to his and Lethington's last letter about Dudley and the succession.

'Nothing but delays, delays, delays,' James raged, 'and now even Lethington says he can do no more because Cecil writes that our perpetual demands are making Elizabeth less rather than more inclined to relent. What if Mary decides to go her own way?'

Randolph said, 'Here, have a cup of wine. You need it. Lethington's right.'

'But the Dudley match *must* go through. Everyone knows I'm personally committed to it. If it does go through, I don't want the credit. Having done my duty to my God and my country is enough for me. But if it doesn't go through, I'll be the one who's in trouble. And ye know how many folk hate my commitment to the English alliance.'

'Yes, but ...'

There was no stopping him. 'And if Mary loses interest and decides to marry someone else, what will that do for my reputation? And if she wants to marry a papist, what then? We either have to put up with it – and we can't – or find ourselves embroiled in another civil war. And I'll be the one who gets the blame!'

Randolph opened his mouth and then, weakly, closed it again. He knew that James valued his reputation. He knew that James saw his own career as indistinguishable from the cause of Protestantism. He knew that James was a godly man inclined to make too much parade of his rectitude. He even knew there must be a streak of vanity in him, because he wouldn't be human otherwise. But until now he had not known how much.

James swallowed his wine, tossed his cloak over his shoulders, and prepared to leave. 'Write to the queen your mistress and tell her we *must* have a reply soon. And tell her what else I've said. I think she has enough respect and friendship for me to take my interests into consideration.'

Randolph might have said – but didn't – 'Don't rely on it, my friend. The only interests Elizabeth takes into account are her own and England's.'

4

To the queen, her Four Maries were friends closer to her than anyone else in the world, closer even than her wilful half-sister Jean, or her half-brothers James and Robert, the first too virtuous to be close to, the second not virtuous enough. Since she had lost François, since she had left France, she had had no one else to love. She felt the Maries were *hers*.

She had, of course, known that she must some day resign at least part of their love and loyalty, so that when a blushing Livingston came to ask her permission to marry, she swallowed her true feelings and responded with the warmth that so much endeared her to people.

Livingston said, 'I know you didn't expect me to be the first. No one did, and I don't know myself how it happened. I'm not the prettiest, and I'm not the cleverest, but oh!' She sighed, her eyes full of stars. 'I love him so much, Madame, and I think he loves me.'

For the queen, marrying for love in the sense Livingston was talking about was an alien concept. Even when she and the Maries had gossiped about possible husbands, the idea of finding a lovable consort had seemed quite unreal. She had loved François, of course, but that had been something different, something almost maternal, and the physical side had amounted to little more than childish fumblings. For François's sake, she had had to pretend that there had been more, because people expected it.

Queens married for political expediency, not for love. From their kings they expected moral support and sufficient intimacy to produce not just one heir – one was not enough, when children died more often than they lived – but two at least. That was all that was required. Now, wistfully, she thought how little it was.

She laughed, 'It must, I imagine, be Sir John Sempill of Beltrees? I

171

have been watching the two of you for months!' and Livingston laughed back, her natural exuberance returning now that she knew the queen would not forbid it.

'Well, Madame, when two people dance together as well as we do, it would be sinful not to take it as a sign! But I won't leave you, Madame, I promise. I will still be one of your Maries for as long as you want me to be.'

Mary said, 'How many children did you have in mind?'

Livingston blushed again. 'Dozens!'

'That is what I thought.' Mary held out her arms. 'But I shall expect you to be with me whenever your dozens of children can spare you. My dear, I don't want to lose you.'

Mallie Fleming, waiting for Livingston outside the queen's door, ran to her as she emerged sniffling and sobbing. 'What's the matter?'

'Oh, Mallie! Madame is being so good, so kind, I can't bear it. She says she doesn't want to lose me, and I know I'm deserting her when she needs us so much. But she says I shall have my wedding gown as a gift from her, and my bridal banquet, and a dowry of £500 a year in land. And she will be a party to the marriage contract and stand godmother to our children. And I am to stay with her between times. Oh, Mallie! *I can't bear it.*'

Mallie Fleming hugged her, and said, 'But that's wonderful!' and thought, 'I must stop dreaming. I cannot desert her, too.'

5

It was a lovely wedding, and the bride's brother, Lord Livingston, somehow succeeded in accommodating most of the court in and around the family home at Falkirk. There was feasting and dancing, at which the bridal couple excelled. There were three days of banquets, and hunting, and a masque in which the participants were dressed as shepherds playing lutes and singing Davie Riccio's arrangement of 'The Lass o' Patie's Mill'. And the queen found herself for the first time in her life in a fishing boat, hopefully trolling a line, and catching something called a haddock which Lord Livingston arranged to have cooked for her right there on the shore. It was unutterably delicious.

Mary, who always enjoyed weddings, was as sentimental as usual about this one. But it was the beginning of an end she did not want to think of, as she watched the bride and groom together, and saw that Fleming was dancing with Lethington and Beaton with the besotted English ambassador, who was forty-two if he was a day. Only Seton, who inclined towards prudishness, had no acknowledged admirer. Only Seton, and Mary herself.

Surrounded by love and gaiety, she had no part in it. Despite her topaz velvet, her pearls, the wreathed gold in her hair, the cloth of state, she felt not like a queen but like a woman alone, lonely and unwanted.

And then she was diverted by Lord Morton's appearance beside her, foetid of breath, stained of doublet, slow of speech, but her lord chancellor nonetheless. She wished he wouldn't bite his nails.

She smiled at him and, as always, he shifted a little as if he were trying to settle his grubby neck more comfortably into his grubby ruff. 'I've just heard something. With us safely out of the way here in Falkirk, Bothwell's had the damned impertinence to turn up in Edinburgh.'

'I thought my cousin Elizabeth had given him permission to leave for France? I certainly wrote to her to intercede for him. Fleming asked me to.'

'Oh, he went all right. But now he's back.'

She shrugged. 'Perhaps he has affairs to attend to.'

'Aye, and so have we. Just because he escaped from the castle jail in '62 doesnae mean he's entitled to come sauntering back again as if he hadnae a care in the world. What's more, there's murder on his mind. He blames James and Lethington for putting him away in the first place and he's breathing fire and smoke against them. Ye'll have to summon him to a day of law. I've looked up the law calendar. What about the beginning of May? There's space then.'

She had always felt it unjust that Bothwell should have been locked up after the Arran affair, in which she was sure he had been innocent – even James had admitted as much – and had felt quietly pleased when he had escaped. But her chancellor was right. She hoped, though she didn't expect, that it would be an opportunity for him to prove his innocence. He was one of the few nobles who had never wavered in his loyalty to the Stewarts, and she needed such men.

'Very well,' she said, and turned back to watch the dancing.

6

Ten days later, Tom Randolph, having presented his credentials to the Master of Requests for the umpteenth time, was ushered before the queen of Scots and her privy council to communicate to them a message from the queen his mistress.

'Whereas her majesty lately said that if her very dearest cousin of Scotland would marry her very dearest subject, the Earl of Leicester, she would thereafter consider advising her parliament to acknowledge her aforesaid very dearest cousin of Scotland as heir presumptive to the throne of England ...' Tom Randolph paused for breath. '... on more mature consideration the queen my mistress now feels compelled to rescind this for the reason that she herself has not yet made up her mind whether or not she herself will marry and, by the grace of God, bear heirs of her body. She is sure that her very dearest cousin of Scotland will understand her decision.'

Scanning the faces of the privy council from under his thick, black brows, Randolph wished, as so often before, that he hadn't come. He waited for the walls of Holyroodhouse to collapse about his ears.

The Earl of Moray, who had so recently made a personal plea to Elizabeth, turned an unhealthy grey-white; the Earl of Argyll, who had told Mary brusquely to marry Leicester and hope for the best, went purple as a thundercloud; Morton was a subtle shade of puce; Châtelherault a tasteful gamboge; and Catholic Atholl, who saw it as a body blow to Anglophile Protestant ascendancy, a satisfied raspberry pink.

The queen's face was white as a sheet and the Four Maries were looking at her worriedly. Randolph took care not to catch Beaton's eye.

Lethington, reflecting that this was the only permutation which had not previously been inflicted on them, said calmly, 'But we have always recognised that, if the queen your mistress were to marry and bear heirs of the body, the question of the queen *my* mistress's succession would fall by the way. Why should this affect the granting of the succession in the meantime?'

If they had been private, Randolph would have said, 'Don't ask *me!* There's no sense in it.' And Lethington would have replied, 'No, nor ever has been.'

7

Mary's lovely amber eyes were swollen with tears of rage and frustration when she summoned James and Lethington to see her privately later in the day.

'I *will* not be patronised. I *will* not be manipulated. I *will* not wed at

174

my cousin's command, to wait forever for her to marry or not to marry, for her parliament to reward, or not to reward me for my meek compliance.'

James said, 'But Mary ...'

'Don't interrupt. You and Secretary Lethington promised me you would win for me the formal acknowledgement of succession to a throne that is rightfully mine, but all you have done is reduce me – *me* – to the level of a supplicant before a woman who has no true right to the throne on which she sits, a woman whose mother, in the eyes of Holy Church, was no better than a strumpet.

'First I was not to marry a foreigner. Then I was to marry an English noble. Then I would have the succession if I married Dudley. Then I was to marry Dudley and Elizabeth would afterwards consider the question of the succession. And now she will not consider the question of the succession at all. After almost four years, you have achieved *nothing*.

'Well, that is the end of it. I want no more of your opinions, your guidance, your promises. Secretary Lethington may continue with his routine duties, but I wish to see as little of him as possible. James, you may do what you wish. I have followed your advice all this time and it has brought me only trouble. From now on, I shall go my own way and choose my own advisers. That is all. Leave me.'

8

Marching back and forth in the confined space of her retiring room, Mary was dictating to Davie Riccio, scribbling away furiously.

'... a matter of urgency ... must know from your master, King Philip, whether Don Carlos recovered from his illness ...'

She said, 'Master Balmerino must leave immediately for London. I want him to go today. He is to take that letter to the new Spanish ambassador, de Silva, and insist that we have an answer as soon as can be arranged. He must impress on de Silva that ...'

The door opened and she turned impatiently, but it was Henry Darnley, who did not need to be announced. She said, 'Harry, I am busy ...'

He smiled a boyish, conspiratorial smile and replied in his light, drawling voice, 'I know it's awful of me, and I have no right to express an opinion to your majesty on such a matter, but I am *so* pleased. You could never have demeaned yourself by marrying that vulgar upstart Leicester,

175

and you should never have been advised to. I have just passed your brother and your secretary, looking as if the heavens had fallen on them, and I hope they did. I didn't like to tell you before, but my mother found out that they had sworn to Elizabeth – *sworn* to her – that they would force you to marry Leicester if only Elizabeth would make one or two tiny concessions. I do hope you've dismissed them, because they deserve it.'

Mary said, 'They what?'

'They swore to Elizabeth ...'

'Never mind. I heard.'

Blithely, he resumed, 'And, of course, everyone *knew* that Elizabeth would never part with Leicester! I mean, they're so *close*. Just a few weeks ago ...'

Fleming said, 'Madame ...' but Mary waved her to silence.

'Just a few weeks ago, Leicester and Norfolk were playing a hot game of tennis with Elizabeth watching, and Leicester snatched Elizabeth's kerchief from her hand without so much as a by-your-leave and mopped his brow with it. And Norfolk reprimanded him, and then Elizabeth reprimanded Norfolk for being impolite to him! Well, you couldn't ask for a more public proof that their relationship is still every bit as close as it has always been, could you?'

Mary said, 'No, you couldn't.'

9

Young Lord Darnley might be deferential and engagingly boyish with the queen but, once he was assured of her favour, his manner towards others began to deteriorate.

It was something his doting mother had not foreseen, the mother who had told him exactly how to approach the queen of Scots, how to address her, how to ingratiate himself with her; the mother who had supplied him with a chestful of small gifts, so that scarcely a day needed to go by on which Darnley did not present the queen with a jewelled pomander, or a book of poems, or a travelling sandglass-clock. The mother who had rehearsed him in intimate smiles and mapped out an acceptable sequence of physical contacts; who had explained to him what an innocent woman might be expected to like or dislike – an explanation that had been necessary because a woman's likes and dislikes were not normally something that interested him. And the mother who had failed to make allowance for her son's innate arrogance.

Even Mary Seton's Christian charity faltered after a time. She had said at first, 'No one who matters is even civil to him, although one would have thought it the merest common sense for some older gentleman to take him under his wing. And with his elders and betters doing nothing but glower at him, he naturally becomes impertinent, as any young man might, and seeks his friends among inferiors who are prepared to look up to him.'

'Most of them toadies and tricksters,' Beaton said. 'Except for Davie, of course. I suppose they both need allies against the dislike of the lords. Have you ever heard them together? Davie addresses Darnley less like a possible king-to-be of the Scots than as king regnant of the world.'

Mallie said, 'Which is how that young man is beginning to behave.'

Beaton sighed. 'Yes. But in the case of his friends, what can we do about it? He is simply a member of Madame's court. She can scarcely dictate to him about who his friends should be.'

'And if he were to become more than a member of her court,' said Mallie, who was engaged, in Livingston's absence, on tidying the rolls of rings in one of the queen's jewel coffers, 'it might be too late.'

They looked at each other helplessly.

10

Lethington said, 'James, you are not listening. I said there is nothing to be done.'

They were sitting on top of the hill known as Arthur's Seat, which loomed high above the eavesdropping ears of Holyroodhouse and Edinburgh, Lethington gazing out across the firth to the lowlands of Fife while James, blind to the early spring sun sparkling on the waters, picked irritably at the wiry stems of a clump of dead heather.

'But we *must* do something. Randolph says Elizabeth probably gave Darnley permission to come north simply to confuse Mary, so that she would swither between him and Dudley and not be able to make up her mind.'

'It's possible. Elizabeth is a careful woman who makes the mistake of judging others by herself. But your sister is much more impulsive and she's done nothing for the last few days except weep and write letters. I am more concerned by the fact that we don't know what is in those letters than about any possibility of her marrying Darnley.'

'What?' James looked up, startled. It wasn't often that Lethington got his priorities wrong.

'Think about it. He's a spoilt and arrogant young man with – as far as I can see – no interest in anything other than pleasure. I have no doubt he wants to be king, but he certainly doesn't want to govern. And that would mean that, if only we could persuade her majesty to begin taking our advice again, we could go on much as before.'

'If only,' James repeated sourly. He had taken Mary's rejection of him very badly indeed. He had never thought she would dare.

'And if Darnley were to give her a son, it would very much strengthen her position in relation to the English succession.'

James scowled. 'A son. Oh, aye.'

Dudley – who was probably infertile – versus Darnley, who was probably not. And an end to James's hopes.

Reverting to the point he had been making, Lethington said, 'Our first priority must be to retrieve our position. Your sister is leaning too heavily on what Riccio says, and he, of course, says only what she wants to hear. We cannot allow her to continue looking for allies and possibly a husband abroad, which is what those letters are almost certainly about. In the present situation the Riccios of this world are more dangerous than the Darnleys.'

'Ye think so, do you? Well, I tell you, the other day my brother Robert was showing Darnley a map of Scotland and pointed out my lands of Moray to him. And he had the insolence to say that my lands – *my* lands – were too wide. What d'ye think about that, eh? Mary made him apologise, but I tell you, I will not be supplanted as her adviser by an ignorant, arrogant, Catholic brat! I will not have my titles and lands questioned by a son of Lennox!'

Lethington, in his youth, had read and been impressed by the writings of Machiavelli and nothing he had learned since had led him to disagree with Machiavelli's view that most men were so ruled by self-interest that a prince needed to take no other consideration into account when dealing with them. 'A man will resent the loss of his patrimony more than the murder of his parent.' He had always been inclined to absolve James of such weakness but was no longer sure.

'No,' James went on. 'I'm not prepared to risk Darnley influencing Mary against me. I'm going to talk to Argyll and Châtelherault and get them to promise me their backing. We can draw up a bond agreeing to support one another in all legitimate enterprises.'

A bond was a contract of honour, a banding together of men who expected to need one another's support in some projected enterprise. It always meant trouble.

Lethington said, 'Châtelherault?' A man who was himself forgettable, but whose position could never be forgotten; a strange bedfellow for James, who had never been other than contemptuous of him. But fear and dislike of a common enemy had a unifying power and family pride was at stake, too, because if Mary married Darnley, the hated Lennox Stuarts would then be able to lord it over Châtelherault and the Hamiltons.

'Yes. And I'm going to talk to Knox. He and I have been at odds for too long. I've never been as keen on the succession business as you have. I've staked my political life on reaching an arrangement between Mary and Elizabeth largely because it would guarantee the supremacy of Protestantism here in Scotland. I've done everything possible to keep my sister's favour, and lost Knox's trust and friendship in the process. And now ... Well, look where it's got me. But I tell you, Mary's cooked her own goose by displacing me as her adviser. I'm going to show her that she either has to give up Darnley or face civil war.'

Pained, Lethington closed his eyes. 'She has not yet given any sign that marrying him has even entered her head, but if you go on like this, you may well drive her to it.'

11

James finally left Mary's court at Easter, head high, declaring that he was not prepared to stay and witness his sister's idolatrous observance of it.

It turned out to be a futile gesture. Not even his co-religionists paid much attention, attributing it to pique at being out of favour, while Mary and her ladies celebrated his departure by dressing up as burgesses' wives and running around the steep streets of Stirling for an hour before arriving unannounced at the English ambassador's lodging and requiring to be fed.

Randolph found it interesting, as he always did, that however tense the queen's relationship with her lords, the common people continued to worship her. On festive occasions, she was spectacularly, gloriously, beautifully royal – everything a queen should be – and it seemed to increase rather than diminish her glamour that she should, now and then, descend mischievously from the throne to the market place in order to talk to, and laugh with, her people. The figure in cloth of gold on a white horse was the more delightful for having been, however briefly, a pretty, high-spirited, slightly rackety young woman.

She could scarcely have appeared more carefree, but in truth she was waiting to hear from de Silva whether there was any remaining glimmer of hope of a match with Don Carlos.

In the meantime, she watched Darnley closely, while her Maries watched her. She obviously enjoyed his company but there was nothing out of the ordinary when the two of them joined their lutes in lighthearted concert or partnered each other at billiards, two tall and gracefully matched figures leaning over with their scoop-shaped cues to tap the ivory balls between the miniature goalposts. One evening, Mary and Darnley lost an agate ring and a brooch worth fifty crowns to Beaton and Randolph, and Darnley bought them back with rueful charm.

She did not always partner Darnley. Sometimes it was Arthur Erskine, or Alexander Ogilvie, or Robert Beaton of Creich. Never Lethington, who was no longer welcome in the royal presence.

There was nothing to put a finger on except that the queen, who had always taken the Maries fully into her confidence, was being less confiding than usual. Mallie found that she was missing Livingston badly, not only because most of Livingston's duties had devolved on her, so that she had ceased to have any private life at all, but because Livingston had a shrewdness that the others lacked.

It was clear, certainly, that the queen was being careful. But she had been a widow for four years and Mallie suspected that, more and more, she was coming to see Darnley as a handsome, agreeable and suitable second husband.

The queen herself, after her outburst at James and Lethington, knew that she needed someone to replace them in her life and counsels and she could see no reason why Elizabeth should object, since Darnley was English-born and noble – the qualifications on which she had always insisted for Mary's husband – and she herself had given him permission to come north.

Considered coolly and sensibly, Lord Darnley was an appealing possibility. He was still of an age to be trained up into a satisfactory consort, a consort whose loyalty would be to his wife alone – because it would be she who gave him everything. Mary felt a little sad that she would have no knowledge of the kind of love Livingston had spoken of, but she was a queen and could not hope for more than an agreeable companion.

At last, on a chilly day in early April, Balmerino returned from London to say that the Spanish ambassador had ruled out, once and for all, any possibility of the Spanish match. Don Carlos, whose sanity was now giving serious cause for concern, had been withdrawn from the marriage market.

It proved decisive.

12

Mary was standing before the pillared stone fireplace in her audience chamber at Stirling, the flames glowing bright and welcoming, when she received secretary of state Lethington on the following day. But there was nothing welcoming in her manner. She showed no sign of relenting either to him or to James. She had ceased to have any interest in what they thought.

Without preliminary, she said, 'I have decided to marry Lord Darnley and I require you to leave for London at once to inform my cousin Elizabeth of it. It will be necessary, I suppose, to observe the formality of asking her consent, since he is of the royal blood and also an English subject, but I anticipate no difficulty there, since she herself sent him to me. You have something to say?'

Despite the line he had taken with James, which had been designed to reduce that gentleman's emotional temperature, Lethington felt no enthusiasm for the match. From Randolph, he knew that it was Cecil and Dudley, more than Elizabeth herself, who had chosen to promote it – which left Elizabeth in the position she liked best, free to disclaim responsibility if anything went wrong, and free to claim responsibility if everything went right. Lethington was less sanguine than Mary about her probable reaction, because whatever she might have said in the past about the acceptability of an English nobleman as a husband for her dearest cousin, Mary's marriage had proved a subject on which she was consistent only in her inconsistency.

It occurred to him, however, that while he was in England he might find the opportunity to investigate a more mature and acceptable alternative to either Darnley or Dudley. England's premier nobleman, the Duke of Norfolk, had recently lost his second wife in childbirth.

For the moment, the coolness in the queen's almond eyes suggested that discretion was likely to be the better part of valour. So he said merely, 'As your majesty commands. May I assume that your majesty will not take any irrevocable step before we have the queen your cousin's response?'

Mary shrugged noncommittally, but Lethington left knowing that, however little she might relish yet another round of negotiations with Elizabeth, she was too well schooled in statecraft to do anything rash.

13

Neither of them could have anticipated what was to happen within a day or two of his departure.

Lord Darnley began complaining of feeling feverish, of having sore eyes, and a raw throat. 'A cold,' he said, gazing at the queen meltingly. 'I think I should retire to my bed and allow it to run its course.'

Mary, always swift with sympathy for those she liked, urged him to do so, sent her apothecary to him, and herself went to visit him in the chamber he had been allotted in the hilltop fortress that was Stirling castle. He looked very young and forlorn as he tossed and turned in the great fourposter bed, with its gilded carvings and heavy green hangings, his face flushed and his eyes bright with fever, and she reached out her hand to him, feeling a rush of protectiveness that she had not felt since she had loved and cared for François during his frequent sicknesses.

When Lord Darnley's cold turned out to be measles, her apothecary forbade her to visit him. Then, when she insisted, the patient himself refused to see her, blotched as he was with the disfiguring rash. It was almost a week before he thought to order his chamber groom to procure him a mask.

It meant that he was on the road to recovery when she entered his sickroom to find him, limp as a plucked blossom, holding the ivory-handled mask before his face and murmuring, 'Mary, my Mary,' as if the seven-day separation had bridged all gaps between them. The boyish vanity of the mask aroused in her only warmth and tenderness as she took it from him and, her eyes grave and sweet, clasped his hands in hers and said, '*My* Harry, you will be well soon.'

Mallie Fleming, who was in attendance, had the curious impression that love and strength were actually flowing from the queen into the young man, although there was no movement, and nothing else was said.

For Mary, nothing else needed to be said. It was François all over again – her husband, her child – although a François taller and more beautiful than the real one could ever have become.

Not for another week did she discover that it was not quite François all over again. She was in Darnley's chamber one evening, playing cards with him on the counterpane as she had so often done with that other, younger invalid, and feeling gently amused by the suspicion that my Lord Darnley was quite well enough to have left his bed if he had not found his royal pampering so congenial. Despite Lethington's mission to Elizabeth, she had not yet said anything of marriage to the young man himself.

She had just sent Fleming off for a hot posset when he threw down his cards, exclaiming, 'These are too old and creased. I can tell simply by looking at the backs of your majesty's hand whether you hold an ace or not. We need a fresh pack. Go and find one, Taylor.'

The chamber groom departed and so, for the first time, they were alone. She had no sense of foreboding, nor of anything other than enquiry, when he extended his hands towards her and murmured, 'Come closer.'

She moved to perch on the edge of the bed. 'Yes, what is it?'

Not until long years afterwards did she recognise, with a distant wonder, how innocent she had been. Reared at the highly sophisticated and none too moral court of France, she could hardly have escaped knowing something about sexual attraction, but she had been shielded from personal experience of it by her own royal situation. No man had ever kissed her, save on her hand or – ceremonially or sometimes frivolously – on her cheek. With François, there had been only an occasional contact of soft lips with soft lips, accompanied by a childishly giggly bumping of noses.

Darnley's lips were soft, too, but not slack, and she had no standards by which to judge how experienced were the arms that encircled her and drew her to him. It did not for a moment occur to her that his mother might have instructed him in the sexual niceties of seducing a possibly resistant and probably virginal queen, or that the tenderness of his lips had its genesis more in calculation than in feeling.

It was a kiss kept brief both by circumstances and by intent, designed to tantalise, not to satisfy. But the effects of the kiss and the physical closeness of the embrace on Mary, twenty-two years old and ignorant until then of what her heart and her body lacked, were cataclysmic. When he released her, she was shuddering lightly from head to toe, her bones like water and an unfamiliar, melting ache radiating through her pelvis.

Mallie Fleming, returning with the hot posset, saw the barely suppressed smirk on Darnley's face and the colour in the queen's cheeks and the dazzlement in her eyes, and thought, 'No! Please, no!'

Lethington, his stockinged knees already deeply embossed with the pattern of Greenwich's rush matting, rose to his feet without waiting for permission, but Elizabeth was so angry that she barely noticed. If she had been acting, she would have noticed soon enough.

She was standing before her chair of state, her hands splayed over her hips, her body rigid with wrath. 'God's death!' she exploded again. 'No, no and *no*! I will not have it. This is no more than another attempt by you Scots – God's death, but I am tired of you! – to take my throne for the queen your mistress. That she should marry a man who has a claim of his own! One of *my* subjects, and a Catholic one! *No.* Far from marrying the queen your mistress, the young man will return to England *at once* and I will deal with him. And his father, too. You will convey to them my express command. I want them both back here immediately. I will hear no more of this nonsense.'

Lethington succeeded in keeping his voice mild and his smile quizzical. 'You are saying, *"Roma locuta est; causa finita est"*?'

Rome has spoken; the case is closed.

There was no purpose at all in arguing with Elizabeth when she was in this mood. It would be days before sensible discussion became possible. Well, he had things to do.

'Augustine of Hippo,' she snapped. 'And you are being insolent.'

'No. It was merely a way of asking whether that was your final word. If it was, then I will take up no more of your majesty's time.'

'Fiddle-faddle! Do not dare to leave this palace until I have consulted my privy council and given you a formal answer to take back with you.'

He had been prepared for some such reaction, though not so sincerely felt. He had guessed that she would secretly welcome the Darnley proposal as an excuse to open up yet another round of negotiating, and procrastinating, and laying down conditions and then changing them. She had not expected to be faced with a demand for an outright yes or no. What he could not understand was why she should be not merely angry, but in the kind of towering rage for which her father had been famous.

Closeted with Cecil afterwards, he said, 'His mother may be a leader of the Catholic community here, but the boy himself seems perfectly flexible.

He has no continental connections, no army at his back, and to imagine such a vain and hollow youth helping Mary lead a Catholic crusade against England is the purest nonsense. Elizabeth cannot possibly see him as a danger. So – why?'

'She is offended. She will not tolerate the queen your mistress trying to manipulate her by presenting her with a virtual *fait accompli.*'

It was almost too much for Lethington who, briefly reviewing the options – to laugh, to explode, or to weep – decided that none of them, alone, properly encapsulated his feelings. So he said merely, 'If that were so, would you not see it as a just return for the queen *your* mistress's manipulations over these last four years?'

Cecil was affronted. 'You talk of just returns? As I recall, it was England that, at your personal request, came to the rescue of the Protestant cause in Scotland five years ago. Without us, Scotland would be Catholic still. Yet you have done nothing since but pester, pester, pester us about the succession. I would have expected better of you, some sign of gratitude!'

'Blessed is he who does not expect gratitude,' Lethington said drily, 'for he will not be disappointed.'

16

His only other possible source of enlightenment was the former Lord Robert Dudley, now Earl of Leicester.

Lethington tracked him down in a wing of the royal stables, irritably muttering, 'Malt and brimstone!' and dressed not in ceremonial whites and greens, not in corals and pale greys, but in practical mud-brown leather.

Leicester greeted him cheerfully. 'Ah, William, my friend! Will you look at these bills for malt and brimstone, for dressings, poultices, medicines for glanders, the stranglion, chafed legs, sore eyes, inflamed bellies? And that's not the half of it. How can I buy brood mares or set up new studs when her majesty barely allows me enough to pay the keeper? Take my advice. Never let yourself be landed with the post of Master of the Horse!'

Lethington grinned and Leicester, grinning back, said, 'Well, what do you want?'

'Darnley.'

'Oh?'

'Mary wants to marry him and Elizabeth is violently opposed. As it happens, I was told by Randolph that it was not Elizabeth but you and Cecil who tossed the boy into the lion pit. May I ask why?'

'Annoyed, are you? Let's go outdoors.' The smell of horse was scarcely less overpowering outdoors than in, but at least there was no unseen audience of stable boys. 'It's simple enough. I have not the slightest wish to marry your queen, beautiful though she may be, and I no longer find the negotiations entertaining. I hoped that Darnley would divert attention from me.'

'I had half guessed as much. And Cecil's motives?'

'Trying to muddy the diplomatic waters by plunging the lady into indecision. Though how any woman of sense could be undecided when offered a choice between myself and that young nincompoop ...'

He was an engaging fellow. 'Even so,' Lethington said, 'it was Elizabeth herself who dealt the new hand by permitting Lennox and then his son to travel north. And I am sure you were very soon warned by Tom Randolph that the young man had found favour in Mary's eyes. So why Elizabeth's extraordinary outburst?'

Leicester cocked a cheerful eyebrow. 'It must be the first time in our acquaintance when I find myself knowing something that you don't. How satisfying! You have James to thank. And Knox. And Cecil, of course. Knox and Cecil have always wanted to see Mary tipped off her throne, and as for James ... Well, if that useless fool, her heir Châtelherault, were to replace her, James would have things very much his own way, wouldn't he? The three of them, combined, have convinced Elizabeth that she made a disastrous mistake in allowing Lennox and Darnley to go back to Scotland. Her majesty does not like making mistakes, which is why she is behaving so excitably.'

'What exactly have they said to her?'

'The usual. That a Catholic husband for Mary will lead to civil war. That she means to force Scotland back into the Catholic fold, and so on. Does she?'

'No, of course not, and James knows that as well as I do.' A man will resent the loss of his patrimony more than the murder of his parent – or the dethronement of his sister? 'She might like to, but her weapon would be persuasion. She is not a Mary Tudor.'

With curiosity, Dudley asked, 'What is she really like? I'm nearer a Puritan than a Protestant myself, though I don't advertise it, but from what Randolph says about her, and Throckmorton when he was in

France, she doesn't strike me as the desperate danger that everyone here insists on thinking she is.'

Lethington allowed himself a trace of exasperation. 'God almighty, Robert! She's a queen and she believes in her divine right to rule. She believes – with justice – that she has a better claim to the throne of England than Elizabeth, but she is prepared to accept the situation as it stands. Beyond that, she is a charming young woman, well educated, artistic, romantic, frustrated, emotional, generous, occasionally unmanageable. But tolerant in religion. To begin with, I had the gravest doubts about her, but no more. I believe that Scotland has been lucky in her. Frankly, if she had a husband and children, I think they would give her the stability and maturity that she lacks. Some women are like that.'

'And some are not. Can you imagine Elizabeth dandling a babe on her knee?'

'Not readily. So?'

'So, you have answered yourself. Tell James – and Knox, if he's tellable – to beg Elizabeth to let the match go ahead, since it appears to be the least risky of the options. She will then be in the gratifying position of being able to do a favour to her good friends, the Earl of Moray and Master John Knox, at no cost to herself. I'll do what I can to help, if only to see the end of this interminable wrangling. Everything *could* turn out for the best, if your queen will only tread gently. Elizabeth doesn't like being bullied.'

'No one does.'

17

He had intended to postpone writing to Mary until he had something useful to say, but within a few days he received a ciphered report from Hay, his assistant in Edinburgh, informing him of 'certain difficulties' which had arisen at home.

Her majesty, it seemed, had fallen in love.

All Scotland was buzzing with the news of her infatuation, a good deal of it exaggerated. It was said that she could not bear to be parted from Lord Darnley and spent hours with him every day to the detriment – although Hay had seen no sign of it – of business of state. The gossips ignored the fact that one or two of her ladies were always in attendance. It was also rumoured that the Maries had taken it upon themselves to draw the queen's attention to the young man's deficiencies and were out of favour as a result. In Hay's judgement, the opposition was having the undesirable effect of making the queen more stubborn, as if she had too long heeded the advice and desires of others and was now determined on going her own way, regardless of the cost. Visitors to the young lord's sickroom found him more arrogant and boastful by the day – he had even dared to threaten Châtelherault – and he was not unfailingly courteous even to the queen herself, but the queen appeared to be blind to his faults.

Unhappily, her majesty's lords were failing to take the long view favoured by my Lord Secretary and were seeing the proposed Darnley marriage solely in relation to their own interests. The queen was thus being drawn into a situation of unusual difficulty, just at a time when neither my Lord Secretary nor the Earl of Moray was there to advise her. Lord Moray had not been seen at court since Easter.

Lethington sat for more than an hour, his cool grey gaze empty, before consigning the letter to the flames. For the first time in his memory, he wondered why he chose to embroil himself in it all. It wasn't as if he needed the employment.

He did the only thing open to him in the circumstances, writing to Mary of Elizabeth's reaction in terms designed to make her stop and think. He also wrote to James, begging him to bestir himself and ensure that his sister did nothing rash.

He could not have foreseen that James would respond by embarking on a course of his own that was ten times more rash and was to start a chain of events that, in the end, would destroy them all.

Chapter Nine

MAY-JULY 1565

1

The queen could barely contain her fury. 'How dare he! How *dare* my brother try to intimidate me! To fill Edinburgh with thousands of armed men! I do not for a moment believe that his only object was to wreck Lord Bothwell's day of law, although that would have been bad enough. He wants to frighten me out of a marriage he fears and detests. Well, we shall see. *We shall see!*'

Fatuously, Mary Seton said, 'I'm sure he didn't mean it, Madame,' but Mallie Fleming was equally sure that he did. And her rash and vainglorious cousin Bothwell had played straight into James's hands. No one other than the queen – who believed Bothwell to be her loyal, if occasionally insubordinate subject – wanted him back in Scotland at all, and certainly not running around tame at court. And so James and his ally Argyll had chosen to settle the matter by doing what John Knox had done eighteen months before, and convocating the queen's lieges to ensure that Bothwell's judges would not dare find him anything other than guilty – or, to put it in the more respectable terms they preferred, to ensure that the judges were made aware of the strength of public opinion.

The population of Edinburgh had very nearly doubled in a few hours as James's men swarmed into the city, most of them wearing swords and leather jacks and conversing in the accents of Fife or the west. Since they had been levied hurriedly and were none too sure why they were there at all, many of the city's burghers had gone hastening home to barricade their windows and doors in preparation for war.

Bothwell had heard about it just in time, and had hastily embarked for France again.

But James and Argyll could have achieved the same end with a force of less than half the size and Mary's conclusion that they had been trying to intimidate her was far from unreasonable in the circumstances. She had, after all, no army of her own beyond a few companies of professional infantry.

Mallie and Seton tried to make light of James's folly; to persuade the queen that there was a world of difference between a display of nervous self-interest and the perils of outright insurrection; to soothe her deep personal hurt that her own brother, on whom she had bestowed title, power and lands, should so betray her.

But they might have saved themselves the trouble. The queen, too, was in revolt.

2

Now, finally and decisively, she rejected all advice except from those who offered her the luxury of encouragement to follow her own instincts and judgement, instead of frustrating her at every turn.

Her father-in-law-to-be, the Earl of Lennox, the inevitable small smile on his small, pouting mouth, said, 'However things may have appeared in the past, your brother James has always wanted the throne for himself. His allegiance has never been to you, my dear, but always to England, because he believes that with Elizabeth's help he can take your throne from you. Believe me, I have lived in England and I know. He has always been in her pocket.'

She had wondered about that when she first returned to Scotland, but had found her suspicions hard to sustain because James had never shown any real sign of wanting to exercise power on his own account. In her present frame of mind, however, she was perfectly prepared to believe that he had been dancing, all the while, to Elizabeth's jealous tune.

They were in Darnley's bedchamber at Stirling where, having recovered from measles, he had been struck by a fever and was confined to his bed again. Now, he moaned, 'I don't feel well,' which he had discovered to be an infallible way of putting an end to discussions that didn't interest him.

Laying a cool hand on his soft and beardless cheek, so like François's, Mary said, 'You will be better soon, my darling.'

His large hazel eyes gazed at her soulfully. 'James is a stupid man, puffed up in his own esteem. He's jealous of me. He doesn't like it that you don't listen to his advice any more.' The light, drawling voice became pettish. 'Really, it's so *silly*. Why should I not be your husband? Why should I not be king?'

'You will be king,' she assured him, and set her mind to devising a

190

means by which she could get the better not only of James, but Elizabeth.

3

A red cross painted on the wall meant No Pissing, and the third courtyard at Greenwich was full of them. Robert Dudley, striding towards a cross-less corner, scooped Lethington up on the way, growling, 'A man could die of desperation!' Then, as he unbuttoned the cod-placket of his breeches, 'You, too.'

Lethington said, 'I don't ...'

'Yes, you do. What could be more innocent than two men pissing together? I have something confidential to say to you.'

'Have you, indeed?'

'I don't think you are going to credit this, but Elizabeth is about to tell you that she has nothing more to say to you, personally, on the subject of your queen's marriage.'

'But ...'

'Wait. What she is about to do, instead, is send Throckmorton to the queen your mistress to announce formally that she is unalterably opposed to the Darnley marriage. Throckmorton is also to tell Mary that she may have any other English nobleman she chooses.' Observing Lethington's raised brows, he went on, 'No, no, my friend, forget Norfolk. Don't waste time feeling hopeful. Because – I can hardly bear to say this – she may have any English noble she chooses, but only if she chooses *me* will Elizabeth consent to look into the succession question again.'

After a moment, Lethington said, 'Well, well. Do you have a certain sense of *déjà vu* about all this?'

Dudley began buttoning up again. 'I cannot imagine how you stay so calm. Your patience is amazing.'

Lethington did not say, 'It has just run out.'

4

He spent the first two days of his homeward journey revolving plans in his mind. Elizabeth had forfeited all right to friendship or consideration, and Lethington – whose acquaintance, when he chose to call on it, was wide and influential – was going to have no compunction in letting it be known, at home and abroad, that Mary was behaving impeccably over a marriage that could be a danger to no one, and Elizabeth like an envious and vindictive child. Whatever Elizabeth might like to pretend, there was a limit to how much pressure she could withstand from France and Spain.

It was, of course, essential that, in the meantime, Mary *did* behave impeccably.

He had reached Newark and was waiting for fresh horses when John Beaton – discreet, unremarkable, unmemorable as a secret messenger should be – rode into the stableyard from the north and said, 'Ah, I'm blithe to see ye, my lord. I hadn't expected to find ye before Greenwich. I've urgent letters for you from her majesty.'

They were letters that caused the famously imperturbable Lethington to come out with a succession of crashing oaths that shocked the eight men of his riding escort to the roots of their beings. Even John Beaton looked startled.

Striding off towards the unmanicured privacy of what the post house called its garden, he read the letters again. Mary, it seemed, had summoned her nobles to Stirling to agree a bond supporting the union of herself and Lord Darnley. On the appointed day, Lord Darnley would take the oath of allegiance to her, and she would clothe him with suitable honours, an unequivocal declaration of her intentions which would effectively undermine any attempt on Elizabeth's part to interfere.

As Secretary Lethington would appreciate, however, it was essential that these events – if they were not to appear unduly provocative – should take place *before* Mary was made formally aware of Elizabeth's opposition, of which Secretary Lethington had already informally notified her. The queen therefore required him to do everything in his power to postpone the setting out of Elizabeth's official envoy from Greenwich, to delay him so that he should not arrive in Scotland until after the 15th May. Secretary Lethington was then to deliver the accompanying letter to Elizabeth, and afterwards to proceed to France, there to announce the queen's forthcoming marriage.

The letter for Elizabeth said that Mary was no longer prepared to submit to her cousin's yea and nay and double dealing, but intended to marry whom she chose.

5

She had to be stopped.
Everything was wrong with her plan and everything, too, was wrong

with the timing, because Sir Nicholas Throckmorton had set out from Greenwich two days before Lethington.

When the fresh horses were brought out a few minutes later, Lethington's mind was made up.

Since courtiers travelling on English royal business and bearing privy council placards were entitled to a priority in requisitioning post horses that was denied to Lethington, it took him a killing four days – four days of hard riding, impatient striding back and forth, and bribery, and very little sleep – before he caught up with Throckmorton at Alnwick in Northumberland.

Amiably surprised, Throckmorton said, 'You are telling me that I must strain every sinew to reach Mary's court before this meeting takes place, so as to ensure that it does *not* take place?'

'Yes. You know as well as I do that if she alienates Elizabeth at this stage nothing but harm will ensue.'

Throckmorton, a sandy man with fine hands and careful eyes, liked Lethington and had always thought Mary a sensible and intelligent young woman. After a moment's thought, he said, 'I found a letter from Tom Randolph awaiting me here. Its news is more up-to-date than anything you are likely to have received. Perhaps you should read it.'

Lethington scanned it and was appalled.

Randolph's emotions were always apt to submerge his judgement, and this time he was wallowing. Even so, the essence of what he had to say was dismaying. He did not know, he moaned, what was going to come of it all. Throckmorton should be warned that Mary, who had always been so worthy and wise, was now so possessed by passion that all wisdom had flown out of the window. Three short weeks of being in love, and she had lost the respect of everyone who knew her. Randolph himself was having an exceedingly trying time, because it was commonly believed that Elizabeth had sent Lord Darnley to Scotland in order to entrap Mary into a politically divisive marriage. In which she was succeeding.

The queen of Scots was furiously suspicious of her brother, the Earl of Moray, and Moray was even more suspicious of *her*, fearing that she might arrest him for trying to intimidate her. Once more hand in glove with Knox, Moray had told her he could not approve the Darnley marriage unless she herself became a convert to the reformed church. The queen, in angry response, was said to have instructed the Cardinal de Guise to go ahead and arrange a papal dispensation for the marriage, which was necessary since she and Darnley were cousins.

Randolph couldn't see where it was all going to end.

Throckmorton, who had never before seen Lethington angry or perplexed, said tentatively, 'Well, you have failed to carry out your queen's instruction about delaying me. What now? I suppose you must return to Greenwich to deliver the letter to Elizabeth?'

'No, I am coming back to Scotland with you, and as fast as our horses will carry us.'

'Dear God! You dare to disobey your queen's commands?'

'Her interests are more important than her commands.'

Kindly, Throckmorton said, 'I will put flowers on your grave.'

6

They reached Edinburgh late on the afternoon of the 14th, but Throckmorton refused to ride straight on to Stirling. 'Dignity forbids that the envoy of her majesty Queen Elizabeth of England should present himself at the court of Scotland in an aura of dust, sweat and haste. Certainly not haste. One would not wish to encourage your sovereign in delusions of her own importance.'

'Would one not?' But Lethington smiled briefly at the other man's diplomatic game-playing. He said, 'You may be right. However, I myself must go on. The day of decision is tomorrow.'

Courteous as always, Throckmorton rejoined, 'I shall be there. At about seven, if I set out at break of day.'

7

Lethington dismounted in the courtyard of Stirling castle, threw the reins to a servant and hurried towards the royal apartments, intent on seeing the queen.

He was refused access to her.

'Her majesty ees busy,' said the ugly little fellow with the taste for lurid satins and velvets. His smile was obsequious but meaningless.

Lethington, who was not a violent man, with difficulty conquered the urge to throttle him. 'I have matters of considerable urgency to discuss with her.'

Riccio held no formal position. He was merely a member of the queen's private household. He should have had no authority at all to hinder the secretary of state in the execution of his duties if the queen had not, in the

194

preceding months and almost by default, permitted him to constitute himself her majordomo, screening who should be allowed to see her and exacting fees for the privilege. The lords, accustomed to easy access to their sovereign and unaccustomed to the continental habit of bribery, had responded with loathing and contempt, but Mary had paid no more than an amused and passing attention to their complaints, saying that she had been trying unsuccessfully ever since she arrived in Scotland to break them of their habit of walking in on her whenever they felt inclined, that it was a pleasant change not to have her days interrupted, without warning, by Lindsay of the Byres shouting about Roman rituals or Ochiltree or Pittarrow laying down the law about the settlement of 1560.

Riccio said, 'I am most sorry, Lord Secretary, but she ees still busy.'

'When will she cease to be busy?'

The little man, his sense of consequence glowing as lustrously on his face as the new-bought satins on his back, beamed lavishly upon him. 'For you, Lord Secretary, never. Her majesty bids me say that she ees already aware of your return from England, and ees also aware that you came in the company of the queen of England's envoy. She says you have disobeyed her and she ees ver' angry. She ees not prepared to receive you.'

Lethington, who had already put almost everything at risk by ignoring Mary's commands, might have hazarded one last throw by forcing his way in. But Davie must have seen it in his eyes. He raised a hand and the royal bodyguard appeared in the archway, pikes at the slope.

Coldly, Lethington said, 'You have no legal authority,' but the ill-shaven little gargoyle, still beaming, replied, 'Ees not so. I have her majesty's authority. There ees no higher authority than that.'

Turning away, Lethington said, 'There is God's.'

8

Next morning – dust-free, smelling strongly of ambergris and myrrh, and in no hurry at all – Sir Nicholas Throckmorton presented himself at the great gate of Stirling castle. The portcullis was up, but the gate was closed and there wasn't even a porter in sight. No amount of shouting or hammering on the inches-thick wood brought any response.

It was some time before Throckmorton could bring himself to believe that it was deliberate. Thereafter, for three hours, he sat his horse grimly and waited, in a silence broken only by birdsong and the shufflings and mutterings of his escort, for the queen to see sense.

Inside, in the magnificent, hammer-beamed Great Hall, Mary sat on the royal daïs with the morning sun streaming in on her through the vast, arched east window and turning her cloth of gold into something rich and molten, her rubies into heart's blood, herself into a shining idol.

The glory was more than external. Not since her betrothal and marriage to François seven years before had she felt such a sense of warmth and fulfilment. And this time there was more. This time she was controlling her own destiny, dependent on no one. She had gambled and won, and it scarcely mattered if the victory were in the end to prove hollow. At this climactic moment, all that mattered was that she had broken clear of the shabby mists of dissimulation and deceit, of huckstering and haggling, into air that was free and fresh and clean.

Her eyes full of love and pleasure, she smiled at the tall, beautiful young man who stood before her, ethereal after five weeks of illness but assured and fashionable in his damasked gold doublet with the high-standing collar and the waist padded into a curve like an eagle's beak. Henry Stuart, Lord Darnley, who was soon to be her husband, whom she had just created Earl of Ross and who had taken the oath of allegiance to her as his sovereign.

Elizabeth would see that as treasonable.

Mary glanced round her assembled nobles, allowing her gaze to rest briefly on James, who was there only because he had been unable to think of an acceptable excuse for staying away. She had made it clear to him that his position rested on a knife edge. He had said nothing since the ceremony began and, indeed, had the air of a man whose lips had been stitched together.

She was tempted to laugh but, instead – now that what was important had been achieved – signalled to Davie Riccio to order the guards to open the gate.

10

Throckmorton was too old a hand to allow his anger to show, but he was perhaps more fluent than usual as he spoke of the unanimous belief of Elizabeth's council that the proposed marriage was 'unmeet, unprofitable, and perilous to the amity between the realms'.

Mary, sweetly and innocently surprised, said, 'But I do not understand why amity should be imperilled. My good sister has often told me that she would be happy to see me married to any English nobleman, and who could be more suitable than one who is a cousin of us both?'

Throckmorton took a deep breath and launched forth according to his instructions, but he had returned from his posting in France too recently to appreciate that, in the matter of Mary's marriage, Elizabeth's objections and Mary's responses had by now become merely a litany, a succession of words and phrases packed with symbolism but lacking any real sense or meaning of their own.

In the end, with the smile that had disarmed Throckmorton in France, and still disarmed him, the queen said, 'Enough. Our new Earl of Ross has been ill and is not fully recovered. I do not think he should be kept standing longer than necessary. In virtue of his new honours, he is about to invest fourteen Scottish gentlemen with knighthoods, but afterwards I will be pleased if you, Sir Nicholas, will dine with us.'

Sir Nicholas, whose stomach was clapping against his ribs with hunger, said he would be honoured.

He did not remain long in Scotland, though by the time he left – richer by the fifty-ounce chain of gold customarily bestowed on ambassadors at their departure – he had sent messages off to Elizabeth reporting that, although the queen of Scots was committed to the path she had chosen, she had consented to send an envoy to London to explain her reasons in full. He understood that the envoy would not be secretary of state Lethington.

In the meantime, he advised that England's border defences should be reinforced, that steps should be taken to monitor the activities of the great English Catholic nobles, and that improved relations with France and Spain should be made a diplomatic priority.

11

In the weeks that followed, with the stimuli of challenge and excitement keeping Mary herself in the highest of spirits, only three other people at her court could fairly have been described as happy.

Among the generality of the Scots lords, of course, happiness was an emotion to which they were not temperamentally adjusted, something they rarely, if ever, experienced themselves and dourly attributed to lightmindedness in others. On occasions when they found her majesty overflowing with gaiety and charm, they might indeed melt slightly – but only around the edges, and only until they began wondering about her motives. Catholic or Protestant, the lords had been Calvinists since long before Calvin was born.

It was different for those who, nurtured in societies that took a less rudimentary view of human nature, knew that other people's moods were instruments to be played upon. Happiness in the queen could bring happiness to those who knew how to strike the right chords.

One of the three happy men was Davie Riccio, who now had position and money and the favour of the young man who would soon be king.

The second was Matthew Stuart, Earl of Lennox, who, though born a Stewart, had spent ten of his early years in the service of France where he had learned gallantry and duplicity and adopted the French spelling of his surname in place of the Scots. Now stout and balding, he was a man of violent temper, large pride and small judgement, whose most conspicuous talent had always been for getting things wrong. Not this time. This time, everything was going right.

The third happy man was his son, Henry Stuart, formerly Lord Darnley, now Earl of Ross and soon to be king of Scots. For him, happiness was synonymous with public recognition of the splendour that was in him. Idolised from the cradle, trained in the courtly arts, taught the correct degree of diffidence to use with his superiors – though needing no instruction in the insolence and offensiveness due to his inferiors – he saw his royal destiny at last assured. His mother had always had her eye on Mary. She had told him what to do, how to behave, and it had worked like a dream. He had successfully conquered the heart of the queen of Scots and for that reason alone he was able to feel quite warmly towards her. He thought that, before long, he must begin persuading her to make him king of England as well as of the Scots.

12

Lethington, clothed not for court but for comfort, subsided onto the bright, springing turf of the river bank and looked out over the fertile lands rolling south towards the gentle greens and blues of the Lammermuir Hills. It was a perfect summer day and the skylarks were singing. He sighed with pleasure.

But his eyes were not wholly focused and his brother John, subduing a grin, murmured, 'Dreaming of love?'

Newly back from France, John was by no means sure, as yet, how far he could go with the brother from whom he was separated by a gap of fifteen years in age and seven years abroad, a brother whom he worshipped only a degree less than he worshipped their father. There was a strong physical resemblance between them, although John's eyes were more darkly grey, his features less sculptured, his mouth less humorous, and his figure still lanky with youth. He could not imagine himself ever acquiring his brother's unruffled stylishness.

Lethington's lips twitched. 'I am immune to provocation. The whole court has been laughing at me for more than a year, now, and it moves me not at all. If Knox, at over fifty, can marry a girl of sixteen, why should not I, at thirty-seven, court my twenty-two-year-old heart's desire? What unfortunately does move me is that the first loyalty of my beautiful Mallie Fleming is to the queen, so that when I am out of favour with the one I am also out of favour with the other. And when I am banned from court, I am banned even from seeing her.' He sighed. 'I wish I knew whether she cared.'

John couldn't begin to understand it. 'You mean, you don't know how she feels about you? Haven't you asked?'

'Oddly enough, no. I don't think of myself as a coward, but I suppose I must be. I am so contented in my heart that I fear to put things to the touch. What, after all, do I have to offer to a girl of the royal blood, who is beautiful and desirable and surrounded by far more eligible suitors?'

'Of all the ... Surely you have *some* idea of her feelings?'

'No. Once she was nervous with me, then we became friends, and now I'm not sure. And since I cannot see her ...'

The queen had never granted him an opportunity of explaining why he had flouted her orders, and pride had forbidden him to persist. She had made it clear that she did not want to know. Now, she consulted him in nothing and when it was necessary for him to approach her on the business of state for which he remained responsible, he had to make an appointment through David Riccio. There was nothing he could do but watch and wait, and he was interested to find that – Riccio apart – it was not at all painful. Not for a dozen years had he savoured the joys of being free of responsibility.

'Will the queen forgive you?' John asked.

'Probably. When she discovers that she needs me. When she remembers that the whole world does not revolve round her marriage to Darnley.'

'You're wonderfully philosophical about it.'

Lethington shrugged. 'I invited her anger. In England, I would now be languishing in the Tower.'

'I suppose so.' John frowned. 'What about Lord James? I've lost count of the rumours I've heard since I returned home. Even father doesn't understand what he's up to.'

Lethington's lips twitched again. 'Neither does he. He has put himself in an impossible position. First, he thought it would be easy to frighten his sister into abandoning the match. Then he thought that Elizabeth's opposition would put a stop to it. And now he's hamstrung. He must either admit defeat, which goes against the grain, or else do something. And he can't decide what. Or how far he dares to go.'

'But surely ...'

'But he has the reputation of being a man of decision? He is, when the choice is simply between A and B. He did not, however, expect his sister to outmanoeuvre him. When he tried to rally the Protestant lords by crying "religion in danger", her majesty simply issued renewed decrees about religious tolerance. In general she is riding high. She has managed things quite cleverly – which is more than can be said for James. I have rarely seen a situation so grossly mishandled. Enough to break one's heart.'

'He should have called you in.'

Lethington lay back, his head resting on clasped hands. 'If that is sarcasm, it has misfired. He tried. But there are too many points on which we diverge. He cannot see that all he has done has been to push his sister into the arms of the Catholic lords and her foreign Catholic household. James's trouble is that he is dedicated to making the worst of things, where I prefer to make the best of them. While the Darnley marriage *may* prove to be a disaster, intelligently handled it *need* not be, and any son of it could well inherit the throne of England and guarantee us peace at last. Which has been my guiding principle for the last dozen years and will be until I die. James, however, can only re-establish his own position by showing young Darnley in the worst light possible. Hence the claim that Darnley and Lennox are plotting to murder him ...'

John said blankly, 'Stop, please! The last thing I heard was that it was *he* who was plotting to murder *them*?'

'That, too,' Lethington sat up again, his eyes gleaming like ice water in the sun, 'although the accepted version is that he was merely proposing to ship them back to England, where Elizabeth could put them on trial for treason. He also needs a legitimate excuse for staying away from court, and the presence there of a brace of reputedly homicidal maniacs supplies it. He is lurking at his mother's castle of Lochleven.'

John said, 'I know I'm only a lawyer, and not a very experienced one as yet, but surely an empty landscape must be a better place for murdering people than in the glare of a thousand candles?'

His brother laughed and rose, running his fingers through the waving black hair that was the only uncontrolled thing about him. 'You may be right. However, we should get back. Father tells me that there is heather to be pulled for the thatching and even secretaries of state are not exempt from such useful toil.'

But John Maitland was nothing if not persevering. 'I don't understand why Lord James *needs* an excuse for staying away from court.'

'Because he hopes that, if he is not under Mary's eye, she will not find out what he is up to.'

'And what *is* he up to?'

'Asking Elizabeth for money and men to start another civil war.'

13

The queen was radiant. Excitement always made her so, and there was excitement in plenty during the weeks before her marriage.

Throwing her arms wide one day, she laughed, 'I think I must be mad. Am I mad, my dear, sweet Fleming?'

She was difficult to resist in such a mood, and Mallie could only laugh back and say, 'Undoubtedly, Madame!'

'I have lost the friendship of England. I have regained the friendship of France and Spain. My brother is showing all the signs of breaking into open rebellion. And I am gloriously in love. At one moment I am in a rage with James, and at the next I am swooning over my sweet Harry. There is no dreary middle state between the two extremes. And it is wonderful. I feel truly *alive*.'

They were walking in the knot garden of Holyroodhouse, with the royal bodyguard – now always present – discreetly disposed at the entrances. The queen's eyes were suddenly caught by the silvery, sun-touched gleam on their morions and breastplates. '*That* is what I need!' she exclaimed.

'What, Madame?'

'One of those steel helmets! I must have one. It will suit me very well, I think.' Then, seeing the mystification on the Maries' faces, she went on a little less gaily, 'I may need it. If my brother continues to disobey my commands to come to court and explain all these secretive meetings and gatherings of his, I may be forced to end by declaring him a rebel.'

'But Madame ...'

'You are thinking of his display of strength in Edinburgh? Well, I have decided to raise an army of my own. I have just authorised a summons to be issued requiring all my subjects to be prepared to turn out in readiness to fight for their queen.' She smiled at Mallie. 'And I have also sent to France for your cousin Bothwell to return to command them. If there is one thing on which I am unalterably determined, it is to bring James to heel.'

Even as she spoke, there came the sound of voices and a scuffle, and she turned sharply to see one of the archers of her bodyguard backing along the path towards her, the flat of his smallsword sloped defensively against the much taller man who was pushing him with one hand and boxing him on the ears with the other.

The unfortunate archer was muttering, 'Mais non, monsieur ...' while the tall young man was snapping, 'How dare you, fellow! How dare you insult the man who is to be your king! Let me pass.'

Mary giggled. 'Oooh, dear.'

She had wanted to be in love, and she *was* in love, and after four long years of bending to other people's wills as if her divine right to rule meant nothing at all, she was at last going to take the course she wanted to take. She remained clear-eyed enough to recognise that Harry was immature and impetuous and arrogant, but his personal attractions far outstripped those of any of the foreign princes she would willingly have married – had tried very hard to marry – for the deliberate political reasons that loomed so large in the matrimonial calculations of royalty. She knew that she could coax him into more responsible, more suitable ways.

Raising her voice, she said, 'That is all right, Duvall. You may let his lordship pass.'

Then she held out her arms. 'Harry, my sweet, kiss me and show that you forgive me. I will see that no one ever bars your way again.'

14

Five days later, the queen elevated Henry Stuart, formerly Lord Darnley and then Earl of Ross, to the royal title of Duke of Albany, and on the following Saturday evening sent three heralds and trumpeters, splendid in their royal tabards with the blood-red lion rampant on a brilliant yellow ground, to read a proclamation at the Mercat Cross.

> Forasmuch as we intend to solemnise and complete the bond of matrimony in face of Holy Church with the right noble and illustrious Prince Henry Duke of Albany: in respect of which marriage we ordain and consent that he be named and styled king of this our kingdom, and that all our letters be in the names of the said illustrious prince our future husband and us as king and queen of Scotland conjointly.

Mary's personal popularity with her people was great enough to raise cheers from Edinburgh's citizens, notably the fishwives for whom titles mattered less than the fact that their lovely queen had found a husband at last – and a tall handsome boy, at that, who would give her what she needed and a quiverful of children besides.

The lords, however, were silent. It was for parliament, not the queen, to bestow the title of king on the consort she had chosen. Those who supported her spoke of royal pride; she had, after all, previously been wed to one of the greatest kings of Christendom and it was right that her second husband should also be a king. But to others the proclamation meant that she cared nothing for her duty, only for the worthless human object of her passion.

Only those closest to her identified the truth of it. She was always generous to those she loved and Darnley desperately wanted to be king, but she was also declaring her own release from the political restraints of the past years. From now on, she intended to have no overweening advisers, but to rule in person and according to her own instincts – a queen, with her king and husband at her side.

15

It was not yet six in the morning, the world still bathed in the freshness of sunrise, when Mary was led into her private chapel at Holyroodhouse by the Earls of Lennox and Atholl.

There was colour in her normally pale cheeks, and her eyes were brilliant with happiness and the knowledge of victory, but, as was traditional for Catholic widows entering on their second bridals, she was dressed in mourning, the black and white that became her so well, with a mourning hood and waist-long filmy veil over a simple black gown, unadorned with embroidery or jewels. Since it was a mourning soon to be symbolically cast off, the four Maries had spent the dawn hour carefully pinning together the sleeves, bodice, veils and skirts that would normally have been hooked or laced.

Mallie Fleming, who was not at her best in the early morning and saw the marriage as an unmitigated disaster, found it hard to remain calm and smiling. Mary Livingston, newly and ecstatically pregnant, had to rush off twice to be sick. Mary Beaton, who had found the turbulence of the preceding months hard to bear, was so grateful to see an end in sight that she was almost as happy as her mistress. And Mary Seton was filled with concern over the fact that the papal dispensation necessary for a marriage between cousins had not yet arrived. The queen had received a letter from the pope two weeks earlier and had allowed it to be generally thought that it contained the dispensation. But her confidantes knew that it hadn't. Her majesty said the dispensation was on its way, but Seton couldn't stop worrying.

And now the four of them, with Jean Gordon, the Countess of Argyll and others of the queen's ladies, stood with her, waiting while the Earls of Lennox and Atholl departed from the chapel to return a few minutes later with the young man everyone now had to think of as king.

He was clad in gold from softly rounded chin to the toes of his long-legged knitted hose, with a short cloak of ruby velvet, trimmed with ermine, slung over his shoulders and enough jewels to fund an expedition to the Americas. He looked superb, as elegant, elongated and highly finished as a painting by Parmigianino. It was a pity, Mallie thought, that they couldn't simply hang him on the wall and be done with him. Behind her, she heard Jean Gordon give a little gasp that had more in it of derision than admiration.

But the queen was suddenly pale and still, as if this climactic moment was almost too much to bear, and she continued to look dazed as the ceremony began, her eyes opaque as honey under the shadows of her cap while the banns were called for the third time. The ceremony itself was brief, with the couple taking their vows and king afterwards placing three rings – the central one a diamond set in red enamel – on the third finger of the queen's right hand, the finger from which, according to Catholic belief, a vein ran directly to the heart. Then they knelt and prayed, and were blessed, and the king kissed his wife and left her to hear the nuptial Mass alone. The Lennoxes might be Catholic in faith, but Darnley had learned from his father to trim his sails as political considerations required and those considerations currently suggested the wisdom of not annoying the Protestant lords more than necessary.

Mary Stewart, who had from childhood signed herself Marie Stuart in the French fashion, was now, by marriage, legally no longer a Stewart but a Stuart, an irony which escaped the greater number of her lords, who barely knew how to read or write and had no notion of spelling.

Only when she led her court out of the chapel and back to her chamber did the queen's liveliness return, and in fullest measure. For it was required of her, now, to cast off her cares and lay aside the garments of sorrow, which meant that, led by the king and prettily resisted by her majesty, every gentleman present was entitled to remove one of the pins so laboriously inserted by the Four Maries three hours before. It was a source of much laughter and gaiety as the gentlemen did their duty while conscientiously avoiding plucking out any pin that might prove a threat to decency. Only when the cap and veil and sleeves had gone, and when the join between bodice and waist was beginning to look unstable, were they chased from the room so that the queen's ladies could dress her in the cloth of gold and jewels that she had decided were appropriate to the occasion. White would have revived memories of François, but gold would be at once an affirmation of change and an emphasis on the harmony between herself and Henry, her husband and king.

Meanwhile, trumpets sounded, largesse was scattered to the crowd outside the palace, and those courtiers who had leisure for it gave themselves up to dancing while the senior officers of the household embarked on the complex preparations for the marriage banquet, where ritual decreed that scarcely a movement should be made, not a cloth spread nor a knife or spoon set on the table, without the accompaniment of three deep bows. As tradition required, king and queen were each to be waited on by three of the great nobles, acting as server, carver and cupbearer. Atholl, Morton and Crawford were to wait on the queen; Cassilis, Eglinton and Glencairn on the king.

If things had been different, the queen's brother, the Earl of Moray, would have taken one leading rôle and her sister Jean's husband, the Earl of Argyll, another. But neither of them was present. This was a marriage that would heal no wounds.

Jean Gordon, observing the Earl of Morton ceremonially wash his hands before being vested with the requisite towels and napkins, murmured to Alexander Ogilvie, the husband she could never have, 'How nice. Clean for once,' and Alexander, watching as the earl went on to taste the royal bread for poison, sighed as the pasty, expressionless face within the huge red beard remained unchanged. 'Harmless. What a pity.'

Brightly, Jean said, 'He still has all the cooked dishes to go.'

There were twelve of them in the first course alone – including calf's sweetbreads sauced with cinnamon, salmon cream with cheese, stuffed pigeons with capers, spit-roasted rabbits with lemon sauce, and almond blamanger with shredded pike – and only when all had been brought in, in procession, and laid out on the table, when the trumpets sounded again and the music soared to an anthem, did the royal couple appear and seat themselves in isolated splendour on their chairs of state under their canopies of state, two figures as svelte and shining, Mallie Fleming thought, as those on the great golden salt-cellar Cellini had made for the French royal table years before. Formal and beautiful and quite unreal.

Her blue eyes sombre, she hoped that the events of the night to come, and the extravagant entertainments that had been planned for the next three days, would give the queen something, at least, of joy to help her face the challenges of the months that lay ahead. Only then did she remember that she herself would need to do something about finding a place to lay her weary head. Ever since the Châtelard affair, the queen had felt safer with her sleeping on a truckle bed in the royal chamber. But now ... Well, Seton and Beaton would just have to move over.

16

In ordinary households, bedding the bride was inclined to be a riotous and less than sober affair, with the last of the revellers having to be forcibly driven from the bridal chamber. It was different with royalty. Even the most light-hearted of courtiers, even those with whom the queen was ordinarily on the easiest and most laughing of terms, were overawed by the sight of the two regal dolls propped up in the extravagantly curtained fourposter under bedclothes suffocatingly drenched with holy water and incense.

While the guests tossed seeds at them, symbols of the fruitfulness which was the divine purpose of marriage, the queen's singers warbled merrily in the background, among them the little Piedmontese bass whose voice had led him stage by stage to a position of power and influence that no one could have foreseen. And then silence was called for, so that the Dean of Restalrig might bless the marriage bed. 'Sow in them the seed of eternal life, that it may spread throughout the length of days and down the ages ...'

After that, they were alone.

Harry said, 'You have been married before, though I hate to think of you in another man's arms. Did François ever succeed in – er – possessing you?' It was not a phrase he would normally have used. It was not a question he would normally have thought to ask. But he had been well taught.

She did not want to remember François, whom she had loved with dedication but without desire. 'We were children. Yours and mine is a different love. Show me what it means. Hold me. Teach me. But be tender with me, please?'

He was gentle and slow and did not force her, and she loved him the more for it because he was not a patient young man.

17

She smiled mischievously to herself throughout the following day, aware that most of those enjoying the dancing and the banquets and the masques were privately wondering how Harry had conducted himself and whether the queen had enjoyed it. It would have amused her greatly to be able to stand up and announce, 'It was lovely!'

There was only one small awkwardness during the celebrations, when Harry was, for a second time, formally proclaimed king at the Mercat Cross and no one cheered except his father. Harry became quite pettish about it.

But it didn't last. When James, having failed to respond to a final summons from the privy council, was declared a rebel and put to the horn a few days later, it restored Harry's spirits wonderfully.

Chapter Ten

AUGUST-DECEMBER 1565

1

'**D**on't do it, James,' Lethington said. It was a wet and windy day, as August days in Scotland so often were, and the long, sandy beaches of the Ayrshire coast were darkly rippled and pitted, the sea iron grey and the rollers capped in furious white.

The two men were sitting their horses on rising ground above the dell where James's levies were encamped awaiting reinforcements. There were only a few hundred of them, although all were mounted, whereas according to Lethington's information the queen had raised an army of thousands, pledging her jewels to do it.

'I must go on,' James replied. 'I have no choice.'

In Lethington's view, there was always a choice, if only people had the strength of mind to confront it. But 'no choice' was the argument on which James always fell back when it was necessary to justify his actions, implying the kind of morality that found it impossible to conceive of evil as an alternative to good, or wrong as an alternative to right. Or common sense as an alternative to stiffnecked stupidity.

Only the habit of a lifetime prevented Lethington from telling him not to be a fool. He said, 'There is still, I think, a possibility that Mary might choose to be magnanimous. It would be the intelligent thing to do.'

James shook his head. 'It is too late.'

'But your object was to stop the marriage, and you failed. It's happened, so why go on? What do you hope to achieve?'

'Ye shouldn't need to ask.' Under the flat-topped steel bonnet, James's long-nosed, weather-beaten Stewart face looked austere. 'I'm disappointed that ye're not with us. Mary's given ye no cause to love her.'

Lethington shrugged. 'I am not one of the landed lairds. I have no men to bring you and no wealth to buy them. And I cannot think that your moral authority needs any reinforcement from me.'

James sniffed. 'The real truth is that ye're not convinced,' he said, and then, with sudden vehemence, 'even though you know better than anyone that I did not mean it to come to this. I've spent four years trying to persuade my sister to banish idolatry from the land, without success, and now she's showing more and more favour to the papists. Darnley's the proof of it. All that's left to us is force.'

Lethington allowed the selectiveness of James's memory to pass without remark. 'I phrased my question badly. What I meant was, if you fight, and if you win, where do you go from there? What happens next?'

'She'll have to agree to outlaw papistry and consent to hand over some of the reins of government ...'

Lethington did not waste his breath by asking to whom.

'... or we'll depose her.'

The Catholic rulers of Europe wouldn't like that, nor the Protestant ones either. It might start a fashion.

'In favour of Châtelherault?' he asked.

With the elderly and vacillating Châtelherault on the throne, it would be James who ruled *de facto* and who might in the end, with the legislative cooperation of a puppet king and his parliament, come to rule *de jure*. It was something of which Lethington would not necessarily have disapproved, except that James, effective though he might very well turn out to be as a ruler, could have no claim to the English throne. Scotland would become no more than an unconsidered satellite of Elizabeth's. Worse, a sycophant, because James himself was Elizabeth's most uncritical devotee.

James said, 'He has the best claim. There's no one else.'

Pulling his monkish hood forward, Lethington gathered his cloak around him and prepared to depart. He had come alone, without even his riding escort, because he had no wish to be seen to be associated with such an ill-judged affair.

There was still one question he had to ask. 'And what happens if you lose?'

'We won't lose. Argyll's collecting his redshanks in the West Highlands. Kirkcaldy of Grange is with us. And Elizabeth has promised us help with money, men and arms. Rest assured, we will not lose.'

Lethington might have said, 'Don't trust Elizabeth to keep her promises,' but James would not have listened.

At Holyrood, Mary also had her mind on men and money, though mainly on money. The Crown's revenues were minimal and most of the gaiety of her court was funded by the income from the estates she held in France as dowager queen.

Now, walking restlessly back and forth across the bedchamber that also did duty as a study, she was dictating – in the French which came most easily to her for correspondence – the draft of a highly confidential letter to the new pope, Pius V, asking for a subsidy. At the table, Davie Riccio scrawled away busily.

It had been far from easy, during the years of making one concession after another to her Protestant subjects, to persuade France, Spain and the papacy that she had not abandoned the Catholic cause. She had become very ingenious at rearranging the facts to suit the reader, but she knew that her credit had waned. It was something difficult to counteract in letters. Her charm, for so long both a weapon and a defence, was reduced to mere effusiveness by its transference to the cool and calculated medium of ink on paper.

In one sense, therefore, James's rebellion was a helpful development.

'... the opportunity now arises to strike at the root of error, at those of my subjects so puffed up in their own insolence that they persecute their queen with demands for her to abandon her own faith and join them in their heresy. This is the cause of the present rebellion which, defeated, will see at last the weeding out and destruction of the thorns and tares of heretical depravity in this country. It is for this purpose, so dear to God, that we beg of Holy Father such assistance as he may feel able to give ...'

'*Momento!*' Davie begged, hastily sharpening a quill. 'Thorns and tares. Ees good. I like that.'

'Thank you.' The queen smiled, amused as always by the little man's candour. 'My uncle the cardinal taught me, long ago, to speak the kind of language that Rome understands. It is just a very roundabout way of requesting a loan. Let me see a fair copy in French before you put it into Latin and encipher it.'

'I do not think I know what is Latin for "tare".'

As Mary laughed and said, '*Vicia*', there came a succession of faint clanking noises interspersed with crashes and smothered oaths from the private staircase set within the wall of the bedchamber. It was a semi-turnpike stair that ascended from her husband's apartments below, and it was rather narrow.

The queen's eyes danced under the delicately arched brows as Fleming sped over to pull back the hangings and open the door to whatever was approaching.

It turned out to be six feet and three inches of exquisitely crafted golden armour which, having bent to negotiate the low door, straightened up to parade itself before its wife. Part, at least, of the preceding noise was explained by the fact that the suit's occupant had left his visor down and couldn't see a thing.

The queen exclaimed, a little unsteadily, 'Harry! How superb!'

From within the gilded shell, his muffled voice replied, 'I thought I'd wear this for the campaign. Oh, God's blood!' He raised a gauntleted hand to open the visor and reveal a fair but somewhat overheated face. 'That is the stupidest staircase! You should do something to widen it.'

Mischievously, she said, 'It was never designed for a king in armour. It was designed for a king in his bedgown.'

But although Harry's courtly training had taught him facility with words and wit, it had failed to teach him humour or grace.

His face bright scarlet, he exclaimed. 'Bed! That's all women ever think of.' Then, ignoring the swift, shocked tears springing to his wife's eyes, he began turning in a clumsy pirouette on his chain-mailed toes and demanded, 'How do I look?'

3

Mary had always been as quick to weep as she was to laugh, and knew it to be a weakness in herself, because the tears too easily washed out even the memory of laughter – the laughter as she and Harry raced their horses round the park at Holyrood, or danced an energetic *volte*, or exchanged the love poems for which both of them had a talent. Harry could be the courtliest of companions, and though he might not always behave considerately to her by day, he was unfailingly considerate by night. She had not expected the marriage bed to be so sweet a place.

But he did have a talent for upsetting her. She had not foreseen how often he would take advantage of the new rank which entitled him, he thought, to fly into a rage if he felt like it. Too often, she had to remind herself that he was still young and irresponsible, and that she must help him to grow out of it.

In the meantime, his anger was sometimes not only disproportionate but politically unwise. When he had decided to go to one of Master

Knox's sermons and been subjected to a two-hour tirade about the woes of a kingdom given over to the government of 'women and boys', he had lost both his temper and his appetite for dinner and, in the end, she had been forced to have Master Knox summoned before an irritated privy council and forbidden to preach for the two Sundays following. Knox had infuriated her, often enough, but never had she gone so far as to ban him from the pulpit.

She herself, she knew, *must* make an effort. Since the days of her marriage to François, she had lost the habit of intimacy. It was true, also, that equality was strange to her; awareness of her own royalty had underlain every word she had uttered since her childhood. If there were flaws in her relationship with Harry, she told herself again and again, they were probably her fault as much as his.

4

Davie Riccio leapt into the breach as she struggled to recover her composure. His dark eyes huge, his voice athrill, his hands clapping together ecstatically, he exclaimed, 'Milanese, *si?* Nowhere in the world do they make armour to match that of Milano. Nowhere in the world but in Milano could they make armour so worthy of your gracious majesty! Is *magnifico!*'

Predictably, Harry was wearing lightweight tilt armour rather than the traditional battle armour which had gone out of fashion for jousting after the horse of an overweight Henry VIII had needed a hedgehog under its tail to goad it into moving. Even the tournament itself was going out of fashion, surviving at Elizabeth's court only as a branch of royal pageantry, and at Mary's as an informal sporting event at which the more youthful courtiers could rid themselves of their surplus energy. Tilt armour was finery for rich young Englishmen who liked to show off both their horsemanship and themselves. In war, it would barely have been proof against a slingshot pebble.

Ignoring the little man who had formerly been his boon companion, but whom he was now finding much too often in his wife's company, Harry said, 'I have decided that, when we march, my father shall command the vanguard, Morton the centre, and I will take the rear.' Then, his vanity warmed by awareness of his style and splendour, he added considerately, 'And although there will be no danger to you, of course, I should prefer to know you safe at Stirling until the campaign is over. I will escort you there before we leave.'

Mary smiled brilliantly through the tears still sparkling on her lashes. 'Oh, no,' she said. 'I am coming with you.'

5

In the last days of August, the royal army marched out westward from Edinburgh towards Glasgow, the king in his golden armour and the queen dressed in doublet and hose, with a steel morion on her head, one of her all-enveloping Highland mantles around her, and a pistol at her saddle bow.

'Now we shall teach James the lesson he deserves,' she declared gaily as the winds blew, the rain came down in torrents, and everyone except herself was reduced to a state of sodden exhaustion.

It was not immediately clear that the campaign was destined to turn into an expensive fiasco, although it might not have done if the numerous but ramshackle foot soldiers of the royal army had ever come face to face with the mounted and far better disciplined rebels. But they did not. All they did was chase them round the countryside until they chased them out of Scotland altogether.

It was James's caution that led him to defeat. With a force of only twelve hundred horse, he waited, hoping to narrow the odds, but found his only reinforcements coming in the form of empty promises. His leading ally, Argyll, having gone off to his estates to collect his wild Highlanders, allowed himself to be diverted into a private war against the Earl of Atholl, while the recruits James had hoped to raise in Edinburgh observed the smallness of his army and shook their heads firmly. When the keeper of Edinburgh castle, who happened to be James's uncle, shot off half a dozen reproachful cannonballs in his direction, he gloomily led his force out of Edinburgh again and beat what he hoped would be only a temporary retreat to the Borders.

Behind him, he left a public letter for his sister.

It said, in essence, that he himself had been unjustly maligned, and that Scotland was endangered by the queen's trusting more to the advice of baseborn foreigners than to the nobility of the realm.

Mary laughed when she heard about it. 'It proves exactly what I thought. It proves that what James wants is not security for Protestantism but power for himself. I shall issue a proclamation to that effect.'

The trouble with amateur armies, she now discovered, was that they had better things to do than trail aimlessly around the countryside at summer's end. On their minds were winter fuel for their homes and chaff and straw for their cattle. Their labour was needed for harvesting or storing the field-peas, barley and oats on which their families' food and ale for the forthcoming months depended. In twos and threes, then in tens and twenties, they began to vanish into the night.

The queen, mildly irritated, summoned new levies from the north, replenished the exchequer through fines and forced loans from James's friends among the Fife lairds, and returned to Edinburgh to see to some of the routine business of state.

She was still in such dazzling spirits that she even smiled at Lethington before she remembered that she was not on smiling terms with him. She had scarcely seen him for months, having required him to send his assistant, Hay, to deputise for him. But Hay had fallen ill.

'Land rights,' she said, riffling through the papers he presented to her. 'Marriage permissions. Kirkcaldy butchers. How dull.'

Then, sitting back, she surveyed him pensively. 'I told you once,' she said, 'that if I chose to trust you, and if anything then went wrong, it would be you I would blame. In justice, I do not think I can blame you for my brother's treachery. You are too clever for that, and I believe you would have advised against it. But I am not sure. If I had not given my word, four years ago, that I would not employ foreigners as my officers of state, you would no longer be secretary. Do you understand me?'

He had known she must be thinking along such lines. His association with James had been too close for too long. But he had received no permission to argue his case, and could not do other than bow his head in acknowledgement. This was not Classical Athens, where intelligent men had been expected to speak their minds; this was sixteenth-century Europe where anarchy was thought to be worse than the worst imaginable tyranny and a supreme monarch was seen as the only bulwark against chaos. It was not permissible to disagree with princes, save politely and only if invited.

Guardedly, he said, 'Your majesty, I *am* your servant.'

The king, who had come sauntering in to lay a possessive hand on his wife's shoulder, said languidly, 'I am sure one of my kinsmen could do the job,' but the queen gave a gurgle of laughter. 'It is *very* hard work, Harry, and *very* tedious.'

'Oh, is it?' The king lost interest and the queen dismissed Lethington with the shadow of amusement still lingering in her eyes.

It could have been worse, but relief was not what sent him out of the chamber with a spring in his step and a delirious sense of wellbeing in his heart. Not for weeks had he set eyes on Mallie Fleming even in passing, and it was five long months since he had been given the opportunity to speak to her. Today, he had been able to cast her only a glance as she sat demurely in a corner busy with some of the endless stitchery that occupied the queen and her ladies. But she had felt his eyes on her and looked up with an expression in her own that he had never seen other than in his dreams. It was an expression that said, if they had been private, she would have wanted his arms around her.

He had no idea why. All he knew was that her heart was engaged. Nothing else mattered.

7

Not until he heard her breathless voice behind him did he know that she had slipped, with a murmured apology, out of the queen's presence.

'Secretary!'

His own breath catching in his lungs, he turned and met her eyes and knew that, in the only sense that mattered, there was nothing they needed to say to each other. Even the most graceful, most elegant, most poetic words would have been uncouth.

It was still necessary to speak, however, because the audience chamber was full to bursting point with courtiers and bodyguards and supplicants, their attention wandering, their gazes inquisitive, ripe for distraction.

He said, 'We must talk. When and where?'

It was possible to be private at court, but only in public places. And while ten minutes on a curtained landing might suffice for purposeful lovers, or half an hour in a corner of the gardens for those whose only desire was to hold hands and innocently kiss, he and she needed a truer privacy in which to open their minds and hearts to each other.

'I don't know. With Livingston away, three Maries are having to do the work of four, and I don't even know when, or if, Madame is setting out again after James. Oh, how I *hate* that man, cousin or not!'

He said quietly, 'It doesn't matter. There will be a time and place for us, even if not here, not now. Just remember that I love you.'

'Do you? *Do you?* Because I have learned in these last months, when I

215

haven't seen you, that I love *you* more than I can bear, but I'm not sure that I know you at all.'

'We will remedy that,' he said, and then had to turn away because Tom Randolph was approaching.

8

Less than half an hour after Lethington had left the queen's presence, Davie Riccio, spectacular in violet satin, popped his head round the door. But before he could speak he was thrust aside by a careless arm.

'Who's this fellow?' demanded the insolent newcomer as he strode forward to bend a muscular knee before his queen.

The king, in turn, said, 'Who's *this* fellow?'

'My Lord Bothwell!' Gratitude surging through her, Mary exclaimed, 'I had not expected you so soon.'

He grinned at her, the loose-tongued, lethal, abrasive Border lord who antagonised everyone with whom he came in contact – except his queen. Who was strong and on whom she could rely as she dared not rely on anyone else. 'I landed at Eyemouth, though the English nearly got me first. I came straight here. You wanted me.'

Before she could reply, Harry said in a tone that even an earthworm might have found patronising, 'You're Bothwell, are you? You needn't have hurried. The queen thought you might command her army in the campaign against Moray, but I decided otherwise.'

Square, strong, dark, explosive with vitality, Bothwell looked up at the willowy figure overtopping him by almost a head and said, 'Well, I hope *you're* not in charge?'

It was not the most felicitous of beginnings.

Mary had not seen Bothwell since the Arran affair more than three years before and she could not at first think who he reminded her of. And then his nostrils flared over the tight yet sensual mouth and the tiny mannerism was enough to bring the memories flooding back, memories of an assurance, pride and power that spoke to her – shouted at her – of her uncle, the Duc de Guise, the man whose presence alone had sufficed to eliminate all doubt in his niece's mind, whose political judgement had been masterly, who had been militarily invincible.

For Bothwell she had little personal feeling, but she needed him, she thought, more than she had ever needed anyone.

She had given in to Harry over the command of her army. To

216

Bothwell, therefore, she said, 'I want you to be my lieutenant-general on the Borders.'

It was an extraordinarily difficult half hour as she tried, unavailingly, to achieve some kind of *modus vivendi* between her slender, fair, almost decadently civilised husband and the Border lord whose animal vitality vibrated through the air like all the Angelus bells of Paris tolling as one.

That night, when Harry came to her in his bedgown by way of the private staircase, his lovemaking, which was usually slow and pleasurable, verged on the perfunctory. He was rough with her, too, and heedless of her comfort. She thought he must still be angry about the delight with which she had welcomed Bothwell.

9

'Ye told me in June that Elizabeth would give her backing to those of us who were determined to defend the reformed faith,' said James.

'Well, she promised,' Tom Randolph replied defensively.

'And in July we asked for money and men and she told us to collect military strength to defend ourselves against all possible contingencies.'

'Yes, but ...'

'And then we wrote formally asking for men, money, arms and ammunition. Especially, we asked for arquebusiers. We asked not once but three times. And she told Lord Bedford at Berwick that she *was* sending us money, which he was to advance to us secretly, as if it came from himself, and that he was to raise men for us, also secretly, as if they came from himself.'

Randolph nodded his head. 'And then she countermanded the orders.'

He couldn't understand why his hair hadn't turned white in these last weeks, when anger and embarrassment had walked with him every moment of every day. And now, after all the promises given and broken, it seemed that Elizabeth was not going to give James any practical help at all; that she expected him to be the loser in this strange little war that was already being known as the Chaseabout Raid.

She had just instructed Randolph to open negotiations with Mary for a pardon for the man whom she had so shamelessly betrayed, which was why Randolph, reflecting that though honour might not matter to his queen it mattered to him, had steeled himself to make a private journey to Dumfries, where James was encamped in a bleak, yellowing field, to break the news that could only mean the end of his friend's hopes.

But James already knew. After the weeks of silence and evasion, Elizabeth had deigned to write personally to him, though not before he had heard rumours of the diplomatic settlement that she, with the help of the French ambassador, was trying to mediate.

Rummaging about, he found the letter and handed it to Randolph.

It was dated the day after Randolph's own instructions and, skimming through it, Randolph felt queasier by the minute.

Nothing that had happened since she came to the throne, said Elizabeth, had grieved her more than to learn about the troubles of the Earl of Moray and his friends. But ...

'As for the aid you require of me, the love I bear you would readily have induced me to give it, had I been able to do so with honour and conscience. I may not, however, enter into open war against my dearest cousin, the queen of Scots, unless that queen give me just cause. This she has not done. If she should offer you terms, I would advise you not to base any refusal of them on the hope of receiving assistance from your most devoted friend, Elizabeth.'

His mouth tightening, Randolph turned the page. 'But if the queen of Scots' indignation should happen to be so great as to place your and your friends' lives in danger, I myself will not omit to receive you into my protection, showing myself a merciful and Christian prince, ever prepared to defend innocent and noble subjects from tyranny and cruelty.'

It was the grossest of insults, in view of all that had gone before, but James did not see it as such. 'I understand her difficulty,' he said, grey-faced more from worry than fatigue. 'Her privy council has advised against helping us, and I have always held that queens should follow their councillors' advice. How can I complain?'

Randolph almost laughed at the thought of the queen his mistress taking anyone's advice unless it suited her. He found it hard to credit that even James, one of the most virtuous men he knew, could be as Christianly forgiving as all that.

In his mind's eye, he saw again the evening just over four years before when Mary, arrived that very day from France and exquisitely clothed in white and rubies, had received her lords for the first time and overwhelmed them with her charm. He and James and Lethington had stood and watched, with James and Lethington planning how to mould the lovely girl into the queen they wanted her to be.

And now, with a helmet on her head, a pistol at her waist, and an army of five thousand men at her back, she was only a few miles away, swearing that she would rather lose her throne than fail to be revenged upon her brother.

Her army might be numerous, but it wasn't impressive. Randolph reckoned it would melt away at the sight of James's disciplined and mounted force.

But when he said, 'What will you do?' James replied, 'I have no choice. I must accept Elizabeth's offer of sanctuary.'

10

Lethington gave his sister, Marie, a peck on the cheek. 'I have brought you a new poem for your collection. It's more your style than father's.'

She looked at him suspiciously and then, glancing at the paper, gave a small hiccup of laughter.

Sir Richard tapped on the floor with a peremptory stick. 'Well, read it aloud, girl.'

> Be governor both good and gracious
> Be loyal and loving to thy lieges all
> Be large of freedom, never covetous
> Be just to poor men whatso'er befall
> Be firm of faith and constant as a wall
> Be ready ...

'Stop!' said Sir Richard. 'What do you mean by bringing such rubbish into my house? I have rarely heard anything more atrocious.'

His son laughed. 'It is an address by our new king to his wife the queen.'

'Saints preserve us!' Marie gasped. 'You mean that green youth is daring to tell her majesty how she should rule?'

'You haven't reached the best bit, about being strong as a lion against rebels and fierce to follow them wherever they be found ... If James had as much sense of humour as a halibut, I would send it on to him.'

Sir Richard said, 'Where is that foolish gentleman now?'

'England, somewhere. Having stood up for his principles and then held back from fighting for them, he is in something of a political quandary, but I fear it is not the end of the affair.'

'No. It cannot be, when he and his friends have always been among the most influential men in the realm. Will her majesty pardon them?'

'Not from choice, but she must be persuaded. Scotland needs them, whatever their failings, and James particularly, because of his unique reputation for integrity.'

Sir Richard shook his head, even his pale and sightless eyes seeming to mourn a more scrupulous past. 'What hope is there for a land whose people can find only one man among their rulers who is worthy of respect?'

Lethington, like most sons, had his own views on the olden, golden days about which his father was prone to sentimentalise. He said merely, 'The queen thinks she has won a conclusive victory because so few supporters rallied to James when he needed them. But, predictably, now that it's all over, opinion is changing. The lords, lairds and burgesses are rejoicing in being able to say, "I told you so," and since not a soul has died or been even slightly damaged, they are coming to regard the whole affair very much as a schoolboy prank. The general feeling is that the Earl of Moray deserves no more than a rap over the knuckles.'

Marie remarked, 'Well, there's nothing wrong with forgiving and forgetting.'

'Nothing wrong with the principle, certainly. The difficulties arise with the practice.'

11

Back in Edinburgh, Randolph found himself regretting James's flight not only for personal reasons – they had always been allies – but because, having been in the habit of picking up most of the gossip that he dignified by the name of intelligence from James, Glencairn, Kirkcaldy of Grange and others of the exiles, he was now faced with setting up alternative sources.

Morton, he wondered? Lennox? Young George Gordon, newly restored to his father's lands and title as 5th Earl of Huntly? Or his sister Jean, whose deceptively serious brown eyes had almost popped out of her head at the news? He was becoming so desperate that he even sounded out his adored Mary Beaton, who was so scandalised that she refused to speak to him for days. In the end, he was reduced to pouring out money like water on the servants of the royal household. Servants always knew everything.

He was rewarded almost at once with the rumour that Mary was Riccio's mistress. They spent too much time together, even allowing for the fact that the queen was one of the world's most indefatigable correspondents. And they were known to play cards together until well into the night, sometimes even after the queen had released her Maries to go to bed.

With immense satisfaction, Randolph reported this to Elizabeth, adding – in a praiseworthy attempt to help James – that the Earl of Moray had found out and had been proposing to hang the fellow, which was why the queen of Scots hated her brother so much.

It was the kind of delightfully shocking *canard* that Elizabeth could not have been expected to keep to herself, so she passed it on to the French ambassador.

12

'I don't *feel* like the king,' Darnley said pettishly, appending his signature to a land grant. 'You always sign first, on the left, and I have to sign on the right, as if I came second to you.'

It was a familiar complaint, and Mary continued running her eyes over a precept to the treasurer as, smiling faintly, she said, 'Never mind, my dear. You always compensate for it by making your signature twice the size of mine.'

His pen took wing across the room, the inkpot splashed its contents across the papers on the table and the chair flew back as his hand snatched the precept from her and tore it in two.

Mildly, she said, 'Harry, that was not necessary,' and, glancing up at Lethington's assistant, expressionless despite the ruin of all his lovely clean, crisp documents, went on apologetically, 'Perhaps you would leave us for a moment, Master Hay?'

He went, and so did Fleming and Beaton, waved out of sight, if not of earshot.

In a voice that could scarcely have been sweeter or more reasonable, she said, 'Harry, you may not feel like a king, but you must learn to behave like one. I know you have no interest in the business of state. I know you prefer to go hawking and hunting ...'

'That's only because I have no responsibilities. Everyone comes to you first. Everyone expects you to make the decisions. You make me feel young and useless. You diminish me.'

'I don't mean to.' Which was true.

'And you spend hours every day with that fellow Riccio when you should be with me.'

221

'I wish I *could* be with you, but I have to govern the realm as well as rule it. And there is a great deal to do.'

He threw himself onto the cushioned chest at the foot of the big, curtained bed. 'You never ask me to sign any of the letters you say you have dictated to Riccio!'

She frowned. 'I "say" I have dictated?'

'Well, how do I know?' He was both defensive and sulky, aware of having overstepped the line.

She tried to make light of things. 'Well, if you *want* to join in signing letters to my *belle-mère* Catherine in France, or my dearest cousin Lisette in Spain, then of course you may. But you are rarely here when your signature is needed. Indeed, your absences are holding up the business of state.'

As happened so often and so suddenly, his manner changed. 'Oh, Mary. My Mary! Come and sit here beside me.' He was like a small boy, wheedling for comfits in the knowledge that the grownups were too soft-hearted to deny him.

She went, but although the arm round her shoulders offered a physical pleasure, there was no longer any pleasure of the heart. He kissed her and she enjoyed it, but now it had neither meaning nor worth. She had needed a husband to strengthen her and help her, but after less than three months she knew that all she had done was double her own burdens.

He took her chin in his long, lax fingers and, gazing into her eyes said, 'I do love you, you know.'

She thought he probably did, though only when for some reason he needed to, or wanted to. In between times, he loved no one but himself and perhaps his mother.

She was suffering from the beginnings of a familiar weariness, and knew that reaction was setting in after the excitements of the spring and summer, but she managed to say teasingly, 'And?'

He wanted something, of course, but it was not something new. 'I know I don't always behave responsibly, the way you would like me to. But I would if I were *really* king. Why can't I be crowned? Why can't I have the crown matrimonial?'

'Harry, I've told you a dozen times, a hundred times! It's a matter for parliament.'

'Yes, I know. But you ordered that I should be proclaimed king, and I don't understand why you can't order that I be crowned.'

It sounded simple, put like that, as if it were merely a matter of a jewelled coronet, trimmed with ermine and padded with ruby velvet. But it wasn't.

Harry would have been no more than the queen's husband if she had declared him king consort, so she had chosen to exceed her authority by declaring him king regnant, which entitled him to share the government with her. But she could not safely go further because the grant of the crown matrimonial would give him sovereignty in his own right. It would mean that, if Mary died before him, he would continue to rule. Also it would mean that, if she bore him no children or only daughters, he could enter on a second marriage whose sons would be entitled to inherit the throne. The crown matrimonial, in effect, would enable him to found his own dynasty.

Granting it was therefore something not to be done lightly, but Harry refused to believe that Mary could not act without the consent of parliament. Besides, she could always force parliament to do as she wished – if she *truly* wished it.

She had thought at first that she did, but no longer.

With patience, she said, 'It's impossible, Harry. The answer is no.'

13

'No,' said Elizabeth.

The Earl of Moray, who had been briefed by Cecil the evening before, bowed his head in shame.

Elizabeth said, 'I have never been more shocked. That you should rebel against your anointed queen, and then dare to come to me for help!'

She was looking magnificently regal, the cream silk of her gown barely visible through the embroidery that covered it, her neck dripping with pearls and her bosom with jewels, her hair startlingly red and intricately curled, her face so thickly painted that even the pockmarks were filled in. She looked as if she were ready to sit for a very expensive portrait.

It was a play, a piece of theatre, with Elizabeth as the leading actor, James as the comic relief, Cecil in charge of the prompt book, and the French ambassador for audience.

'I have,' Elizabeth went on, 'invited Monsieur de Foix to be here so that he may report to my good sister in Scotland that England has given her no cause for hostility. I am distressed beyond measure to discover that there is a wicked rumour circulating to the effect that I gave you encouragement in your rebellion.'

It wasn't only that backing losers was poor tactics. She couldn't afford such rumours to gain currency because she couldn't afford to forfeit the precarious goodwill of France and Spain, which had given their blessing to Mary's marriage and might well rally to her in case of need – especially if, as was rumoured, Mary had joined the secret league of Catholic nations believed to have come into being at Bayonne a few months earlier, dedicated to uprooting heresy with fire and sword.

James, as instructed, said nothing.

Cecil, whose two-year-old son Robert was remarkably forward for his age, wondered whether the boy's daily curriculum might usefully be widened to include cosmography.

M. de Foix, a well-informed gentleman with a shrewd idea of what the charade was actually worth, stood and looked reproachful, while longing for his dinner.

'What do you have to say for yourself?' Elizabeth demanded. 'As I understand it, your rebellion was stimulated by fear of the political and religious implications of my good sister's marriage to my own disloyal subject, the Lord Darnley?'

Without so much as a blink, James replied, 'I will admit that such considerations did weigh with me, but the queen my mistress has always behaved kindly towards me and I would not like ye to think that my actions were directed against her personally.'

'Indeed?' said Elizabeth. 'Then if her marriage was not the deciding factor in your rebellion, what was?'

There was a thick mist outside, hanging over the wide, evil-smelling brown waters of the Thames, but it was no river mist that contaminated the royal presence chamber at Westminster. Even de Foix, bred to deceit from the cradle, could taste it in the air and found it unpleasant.

'It was the Lennox plot against my life. I could not prove what I knew, because I had to protect those who had informed me of it, and the whole thing developed from there. In the end, I was *harassed* into rebellion.'

Cecil, watching de Foix stroke his short, silky beard, could make nothing of his expression but it scarcely mattered. The ambassador could be as suspicious as he liked, providing he reported back to France the actual words that had been uttered.

James went on, 'I am ready to admit that I was in the wrong, and I want to make my peace with my sister. Ye'll understand when I say that I have no hope of her listening to me. But she would listen to your majesty and I am here to beg you to intercede for me.'

'I? Why should I?'

To the relief of everyone present, she did not wait for an answer. Even a farce could run too long.

'I do not see how I can, but I will consult my council. You may go now. But I will say again how shocked I am that any subject should rebel against my good sister and his rightful queen. Consider yourself fortunate that you do not find yourself consigned to an English prison.'

And that, thought de Foix – who had always had a soft spot for Mary – would have been the perfect answer. James Stewart, Earl of Moray, was not only a troublemaker but a righteous one, which was the worst kind.

14

Elizabeth's strength of personality, like Mary's charm, carried her a long way, which made it all too easy for her to forget that its impact faded with the miles.

Pleased with her performance, and having regaled the Spanish ambassador with every tiniest detail of it, Elizabeth went on to send an account to Edinburgh for Mary's delectation. She had given Moray *such* a telling off, she said. She wished her good sister had been there to hear it.

Mary enjoyed it greatly and gave it the widest circulation.

It was the end, for many of James's supporters, of amity with England, which had been the enemy for centuries and a friend for little more than a decade. Elizabeth's double dealing enraged them into declaring England's friendship to be as dangerous as England's enmity, and far more humiliating. It was not right that Lord James should have been so demeaned.

The most extreme convert to this view was Argyll, still lurking in his Highland fastnesses. His own failure to supply James with the reinforcements he needed might have had something to do with it, but his hostility to Elizabeth now became so bitter and so deep that he was prepared to see any opponent of England as an ally of his. He even began to look kindly on Mary.

There was a less direct sequel, too. Mary, misjudging the situation as Elizabeth herself had done, thought James now wholly discredited and began making open concessions to those of her subjects who adhered to the old religion. As a result, both James himself and his cry of 'religion in danger' were revitalised. The mildly censorious sympathy that had ruled in the middle of October was magically transformed by mid-November into strong partisanship and Lord Moray himself into the martyred guardian of the Protestant cause.

Lethington watched and listened with interest. Months before, he had lost all trust in Elizabeth, but Elizabeth was not England, although she liked to believe she was, and he remained dedicated to the English alliance of which he had been one of the architects.

James wrote to him privately from Newcastle, where he had found a lodging, claiming to be still on sufficiently good terms with Elizabeth to have been able to rebuke her privately after their interview for forcing him into such an embarrassing position. But he was not, it seemed, on sufficiently good terms to wring any money out of her. He was suffering from a serious shortage of funds and, since his wife's messengers were being stopped by Bothwell, Mary's lieutenant-general on the Borders, before they could cross into England, he was hard put to it to pay for his bread. Was there any way in which Lethington could help?

Something had to be done.

A diplomat in every fibre of his being, Lethington was used to shuffling the cards anew, year after year, as the political situation changed. He supposed, as he set his mind to yet another shuffling of the cards, that he must be a gambler at heart. But although the fall of the cards might differ, the game for him was always the same, because he never lost sight of his end – a country settled and safe enough to begin to realise its potentialities and explore its own genius.

15

'If I had ever doubted,' Mallie Fleming said, 'the value of a love based only on desire, I would know better now.'

It had taken more than six long weeks of arrangements and postponements to set herself and Lethington free to walk together on the hill called Arthur's Seat, looking as if they had met by chance – although what chance should have taken two such people out in a howling November gale might have puzzled even the most disinterested observer.

'The queen?'

'Yes.'

But he sensed that she was not speaking only of the queen, and waited. It was not a time for him to take the lead. He himself had no doubts or hesitations of any kind but he thought, from what she had so briefly said in the audience chamber, that for Mallie the long emotional step from a love cherished privately within the heart to a love shared might not seem quite so easy or so simple. And he guessed that, until the step had been taken, the physical attraction between them, intense though it was, could not be fulfilled.

She turned to him suddenly, and it was not the cutting wind that brought the tears to her eyes. 'You can't imagine how hurt she is to have been betrayed for a second time. I know James is a friend of yours, but to have accepted so many gifts and honours as if they were his due, and then to try to raise her subjects against her! He is my cousin and I have always disliked him, but I never expected that of him. And then to have the king, whom she married for love, let her see that he married her solely because he wanted the crown ...'

'She must have known that.'

'Yes, but she persuaded herself that he loved her, too. Perhaps he did. But now he cares about only one thing.'

'I'd guessed, but I wasn't sure. Thanks to Riccio, I have little access to either of them.'

'Davie? I don't know why everyone seems to hate poor little Davie. He is competent, and amusing, and far from a fool. And she can trust him absolutely. If you can tell me of any other man at court of whom one can say as much, I should like to know.'

Ignoring his ruefully raised eyebrow, she hurried on, 'Yes, he is a lowborn favourite and, yes, he has the faults of such men, but he is really quite harmless. It cannot be beyond your ingenuity to come to terms with him?'

He shook his head, smiling. 'What may look possible from inside the royal apartments is not always possible from the outside. And, you know, every time such a man intervenes between the queen and her lords, he widens the divide between them. That makes him dangerous. However, it is hardly your concern. Is her majesty still confined to her bed?'

'Yes. As always, she meets crises and challenges splendidly, but has to pay the price afterwards. She has the usual pain in her side and we are all concerned about her, but the apothecary says it will pass.'

'If his remedies do not kill her first?'

She gave him a darkling look. 'Exactly. And the king has not even visited her. He has been away for nine days, hunting.'

'At least, for him, it's a relatively harmless occupation.' Lethington said it a little absently. He was a patient man but his interest in the queen and her problems was waning rapidly.

They were approaching the deserted hermitage known as St Anthony's

Chapel when a great gust of rain-laden wind swept across the hillside and he drew Mallie hurriedly into the shelter of the walls, both of them laughing breathlessly with the relief of it. After a moment, because they were no longer walking side by side but able to look fully into each other's faces, their laughter died.

For the first time, he took her in his arms and, saying, 'I love you so much,' laid his lips lightly on hers. Her gentian eyes were watering, her elegant nose was pink at the tip, and they were both shivering almost uncontrollably from the wind, but their kiss could have been no sweeter if they had been in a paradise garden, full of the scents of sun and summer.

Afterwards, she laid her cheek on his chest and he drew his arms and his cloak more tightly around her. Sounding almost surprised, she murmured after a moment, 'I can hear your heart beating!'

'Well, thank God for that. Will you marry me?'

She did not move, but he felt her indrawn breath and her voice was hesitant as she said, 'That is what we should be talking about, isn't it? My senses have no doubts. I do love you. I always have done, although at first I think it was more like a fascination for something – not someone – unattainable. Do you understand?'

'No.' But then he remembered the masque, when his lifelong self-sufficiency had been shattered by a vision of silver and moonlight, a vision from a world that had never been his. He said, 'Yes. I think so.'

'And now, even in those brief moments when we are together, there is something invisible and powerful flowing between us. It should be enough, but ...'

She raised the serious, flowerlike eyes to his. 'I love you, but I don't know you. When everyone began gossiping about your interest in me, I tried to ignore it because in this last year or two quite a few men have found me desirable. And that is *not* vanity speaking! I was terrified that, for you, desire might be all it was. That it was only my looks that attracted you, not *me*.'

'My dearest darling ...'

'No, let me go on. I couldn't bear that you should love me less than I love you, but you have been away from court so much, and you have never said anything ...'

'That was partly because you gave me no hint of how *you* felt.'

'I suppose not. Oh, what fools we are! But it's still true that I have no idea how you think or feel, not only about me ...' He moved slightly and she gave a watery chuckle. 'When we are apart. No, please let me finish!

When we are apart, I can only guess at how you think from what you do, and ...'

'And much of what I have done in this last year has seemed either disloyal or incomprehensible to her majesty, and therefore to you.'

Gratefully, she nodded.

Lethington envied his father sometimes. Sir Richard Maitland was a man of great gentleness, political moderation and unshakeable integrity who, since his blindness, had virtually withdrawn from public affairs, pouring his despair at the state of Scotland into poetry that distilled the wisdom of seventy years of thoughts and dreams. But his son was committed to a world that dealt not in poetry but in prose, where distillations of thought and dreams were neither required nor appreciated, where everything had to be spelt out and explained and defended. He had learned not to expose the private patterns of his mind to men who could never understand them.

He could not imagine sharing them.

But now ...

When he said, smiling, 'Then we must find time to talk, and I will reveal all to you,' he was making, although the girl he idolised did not know it, one of the greatest commitments of his life.

16

On the eve of her betrothal to François almost eight years before, Mary had signed not one, but two marriage contracts. The second had been a secret one, and although she had been successful in forgetting it for most of the years since then, it still returned sometimes to haunt her.

As she lay drowsing in her bed at Holyrood, grateful for the cessation of one pain and preparing her mind for a new one to which she looked forward with disbelieving joy, she remembered the scene with her Guise uncles, duke and cardinal, the only fathers she had ever known, whom she had loved greatly for the care they had lavished upon her and the wisdom she knew they possessed.

'There are three deeds in the secret treaty,' Duc François had said, 'and they must be signed privately, in advance of the official treaty.'

At fifteen, she was old enough to ask, 'Secret from whom?'

Smoothly, the cardinal had replied. 'Not "from". Secret *to* you and to France.'

At fifteen, she was also old enough to say mischievously, 'Ah! That is *quite* different. But why?'

Her uncles had glanced at each other, and it was Duc François who said, 'Before we explain, you must understand that, unless you sign the secret treaty, his majesty of France will not permit your marriage to the dauphin to go ahead.'

The shock had been appalling. Her whole life – or all of it since she was old enough to remember – had been directed towards becoming queen, some day, of France as well as Scotland. At fifteen, she knew France to be her life and her true destiny. Nothing could justify the threat to take it away from her. Nothing could be worth such a sacrifice.

She had still been too innocent to appreciate just how many of her Guise uncles' ambitions, how much of their influence in France, depended on her rôle as its future queen. It had been clever of them to warn her, first, of what would happen if she failed to cooperate. It had made the terms of the secret treaty seem painless by comparison.

Aware that they were watching her like the hawks they so much resembled, she had gathered herself together and, justifying her years of training, smiled regally and said, 'We cannot allow that to happen. Tell me about the treaty.'

The first of the deeds said that, if she died without children, possession of the realm of Scotland, together with her claim to the throne of England, would pass automatically to France. The second deed, in which her death did not figure, laid down stringent terms under which France was to be repaid the moneys spent in Scotland's defence. And the third guaranteed that, whatever happened, whatever Mary might later decree as queen of Scots, whatever documents she might some day ratify, the terms of the secret treaty would supersede them all.

The terms had not seemed so very terrible in comparison with the alternative. Even so, she had hesitated. What she knew of Scotland suggested that the country would be far more prosperous as a province of France than left to its own devices, but ...

'But I can't just give my realm away, can I?'

Suavely, the cardinal had said, 'You will not be doing so in any irresponsible sense. The first deed, the one that seems to concern you, is no more than insurance against any delay in granting François the crown matrimonial of Scotland. The effect in both cases is the same. If you were to die childless, he would become king in his own right.'

She was trying to behave as the queen of Scots should. 'Yes, but the formal treaty doesn't promise him the crown matrimonial the instant we are married, does it? Not until his father dies and he himself becomes king of France.'

'Does it matter? It is merely a question of timing.'

It wasn't, quite. 'I suppose so. But ... No, I am sure you are right! In any case' – she had laughed, all her happiness over her forthcoming betrothal resurfacing – 'I don't intend to die childless. I intend to have a whole nurseryful of children!'

And so, since the only alternative was unacceptable, she had signed all three of the deeds and had been married soon after.

She had never been sure whether François's death had invalidated the secret treaty. It had not been part of the marriage contract but a separate commitment, and potentially explosive. If she died childless, it had said not that Scotland would pass to her dear, dead little François but that it would pass to France.

Once she had left France, there had been no one she had dared to ask, because, reminded of it, even the cardinal – playing three simultaneous games of diplomatic chess with his right hand and three with his left – might see a use for it in one of his gambits. He was still fond of her, as she was of him, but she had ceased to be politically important to him.

Seven months from now, however, a few days more or a few days less, she would be childless no longer, haunted no longer by guilt over what might happen if she died. She had tried her best to love Scotland, and had succeeded for a while, despite the long, hard winters and the long-faced, hard-headed lords, until the endless grey days had begun to bear down on her spirits and she had learned to like or trust no one whose native tongue was Scots or whose interests might run contrary to her own.

Even so, she could not now abandon her people – the ordinary people who loved her – to the rule of a France which they had somehow come to hate. If she had known the depth of that feeling when she returned to Scotland just over four years before, many things might have been different.

Sighing, she turned on her side. Although her husband, as yet, did not know she was with child, because she had not seen him privately for two or three weeks, the Maries knew and the servants must know it too. Perhaps that most ardent of gossip collectors, Master Randolph, might already have sent rumours racing on their way to London, to Elizabeth, who was thirty-two years old and still a virgin.

Contentedly, Mary drifted off to sleep.

The king, summoned to meet his wife and celebrate her birthday at the palace of Linlithgow, where she had been born twenty-three years before, was on his best behaviour.

It was a restful place, unusually large for a Scots castle, square-built, set in an open landscape and on the edge of a loch full of fish. Mary had never cared for it much, but Harry was seeing it for the first time, which gave him an opportunity to display his sophistication, to compare it with the *châteaux* of France – not altogether to Linlithgow's disadvantage – and make a great many pretty speeches about its special beauty as the place of his wife's birth.

As she still too easily did when he was behaving like a civilised human being, she found herself beginning to melt towards him, to remember why she had fallen in love with him. There were some men, she knew, who were transformed by fatherhood, brought to understand the meaning of responsibility. She thought there might be hope, yet, and even blushed a little as she told him of her condition.

They had been riding sedately in the park and he slid off his horse and came to stand by her saddlebow and say 'Mary, my Mary!' with every evidence of surprise and delight.

She did not know that it was more than a month since he had heard the first rumours, a month of waiting during which his resentment had worked up to fever pitch, fed by her silence and the rumours about Riccio being so assiduously spread not only by Master Randolph but by Darnley's own kinsman, the Earl of Morton.

And by his father, who had told him, 'Flatter her. Abase yourself to her. Do anything, anything at all, to revive her love for you and force her to grant you the crown matrimonial. It must be done soon, because if she were to bear a son and die in childbirth, it would be the child who would succeed her, not you.

'It would mean that you could never rule in your own right. You could never be more than the father of the king.'

Chapter Eleven

DECEMBER 1565-MARCH 1566

1

Everyone knew that Darnley went drinking and whoring around Edinburgh of nights, that he daily demanded the crown matrimonial, that he flew into a passion at every imagined slight, that he counted himself superior to his wife simply because he was a man, that he complained that she would not go to bed with him and accused her of going to bed with Riccio instead. By the end of the year, there were few people who continued to refer to him as 'the king', except in his presence, and even fewer who thought of him other than with contempt.

The queen herself, her natural optimism reasserting itself as she recovered her health, was no longer interested in what her husband did or said; she simply laughed at the Riccio gossip, because it was so ridiculous. Although her marriage might, in human terms, be proving a disaster, her successes in getting the better of both Elizabeth and James combined with the knowledge of approaching motherhood to give her an invigorating sense of personal achievement, almost of invincibility.

Governing the country without the advice of the exiled James and discredited Lethington was an exacting task and, absorbed in it, she was unaware of how out of touch she was becoming. She scarcely noticed – except at Christmas and the New Year, when it was easily explained by the appalling weather – her lords' increasing disinclination to show their faces at court. Nor did anyone tell her that, when they did appear, they no longer conversed indoors but only in the open, where there was no danger of being overheard.

2

The Earl of Morton, swinging his golf club, said, 'We have tae get James back,' and watched morosely as his ball trundled off its miniature hillock of sand and rolled to a halt a few inches away. Hitting wee balls into holes was, in his opinion, no occupation for a grown man. 'You're supposed tae be the clever one,' he went on, teeing up again. 'Have ye not got any ideas?'

Lethington shook his head. 'I have run out. I invited, all too successfully, a crushing rebuke from her majesty for suggesting that she might permit some of the income from James's estates to be forwarded to him. I defended John Knox – not only his argument but, God help me, his language – when he called for royal forgiveness for the exiles. And I have this very day written to Cecil, who is as concerned as I am over the bad relations between our queens, to say we must strike at the root of the problem, which is Elizabeth's determination to force Mary to pardon James. If Elizabeth would cease to be so dictatorial and relent, even a little, over the succession, Mary might begin to relent over James.' He shrugged. 'What more can I do?'

'I didnae mean that kind of thing. Guidsakes, man, we need deeds, not words.' Morton gave his ball a whack that would have sent it well on its way to the hole had not its seams been weakened by too much intimacy with wet grass. Rising a sluggish six inches into the air, it descended to earth again with a thud, the leather splitting wide and the feathers bursting out.

His face as red as his whiskers, Morton began beating at it with his club until the head of the club broke off. Then he stabbed the shaft viciously into the turf.

Lethington, his eyes politely averted, said, 'Do *you* have any ideas?'

'Aye. But I'm not telling you. Not yet, anyway.'

Lethington thought he knew. James and his fellow rebels had been required to present themselves before parliament in Edinburgh on 12th March, there to be attainted and have their property forfeited, and he guessed that Morton intended to resort to the familiar practice of convocating the queen's lieges, turning out his Douglas followers in their thousands so as to terrorise parliament into finding the rebels innocent. It might work, since parliament was already that way inclined.

But he was underestimating Morton, who had an economical turn of mind and expected maximum returns from his efforts.

Jean Gordon said dispassionately, 'Well, I hope her majesty's husband is not going to get drunk at my wedding.'

'Or get everyone else drunk, which is what he really likes to do.' Mary Seton, plaiting a long silver hairpiece in with Jean's chestnut locks, cocked her head approvingly. 'Yes, that's what you need. It makes a link between you and your gown. Madame sometimes forgets that cloth of silver does not suit everyone.'

There had been twelve yards of cloth of silver and six yards of white taffeta to line the sleeves and train. Jean said, 'It was a most generous gift,' and then, 'I'm not sure about the hairpiece, though. It looks lovely, but it might give me a headache. Or even more of a headache than I expect to have before the day is out.'

'Nonsense. They're perfectly comfortable. Everyone wears them. The queen has dozens.'

'The queen isn't marrying my Lord Bothwell.'

4

Jean sometimes wondered whether tears would have come more readily to her if she had been born into a civilised family. But, being possessed of a commonsensical disposition, she had found it more irritating than heartbreaking to live with a father and brothers who had spent most of their days actively inviting, and in three cases successfully achieving, violent death. Even her mother consorted with witches, and one of her sisters was becoming really rather eccentric.

She had thought her brother George to be more sensible, but as soon as he had been freed from ward and restored to the earldom of Huntly, he had entered into an alliance with Bothwell. It was understandable enough, because George hated the Earl of Moray, who had been responsible for all his family's recent troubles, and Bothwell hated him even more. By allying themselves against the earl, however, they were allying themselves against most of the rest of Scotland.

When Jean had become aware of how much time they were spending together, she had said to Mallie Fleming, 'I don't know what to do. Even Lord Moray's most lukewarm friends seem to want him back in Scotland, but I'm *sure* my brother and Lord Bothwell are plotting to prevent it. Really, I wouldn't put it past them to be thinking of murdering him!'

'Bothwell isn't as bad as he's painted,' Mallie said a little defensively. 'He was born a wild Borderer, and Borderers like their crimes to be open and above board. Given the opportunity, he'd probably be very happy to kill James if they met face to face, but I can't imagine him sending someone off to Newcastle to pop some poison in his soup. In any case, I believe that he's trying to mend his ways.'

'Truly?'

'The queen is very satisfied with the work he's been doing for her on the Borders, and being approved of – for once – is doing wonders for his temper. He is even sitting on the artillery committee and saying quite sensible things. All he needs is the love of a good woman to turn him into a model citizen.'

Jean had giggled, until she learned that she was fated to be the good woman.

Her brother George had said, 'It's time you were wed. You're getting on. You're – what age are you?'

'Twenty.'

'Well, there you are, then. Now that I've been reinstated, I can give you a dowry, and Bothwell's short of funds and needs a wife. So I've arranged it.'

Jean's normally level head had seemed to be gyrating in her brother's draughty and yet stuffy business room in the Meal Market. 'Do I have no say in the matter?'

George had looked at her as if she were speaking a foreign language. 'Why should you?'

The queen had strongly approved the match, uniting as it did the families of Gordon, her most loyal supporters in the north, and Hepburn, her most loyal supporters in the south. She liked Jean, too, and thought she would be a steadying influence on Bothwell, who had, she pointed out, a great many excellent qualities which too often went unappreciated.

Mallie Fleming had said, 'The queen is right, but I'm afraid his excellent qualities don't include gentleness,' and Jean had answered calmly, 'Whose do? This is Scotland. And I do not come from a gentle family.'

She had always known that she would never be permitted to marry Alexander Ogilvie and was vaguely surprised when, after the Bothwell contract had been signed, she had found herself weeping all through the long, cold winter night. In the morning, however, she had dried her eyes, blown her nose, and reminded herself that women were no more than dowry bringers, occasional bedfellows, child bearers, and high-class housekeepers, and why should she be any different.

But when, during the exuberant celebrations that followed her bridals at the Kirk of the Canongait, Mallie Fleming gave her a convulsive hug and assured her that the silver strand was wonderfully flattering, she could not forbear to murmur, 'Why is it such a horrible world?'

The queen's husband did not attend, which meant that, for once, there were no public quarrels about his drinking, his jealousy, the queen's refusal to grant him the crown matrimonial – or to come to his arms. The presence of an audience never shamed Darnley into reticence.

Jean rather regretted it, after all, because there was nothing to take her mind off the night to come. The only consolation was that her husband was reputed to have such a vast and varied experience in bed that it ought to be interesting, at least.

5

With rare expansiveness, Lord Morton said, 'We havnae got tae know each other awful well yet, your majesty. Why d'ye not come and visit me at Aberdour? We're kinsmen, when all's said and done.'

Darnley, whose mother was a Douglas but who had so far found Morton, the head of the family, vulgarly repellent, was about to refuse when he remembered that Mary had recently relieved Morton of the Great Seal because he'd dug his heels in over a piece of property that Mary had wanted to give to her lover Riccio. At least he would be a sympathetic audience.

'Oh, very well. I'll dine with you tomorrow. I might stay. We'll see.'

It proved to be very rewarding for both of them.

Clamping one hand over the breastbone of a wild duck and tearing a leg off with the other, Morton said, 'I think it's a right shame that her majesty should behave as if she's better than you. It's against nature for the hen tae crow before the cock. There's many folk that thinks it should be you that rules.'

Darnley, who did not like getting his hands greasy, summoned a servant to carve for him. 'If I had the crown matrimonial, I could.'

Morton, chewing, gestured to his cup bearer and then drank long and deep. 'She doesnae give you the respect ye're due. Mind you, that fellow Riccio's to blame for a lot of it.' He shook his head mournfully. 'And these rumours about the pair of them ...'

It was like opening the flood gates.

Darnley had neither discretion nor sense, and the cup bearer, who earned a generous shilling for every interesting piece of gossip he was able to pass on to Mr Randolph, listened avidly.

When Darnley had finished, Morton said, 'Aye, I can understand your feelings, and it's a tempting notion. We'd better have a wee thought about it. Here, try some of this mortrews. It's got pigeon in it.'

Not until the board had been cleared and they were sitting over spiced wine and wafers did Morton come to the point. Before Darnley's outburst, he had known he held one trump card. Now he had two.

'This business of the crown matrimonial. Speaking personally,' he managed a tight smile, 'I'd like tae see ye crowned king in your own right – for the Douglases' sake as well as your own. Having royal connections never did anyone any harm. And I've a notion that maybe we could arrange a wee bargain.'

Darnley lay back on the settle and tried to look bored. 'Yes?'

'It's like this. There's many of us want the Earl of Moray pardoned and allowed to come home ...'

'Moray? After he rebelled against my marriage? Never!' Darnley sat up. 'He's my worst enemy! I *hate* him.'

'Wait a bit. The queen's not very partial tae him, either. Just like she's not very partial tae letting you have the crown matrimonial. But there's one way we can all get what we want, whether she likes it or not.'

'And what may that be?'

'Well, when parliament meets next month she means tae have Moray, Argyll, Glencairn and the others formally confirmed as rebels and then tae have their lands, titles and possessions taken away from them. But it wouldnae be legal without the royal assent.'

'Well?'

Morton smothered a sigh of exasperation. 'Royal assent means both of you. If ye want tae, ye can stop the whole thing just by refusing tae sign. It would be the same as finding them not guilty. They'd be reinstated and they could all come home again.'

It was a summary of the situation which left so much out of account that someone like Lethington would barely have recognised what Morton was talking about, but Darnley didn't question it.

Petulantly, he said, 'But I *don't* want to. I don't want them home. I *want* them forfeited. They're traitors.'

One of Morton's dogs was sniffing around the long booted royal legs sprawled out in front of the fire, as Morton said, 'I mentioned a bargain.'

Darnley loosed a drunken kick at the dog. 'It'll have to be a good one.'

'Oh, aye. It is. Because in return for you helping to get them reinstated, they'll make sure that, at the following parliament, ye'll be granted the crown matrimonial.'

The wine had done its work. It didn't occur to Darnley that any such grant would still need a royal assent – this time with his wife's signature as well as his own.

His fair, flushed face intent, he said slowly, 'They'd have to agree a bond with me beforehand, swearing to do it.'

'Oh, aye. And you'd have to swear a bond yourself, too.'

'I would have thought my word should be good enough!'

Morton said nothing, and after a moment Darnley giggled. 'Moray's stuck, isn't he? And I'm the only one who can get him out of the mess. I like that. But it could be a long time before the parliament after this one meets, so he's going to have to pay me something substantial on account.'

6

Tom Randolph was having one of the most exasperating months he could remember in an aeon of exasperating months, because his spine was still crawling at the news the cup bearer had brought him when the queen of Scots summoned him to her presence.

It was snowing in an inconsequential way, fat white flakes drifting down from an iron-grey sky and rimming the sills of the windows in the royal audience chamber. Every candle in the place had been lit and the queen was seated in her chair of state with two Maries at her side and a number of privy councillors and officers of state in attendance.

There was someone else, too, whom Randolph observed with a sinking heart.

The queen gestured towards the man. 'Master Johnstone here has a statement to make.'

The fellow was an Edinburgh lawyer with a whey-coloured face and ink-stained hands, one of the kind who was not above carrying out special commissions which had little to do with the law but could be loosely classed under the heading of business dealings.

Master Johnstone cleared his throat. 'Whit I say is said on my conscience and as I should answer afore God. During the late rising of James Stewart, Earl of Moray, when the said rebellious earl was riding the countryside with his followers, I was sent for – as a man of business in good repute, ye understand – by Master Thomas Randolph, the English ambassador here present. With another English gentleman as witness to the transaction, Master Randolph handed to me three sacks each containing one thousand golden crowns which he required me to convey to the residence of Lady Moray in St Andrews in order that she might forward them to her rebellious husband for the payment of his followers. I fulfilled this task as required, being paid three crowns for my trouble.'

The queen said, 'What have you to say to that, Master Randolph? Do you admit aiding and abetting those who rebelled against my royal authority?'

To begin with, he flatly denied it. Then he blustered. Then, since the queen of Scots had no legal jurisdiction over him, he offered to prove his innocence in an English court of law.

Carefully, no one raised the question of who had supplied the money in the first place, although Randolph could see that everyone suspected Elizabeth. In fact, it had been the Earl of Bedford who had sent it, in the mistaken belief that Elizabeth would reimburse him. But the money was only part of it. The truth was that Mary had become tired of Elizabeth's domineering ways and it was Randolph who was going to have to pay the price.

Sweet and inexorable, the queen of Scots said, 'If your sin had been less, I might have done no more than reprimand you and send an official complaint to my cousin's Secretary Cecil. As it is, however, I have to tell you that, as England's ambassador, you are no longer welcome here. I require you to leave the country as soon as may be arranged.'

It came at the worst possible time. Hurrying back to his lodgings to prepare a report for Cecil, Randolph decided not to leave Edinburgh a minute before he had to. He would shut himself up in his quarters and refuse to move.

In the end, it took one of Bothwell's lairds and an armed escort to see him on his reluctant way.

7

James's lodging, a house in one of the steep streets above the river Tyne in Newcastle, was ceaselessly loud with the sea birds from the estuary. On the second day of March, when Lord Darnley's father, the Earl of Lennox, arrived bearing a bond for his and the other exiles' signatures, the gulls were noisier than usual and James found it hard to concentrate. After four months of unendurable tedium and increasing desperation, it was as if his brain had become rusty.

He said, 'I don't know about this', and glanced round the table at Glencairn, Rothes, Boyd and Ochiltree. 'What d'ye think?'

Glencairn said, 'We need someone with a legal mind. I wish Lethington was here. Is he coming?'

'He sent a message to say he would, if he could find an excuse for absenting himself from court and if Randolph was still there to give him an English safe conduct. But we weren't to rely on him.'

Jovially, Lennox intervened. 'Why should you need Lethington? The bond's straightforward enough.'

'Aye, a bit too straightforward, in my view. If anything went wrong, we'd be in worse trouble than we are now.'

Lennox spread his hands in one of his occasional Frenchified gestures. 'How can anything go wrong when there are so many of the lords already committed? Argyll, Morton, George Douglas, Ruthven and Lindsay have all signed in Scotland. They didn't complain about the terms.'

'Ye don't mention Lethington?'

'As secretary of state, he doesn't have a vote in parliament and he's a servant of the Crown, whoever wears it, so there would be no purpose in him signing. That's what he says, anyway.'

Ochiltree, whose formerly amiable disposition had taken a turn for the worse when he had acquired John Knox as a son-in-law, muttered, 'He's a right politician, yon one. A proper Mackyvelly.'

An hour later, the proper Mackyvelly rode into the courtyard, tired and dusty and as parched, he claimed, as one of the Desert Fathers. Although he and James were no longer in complete political accord, their old friendship remained. James still valued both the man himself and the extraordinary breadth of his mind, while Lethington felt an irrational compulsion to save James from the pit he had so obstinately dug for himself.

He knew about what was planned, and about the bonds and how many people were involved. Being a sensible man, he also knew that there was nothing to be gained by declaring himself to be a minority of one. All he could do, as he had done so often before when the lords took the bit between their teeth, was try and minimise the damage.

When he had swallowed a long draught of ale, had some food, and assured himself that his knees were not permanently bent to the stirrups, he ran his eye over the bond.

'You're swearing to support the king, stand up for his honour, maintain – with his help – the queen's 1561 proclamation about religion, get the crown matrimonial for him and uphold the right of the Lennox Stuarts to the crown if the queen dies childless. Yes. I think one or two small amendments are needed.'

Lennox argued, of course, but, however much he would have liked to, he could scarcely argue against such additions as supporting the king 'in all lawful and just actions', or standing up for his honour 'according to the word of God'.

He had brought with him a copy of the bond which his son was to sign, once he was assured that the lords had signed theirs, and it was satisfactory enough. Darnley swore to grant the exiles remission for all crimes they might have committed, to ensure that parliament would not forfeit them, to restore their lands to them, to stand by them in all just quarrels, and to confirm the religious settlement of 1561.

Lethington said, 'That looks all right. And what about his second bond?'

'His second bond?' Lennox asked.

'The one with Lord Ruthven.'

'I know of no such bond.'

Perhaps it was true, and Darnley had kept it secret from him. Lennox had very little sense but, if he had known of the bond's contents, he might have had enough to try and put a stop to what his son was planning.

8

Lennox left in mid-afternoon, but Lethington stayed overnight, and not only because he had already ridden far and fast that day. Perhaps his thirty-eight years were beginning to tell, or perhaps he had covered too many thousands of miles in the course of his life. His muscles, now and then, were apt to complain.

He stayed, however, mainly because he had questions to ask. Late in the evening, alone with James, he said, 'Why? How do you justify all this?'

'What d'ye mean "justify"?'

'Less than a year ago, you rebelled against your sister and sovereign, did your best to start another civil war because you thought Darnley, even though he appeared to be a lukewarm Catholic at best, was an unsuitable husband for the queen. And now, when he has proved himself not only unsuitable but irresponsible, vicious, and a far more devoted Catholic than Mary herself, you are prepared to sign a bond guaranteeing to support him in everything – even to the extent of founding a new dynasty in place of the Stewarts – if only he will give you back your estates. Some might think that cynical, a betrayal of your principles.'

James's face was long and earnest. 'It's not like that at all.'

'Isn't it?'

'Last year, Mary was using Darnley as a tool in her campaign for the English throne and her plan to restore Catholicism. But now, with these bonds, he's come over to our side. Don't ye see? He's committed himself to the Protestant settlement. He's not *her* tool any more. He's ours.'

Lethington, who had a logical mind, always had difficulty with James's personal brand of reasoning. He shook his head slightly, trying to clear it. 'Is he?'

James grinned. 'Those amendments you suggested to the bond were just what we needed to eliminate any possible doubt.'

'Were they?'

'Well, we've never meant to honour the bond. Ye must see that. None of us wants him to have the crown matrimonial.'

Lethington, staring into the heart of the fire, said, 'Don't I remember something about bonds being inviolable? Good faith, *noblesse oblige*, morality – that kind of thing?'

'Och, in an ideal world, maybe, but this isn't an ideal world. Anyway, the bit ye put in about supporting him in "all lawful and just actions" settled any possible arguments of that kind very nicely. We can retract our oaths with a clear conscience the minute he resorts to *un*lawful and *un*just actions.'

'And, of course, he will have done just that when the second bond, his bond with Ruthven, is fulfilled ...'

The lethal bond Darnley's father didn't know about, but James did.

'Just so.' James grinned.

It was rare for Lethington to be hoist with his own petard, but it was not that which most concerned him. Although he was not entirely opposed to the object of the Ruthven bond, the way it was to be fulfilled concerned him deeply. He had hoped, at the very least, to modify it. But that, it now seemed, was impossible.

9

Davie Riccio, who had been seated at the end of the supper table, hopped to his feet.

'Ees like this, see! You go in the barber's shop to have your beard trimmed and he say, "How your honour wish to look, eh?" and you think, "How I wish to look?" and you say, "Tall and handsome, maybe?" '

He beamed happily and everyone round the table laughed.

'So the barber say, "Ees not what I mean. I mean you wanna look fearsome to your enemies or amiable to your friends? You wanna look grim and stern, or modest and retiring? I have trims for all these." So you say, "I wanna look modest and retiring." '

Sir Arthur Erskine, Mary's Master of the Horse, let out a shout of mirth. 'And the barber says, "Sir, you ask the impossible!" '

Davie, flinging open his fur-trimmed damask overgown to display the blinding sheen of the doublet and hose beneath, replied austerely, 'Not so. To such a genius as thees barber, all things ees possible.'

Mary said, 'Davie, sit down. I cannot eat and laugh at the same time.' She was almost six months pregnant and, laying her hand on her stomach, smiled. 'My baby is telling me that he does not like it.'

'But Madame, he must learn to laugh, too. And I have still to tell you about curling mustachios into little horns, and the pomades to use, and ...'

Mary looked at him and he sat down.

More and more, because of her pregnancy, she had been choosing to spend her evenings in the company of half-a-dozen close friends and members of her private household, holding intimate supper parties, gossiping, making music or playing cards until beyond midnight. This Saturday evening was very much like any other, with Arthur Erskine, Robert Beaton of Creich, and her half-brother and sister, Lord Robert Stewart and Jean, Countess of Argyll. And, of course, Davie, in the rôle not of bass singer, majordomo, correspondence secretary or confidential servant but because he was a merry and entertaining little fellow whom the queen liked very much.

Thoughtfully, her sister Jean said, 'I wonder if babies *can* learn to laugh before they come into the world. It would be ...'

Abruptly, she stopped and, pushing back her chair, dropped into a curtsey, while all the men rose and bowed.

Darnley, standing in the doorway, nodded acknowledgement and then crossed the room to sit beside his wife on the daybed.

He put his arm around her waist and she was aware of tension and a hint of breathlessness in him, but since he appeared to be on his best behaviour she smiled at him and asked, 'Have you supped.'

'Yes.'

'I didn't know you had returned from Leith. You missed the state opening of parliament.'

He pouted. 'I am not interested in parliament until it gives me the crown matrimonial.'

The temptation to pat him on the shoulder and murmur, 'There, there!' was great, but Mary resisted it. 'You will attend on Tuesday, though? That is when James, your favourite enemy, is to be dispossessed.'

As she spoke, they all heard, as Mary had heard once before, the clatter of an armoured man ascending the private staircase from her husband's bedchamber to her own, which lay next door to the supper room. Darnley's arm tightened around her.

Frowning, Mary said, 'Who – what –'

All eyes were on the doorway when there materialised in it the startling vision of Patrick, Lord Ruthven, hanging onto the frame for support, his eyes feverish in a face skeletal, grey and ghastly. He looked as if he were dying on his feet and, indeed, for three months there had been rumours of it. Few would have mourned him. Protestant though he was, he was also generally believed to be a practitioner of evil magic who numbered his victims in dozens.

But dying men did not appear, uninvited and unannounced, in the queen's retiring room, with steel caps on their heads and full armour showing under their overgowns.

Everyone stared at him.

Disguising her sudden uneasiness, Mary said coldly, 'Lord Ruthven! What do you mean by this intrusion?'

He took a step into the room and, raising a mailed fist, pointed it at David Riccio. 'Let it please your majesty for yon man Davie to leave your private chamber. He has been here too long.'

She frowned and, on a rising note, exclaimed. 'You are out of your senses. Leave us at once, or you will be dealt with more harshly than I would choose to deal with a sick man.'

'I will not go without him. He has offended against your majesty's honour in ways I will not name. He has persuaded your majesty against giving your husband the crown matrimonial that you promised him ...'

Mary's head flashed round at the husband still sitting motionless beside her. 'Is this your doing?'

He mumbled something she did not hear, because at that moment Ruthven made a lunge at Davie.

The spell broke and Erskine and Creich jumped to their feet, daggers drawn, while Davie fled to the end of the table to crouch behind the queen, and Ruthven shouted, 'Lay no hand on me!'

It was the beginning of the nightmare.

The place was suddenly filled with Ruthven's followers, armed and ugly, surging across the room, holding Erskine and Creich at swordpoint, knocking over the table as Mary struggled to her feet. Everyone was shouting or screaming, and Harry had her pinioned in his arms, and Davie had taken a vice-like grip on her skirts, and as she fought wildly to free herself two of the men pressed the muzzles of their pistols to her stomach. They were men she knew, which made it all the more horrible.

Shrieking, 'Harry! Harry!' she turned desperate eyes towards him, but there was no help or comfort there and, even as she sought it, she saw the hand of another man she knew, one of the Douglases, snatch her husband's dagger from its sheath and raise it to strike. But not at her, although she felt the wind of its passing as it flashed down over her bare shoulder in the brief, hideous moment before Davie screamed out in pain and terror.

They tore the little man away from her and dragged him from the room crying, '*Giustizia! Giustizia!* Madame, save me! *Sauvez moi!* Madame! Madame ...'

His cries became wilder as the sound of them faded across the bedchamber. And along the length of the audience chamber. And out to the landing on the great turnpike stair. But by that time, they had become no more than a weak and spasmodic whimpering. Then, suddenly, they stopped.

10

For the handful of people remaining in the supper room, every sense concentrated on the tragedy that was being played out, it was as if the world had been holding its breath.

But then the false silence gave way to commotion, as more murderers crowded up the great turnpike stair crying, 'A Douglas! A Douglas!' and Mary could hear her servants and guards shouting, and blows being exchanged, and Mallie Fleming's voice, clear as a bell, exclaiming again and again, 'How dare you! Let me through. Her majesty needs me,' and then Mary Seton's, 'You will burn in hell for this! Let me through. If you have so much as laid a finger on the queen ...'

Mary's sister Jean had succeeded in slipping out of the supper room during the affray to summon the help that had come too late for Davie, and Erskine and Creich now hurried out to see what they could do.

Mary found herself alone with her husband in the wreck of her supper room.

He released her at last, his face almost as pale as hers, his breathing light and rapid, his mouth slack, and his eyelids, their lashes as long as a girl's, fluttering. He was excited – and not unpleasantly.

Mary herself was shuddering violently, drawing great tearing breaths as she tried to control her rage and her distress. Her back ached horribly and she put a hand briefly to it for support. When she brought the hand forward again it was streaked with blood, though not hers.

Davie's blood, from that first blow struck over her shoulder by George Douglas, using her husband's dagger.

She made only the smallest of sounds.

After a time, her husband said, 'This place is a shambles. We should go into your bedchamber. Perhaps you should lie down?'

Beneath the artificial sympathy in his voice she detected something that – chillingly – hinted at hope. Straightening up, she said, 'Do not think for a moment that I shall miscarry, or die, from this night's work! But by all means let us go next door.'

The bedchamber was warm and pleasant, with its carved and coffered ceiling, its elegant French tapestries, the cushions that she and the Maries had spent so much time embroidering. The fire was still blazing merrily, although it must have been an eternity since a servant had been in to replenish it. And then she thought, not an eternity. No more than twenty minutes could have passed since the peace of her mind had been shattered forever.

There were bloodstains on the floor.

Somehow, she brought herself to turn and look in Harry's eyes and say, 'Why? What have I done to deserve this of you?'

She could see him trying and failing to decide whether to deny responsibility or preen himself for having demonstrated that he was not, after all, a spineless boy but a man capable of taking action when the situation required it. Instead, he launched into all the festering resentments of their life together, so that even what in the early days had been loving and joyful became sordid and distasteful. She had heard most of it before – her disregard for his dignity and his opinions, her objections to his friends, her refusal of the crown matrimonial. Some of his complaints were true. When she had discovered that his courtliness was the obverse of a coin whose other face was decadence, she had at first been disbelieving, then repelled, and finally contemptuous. And publicly so.

What she had not known was how deeply sexual jealousy had eaten into him. She had been amused when she first heard of the gossip about herself and Davie. The queen – and a baseborn servant! It had been too ludicrous to take seriously. It seemed now that she had been wrong to ignore it.

A shadow darkened the door from her audience chamber and she started nervously, and turned.

Ruthven.

She had not had time to experience the fullness of fear during the chaotic scene earlier. Now, she did. Now, with a cold rush of terror, she thought, they hate me and they could kill me easily. If this is a revolution, a real revolution, they have no reason not to.

Her baby kicked inside her.

It was enough. Drawing herself up to her full height, she looked down at Ruthven with contempt. 'My lord,' she said. 'I did not expect to see you again. You look no better than you were, although I have always understood that a draught of blood is an excellent restorative.'

'Wine is better. I have told one of your servants to bring me some.' And then he collapsed into a chair.

She had always recognised her need to live on two levels. As a person, she laughed easily, and wept easily; liked people willingly, and disliked them unwillingly. As a queen, it was different. Charm and authority were weapons, self-discipline an intrinsic principle. It was rare for the two sides of her to collide.

They had done so on the occasions when she had confronted John Knox. Now, they did so with Ruthven. To seat himself, uninvited, while his queen remained standing; to order his queen's servants to cater to his needs ...

11

The torrent of her rage was still sweeping hysterically over her hearers – the threats of vengeance from the kings of France and Spain, the princes of Italy, the might of the papacy – when Lord Gray came hurrying to tell Ruthven that Bothwell, Huntly and Atholl, all of whom had been in other parts of the palace, were trying to fight their way up the outer stair towards the queen.

Mary's heart leapt as Ruthven dragged himself, groaning, from the room, but the clash of arms ceased almost at once, as if a truce had been called. Her heart leapt again when the alarm bell of Edinburgh was rung and the townspeople appeared under her windows demanding to see the queen and be assured of her safety. But by that time her bedchamber was once more full of armed men, and when her husband went to the window to reassure the people and she tried to push him aside and cry for help, Lord Lindsay of the Byres brandished his dagger before her eyes and threatened to cut her in collops and throw her to her people, like meat to the dogs.

They went away, in the end – the townspeople, and the murderers, and even Harry who said, yawning, that he could do with some sleep.

She was sitting limply in a chair by the long-dead fire, her mind skittering about like a rat in the wainscotting, when Fleming and Seton – the old Countess of Huntly trailing behind them, tut-tutting – were at last allowed in to fuss over her and help her prepare for bed. Seton told her that Davie was dead from dozens of dagger wounds, but she was too weary even to weep, although she felt the tears welling up behind her eyes. Bitterly, she said, 'What is the use of weeping? I will pay them back for this.' Then she remembered something and sent Fleming to Davie's room to bring back the little coffer with her ciphers in it and secret letters.

There were guards on her door, and she had no company in the night save for Lady Huntly, whom the murderers thought old enough to be harmless.

She slept the sleep of exhaustion for two hours, and then awoke, reliving everything that had happened and everything that had been said, but no nearer to understanding it. What was very clear was that poor little Davie's murderers would not – could not – simply pack their saddlebags and ride peacefully off in the direction of their homes.

She must escape. She must escape before they decided to kill her too.

Lying lethargically in the stuffy darkness, listening to the sound of Lady Huntly's snoring, she was hampered by her inability to predict what they would do next. She wondered if they even knew themselves.

She did not guess that they were waiting for James to come and tell them.

12

Lethington said, 'Unofficially, I would advise you to leave.'

Bothwell, who both hated and distrusted him, said, 'Why?'

'Because when you tried to fight your way in to rescue the queen,

Ruthven told you that getting rid of Riccio was the sum and substance of the plot and that you should just go back to your supper. And you believed him and you did.'

Huntly, who shared his looks with his sister Jean but not her brains, said, 'Well, what's wrong with that?'

Anxious to get them out of Holyroodhouse as soon as possible, Lethington said, 'We are all grateful to be rid of Riccio, but our dagger-wielding friends did not look to the consequences of killing him in the way that Darnley wanted him killed. A quiet, anonymous little ambush in one of the wynds off the Highgait would have been much more satisfactory. Instead, they have left themselves with no room for manoeuvre. One cannot murder the queen's servant and lock up the queen, and then just walk away.'

'No. What will they do next?'

'That is a question they have not yet resolved. The more optimistic among them think the answer is to hold her prisoner until she consents to pardon them. As for the others, you may guess. That is why I suggest you make good your escape now, before it occurs to them that they cannot afford to leave two of her most powerful adherents free to raise an army to rescue her.'

Bothwell stroked a stubby-fingered hand over his jaw. 'You're saying they'd murder us, too?'

'It's possible.'

'Why the warning? You like me no more than I like you.'

'We both, however, like the queen.'

Whatever his faults, Bothwell was quick to make up his mind. 'Right. We'll climb out of one of the back windows. Are you coming, Huntly? We can be in Dunbar by soon after dawn and I can start getting my mosstroopers together.'

13

Just before daybreak, Mary drifted up from a restless doze to the awareness of someone sitting on the edge of her bed. She did not at first open her eyes, not until she was sure that there was no expression in them.

It was Harry, as she had guessed, and he was full of remorse for what had happened the night before and begging her to forgive him.

And expecting her to believe him.

250

He was once again the disarming, soft-faced youth with whom she had fallen in love – and as untrustworthy now as she supposed he must have been then.

'Oh, Mary! My Mary. I meant no harm. I swear to you, I did not know it was going to be like that.'

'No, Harry. I am sure you didn't.'

His hazel eyes were large and melting, and his girlish lips unsteady, but Mary did not believe for a moment that it was remorse that possessed him. Nothing in the nineteen years of his life had prepared him for the crude violence of the evening before. He had enjoyed it, almost pantingly, at the time, but in the solitary darkness of the long March night it must have been borne in on him that he was out of his depth. He was afraid.

She didn't know, or very much care how deeply involved he had been. Even a little was too much. All that interested her was that she could use him, could turn his desire for a reconciliation to account. She was prepared to make use of anyone and anything that would help her to escape from the men she thought she had known, but knew no longer.

Lady Huntly, helping her dress after Harry had departed for his own rooms, proved to be full of clever schemes. She was a little huffy when Mary rejected her suggestion of a rope ladder, but Mary said, 'It's not my dignity that worries me. It's the size of my stomach and the size of the window and the twenty feet of space beneath it. Now we know that your son and Lord Bothwell have escaped the palace, what I need is for you to smuggle out a letter to them.'

Soon after, tucking the letter between her chemise and her skin, Lady Huntly said, 'They'll maybe search me but, if they ettle tae search me as close as yon, I'll give them a skelp round the lugs they'll not forget for a while.'

Mary laughed, a little weakly. 'In case they don't let you come back, I should tell you that I intend to be very unwell this afternoon.' If she could only convince the conspirators that she had neither the desire nor the ability to try and escape, it was possible that they might remove the guards from her apartments; even if they didn't, the guards might become careless. 'Do you think you and the Maries could set up a commotion – you could even skelp a few more people round the lugs – just to make it more convincing?'

Three hours later, she gave such a superb rendering of a terrified woman on the brink of a miscarriage that even the hastily summoned midwife believed her.

It was a beginning.

James had taken care not to know the finer details of how Riccio was to be killed. He had also ensured that, when it happened, he himself would be very publicly elsewhere, riding from Newcastle to Edinburgh with a large and formal escort. Having been commanded to present himself before parliament on the following Tuesday in order that his objections against his forfeiture might be heard, he had a foolproof excuse for the journey.

He was disapproving when he arrived on the Sunday evening and discovered how the business had been handled, and much concerned over the shock to his sister, although he felt no compulsion to rush to her side to sympathise. Instead, after supper, he and Rothes joined in the second conference of the day between Morton, Ruthven, Lindsay, George Douglas and young Darnley who, this time, had brought his father with him for moral support.

If he had been intimidated earlier by Morton and Douglas, who were kinsmen of his, Darnley was completely overawed by the new arrivals, all very much older and more experienced than he was, and whose dislike and distrust of him – bonds or no bonds – were clearly as great as they had ever been. Morton also happened to mention, in passing, that it had taken fifty-six stab wounds to despatch David Riccio, and that by a queer oversight someone had left Darnley's own dagger in the body.

If his mother had not been so far away, he would have run to her. As it was, he hurried home to Holyrood and his wife.

15

Tears in his eyes, his golden curls becomingly ruffled, he stood at the side of the bed where she lay looking as weak and ill as she could contrive and said, 'I have let you down. Will you ever forgive me? If I confess everything to you, will you shrive my soul?'

'Only a priest can shrive your soul,' she said, rebuke and encouragement exquisitely blended in her voice. There was nothing she wanted more than to discover what he had to confess, because although she knew that the Douglases, with some help from her husband, had been responsible for killing Davie, she still had no idea why they should have been involved. All she knew was that the murder of her servant and her own imprisonment could not be isolated incidents, but must be part of some greater design.

'It was the crown matrimonial,' her husband muttered. 'I wanted it so much. And they promised me that, if I agreed to letting Moray and the others come back, they would get it for me. So I did.'

'Oh, Harry!'

She did not yet see how Davie's death fitted in, but because it would have struck a wrong note if she had asked, she merely said, '"They" promised you? Who were "they"?'

He shrugged. 'All the usual people. Moray and his friends, Morton and Glencairn, Ochiltree, Argyll, Lethington, Boyd ...'

'Did they make you sign anything?'

'Yes, but I made *them* sign, too.' Almost eagerly, proud of having been so businesslike, he produced copies of his bond with James and his friends and theirs with him. She read the documents carefully, and noticed that the signatures, most of them barely legible, did not include Lethington's neat and elegant 'W. Maitland'. It made no difference; it was inconceivable that he had not been involved in the affair. Also missing was any mention of Davie.

Darnley said, 'Your brother and Rothes and Glencairn and the others have just arrived back in Edinburgh. I've been at Morton's house and seen them and it's shocking – they mean to imprison you until the child is born.'

It was better than being murdered.

After a moment, she said, 'Indeed? And who will rule the country in the meantime?'

'They say me, under their guidance, but I don't believe them. I think they hope you'll die in childbirth. Women often do, and your health isn't good. And I've just thought – if you die and the child survives, they won't need me any more. They'll kill me too and then they can be regents for the child, and have all the power for themselves.'

Why? Why had she married him? How could she ever have been in love with him? Such a weak, inconstant, *stupid* boy. There was no more lethal combination than youth, ambition and stupidity.

His imagination had been running ahead of him, but she recognised that what he said was a possibility, though only if they were able – in these next few weeks – to surmount the diplomatic and political problems of keeping a queen regnant in forcible confinement.

He was tugging childishly at her hand. 'You have to stop it.'

253

Not 'I', not 'we', but 'you'.

She would not have expected anything else. She said, 'Yes. But first we must escape from here, and this is how we will do it.'

16

James came to see her next morning and Mary threw herself in his arms, crying, 'If only you had been here, no one would have dared to treat me as they did.' She even believed it until James, at his most irritatingly consequential, lectured her on her own sins of omission and commission. His rebellion, it seemed, had been all her fault.

He came again in the afternoon, in company with Morton and Ruthven, both of them on what passed for their best behaviour. They had intended, they said, only to lock Davie up for a night or two before putting him on trial for dishonouring the queen's majesty, but there had been a lot of men milling about on the staircase, and some who were badly disposed towards him had stuck their daggers in him. These things happened.

Mary, like Lethington, was familiar with the works of Machiavelli, although, until she had become acquainted with her Scots lords, she had seen no particular reason to credit the Florentine's thesis that all men were selfish, treacherous, cowardly, greedy, gullible and witless. Now, remembering the corollary that a prince should keep faith with no one, since no one would keep faith with him, Mary raised her chin regally and said she was prepared to forgive and forget. If the lords cared to draw up a bond to that effect, she would sign it.

It was an assurance that, punctuated by some well-judged gasps of pain and an occasional clutch at the waist of her quilted bodice, achieved its object of persuading them to withdraw their guards, 'so that she might be comfortable again'. She was even allowed to have her chamber woman, Margaret Carwood, with her.

At midnight, the queen, Darnley and Margaret Carwood crept down the privy stair into a pantry in the undercroft and, from there, squeezed out through a broken-down door into the burial ground of the old abbey church of Holyrood. Beyond the graves were waiting Mary's Captain of the Guard, her Master of the Horse, and a handful of loyal soldiers.

Born to a crown and reared at the court of the Valois, where the other side of the divine right of kings was an equally divine insistence on stamina, Mary had early learned physical endurance.

Despite her pregnancy, therefore, and despite the cold and the darkness and the thirty hard-riding miles, with a panicky Darnley flogging Mary's mount as wildly as his own, when the little party reached Dunbar castle five hours later she did not give way to physical collapse. Instead, surveying the comfortless keep perched on its rock above a grey and wind-tossed harbour, she demanded eggs for breakfast and cooked them herself, then launched into discussions with Bothwell and Huntly.

Bothwell, a tower of strength, had already begun summoning his mosstroopers, and within the next few days the Lords Atholl, Fleming, Livingston and Seton arrived with reinforcements. By the end of the week, Mary had decided to order a general muster at Haddington on the following Monday.

Harry, his opinions unsought, went riding by day and drank himself insensible by night.

By the Friday, still unsure of how the situation would develop, Mary was writing to France, Spain, Italy and England asking for her friends' support. Her letter to England was unusually long and emotional, describing the harrowing death of her 'most special servant' and her own captivity, and begging her good sister Elizabeth, from the love she bore her, to be ever fearful of the danger of betrayal by men she trusted.

The letter, as it happened, came as something of an anticlimax to Elizabeth, who had heard from Randolph as early as the middle of February that Davie was soon to have his throat cut and that there was word also of a threat to Mary's life. By the day of the murder she had even been provided with the agenda of the conspiracy, the names of those involved, and the full text of the bonds that had been signed.

Although she had felt no compulsion to warn Mary of what was afoot, it was mildly interesting to hear her side of the story and Elizabeth was – of course – pleased that her good sister had survived.

'De'il take it!' had sworn Morton when he heard of the royal couple's escape. Stamping around the room with such vigour that the horses in the stables below whinnied in protest, he went on, 'I told ye – did I not tell ye? – that they were no' tae be trusted? But she was the queen and Darnley was my kinsman – dod! I'll kill the wee rat! – and "I've signed a bond", says he, and "I give ye my word", says he, and we believed him. And now they've gone. What's a bond for, I ask ye, if ye cannae trust what it says?'

'How true,' agreed Lethington suavely. 'The question, however, is what are you going to do now?'

Morton gave up stamping. 'You're supposed to be the clever one. You tell us.'

Lethington shook his head. 'If you remember, it wasn't my plot. I am merely an interested bystander.'

'Huh!'

'Very well. Looking at it coldly, your options are either to give in or to fight. But you should remember that, although her majesty may not be popular with you, she still has a remarkable grip on the hearts of her people. Also, I would guess that she is on her way to join up with Bothwell, who is probably raising an army for her. That means you will need one too. Can you raise one in a hurry? Are you prepared to start a war? And all for the sake of Davie Riccio?'

James said, 'Come on, now. That's not what it's all been about.'

'No, but that's what it looks like. Morton, Ruthven, Lindsay and George Douglas, here, will *appear* to be fighting simply to save their skins and although you, Argyll, Rothes and Glencairn are lily-white innocents with no reason to become involved, if you *don't* become involved the battle's lost before it begins.'

George Douglas said, 'What's wrong with starting a nice wee war? It'd clear the air,' but his was a lone voice.

James said, chewing his lip, 'There must be some other way.'

But they had failed to think of one when they heard that the queen was proposing to ride back into Edinburgh in triumph next day at the head of an army of eight thousand men.

In the resulting diaspora, with the guilty parties departing hurriedly for England and even the innocents prudently finding themselves with things to do elsewhere, James went to Linlithgow and discovered that Argyll was there ahead of him, while John Knox, who had noisily applauded the murder, fled to Ayrshire amid the lamentations of the godly.

Even Lethington, warned by Atholl that her majesty counted him among the guilty, accepted his friend's invitation to make himself at home at the earl's Highland fastness of Dunkeld until everything settled down.

If it ever did.

Chapter Twelve

MARCH 1566-JANUARY 1567

1

Mary rode back into Edinburgh in triumph with Bothwell at the head of his four thousand Border spearmen and four companies of professional infantry. In her train, too, with their followers, were the predominantly Catholic earls and lords of Atholl, Sutherland, Crawford, Cassilis, Caithness, Marischal, Seton, Fleming, Huntly, Livingston and Home.

It was just six days since she had fled Holyrood on her wild night ride to Dunbar, with only a handful of followers, and the speed and very different style of her return were due in part to her own feverish energy, in part to Bothwell's military effectiveness, but mainly to a growing alchemy between the two. When action was in prospect, they shared the same dashing and reckless spirit.

Riding by her side was Harry, a Harry sulkily aware that all the cheering was for her and none for him but nevertheless behaving well, smiling and bowing as a king should do. She had almost succeeded in persuading herself that he was too contemptibly weak for his part in the murder of Riccio to have been other than a passive one. She could not afford to believe otherwise.

She remembered, with a twist of irony, discussing potential husbands with the Maries years before, and Fleming saying how heartbreaking it would be to marry some member of a foreign royal house for love and then be kept apart by the need for him to rule his own country while Mary continued to rule hers. And Mary had giggled and said, 'Whereas if I married from policy and found my husband unlovable, it would be a positive blessing!'

But Harry was her husband, and her king, and nothing else. He had nowhere else to go, and there was nothing to separate them except themselves.

257

Her flesh crept at the thought of returning to Holyroodhouse, where assassins – and husbands – could come and go at will, so she spent her first nights back in Edinburgh at the house of the Bishop of Dunkeld and needed little urging when her privy council recommended that, at least until after the birthing, she should stay in the long, low palace block her grandfather had built within Edinburgh castle more than half a century before. Beds and hangings were hastily brought, carved oak tables, chairs upholstered in gilded leather, tapestries for the walls and carpets for the floors of the private apartments. They did not have the beckoning comfort that almost five years of residence had given to Holyrood, but neither did they have the memories.

She was just beginning to feel more tranquil in her mind when the conspirators, revenging themselves on the youth who had betrayed them by helping his wife to escape and thus bringing about their ruin, sent her a copy of the bond he had made with Ruthven.

It proved that it had been Darnley himself who had insisted on Riccio being murdered in his wife's presence and who had devised the manner of it. Lord Ruthven had at first disliked the idea, fearing the blood feuds that might ensue if anyone other than the unfortunate Davie should be killed or wounded in the affray. He had demanded some kind of indemnity. And so Harry, to protect the murderers and their families, had arrogantly signed a bond assuming responsibility both for the murder and the way it was to be carried out.

There was no mistaking the wording of the bond. 'A stranger Italian called David ... who might happen to be killed ... which might chance to be done in the presence of the queen's majesty ...'

Nor was there any mistaking the signature.

3

She didn't tell Harry. She tried very hard to convince herself that what had brought him to her after Davie's death, what had persuaded him to escape with her, had been a true revulsion of feeling. But she could not rely on it. After her child was born, she would think what to do, but until then they must seem to be reconciled.

So, when he insisted on declaring his innocence before her privy council, swearing that he had never 'commanded, consented, assisted nor approved' the death of her majesty's Piedmontese servant, she listened sympathetically to his lies and agreed that a signed declaration stating them might be posted, as he wished, at the Mercat Cross.

It was necessary to bind him to her, in case resentment, spite or ambition suggested to him that he might deny having fathered the child who would be heir to her throne.

4

Her new surroundings in the castle, she soon discovered, were only marginally stranger than her new privy council and a good deal quieter, the clash of arms less deafening than the clash of personalities.

Little though she had wanted to reinstate James, she had been left without a choice, since his six months' absence seemed to have attracted to him a greater following than his presence had ever done. And if she reinstated James, then Argyll and Glencairn had to be reinstated, too. She trusted none of them, but her victory over their murderous friends had put her in a strong enough position to decree that they must pay what was for them the bitter price of sharing the government with three men of whose loyalty she had no doubt – Bothwell, Huntly and Atholl.

To Bothwell alone, in gratitude for his strength, decision and resourcefulness, she gave her trust and confidence.

There had always been personal undercurrents among her councillors – Argyll and Atholl had been at feud for years – but there had been a tacit agreement to keep them out of the council chamber as far as possible. It was different now. Although they swore to Mary that they would reach some kind of *modus vivendi*, their promises were like their bonds, statements of goodwill rather than pledges of intent. James made no secret of his hatred for Bothwell, just as Bothwell and Huntly made no secret of theirs for him. Even Argyll, James's oldest ally, was at odds with him because he could no longer stomach the English alliance to which James was still committed. He had, indeed – or so Huntly later reported to an unsurprised Mary – turned a worrying shade of purple when he heard that, before leaving England, James had written to the double-dealing Elizabeth to thank her for her many kindnesses and assure her that she had not within Europe a more affectionate servitor.

By the middle of May, lacking anyone to keep them in order, the privy

259

council found its meetings becoming ever more irritating and unproductive. After one particularly frustrating morning when nothing had been agreed except that it should be made illegal to shoot deer with cannon and that foreigners should be forbidden to fish in Highland lochs, James said, 'We need Lethington back. He's got a knack of putting things in perspective.'

Bothwell, who did not like subtle men in general and Lethington in particular, sneered. 'You mean talking folk into doing what *he* wants them to do.'

'No, that's not what I mean. What I mean is that, though he and I don't see eye to eye the way we once did, he's got a knack of putting his finger on the essentials. If he were here, we'd spend a damn' sight less time arguing round in circles and more time making decisions.'

'The wrong ones.'

Languidly, Huntly asked, 'Where is he, anyway?'

James said, 'My sister told him to go abroad, then changed her mind and said he was to ward himself in Caithness. I still don't understand why she's so convinced that he was involved in the Riccio business but, from what I hear, her change of mind probably saved his life.' He stared at Bothwell. 'I'm told our hereditary Lord High Admiral here had ships waiting for him at sea.'

Bothwell didn't deny it but merely went on whistling under his breath. It was one of his most aggravating habits.

Tight-lipped, James said, 'Anyway, he's in ward in Caithness until she's prepared to pardon him.'

'Which will be never,' Bothwell said.

'Aye, if you have anything to do with it. Ye'd have to give him back those lands at Haddington that the queen's taken from him and given to you.' Ignoring Bothwell's darkening countenance, he went on, 'But I tell ye, I won't rest until Lethington's restored, and Morton, too.'

'Funny, isn't it?' Bothwell said savagely. 'Just think – only a couple of months ago, it was Lethington and Morton who were working their balls off to get *you* reinstated. How the world turns! But don't be too sure of yourself.' Rising, he strode to the door. 'There's one or two of us have advised the queen to put you under guard when she's confined with the child. It would never do for you to bring Lethington and Morton home when she's in no state to stop you.'

The door slammed and James, through gritted teeth, said, 'I'll see the end of that man, if it's the last thing I do.'

Late on the morning of 19th June, in a roomful of witnesses and after a long and painful labour, Mary gave birth to a son who was miraculously strong and healthy.

His father came to see him in the afternoon – and to discover for the first time what his wife truly thought of him.

Propped up in the huge bed which, with its hangings of blue velvet and taffeta, dominated the small, dark-panelled lying-in chamber, she stared at him exhaustedly for a moment before gesturing to Lady Reres to give her the swaddled little bundle that was her son. Then, drawing the coif aside from the baby's sleeping face, she spoke in a voice that was weak but disastrously clear, her words addressed not to her husband alone but to all who were present.

'I swear to God, and will so swear at the Judgement Day, that this is your son, and no other man's. And I wish everyone here to bear witness to it, because he is so much your son that I fear it will be the worse for him hereafter.'

Then she turned her head away, as if she had no further interest in him, and said with a faint smile to one of the bystanders, 'This is the son who will first unite the two kingdoms of Scotland and England.'

' "First", Madame? Surely your majesty and your son's father will do that?'

'Not his father.'

Into the silence that had fallen on the suffocating little room, her husband foolishly stammered, 'But you promised to forgive and forget!'

'I have forgiven, but how can I forget!' She drew a harsh breath. 'If the flint and steel had met when Fawdonside pressed his pistol to my stomach, what would have become of my child, and of me!'

'That's all over. It's past.'

Was it? She didn't know.

Five hundred bonfires were lit in Edinburgh on the night of the little prince's birth. Lords and commoners alike gave thanks at St Giles for the arrival of an heir. Both the queen and her infant son were startled into tears of fright when all twenty-five of the castle's great bronze cannon were fired off in ragged unison.

By that time Sir James Melville was already at Berwick en route for the court of Elizabeth. His mission being urgent, the weather fine and the post horses feeling their oats, he reached London only four days later.

It was, however, not he but Secretary Cecil who broke the news to Elizabeth, an Elizabeth who, furious with jealousy over Robert Dudley's flirtation with her own voluptuous cousin, Lettice Knollys, and in a torment of indecision over the renewed negotiations for her own match with the Archduke Charles, had become prone to uncomfortably frequent Tudor tantrums.

She had been dancing after supper, cheerfully enough, when Cecil murmured in her ear and she sat down suddenly in a chair, head in hand. The music stopped just as she raised her voice above it, so that not only her ladies but everyone else in the room heard the eruption of her anger and frustration.

'The queen of Scots is lighter of a fair son. While I am still barren.'

7

Mallie Fleming, released for a few days from serving a mistress who was kind and generous but more demanding than she knew, fled from Edinburgh, leaving in charge Mary Livingston, whose own proud motherhood had transformed her from a merry, scatterbrained girl into an alarmingly respectable young matron.

The Dowager Lady Fleming took one swift look at her daughter when she arrived at the family home in Ayrshire, and exclaimed, 'Sweetheart! You look quite tired and drawn! What has been going on to make you so worn out?'

After a moment of helpless disbelief, Mallie sat down and began to laugh. If her mother had been eighty years old and ignorant of courts and kings, her question might have been reasonable enough. But Jenny Fleming was still plump and seductive, even in her early fifties, and her youngest son had been fathered by King Henri II of France. Mallie would never forget the scandal of it all.

'Mother! How can you! You *must* know what has been going on?'

'That poor little man being murdered, you mean, and all those political comings and goings? Oh, well, I take no account of that kind of thing, especially when my saintly nephew James is involved. I have often wondered why someone does not murder *him*. No, let us have a cup of hippocras and you can tell me about her majesty and the baby. Though goodness knows how long we will be able to afford to go on drinking hippocras. The cost of spices, my dear! And then you must tell me all your troubles, because I can see that you are not yourself at all. You need your mother's advice.'

Though Jenny Fleming was a darling and by no means as silly as she sometimes chose to sound, none of her children would have dreamed of taking her advice on anything – other than, perhaps, seduction or spices. Mallie said, 'All I want in the world is to sleep, not on the floor, not on top of a chest, not even in a truckle bed, but privately, in my own feather bed, in my own room, for days, and days, and days.'

Jenny, mildly surprised, said, 'If you wish, my love. But when you wake up we must talk about your future. I am becoming quite concerned, because you are twenty-three years old and most girls have been married and widowed at least twice by your age.'

Two days later, Mallie Fleming sat down in blessed solitude and began to compose a letter.

My lord,

If you were here, I would be in your arms and nothing else would matter. But you are not here. It is six months since I have seen you even in passing, and more than four months since I have seen you at all. I still do not know your mind. Your letters have told me why my cousin James had to be brought home regardless of the cost, and I think I understand, although Madame does not and never will. I also understand why poor Davie had to be removed although truly his influence was less weighty than you thought. And my head understands, though my heart does not, why, knowing so much, you uttered no word of warning to me. But, but, but ...

You have explained your reasoning to me, but I know that reasoning is sometimes only a veneer on the surface of a different truth. I cannot tell. Some day, perhaps, when we can spend hours together rather than minutes, it may be different.

Why do you love me?

The queen has been quite unlike herself since the little prince's birth, tearful and indecisive. She continues to forbid the king her bed, and he does not understand that this is common with women after childbirth. He has gone back to drinking and whoring again. If he were merely dissolute, it would be bearable, but he treats her majesty harshly and his head is full of wild plans to get the better of her. I sometimes think he is as mad as poor Don Carlos.

It seems a very long time since the court was a cheerful place.

Did you know that, in April, Mary Beaton married Alexander Ogilvie? It was an arranged match, of course, with a quiet wedding at Beaton's home in Fife. No cloth of silver, but her majesty gave Beaton a lovely diamond and ruby carcanet instead. Jean Gordon – whom I *cannot* think of as Lady Bothwell – was not among the guests and, being Jean, would not have wept if she had been. But, somewhere inside me, I wept for her and for Alexander, too. Never mind, at least Beaton is happy, and they make the most amazingly handsome couple.

Jean, I should tell you, is not at all pleased with her new husband, who has already betrayed her with one of her sewing maids. I report this to you only because it may amuse you as, sardonically, it amuses Jean, that my cousin – with whom I am losing all patience – seems invariably to have chosen church steeples and cloisters for his assignations.

James has been reinstated as one of Madame's leading advisers and I feel almost warmly towards him, because he gives her majesty no respite from his demands for your restoration. I make my own small contribution to his campaign by looking lovelorn, as if I am wasting away for need of you.

As indeed I am.

She signed it with a little flourish of initials and, next day, sent one of the grooms off on the long and testing journey to Caithness, the most northerly tip of Scotland, to deliver it. She had no need to wonder what Lethington was doing in that lonely wilderness. He would be thinking – thinking – thinking.

8

Mary felt, sometimes, as if she would scream if one more angry voice were raised, one more harsh word spoken. It was almost impossible to believe that, until just a year before, no one in her life had ever shouted at her or even raised his voice in her presence. Except John Knox, who was a special case.

Two evenings before, 'I'll kill him!' Harry had raved for no good reason that she could discover, and, helplessly, she had seen nothing for it but to tell James, little though she loved him.

The August sun was sinking, its warmth giving a rosy sheen to the unnaturally calm silken waters of the firth, as she strolled along the parapet walk of the castle after a late supper in the company of some of her ladies and gentlemen, James among them. And then Harry came

264

stalking out, his face like thunder as he observed her surrounded by the friends and intimates who saw so much more of her than he did.

Before he could speak, James stepped forward. 'Ye're threatening to kill me, I'm told?'

It was so easy to read the expressions chasing one another over Harry's face – the desire to run his sword through the man who wielded far more power than he himself had ever been granted; the knowledge that he dared not; the shiftiness as he tried, and failed, to think of something crushing to say.

His only advantage that of height, he looked down, face flushed, on James and said, 'Perhaps.'

'Why?'

'I'll trouble you to address me correctly.'

Mockery was not James's style, but there was a curl to his wide, thin-lipped mouth as he replied, 'May it please your majesty to condescend to tell your most obedient subject in what way he has erred?'

The hatred between the two men was almost palpable.

A shudder passed through Harry's tall, slender frame as he succeeded in saying, 'I was informed that you bear ill will towards me.'

And then he glanced round and became aware of all the eyes watching him. If he had been drunk or in a rage nothing would have stopped him. But he was neither. He was twenty years old, inexperienced and a coward at heart, and to face down a man fifteen years his senior in age and assurance was beyond him. When James made no reply, he added, 'If this is not so, I … If I was misinformed, I repent of what I said.'

Mary said, 'Thank you, Harry. Please understand that I will not permit you or anyone else to be at odds with Lord Moray. I will have no feuds and no raised voices at my court. Remember that.'

9

A year before, she would have been obeyed, for a time at least. Now, not even James paid much attention. Pompous and overbearing he had always been, but never loud and never undignified. He had always behaved as if it was beneath him to lose his temper. But the very next day he invited a vicious row with Bothwell. She thought, for a moment, that slaughter would be the end of it.

She and James had been discussing the problem of Harry, and not just the stupid, dangerous things he was doing, like ranging Edinburgh's dark wynds with only one or two servants for company, drinking himself insensible, demanding to have the castle gates opened to him at dead of night, swimming in lochs and rivers unarmed and unattended.

Mary's recurring nightmare was that he would snatch their son from her. From almost the moment he was born she had feared desperately for her child. She could not bear for him to be out of her sight, kept his cradle in her room, watched over him in the hours of darkness. It was not only maternal love for a helpless scrap of humanity; it was also that princes were exposed to more than the ordinary dangers of infancy. Whoever held the child held power.

'What would I do if he held him to ransom? He cares far more for himself than the child. He might threaten to kill him if I don't grant him the crown matrimonial! Or he might crown the child and depose me, and then rule as regent.'

James said, 'Ye're letting your imagination run away with you.' But he looked thoughtful.

'Monsieur du Croc tells me he is continually trying to discredit me with the Catholic powers. And now I hear that he has some wild plot to raise a rebellion of English Catholics in order to turn Elizabeth off her throne. If Elizabeth were to discover it ... We must do something. You are one of my chief councillors – *you* must do something.'

'I can't, Mary,' James said, at his most sanctimonious. 'Where Elizabeth's concerned, my conscience wouldn't allow me to tell her he *isn't* plotting against her if he *is*. And as for the Catholic powers, they've no time for me. They think I'm a worse threat to the church of Rome than Knox himself.'

Drily, she said, 'Which you find not unflattering.'

He ignored it. 'I've said it before and I'll say it again, what ye need ...'

She knew. On a rising note, she forestalled him. 'Yes, yes, yes. I need Lethington back.' She had fought against summoning him back because he was charming and civilised and accomplished, and it was dangerous to feel too personal a warmth for a man one could not trust. She had no idea what underlay the charm, what went on in the private depths of the brain she had learned to admire.

'Well, ye do need him. I swear to you, he did no more than give me some lawyerly advice about my bond with your husband last March and yet ye've taken Darnley's unsupported word that he was one of the ones responsible for killing your wee singer.'

It was at that point that Bothwell swaggered in, swarthy and muscular, invincibly arrogant, knowing himself favoured, never doubting his welcome.

'Lethington?' he exploded. 'Over my dead body.'

She had thought, at first, that it had to do with Lethington's long-standing alliance with James, but in the climate of tension that had been growing at court for the last months, she had come to see that what had once been a mild discomfort over Lethington's cleverness was developing into something closer to suspicion. And not only on Bothwell's part.

In the lords' view, you were either for them or against them, and Lethington's detachment was alien to their way of life and way of thinking. He was the egregious one in the wild and undisciplined flock of her subjects, a *politique*, one of those whose belief in tolerance and compromise would always be scornfully rejected by others in the certainty that their own truth was the only truth.

Even so, James was right. Through the dragging tiredness of the mind that had possessed her since the birth of her son, she knew that it was necessary to restore some semblance of calm and rationality not only to privy council meetings at home but to affairs abroad. Lethington was the only man capable of handling the situation and, since everyone was suspicious of everyone else, stirring another ingredient into the brew could hardly make things worse. It was ironic that the subtle Lethington should be mistrusted for making too many concessions, and the unsubtle Bothwell for making too few.

She was opening her mouth to try to explain to Bothwell why she needed Lethington back when James snapped, 'Shut your mouth, man! Ye're in her majesty's presence and it's her majesty who decides what's what, not a lout like you.'

Mary's hands flew to her mouth, the easy tears all too close, as Bothwell turned an ugly colour and took three swift steps forward. Before James could move, he had sunk his fingers in James's shoulders, thumbs and figures gouging into the muscles, front and back, until it seemed as if they must meet through the flesh. Then he picked him up and shook him, like a wild animal shaking its prey. And then dropped him back in his seat.

Mary shrieked, 'No, James!'

He was on his feet, his sword half out of the scabbard and Bothwell was standing back, arms curved ape-like, grinning as if he needed no other weapons. He was inches shorter than James, but miles more frightening.

And then James slammed the sword back in its scabbard and said,

'You'll pay,' and Bothwell grinned even more widely and said, 'Who'll make me?'

Mary sank back in her chair. She should have rebuked Bothwell, should have sent him away for a time at least, but she couldn't. Her voice shaking, she said, 'Lord Bothwell, I know you are opposed to the return of Secretary Lethington and I know you would like to keep his lands at Haddington. But I have made my decision. Don't you understand? Somehow, we must restore my realm to sanity. Help me!'

At once, his face changed and he stepped forward, and knelt, and kissed her hand. He was perfectly civil with people who were civil to him.

He was also the only solid rock in the terrible, shifting sea around her, the only man on whom she knew she could unequivocally rely, and for that she would have forgiven him anything. He was ambitious, but who was not? His political judgement was not reliable, but whose was? He was difficult. He was rough. But he was an honest man with many good qualities.

She was becoming dependent on him, and knew it to be dangerous. By showing him favour, giving him power, she was also bringing down on him the envy and hatred of others. In the long, fear-racked nights when, hour after hour, she rose to look to the baby and could not sleep afterwards, she remembered the fate of the other man who had been servant, friend and adviser to her.

But she could no longer live, she thought exhaustedly, without someone to lean on.

10

Nothing improved.

She began taking exercise again, hoping to overcome her lethargy and depression. She went sailing round the coast, accompanied only by her ladies, and the freedom and the cool, salt, refreshing breezes gave her a brief sense of wellbeing. But afterwards she and Harry went hunting at Traquair on the Borders, where Harry made an unspeakably vulgar public scene. And then, at the end of the month, he announced, in the presence of the French ambassador, that he was leaving the country because the queen did not permit him the intimacy that an honest wife should and that he was not honoured and trusted as a king should be.

After that, she sent the baby Prince James – her dearest 'little man' – to the safety of Stirling, with a guard of five hundred arquebusiers.

By October, riding to Jedburgh on the Borders to hold a justice sitting, she was so weary and discouraged that she feared it might prove beyond her to pronounce on the guilt or innocence of poachers and coin-clippers and Border reivers. And bad was made worse when she arrived to be met with the news that Bothwell, sent ahead to round up malefactors for her, had run foul of one who had no intention of being rounded up. He had been severely wounded and was said to be unlikely to live.

She struggled through the week, the all too familiar pain griping at her side, and then set out for the south-west and Bothwell's fortress of Hermitage with James and members of her court to discover whether her Lieutenant of the Marches was alive or dead.

There was no accommodation for women at Hermitage and little enough for Mary's privy councillors and escort, so the journey there and back had to be made in a day, a ride of something over fifty miles. It did not sound too taxing.

The countryside, its shallow rivers running fast and full of fish, was gloriously autumnal with vivid green patches of grass and moss, fiery gold bracken, the purple of heather sheeting the drier hillsides, and copper-coloured reeds marking the bogs. Mary was sad to see the derelict churches – roofless, empty of windows, fonts and vestments – but she knew that the harm had been done more by the old church's negligence and the destructiveness of English armies than the depredations of John Knox and his followers.

They had set out at sunrise, but a roadless landscape with much scrambling up steep braes, skirting of bogs and fording of flooded burns made for poor speed and it was almost midday when, half-soaked and splashed with black peaty mud, they came at last in sight of the vast grey arch that gave admission to Hermitage.

The queen's Lieutenant of the Marches turned out to be convincingly alive and on his feet, even if his temper was as ragged as his multitudinous bandages and his complexion more sallow than swarthy.

Mary's relief was enormous. 'Scotland cannot afford to lose you,' she said.

Lethington, recently reinstated and acutely sensitive to new resonances, noted that there was no echoing chorus from her privy councillors. Huntly's allegiance to Bothwell was apparently unchanged, but James, who would once have taken care to guard his expression, was allowing his annoyance to show. 'Pacifying' the Borders had always, of course, been one of his favourite hobbies and he had resented having to hand the task over to Bothwell. The lieutenancy carried as great powers as could be granted to any subject, entitling its holder not only to pursue and besiege, to use fire and sword, but to direct letters in his sovereign's name and command assistance from others on pain of death.

'What happened?' Mary asked when they were seated before the traditional Borderer's dinner of barley porridge, milk and meat. Hermitage had not been designed for the entertainment of queens and their courts.

Bothwell swore. 'Elliots, damned Elliots! We were chasing Jock o' the Park and caught up with him by the Liddel Water. It's marshy and he dismounted and took to his heels. I'd outdistanced my men and I shot at him, then I tripped over a stump and measured my length. I was just turning to get up when he came back at me with his big two-handed sword. I couldn't get at my own sword so I could only stab up at him with my whinger. He got away just before my men arrived' – his lips twisted in grim humour – 'to find their invincible leader, bleeding profusely from head, hand and hip, in a dead faint at their feet. They had to drag me home on a sledge.'

The queen shuddered. 'You must rest until you are fully recovered.'

Her host snorted. 'Rest? Just give me two days more and I'll perforate any Elliots, Armstrongs or Johnstones who come my way so thoroughly that your majesty will be able to strain your broth through them.'

They talked briefly about privy council business, and Bothwell's immediate responsibilities, and then left in order to complete their return journey by a nightfall that, in October, came not long after five in the afternoon.

11

Mary collapsed out of her saddle when they arrived at the small house she had rented for her stay in Jedburgh, and by next day she was vomiting until it seemed there could be nothing left inside her, the pain and misery so severe that she lost consciousness and, even when awake, was unable either to speak or see but fell into convulsions. On and on it went for days, without respite, until it began to seem that death was something not to be resisted but prayed for.

By then, the news of her illness had spread and the vultures had gathered in the little town – the ambassadors and envoys, the thieves and cutpurses, the astrologers and alchemists, the healers and witches' familiars – the sound of their gossip and spells a macabre counterpoint to the prayers being said in the churches.

Within the house there was no rest for anyone, and little space to move. The servants' quarters on the ground floor were as full of ambassadorial messengers as of servants. The hall on the first floor was crammed with councillors and courtiers, gossiping, speculating, trying to reach decisions, while the small retiring room next to it had been taken over by the queen's physicians and apothecaries. The queen in the bedchamber above was surrounded by ladies and chamber women, priests and surgeons, all of them invading the Maries' small space under the roof for a few snatched hours of rest. The owner of the house was one of the Kerrs, a famously lefthanded family whose turnpikes always wound the wrong way to allow their sword arms freedom of movement. Not a day passed without two or three of the royal entourage misjudging the treads and tumbling down the stone stairs.

In the early morning of the ninth day the queen had a seizure that paralysed her whole body, so that it seemed to those present that, this time, her loss of consciousness was for ever. Her chamber women, weeping and sobbing, threw open the window to allow her spirit to fly free, while the Earl of Moray providently began to collect up his sister's silver and her rings.

But her French physician refused to be defeated, massaging warmth back into her limbs, forcing wine down her throat, and administering an enema. Slowly, slowly, she came back to life. The physician said she had been suffering from a blockage in the intestine.

But Mary and those closest to her knew that to have been only part of it. The greater part of it, what had given the attack its virulence, the reason why she had almost died of it, had been despair.

12

'January?' Mallie Fleming said, startled.

'Twelfth Night?'

'No, thank you. I don't want my wedding to be mixed up with a masque. Anyway, why that date in particular?'

Lethington had made no formal offer of marriage, and Mallie no formal acceptance. Their six months' separation had asked and answered

271

all questions without a word having to be spoken. When Lethington had been summoned by the queen to return from Caithness and present himself before her, Mallie had been in attendance and their eyes had met. It had been enough.

They had had neither the time nor the opportunity for more than a few hasty and noncommittal words since then, but now they were able to ride a little apart from the company that surrounded the queen, who had recovered sufficiently to embark on her journey back to Edinburgh, taking the long coastal route in slow and easy stages. With her, as well as her household, were her privy councillors James, Huntly and Bothwell, and an escort of a thousand horsemen. Although the east was not Lennox territory, no one knew what Darnley might attempt. He had visited Jedburgh to see his wife once during her illness, and had not been welcome.

'Twelfth Night,' Lethington said, 'would make it three years exactly since I was moonstruck by the Queen of the Bean.'

She sighed. 'What a lovely evening that was. Will the court ever be as happy and brilliant again?'

'Not until we find some means of resolving the queen's heartache, which means doing something about the king. If not Twelfth Night, then the day after?'

'It's interesting,' she said, cocking her fair head. 'Have you noticed? Everyone at court seems to marry in the depths of winter. I wonder why?'

'Too cold for there to be anything better to do. Will you stop evading the question, woman! Now that we have had endless opportunities to talk, if mostly on paper, now that you know my mind, now that you have admitted a desire to know the rest of me – will you marry me at Epiphany?'

She hesitated. 'Are you sure, are you *truly* sure that you don't mind us being married according to the Catholic rite?'

'My darling, we worship the same God. I have never, myself, been convinced that the forms matter so very much, but I know you would feel your soul in jeopardy if I refused. No, I don't mind.'

'I'm not sure that you worship God at all,' she said doubtfully.

He was shocked. 'I? Who would never willingly miss one of Master Knox's sermons!'

'You're incorrigible! But you're talking of a date barely six weeks away. Why such a hurry?'

'I am getting old.'

She giggled. 'So am I. My mother says I should have been married and widowed at least twice by now.'

Suddenly serious, he said, 'I am thirty-eight years of age, and few men live much beyond forty-five. We can have only a few brief years together. That is why I am in a hurry.'

He could almost see the chill run down her spine. 'Don't! I don't want only a few brief years. I don't want our love to be brief. I want it to be for ever. Your father is still alive at seventy, and I insist that you do better.'

'I'll try.'

Rational man though he was, returning to Mary's court after six months' absence he had recognised new undercurrents of violence and the nearness of danger. He was not a Highlander and had no gift of second sight, yet he had a certainty that his doom would be sealed by the events that were to come. Not now, not even next year, perhaps. But, as one grew older, the weeks and months passed ever more quickly and seven years would vanish in the twinkling of an eye. He was possessed by a sense of urgency that he had never known before.

He smiled into the brilliantly blue eyes fixed on his, and said again, 'I'll try. I swear it.'

13

The castle of Craigmillar belonged to Sir Simon Preston, occasional provost of Edinburgh, Catholic of sorts, and husband to one of Lethington's four sisters. It stood only a mile or two from Edinburgh and was set high enough to have wide prospects of moorland and mountain and shining sea. Its fresh breezes were generally held to be salubrious. It was an admirable resting place for a convalescent queen, her last before the return to the Edinburgh and the routines she dreaded. Although privy councillors and business of state always travelled in company with their sovereign, there was an informality during the journeying that made it seem almost like freedom.

Certainly, she could not have imagined sitting in Edinburgh or Stirling discussing with her privy councillors, against a sweet, subdued background of lutes and viols, how to be rid of an unwanted, detested and dangerous husband.

'What *will* he do next?' she had wailed, when she heard that, yet again, he had been trying to undermine her position with her friends in Europe, writing to the kings of Spain and France, to the pope, even to her uncle the Cardinal de Guise, to tell them that she was 'dubious in the faith'.

Her councillors had no interest in maintaining her good relations with the Catholic powers – far from it – but were all too conscious of what a liability Darnley had also become at home.

When she said, not for the first time, 'I wish I were dead,' they exclaimed simultaneously, 'Your majesty!'

James and Argyll, Huntly, Bothwell, Balfour and Lethington. She knew that they must have been discussing it amongst themselves. Lethington had been appointed spokesman. Of course. He had the clearest brain of them all and was least guided by self-interest. She said, 'Yes?'

The clear grey eyes smiled reassuringly at her. 'With the situation as it stands, your majesty will never know contentment and we are all agreed that something must be done. You have your son. We have our prince. It seems increasingly possible, now that you have an heir, that Elizabeth of England might be prepared to reconsider the question of the succession. The little prince who will be King James VI of Scotland may well, some day, become King James I of a united kingdom. It is in all our interests that there should be no more dissidence in your realm. The first thing your lords would recommend is that you pardon those who were involved in the unfortunate matter of the death of David Riccio.'

She thought, poor little Davie, but said, 'I will consider it.'

After an almost imperceptible pause, he went on. 'Connected with that is your lords' wish that you should be freed from your present cares, which trouble them also.'

It was, she supposed, one way of saying that they were prepared to strike a bargain.

'The difficulty lies in discovering a means of achieving your freedom.'

If to die, in despite of God's will, had not been a sin, she would have achieved it by giving in to death at Jedburgh. 'Yes?'

'The obvious solution is divorcement.'

Obvious it might be, but she knew it to be fraught with complications.

Lethington knew it, too. Experience had given him facility in the law, but, aware of his limitations, he had paid a hasty visit home to the tower just outside Haddington, to consult with his more recently qualified younger brother.

John had said, 'D'you know, I'm not sure I can tell you the answer. The queen was married by Catholic rite, so you have to take Catholic law and the tables of affinity into account. But she's also queen of Scots, so at the same time you need to look at it in terms of our own recent legislation, which is Protestant. Roughly, what you've got is canon law versus civil law. It's something that hasn't been tested yet, but it'll have to be. You can't have two clashing sets of marriage and divorce laws in the one country.'

'Start with the Catholic position.'

'The first point is that, if the pope were to annul the marriage – which is the easy way out – the little prince would be rendered illegitimate.'

'That won't do.'

'Divorcement, then. According to what your future wife tells you, the papal dispensation permitting cousins to marry wasn't issued until weeks after the wedding.'

'No, but it was backdated and only a handful of people know of the delay.'

'Normally, that would be good enough, but not if the legitimacy of the heir were ever called into question. When was Prince James conceived?'

'How in God's name should I know?'

Mischievously, John said, 'You could ask,' and then, dodging a friendly blow, went on, 'If the dispensation were issued on, say, the twentieth of the month, it would make a difference whether the child was conceived on or about the tenth, or on or about the thirtieth.'

Lethington groaned. 'Yes, I see that.'

'Leaving that aside, with a divorce, the prince would be legitimate but the queen couldn't marry again.'

Lethington's impression was that the last thing the queen wanted to do was marry again. On the other hand, one prince was not enough. Children died, all too easily, and a Scots queen without an heir and no possibility of an heir was of no use in the grand design.

John had added, 'I *should* say, she couldn't marry again while Darnley was still alive. As for the Protestant view ...'

Whereupon Lethington had flapped an exasperated hand and said, 'Don't tell me.'

Now, her majesty repeated, 'Divorcement? I suppose it might be the answer, but ...' Her face had lost much of its youthful bloom in the course of the year, and she looked almost haggard as she went on, 'Whatever the solution, it must not prejudice either my own honour or the position of my son.'

'My parents,' Bothwell intervened, 'were divorced, but I succeeded my father without question.'

275

She might have pointed out that he was neither a Catholic nor a prince of the blood, but instead the queen smiled at him gratefully.

Lethington, suppressing a mild irritation, said, 'Don't concern yourself unduly, Madame. We understand.' Since there seemed little purpose in prolonging a discussion which was being inhibited rather than helped by the queen's presence, he added in tones of finality, 'Be assured that we will find some way to see you quit of your husband without prejudice to your honour or your son.'

James said, 'Aye, that's fine and easy to say, but if ye rule out divorce, then we're getting into deep waters ...'

Lethington silenced him with a lightly sardonic glance, and Mary was reminded why Fleming was so much in love with him. He said, 'The Lord Moray may have doubts about the means but, in the end, he will look through his fingers and say nothing. Leave it to us. We will resolve it. Your grace will see nothing but good, nothing that is not approved of by your parliament.'

She said, 'I will leave it all to you, then. And now, I bid you good night.'

14

Bothwell – the scar on his forehead still raw and his left hand still stiff from his encounter with Jock o' the Park – said, 'We have to kill him.'

It was the simplest solution and had been in everyone's mind for months, especially since it emerged that Darnley had told the papal legate that he intended to have Moray, Argyll, Morton, Lethington, Justice Clerk Bellenden and Clerk Register MacGill executed as a preliminary to restoring Scotland to Holy Church. The difficulty was that no one other than Bothwell was prepared to talk outright of killing, far less to do the deed.

James shook his head. 'I'll not be party to cold-blooded murder!'

Lethington, who had always admired James's capacity for self-delusion, transferred his questioning gaze to Argyll, who turned his mouth down at the corners, and then to Huntly, pale-skinned and elegant, who did the same. Only Sir James Balfour, an ingenious lawyer and morally mobile gentleman whose current, if probably transient, allegiance was to Bothwell, wore an abstracted look.

Argyll, his big nose wrinkling, said slowly, 'Maybe the lords could be putting him on trial for treason. It iss likely he would be trying to escape

276

when we went to arrest him, and I haff heard of accidents happening in situations like that.'

Balfour shook his head. 'He's the king. It would be illegal for the lords to arrest him for treason in the first place, even if the right kind of accident did happen. I don't know that anyone would choose to make an issue of it, mind you.'

'Lennox would,' James pointed out sourly.

Huntly stroked his slender chestnut moustaches. 'He's fond of swimming. That's a dangerous thing to do.'

'It'd be a damn' queer thing to do, too, in the depths of winter,' said James.

'Riding accident?'

Bothwell, who had been listening with growing impatience, exploded. 'Her majesty's desperate and you sit here like a flock of bloody sheep, bleating about "accidents". We need something surer than that.'

Amiably, Lethington said, 'You're the expert,' and then, as Bothwell's fleshy brows drew together, raised a placating hand. 'By which I mean that, unlike the rest of us, you are inclined to prefer action to words.'

'What's wrong with that?'

'Nothing at all. Just at the moment, however, I believe it would be unwise to make any firm decisions about a matter of such importance. We need to reflect for a week or two.'

'Well, maybe.' And then, with a terrible inevitability, Bothwell went on, 'But we must all sign a bond confirming that we're agreed Darnley must go and that we'll all support each other if we get into difficulties. Balfour can draw it up.'

'Don't look at me,' James said. 'I'm not signing any bond.'

But Lethington, who had a constitutional dislike of useless pieces of paper, for once made no demur. Returning to court, he had been much struck by the development in Mary's and Bothwell's relationship. She was dependent and he was ambitious, and his desire to be rid of Darnley was suggestive. According to Mallie, Jean Gordon said she'd be delighted to divorce her husband any day; the queen could have him and welcome. But although Jean might like the idea, Lethington knew that it would be politically disastrous. On a personal basis, too, he found it difficult to view with equanimity the possibility of being ruled over by a man who had, on more occasions than he could remember, threatened his own life.

He had the beginnings of a plan that might resolve everything, one that made it desirable for Bothwell to be encouraged to feel that he was in charge.

He was also in charge, at the queen's command, of arrangements for the baptism of the six-month-old Prince Charles James at Stirling. Elizabeth of England had agreed to be a godparent and sent the Earl of Bedford to represent her. She even overcame her accustomed parsimony to the extent of sending with him a massive and splendid gold font weighing more than twenty pounds and liberally decorated with enamel and jewels.

Mary insisted on the baptism being celebrated with full Catholic rites, which had the incidental effect of ruling out any overcrowding within the Chapel Royal. The English envoys remained outside with the Scots Protestant lords, colourfully clad by Mary at her own expense – James in a cold-toned green, Argyll in a red that accorded better with his temper than his complexion, and Bothwell in the blue that, in heraldry, represented loyalty and fidelity. The baby himself had a canopy of state made from gold-fringed crimson velvet, and a crib lined with figured cloth of silver.

The dark December afternoon was ablaze with wax candles and loud with the sound of trumpets, but the little prince's father, who was to have cast everyone else in the shade with his cloth of gold, failed to turn up. He was not prepared to risk having his dignity slighted, and remained unreconciled to the existence of a son who was more important than he.

There was a banquet afterwards, during which the Maries were strategically seated as buffers between the ambassadors of warring nationalities, and a masque, and supper and dancing and, next day, a chase in the park, and another banquet, and fireworks. Throughout the bangs, shouts, music and laughter, the queen sparkled relentlessly while the king lurked in his apartments, alone except for his servants.

Not until three days afterwards was Lethington able to snatch a private word with his beloved Mallie, who said, limply, 'It was almost as it used to be, but I don't think I have ever worked so hard in my life. Having to perform in masques is all very well, but *not* immediately after a banquet. And I wish Master Buchanan would cast the words in Scots and in rhyme, rather than in Latin. They would be *much* easier to memorise. Do you think the ambassadors were impressed?'

'I hope so. We had to raise £12,000 in taxation to subsidise the affair.'

'You mean the state paid for it all? Ah-h-h-h. Perhaps that is why her majesty – when she isn't sunk in thought or tears – is feeling so kindly towards you and James. I think she may even be going to pardon Lord Morton and his friends. On Christmas Eve, if you please. I can't imagine why she is feeling so forgiving. Peace on earth and goodwill towards men is all very well, but *Morton*!'

He kissed her on the tip of her indignant nose. 'Excellent,' he said.

16

They were married in the Chapel Royal at Stirling. It was a quiet affair because it was so important to them. If it had been possible, they would have had no one there but themselves.

Sir Richard Maitland, his blind hand on his younger son's arm, murmured, 'I would not have believed ... Pray God that they have time together.'

Jenny Fleming, who had borne seven children without her heart ever being touched, recognised that she was in the presence of something sensitive and strange, and thought, 'Goodness gracious!'

The queen was wonderfully vivacious until, returning to the royal apartments after the wedding banquet, she collapsed on her bed and wept from weariness, despair and loneliness. Once, she had had Four Maries and they had been hers, and hers alone. Now only Seton, the most pious and least loved, remained.

17

The Earl of Morton set foot again in Scotland on the eleventh day of January 1567, free save for the proviso that he was not to come within seven miles of the court.

Four days after that, Bothwell turned up at the tower house of the Maitlands of Lethington, and commanded the secretary of state to accompany him to Whittinghame, half a dozen miles away, nestling in the valley between Trapain Law and the Lammermuir hills, where Morton was visiting one of his Douglas relatives.

The secretary of state who, with his new bride, was trying to decide how to introduce some comfort into their spartan private apartments, was not pleased, but Bothwell's influence with the queen was now so great that he was in no position to refuse. He had, in any case, a better reason for agreeing to go. It was not that one of his sisters happened to be wife to the Douglas in question. It was that he had a good and cogent desire to know what Bothwell wanted to talk to Morton about.

By the time they reached Whittinghame, he had a fairly shrewd idea.

Morton was exceedingly wary. Although there had been snow in the night, he said, 'I take ye're not here just for a gossip. We'll go outside in the courtyard.'

Bothwell said, 'We've a bond we want you to sign.'

'Oh, aye?'

Bothwell looked at Lethington, but this was not a discussion in which Lethington was prepared to participate. He shook his head. 'You're in charge.'

The other man nodded and turned back to Morton. 'We had a meeting with her majesty at Craigmillar a few weeks ago. She's desperate to be rid of Darnley, and we discussed the obvious possibilities, and they're too complicated and too slow. There's a notion that he might be taken and put in ward, but nothing's decided. Anyway, whatever we do, it would need the support of as many of the lords as possible to make it legal. So we drew up a bond.'

Abrasive and rash Bothwell might be, but he had a certain native cunning. Lethington couldn't have put it more harmlessly himself.

'Well, let's see it,' Morton said.

Balfour's much-amended draft ran, 'Forasmuch as it is thought expedient and most profitable for the common weal by the whole nobility and lords undersigned, that such a young fool and proud tyrant should not reign or bear rule over them, they have all concluded that he should be put off by one way or another.'

The signatures of Argyll, Huntly and Bothwell at the top were followed by space for other noble signatories, while that of Lethington – a lord only by courtesy of his secretaryship – appeared at the foot.

Morton, having read it through three times, said, 'Put off?' then handed it back. 'No, thanks. I've just got out of one load of trouble. I'm not getting intae another.'

'Trouble? If you lend your help, I'd guarantee you the queen's favour!'

' "Help"? Yon's a dangerous wee word. What dae ye mean by it?'

It was exactly what Lethington had been thinking and, since he had no wish to be a direct witness to the answer, he chose strategic withdrawal. 'You don't need me,' he said. 'I'll leave you for a few moments. I have a message from my wife for Lady Douglas, and I am a sufficiently new husband not to dare to forget.'

When he returned half an hour later Morton was saying, 'Well, I've nae objection in principle. Kin to the Douglases he may be, but I wouldnae lift a finger to protect him considering the way he let us down after the

Riccio business. Mind ye, I'm not getting in any more bother with the queen. I'd want something in writing from her, giving her consent.'

Bothwell said, 'One of your men can come back with me now. If she agrees, he can bring it to you.'

'My cousin Archie Douglas can go.'

Lethington was left alone with Morton when Bothwell went off to the garderobe, complaining of an attack of the bloody flux.

Morton looked after him thoughtfully. 'James was writing tae me that yon one was getting too big for his boots. Dangerous, he said. Too much influence. Needs to be slapped down. A wee bit like Davie Riccio.'

'Perhaps.'

Morton chewed his lip. 'I'd have expected James or Argyll tae be the one tae come tae me wi' such a bond, not him.'

'No. Bothwell's in charge.'

They parted soon after, Morton wondering why Lethington had found it necessary to make such a point of the affair being in Bothwell's hands, while Lethington reflected on Morton's demand for something from the queen which he assuredly knew she would not provide. Only as he turned off for home, leaving Bothwell and Archie Douglas to ride on to Edinburgh, did he remember what a rare talent Archie Douglas had for picking up information.

Which meant that Morton was more interested in what Bothwell had in mind than he had pretended. It was a satisfying thought.

18

Darnley – swearing truthlessly, as so often before, that he would leave the country and that his wife would never see his face again – had left Stirling at Christmas to visit his father in Glasgow and fallen ill on the way. The first rumours were of poison, as they always were when an important personage was taken ill unexpectedly, but his father's doctors diagnosed smallpox.

He should have been on the mend in two weeks but he was not, so Mary, sighing, sent her French physician, Arnault, to him. Little though she loved him, she could not have his life on her conscience.

Arnault returned one morning when her eyes and her mind were on a letter the clerk of the council had just brought to her. She found it hard to concentrate nowadays. Absently, she asked, 'Is the king improved? Have you cured him?'

'*Non*, Madame. I fear that I cannot.'

Tiredly, she raised her head. 'You cannot? What do you mean? What is wrong with him?'

He glanced uneasily at Mary Seton, stitching in a corner of the room, and the queen said, 'Seton, leave us.' Then, 'Well?'

'I cannot be sure, but I believe that the king your husband is suffering from – he is suffering from the pox.'

'Smallpox. Yes, I know.'

'No, Madame. Not the smallpox but *la vérole*. The Neapolitan malady. It is a disease that has become epidemic. It is sometimes called *morbus venereus*, sometimes syphilis.'

'Explain.'

Although men of medicine were accustomed to dealing in unpleasant facts, he hesitated. He was a wispy little man, but Catherine de' Medici's personal physician, M. Joubert, had recommended him and Mary had found him reliable. He had saved her life not very long ago, even if against her will.

She said again, 'Explain.'

'It is a disease transmitted through the – ah – shameful parts. It takes many disguises, but in general it progresses through three stages. The third one may begin two or three years after the first, or as much as twenty. It rots the nerves and the brain, and ends in madness.'

She had said, often enough in the last few months, that Harry must be mad, but it had been no more than a figure of speech. Her hand to the pearls at her throat, she stared at the man. 'Is there a cure?'

'In the early stages, yes, although the treatment is painful, but ...' He looked even more nervous. 'Before you married the king – before I myself entered your service – he suffered an attack of measles and then a high fever?'

She nodded.

'Because of the fever, I think now that it may not have been measles. It is easy to be mistaken. It may have been the second stage of the Neapolitan malady. If that is so, he is entering the third stage. May I ask, has he been behaving strangely? Do his moods change suddenly? Does he swing from intense piety to extreme dissipation? Does he have – how does one say it? – grandiose illusions?'

They were easy questions to answer. 'Yes.'

'I had indeed heard some gossip of the sort.' He twisted his hands together. 'And Madame, have you had – ah – marital relations with your husband?'

282

She stared at him. 'Of course. I could not have borne him a son otherwise.'

'I fear you should not have them again, ever. You are fortunate that he has not infected you. You are fortunate that your babe was not stillborn. You are fortunate that the little prince is healthy.'

There was a cold, crawling feeling in her spine. She could not take it in, and did not want to.

After a time, she said, 'I had heard of the pox, but knew nothing of it.'

'Respectable ladies should not know of it. Men know, because it is a common disease among those who consort with whores, but respectable ladies consort only with their husbands.'

Her head was full of a thick grey fog. Somewhere inside her, she was aware that God required her to feel compassion for the beautiful boy and the fate that lay in store for him, but one thought was paramount. She said, 'You are telling me that my husband knew? He knew that he was putting me and my child in danger?'

Arnault was terrified, she suddenly realised, doing his duty to her but aware of the retribution he would meet from the Lennoxes if they ever found out. Briefly forgetting her own troubles, she smiled. 'Don't worry, Arnault. I will tell no one.'

'Thank you, Madame. In answer to your question, I cannot judge whether the king knew. He should have done, but perhaps he closed his mind.'

It would be like him.

As if in extenuation, Arnault said, 'He may have wished not to hurt the lord his father, who talks of him as "my innocent lamb". And his own physicians speak only of smallpox, although they must know better. Scotland has been familiar with *la vérole* for seventy years. I believe that Edinburgh once tried to isolate sufferers by confining them on the island of Inchkeith ...' He stopped, because she was no longer listening.

'Thank you, Monsieur Arnault,' she said. 'You may go.'

For the better part of an hour, she sat with nothing in her mind at all, because there was no thought she could touch on that was bearable. From outdoors, she could hear the wet January wind soughing round the palace, and occasional voices, and even laughter as someone ran for cover. Indoors, from her audience chamber, came a quiet bustle of activity, low commands, and the clatter of silver as the table was laid for dinner, the dinner she could not imagine eating. Behind her, the logs settled in the fireplace. The only other sound was of the breath beating in her chest.

At last, with infinite slowness, her mind began to come back to life, but wherever it looked, there were signs saying, 'Here be dragons'.

She sent for the nurse to bring the baby to her and, taking him in her arms, hugged him convulsively. He wailed from the extra pressure on the swaddling bands that would make him grow up straight-limbed and strong, but stopped as he caught sight of the carved and painted panels on the ceiling and gurgled instead. He was a normal, lively-minded and inquisitive infant.

She had wanted him so much, but since his birth she had been quite unlike herself. In public she was able to appear as no more than a little subdued; she had always been queen, and her regal instincts seldom failed her. But in private she had been sleepless, and restless, and tearful. For hours at a time, she had been scarcely aware of what was going on around her. And at Jedburgh she had nearly died. She, who had always been full of energy, now had to struggle through each day except when there was some activity to encourage in her a semblance of vitality. At the celebrations for her baby's baptism, she had felt almost well, as she did when she went hunting or hawking, but such occasions were rare.

The worst part was having to struggle alone. She could no longer trust her own judgement, because she had lost the power of her mind. She couldn't think. Nor did a day pass, or so it seemed, without a rumour of some plot against her or the baby, so that she was haunted by worry and suspicion. It was like spinning in a vortex. It could not go on like this. Even before Arnault had told her about Harry, she had known it could not go on like this.

Seton came in and found her lying on her bed, drearily weeping, but Seton, of all the Maries, was the one she could least confide in.

'Go away! Go away!'

She went, and came back with Arnault, who talked of drawn curtains and soothing draughts.

And then the door was flung open and it was Lord Bothwell, who looked quite unlike that second father of her childhood, the Duc de Guise, but had the same power of personality, the strength of will, the decisiveness. Who physically pushed Seton and Arnault from the room, and then came to her and said, 'Your majesty? This will not do.'

She submitted to the hard hands clamped about her wrists, pulling her up, as he went on, 'Tell me, and I will put everything right.'

Staring up into the swarthy face with the heavy brows, the broken nose and the hot brown eyes, she knew it was true.

She told him why she was weeping. She told him about Harry.

He had nothing but contempt for Harry. He himself had had whores by the dozen, and he'd had to take the mercury cure twice – and bloody painful it had been – but he had recovered.

It had been obvious for months that getting rid of Harry was a public duty. Now, it seemed, it had become urgent.

The first thing was to get him back from Glasgow to Edinburgh. At Glasgow he was too closely protected by his Lennox kin.

Only the queen could manage it and Bothwell found himself in a difficulty, because he could not tell her the true reason and couldn't think of any other that sounded convincing. He needed that clever bastard, Lethington, who, after Darnley and Moray, was top of his list for extermination.

It was always a challenge, being a peaceable man in a violent age, but Lethington was also a realist. There were times when death was the only solution to an intractable problem, and this was one of those times, though he could never have brought himself to wield the knife.

He remembered once publicly arguing the question of responsibility with John Knox, who was still keeping his head down in darkest Ayrshire.

Lethington had said that, while he would not obey the queen if she ordered him to slay John Knox, was he bound to save the preacher if she ordered others to do it? And Knox had replied, 'The Word of God says that, if you believe me innocent and have the power to save me, you would be criminal and guilty of my blood if you did not.' It was a view of responsibility that ran completely counter to the traditional moral code, and even Knox's most fervent adherents had thought he was going too far. Certainly, if merely knowing about a crime carried as much guilt as participating in it, then half of Scotland lived in a state of sin.

Knox had probably been right, Lethington thought, but shrugged it off as he prepared to give Bothwell the help he required. Bothwell's purpose was simple, whereas his own was more complex, having less to do with his unhappy queen's peace of mind than with the need to restore the country, by whatever means, to stable and responsible government.

Since Bothwell's plan was part of Lethington's own, Lethington was ready enough to suggest to the queen that it would be wise for her to bring her husband back from Glasgow to Edinburgh, where the young man would be under her eye in the political as well as the prophylactic sense. His and his father's endless plotting against her – real or rumoured – would be frustrated, her physician could look after him, and she would be seen as behaving to him in the way that a good wife should.

She said, 'Yes. Yes, of course. I am sure you are right.'

21

Mary set out for Glasgow with a guard of mounted arquebusiers, a litter for her husband to travel in, and the Lords Bothwell and Huntly for company as far as Falkirk. Next evening, two days in the saddle having partially revived her, she arrived in Glasgow in regal style and with a temper sharpened by foreboding about the ordeal to come.

It was as distasteful as she had expected. She found her husband wearing a taffeta mask to hide his disfigurement and alternately reproaching her for her cruelty to him and begging her to forgive him for the very small faults which he had committed because he was young and lacked wise counsel. They talked a great deal, Mary trying to discover the truth of his rumoured plotting against her, while Darnley threw out hints about having heard of the conference at Craigmillar and the threat that he might be put in ward.

'I know of no such threat,' she declared with perfect truth, whereupon he hastened to say that he knew she would do him no hurt.

It took time to persuade him to return with her to Edinburgh, and he agreed only on condition that when his cure was complete they should live together again as man and wife.

All she wanted was to settle things and forget about them, so she was impatient when he raised the question of where he was to be lodged in the meantime. Holyrood was impossible because the baby was there and must not be exposed to the danger of infection. She suggested Craigmillar, not too far away, where the air was fresh and it was easier to find water for the baths necessary to his recovery than within the crowded confines of Edinburgh.

He didn't like the idea of Craigmillar, and the only practicable alternative was an unoccupied house at Kirk o' Field, which was just within the town wall in grounds that, for Edinburgh, were considered spacious. It was less than three-quarters of a mile from Holyrood. He said yes, and no, and maybe, and since she had letters to write to Bothwell and

Lethington she suggested asking them what they thought. By the time her messenger returned with their recommendation of Kirk o' Field, Darnley had himself come to the same conclusion.

And so, on the last day of January 1567, the royal procession made its way back to Edinburgh and the king was installed in his lodging at Kirk o' Field.

Chapter Thirteen

FEBRUARY-APRIL 1567

1

'What could be cosier or more inviting?' Mary exclaimed, surveying her husband's chamber in the Old Provost's Lodging. But he, like a tired child resisting his mother's coaxings, scowled around him and, his eyes lighting on the figured black velvet hangings of the fourposter, said with a shudder, 'Horrible, gloomy things. I want my own bed.'

'Of course, my dear. Tomorrow, everything shall be done as you wish, but now you must lie down and rest after your journey while I go on to Holyrood.'

The Old Provost's Lodging – which with the house next door belonged to Robert Balfour, brother of Mary's privy councillor and Bothwell's adherent, Sir James Balfour – was a handsome place, forming part of a quadrangle attached to the pre-Reformation collegiate church of St Mary-in-the-Field, now in disuse, which had given Kirk o' Field its name. Its rooms were larger than most of the private apartments at Holyrood, and Darnley's mood improved greatly when, on the following day, richer and more kingly furnishings were brought from the royal store – fine tapestries for the walls, red velvet cushions, a Turkish carpet, a double commode chair under a canopy of yellow taffeta, and a bath to be set beside his favourite bed, one that the queen had given him, hung with violet velvet embroidered with ciphers and flowers and trimmed with gold and silver braids.

A pleasant little gallery projected from his bedchamber, resting on the town wall itself and giving a view over the orchards beyond, and there was another window overlooking the east garden of the house. Below his own chamber was another, less lavishly furnished, for the queen's use if she should need it, while on the ground floor there was a large room designated as his audience chamber. Cellars ran below the whole house.

He was disappointed that his wife preferred, on most nights, to sleep at Holyrood, but his time at Kirk o' Field was merry and he even began to feel like a real king again, because the queen visited him every evening and brought half the court with her, so that he was the centre of attention as he had not been for many months.

It did not occur to him, or indeed to anyone other than his wife's closest confidants, that she brought the court with her because she could not bear to spend time alone with him. He had become once more as soft and dependent, as appealing to her maternal instincts, as he had been when he was sick with measles before their marriage. Knowing now how untrustworthy he was, she did not want to find her heart touched, or to be reminded of those brief weeks when she had been in love. The depression underlying her gaiety was deep enough already.

It was an almost idyllic week, during which most of Edinburgh sensed that something was about to happen, although not even the queen, living as she now did only from day to day, knew what.

2

There were some, of course, who did know.

Archie Douglas, who had become surprisingly close to Bothwell in the space of no more than a week or two, occupied himself in spreading a number of inchoate rumours on the principle that, if he gossiped inaccurately about what might be afoot, he wouldn't be suspected of being involved in what *was* afoot, when it happened. That was how, by a natural process of diffusion, Darnley had heard of the Craigmillar bond. That was why Archie had paid a visit to his cousin Morton, to allow eavesdropping servants to hear them say, 'Tut, tut! How shocking!' What they said in private was rather more intricate.

Argyll knew Bothwell was up to something, but shrugged his shoulders.

Huntly knew and didn't greatly care, although he could see problems ahead. His sister was Bothwell's wife, and Bothwell, if everything went as intended, was going to need a divorce. But Jean wouldn't object, and it didn't matter if she did.

James knew, but had no intention of doing anything other than look through his fingers, which meant that it was politically convenient – if privately regrettable – when his wife chose to have yet another miscarriage at just the right time, so that he had a perfect excuse for departing

Edinburgh for St Andrews.

Lethington knew, because he had made it his business to know. He was taken aback, at first, by the sheer vulgar ostentation of Bothwell's plan, but the more he thought about it the more he liked it.

Two birds with one stone.

3

Bothwell had been attracted by Argyll's original notion of arresting the king and killing him accidentally when he tried to escape, but Balfour had been discouraging. If the bond were signed by *all* the leading lords, he had said, their combined power would make a farce of any subsequent attempt to charge them with treason; otherwise, there could be much settling of old scores. And since everyone Bothwell approached was showing an unaccountable reluctance to sign, conveying that they were perfectly content to leave everything in his hands, he had given up that idea in favour of one surer and simpler in the deed, and harder to pin on the doer.

His first problem had been laying his hands on the gunpowder at short notice, because Darnley was not going to be at Kirk o' Field for ever. But since Edinburgh castle was the nation's arsenal and there was enough gunpowder in it to blow up the whole city, it was only a question of finding the right men to bribe or, more economically, blackmail. To James Hepburn, Earl of Bothwell, Lieutenant of all the Marches and Sheriff of Edinburgh, that presented no great challenge. Then it was a question of transporting the gunpowder secretly from the castle to Robert Balfour's second house at Kirk o' Field to be transferred, when opportunity offered, to the cellars of the Old Provost's Lodging. That was the kind of thing servants were for, and since French Paris, a former man of Bothwell's, was now in the royal service, even the keys presented no problem.

Supervising the preparations might have been difficult, since Bothwell himself was committed to his duties at court for almost every hour of the two appointed days but, fortunately, Sir James Balfour was not so busy.

4

By just over a week after his arrival in Edinburgh, Darnley was sufficiently recovered to declare himself cured and ready to move back to Holyrood-house on 10th February.

The previous day happened to be the last Sunday before Lent, and although for the queen's Catholic adherents this represented the last opportunity to enjoy themselves before their forty days of abstinence, her Protestant lords – who claimed to be abstinent not just for forty days in the year but for three hundred and sixty-five – were perfectly willing to join in the festivities.

Mary's court was therefore well attended on a day that began with the marriage of one of her women, Christian Hogg, to her favourite valet and Master of the Revels, Bastien Pagès; continued with their wedding dinner; and was to end with a masque devised for the occasion by the indefatigable Bastien himself.

In the interval between dinner and masque, Mary and her senior lords – Argyll, Huntly, Bothwell and Cassillis among them – set out for another and more formal dinner given by the Bishop of the Isles in honour of the departing Savoyard ambassador, and when that was over rode down to Kirk o' Field to spend the first part of the evening with Darnley.

It was a pleasant evening of music and talk, dice and cards, and it was late when someone reminded Mary about Bastien's masque. She had spoken of returning to Kirk o' Field afterwards, to sleep in the bedchamber below her husband's as she had done on two previous nights, but the long day, the lateness of the hour and her husband's imminent return to Holyrood led her to hesitate, and when Bothwell reminded her that she had planned to ride out to Seton next morning, she changed her mind.

She was grateful afterwards that she had done so, even though it had been at the cost of soothing a disappointed husband with lying promises, because even after the masque and the bedding of the bride the day was not over, since Lord Bothwell and her Captain of the Guard needed to consult her on something that could have been dealt with in the morning, had she not been intending an early start. It was after midnight before they left her.

5

The palace of Holyroodhouse had settled into sleep when Bothwell, clad now not in silver and black velvet but in a canvas doublet, plain dark hose, and neutral-coloured riding cloak, set out with four of his servants for

Kirk o' Field. It was a cold night powdered with snow and with dark clouds swimming across a sliver of new moon. Edinburgh's only lighting was the torches at the ports of the town wall and the lanterns of the ten bored night watchmen rambling separately about the streets.

Even so, Bothwell and his companions took the long way round. By following the town wall along its outer face, they were protected from view for most of the way and able to move rapidly despite the rough ground. Only when they reached the Cowgait did they move more circumspectly.

Others were waiting for them when they arrived at the postern gate that led through the wall across a yard of open ground to the door that gave directly into the cellars of the Old Provost's Lodging at Kirk o' Field.

John Hepburn, a kinsman of Bothwell's, whispered, 'The powder's a' set and tamped down. There's two trains laid.'

The earl swore. 'Here? You were supposed to lay them through the house door into the east garden!'

'Aye, but then we would have had to go into the main house to lay the trains. This way's more direct and we can get off as soon as we see the powder well alight. In the east garden, we might have the house down on top of us.'

Grudgingly, Bothwell conceded, 'Maybe. Where's Balfour?'

'We've no' seen him. Probably tucked up in his bed wi' his fingers stuffed in his ears. He's a careful one, yon.'

'Well, let's get on with it. Where's the flint and tinder?'

'Sakes! Have ye no' brought your own?'

There were nine of them in all, milling around in the alley outside the postern gate. They thought they were being quiet, but they weren't. There were footsteps and shufflings and murmurings, and then the flint and tinder wouldn't strike. And after that it seemed as if the powder hadn't caught, and Bothwell was moving forward to inspect it when it flared suddenly and Hepburn dragged him back, muttering, 'It's corned powder, it'll burn fast.'

6

Shielded by the trees, Archie Douglas and his followers lay in ambush in the east garden, where the train was supposed to have been laid. They were wearing armour and steel helmets, and waiting for the unmistakable smell of burning gunpowder.

Inside the Old Provost's Lodging, Darnley woke abruptly in his violet velvet bed. It was a moment before he identified the sounds that had roused him, and the direction they came from. Kicking awake his chamber groom, Taylor, snoring on a mattress on the floor, he ran to the gallery overhanging the town wall, from whose window, once his eyes were adjusted to the outer dark, he could see a host of stealthy figures.

With terror clawing at his throat, he remembered the hinted warnings he had received but, in the last halcyon week, had chosen to dismiss. Murderers.

He had heard tales of the Scots burning the houses of their enemies down about their ears. But this house was of stone. Surely it wouldn't burn?

The dagger, then? With an hysterical gasp, he remembered the fifty-six dagger strokes that had ended the life of Davie Riccio.

It was clear that his chamber groom was no less terrified than he, while his second groom, sleeping in the gallery itself, hadn't even stirred. There were no more than two or three other servants in the house.

He didn't dare shout for help in case the assassins reached him before his servants did.

Taylor, his wits unnaturally sharp, fled to the east window and looked out on a walled garden sunk in wintry peace.

'My lord! My lord! This way. It'll be safe here, if we're quiet.'

While Darnley stood frozen, Taylor tied a pair of sheets together into a makeshift rope and wound one end of it round the back of a chair to anchor it while he threw the other end out of the window. He was holding Darnley's furred velvet gown out to him, and the king saw that he had a dagger in his hand. 'My lord! My lord! You must escape! Now, while you have the chance.'

The sight of the dagger rendered Darnley's panic complete, even though he knew that Taylor was no traitor.

Flinging himself onto the rope, lowering himself hand by shaking hand, he landed in the quiet, seemingly empty garden with Taylor just behind him. The chair fell out of the window after them.

8

After that, everything happened at once.

Archie Douglas and his men were there to catch the king's assassin, with the marks and the smell of gunpowder still on him – though not until it was too late to prevent the explosion. Two birds with one stone.

But here was one of the birds trying to fly away just as the smell of the gunpowder began spreading its taint on the cold night air.

'Take him!' Archie snapped.

They rushed forward, and as one of them threw Darnley's own, furred gown over his head, the king screamed, 'Have pity on me, kinsmen! Have pity on me!'

But they could not afford to have pity on him, and they could not afford to wait. They would need almost to brush against the walls of the house itself in order to gain the alley beyond and lay hands on Bothwell – if the scream and scuffle had not already warned him. Time was getting tight, and to be blown up with the house was not part of their plan. If anything was to be salvaged, they had to go instantly.

When it had first dawned on Archie Douglas that he was in the wrong place, he had decided that the answer was to leave it until the incriminating moment and then lead his men through the narrow postern as if they were there to give Bothwell a hand and watch the fun. He needed only to distract Bothwell for long enough to let all the Douglases through the gate, then they would turn from friend to foe and take him in the act.

Of Bothwell's adherents, only Balfour might be clever enough to wonder why the Douglases should have turned out in full armour merely to watch a slender youth and a handful of house servants being blown to eternity.

But when they reached the alley, it was too late. The delay and the scuffle had done their work. Bothwell and his men had scattered.

Archie hesitated only for a moment. One bird was better than none. Dragging along with them Darnley and his servant – still tangled in rope and chair, still kicking madly and trying despairingly to scream – the Douglases ran across the alley beyond the town wall into the orchard on the other side.

There they tightened the smothering velvet cloak, until it had done its work. A moment later, the house blew up.

9

It woke the entire city. It was like the evening of little Prince James's birth, when all the cannon of the castle had been fired off at once.

Pulling on overgowns and cloaks against the chill, those who lived nearby rushed towards the scene of the explosion. Those who lived further away, like the queen at Holyrood, first had to enquire about the site of it. Lord Bothwell slept through it all and had to be rudely shaken awake half an hour later to be told that the king was dead.

Kirk o' Field had been reduced to rubble. At first, it was thought that the king must be buried in the ruins, but then someone heard a feeble cry for help from the top of the town wall. It was the king's second groom, Nelson, who had been blown, unconscious, out of the gallery in which he slept.

If he had survived, so might the king.

When they had begun casting around, they had found him. But they found him dead, naked under his disordered nightshirt, lying under a tree in the orchard beyond the wall with his equally dead servant beside him. To those who had known him only as a ceremonial figure, as their queen's estranged husband, there was pathos in the sight of a young man who had lived in cloth of gold and jewels and royal dignity being sent precipitately to meet his Maker clad only in his nightshirt. He had been a wonderfully handsome young man, too, and only twenty years old. Whatever his sins, he had not deserved to die so.

10

The awakened Bothwell, as sheriff of Edinburgh, went with a party of soldiers to the scene of the explosion and it was under his supervision that the king's body was carried into a neighbouring house and examined by surgeons in the presence of members of the privy council, then exposed to the public view before being carried back to Holyrood.

The surgeons shook their heads. There was no trace of violence on the body, no fracture, wound, bruise or burns. No singeing or blackening, no smell of fire.

Bothwell was as mystified as they were.

11

A few hours later, fifteen members of Mary's privy council – Bothwell and Lethington among them – subscribed a letter to Catherine de' Medici, regent for her son, King Charles IX of France, informing her of the tragedy and claiming that the explosion had been designed to kill not only the king, but the queen, whose intention, until a last-minute change of plan, had been to sleep at Kirk o' Field herself. Mary wrote to her ambassador in France, Archbishop Beaton, in similar terms if more emotional language.

She, at least, believed it at first. She agreed that the privy council should offer a reward of £2,000 and a free pardon for information leading to the discovery of the murderers. She ordered the court into mourning. She authorised the purchase of embalming spices for the body of her husband. She made the correct preparations for her own forty days of retirement into a black-hung mourning chamber, although she emerged briefly next day to fulfill her promise of attending the wedding of Margaret Carwood, the favourite chamber woman who had been with her when she had fled from Holyrood just eleven months before.

She was in a trance throughout.

12

'I can't tell you!' Mallie Fleming almost shrieked. 'I have no idea how she feels, other than ill. Arnault is going to ask the privy council to agree to her leaving that awful, suffocating room and going to Seton for fresh air. He thinks that, otherwise, not only her health but her life may be in danger.'

'As bad as that?'

'She's distraught, and that always makes her ill. I think she realises now that she herself was not intended to be a victim, but she said something very strange today. She was walking about, with her fists to her mouth, when she suddenly burst out with something that sounded like, "Who will rid me of this turbulent priest?" Does that make any sense to you?'

'Ah.' Lethington frowned. 'Yes.'

'Well?'

'Centuries ago, King Henry II of England became impatient with his Archbishop of Canterbury and exclaimed, "Who will rid me of this turbulent priest?" Four of his knights took him more literally than he had intended, and murdered the man in his own cathedral.'

'You mean that's what's happened now? And that she feels responsible?'

'Perhaps.' He still had not disciplined himself into sharing his mind fully with the wife he worshipped, and she knew it. And he knew that she

296

did. But they had reached an unspoken truce, because she recognised that she could not, after all, expect him to put hours of deep and complex thought into the explicitness of words. Especially when they might be dangerous words.

It did not matter now that she had come to love and trust him so completely.

This, however, was something of which she needed to be sure in her own mind, if she were to help the unhappy queen who was also her cousin. 'So she made it clear at Craigmillar that she wanted rid of her husband, and then closed her eyes and her mind and hoped for the best? And now someone has obliged her, though in a way she would not have wished, and she doesn't know how much of the guilt is his and how much is hers?'

'Very neatly put, my darling.'

She did not say, 'And you knew about it.' She said, 'And it worries you, the way she is behaving?'

He sighed. 'If she were behaving naturally, she would recognise that she dare not stand aside, that she must be clearly seen to pursue the criminal or criminals in order to damp down speculation that she herself might have been involved. Then everything would be all right. But she isn't behaving naturally.'

'No. She has been weary and lost for months. And now she's shocked, and doesn't know what to do. You will have to behave naturally *for* her.'

'If only it were as easy as that.'

Bothwell's luck in escaping the trap had been the worst possible outcome. His influence with the queen was undiminished. He would take care to ensure that the explosion at Kirk o' Field was not too rigorously investigated. That he had not himself murdered the king would undoubtedly encourage him, privately, to try and find out who *had* done, and why, and what secondary motives there might have been. And to top it all off, Darnley's piteous death had turned the queen's husband, in the eyes of many, into a martyr.

He had been dangerous young man alive, and unless something were done soon, he might prove to be even more dangerous dead.

Lethington couldn't see where it was going to end.

13

Edinburgh's night watchmen were paid, if not over-generously, to keep an eye on what went on in the streets during the hours of darkness, but none of them knew whose were the hands that, just one week after the king's murder, nailed up a placard on the great wooden door of the Tolbooth. As they explained apologetically, the light of their torches was apt to signal their approach to miscreants, and the new Tolbooth was, of course, slightly off the Highgait and sheltered by St Giles. They were not interrogated further because the burghers were, in truth, not unsympathetic towards these particular miscreants.

The placard declared, in an educated hand, that the anonymous author had 'made inquisition into them that were the doers of the horrible and abominable murder of the king' and was able to affirm that the leaders were the Earl of Bothwell and Sir James Balfour, and that the queen, having been bewitched, had consented to the deed.

There was another placard two nights later, naming the queen's valet Bastien Pagès and her French secretary Joseph Riccio – brother of the late Davie – and from there everything escalated, with the night watchmen remaining so blind and deaf that they might justifiably have been sacked for incapacity.

Bothwell's name began to be cried in the streets in the hours before the dawn. Placards in increasing numbers appeared not only on the Tolbooth, but on churches and trees around the town.

> Is it not enough that the poor king is dead
> Without the méchant murderers occupying his stead
> And double adultery has all this land shamed ...

When Jean Gordon, Countess of Bothwell, fell so ill towards the end of February that she was reported to be at death's door, even the least cynical found themselves thinking of poison and giving credence to the rumour that the queen and Bothwell were lovers who had conspired to rid themselves of, first, an inconvenient husband, and now an inconvenient wife.

On 1st March, the most savage of all the placards appeared, one bearing a vaguely heraldic image showing a mermaid and a hare. The mermaid was a symbol of prostitution, and the hare happened to be the crest of the Hepburns. The artist, to insure against misunderstanding, had inscribed the letters M R – Maria Regina – beside the mermaid.

No one knew how it had all started, since before the king's death there had been no hint of salacious gossip about the queen and Bothwell, but the placards were so widespread and so similar in content that they might have been orchestrated.

By whom?

Interestingly, although no more than a few literate souls among Darnley's acquaintance – Bothwell among them – were aware of it, the mermaid and hare image bore a close resemblance to one of the images in a book which had belonged to the young man himself. If Darnley's distracted father, Lennox, had not been in Glasgow while the book was still in the late king's apartments at Holyrood, it might well have been thought that Lennox was behind the placard campaign.

Bothwell, swaggering through the town with his hand on his dagger and fifty of his adherents surrounding him, swore that, if he could find the culprits, he would wash his hands in their blood. He had his own views on who the culprits might be, and one of the chief among them was Lethington.

14

He was wrong, as it happened. The last thing Lethington wanted to do, however strong his desire to see the last of Bothwell, was to implicate the queen in the affair. Not only did he need her for his darling design of union but his sense of justice and the personal loyalty, in which Mary herself did not believe, committed him to her side. His support, as he knew, might appear devious to the superficial mind, but there was nothing new about that.

In any case, he had no time to waste on placards. All the monarchs of Europe, and most of their minions as well, were writing to tell the queen what she ought to do and not one of them failed to mention Mary's honour, as if they knew what 'honour' meant.

Even after a dozen years of experience, he was still astounded at the speed with which gossip spread. Catherine de' Medici wrote with ill-concealed delight to say that she was sure it wasn't true that Mary had ordered her husband's murder, but she must instantly catch the murderers, or else ...

The Spanish view, though expressed somewhat more opaquely, was that unless she were able to prove her innocence she would be useless as a weapon against England and therefore of no more interest to Philip.

Elizabeth's response was a masterpiece.

Madam,

My ears have been so astounded and my heart so frightened to hear of the

299

horrible and abominable murder of your late husband and my slaughtered cousin, that I have scarcely spirit to write. Yet I cannot conceal that I grieve more for you than him. I should not do the office of a faithful cousin and friend, if I did not urge you to preserve your honour, rather than look through your fingers at revenge on those who have done you such a kindness, as most people say ...

It was sound advice, for all that, but Lethington, who a year or two before would have been no more than amused by the hypocrisy of it all, found as he dictated suitably smooth replies that amusement had died in him.

15

If the reaction abroad was bad, it was worse at home. The placards increased in number and virulence. The commoners thought the whole nation shamed that the king should not be avenged. John Knox, still in Ayrshire working on his great *History of the Reformation in Scotland*, demanded blood in atonement for blood. Which came as no surprise.

The fact that Bothwell might have been responsible for the pyrotechnics but not for the king's death was overlooked by everyone. No one even hinted that Morton, via his family connections, might have been involved. The names of Argyll and Huntly, Cassillis and Glencairn, Lindsay and Ruthven, were never mentioned. Argyll even presided over the first, formal enquiry into the affair.

Hagridden by fear and self-interest, Mary's lords could not decide what to do. Although half of Scotland held Bothwell guilty of regicide, he himself, by proven loyalty and force of personality, had persuaded the queen that he was blameless.

She desperately wanted to believe him.

Once, when her world had still retained some semblance of sanity, she had spoken to him about his relationship with the rest of her privy council and her desire that he and they should be reconciled.

He had been in what was, for him, a subdued mood, although he was seldom less than respectful to her even when he was arguing a course of action or debating some political point. His fleshy brows had drawn together, emphasising the twin vertical frown lines between them. 'It's not all me, your majesty,' he had said.

'No, I recognise that.'

'There's a gulf between us, and it's more than a matter of us not seeing eye to eye over a few awkward episodes in the past.'

She had waited and then said smilingly, 'I am told you go out of your way to make enemies.'

He shook his head. 'Why should I? Enemies cost money that I haven't got. Friends are cheaper.'

'You mean you don't have to pay for a bodyguard to protect you from your friends?'

'Sometimes I wonder. No, the difficulty is that I'm a Borderer and we Borderers like things out in the open. We've no time for backstairs intrigues.' He had chuckled. 'Most of our homes don't have any stairs at all. I say what I think, honestly, and I don't change my opinions to suit the political situation. I know what's right and what's wrong.'

Wryly, she had remarked, 'My brother, the Earl of Moray, is also famous for knowing what's right and what's wrong. So why can you and he not agree?'

Another man might have passed it off with an evasion, but Bothwell, though clearly taking care over his words, in the end had said, 'There's a difference between knowing and observing.'

Since Mary knew, all too well, the deviousness that underlay the public rectitude of James and her other lords, she had not been offended by his forthrightness. It had led her to trust him more.

It meant that in the agonising darkness of the weeks following her husband's murder, she was ready to accept it when Bothwell told her that there was a conspiracy of the lords to blacken his name. By then she was so dependent on his strength, decisiveness and loyalty, that to disbelieve him would have killed her.

At court and in council, therefore, Bothwell became supreme while the lords kept their heads down. When Mary – or Bothwell – commanded, they obeyed because if Mary – or Bothwell – was looking for someone to sacrifice on the altar of public outcry, it was not going to be them.

16

If James, widely trusted and respected, had been there to give them a lead, if he had seen fit to return to court and take the situation in hand, everything might have worked out. But he stayed away, just as he had done in the weeks before his sister's marriage to Darnley. He did not want to be involved, was not prepared to make a move, and his absence was publicly seen as a condemnation of Mary as much as of Bothwell.

Not until a month after the murder did he even show his face in Edinburgh and it was not to resume his position as one of the senior advisers Mary so badly needed but to arrange for the issue of a passport.

Lethington said, 'What do you mean, you're going abroad for a few months?'

James said, 'It's unworthy of my position as the queen's brother and chief minister to remain in a country where such a crime goes unpunished.'

Even from James, that was a bit rich. 'You don't feel that, as the queen's brother and chief minister, you might do something about it?'

'Bothwell's too strong, and my sister isn't going to sacrifice him.'

There was a distaste on his face that suggested he was thinking more of the seventh than the sixth commandment. It wasn't simply a matter of 'Thou shalt do no murder'. Lethington said, 'Ah. You've seen the mermaid-and-hare placards, have you?'

'I was never more shocked!' James had put on flesh in the last year, not very much, but enough to coarsen his features. 'And to think I never even suspected!'

'There was never anything to suspect.' Mallie would have known, if anyone had. 'James, your sister needs you.'

'Well, she knows what to do about it. I'll not share power with Bothwell again. D'ye know, he's even been spreading rumours that I had something to do with Darnley's death. Me!'

'No!'

'Ye think that's funny, do you? Well, Cecil's heard them and so's the Venetian ambassador in Paris.'

'Then your best course is to encourage Mary to set up an investigation and bring the real guilty party to book. She'll be forced to do it in the long run, and you might as well take the credit.'

James wasn't even tempted. 'Why don't you do it?'

'Because,' Lethington replied caustically, 'I am Mackyvelly, remember? I am too clever for my own or anyone else's good. If it's a question of trusting me to get them out of a difficulty or looking to their own self-interest, no one even sees it as a choice. Anyway, my primary rôle has always been in foreign affairs.'

'Yes. No. Well ... I wouldn't disagree. But as I see it, the truth's bound

302

to come out in the end, though not until after there's been some kind of upheaval, and I don't want to be involved. I'm off to Italy to further my education.'

Lethington studied him for a moment. 'And when somebody else has eliminated Bothwell, *then* you will come back with your hands clean and take over political control again?'

'Aye. Well, it's common sense, isn't it?'

They had known each other for years, worked well together, been friends – even when they disagreed, even when Lethington had become suspicious of him. And that, Lethington supposed, was why he had never before seen the full truth of James, that, although he was a tower of strength, a fine administrator and an effective statesman when he had the upper hand, he had no moral stamina at all when things went wrong. He either floundered, as he had done over the Darnley marriage, or, as now, sacrificed everything to his own self-interest. Just like everyone else.

'Yes, it's common sense,' Lethington agreed. 'But won't you change your mind?'

By the end of the month, Mary had been forced by pressure from her fellow sovereigns abroad and Darnley's extravagantly grieving father at home to set a date for Bothwell to be brought to trial, but it didn't change James's mind. He wouldn't even put off his departure for the four days that would have enabled him to attend.

17

It was unfortunate in that it deprived him of the opportunity of saying, 'I told ye so.'

A criminal prosecution would normally have been initiated by the Crown, but the Earl of Lennox, repetitively demanding it, made the mistake of begging the queen to bring to trial the people named on the anonymous placards. This raised a number of difficulties, not least that her majesty was being required to try the alleged murderers on the word of accusers whose identity, like the worth of their accusations, was unknown.

Since Lord Lennox was anxious for swift action, it seemed best to the queen, or so she wrote, that he himself should institute the prosecution, naming names and being responsible for producing witnesses. The trial would be set for Saturday, 12th April, when Lord Bothwell would be tried – or so she understood from Lord Justice Argyll – for being 'art and part of the cruel, odious, treasonable and abominable slaughter of the late, the right excellent, right high and mighty prince, the king's grace, dearest spouse for the time to our sovereign lady the queen's majesty, under silence of night in his own lodging beside the Kirk o' Field, he taking the night's rest.'

Lennox found nothing amiss with the charge but, his disposition never having been trusting, took three thousand men with him when he set off for Edinburgh – a city already swarming with Bothwell's men – only to be forbidden to enter it with more than six personal followers, the number prescribed by law. His desire for retribution much dimmed, he delegated one of his clerks to represent him and beat a prudent retreat back to the safety of Glasgow.

The trial went ahead without him. A little before noon on the appointed day, the queen stood at an upper window at Holyroodhouse watching Bothwell emerge below her and ride off up the Canongait and the Highgait to the Tolbooth, flanked on one side by Morton and on the other by Lethington, and with Hepburn supporters converging from all directions to bring up the rear.

She sighed. 'It seems to me very cowardly of Lord Lennox not to appear. If his faction and Lord Bothwell's had been allowed to meet in open war, his life would have been in much greater danger than if he had come as a private person, as he was told to do. Oh, dear, I think I ...'

Mallie Fleming said, 'Madame, you *must* not faint!'

'No, I ...' She had fainted times without number in the previous week, and still felt weak and helpless. To submit to rising this morning, and being gowned and coiffed and jewelled had been almost beyond her, but on public occasions she had no choice. 'What will happen? Lethington says that without verification or testification of the indictment, the court must find Lord Bothwell not guilty, but I am not sure. I am sure of nothing any more.'

Gently, Mallie led her to a chair, wondering whether her sickliness and melancholy would ever be healed. 'It will be all right,' she assured her. Two thirds of the assessors and jury, she knew, were active enemies of Bothwell, but her husband said that, without evidence, even they would have to judge in his favour.

And so it fell out.

His innocence vindicated, Bothwell sent criers around the town proclaiming it. But no one believed it for a moment.

Parliament opened on the following Monday, and on the Wednesday Mary attended with full ceremonial, Bothwell bearing the sceptre and Argyll the crown. This year, for the first time, the queen felt the need for a guard of arquebusiers around her.

Lethington, too busy to attend the sitting, was patiently working his way through a budget of papers that never grew smaller when he was confronted by a wife in a flame of anger – no moonlight goddess, but a woman infinitely beloved, at the unexpected sight of whom his heart still leapt, and would do for ever. He had barely seen her for three weeks because she been in attendance on the queen day and night.

Bursting unceremoniously into his sanctum at the palace, she demanded, 'Can you not do *anything*? She is exhausted in her very bones. Yesterday she fainted clean away on three separate occasions. She can't even think for herself and, what's worse, doesn't want to. I believe she is really, truly bewitched. All those years when you and James tried to persuade her, for good and rational reasons, that she should legally acknowledge the reformed kirk ... All those careful years, and now, if you please, *quite* out of the blue, an Act taking the reformed kirk under the protection of the Crown! And all because my vile cousin Bothwell has overridden her own judgement and has simply told her she must! He means to marry her. I know he does. Not because he loves her but because he wants power.'

Lethington had no doubt that she was right, but how to control the man he did not know. Evading the issue, he said, 'Bothwell is a good Protestant, and the Act was a necessary one.'

'You cannot think that his motives were pure? It would be the first time in his life that anyone has said that of him!'

'Perhaps not. But he is trying to buy support, and if the end is good then I'm not sure that the motives matter.'

His wife flounced, and he could not resist taking her in his arms and saying, 'Don't be upset, my darling. It cannot be good for the baby.'

The flame died from her eyes, and with a sigh she leaned her forehead against his shoulder. 'Oh, what a mess everything is. I pray God grants me a more peaceful pregnancy than He granted Madame. But He will. I know He will. And I have you to protect me.'

He had no need of the reminder. He had always valued his life, as all sane men did, but he had not always been careful of it. The time had come to change that. If he could.

The air in Ainslie's tavern was thick with noise and sweat and wine and meat, although it was no common Saturday night. Never before had Master Ainslie kicked his spit boys so constantly back to the fires of their own particular hell; never before had Mistress Ainslie clouted the kitchen scullions' ears so hard that she rendered them deaf to her screeched commands; never before had the serving wenches smiled so warmly as drunken hands fumbled at their breasts; never before had the fiddlers put so much energy into 'The wowing o' Jock and Jenny'.

Never before had a king's murderer entertained eight bishops, nine earls, and seven barons to supper.

The Earl of Morton, peering out from the riotous red jungle of his whiskers like a wildcat out of a whin bush, discovered that his wine cup was empty and upended it on his head, saying, 'I wouldnae mind a hat this shape. What d'ye think, Cassillis?'

'Needs a brim. Why's Bothwell paying for all this?'

'Won't pay. Never does. Doesnae have any money.'

Huntly said solemnly, 'Wants to tell us something. He's a witch. My mother's got a tame witch. Tells her all sorts of things.'

Even Argyll, who normally had a head like a rock, was a little the worse for wear. '*Dia*! It iss four years since we wass making witchcraft a capital crime. Maybe we could be catching him there.'

Huntly said, 'Shouldn't talk like that. He's a friend of mine. Anyway, 'tisn't reasonable to expect someone to stop being a witch right off, jus' because parliament says so ...'

He was interrupted by their host, who had mounted the table and was standing feet astride, head thrown back, yelling for silence at the pitch of his powerful lungs. In one hand he held some sheets of paper.

'We've had a good week,' he declared, 'and you should all be pleased – except Sutherland and Eglinton there – at the kirk laws we passed today. You've me to thank for those, as no doubt you know. Now, I've a bond here I want you to sign. There's six copies, and I'll pass them round so you can read it between you, then you can write your names on the main bond. I'll not take refusal kindly.'

And neither, Argyll thought sourly, would the arquebusiers surrounding the tavern. Bothwell's guests had attended the supper from a mixture of motives, some because they were stupid, others because they were bootlickers, but most because they were inquisitive. As far as he knew, the only men who had declined the invitation were Atholl and Lethington.

Argyll had thought, himself, that it was just Bothwell showing off, proving that he was able to command the chief men of the kingdom to sup with him, but when he read the bond, with Sutherland looking over one shoulder and Rothes over the other, he discovered how wrong he had been.

It began, which came as no surprise, with a long-winded pledge by the signatories to support Bothwell against any further accusations relating to the death of the king, but what followed was less predictable. After pointing out that, in the interests of the common good, the queen should not remain destitute of a husband, it went on by way of Bothwell's 'affectionate and hearty service', his noble blood, and the desirability of her choosing a native-born rather than foreign subject as her consort, to its outrageous conclusion – which was that, if the queen was moved to take the said Earl of Bothwell to husband, all the signatories swore 'to further the marriage by vote, counsel and assistance.' Any who went back on their oath would 'never have reputation or credit in no time hereafter, but be accounted unworthy and faithless traitors.'

Morton, across the table, muttered, 'Guidsakes!' and looked up to catch Argyll's eye. 'Am I reading this right?'

Considerably sobered, Argyll nodded. There had been rumours of such a plan, even that Bothwell had proposed marriage to the queen and been rejected. And now Bothwell, who did not lack cunning, had thought of a way round the problem. The queen had married Darnley against the wishes of almost all her lords; this time, she could fall in with their wishes by marrying the man they unanimously approved, none other than James Hepburn, Earl of Bothwell.

King James Hepburn.

Argyll didn't like the sound of it.

In his ear, Rothes murmured, 'Well, I'll sign it with pleasure. If she marries her husband's murderer, we'll soon see the end of both of them.'

Further along the table, he could hear Seton, Mary's frequent host and most devoted admirer, saying with conviction, 'It's all right. She'll never agree.'

In the end – since, as Morton muttered, there were some bonds ye couldnae expect folk tae keep – everyone signed except Eglinton, who contrived to slip out to the privy and never returned.

Chapter Fourteen

APRIL-JUNE 1567

1

The queen had her own set of apartments at Seton House, a splendid mansion about ten miles along the coast from Edinburgh, which meant, as Lord Seton – her Master of the Household and Mary Seton's brother – had said when he first suggested it, that she could come at any time, without warning and without ceremony. It had become one of her favourite retreats, a friendly and happy place on the southern shore of the Firth of Forth where she always felt at ease.

On the day after the supper at Ainslie's tavern, she was walking in the garden with Lady Seton and three of the children when Lord Bothwell arrived, accompanied by justice clerk Bellenden and secretary of state Lethington. As the three of them uncovered their heads and bowed before her, she noted that Bothwell was bursting with vigour, as always; Bellenden tight-mouthed; and Lethington so extravagantly bland that she wondered if something had happened to anger him. It seemed unlikely, since his even temper was proverbial.

But such considerations fled from her mind as Bothwell, with the courtesy he always showed to her, if no one else, begged that they might sit formally round a table since this was a formal meeting and they were here as her privy councillors. Vaguely worried, Mary tried to think if there was anything urgent she had forgotten. It was not unlikely, since her mind, these days, constantly skittered away from anything on which she might have to make a decision.

Smiling with absent politeness, she led them up to her audience chamber, and they sat round a table, with Mary Seton and Lady Reres – who was Mary Beaton's aunt and now shared her duties – settled in a corner with their stitchery. Then Bothwell told her that she needed a husband, and that all her leading nobles had signed a bond recommending him as the best candidate, and here it was.

The room whirled about her, and she had to close her eyes because the windows were sliding over the wainscotting and the ceiling medallions wafting to the floor like autumn leaves. For the briefest of moments, the thin spring sunshine gave way to darkness.

All she could say was, 'But the scandal!' There was no other thought in her head, and no feeling in her heart. No pleasure or displeasure. Nothing.

'What scandal?' demanded Bothwell. 'All your lords agree that I'm innocent of your late husband's death, and I told you myself I had nothing to do with it.'

'I know,' she said hastily. 'But ...'

She stopped, because she couldn't think what to say after the 'but'.

Lethington's cool voice intervened. 'This has come as a surprise to your majesty. Indeed' – he smiled quizzically – 'it has also come as a surprise to Bellenden here, and to myself. We only heard of the bond this morning, when Lord Bothwell asked us to accompany him here. But it is very true that something must be done to rectify the state into which public affairs have fallen in these last weeks, lacking guidance. A strong husband would give your majesty the support you need.'

With a spurt of temper that surprised herself as much as her hearers, she snapped, 'My cousin Elizabeth seems to manage very well without a husband to support her. But she, of course, has Secretary Cecil.'

Without a flicker, Lethington agreed, 'Who is a model to us all. I am one of his greatest admirers. The situation is not, however, the same.'

'No.' She scanned the list of signatures to the bond. Atholl was missing, and Eglinton, and James, of course, who was probably in London by now, ingratiating himself with Elizabeth. She should be angry, should be saying how dared her lords discuss her affairs in her absence, how dared they dictate to her! They had always thought that, because she was a woman, they were entitled to tell her what to do. She would marry again if she chose, whom she chose, and when she chose.

But she did not have the energy to be angry, just as she did not have the energy to think about the contents of the bond. She said, 'I will consider the matter. You may leave me now.'

As they were bowing their way out, she remembered something. 'Secretary Lethington, I will be returning to Holyrood this afternoon and leaving at first light tomorrow for Stirling. It is almost six weeks since I have seen my son. You may tell the privy councillors whose turn it is to accompany me that I do not expect the visit to last for more than a day or two.'

Her little man was ten months old now and she had forgotten how quickly babies developed, because now he could not only stand with confidence but was almost ready to walk without holding on to the furniture. She laughed and wept at the same time as he abandoned his reassuring chair leg and took three scrambling, panicky steps towards her outheld arms and the safety of her skirts. She read aloud to him and showed him some of the miniatures in her prayer book, and although he could not possibly have understood them, he made guggling noises as if he were trying to imitate her words. She played ball with him, and he loved it. Sitting on her lap, he grasped her pearled and jewelled pendant in two chubby little fists and began gnawing on it as if it were a teething stick.

She would not allow the nurse to take him from her when he sank into sleep in her arms, cradled in tenderness. It brought so much back to her, the wonderful, glorious days of her own childhood, when as the youthful eldest in the Valois nursery she had loved and cherished the succession of royal babies, and discovered her own maternal instincts. So long ago, it had been. So far from this violent, frightening world of which she was queen.

It had been a golden time, endlessly exciting, endlessly delightful. Even in the formal clothes that children had to wear from the age of eight, when they began to be seen as miniature adults – the expensively embroidered outer garments, the restricting undergarments, the stiff little bonnets and the serge stockings – it was still possible to have ordinary childish fun, to play catch-me-who-can up and down the unfinished marble staircase at St Germain when no one else was in residence, to slide as smoothly as on ice from one end to the other of the magnificent, half-painted ballroom at Fontainebleau, to play racquets across the king's very own bed in his official mistress's *château* at Anet. François had even slept in the bed because, however undersized the heir to the throne, if he happened to be in a stubborn mood – and François could be very stubborn – there were few people with the authority to say him nay.

She had forgotten what it had been like.

Only now, with her son in her arms, did she understand what it must have meant to her own mother to give her five-year-old child into the keeping of others, far away. To see her again, for an extended visit, only once more in her lifetime. When her mother had died, Mary had wept her heart out from grief and from guilt, because theirs had been a love without intimacy. She had thought, 'Things will be different when I have children. I will *never* let them be separated from me.'

And now she had one small son whom she saw rarely, and there were no marble staircases and no ballroom floors, and she was so weary from the blood and strife of this savage land, where all her careful training in courtliness and statecraft had availed her nothing, that she did not know what to do for the best.

3

But there was no escape from being queen.

She set out from Stirling next morning to return to Edinburgh. Still tired from the forty-mile ride of two days before, a ride that would once have stimulated rather than tired her, she chose to break the journey with a night at Linlithgow, the lochside castle where she had been born. Even before she reached it, she had to stop at a wayside cottage because the pain in her side was troubling her so badly.

And next day, everything – her whole present, her whole future – was taken out of her hands.

Her party was a small one with a guard of only twenty horsemen. As well as Mary herself, with two valets and her two favourite chamber women, there were her three privy councillors; Lethington with his clerk, his bodyservant and his groom; Huntly with his usual two bodyservants and two grooms in full livery; and Sir James Melville, slender and elegant, with his equally slender and elegant bodyservant and groom. And that was all.

It meant that she could not resist, even if she had had the energy or the desire, when Lord Bothwell appeared at the head of eight hundred men and told her that danger threatened her in Edinburgh and he would take her to the stronghold of Dunbar, where she had found refuge after the murder of Riccio.

Lethington said, 'Danger? What danger? Where is your proof of it?' but Bothwell ignored him.

Swords were drawn among her escort, but she gestured them back into their scabbards. Too much blood had been shed already.

It was late in the evening when Bothwell lifted his fainting queen out of the saddle and carried her indoors at Dunbar, his men hustling Lethington and Melville along after her. Huntly, who had known about the abduction beforehand – for abduction was what it was – remarked

311

languidly, 'What we need is a drink.' It was the most sensible statement anyone had made all day.

Lethington, his grey eyes ice-cold, turned to Bothwell. 'This is not the way to do it.' And Bothwell looked back at him, his brown eyes hot, and said, 'I knew you would say that.'

The Great Hall of the castle was cold and unwelcoming despite the huge logs burning in the fireplace and the stands of candles that had been set out in advance of their coming; tallow candles, smoky and smelling of mutton. Outside, the North Sea beat relentlessly against the rocks on which the castle stood and a rising gale howled around its walls. A servant brought some cold meat and wine, which they were all in need of.

'If that bond means anything at all,' Lethington said, 'you can do things decently and respectably.'

'Why should I? Decency and respectability take too long, too much negotiating. The queen needs a husband *now*.'

Lethington hadn't foreseen anything like this, although he supposed he should have done. That was always the problem if you happened to be a civilised man dealing with uncivilised ruffians.

Huntly, subsiding onto a carved oak bench and stretching his booted feet out comfortably, drawled, 'You're being tedious, Secretary. Bothwell knows what he's doing.'

Lethington barely glanced at him. It had always been a mystery how such a likeable, wise and down-to-earth young woman as Jean Gordon should have a brother like this, a brother lacking all judgement and consideration, who had forced her to give up the man she loved in order to marry Bothwell. Whom he would now instruct her to divorce.

'Does he?'

Only because the queen was present, although limp, shivering and barely conscious in her cushioned chair beside the fire, did Bothwell deign to provide an explanation of sorts. 'If I do it this way, I can take all the blame. By kidnapping the queen, I, and only I, am responsible. I can hold her until she agrees to marry me. It means that her reputation remains unsullied.'

It was hard to believe that any man could be so arrogant and so stupid.

Turning to Mary, Lethington said with all the intensity of which he was capable, 'Your majesty, this will not do. You must tell Lord Bothwell, here and now, that you cannot approve such doings, which can bring nothing but disaster. If you make it clear to him that you will *not* be forced into marriage, we can cover up this day's work somehow.

'Don't believe, for a moment, that the bond he showed you has any meaning. Don't believe, for a moment, that the signatories will continue to favour the marriage after such an episode as this, if they ever favoured it at all. From what I know, most of them signed because they thought it didn't matter, that nothing would come of it. Others hoped that something might come of it and that the sequel would be a rebellion against you. You *must not* submit.'

He had gone too far. The tension, already palpable, erupted into violence. He felt his arms gripped by two of Bothwell's men, and Bothwell was within a foot of him, red hatred in his eyes. He knew that there was a cold and corresponding hatred in his own – in the eyes of William Maitland, laird of Lethington, who had never before condescended to hate anyone.

The dagger went in with a deliberate slowness, piercing his dark blue doublet over the ribs, penetrating his shirt, touching his flesh and entering it, twisting, grinding, until he could feel on his skin the first invisible trickle of blood that would soon become a stream and then a torrent.

He was scarcely aware of the pain. Pain was as much a part of life as effort and despair.

He had come to love too late. He should have been thinking of his wife, his unborn son, his promises, but all that possessed his mind was anger at the thought of dying defeated.

Over Bothwell's shoulder he could see Melville watching, his face strained but resigned, a man who would not intervene because he wanted to go on living. And that was the tale of sixteenth-century Scotland in a nutshell. Lethington could not understand why he himself had spent so much of his existence trying to change things.

It was the queen who saved him, dragging herself out of her chair, overcoming her apathy for long enough to gasp, 'No! No! I will have no more killing.'

After that, they threw him in one of the dungeons and locked him up.

4

Next morning, they allowed Melville to see him.

Melville said, 'I'm told he raped her last night, though she looked so exhausted that she probably slept through it. And now he's given me my servants and horses and told me I can go. I imagine I'm expected to spread the news.'

313

Through the searing agony the night had brought, Lethington managed to say, 'I imagine you are.'

5

Melville did his work well. It was unfortunate that Huntly had given the abduction plot away in advance to one or two of the lords, so that it was widely suspected that Mary had gone with Bothwell quietly because she, too, had known about it in advance. Melville discovered that he was wasting his breath pointing out that eight hundred men were an argument not to be gainsaid, but he did succeed in persuading most people that the rape had been against the queen's will.

Within two weeks of the abduction, Jean Gordon successfully petitioned 'to be no longer repute bone of her husband's bone, nor flesh of his flesh' in view of his adultery with one of her maidservants, and the Earl of Bothwell applied for and was granted a nullification of their marriage by Archbishop Hamilton.

By that time, to the surprise of no one, most of the signatories to the Ainslie's tavern bond had signed another, very different bond.

'It's a scandal!' Morton had declared. 'An outrage against public decency. I never heard the like. We'll have tae do something. We'll have tae rescue her majesty.'

The lords who had been keeping their heads down since the Darnley murder had excused their inaction by claiming that they did not wish to be accused of envying Bothwell's increasing power. That was something they could forget about now. This time Bothwell had committed high treason, and very publicly indeed.

Morton scarcely needed to point all this out to Argyll, Atholl, Mar and Kirkcaldy of Grange, but that did not stop him. What he did not mention was the other considerations he had in mind. This time there were going to be no rigged trials. This time, Bothwell was going to finish up dead. And this time, Morton, for one, wasn't going to be bothered if the queen lost her throne in the process.

'Right, then,' he went on, rubbing his hands. 'What are we going tae put in the bond?'

Liberating the queen was obviously the first item, but the Earl of Mar, official guardian to the infant prince, suggested, 'We should have something about keeping the boy safe from such a man.'

314

It was agreed. Then Atholl offered, 'And we should commit ourselves to punishing the king's murderers.'

That, too, was agreed. It seemed unnecessary to add anything more.

It looked a very responsible and honest bond, guileless enough to attract many signatories; guileless enough to persuade Elizabeth of England to honour it with her support; guileless enough to warrant raising an army.

Morton, Argyll and Atholl went off to do just that.

James Stewart, Earl of Moray, who was still in the south of England when the news of his sister's abduction and rape became known there, did not allow it to change his plans. On 1st May, the day the bond was drawn up, he crossed to France.

6

The eight hundred men encamped round Dunbar were the only sign that the queen was being held under duress. Indoors, they might not have existed. Bothwell was shrewd enough to recognise that it was necessary for the queen's government to continue to function in proper legal form, and it was made possible by the fact that there were three privy councillors – himself, Huntly and Lethington – there to advise her. Lethington's clerk was a tower of administrative strength and Lethington himself, although heavily bandaged and barely cooperative, was permitted to send messengers back and forth to Edinburgh to keep in touch with his assistant, Alexander Hay.

The queen herself mystified him by behaving exactly as she had been behaving for months – apathetic and melancholy by turns, showing a rare flash of the old charm and an even rarer flash of the old spirit. He could not believe that a young woman whose virtue had never been questioned by anyone who knew her well and who was, indeed, inclined to be straitlaced in her attitude towards sexual laxity, had been able to take rape quite so much in her stride. Even the fine skin of her face showed no sign of contact with the roughness of a Borderer's beard. He instructed his bodyservant and groom to make enquiries but, although there was gossip, none of it was conclusive.

And then, one afternoon, Mary's apathy vanished and she and Bothwell quarrelled loudly, violently and at length.

No one knew the reason for it but the servants reported that her soft voice had several times risen to a scream. 'How dared you? How dared you?' But Bothwell's voice was deep and did not carry. All anyone heard was a single shout of, 'It was the best answer.'

The queen had been distraught afterwards but, next day, lifelessly calm again, she called her three privy councillors together to inform them that, since she understood that the entire world now believed Lord Bothwell not only to have abducted her but ravished her, it seemed that she no longer any choice open to her.

'I have no strength left to deal alone with these endless crises, and I need a consort to support me. Many members of my privy council were signatories to the bond Secretary Lethington so much distrusts, but what is the purpose of a bond if not to be honoured? I have therefore agreed to marry the Earl of Bothwell. We will return to Edinburgh in the coming week and the marriage will take place soon after.'

Lethington met Bothwell's gloating eyes, no expression in his own.

7

Before the minister at the parish church of Edinburgh would consent to read the banns, he demanded a written assurance from the queen that she had neither been violated nor kept in captivity.

She gave it to him, but the placards of March and the rumours of April had had their effect. In her subjects' eyes, if what she said was true, then whatever she was doing, she was doing voluntarily. The kindest interpretation was that she had been bewitched into taking her husband's murderer as her lover and now as her new husband; Bothwell had always been suspected of practising witchcraft.

Mallie Fleming, lady of Lethington, was never to be able to look back without a shudder on the weeks that followed.

The queen's marriage to François nine years before had been a pageant of dreams, an affair of white and gold and diamonds, of grandeur unimaginable. And when she had married Darnley just two years before, there had been cloth of gold and jewels and dancing, feasting and masques. But now ...

'Perhaps if we stitched some gold braid to one of my old black gowns, that would do. And a new white taffeta underskirt for the yellow gown with the paned sleeves? I don't need more than that, do I, Fleming?'

'No, Madame. What wedding gifts were you thinking of giving Lord Bothwell?'

'What did I give Harry?' the queen said. 'I don't remember.' And then she heard her own words and her eyes filled with horror.

It was unbearable. Not since they were children had Mallie Fleming embraced the queen or called her anything other than Madame, but now she dropped the silks and velvets she was holding, and threw her arms round her and said, 'Cousin, don't. Oh, my dear, don't! Don't think of it!'

'How can I help it? What have I done? What am I going to do?' And then, even through her tears, she saw Mallie's expression and exclaimed, 'No, you are going to say what Lethington says. You are going to tell me I don't have to marry him. But I don't want to hear it. Neither of you knows what I have been through. I *must* marry Bothwell, because he is strong and without his strength I shall die. If it were not for my son, I would *want* to die.'

Frowning a little, Mallie stepped back, aware that there were few occupations less rewarding than trying to reason with someone who was not only miserable, but revelling in it. And it was not for a subject, even for a cousin, to slap a beloved queen hard and tell her to pull herself together. So she said, 'There were jewels and lengths of velvet, as I remember, and a cabinet for perfumes, and ...'

'No, I can't give thought to such things. Some furs for his bedgown will be enough.'

The wedding was held according to the Protestant rite in the Great Hall at Holyrood and the marriage contract included a clause stating that one of the objects of the union was to produce heirs of the queen's body. But there was no lighthearted sequel during which the bride exchanged her widow's weeds for cloth of gold. There were no masques and no dancing, only a chill dinner consumed in chill formality by bride and groom, watched by a handful of guests and some mildly interested spectators from among Edinburgh's citizens.

8

It was the third wedding night in Mary's twenty-four years of life. On the first, there had been nothing sexual. On the second, she had been romantically, determinedly in love, and her husband – although she had not known it at the time – had been careful with her. Even when he had ceased to be careful, he had never been animal. She had never felt less than the queen she was.

But Bothwell was different. A man who expected her not to be a queen, but a woman. A man who tried to arouse her with words whose coarseness she recognised but whose meaning she did not understand, who invaded her tender body with rough-skinned fingers and then swore savagely as he forced himself into her. Whose only interests were in his own physical release, and in begetting a son who might some day found a Hepburn dynasty.

She was aching, heartbroken and hysterical by the time the night was over, and the skin of her breasts and thighs was raw and scarlet from the roughness of his beard.

9

The tears of repentance for the Protestant rite and shame over the demeaning marriage began publicly and in earnest on the day after the wedding, so that every minute, every hour, certainly every document, seemed to be watered by them. Lethington found himself almost sympathising with Bothwell until the new Duke of Orkney's temper became so exacerbated that violence hung in the air like a thundercloud from which lightning might at any moment flash through. Three weeks after the wedding, with his Dunbar wound not yet healed, Lethington found himself gazing again at the point of Bothwell's knife. This time, fortunately, there were too many people present for even Bothwell to do what he so savagely wished to do.

For the queen's sake, Lethington had stayed as long as he could, far longer than some thought reasonable. For the queen's sake, he had tried to moderate the plot that was forming against her new husband, so as to save her from the worst consequences. But there were limits. She was, after all, an adult and responsible for her own life.

As he prepared to make his escape from court, his wife said, 'I remember asking you once whether you would die for her, and you thought about it and said, "Perhaps." Don't think I *do* want you to die for her, or for anyone, but what has changed?'

He looked at her almost abstractedly, his eyes in the thin candlelight as darkly grey as the northern seas. 'I would give my life in the hope of achieving a worthwhile purpose,' he replied after a moment, 'but I will not waste it uselessly. I must go now, and see what is to be done about that purpose. Goodbye, my dearest love.'

Her hand to the child within her, Mallie Fleming, lady of Lethington, said, 'Come back to me,' and then, under her breath, 'but try not to let her be hurt any more than she has already been hurt.'

10

During those same three weeks after her wedding, the queen discovered that she had alienated almost every sovereign in Europe by marrying the man who was generally believed to have been her husband's murderer.

Despite endless, carefully drafted, sometimes apologetic letters written not only by herself but by an unexpectedly statesmanlike Bothwell, and despite the uneasy excuses of her ambassadors, the general consensus was that she must have run mad. Her Protestant marriage ceremony and the subsequent proclamations designed to reassure her Protestant subjects cut her off finally and it seemed irrevocably from France, Spain and the papacy, while completely failing to silence her lords. She conceded almost everything to them. John Knox should have been proud of her – the man who had made her life a misery and taught her subjects to hate her, and who had then gone off to Ayrshire to write his book and beget a new family of daughters and behave as if the queen no longer mattered. The truth, it seemed, was that although her lords had hated her Catholicism for years, they hated Bothwell more.

By late May, before he and the queen had been married a month, Bothwell recognised that serious trouble was brewing, though he was not sure how widespread it was. Since he had dispersed his army after Dunbar, he needed to muster a new force and it seemed a good opportunity to test loyalties. On the pretext of a raid against the incorrigible miscreants of Liddesdale, he therefore summoned all earls, lords, barons, freeholders, landed men and yeomen from districts immediately to the west and north of Edinburgh to meet on the Borders at Melrose, with arms and provisions, on 12th June.

It precipitated the crisis, because the men who had begun to call themselves the confederate lords saw his move as a declaration of war.

11

Two days before the appointed date, Bothwell rode the twenty miles to Melrose from Borthwick castle, where he and Mary were staying as guests of the laird, to return with the news that there was no sign at all of a gathering army.

Or not at Melrose.

On the very next morning, an army, though not a friendly one, appeared outside the walls of the high, stern, twin-towered keep known as Borthwick, which was set on a shallow hillside in a river valley.

Soon after first light the disbelieving watchmen on the battlements saw a seemingly endless column of horsemen approaching, arms glinting in the newly risen sun. Within minutes, hurrying into the queen's chamber, strapping on his armour, Bothwell snapped, 'There's at least a thousand of them. Can you make out who's at their head?'

Mary, still in her shift, ran to the window. The head of the column had slowed to allow the rear to fan out into a long and ragged line and although there was a banner, hanging limp in the windless air, it needed no banner to identify the black clothing and full red beard of the leader.

In a flat voice, she said, 'It's Morton.' Lethington, it seemed, had been right, and the Ainslie tavern bond had meant nothing.

She snatched at her bedgown as Lord Borthwick appeared in the doorway. 'This isn't just an ordinary raid. I sent one o' my men out, and it's you they're after, Hepburn. They're demanding that you give yourself up.'

'They can demand as much as they like! What force have we got?'

'With your men and mine? Two hundred or so.'

'Can we stand a siege?'

'Oh, aye, if it's the old-fashioned kind. We're long used to that. We've got weapons and supplies and a well of fresh water. But if they bring up cannon, we're too exposed. It'd be all over in a day.'

Bothwell stood chewing his lip, and then grinned. 'Single combat, then. I'll send out a challenge to Morton.'

'You will do no such thing!'

He turned, his swarthy face flushing, his mouth opening on a hectoring reply.

But his wife's temper had also risen. Morton, she had seen, was accompanied by a number of men to whom she had shown favour, whose loyalty she had bought on what she now saw to have been a very short lease. Her anger giving her vigour, she said again, 'You will do no such thing. You are my husband and also my military commander. If this is a rebellion against the Crown, it cannot be settled by single combat. I need you to be free. I need you to raise an army for *us*, so that we can settle these outbreaks of disaffection once and for all. It is not possible to rule a realm constantly riven by faction. I want my son to inherit a peaceful kingdom.'

Bothwell, who had not seen his wife in such a mood since the days of the Earl of Moray's Chaseabout Raid, stared at her as, glancing out of the window again, she said, 'I think the flanks are moving to surround the castle. There is still time for you to get away. I will keep them occupied and, if I can, come and join you later. Where?'

Reluctantly, he said, 'I'll make for Hailes, and then Dunbar.'

He bowed to her formally as he always did in company, however roughly he might behave in private. She did not love him. She had almost forgotten that she had once liked him a little. But she still needed and trusted him. To her own surprise as much as his, she leaned forward and kissed him, and said, 'Go, now. I depend on you.'

12

From where she stood on the battlements, she could just see the roof of Bothwell's own castle of Crichton, two miles away. When he had married Jean Gordon, the contract had given her a life rent in it and she was still there, convalescing from the illness that had nearly killed her. Life was full of ironies. Mary liked Jean and hoped she would return to court some day, when everything had settled down.

Morton was shouting up at her, keeping his distance from the castle and the archers and arquebusiers who might be lying in wait behind the slit windows. 'We want Bothwell. We've come tae save ye from him. Give him up tae us and we'll go away peacefully.'

Although her voice was naturally soft, training had given it the carrying quality required of royalty. Leaning through one of the embrasures, she called down, 'The Duke of Orkney is husband to the queen, who has no need to be saved from him. Nor is he here. I warn you, my Lord Morton, that I will have you and your friends tried for treason unless you disband your force and return to your homes.'

'We know he's here.'

'I assure you he is not. Do you dare doubt your queen's word?'

'I'll dare right enough. She's told us enough lies in the past.'

With a thousand horses tossing their harnesses and pawing the earth, it was not easy to make out what Morton was saying, and Mary could not at first believe she had heard aright. But her instinctive fury at the untruth of it was at once lost in the realisation that this was, at last, a full rebellion against the Crown. No man called his sovereign a liar if he might be called to account for it.

As she leaned out again to cry, 'You will pay dearly for that,' there was a shout from one of the horsemen, followed by another, and then there was a forest of pointing arms raised, and cries of, 'It's him!' and a group of about fifty horse wheeled away to ride fast uphill past the castle.

Mary fled round the battlements to watch the pursuit. But Bothwell was well mounted on a horse fresher than his pursuers' and he was disappearing from sight even as the chase began. Half an hour later, Morton's men came straggling back.

After that, when Mary with a scornful laugh had refused Morton's offer to escort her back to Edinburgh, he held a conference with his supporters. If it was truly Bothwell they were after, they had no justification for remaining. At a little past nine o'clock in the morning, a triumphant Mary saw them turn away and vanish whence they had come.

Or so it seemed. But it turned out that Morton had left two hundred men lying hidden around the perimeter, so that Mary had to wait until after midnight before, dressed in doublet and hose belonging to one of the Borthwick sons and escorted by another of them, she was able to slip unobserved out of the keep and away, to be reunited more briefly than she yet knew with the third husband in her twenty-four years of life, the man whose strength and purpose still reminded her, just a little, of the dark, harsh-featured, beloved second father of her youth, the Duc de Guise.

13

It was not true to say that whoever held Edinburgh castle held Edinburgh, but twenty-five cannon and a clear field of fire down the Lawnmarket and the Highgait normally served to discourage rebel armies from marching blithely in. And since the current captain of the castle was Mary's privy councillor and Bothwell's avowed adherent, Sir James Balfour, Morton and his men, returning from Borthwick, might have been expected to hesitate.

That they did not was because Sir James had an educated eye for fashion and knew when it was time to turn his coat.

The confederate lords were proposing to call on all lieges to join them in delivering their queen from captivity and bringing to trial the murderer of the late king, and Sir James had no doubt that the lords were going to win or that they would then ritually sacrifice a few selected victims to the memory of Darnley. Since he had no intention of being one of them, he had entered into negotiations to sell the lords both his allegiance and the castle in exchange for an indemnity against past misdeeds, whatever they might be. Which would neatly dispose of his involvement in the preliminaries to Darnley's murder.

14

Bothwell had not intended to march out of Dunbar until he had a force strong enough to face anything that the confederate lords might muster, but Mary was impatient. It was not for a queen to hide in a coastal fortress, her royalty and her authority diminishing daily as she stayed away from the city that was the centre of her rule. It was an admission of defeat even before battle had been joined.

Bothwell, who had experience in and an instinct for war, succeeded in overriding her until the message arrived from Sir James Balfour, recommending that her majesty and the Duke of Orkney should return to Edinburgh where they would be under the protection of the castle and its guns.

'Yes,' said her majesty. 'He is quite right.'

'No. We have only two hundred arquebusiers, sixty cavalry, and three field guns. That's not enough even to protect us on the journey. Wait until I have collected my mosstroopers.'

But Mary laughed, remembering the Huntly expedition, and the Chaseabout Raid, and the days after the murder of Davie Riccio.

She said, 'You don't understand. My subjects love me. All I have to do is ride among them and tell them I need them, and they will join me in their hundreds. In their thousands. And confess, although I may not at present be royally dressed, my borrowed rags are most becoming!'

She twirled and, reluctantly, he smiled. She was not the kind of woman he would have chosen as a wife, too elegant, too mannered, too literary, too conscious of her royalty. And too cold in bed. He almost regretted Jean, who had complained that he treated her like a whore – but admitted that it was fun, as long as he didn't make a habit of it. Mary's only real attraction for him was that she was the queen. But she was goodlooking enough, if you liked the type, and the short red petticoat, the velvet hat and the bow-tied sleeves borrowed from a local fisherman's wife made her look younger than her years.

She said again, 'My people will join me in their thousands. You'll see!' She did not know how their attitude to her had changed.

All too soon it became clear that her people were not going to join her, although Lord Seton arrived with reinforcements and a handful of Border lairds. It was left to Bothwell, belatedly wise, to guess that Balfour and Morton had tempted them out of Dunbar in the certainty that they would never reach the safety of Edinburgh.

15

It was a week before midsummer, and dawn came early. At two o'clock on the morning of 15th June, the confederate lords marched out of Edinburgh with their army and drew up on a hill near Musselburgh to offer battle to their queen.

Each of the lords moved under his own banner, but there was another banner carried in the vanguard – a white one with, sketched upon it, the corpse of the late king under a green tree. There was an image of the infant prince, his son, kneeling before him, from his mouth issuing a streamer bearing the words, 'Judge and revenge my cause, O Lord.'

Riding with the confederate lords but, like the French ambassador du Croc, not one of them, Lethington was cold with foreboding.

It was several hours before the royal army appeared and accepted the challenge by taking up position on Carberry hill, but even then the battle was not joined. On the advice of Kirkcaldy of Grange, the lords waited for the hot-headed Bothwell to make the first move, while Bothwell, who also knew something of military science, refused to abandon his hillside in order to rush the enemy. It would have been a suicidal move, in view of that enemy's superiority in position and strength.

Both sides decided to wait and hope that the opposition would grow bored first.

The sun rose steadily higher in the heavens, but still nothing happened. The lords' banners flapped lethargically on one hot and thirsty hillside, and the cross of St Andrews on the other. Where the queen sat her horse, there was the lion rampant. She tried to keep her eyes averted from the Kirk o' Field banner, but they strayed constantly back to it like a tongue to an aching tooth. It was outrageous, when the lords had signed the Ainslie bond only weeks before, swearing to Bothwell's innocence.

After a time, du Croc, who had been telling Mary for four weary years what France thought she should and should not do, went spurring across to her to tell her yet again.

Doffing his cap, he said, '*Majesté!*'

Hot, hungry and parched, she could still manage to smile at him. But when he told her that he had come as a mediator and that, if she would agree to abandon Bothwell, the lords would restore her to her throne and once more become her loyal subjects, her face changed.

'Loyal! What do they know of loyalty? There is only one man in whose loyalty I have ever been able to trust, and that man is now my wedded husband, the Duke of Orkney.'

'You must give him up, Madame. Otherwise there will never be peace with your lords.'

Angrily, uncomprehendingly, she cried, *But it was my lords who wanted me to marry him!*'

'Yes, Madame, but ...'

'You may tell my lords that I will not abandon my husband merely because they have changed their contemptible little minds.'

Bothwell gave his own answer. Sitting his black charger easily and in a voice that rang out so that his men might hear, he demanded, 'What harm have I ever done them? I never wished to displease any. I have sought to gratify them all. No, their words and deeds arise out of envy at my favour. There is not a man of them but wishes himself in my place!'

The queen smiled at him, and for the first time du Croc found himself impressed by the man. Action was what he had been born to, not the secretive action of palace corridors but that of the open air and the open landscape. Rash and vainglorious he might be, but here he appeared in command and almost debonair. The right man in the right place, but at very much the wrong time.

Bobbing his head again, du Croc turned away to rejoin the lords. As he went, he was aware of Bothwell behind him, not quite under his breath, mischievously breaking into one of the wild Border songs that to the uninitiated sounded like some masterless dog howling in the night. *'Fy lads! shout a'a'a'a'a' ...*'

The minutes passed, and the hours, and the lords suggested single combat. Bothwell would have accepted gladly, but Mary stopped him, saying, as she had said four days before, 'No. You are my husband and my general. I need you to be free.'

Fighting men were always prone to melt away, and after a time it became clear that the royal army was shrinking by the minute, lacking both a sufficiency of leaders and any great dedication to a cause. It was different for the men on the other hill, who had not only a banner of righteousness to persuade them to stay, but Morton, Home, Atholl, Mar, Glencairn, Lindsay and Ruthven to force them, leaders who had everything to lose unless they gained the victory.

Mary had no premonition of how much she herself had to lose.

With evening coming on, Bothwell finally said to her, 'This is purposeless. We must retreat. We'll go back to Dunbar. It's impregnable, and we can rally new troops from there.'

But she wasn't listening, because Kirkcaldy of Grange, whom she knew to be a kindly and honourable man, was riding towards them to parley. His message was the same as du Croc's had been.

There had been time enough for thinking during the long, draining day. Mary raised her exhausted head. 'I will have no useless slaughter. Your confederate lords wish to "save" me from my husband. Well, I will come with you, to show you that he is not holding me captive and is not guilty of that crime. I will agree that parliament should meet to investigate the murder of my son's father. If they find the Duke of Orkney innocent – as I know him to be – I will be his wife once again. If not, it will be an endless source of regret to me that I should have ruined my honour and my reputation in such a cause. If you will now give him a safe conduct to leave the field, I will entrust myself to you and to my subjects.'

Not from love, but from pride, she embraced Bothwell in view of the assembled lords and armies before he galloped, free, back along the road to Dunbar, the sinking sun's light casting his long dark shadow before him.

Then Mary gave Grange her hand to kiss and was led across to the opposite hillside and the respectful welcome Grange had promised her.

She had not expected Morton or Glencairn, Lindsay or Ruthven, to bow to her and smile and beg her pardon, and they did not.

But neither had she expected their men – those ordinary subjects whose love had never failed her – to howl and jostle her, to tear the hat from her head and the gown from her shoulders, to jeer and spit at her.

To shout, 'Kill her! Burn her! Burn the whore!'

Chapter Fifteen

JUNE 1567–MAY 1568

1

He could hear the heartbroken cries of, 'Lethington! Lethington!' from the window above his head, but could not bear to look. Helplessly, he had witnessed the terrible ride back to Edinburgh, with the hands pawing at her, tearing at her clothes, and the coarse voices shouting, 'Burn her! Burn the whore!' He had seen her shift ripped open, and her auburn hair descend into tangled strands; he had seen the lovely almond eyes become swollen and red, and the rivers of tears paint themselves through the dust on her cheeks.

He and Grange had tried laying about them with the flat of their swords, but it had only made matters worse and they had been forced to desist.

And now she was in a heavily guarded bedchamber in the house known as the Black Turnpike in the Highgait, which belonged to Edinburgh's provost, Simon Preston, who was also Lethington's brother-in-law and owner of Craigmillar, where today's troubles had had their genesis.

With deep distaste, he crossed the threshold to see if he could salvage something from the wreckage.

2

'And about time,' Morton said. 'Where've ye been? We're having a wee bit argument as tae what happens next.'

They were all seated round the table in the hall, and there was an appetising smell of roasting meat.

Lethington said, 'Has her majesty had something to eat and drink?'

'Didnae want anything.'

He guessed that she must have been afraid of poison, although even

Morton was unlikely to carry a poke of deadly nightshade around in his trunk-hose pocket. 'What about a basin and ewer? Have you sent her a chamber woman?'

'Och, sit down, man. We've more important things tae worry about. We've separated her from Bothwell ...'

'Aye, and let him escape,' interrupted Glencairn. 'A damned silly thing to do. It's him we want locked up, not her.'

Morton gestured with his capon leg. 'A bird in the hand. She's the queen and she would still have the power tae free him, but there's not much he can do wi'oot her. There's time enough to hunt him down and make sure he gets killed in the process. But we cannae have her escaping and foregathering with him, or we'll have a proper war, so we have tae keep her locked up until we've sorted him out.'

Lethington said, spearing a slice of mutton, 'And afterwards?'

'Aye, that's the problem.'

Which it undoubtedly was. Because if the queen ever went free again, most of their days would be numbered.

Morton said, 'Atholl here thinks she should abdicate in favour of the wee laddie and appoint a council tae rule in her name. Then she could go off back tae France and live there, if she wanted.'

'And?'

'And Lindsay's for putting her on trial and condemning her to death.'

It was just what the brutish Patrick Lindsay of the Byres would be for. Mildly, Lethington asked, 'On what grounds?'

Morton tossed his chewed capon leg to the dogs. 'Does it matter? If a woman marries her husband's murderer, she must have been a party tae the deed. Everyone knows that.'

Lethington restricted himself to saying, 'Knowing is not the same as proving.'

'Och, we can manage something. But Mar and Home and Sanquhar and the rest say we should just put her in confinement and keep her there. No need tae try her, or condemn her. I think maybe they're right. England, France and Spain would get a bit excited if we executed her. So what's your view?'

Lethington twirled his wine cup thoughtfully, as if he were reviewing the possibilities. 'Speaking as secretary of state, I'd say you're right about the reaction of the foreign powers if we executed her. If she were to abdicate voluntarily, they might accept it. Certainly, she mustn't be allowed to rejoin Bothwell. But I have to say that, once he has been disposed of, I would myself be inclined to recommend her restoration –

under the most stringent conditions, of course, including a full pardon for everyone involved in the present affair.'

The quality of the silence told him that, with one ill-judged sentence, he had forfeited his position with every man at the table, so, his expression and tone unchanged, he went on, 'But that is only a personal view. As an officer of state, I am entirely at your lordships' command.'

Morton said, 'Aye, that's better.'

Atholl grinned. 'Och, we must not be blaming the poor fellow too much when he is not long wed to a favourite of the queen's and still at the stage of listening to what his wife says. He will be getting over it soon enough.'

He and Lethington had been friends for years and Lethington was grateful for his intervention, if not for the form it took. He wished very much that Mallie were here in Edinburgh, but she had gone to Dunkeld to spend a few days with her sister Margaret, Atholl's own newly wedded second wife, whose predecessor had been Jean Gordon's sister Elizabeth. It was little wonder that outsiders found it hard to grasp the intricacies of Scotland's family alliances.

Everyone laughed, if with no great conviction.

Even Morton managed a smile – Morton, crude and shrewd, who had inspired the murder of Riccio in order to buy a pardon for James. Who had – as a result of Lethington's own intricate contrivance – manipulated the murder of Darnley in order to bring Bothwell down at the same time. And had made a mess of it. And who then, like all the other lords, had done nothing while the queen, who had always needed someone to lean on, had been reduced to leaning on the one man they all hated and feared.

Carberry Hill, today, had been both a climax and a turning point. It was time to rebuild, not to embark on further destruction, but the lords would not understand that. Lethington, in a minority of one, could not think how to bring the queen's restoration about except by slow and subtle ways.

3

He contrived to see her briefly on the following evening, after nine of the lords had signed the warrant for her sequestration.

She was wild-eyed, haggard, unwashed and despairing, the lovely queen who had once been the darling of Europe, and he now discovered that she had not had a moment of privacy since her arrival. There had been guards in her room at all times.

'Yes, I can imagine how you feel,' he said, low-voiced. 'But listen to me, please. I must be quick. I can do nothing to help you unless you swear to the lords that you are ready to reject Lord Bothwell completely and are prepared – anxious, even – to have your marriage annulled. If you do not, your subjects will never be persuaded of your innocence of the events surrounding the king's death. Agree to it now, before the lords are irrevocably committed, and you will take away most of the justification for their treatment of you.'

The scantily furnished bedchamber faced north, and the June sun was sinking somewhere to the south-west, lighting the windows across the Highgait with flame. In the reflected glow, he could see the misery in her eyes as she moaned, 'How can I? How can I? I am – I think I may be carrying Bothwell's child, and if I reject him then that child will be born a bastard.'

4

Morton walked in without knocking, although he at least had the grace to uncover his head.

'We're taking you down tae Holyrood, your majesty.'

It was painful to see her face light up, but Lethington could not do other than hold his tongue as she was taken from the room and, with Morton on one side of her, Atholl on the other, and guards all round, marched on unsteady legs down the half mile to Holyroodhouse through hostile crowds.

Mary Seton and Mary Livingston were there, Seton as pale as Mary herself and Livingston swallowing her emotion as, treating the queen as tenderly as her own small son, she made her sit down, and washed the grime and tears from her face and hands, and began to brush her hair until Seton, returning from the kitchens with a cup of wine and a promise of supper, said, 'Let me do that.'

When they discovered that she had neither eaten nor slept since dawn on the previous day, Seton said, 'You shall have supper first, and then we will put you to bed.'

Lord Morton stood behind her chair in the little retiring room while she struggled with the food she needed but did not want, her nerves strung so tight that she could barely swallow. She was scarcely halfway through when, impatiently, he sent one of the soldiers guarding the doorway to find out if the horses were ready.

Sharply, Livingston asked, 'Horses?'

'Aye, well, we're no' leaving her here. We have tae keep her safe somewhere.'

'She will be perfectly safe here!'

'No.'

Seton said, 'Then you must wait while I go and pack some fresh clothes for her majesty and for Livingston and myself.'

'You're not coming and the queen's got nae need for fresh clothes.'

The Maries stared at each other in horror, the same thought springing to both their minds. There could be only one reason why the queen should not need fresh clothes.

Livingston gasped, 'You wouldn't dare!'

Morton was not a notoriously quick thinker, and the fact that he understood at once what was in Livingston's mind was the clearest confirmation that the possibility had already been raised, and not too long ago. Brusquely, he said, 'She can bring a chamber woman or two, if she's so handless that she cannae look after herself.'

Mary was too exhausted to take in what was being said, or understand the implications. And when she trudged out of Holyrood again, her supper half eaten, and the cavalcade set out westward, she thought perhaps she was being taken to Stirling castle, where she could be with her son.

Instead, after crossing the firth and riding pillion behind a common soldier for thirty barely conscious miles, she found herself at Lochleven, the towered island keep that belonged to Sir William Douglas, whose mother was also mother to James Stewart, Earl of Moray. It would not be the first time in the four hundred years of its history that Lochleven had been used as a prison.

Sir William was to be her jailer, but not the only one. There were to be two others as well – Lord Lindsay of the Byres, who had threatened to cut her in collops on the night of Davie Riccio's murder, and Lord Ruthven, son and successor to that Ruthven who had dragged Riccio from her supper room to his death.

5

On the day after the queen's journey to Lochleven, Morton, who had elected himself head of the provisional government, summoned a reluctant Lethington to dine with him at Edinburgh castle.

'You're the one who knows about proclamations. We have tae put one out offering a reward for Bothwell's capture. I thought maybe a thousand crowns would be about right. We can melt down some of the queen's silver plate tae pay for it.'

'On what grounds?' Lethington had said it so often that it was beginning to sound like a cliché.

'What?'

'You have to specify grounds for wanting him caught, and having held the queen captive will hardly do, now that it's become less of a crime than a popular recreation.'

'Very funny. No, the king's murder.'

Slowly, Lethington said, 'If you capture him and if, by some oversight, he survives the experience and is brought to trial, you will need evidence and witnesses.'

'We've laid hands on one of his underlings, a man called Powrie. He was in the crowd in the Highgait after Carberry and someone pointed him out tae Ochiltree. We're persuading him tae name names.'

Lethington raised an eyebrow.

'Och, don't worry. Just the names of the folk who got their hands dirty.'

'Let us devoutly hope so.'

Lethington was rising to leave when Sir James Balfour, still captain of the castle, appeared, his hollow-cheeked face very slightly heated and his thinning hair dishevelled.

'Bothwell's tailor,' he said succinctly. 'A man called Dalgleish. We've just caught him here inside the castle. He says Bothwell sent him from Dunbar to fetch some clothing, but I'm not convinced. Do you want to see him?'

They saw him, and he stuck to his story.

But then Morton said, 'Never mind. We wanted tae see you on other matters, anyway. We've got Powrie, a friend o' yours, and he's been talking. About the king's murder at Kirk o' Field. I'm told ye were there yourself.'

He had not been told any such thing, but Dalgleish stuttered, 'Ah dinnae ken! Ah wasnae there, yer honour. I wasnae. Honest tae God!'

Morton turned to Balfour. 'We've got a nice wee rack in the dungeons, have we not? And some thumbscrews? Take him down and show him.'

The man was chalk white and shaking when he was brought back, the

332

spine of his doublet soaked with sweat. Balfour, it seemed, had interpreted the word 'show' as meaning 'demonstrate'.

Yes, he *had* been forced to go with his master to Kirk o' Field. There had been about nine of them. Yes, he had seen the powder train laid and, yes, he had seen my lord fire it. But that was all.

With an amiability that was all too obviously artificial, Morton said, 'Good. Now, just one other wee thing before we clap ye in the jail. What did ye really come to look for in the castle today?'

'Naething but clothes, yer honour, I swear tae God.'

Balfour, who was enjoying himself, said, 'Shall I take him down and stretch him a bit more?'

It was enough. Lord Bothwell, it appeared, had also wanted the man to find and take back to Dunbar a small casket, which was hidden away in a house in the Potterow.

6

Morton leaned his elbows on the table and surveyed the casket thoughtfully.

It was silver, badly tarnished, and about a foot long with an arched lid heavily decorated with wire filigree and ornamented with the crowned letter 'F'.

Lethington said, 'The "F" is for "François". I've seen it before. It belongs, or belonged, to the queen.'

'Pity there's nae key. What d'ye think's in it?'

'Embroidery silks?'

Morton glowered at him. 'Could we prise it open, d'ye think?'

With a conscious effort, Lethington reminded himself of the importance of staying on terms with Morton; of the need, too, to know everything that was going on. So he said, 'Not with a dagger. The silver's too soft.'

Balfour said, 'Let me have a look. There's no sense in having a complex lock on something small enough for any thief to pick up and walk away with. A thin blade used as a lever along the length of it might do. I'll see what they have in the kitchens.'

Twenty minutes later, he slid the casket back to Morton again.

'Well, well,' said that gentleman, his lower lip trapped between yellowed teeth.

If he had been expecting jewels, he was disappointed. 'Papers.' He picked up the one on top and held it out to Lethington. 'It's in French, but that's the queen's writing, is it not?'

'Yes, she always writes in French.' He took it and scanned it. 'It's to Bothwell, when she was at Stirling in April.'

His hands together in an attitude of prayer, Morton breathed, 'A love letter?'

'No. Merely some practical instructions.'

After the third innocent epistle that Morton's French wasn't up to, he began scrabbling further down in the casket. 'Oh, here!' he said. 'This is better. See what I've got!' Triumphantly, he held up the Ainslie tavern bond. 'Well, we don't need tae keep this, do we? It wasnae our fault that she took our advice and married the fellow.'

It was a chill day, after the brief heat wave, and there was a fire burning in the great marble fireplace in the hall. Crossing the room, Morton consigned the bond to the flames.

Lethington, who had not signed the Ainslie bond, was more interested in another and far more dangerous bond which he *had* signed. He still had no idea what had possessed him. He said, 'I don't suppose the Craigmillar bond is there, too?'

'More letters. What look like marriage contracts. Poems, for guidsakes. Man, ye're in luck.'

And there it was, the bond signed by Argyll, Huntly, Bothwell and Lethington, agreeing that the king should be 'put off'. It might have meant anything – it had been intended to, at the time – but the events of the last seven months had purged it of any innocent interpretation. For Argyll and Huntly, signing the bond had been the end of it, and both were in any case too rich and powerful to need to fear repercussions. It was not so for Lethington.

He took it from Morton's hand, read it through, and then walked over to the fire and watched it brown and curl and turn to crinkling tissue in the flames.

Morton, still rummaging, said, 'I cannae read this stuff, and there's an awful lot of it. Some of it's in secretary-hand and some's in Roman. But I suppose Bothwell wouldnae have kept it if it hadnae been important. Here, Balfour, you can look after it all until Friday. We've a privy council meeting and I'll open the casket formally then.'

Bland as butter, Sir James said, 'Would you like me to go through the casket for you? If it contains evidence that her majesty and Lord Bothwell were having – er – an illicit relationship before their marriage, or that,

God forbid, her majesty was aware in advance of the plot to murder the king, it might affect the privy council's deliberations.'

The beady brown eyes stared at him from the wild red jungle of beard and whiskers. 'Aye, it might.' Morton said. 'See what ye can do.'

Lethington said nothing, because there seemed to be nothing he could acceptably say. He would much have preferred to skim through the letters before Balfour made off with them, but dared not arouse in the other men even the shadow of a suspicion that he trusted them even less than they trusted him.

7

Eleven of the lords were present at the privy council meeting when the casket was produced, and only three of them were fluent in French, and another three weren't fluent at reading at all.

Morton waved a handful of the papers in the air, saying, 'These are things the queen wrote tae Bothwell before the so-called abduction. I'm not going to pass them round, because if ye all take time tae read them, we'll still be here next week. And even if Balfour or Lethington reads them aloud and translates as they go, the day'll be gone. So I've asked Balfour just tae give us a wee taste.'

There were a number of extracts that would have mystified Lethington if he had not already had cause to doubt. When she had been in Glasgow with the invalid Darnley, the queen had apparently written to Bothwell, 'I remit myself entirely to your will. Send me notice of what I should do, and whatever comes of it I shall obey you. See if you can find some secret means by medicine ...' There was another reference to herself as 'the most faithful lover that ever ye had, or ever shall have.' And one of the poems began, 'Into his hands and fullness of his power, I place my son, my honour and my life, My country, people, my subjected soul, All is for him ...'

'It's shocking,' Sanquhar said, and meant it. Tullibardine wore a heavy frown. Sempill, puzzled and distressed, exclaimed, 'I wouldn't have believed it.'

And rightly not.

Lethington, his mind racing, recognised that Balfour, as captain of the castle, could with perfect freedom have searched the royal apartments for material to interpolate among the genuine contents of the casket. A few discarded drafts of the sonnets the queen wrote for her own amusement;

scraps of letters to Bothwell from past mistresses; an amorous phrase inserted here or there ... Even imitating her majesty's writing would have offered no great challenge, since many of her privy councillors never saw it except as a signature appended to letters written in secretary-hand by her clerks. Balfour, having already betrayed the queen by tempting her from impregnable Dunbar to capture at Carberry, had very good reason for contributing to her ultimate downfall.

Lethington held out a hand, but Morton said, 'No, we havnae got time now. Let's get on wi' more important business. We need tae write to Elizabeth and see if she'll lend us some money.'

8

James had been on his way to Italy when, late in June, a messenger from Catherine de' Medici caught up with him, requiring his immediate return to Paris. His sister, the queen of Scots, who was also Catherine de' Medici's daughter-in-law and the second of France's dowager queens, had been defeated in battle against her rebellious lords at some place near Edinburgh and had then been imprisoned by them in an island fortress. One could not have the Scots setting such a regrettable example to one's own nobles. What did M. le comte de Moray propose to do about it?

M. le comte de Moray, annoyed, was disinclined to do anything about it. He had anticipated some kind of revolution that would ruin Bothwell, but not one that would bring Mary down as well. He had expected to go home and take the reins of government gravely out of her hands, so that he might put the country to rights again.

To Catherine, he said that he would send a messenger home to discover the truth of the matter. She said, 'Pray do. But do not leave France until you – and we – have had an answer.'

9

It was not only France that was disturbed.

Elizabeth, who, when the lords had first notified her of their intended proceedings against Bothwell, had followed her usual policy of making promises whose equivocal nature only became apparent when it was time to fulfil them, was so scandalised by Mary's imprisonment that she executed an immediate *volte face*. Whereas formerly she had rebuked

Mary for marrying a man generally believed to be the murderer of her husband, now she swore that nothing in the world was dearer to her than her good sister Mary's honour and life. To Morton, she wrote that she was proposing to send Throckmorton to Scotland to ensure that Mary was restored to her throne, mentioning, not quite in passing, that it would be a good idea for the little Prince James to be sent to England for safe keeping. Catherine de' Medici, her mind working along similar lines, had already suggested that the boy be sent to France.

Throckmorton would have preferred to be going anywhere other than Scotland. Cathay would have done. It was all very well for her majesty to instruct a mere ambassador to tell the *de facto* rulers of a foreign country what to do and to supervise them while they did it, but an ambassador's life was not like that.

It was Lethington, he discovered as soon as he crossed the border, with whom he had to deal; Lethington who, riding with him to Edinburgh, explained how the lords, many of them anti-English out of long habit, felt not only about Mary's sins but about Elizabeth's interference; Lethington who thought it an excellent idea that the little prince should be released into Elizabeth's keeping – in exchange, of course, for a formal guarantee of his right to the English succession and suitable financial provision for his royal state and entourage.

Throckmorton said, 'Be realistic, Lethington!' and Lethington said, 'It would be a good bargain.'

It was several days – days during which Throckmorton was politely but absolutely forbidden by the lords to see or communicate with the imprisoned Mary – before he had the opportunity of talking privately to Lethington again.

Lethington said, 'Let us sit peacefully in the gardens. I take it that you now understand not only our difficulties but your own?'

Conversations between diplomats never made allowance for ordinary human truth. Throckmorton said, 'Difficulties? I am not aware that I have any difficulties.'

'Of course not.' Lethington's cool grey eyes were smiling, but Throckmorton sensed that he was weary of it all as he went on, 'The queen your sovereign, however, thinks she has the right to tell the Scots what to do. We don't agree. And while we are grateful for her advice that, instead of using force against our own queen, we should have commended our cause to God, it seems unlikely that His intervention would have achieved, with sufficient rapidity, what the lords saw as needing to be

337

achieved. I fear that we are no longer prepared to heed the queen your sovereign's words, either political or spiritual.'

Throckmorton – tall, sandy, clever – exclaimed, 'That is not what Morton says. You are speaking only for yourself!'

'Oh, no. But I will, if you wish. I will talk more frankly to you than I would to any other Englishman except Leicester or Cecil.'

And that would be a new experience, Throckmorton thought.

'It is not in my power to have the queen my mistress restored to her rightful place. The lords are fearful of what she would do, but I think that could be overcome. What cannot be overcome at present is her subjects' loathing of her. I have never seen such a violent revulsion of feeling. I suppose that, having been charmed by her for so long, they see her so-called betrayal as all the greater. And now John Knox is back in Edinburgh demanding her execution and ranting about a queen having no more privilege to commit murder or adultery than a private person.

'Believe me, she is in peril of her life and the balance is very delicate indeed, so delicate that I myself dare not do or say anything to help her in case it precipitates a crisis. And I tell you bluntly that, if Elizabeth goes on threatening war unless she is restored, the effect on Mary is likely to be fatal. Loch Leven is wide and deep.'

Gloomily, Throckmorton dropped his diplomatic mask. 'I know. And if anything happened to her Elizabeth's enemies would say that disposing of Mary was her real objective all along. Cecil has warned her, Leicester has warned her, I have warned her, but she won't listen. What is likely to happen next?'

'In a few days, the lords hope to persuade her to abdicate in favour of her son.'

Throckmorton groaned.

'Yes. But it is better than dying,' Lethington said.

10

James had now been in Paris for three weeks, a guest discouraged from going home by his hosts' insistence on knowing what he proposed to do when he got there. He said that he had no idea at present, but nothing, certainly, that would constitute an attack on his sister's right to rule. He would travel back to Scotland by way of London in order to ask for Elizabeth of England's help in setting her free. But that, of course, did not diminish the value he placed on the friendship of France.

Graciously, Catherine de' Medici said, 'Excellent. I shall send Monsieur de Lignerolles with you to negotiate a new Franco-Scottish alliance. *Bon voyage, Monsieur le comte.*'

<h1 style="text-align:center">11</h1>

Mary had visited the island castle of Lochleven several times in the past as a guest of her brother. It was an excellent base for a few days' hawking in Kinross, and she had apartments there, richly furnished with tapestries and velvets and with charming views over the water to the wooded hills.

But when she was half carried and half dragged into the castle after Carberry, she found that she was not to lie in her own green-curtained bed with its green taffeta counterpane, but in the laird's room, a barren, masculine place with no comforts of any kind.

For the first two weeks, she lay in a state of suspended consciousness, speaking to no one, eating and drinking no more than would have sustained the chaffinch that sang on her windowsill every morning at first light. There were those in the household who thought she would die. There were those who would have been happy if she had.

The retreat from reality, however, was what she needed, both in body and mind, and when at last she began to emerge from it she found that, although her limbs were weak, her mind had become clearer than at any time in the year since her son's birth – that long, terrible year when the world had gone by like some moving landscape to which she did not belong; when making decisions, taking responsibility, had been beyond her. Instinct, training and habit had carried her through where it was possible for them to do so, but they had not been proof against murder, abduction, betrayal and battle.

She had not forgotten those, and never would, but the edge of her memories had been blessedly dulled. As she took her first few unsteady steps outdoors, savouring the sun and the breeze from the loch, she was, she thought, on the road to recovering her true self.

Even so, her nerves were still raw as an open wound, and the constant, threatening presence of Lindsay of the Byres meant that she could never feel safe. Scarcely less intimidating, if in a different way, was the mistress of the castle, Lady Margaret Douglas, who had once also been mistress to Mary's father. To him, she had borne the son who was now Earl of Moray before returning to her wifely duties and presenting ten children in succession to her legally wedded husband.

As royal mistresses went – and Mary had met a representative sample at the court of France – she was a very odd specimen indeed. Dour, disapproving and relentlessly pious, she resembled nothing so much as a female version of John Knox, though without the oratorical skills, and was quite as impervious as he to Mary's reawakening charm. She had made it her mission to superintend the prisoner at all times, and she was anything but a soothing companion.

Mary concentrated on regaining her strength, aware that she needed it not only for the dangers that seethed around her, but for the political battles that – if she survived – must lie ahead. She was not wholly cut off from the world, even if her own communication with it consisted of repeated refusals to divorce Bothwell and repeated demands to be permitted to address her Three Estates. Otherwise, save for threatening letters in reply, she received occasional scraps of news in notes smuggled in among the stockings and chemises and sweetmeats that the Maries, whose perseverance had begun to wear Morton down, succeeded in having sent to her.

Atholl wrote to warn her of an approaching attempt to enforce her abdication, and when Throckmorton arrived in Edinburgh, he repeated the same warning. She should sign any papers presented to her, he said, because otherwise her life would be in danger; he assured her that papers signed under duress could have no legal validity.

But what brought warmth, however fleeting, to her heart was a token from Lethington who, with it, sent a message similar to Throckmorton's though only by word of mouth. The token itself consisted of a small oval gold brooch, enamelled with Aesop's fable of a mouse gnawing through the net in which a lion was entrapped. There was a legend surrounding the image. *A chi basto l'animo, non mancano le forze.* 'Who has spirit enough will not lack strength.'

She thought, 'He is right. I *will* not despair.'

Much of her time, too much, was taken up with thoughts of the child growing within her. She was sure now and found herself, for lack of books, music, embroidery – anything to occupy the long, long days – listening to her body as if it were an instrument, marking every tiny physical development in her pregnancy. She had no Arnault to advise her, and her chamber women were ignorant, so in desperation she turned to Lady Margaret.

'I want nothing to do wi' it,' said her ladyship. 'Yon Bothwell's a son of Satan, and it's obscene that any God-fearing woman should be carrying his seed. It'll be a monster, mark my words. Two heads and a tail, most like. It would be against my conscience to help ye bring such an unnatural being into the world. Aye, one that should never be born, that would be better dead.'

Tears still leapt easily to Mary's eyes. 'And so, I suppose, would I? Is there no Christian kindness in that pious heart of yours?'

Lady Margaret clasped her hands primly over her own stout stomach. 'The Lord commands destruction of all the seed of Satan. Ye've brought your woes on yourself.'

Shivering with a chill of the spirit, Mary turned and left her.

In France, there had been a young doctor from Montpellier who had attracted Catherine de' Medici's attention, something of a pedagogue and a great writer of treatises, especially on pregnancy and childbirth. It was he who had recommended Mary's own physician, Arnault, to her. Mary, smoothing her hands across her stomach, wondered if she were merely imagining the signs that, she remembered M. Joubert saying, often indicated that a woman was carrying twins – a depression in the centre, and a slight swelling on either side. It was too soon to tell, surely, and yet ...

Then, ten weeks after her marriage and something over five weeks after the battle of Carberry, she was gripped by an agonising pain and began bleeding as if she would never stop.

12

More than a hundred miles to the north, her husband had retreated to the episcopal palace at Spynie, which stood a little inland from the sandy shores of the Moray firth. The bishop was his uncle and Bothwell had spent some of the happiest days of his childhood there, in the great tower smelling of the sea and loud with seabirds.

He had had high hopes of raising an army to restore the queen to her throne. Indeed, within ten days of Carberry, he had wrung promises of support from Hamilton, Huntly, Seton, Fleming, Argyll, Boyd and a number of other lords. But Morton had issued a decree that anyone aiding Bothwell, now declared an outlaw and rebel, would be judged as guilty as he of the 'horrible murder' of the king. It had dimmed their enthusiasm and ruined his own hopes. And so, frustrated of an army on land, he had retired to Spynie to begin creating an army on the sea.

By a curious chance, an elderly English spy had been installed there for some months and Sir Nicholas Throckmorton in Edinburgh was much surprised to receive from him, a little after the middle of July, a letter enquiring whether he would prefer Bothwell to be murdered or merely taken into custody.

It was not a decision Sir Nicholas felt competent to make. Although the queen his mistress would have been delighted to see the end of Bothwell by God's hand, he did not feel it would be agreeable to her princely nature to consent to murder. Having no such reservations where the Scots lords were concerned, he passed the question over to them.

But the lords had other matters on their minds.

13

Lindsay of the Byres, summoned to Edinburgh for a meeting, reported to the lords with grim satisfaction, 'She's miscarried.'

'Dearie me,' said Morton absently. 'That's sad. Well, now, we're all here and I've got the deposition documents that she needs tae sign. The first one's right touching. She says she's so vexed, broken and unquieted by the toil of governing the country than she cannae go on and wants tae abdicate in favour of her son. The second's tae appoint the Earl of Moray as regent. And the third's tae set up a commission in case the Earl of Moray doesnae want to act alone.'

Glencairn said caustically, 'I can just see that happening!'

There wasn't one of the lords who wouldn't have been delighted to act as regent to a year-old child, with many years of power and profit ahead. In Scotland, sovereigns did not come fully of age until they were twenty-five, although they were apt to take the reins of the realm into their own hands well before then and to begin settling a few old scores – usually with the regent. The first fifteen years were safe enough, though.

14

That same night, Lindsay returned to Lochleven, accompanied by Sir Robert Melville, a pleasant man who had once been Mary's ambassador to London and was now the lords' most regular messenger to Lochleven.

Mary was lying in bed, weak from loss of blood and distress over the loss of her twins. Lady Margaret, who had come to see what the seed of Satan looked like, had told the chamber women, 'Rubbish. Those were never twins. They're no more than blood clots!' but Mary clung to her conviction.

Lindsay said, 'You've to sign these.'

His crude disregard for her rank, her femininity, her condition, would never become easier to bear. Faintly, she said, 'What are they?'

Robert Melville explained them to her. 'But your majesty should read them before you sign.'

She had been forewarned and knew she would have to give in, but not easily. 'I will neither read them nor sign them.'

'Ye will,' Lindsay said.

'No.'

'Yes.'

There was a dagger in his hand and his eyes told her he was quite prepared to use it. They could toss her in the loch afterwards, and say she had been drowned, trying to escape.

She remembered playing a friendly golf foursome with him at St Andrews once. She and he, Beaton and Lethington. She remembered, too, how often she had said in this last year that she wanted to die. But she didn't; not any more. She wouldn't give them the satisfaction.

Summoning all her courage, she smiled. 'Or you will cut me in collops?'

'I'd like that fine.'

Painfully, she dragged herself up in the hard, lumpy bed. 'If you cut me in collops, I won't be able to sign.'

'If I cut ye in collops, we won't need you to sign.'

Whether I sign or not, she thought, what will my life be worth afterwards? But at least it would give her time – time, perhaps, to escape. The lion, the mouse, and the net ...

It was not easy to be regal with her hair falling down her back, her lips colourless and the bedchamber still thick with the smell of her own blood. But she said, 'Give me the papers. I will sign them, but I will neither read them nor be bound by what they say.'

She was twenty-four years old and sick and frightened.

She could not believe that she was signing away her throne.

15

James was in London when his small nephew was crowned at Stirling according to the Protestant rite. John Knox preached the sermon, likening the child to Joash, whose mother Athaliah was slain with the sword.

The lords stood around, looking staunch and sincere, their palms fairly itching at the thought of all the give and take that went with a regency; Châtelherault, in the years of Mary's infancy, was believed to have profited to the tune of 300,000 livres. Sir William Douglas, at Lochleven, told his servants to light bonfires in the garden. And Kirkcaldy of Grange, somewhat belatedly, girded on his armour and set off for the north in pursuit of Bothwell.

At Greenwich, Elizabeth told James in the most offensive language what she thought of the lords' proceedings, and James replied that his sister's continuing passion for Darnley's murderer justified everything the lords had done. As regent-to-be, for the first time in all his dealings with Elizabeth he was meeting her on almost equal terms and it made a pleasant change to be able to repay harsh words with equally harsh words, although he, of course, would never have permitted phrases like, 'God's death!' to pass his lips. They parted on bad terms, which did not worry him at all. He knew that Elizabeth really liked and respected him at heart.

He took his time on the journey back to Scotland, stopping for a night or two at Apthorp and then at Berwick. Not until 11th August did he ride into Edinburgh to a saviour's welcome that warmed even his cold and sanctimonious soul. He had never doubted the wisdom of staying away throughout the troubles, but it was satisfying to have his judgement confirmed.

He had been meditating on the tone of his regency and decided that he would be stern but just, a man of principle. Which, of course, was what he was.

The privy council greeted him not only formally but reverentially. Even Lethington took care not to smile as he doffed his velvet court cap and said, 'Welcome home, your grace.'

16

Four evenings later, James rode with Morton and Atholl to Lochleven.

Mary knew that they would have preferred to find her frail and submissive, as distracted in mind as she had been, in one degree or another, for so many long months. They would have known, then, that they had won.

But her health and, therefore, spirits were so much improved that her immediate reaction to the sight of them stepping out of the rowing boat was, 'Ah! I have a great deal to say to you gentlemen! Pray come indoors.'

They had barely crossed the threshold of the Great Hall when she swung round and said, 'Before we talk of your outrageous rebellion against your anointed queen, I propose to tell you exactly what I think of the conditions under which I am being kept here. I could see no reason at all, at first, why I should not have remained at Holyrood, where I might as easily have been incarcerated, but I now realise that, if I had been there you would not have dared, as I hear you have done, to make free with all my possessions – to steal my gowns, my furs, my jewels, my embroideries, my tapestries – or to melt down my silver into coin. Nor would you have dared to wreck my private chapel.

'Here I am not even permitted to occupy my own royal apartments but have to sleep in a curtainless bed, with bare stone walls and not even a cushion on the chair on which I must sit. And I have no servants beyond two chamber women who have little talent for dressing hair or carrying out any of the other tasks to which I am accustomed. And it was days after I arrived before anyone was permitted to send me even a pair of shoes or a petticoat. Furthermore ...'

They stood and listened like schoolboys being scolded, Morton surly, Atholl embarrassed, James offended that her flashing eyes should pass so impersonally over the brother she had not seen for more than four eventful months. She hadn't said a word of welcome.

In the end, however, she turned towards him. 'Well, James? Did you have a pleasant holiday? You have the look of a man who has been enjoying the delights of French cuisine.'

But James was not prepared to be provoked. He did not lose his temper. He didn't need to.

He said, 'We did not come to talk about beds and shoes and cooking. We have come to talk about why ye're here. I hoped, when I returned, that ye might be showing some elementary sense of shame for the folly and wickedness of your conduct, for your compliance in the murder of the king ...'

'I had no part in that!'

'... and your disgraceful connection with his murderer. But it seems that ye remain steeped in sin. Your misgovernment ...'

It was a long time before his speech wound to its close, a speech designed – although there was no reason why Mary should have known it – as much for Morton's benefit as her own. There was no harm, James had decided, in demonstrating that family feeling came appreciably lower on the regent-elect's list of priorities than fidelity to the Protestant cause.

There was no stopping him as he reviewed every one of his sister's

345

faults, real or imagined, during the years of her personal rule, her carelessness of her reputation, her failure to recognise that being seen to be innocent was as important as being innocent, and, of course, her obduracy in the matter of religion. He was as stern, pitiless and certain of his own righteousness as an Old Testament prophet, although it was less his severity than the injustice of so many of his accusations that ultimately reduced Mary to hysterical tears.

When they separated for the night, he recommended her to think on God's mercy, but all she could think on during the darkest hours was that her death had been decided. James had been speaking as both prosecutor and judge.

She was a great deal more tractable in the morning. She even begged James to accept the regency, and he saw no necessity to tell her that he had already done so.

'I will do my best to save your life,' he said, 'though it is a decision that does not rest with me alone. But ye must not look for liberty. Ye must not try to escape, either, or intrigue against my government, or bear your lords a grudge. Ye must give up this inordinate affection for Bothwell.'

'It is not ...' She stopped, fearful of angering James by pointing out that it was Bothwell's loyalty for which she felt an inordinate affection, not his person.

In the end, James said, 'Is there anything ye want?'

She made a strange little sound, part way between a laugh and a moan. 'Anything I want?' But James saw nothing ironic in the question, so she said only, 'I would appreciate a little comfort, a few gowns of my own to wear, some embroidery silks to keep me occupied, and perhaps Mary Seton to keep me company. And I'm concerned that my jewels should be kept safe. Where are they? I have always meant some of them to become part of the inheritance of the Crown, but others were given to me by François and I am sentimentally attached to them.'

James said, 'Don't worry. I'll look after them for you.'

17

He left her in a state of renewed despair. If James, who knew the truth, had really brought himself to believe everything that he had been saying, then other people must, too. James had always been convincing.

And then Mary Seton arrived, with love and moral support and all the gossip Mary had yearned for, and she learned that she did have adherents

346

still, even among the Protestant lords, although they had been forced to make temporary terms with James. And the Hamiltons would be delighted if her abdication were overturned, because then, if any misfortune were to overtake her son, the head of their house, Châtelherault – the vapid old man she had banished to France after his involvement in the Chaseabout Raid – would once more be heir presumptive to her throne.

Lethington, too, was at odds with James. 'Fleming says that he has always seen your majesty's imprisonment and abdication as temporary expedients, necessary because the alternative would have been worse. But the regent has become very aloof. He will not take advice, and he will not listen to any opinion that does not agree with his own.'

Almost as an afterthought, Mary asked if there was any news of Lord Bothwell, who had dominated her for a year that had felt like an eternity, but for whom all feeling had been swept away with the embryos she had conceived by him. She knew now that no army of her nobles would ever rally to him, and that she could not look for rescue at his hands.

'Poor man,' she said. 'What a talent he had for getting into trouble. I wonder if he still whistles under his breath in that irritating way.'

18

Bothwell's talent for getting into trouble had already set him off on a course that was to end in his own protracted tragedy.

James, immediately after he was installed as regent, had reinforced Kirkcaldy of Grange with four large ships and instructions to pursue Bothwell's own small fleet with 'fire, sword and all other kinds of hostility'. There had been a battle during which Grange had very nearly drowned, but which had ended with Bothwell limping with his two remaining ships to refuge on the coast of Norway, a dependency of Denmark and a country he knew from his earlier travels.

Unhappily, he had sailed straight into the orbit of a pirate-hunting Danish warship, whose commander demanded to see his credentials. He had none and, in the end, finding himself and his crews under arrest, had to reveal himself.

'Who can give me credentials? Being myself the supreme ruler of the land, of whom can I receive authority?'

In Bergen, they were unimpressed. He did not look like a supreme ruler in his worn and salt-stained Borderer's doublet, wore no jewellery, had no papers to prove that he ranked higher than an earl. Since there was talk of piracy and the true ownership of one of his vessels, he was required to appear in court.

He might have walked free, if gossip had not spread news of the impending case around the countryside; if it had not reached the ears of a mistress to whom he had once promised marriage; if she had not sent representatives to the court to demand repayment of money she had lent him seven years before.

After that, a portfolio of papers was found in the ballast of one of his ships, papers that included a copy of the proclamation branding him murderer and outlaw and putting a price on his head.

At the end of September 1567, just when his wife had shaken herself free from the dependence that had given him power and taken it from him again, he was sent under guard to Copenhagen and an initially courteous imprisonment. The king of Denmark looked forward, with pleasure, to exploiting the queen of Scots' husband as an asset in future negotiations with Scotland's regent, England's queen, and the effective ruler of France, Catherine de' Medici.

Political pawns were useful things, as long as one did not permit them to slip from one's grasp.

19

The first business of the parliament that met in Edinburgh in December was to justify the confederate lords' rebellion against their anointed sovereign.

The first two objects of their rebellion – saving her majesty from Bothwell and protecting the infant prince – had been achieved to everyone's satisfaction, but the punishment of Darnley's murderers remained outstanding.

Although James had been conscientiously working his way through Bothwell's servants, executing one after another, there was increasing popular disapproval over ordinary men being hanged, drawn and quartered while the great went free. Men doomed to the scaffold, with nothing more to lose, also had an inconvenient habit of following extorted confession with public accusation. Names were beginning to be bandied about – including those of Morton and Lethington, Huntly and Argyll and James Balfour.

Not even James could afford the political destruction that would ensue if the gossip went much further. If all those who had known in advance of, and in one degree or other assented to, Darnley's removal, were to be brought to trial, not a lord in the land would escape the odium of it. Although James himself had not subscribed to the Craigmillar bond – the bond that Bothwell had shown to too many people – he had been there at the time and it made no difference that he had afterwards, in Lethington's words, 'looked through his fingers'.

It was clear to James and to Morton that they must buy all the public support they could, and the most influential merchants of it were John Knox and the Protestant kirk. All that was necessary was to abolish Catholicism and make a sacrifice of Mary. It was not a transaction that caused them any qualms.

Months before, the French ambassador had been told informally of the incriminating nature of the letters found in Bothwell's silver casket, and so had Throckmorton. Now, although the letters themselves were not produced in verification, it was announced to parliament that documents existed which proved that the queen had been 'privy, art and part of the actual devising and deed of the murder of the king her lawful husband'.

If the queen was a criminal, the lords had been entirely justified in deposing and imprisoning her. It was, indeed, a more merciful fate than she deserved. For the regent and Morton, it was a satisfactory outcome. Now, they could forget about her.

Mary, when she heard what had happened, said blankly, 'Incriminating letters? I don't understand.'

20

Mystified though she might be by the reference to letters, what concerned her far more was that parliament's approval of the lords' proceedings meant that her imprisonment was no longer negotiable, if it ever had been, but a sentence for life. To escape now became her obsession and, in the months that followed, she smuggled out letter after letter to France and England, begging for armed help to set her free.

She had always been an enthusiastic writer of letters, long, friendly, gossipy ones that strove to project the charm that served her so well, face to face. Now, with little else to occupy her, they became a lifeline.

The most impassioned of the endless stream of occasionally angry but more frequently blandishing epistles she had sent to Elizabeth over the years arrived on the very day when Elizabeth – still officially refusing to grant recognition to the government of Regent Moray – was inspecting, with a view to purchasing, Mary's famous pearls, perhaps the finest of the superb jewels that James had promised his sister that he would 'look after' for her. Catherine de' Medici, who had always coveted them, went into a full-blooded Florentine rage when she found out. She had wanted the jewel-encrusted narwhal tooth, too, which, dipped in a wine cup, neutralised the poison of which every ruler always went in fear.

Cecil, interpreting the offer of the pearls as a sign that James was anxious to restore good relations with Elizabeth, was mildly entertained. He ceased to be entertained when news came that Mary had escaped from Lochleven.

21

Mary had never had any difficulty in enchanting men – unless their names happened to be Moray, Morton or Knox – especially men who were youthful and romantic. At Lochleven, her charm and fragility, combined with the almost mystical allure that went with being victim of a cruel fate, had within two or three months begun to soften the hearts of several male members of the household, among them Geordie Douglas, one of the younger sons of the house.

She was aware of it, but at first forbore to take advantage of it. Year after year since 1562, the month of November had seen her ill, twice almost to death, and now she waited superstitiously to discover what the November of 1567 would bring. Unbelievably, it found her in better health and spirits than she had known since her son was born. The transformation had begun when she was permitted to move from the spartan quarters of her first weeks into the royal apartments, a pleasure which even sharing her bedchamber with two spying Douglas daughters failed to dim. After that there arrived a number of small luxuries and comforts that James was too occupied or uninterested to forbid her – sweetmeats and stockings, soap and pins, embroidery threads and lengths of dull fabric for dull gowns – and eventually a box containing the hairpieces and accessories that Mary Seton needed to arrange her hair in the styles that suited her best. The miracle was complete. She was herself again.

Escape ceased to be an empty dream and became something that might be possible to achieve with planning and determination. But, if she were to attempt to cross the water that imprisoned her more effectively than bars, she had to know whether she would meet friends or only enemies on the further shore. She could do nothing without help.

Geordie Douglas was a gallant, goodlooking and likeable young man and she set about making him her slave.

She invited him to walk in the gardens with her and dazzled him with tales of the court of France. Gracefully, one evening before supper, she danced a measure with him and, so perfectly did their steps match, insisted that he should always partner her. She borrowed his lute and, with it, made eloquent music. She played merry games of cards with him and taught him some of the wicked tricks she had learned from Davie Riccio.

She went too far – or seemed to. His brother, Sir William, became uneasy and rebuked him and when Geordie resentfully shouted back at him, ordered the young man out of the house and off the island. Nothing could have been better, because it freed him to make arrangements for Mary's flight. He had no thought for his own future. Young lovers rarely did. Steeped in the romances of chivalry, his only thought was to serve his *princesse lointaine*.

The day came at the beginning of May, with Geordie Douglas on the mainland and his orphaned cousin Willie on the island.

Willie was a bright and clever boy, who adored Mary no less than Geordie did. Like old Lady Huntly when Mary had been held captive after the murder of Riccio, however, he was full of ideas that were less than practical. Lady Huntly had suggested that the heavily pregnant queen should climb out of a window. Willie favoured her scaling a seven-foot wall.

She said, 'Willie, I can't. And I can't crawl through tunnels. I can't swim, either. You must think of something else.'

He was disappointed in her.

He wrinkled his button of a nose. 'It must be tomorrow because Geordie's got everything arranged. We could play May Day games, maybe. Usually, everybody's doing the same thing at the same time in the same place, and they'd spot anything by-ordinar straight off. We need to get them fleeing around in all directions so that they don't notice. If I played the Abbot of Unreason, would it be too much to ask your majesty to follow in my footsteps all day? Uphill and down dale and that kind of thing? It would be a start.'

She didn't laugh. It was too important. 'I am in your hands.'

Willie had a natural talent for mimicry and by the time Mary had raced around in his supposedly drunken footsteps for several hours, her jailers in increasingly breathless pursuit, everyone except Willie was exhausted.

It meant that, when the Lady Margaret glanced across the water and saw horsemen on the far shore, Mary was able to divert her by exclaiming, 'What an enjoyable day! James would never have allowed us to have such fun.' It was enough to cause Lady Margaret to leap to her son's defence. 'James has no objection to rational entertainment ...'

And then, at dinner, Sir William saw young Willie engaged about some mysterious business in the boats on the island's shore, and Mary was able to divert him, too, by exclaiming, 'So much excitement! I think I am about to faint,' and having to be revived with a glass of wine.

The laird, as usual, served the queen her supper, which she had the greatest difficulty in swallowing, and then crossed the courtyard to sup with his family, while Mary retired to her tower to pray, not only for her soul but that Willie should have succeeded in purloining the laird's keys.

It was dark when she had finished, dark enough for her to change into a countrywoman's dress and hood, so that she might be mistaken for one of the washerwomen who came and went daily from the mainland village of Lochleven.

Then she went downstairs to wait in the shadows of the courtyard.

She felt a movement beside her and her heart leaped to her throat, but it was Willie.

'I've got the keys, and I've spiked all the rowing boats but the one, and here's a laundrywoman's basket to carry on your hip. If you bend over it a bit you won't look so tall.'

She could have hugged him.

Together, without haste, they walked forward to the gate. Willie unlocked it as if it were the natural thing to do, and when Mary had passed through, locked it again and threw away the keys.

Lying down in the only seaworthy boat, the queen was rowed across the water to freedom.

Geordie Douglas was waiting for her. As Mary mounted the lively pure-bred mare he had brought for her, he said with a grin, 'It's the laird's.'

She laughed, not only with the wild delight of being free, but because there was piquancy in the thought that the mare had not been borrowed or bought, but stolen from the stables of the man who had been her host for too long, and against whose brother, who was also her own, she was about to take up arms.

James was in Glasgow holding a justice sitting when a messenger arrived and, bowing as was expected of him, announced breathlessly, 'Your grace, the queen has escaped from Lochleven and joined with Lord Seton and the laird of Riccarton. She is on her way to Hamilton and there is much cheering from the common people as she passes.'

Lethington did not remember ever having seen James's jaw literally drop before – James, who had believed that his sister, having been publicly branded a murderess, had been rendered harmless for ever; who had given her scarcely a thought since that day; to whom it had never occurred that a beautiful, if sinful, queen might now have an attraction for her subjects that was lacking in the equally sinful but far less beautiful lords, whose cantankerous activities and attitudes over the last months had done little to endear them to anyone.

James, rattling his fingertips on the table, said, 'She won't get any real support, will she?'

'Seton, the Hamiltons, Herries, Maxwell, Argyll, Huntly, maybe Atholl ...' Lethington suspected that Atholl would feel as he did, that the time was not right. And if Mary allied herself too openly with the Hamiltons, the realm would be brutally divided.

Looking back, he remembered how peaceful life had been, even if it had not seemed so, before the Darnley marriage. It had been only two years ago, but he himself felt at least ten years older, and ten years less able to view the ever-darkening world from the Olympian standpoint that had once been his.

'I'll get proclamations out to summon the lieges,' James said.

'Wait,' Lethington said. 'She'll negotiate. We can persuade her to compromise. Don't *invite* civil war, James ...'

James looked at him.

Correcting himself, Lethington said, 'I meant, of course, "your grace".'

23

Ten days later, the two armies met at Langside, to the south of Glasgow.

It was not like Carberry, although Mary once more sat her horse on a hill, the lion rampant flapping above her. This time, Mary's force was vastly superior in numbers to the lords'. This time, the pikemen and the arquebusiers did go into action. This time, bodies of horsemen ranged about the field. This time, there was a pitched battle. This time, men were killed. This time, the affair lasted not a day, but an hour.

But the result was the same. Mary lost.

Argyll had been in command of her main body, which consisted largely of his own Highlanders, but he became suddenly ill and incapable of leading them. Without him, all was confusion, because most of his men did not understand Scots and none of Mary's other lords had the Gaelic. Nor were the Highlanders, whose own wars were fought in a guerrilla landscape, accustomed to facing such disciplined fire as that of Grange's arquebusiers or the charges of his pikemen. They began to break away from the battle, congregating into quarrelsome factions – to stay or to go? – leaving Herries and the Hamiltons without the support they desperately needed.

Mary spurred down to the field and would have led them herself except that they were not prepared to be led.

It was the second battle she had witnessed in her life. The first one, against Huntly almost five years before, had been very different. Her brother James, then, had been on her side, and she had been far enough away not to see the blood.

In the end, Lord Herries came to her and said, 'Your majesty, it is time to go.'

And since she could see through her tears that indeed it was, she turned and went with him.

24

They should have gone to Dumbarton, the impregnable fortress to the west of Glasgow that was still held for the queen by Lord Fleming's men, but the way was blocked by James's army. And so the little party turned south on a wild ride to the Borders, a ride during which, hour after hour, the desire for haste was frustrated by the terrain itself, by the rough tracks and unfrequented passes that offered secrecy at the cost of speed. It took three nerve-stretching days and two nights, sustained by milk and oatmeal begged from isolated cottagers, with halts only to rest the horses and snatch an hour or two's sleep on the bare ground, before they came to a halt at last in the far south-west, at Lord Maxwell's castle of Terregles.

'I shall go to England,' Mary said.

Herries exclaimed, 'No, Madame! On no account!'

'My cousin Elizabeth will give me shelter. She will give me help. She is shocked and horrified over how my lords have treated me.'

'No, Madame,' Herries said again. 'She is not to be trusted. How often has she seemed to promise help to some or other of us in these last years, and how often has that help materialised? She can always be relied on for promises, but not for fulfilling them. Please, Madame!'

Lord Fleming added his voice, and so did Lord Maxwell, but Mary – always at her best when facing a challenge – laughed as gaily as if the last disastrous days had never been. 'I shall go, and I shall return within the month with an English army at my back.'

'No,' Herries said again. 'We can hold out here for forty days. We don't need an English army. We can raise a new one of our own.'

Lord Fleming, as fair and blue-eyed as his sister, said, 'If you must seek help elsewhere, then go to France, where you have friends and money and estates. You can sail from the Solway, from here. France's religion is yours, and it is in France's interest for you to be restored to your throne. It is not in Elizabeth's, however friendly she may appear. When you were at Lochleven, the only help she sent you was words. Why should she do more now?'

'Jesu! How unadventurous you are! No, I shall sail not *from* the Solway but across it, and I will have no more argument, if you please.'

And so, on the following afternoon, accompanied by Lords Herries, Maxwell, Fleming, and seventeen others including her young rescuers Geordie and Willie Douglas, Mary Queen of Scots – once more in borrowed clothes – stepped into a fishing boat and was rowed across the wide silver waters of the Solway to the flat, sandy shores of England.

PART THREE

ENGLAND 1568 – 1603

Chapter Sixteen

MAY 1568-JANUARY 1570

1

Elizabeth was not pleased to hear that her good sister, the queen of Scots, had landed on England's shores. 'God's death! As if I had not troubles enough. If I give her what she wants, it will ruin my reputation – a Protestant sovereign re-imposing a Catholic queen on a Protestant people by force of arms! – while if I do *not* give her what she wants, my reputation will still be ruined. Because if I send her back without support, and her subjects choose to execute her, I will get the blame. So what can I do? Because I do not want her here.'

Cecil said, 'She is exceedingly anxious to meet and talk to your majesty ...'

'I imagine she is. And if she is as talkative in the flesh as she is on the page, I shall scarcely be able to get a word in!'

'... but I would not advise that you should receive her in London, certainly not until you have decided what to do about her demands.'

Afterwards, long afterwards, Cecil was to think that perhaps he would have done better to advise his mistress otherwise. Mary's looks and charm would have infuriated Elizabeth, who did not like women very much – especially beautiful ones – and what was to develop into a seemingly endless saga might have been cut off, incontinent, at the very start.

The quiet, spiteful voice of Francis Walsingham intervened. 'If your majesty permits? Might I humbly suggest that, in the meantime, since your subjects in the north of England have not yet been fully weaned from worship of the Antichrist, the queen of Scots should not be left at Carlisle, where she might be tempted to try – unsuccessfully, of course! – to stir up your majesty's subjects against you?'

Elizabeth looked at him with disfavour. He was a newcomer to her councils, but she had been acquainted with him when she was a child, and had not cared for him much even then. He had been a fat boy who was bidding fair to be a fat man, and she did not like fat men. He was also sycophantic, which she expected and approved on public occasions but found tedious in the council chamber. He was skilled, however, in his chosen rôle of spymaster and would be even better in time.

Cecil, on whose toes Walsingham had already begun surreptitiously treading, said dismissively, 'Let us not imagine dangers where none exist.'

'If I may say so, it is safer to fear a danger that may not exist than to dismiss the possibility that it might.'

Cecil, whose caution was proverbial, ignored him. 'Perhaps your majesty should temporise.' It was a reasonable suggestion, since her majesty rarely did anything else.

'Yes, let us wait and see which way the winds are blowing. In the meantime, we can send Knollys to keep her quiet. He is a sensible man.'

To her annoyance, the sensible man, elderly and Puritanical, was much impressed by Mary at her intelligent, friendly and most spirited best, and as unhappy as she that the windows of her apartments were barred, the antechambers full of soldiers, and all but three or four of her little court required to leave the castle at sunset.

The truth of the matter was that, within three weeks of escaping from Lochleven, she was a prisoner again.

2

It was years since the queen of England had appeared in Mary's dreams, dreams that in those years had been largely inhabited by violent men and violent deaths. But at Carlisle she dreamed of no one else.

The figure that appeared beside her bed was as erect and arrogant as ever, the face as hard, the clothes and jewels as vulgarly excessive.

Mary, who was lying on top of the coverlet in a plain black gown, taking an afternoon nap, sat up and said angrily, 'Oh, there you are! You have taken your time, haven't you?'

Elizabeth's invisible eyebrows rose in a patronising way, but Mary had no intention of being patronised. She slipped off the bed to stand facing her dearest cousin and sister, forcing the other woman to look up to her, and said imperiously, 'I wrote and begged you to send and fetch me to your presence as soon as I landed in England, when I was in a sorry state with nothing in the world other than the clothes I stood up in. But instead you had me installed here in Carlisle in a chamber with bars on the windows. Perhaps you will explain yourself?'

Obviously taken aback, the figure in the viola-embroidered gold and amber satin said, '*Explain* myself? You must see that I cannot receive you at court in the present circumstances.'

'Which circumstances?'

'Knollys must have told you.'

'You mean that stupid slander about my husband's murder? That I knew about it in advance?' Mary laughed. 'I pay no more attention to that than you paid to the gossip when the wife of your Master of the Horse died so conveniently.'

The other woman turned scarlet. It matched her hair beautifully. She snapped, 'Take care!'

Meditatively, Mary went on, 'I remember thinking at the time how extraordinary it was that the queen of England should be considering marrying her horsekeeper.'

'Yes, and you not only thought it but said it. It was reported to me and I did not take it kindly.'

'Good heavens, cousin! Can't you recognise a drollery when you hear one?'

Elizabeth was always said to be witty, but that was not the same thing as having a sense of humour. She was clearly not amused; her breath was coming fast and her fists were planted belligerently on her hips.

The trouble was that Mary was not amused, either. She was so angry that, although she knew that deliberately provoking her cousin was not her wisest course, she could not stop herself and did not want to.

After a long moment, it was Elizabeth who gave way, who unclenched her fists and laid her palms flat against her skirts in the approved fashion, and then moved towards the window, putting a space between herself and Mary. Turning, her back to the bars, she said without expression, 'As Knollys should have told you, I am myself sorry and much grieved that I cannot receive you while any doubts remain about these slanders.'

Mary was always generous in her responses, quick to forgive except in the case of people who were beyond forgiveness, which Elizabeth was not – or not quite, not yet. Her head gracefully bent towards the smaller woman, she said, 'If you would only let me come to you and explain everything, you would understand. *Please*, don't do as the serpent does, and stop your ears! You must not listen to the lies you are told. I am not some wicked enchanter but your sister and natural cousin. And even if I *were* as dangerous and accursed as men say, you would be sufficiently armed against me in the loyalty and constancy of your own subjects.'

'Perhaps. But you know very well that queens are not their own mistresses. I am not the only one who must be convinced of your innocence. We must make some enquiry into it before I can receive you.'

Mary's goodwill vanished. 'So Knollys says, but I had hoped you might say otherwise. How *dare* you presume so? I am a queen. *I have no other judge than God.*'

Soothingly, as if to a child, her cousin replied, 'Don't concern yourself. I am sure Knollys must also have told you that, even if you are unable to establish your innocence, you can rely on me to help you back to your throne.'

It was then that Mary's precarious control snapped and the furious tears came flooding. Beating her fists wildly against her thighs, she screamed, 'You don't *believe* I am innocent. You don't *want* me to be innocent. What you want is to send a tarnished queen back to a tarnished throne! That would suit you very well, wouldn't it? You could sit back and laugh in everyone's face. You are evil, evil, *evil!*'

The other woman's stare was like a basilisk's. 'How dare you say such things to me!'

'Because they're true!' Then, in a despairing wail, 'Let me go! Please let me go! What have I done that you should treat me so?'

'What have you done?' There was a world of contemptuous astonishment in Elizabeth's voice. 'You exist. You are a threat to me. You will always be a threat to me. And as for letting you go, where *would* you go? They would kill you if you went back to Scotland. And if you went to France and they helped you back to your tarnished throne, they would have to leave an army behind to keep you on it. I *will* not have a French army on my northern doorstep again.'

Mary laughed hysterically. 'I shan't go to France. How could I possibly go to France in *these* hideous clothes?'

The other woman blinked. 'What? What have clothes to do with it? In any case, they are not hideous. Out of the goodness of my heart, I sent them to you from my own wardrobe. I chose them myself, with the greatest of care.'

'Oh, *did* you! Because even Knollys was so embarrassed at their dowdiness that he said one of your maids had chosen them, believing them to be for one of my waiting women.'

Viciously, Elizabeth said, 'You dare complain? You dare complain about *anything*? You stupid woman! You should be on your knees thanking me for my charity.'

It was too much. Mary flew at her, hands outstretched to tear at the filmy gauze over her bosom, to pull at the bright red artificial curls, to

362

scratch at the polished paste that hid the smallpox scars, to claw at the domineering eyes under their invisible brows.

'I hate you, I hate you!'

Mary woke up as they fell to the ground struggling.

She was startled and shocked by the violence of her feelings. Never in her life – or in her dreams – had she ever raised her hand to anyone. But, lying on her hard bed under her barred window, she could not be sorry.

3

'On the word of a prince,' Elizabeth wrote, 'nothing shall ever persuade me to endanger your life or honour. I will do all I can for you.' The only small difficulty was that her councillors were determined on something more than a private enquiry; they wanted a formal investigation into the regrettable scandal of Darnley's death and Mary's subsequent marriage to the chief suspect. Elizabeth was sure that her good sister would understand.

Her good sister understood only that it was an outrageous suggestion, since Elizabeth could have no jurisdiction over a fellow sovereign. Furiously, Mary set about writing letters demanding help from Catherine de' Medici, Charles IX, her uncle the cardinal, the Duc d'Anjou, and a great many others. When she sent Lord Herries to London, however, he returned with the reassuring message that, whatever happened, Elizabeth was determined to see Mary restored to her throne.

Elizabeth, meanwhile, was telling the Spanish ambassador that she thought Mary might be restored to her throne in name only, with the Regent Moray ruling *de facto*. She also wrote to James to assure him that, if the investigation found Mary guilty of involvement in Darnley's murder, she would not insist on Mary being restored at all.

Privately, she hoped that the investigation would give her an acceptable international pretext for keeping Mary under her own eye and her own hand.

4

It was a beautiful evening in the countryside around Haddington, the grass faintly gilded, the bracken beginning to turn to amber, the far hills rough-edged but kindly, like broken amethyst. The sun had the amiable warmth of September and the martins were swooping low over the cattle grazing in the fields.

Lethington saw none of it. Sinking his head in his hands, he said, 'I have lost my way.'

It had been hard for Mallie Fleming, in these last months, to pretend that she had not been aware of it. Her concern had been not to intrude, whatever they had once said about sharing each other's minds. When he asked her views about the queen, she told him as honestly as she could, but whereas her own attachment to Mary was human and personal, she knew that his was more complex, personal sympathy and personal loyalty subservient to greater ends. She knew that, if he had been just an ordinary laird and she just an ordinary wife, life would have been wonderfully simple. But in that case she would not have loved him so much, or at all.

Shocked, she said, 'Secretary Lethington losing his way? Impossible.'

Normally, he would have let out a puff of laughter, but this time he did not. At this moment, she thought, she was not the wife he adored, the wife who worshipped him, the mother of their infant son James – named, as everyone's son was, in honour of the little king – and heavy with their second child. She was only a sounding board for his thoughts.

She stretched out a hand and he took it and held it against his cheek. 'No,' he said, reading her mind. 'You *are* here. You are always here.' And then, 'Peace is what I want, what I have always wanted, but not at the price of Scotland's self-respect. If Mary remains in English hands, Elizabeth will always be able to use the threat of releasing her as a weapon against James. Which means that he will finish up ruling, not as regent for a two-year-old king but as England's lieutenant in the north. It seems to be a price he is prepared to pay.'

'I suppose he sees it as preferable to holding the queen here. Out of sight, out of mind, not only for James but for her supporters.'

'Those who remain.'

After Mary's flight to the false haven of England, James had set about doing what he did best, forcibly imposing peace on the disaffected. Having been privately warned by Cecil that he should take action against Mary's adherents before Elizabeth told him not to, he had swept through the south with an army of seven thousand men, burning, destroying and forfeiting without mercy.

'There's something else. In England, the queen might "happen to die" more easily than here, with fewer questions asked. James has always felt – although it took me years to recognise it – that *he* should have been king, and with Mary permanently out of the way, the possibilities would open up. If her son were to die, too ... Well, James himself is the son of a king, and it would need only a small change in the law to override his bastardy. He could probably buy enough support in parliament and in the country to achieve it.' He shrugged. 'He might make quite a good king, if one could stomach his methods. But, unlike Mary, he has no claim to the English succession, and there could be no union of the crowns and therefore no security for lasting peace.'

He moved uneasily on the heathery bank, a slight frown on his forehead.

She tried not to sound anxious, because she knew how he hated it. 'Are your legs paining you?'

'A little, but it's not important. I am paying for having ridden too many miles over too many years, that's all. Though I would prefer not to have to go to York next month.'

'Must you?'

'Yes. I don't know whether I will be able to do anything, but I must try. James is set on blackening Mary's name so irrevocably that any possibility of her restoration will be ruled out forever. If he succeeds, he will have no more trouble with Argyll or Huntly, Eglinton, Crawford, Cassillis or the others here at home. The queen's party will cease to exist. I cannot imagine,' he exclaimed with rare savagery, 'why she has consented to submit to the enquiry at all. She has Herries and Bishop Leslie there to advise her and even if *she* continues to think of Elizabeth as a friend and James as a brother, however undutiful, *they* should know better.'

With forced lightness, his wife said, 'Don't make an enemy of James, my dearest love. You're not like Argyll and Huntly, able to raise thousands of men to defend you.'

And to defend you, too, he thought, and the little ones, and my father, and my brother and sisters ... That was what had caused him to lose his way.

He smiled back at her. 'We have friends.'

5

The investigation opened at York in a room within a room, a large, panelled open-topped booth with most of the space occupied by a table, and benches along the sides for the judges and commissioners. There was a canopy at one end bearing the royal arms of England, under which sat the chairman, the Duke of Norfolk, with the Earl of Sussex and Sir Ralph

Sadler beside him, while the Regent Moray's commissioners occupied the bench to their right and the queen of Scots' commissioners that to their left. At the foot of the table were the clerks, and milling around between the booth's high-backed benches and the stone walls of the great vaulted chamber in which it was set were all the messengers, serjeants and inferior beings whose presence might, or might not be required to further the course of justice.

The declared purpose of what had been officially designated as a 'conference' was to enable the English commissioners first to hear the complaints of the queen of Scots against the regent and his government, then the arguments of the regent, and then to adjudicate between them. Mary, who was not permitted to be present in person, had been assured that it was in no sense a trial, but anyone unwittingly stumbling into it might easily have mistaken it for one.

Elizabeth's commissioners took an oath to proceed sincerely, uprightly and impartially, and Mary's and James's to conceal nothing that might be requisite to the discovery of the truth. After this impeccably lucid beginning, however, things deteriorated badly, since there were too many misapprehensions chasing too few facts.

On the second evening, when the queen's commissioners – Lord Herries and the Bishop of Ross – had charged the regent and his associates with treason and rebellion, and the regent had requested time to study the charges and prepare his answers, James retired to a tavern with Morton, Lethington, Lindsay of the Byres and the Bishop of Orkney, and said bitterly, 'What am I supposed to do? Norfolk claims that Elizabeth's instructions to him confirm what she's told me, that if Mary's guilt is plain and manifest, she'll consider her unworthy of being restored to the throne. But Herries says she's promised Mary herself that she'll be restored whatever happens.'

Morton said, 'That just Elizabeth being Elizabeth. She doesnae want Mary back on the throne.'

'Maybe not, but Norfolk's also been told that if her guilt isn't proved beyond doubt, he's to negotiate a reconciliation between her and us.'

Morton guffawed.

'The proposal,' James said repressively, 'would be that we would have Mary back on the throne, but the country would be ruled by a Great Council equally divided between Mary's supporters and ours, with Elizabeth as arbiter in all disputes.'

'Well, we're no' having that!'

Lethington rose to stretch his aching legs. It was easy to recognise

366

Cecil's fine Italian hand. He had always wanted Mary out of the way, and now he was suggesting a basis for reconciliation so absurd that James either had to destroy Mary's reputation beyond hope of repair or else accept Elizabeth formally as Scotland's overlord. And parliament would never let him get away with that.

James said, 'No, it's not acceptable. So I'm afraid we'll have to produce the *Book of Articles* and the contents of Bothwell's casket.' He managed to sound as if that had not been his intention all along.

'I don't know why ye're hesitating,' Morton complained. 'Your sister's a wicked woman and it's time she was put away for good.'

'D'ye think so?'

'Yes,' Morton said.

'Yes,' Lindsay said.

'I suppose so,' said the bishop.

James looked at Lethington, who sat down again. He was moderately sure that he had been required to attend the conference because James, who no longer trusted him, preferred not to leave him running loose in Scotland, where he might be tempted to reconstruct the queen's party. Suspicious of everyone who did not unfailingly agree with him, James now had to be handled with extreme caution.

When Lethington spoke, therefore, he spoke in the tones of one to whom an idea had just occurred. 'I think,' he said, meditatively, 'that we need to know exactly where we stand before we commit ourselves. As we all know from experience, Elizabeth is inclined to say one thing and mean another.'

'That's true,' James admitted. 'So what d'ye suggest?'

Lethington hesitated convincingly. 'You could, perhaps, ask for guarantees. Insist on knowing whether Norfolk has full royal authority to pronounce a verdict of guilty or not guilty, and what exactly they propose doing if the investigation finds Mary guilty. Will England hold her, or return her to us? Will Elizabeth finally approve our past proceedings and grant recognition to the regency?'

Morton said, 'There's something in that. Everything's a wee thing imprecise as it stands.'

'Very well,' James agreed.

6

As Lethington had hoped, Norfolk did not feel qualified to answer

James's questions and had to refer them to London. To his annoyance, however, James took the opportunity, in the meantime, of informally showing the duke the letters that had been found in the Bothwell casket, the evidence that Mary had betrayed the king her husband with Bothwell, and been instrumental in the king's death.

Carefully, James pointed out the incriminating phrases, which was necessary since the letters were long – one of them impossibly long in view of the occasion on which it had supposedly been written – and the phrases few.

'For sure, he suspects of the thing you know, and of his life ... Burn this letter, for it is dangerous, for I am thinking of nothing but trouble,' said one. And another, 'Now if to please you, my dear life, I spare neither honour, conscience, nor hazard, nor greatness, take it in good part ... the most faithful lover that you ever had or shall have.'

James said, 'It's just to give ye a notion of what's in the letters. I wouldn't want ye to think we're holding things up for lack of evidence. And now ye've had a look at them, maybe ye could ask Cecil whether he'd see them as the kind of manifest proof of guilt we've been talking about.'

The Duke of Norfolk was in his early thirties, an experienced administrator but an anxious man, whose long face, hollow cheeks, full lips and pouched eyes wore a perpetually harassed expression. He had a habit of rubbing his brow and disturbing his court cap so that it developed an independent tendency to wander. It did so now, tilting so steeply towards the back that it looked like an elegantly ruched dark blue halo.

'They do appear to be somewhat incriminating. Dear, dear. How unfortunate! What a coil!'

7

Lethington, who had been hoping to discredit the letters before anyone saw them, gave Norfolk five days' grace before riding out to the hunt with him. Norfolk, England's greatest nobleman, had always seemed to him the ideal husband for Mary. Since he was a Protestant, he would be acceptable to Scotland; and the match would be sufficiently acceptable in England to guarantee the succession to any children of the union.

The problem had always been catching Norfolk between wives, but his third wife had recently died in childbirth, like her predecessors, and he was available again. Since, however, he might reasonably be expected to hesitate over taking as his fourth wife a young woman who, queen or not, had a proven predilection for adultery and murder, Lethington's task was to cast doubt on the trustworthiness of the letters without, at the same time, casting doubt on the trustworthiness of the Scots commissioners who were offering them in evidence.

There was no need for him to raise the subject. Norfolk did it for him as they cantered over the autumn fields.

'I had heard such excellent reports of her,' he said sadly.

'She is a very charming and intelligent young woman.'

'But such wickedness! Those letters and poems!'

Lethington said nothing and after a moment Norfolk cast a glance at him and saw the faintest of frowns in the clear grey eyes. He had known Lethington personally for several years and by reputation for very much longer, so he said, 'You may speak with perfect reliance on my discretion. Is something troubling you?'

'No. Yes. There is a doubt in my mind, but one so insubstantial that I have not mentioned it to anyone. My colleagues would simply dismiss it as a product of my imagination.'

Norfolk's rather slack mouth curved. 'Certainly, the regent and my Lords Morton and Lindsay are of a down-to-earth persuasion. I think, however, that I might understand where they do not.'

'I believe you might,' Lethington said gratefully, and looked as if he were collecting his thoughts. 'You've heard from Morton how the casket was discovered. I was present, and the contents appeared to be damning. It was some little time before it occurred to me to wonder why *all* the contents should be damning.'

'I beg your pardon?'

'Consider. If you yourself chose to keep every document relating to one particular correspondent in the same box, the earliest letter would probably be at the bottom and the most recent at the top. In between, the letters would reflect the passing of time, different moods and different subjects?'

'Yes.'

'Now, as her majesty's secretary of state, I know that she wrote a good many entirely innocent letters and memoranda, in her own hand, to Bothwell. But there were no innocent letters in the casket. What does that suggest to you?'

'That he kept only the guilty ones! I *see*. But a man might choose to preserve love letters, and not others. And what about the poems?'

'Some of the letters have no mention of love, only of plotting. And writing poetry is one of the queen's favourite amusements. The poems could have been addressed to anyone, or to no one.'

'I *see!*' Norfolk said again. Then, after a moment, 'You must be thinking of blackmail?'

Lethington nodded. 'I wondered at first whether Bothwell had kept the documents as insurance against being brought to trial for a second time for involvement in the king's murder. His argument, in that event, would be that the queen would not dare try him because then she would incriminate herself. Another possibility was that he might use the threat of publishing them as a way of forcing the queen to marry him if he could not persuade her by other means.'

'It's possible,' Norfolk said, 'but none of it invalidates the *contents* of the letters and poems.'

'This is the difficult part,' Lethington said – and meant it. 'I am in a position to know her majesty's hand better than anyone, and I know her cast of mind and turns of speech. There are occasional pages in the letters that are not quite in her usual hand, and others with insertions in the margins.' He shrugged. 'I might have missed it, because her writing varies a good deal depending on her mood and whether she is in haste, if it had not been that the uncharacteristic pages happened to be those that contained the implications of guilt.'

'Dear, *dear*. Forgery?'

'Yes, and good forgery. But anyone who has lived in France, where the Roman hand is common, could do it.'

'Bothwell himself?'

'Possibly. He spent some years there in his youth.'

They were supposed to be after hare, but Norfolk had lost all interest in the chase. Their horses had slowed to a walk and their companions were out of sight. 'You are saying that you believe your queen to be innocent? If that is so, why have you allowed yourself to be associated with your fellow commissioners, who are convinced of her guilt?'

Lethington shrugged. 'As I say, I have no proof at all. It is purely a matter of impressions. Though of suspicions, too, because the incriminating parts of the letters contradict everything I know of her.'

Norfolk, though a fool in some ways, was not stupid. 'You are telling me that I must either believe the letters, or believe you.'

Lethington smiled at him with the brilliance that had once come naturally, but no longer. 'It is for you to decide.'

Next day, in the most roundabout manner, the Duke of Norfolk hinted to the Earl of Moray that the whole regrettable business of the investigation could easily be resolved with a little goodwill on both sides – if, for example, the regent dropped his charges and the queen confirmed his regency. She would be harmless to Scotland – would she not? – if she were free to marry an English husband who would keep her in order. And, of course, any children she bore that husband would help to distance Châtelherault and the Hamiltons, no friends of Lord Moray, from the regency and throne of Scotland. The present little king was a very frail bulwark in an era when children died so readily.

James said, 'It's an interesting notion, but she's still married to Bothwell.'

Elizabeth had the strongest dislike of being presented with ultimata, even from people she approved of, such as James. Furthermore, Cecil was receiving private information from York which suggested that too many of those involved in the conference were doing their best to avoid discussing the real issues. The Earl of Moray, it appeared, had wasted days arguing the constitutional case for his own claim to the regency as opposed to Châtelherault's.

At the beginning of November, therefore, Elizabeth's privy council declared the conference in recess, and instructed it to resume its deliberations at Westminster.

'She does not allow herself to become discouraged,' Mary Seton wrote to Mallie Fleming, 'because she knows very well that the regent and the lords are guilty of the charges she has brought against them, whereas she herself is blameless of all she is accused of. She continues to believe that Elizabeth will stand her friend, although I cannot myself like the proceedings. Having been removed to isolated Bolton we are starved of information, although Sir Robert Melville has been here once or twice with messages from the commissioners, and Madame's own commissioners, Lord Herries and Bishop Leslie, have ridden over to consult with her.

'Thanks to the good offices of your husband, we know something of these mysterious letters that the regent considers so important to his case, but we have not seen them, and neither have Lord Herries or Bishop Leslie, which I think very improper. How can Madame answer allegations if she does not know what those allegations are? And how can she remember what she wrote in letters from years ago? But if they talk of poison and passion, then she never wrote them at all and they must be forgeries.

'And now the conference is to be moved to Westminster and Elizabeth says there is no need for Madame to attend, because no proof has yet been shown against her and there might be no need for her to attend at all. Westminster is two hundred and fifty miles away and the snow here is already thick on the ground. Madame has told her commissioners, yet again, that they must refuse to take part in the conference if she is not permitted to attend, but I fear that they have not the strength of purpose, nor the cleverness, to obey her.

'Life here goes on pleasantly enough in our little court. Lord and Lady Livingston are here, and your brother Lord Fleming and his lady, and Geordie and Willie Douglas from Lochleven. John Beaton and Bastien look after the household as well as they may. Sir Francis Knollys still holds sway as Elizabeth's envoy, and has been endeavouring to teach Madame to become a Protestant and also to write in English, in which she tries hard, to please him. But in the evenings, when she is not embroidering, or playing cards with young Willie, she spends little time writing in English and a great deal writing in French – you may guess to whom, and with what result. Do you remember what a scheming, spiteful woman Catherine de' Medici was? She has not changed.

'At least my arrival has helped to restore Madame to the perfection of appearance which has always been hers. Knollys is quite lost in admiration at all the new hair styles I have contrived for her – a different one every day. I almost wept when I found how much pleasure it gave Madame herself.

'Only God knows what will come of it all, and we can but commit ourselves to His mercy. As you know, I have always found comfort in prayer, but I have never needed it as much as now.

'God's blessing be with you, dear Fleming, and your son and new little daughter. How much I envy you.'

When the conference reassembled, there were no more of the amiable maunderings that had taken up so much time at York. Now, Elizabeth's commissioners were joined by the formidable Cecil, Leicester, Bacon, Clinton and Arundel.

James was given all the assurances he had requested at York, and could no longer play for time – the time that Lethington had privately desired and made such good use of. Now, it was necessary for James to produce the evidence.

He did it beautifully. Whatever Mary Stewart's crimes, she was his sovereign and his sister. One could almost see the tussle between love and duty as he hesitated to reveal the damning summary of evidence. But then the Bishop of Orkney snatched it from the clerk's hand and tossed it on the table to cries of, 'Well done, Bishop Turpy!'

James's distress and embarrassment were clear for all to see.

The *Book of Articles* had been prepared by the same George Buchanan who had been the queen's Classical tutor but, as an adherent of the Lennoxes, had become one of her most virulent detractors after the Darnley murder; a man so steeped in scholarship that he was incapable of distinguishing life from learning or a Mary Stewart from a Clytemnestra. According to him, Mary and Bothwell had been lovers since a few days after the birth of her son, and had conspired together to bring the king to Kirk o' Field and there to murder him. One of his choicer inventions had a half-naked Bothwell being hauled up on a rope, by little Prince James's wet nurse, straight from his mistress's bed into that of the queen.

The Earl of Leicester said to Lethington afterwards, 'I had not thought Edinburgh such an exciting place. You don't look well. Why are you walking with a stick?'

'My past is catching up with me. A little rest and I will be myself again. Are you implying that you find the evidence unconvincing?'

The man who had once been Robert Dudley grinned. 'We all know what this conference is about. Elizabeth wants Mary out of the way and forgotten. She is having enough problems with Spain and France at the moment without being accused of illegally imprisoning an innocent Catholic sovereign as well. If she can do it with an appearance of legality, that's another matter. Whatever your own attitude to Mary, remember that she is of no importance as a person, but only as a pawn, a symbol. As one of the most experienced diplomats in these islands, you must know that.'

Once, Lethington would have conceded it, but no more. His love for his wife and his small son and the daughter he had not yet seen had changed all that. But the game had to be played out to its end. He smiled with his old dry charm. 'Perhaps. But what about the evidence?'

'Most of it appears to be salacious nonsense. I'm surprised at James even offering it, although he is such a moral man himself that he may not see what strikes the more sinful among us as – how shall I put it – improbable. God knows, I'm no angel, but going from bed to bed by way of a rope? These letters we are being promised, however ... Tell me about them.'

'What have you heard?'

'Incriminating on the surface, but Norfolk has privately confided to me that he has reservations about them.'

'Has he? Well, well. How interesting.'

12

The rumour went round. And round. And round.

Early in January, Secretary Cecil – annoyed because Leicester, with whom he was forever at odds, had won – summoned the Regent Moray and his colleagues to inform them that nothing of which they had been accused by the queen of Scots' commissioners was considered to have impaired their honour. Similarly, nothing that had been said by the Earl of Moray and his confrères had convinced her majesty Queen Elizabeth of England that her cousin and good sister Mary of Scotland was guilty of the charges levelled against her.

Both sides, it seemed, were innocent.

Lethington's own private enterprises had gone far towards discrediting the so-called evidence against Mary, but the decisive factor was that Elizabeth had developed cold feet. And not before time. If the York-Westminster conference had found Mary guilty of murder, the English parliament – which violently disliked the possibility of having a Catholic foreigner, which to them Mary was, succeed to Elizabeth's throne – would have pressed hard for her execution. And Elizabeth had no intention of setting a precedent in executing anointed queens. Nor could she afford the disturbance that would result among her still numerous Catholic subjects, or the diplomatic uproar such a deed would have provoked abroad. And so a deeply dishonest and discreditable affair came to an equally dishonest and discreditable end.

James was anxious to get home, because the Borders were in chaos again and Argyll and Huntly raising the west and north in Mary's name. Elizabeth gave him a large escort to see him safely on his way and a contribution to the exchequer of £5,000, which was even more welcome. Before he went, however, he took time to meet the Duke of Norfolk privately and tell him that he had been forced to accuse Mary in order to save himself, but that he had nothing but affection for his sister and could wish her no better husband than Norfolk. On the understanding, of course, that such a marriage had Elizabeth's consent.

James went free, but Mary did not, although she ceased to be a guest at the castle of Bolton and became a guest at the castle of Tutbury in Staffordshire, further away from Scotland than ever.

It might have been worse. Although gossip about her guilt was to swill back and forth across Europe like an insalubrious tide, Elizabeth's failure to declare it explicitly left a faint ray of hope for the future. Scandals could fade in a surprisingly short time. Only eight years before, Robert Dudley, now Earl of Leicester and one of England's leading privy councillors, had been almost universally believed to be Elizabeth's lover and to have murdered his wife for her sake.

13

Tutbury was huge, rambling, ruinous and damp, perched on top of a hill above an evil-smelling marsh. The journey from Bolton had taken days, the weather had been bitter and the tracks icy, so that first Lady Livingston had fallen ill and then Mary herself. When they reached Tutbury, which was seldom occupied, it was to discover its borrowed hangings and furnishings fighting a losing battle against the damp, the chill and the smells that had, over the years, become part of a castle in such poor repair that the wind seemed to whistle as bitingly indoors as out.

Since Elizabeth had prevented Lord Fleming from going to France for money from Mary's estates there, her household was destitute and Sir Francis Knollys had to write to London to beg £500 to maintain it. It was in anticipation of other such unwelcome demands in the future that Elizabeth had decided to transfer Mary into the hands of George Talbot, sixth Earl of Shrewsbury, one of the richest men in England and well able – in Elizabeth's view – to afford the inconveniences and the costs of becoming Mary's jailer. Tutbury was only one, and the least favoured of the great string of his residences, and his newly-wed wife, Bess of Hardwick, whose fourth husband he was, owned several more on her own account.

In due course, the Shrewsburys paid a visit to Tutbury, the earl himself mild, nervous and finical, the countess a formidable and much older woman in a carrot-red wig and enough pearls to restock the fisheries of the orient.

The earl, anxious above all to have a well-behaved prisoner, made no demur over Mary having her cloth of state erected over her chair, and even closed his eyes to the introduction of a Catholic priest into her household. The countess, though unable to see any immediate profit in association with a queen who lacked throne, money or possessions, nevertheless recognised the uncertainty of fortune and, for a time at least, made herself pleasant to her unwanted guest.

Together, they sat and gossiped over their embroidery, saying little that touched on the outside world although Mary learned an amazing amount about the countess's properties, her children, and her previous husbands.

She exchanged letters with all her old correspondents and a few new ones, including the Duke of Norfolk. She received occasional visitors and charmed them as she had always done. She knew a little of what was going on beyond the walls of her prison, but not enough. Never enough, and always at unreliable second or third hand. She became certain that her correspondence was being tampered with.

Before long, her health deteriorated, the pain in her side becoming ever more familiar and gastric attacks more frequent. As the weeks passed, and then the months, the news from Scotland of James's ruthless campaigning against her supporters began to depress her so deeply that she went into a decline that led to fears for her life.

14

By mid-May, James had received formal submissions from Argyll and Huntly, Crawford and Ogilvie, Caithness, Sutherland and Lovat. His only failures had been Châtelherault and Herries, who agreed to a reconciliation and then, following pleading letters from Mary, changed their minds. Within the hour, they found themselves in jail.

James was feeling justifiably satisfied with himself when he received a communication from Elizabeth throwing the whole question of Mary wide open again. He could scarcely believe it, although he should, of course, have foreseen that Elizabeth would find an imprisoned and uncondemned Mary scarcely less of an embarrassment than a condemned one would have been. She herself, as accepted patron of all the Protestant heretics of Europe, was already unpopular enough with France and Spain; she did not need a Catholic martyr on her hands.

She wanted rid of his sister.

15

Lethington had known for almost a year that there would be no bettering of the pain and weakness in his legs, and had resigned himself to it. But he had not anticipated that his body, too, would begin to fail him. Nothing, however, would have kept him from the convention James had called at Perth to discuss Elizabeth's ultimatum.

His wife, with the anger of love, demanded, 'And how do you propose to get there?'

He could still smile, though the lean and handsome face had become gaunt and the thickly waving black hair was streaked with grey. 'I shall ride pillion, like a lady. This may be the last opportunity to have Mary restored without civil war. Elizabeth has proposed three options, the first that she should be restored to her throne under guarantees for the safety of those who rebelled against her, the second that she should rule jointly with her son ...'

'Who is three years old.'

'Precisely. It would mean ruling jointly with James. The third option is that she should ratify her abdication and be released to live in England.'

His wife said, 'I cannot imagine James favouring either of the first two.'

'No, although I intend to argue for the first of them. But he is so full of self-confidence that he may also refuse to consider the third, and that would mean an end to the Norfolk marriage plan on which her majesty's freedom – and perhaps the succession – could depend.'

She shook her head. 'Will you never give up?'

'How can I? Come, help me up so that we can go and see the children.'

She gave him her arm and he gripped it with sudden intensity. 'My dearest dear, how could I have lived for so many years without you?'

And how many years, she thought desolately, shall I have to face living without *you*?

Because his influence depended solely on power of personality and because his mind was intricate, Lethington had always tried to hold back from public commitment, believing that he could accomplish more by subtle ways. But now, at last, he committed himself openly to Mary's restoration – and found that he had left it too late.

Where once reasoned argument had been possible, it was no longer so, because James was not now prepared to brook any hint of disagreement with his views and certainly not a perceived attack on his right to rule. As a result, the Perth assembly was packed with his own time-serving friends and Mary's enemies.

Although Huntly, Atholl and a few others supported Lethington, they were heavily defeated. The convention also angrily turned down Mary's request for assent to her proposed divorce from Bothwell, still in his Danish prison. Sardonically, Lethington congratulated them for refusing, now, what they had imprisoned the queen for resisting two years before.

Treasurer Richardson noted that Lethington, with his brother John Maitland, had opposed the king's authority and that whosoever did so in the future would be deemed a traitor.

James was clever about his priorities during the month that followed. Not until Argyll, Huntly, and Mary's more powerful supporters among the Border lords had been neutralised by means of bribes or threats did he turn on Lethington, now left isolated and fatally exposed.

Aware of his danger, Lethington had retreated with Mallie and the children to Atholl's stronghold at Dunkeld but, summoned to a privy council meeting at Stirling on 3rd September, he went – and found himself formally charged with complicity in the murder of the 'young fool and proud tyrant' of the Craigmillar bond.

It was an adherent of the young fool's father, the Earl of Lennox, who knelt before the council and demanded justice on the basis of proofs newly discovered.

'Proofs?' Lethington asked. 'What proofs?'

'I have laid before the council copies of the confession of Nicholas Hubert, known as "French Paris", the former servant of the Earl of

Bothwell, who was present on the occasion of the horrible and abominable murder of the young king.'

'And is Nicholas Hubert here to swear to his confession?'

Carelessly, James intervened. 'No, he's been executed.'

'When?'

'I don't see that it matters. A fortnight ago.'

Lethington knew about Nicholas Hubert. Knew that he had been captured in Denmark in October of the previous year. Knew that he could have been brought back in plenty of time to give evidence at the York-Westminster enquiry into Mary's guilt. Knew that he had not been, because James had not dared to produce a possibly loose-mouthed witness who might have incriminated some of the great and powerful.

He said, 'I see. You executed him two weeks *after* our assembly at Perth and two weeks *before* this impeachment?'

James shrugged. 'Obviously.'

'And the circumstances under which his confession was made?'

'We interrogated him on two successive days.'

Lethington might have asked, 'Rack or thumbscrews?' but the question would have been superfluous. He contented himself with, 'We?'

'Wood, George Buchanan, and Ramsay.'

In spite of everything, Lethington laughed. Wood and Ramsay were James's own servants, and George Buchanan the Lennox supporter whose libels on Mary had been so colourful as to cause even Robert Dudley to raise an eyebrow.

He said, 'I should have liked to question him myself. I am sorry that you did not see fit to keep him alive for a little longer.'

'There was no need.'

'That depends on one's viewpoint.'

There was a gale whirling round the castle, high on its crag, gusting down the great chimneys and sending smoke billowing from the marble fireplace. Lethington remembered Mary standing before that very fireplace on the morning less than four years before when she had instructed him to leave for London and tell Elizabeth that she proposed to marry Lord Darnley.

'May I hear the confession?'

Lennox's man read Hubert's words from the paper in his hand. 'The Lord Bothwell was suffering as he often did from the bloody flux and was relieving himself in a corner at Kirk o' Field while I, who had been his servant and was now the queen's, stood by to shield him from intruders. The Lord Bothwell said that he had in mind to kill the king, and I said,

"Good God, my lord, that would be something that might bring much danger to you", but he said I was a fool if I thought he would enterprise such a deed without the support of others. I asked what others, and he spoke of the laird of Lethington.'

The voice stopped as if the evidence had come to an end.

Lethington said, 'And the rest, please.'

Lennox's man glanced at James, who frowned and then nodded. It would have been too blatant, in the presence of the rest of the privy council, to forbid it.

'... the laird of Lethington, the lords Argyll, Huntly, Morton, Ruthven and Lindsay. I asked him about Lord Moray, but he said that Lord Moray was neutral in the affair.'

'I am sure he did,' Lethington remarked drily. 'And that is the sum and substance of the confession?'

'Yes.'

'Then I wonder why I do not see the lords Argyll, Huntly, Morton, Ruthven and Lindsay lined up beside me to answer to the indictment?' He smiled blandly at Morton, seated with James among the righteous.

'They have no need to answer. Their innocence is beyond doubt.'

As were their power, their influence, and the number of their bondsmen.

James said, 'Your day of law will be set for 22nd November when you will be required to answer to the charges.'

'Yes, your grace. What sureties does the council require for my appearance before the court on the due date?'

James glanced at the faces round the table, then shook his head. 'No sureties will be acceptable. You will be taken under guard from here to Edinburgh, where you will be kept in custody until the day in question.'

Despite the rage in his heart, Lethington had too much pride to say other than, 'As your grace commands.'

18

James was riding high, but there were one or two incidents that should have warned him that his regency and his methods were not universally acceptable.

Kirkcaldy of Grange, though long devoted to him, went to the length of forging James's signature in order to have Lethington released from his close detention in the house of one of James's adherents in the Highgait into his own less rigorous custody at the castle, of which he was now captain. In part, he was moved by personal sympathy for Lethington, but more by the knowledge that the accusations against him were far too politically convenient for the regent. Grange, that rarest of beings among the Scots nobility, an honest man with a sense of justice, could not stomach them.

And so Lethington spent the next few weeks in Edinburgh castle in company with Mary's supporters, Lord Herries, and Châtelherault, head of the Hamiltons.

As his day of law approached, he was confirmed in the belief that he still had many friends. In the old tradition, he wrote to convocate the queen's lieges and they came armed, and in formidable numbers.

But James, who would have done precisely the same thing himself, had foreseen it and had another army standing by under Morton's command.

He was displeased to find that many of those who had turned out to support Lethington were traditional supporters of his own but, being James, did not pause to wonder why. Instead, he called their leaders together and rebuked them in terms that were a masterly blend of hypocrisy and self-deceit.

'When ye declared your desire to avenge the king's slaughter, I was in France. Ye required me to come home and take the government upon myself. Ye required me also to swear to revenge the murder of the king and swore in turn to give me your support. Now, a gentleman stands accused of this murder, but ye have convocated to hinder justice. I will therefore prorogue his day of law to another time. If he is clean, he will suffer no harm. If he is guilty, it will not lie in your hands to save him. In the meantime, he will return to his prison.'

19

It was to be James's last victory but one.

The last one came soon after. The Duke of Norfolk, already seduced by the idea of marrying the queen of Scots, had gradually come to view the attractions of a reigning queen as superior to those of a deposed one and had become – if somewhat indecisively – involved in a plot for a Catholic rising in the north of England whose object was to free Mary and place her on Elizabeth's throne. The plot having been discovered, Elizabeth went hastening to the safety of her most defensible castle, Windsor, while the Duke of Norfolk was despatched to an equally safe haven in the

381

Tower. The northern Catholic lords, however, went ahead with their rebellion.

It was ruthlessly suppressed, but several of its leaders escaped and, just after the middle of December, the commander of Elizabeth's army wrote to Regent Moray to say that the earls of Northumberland and Westmorland were believed to have crossed the border into Scotland and would he be so obliging as to lay hands on them and return them to safe keeping.

It was the kind of enterprise that James enjoyed, and on Christmas Eve he duly laid hands on Northumberland.

He was not prepared for the fury this aroused on the Borders, where there was an age-old tradition that political offenders, from whichever side of the dividing line, should be granted automatic refuge. Even Morton was scandalised at the thought of returning Northumberland to England and a traitor's death. Argyll and Huntly, as usual, threatened to rise against the regent, and Kirkcaldy of Grange said he would abandon the regent's cause and release Lethington, Châtelherault and Herries from imprisonment if James dared to hand the earl back to Elizabeth.

James sighed in exasperation and wrote to Elizabeth to say that he was having a few difficulties. However, he thought he could arrange to let her have Northumberland back if she would pay him £1,000 to relieve his immediate debts, a further annual subsidy of £1,000 to maintain his army, if she would recognise the infant king, guarantee his throne, and do something about Mary.

20

The unobtrusive little man, a Hamilton who had been paid in advance by Châtelherault's brother, followed the regent about for several days until he reached Linlithgow. The Hamiltons had a house there, with a convenient second-storey room overlooking the street.

He laid a mattress on the floor to smother his footsteps and draped the walls with black, so that no shadow would show. He removed the keystone of the arch of the back garden gate, to accommodate the height of escaping horse and rider. Then he settled down to wait.

In the two years of his regency, James had taken a sufficiently arbitrary line with the opposition to make himself a goodly number of enemies and was not, therefore, unaccustomed to receiving death threats. On this January day, he paid no more heed than usual to a warning that he should avoid the street outside the Hamilton house although he would have done as advised if the thickness of the crowds gathered to see him had not prevented him from making alteration to his planned route.

When the shot struck him, he appeared barely to feel the wound, and dismounted easily enough. The surgeons said, at first, that the injury was not mortal.

But it was.

21

The manner of James's death was to be the making of him. As with Darnley, martyrdom became him well, and it helped that those who had been opposed to him in life had learned enough from the aftermath of the Darnley affair to express their reaction to his murder in terms of unequivocal horror. No man criticised him. No man questioned his integrity. No man raised an eyebrow when others took to referring to him as the Good Regent.

It might have been a Hamilton who had done the deed – and made a successful escape – but every man feared the whispered accusation of foreknowledge.

There was scarcely a dry eye among the three thousand mourners in St Giles cathedral when John Knox, old and tired in body but not in rhetoric, delivered the funeral oration.

'O Lord,' he prayed, 'in what misery and confusion found he this realm and to what rest and quietness he swiftly, by his labours, brought it. Thy image, Lord, did so clearly shine in him that the devil himself could not abide it. And so, to punish our sins and ingratitude for failing rightly to esteem so precious a gift, Thou hast permitted him to fall into the hands of cruel and traitorous murderers. He is at rest, O Lord, and we are left in the extreme of misery.'

Queen Elizabeth of England who, when the news arrived from Linlithgow, had just finished writing a sharp letter to James ticking him off for trying to blackmail her, publicly succumbed to such a fit of weeping and sobbing over the loss of someone she suddenly discovered to have been the best and most useful friend she had in all the world that an irritated Robert Dudley finally told her to pull herself together lest the French ambassador – a fascinated witness – should draw the wrong conclusions.

When the news reached Mary Stewart, however, in her cold, damp prison at Tutbury, she wept not a tear. Indeed, she was so grateful to the assassin that she offered, if he could be found, to arrange to pay him a pension that would keep him in luxury for the rest of his life.

Chapter Seventeen

1570 – 1573

1

Tom Randolph had not been idle since Mary, almost four years earlier, had expelled him from her realm. Indeed, he had enlarged his experience considerably on a trade mission to Muscovy, so that, rediscovering the cold, wet and windy world of Edinburgh after James's death, he found himself comparing the Earl of Morton with Ivan the Terrible and concluding that there was little to choose between them, except that Ivan was cleaner and better dressed.

Elizabeth had chosen Randolph to go north because of his long acquaintance with the Scots lords, but he soon discovered that the lords of 1570 were not the lords he had known in 1566. They had always been hard men, and self-interested, but, although courtly smiles rarely creased their weatherbeaten faces, there had been a rough joviality about them that he had found congenial. That, now, had gone, to be replaced by surliness and suspicion, and there was a darkness in the air that had little to do with the absence of lights, laughter and music from Holyroodhouse.

Randolph was just old enough to remember the days when politics had been one thing, and religion another. Now, they were interchangeable, among the Scots as elsewhere in Europe. But it seemed to him that, in the clear and vindictive divide which had opened up between the little king's sour-faced supporters and the revivified queen's party in Scotland, the leaders of the factions were moved almost entirely by personal interest.

It was very obvious that Morton, inheritor of James's mantle as leader of the king's party, would never dare agree to the return of a queen against whom he had consistently and brutally sinned, while Lethington – or so Randolph supposed – having once committed himself to Mary, would never concede victory to the king's party because it would put an end to his own political influence.

Elizabeth, still anxious to solve the problem of Mary, had told

Randolph to find out whether a compromise was possible, or, if not, which party was going to win, so he went to Morton first, Morton being one hundred per cent easier to negotiate with than Lethington.

'No,' Morton said flatly. 'There's nae hope of compromise. Ye wouldnae believe it – I get Lethington released from jail, I make sure he's cleared of the Darnley murder, and what thanks do I get? He's arguing that Mary only stepped down on condition that James became regent, so we've no right to appoint another regent to replace him. He's managed to talk half the lords intae agreeing she should be let back, under conditions. Well, I tell ye. There are no conditions on earth that would be acceptable tae the rest of us, and we've got the barons, the lairds and the burgesses behind us. They're all solidly Protestant, and we're making sure the wee king's being reared as one.'

And that, Randolph thought, could be the deciding factor. The new bourgeoisie was increasingly a force to be reckoned with.

Morton went on, 'What we want, and what we're determined on, is tae have everyone recognise the wee king as our legitimate sovereign, and tae have an honest regent ruling in his name until he comes of age.'

Randolph liked the word 'honest'. The Scots lords, with a century and a half's experience of royal minorities, knew how to extract the last drop out of the buying and selling of favours on which a regent's power depended. An honest regent was a contradiction in terms.

He opened his mouth and said decisively, 'My queen is anxious to maintain the true religion and amity between the two realms.' Then he closed his mouth, equally decisively.

Morton's boot-button eyes stared at him. 'Is that all ye've got tae say?'

It was all Randolph had been authorised to say, or all that was diplomatically tactful rather than downright dictatorial. 'I have been instructed to discover your views.'

'Well, ye've discovered them,' the other man said shortly. 'And what *we* need tae do is discover Elizabeth's. There's none of us in the king's party prepared tae take on the job of regent without being assured of England's support. We need tae know who she'd approve of.'

Randolph's eyebrows drew together, brows that remained black and thick although his hair was grey and thinning. Morton's statement of submission to Elizabeth might be professionally satisfactory, but he found it unedifying. Even James, committed anglophile though he had been, had never gone quite so far as to ask Elizabeth for orders. Just for money.

'Very wise,' he said a little curtly. 'England's attitude towards the king's party, and indeed the queen's party, obviously depends on a number of factors. If you were to return the Earl of Northumberland to face English justice' – a phrase which, in the present instance, was synonymous with the headsman's axe – 'and if you were to make an effort to stabilise the Borders, which have been in chaos since the Earl of Moray's death, I am sure my queen's response would be favourable. And perhaps you might like to submit a list of candidates for the regency?'

2

He had heard that Lethington was ill, but the shock when he saw him was almost physical. The lean, elegant, humorous man he had known had become a skeleton, someone who lay in his bed as still as a corpse and could go nowhere unless he were carried in a litter. But his eyes were as clear as ever, despite the suffering that ringed them.

'It's the muscles,' he said. 'My brain, heart and stomach still function perfectly. The most exquisite torture is sneezing, so if you wish to wreck the queen's party at a blow, I suggest you scatter some pepper around.'

Randolph said, 'You're paying the penalty. I always said you would.'

'Penalty?'

'For marrying a beautiful wife twenty years younger than yourself.'

'Fourteen years. Don't make me laugh. It's as bad as sneezing. On that basis, though, you should be grateful that Mary Beaton refused you.'

Randolph was silent for a moment. Even after four years, the memory was painful. 'She married Alexander Ogilvie just after Jean Gordon was wed to Bothwell. If only Ogilvie had waited a year, we could all have been happy. Him with Jean and me with Mary Beaton. What's happened to Jean?'

'She isn't repining. Her brother means to marry her off again to young Sutherland. My wife tells me that she already has Sutherland firmly under her thumb and she has some idea of starting a local saltworks and a coal mine. She always was a positive young woman.'

'It must be terrible,' Randolph said suddenly, as if the idea had just occurred to him. 'Being a woman, I mean.'

'What? Being legally owned by your father, and then your brother, by your husband and then by your son? In abstract, yes. But Scotswomen seem to have a natural talent for rising above it. Look at Jean Gordon. Look at my ...' His voice stopped, of purpose, not of weariness. He was coming too close to intimacy.

Randolph had thought himself immune to tragedy, but he remembered the stylish Lethington and the exquisite Mary Fleming and was sad. He was not very imaginative, and had no idea how they must now feel.

But the silence made him uncomfortable and after a moment he ventured, clumsily, 'I don't understand. How can you go on? Why do you go on?'

The grey gaze flickered. 'Why do I not just lie here quietly and die? Well – would you?'

Randolph had always been envious of Lethington, his friendship towards the other man tinged with spite, but now he felt shamed. He said, 'Yes, I think I would.'

Lethington might have told him that harrowing pain and endless indignity were not enough to kill a man; that the exercise of a fertile and agile brain offered an escape, the only escape from the torments of the body. Instead, he asked, 'Why are you here?'

When Randolph had told him, Lethington was silent for a while. Then he said in the light, pleasant voice that was still his, 'There are three points I should make. The king is little more than a baby, so the king's party is the regent's party, not the king's, and there is not one among its leaders whose hands are not a hundred times bloodier than those of the child's mother. Believe me, Tom, if you can. Mary was sick, and foolish, but her guilt went no further than that.

'Secondly, I believe there is no hope for a nation that dishonours itself, and that is where the king's lords are leading us. At Carberry they took arms against the queen, ostensibly to free her from Bothwell, to safeguard her son, and to bring the murderers of Darnley to justice. The first two objects were easily achieved, and Bothwell's flight abroad might have been said, in public at least, to resolve the third. But because James wanted power and Morton – and his kinsman Archie Douglas – wanted protection, Mary had to be sacrificed. There were many of the lords who could have said, "Enough!" but no one did, and that, as I see it, is a dishonour that has contaminated the entire country.'

Subdued, Randolph asked, 'And your third point?'

There was a quizzical gleam in Lethington's eyes. 'It is one in which I have no great interest, since it concerns your own queen's wellbeing. She no longer approves of me, does she, despite the charming letters she sends me? Because I have dared to disagree with her whereas James gave in to her every whim and Morton will do the same. Dear God, I cannot tell you' – even the sudden vehemence of his words was enough to bring a shudder of pain to his eyes – 'I cannot tell you how it breaks my heart to see Scotland yield so readily to Elizabeth's will.'

Randolph made to deny it, but the words stuck in his throat.

Lethington's mouth curled. 'Don't waste your breath, Tom. Let me return to the main point. I hear that the pope has issued a Bull excommunicating Elizabeth and calling upon all loyal Catholics to depose her. And that is dangerous. It means that everyone who dislikes Elizabeth, for whatever reason, now has the justification of faith for attempting to bring her down – not only English Catholics but France, Spain and the papacy, their territorial ambitions sanctified by God's decree. You know and I know that, for as long as Mary remains Elizabeth's prisoner in England, she will be a focus for Catholic plots. In religion, no one has more appeal than a martyr. So it would be safer for Elizabeth to be rid of Mary. If she were back in Scotland, under the control of Protestant advisers, the problem would disappear.'

Sourly, Tom said, 'She was a problem for Elizabeth long before her imprisonment or the excommunication.'

'Only in Elizabeth's imagination. Mary has never been a real danger to her until now.'

The door opened, but it was not the exquisite Mary Fleming. It was Lethington's cool, controlled, wary younger brother John.

He said, 'William, this has gone on too long. You must rest.'

Lethington, it seemed, was resigned to being told, out of love, what to do and it did not seem to anger him. He smiled and said, 'Soon. But there is something, first, that I must clarify to Tom, and also to you, because the future will be in your hands when I go.

'However much I may have been diverted over the years, however great my personal sympathy with Mary, I have always had one overriding purpose, to see the establishment of peace between Scotland and England. But not a peace founded on English supremacy. God knows what may happen in centuries to come, but if we can put a Stewart on the united thrones of Scotland and England, we will at least start on the right footing. Scotland is not, and must never be, a dependency of England.'

John, with a curious desperation, exclaimed. 'Enough, William. We know.'

'Randolph doesn't.' The grey eyes turned towards him. 'Tom, you must tell Elizabeth that it is in her power to resolve all our, and her, problems – now – by acknowledging our infant king as her heir. If she does, the queen's party will withdraw from the fray. We, and Mary herself, will be satisfied with the promise that King James VI of Scotland will, when Elizabeth dies, become King James I of a united kingdom.'

In the ten years of their acquaintance, Randolph had never known

Lethington other than witty and urbane, had never guessed that there might be passion behind the imperturbable exterior. He had always thought of him as fascinated more by the challenge of the means than any vision of the end.

Slowly, he said, 'I'll tell her.' But he knew, as he thought Lethington himself must know, deep in his heart, that not until Elizabeth was on her deathbed – if then – would she name her successor.

3

To Cecil, who was not interested in visions, Randolph reported that the queen's party was an aristocratic alliance held together largely by the personality of one man who had not long to live, whereas the king's party was more widely based and more convincingly united – not only by the staunchness of its Protestant convictions but by growing opposition to the belief that the aristocracy had a God-given right to rule. Although Lethington was trying to bring about a reconciliation, neither party was prepared to give ground. It seemed to Randolph that the king's party would win – and it would win sooner with some help from England.

Elizabeth, who did not believe in backing losers, could see only one small difficulty, other than the usual financial one; France and Spain wouldn't like it. They could hardly complain, however, if she took steps to settle her own northern troubles, for which the primary responsibility lay with the Scots Borderers who, in the absence of a strong government in Edinburgh, were having the time of their ruffianly lives, raiding and reiving. It was entirely coincidental that most of the offenders happened to be adherents of the queen's party.

In April, therefore, the Earl of Sussex entered Scotland on a punitive expedition which left every house, village and town in Liddesdale a smoking ruin. The king's party sent an envoy to Elizabeth to thank her, to ask for more help and, true to form, money. They also wondered whether she yet had any views on who should become regent.

In May, another thousand-strong English army – accompanied by the Earl of Lennox, the little king's grandfather – crossed the border to join up with one led by the Earl of Morton. The declared object this time was to punish, not the reivers, but those who had encouraged them in their wicked ways. Which meant the Hamiltons, whose head was the fifty-five-year-old Châtelherault, who, if anything were to happen to the four-year-old king, would once more become Mary's heir presumptive. Who also

390

had the best legal claim to the regency. Who had to be discouraged from insisting on it.

This was duly achieved by the burning of the town of Hamilton, including Châtelherault's palace there, his castle at Kinneil, his house at Linlithgow, and the homes and lands of as many Hamilton adherents as came within range of the striking force. Two weeks saw the satisfactory conclusion of the operation, after which the king's party once again asked Elizabeth for her views on who should become regent.

This time she replied, at discursive length, to the effect that the Scots knew better than she who should be chosen but, if they absolutely insisted on having her opinion, she had to say that if they were to name the king's grandfather, the Earl of Lennox, no one would be more meet for the task. By saying this, of course, 'we do not mean to prescribe to them this choice, except they shall of themselves fully and freely agree to it.'

And so the Earl of Lennox became regent of Scotland. His predecessor, the Earl of Moray, would not have approved.

4

Blair Atholl, set deep in the heart of a green and purple glen, had for many years been a second home to Lethington and more than once a refuge, when his own home in the open, rolling countryside of Lothian had become too dangerous for him. The Earl of Atholl, though a Catholic, had always been a loyal friend and their friendship had deepened when Lethington had married Mallie Fleming, and Atholl her sister Margaret.

Now, twelve destructive months after Elizabeth's military intervention in Scotland, Mallie Fleming stood with her sister in the kitchen of the castle and said, 'You must give me something for him.'

'No!'

'But you must.'

The queen's party had lost. Elizabeth had made sure of that. But although everyone knew it and some of its most powerful supporters had deserted or were temporising, not everyone was prepared to give up. Kirkcaldy of Grange still held Edinburgh castle, which meant in effect that, with his fortifications and his cannon, he also held Edinburgh itself.

Lethington was about to join him there. If ever there was a time, he had said with a smile, when one could afford to stand up for one's principles, it was surely when one's back was against death's door.

His wife, who every night prayed passionately to God to give him release, had said prosaically, 'Obviously, you must be in the castle. I should be a hindrance there, so I shall stay in our house in the Meal Market.'

'No. You and the children must remain here. Danger means nothing to me, for myself, but for you ...'

If she had loved him less, she could have defeated him. As it was, she had given in.

Margaret, who had always had an interest in witchcraft, said again, 'No. You are asking me to give you something that will allow him to take his own life, to commit the greatest of sins!'

'Yes.' She had, she supposed, become infected by her husband's scepticism, but she could not believe that a just God would count suicide a mortal sin in circumstances such as these. 'Meggie, you have watched him, day after day, throughout all these terrible months. You have seen the pain become inconceivably worse. You know he survives only through his mind.'

She herself, somehow, had kept her emotions in check, but now it became too much. The misery tearing her apart, the tears pouring down her cheeks, she sobbed, 'Must I go on my knees, Meggie? Please, *please* find him a way out. Even if he scorns to use it, I cannot bear to think of him left without choice.' Then, seeing her sister still hesitate, she controlled her tears and, her voice almost inaudible, said, 'He does not even have the strength to drive his dagger into himself. And I may not be there to do it for him.'

After a long silence, Margaret said, 'I know of something that would stop his heart.'

They climbed up into the hills, stumbling through bog myrtle and mud, to where the wise woman known as Jinty lived in a windowless stone hut floored with earth, thatched with heather, and wreathed in a suffocating smell of peat smoke and midden. The advent of two fashionable ladies did not disturb her, and she showed neither respect nor gratitude as the Countess of Atholl presented her with a basket of food. Only when, peering and poking inside it, she discovered a twist of peppercorns, a nutmeg in a bottle, tallow candles and some silver coins did a gleam come to her watery blue eyes. She said, 'It iss good. What iss it you are wanting from me?'

She knew everything that went on for miles around and had heard about the poor laird at the castle, so it was less difficult than Margaret had expected to persuade her to provide them with what they wanted.

The light from the open door showed a chair, table and bed varnished brown by decades of peat smoke. A hoodie crow glowered from the back of the chair at a huge grey cat sprawled by the hearth, a cat whose bottlebrush tail spoke of its wildness. Jinty, nudging the cat away with her foot, filled a small three-legged cauldron with water from the burn and set it on the glowing peats.

She said, 'I will giff you something that iss as old as knowledge. My mother, and her mother before her, and generations before that, learned of it from the Romans who came here before the days of Jesus Christ. It iss something you can be sure of.'

When the water began to come to a boil, she went to a woven cage in a corner so dark that neither Margaret nor Mallie had seen it, and crooning endearments, coaxed something out and held it in her hands to show them.

It was a large, goggle-eyed, warty toad and, even as the women gasped and recoiled, she tossed it living into the cauldron.

Conversationally, she said, 'If you wass wanting something chust to make you fly in the air or haff visions, I would stew him in fat and make a salve for rubbing on your wrists or throat, but this way iss better for a potion. Ah!' There was a milky foam rising to the surface and she picked up a spoon and began to skim it off. 'That iss the venom, do you see?'

Mallie, choking with disgust and horror, turned and fled from the cottage, and did not stop until she had reached the foot of the hill.

Margaret found her there an hour later and held out to her the little bottle that had contained the nutmeg, a bottle now full of white liquid and sealed with a scrap of cloth soaked in tallow. 'We have to let it dry out until it becomes a powder,' she said. 'Then it can go in a gold locket that William can wear under his shirt, always. You were right, and I was wrong. Where life and death are concerned, you and I have many choices. But he has none, unless we give him this.'

5

In the very week during which Mary's supporters in Scotland were being forced to retire into Edinburgh, Sir William Cecil in London – not yet accustomed to his new title of Baron Burghley, which had been bestowed on him by Elizabeth a few weeks before – was exercising his mind over the rumoured activities of certain others of Mary's supporters in England

and abroad, supporters encouraged by the papal Bull to believe that to obey Elizabeth was a sin and to rebel against her a duty.

His suspicions aroused by some ciphered documents intercepted at Dover, he first tried torture on the courier and then trickery, and was not surprised to find that there was, indeed, something suspicious going on and that a certain Roberto Ridolphi, a meddlesome Florentine banker and merchant who was already well known to him, was involved. But in what? Questioning the Bishop of Ross, now the queen of Scots' informal ambassador in London, with no great success, he nevertheless found the name of Ridolphi cropping up again. Being a careful man, he placed the bishop under house arrest with England's own Bishop of Ely.

For some weeks after that, the trail seemed to have petered out. And then the English navigator John Hawkins discovered in the course of some devious Spanish dealings of his own that the Duke of Norfolk had consented to a scheme for a Spanish invasion of England. Within days, Cecil's agents intercepted a bag of money and ciphered letters sent by the Duke of Norfolk to the queen's party in Scotland.

It was almost enough, but not quite – or not until Cecil bluffed the Bishop of Ross, whose skin mattered more to him than loyalty to his mistress, into confessing that Ridolphi had been coordinating a scheme which entailed landing Spanish forces in the east of England to act in concert with an English Catholic uprising. That achieved, so the theory went, Mary would marry Norfolk and reign in Elizabeth's stead.

Norfolk, who had been released from the Tower after the collapse of the Northern rebellion, found himself, in September 1571, back there again, while Cecil devoted his energies to preparing a case against him that, this time, would be irrefutable.

6

But not all of his energies. Two days later, the news arrived from Scotland that the queen's party, now under the active leadership of Kirkcaldy of Grange, had made a daring raid on Stirling, with the object of capturing Lennox, Morton, Glencairn and Ruthven in their beds. The raid had been foiled, but Lennox had been killed.

In the interests of French and Spanish goodwill, Elizabeth and Cecil had for some months been successfully confusing everyone except Lethington – who knew them too well – by making desultory efforts to arrange a compromise between the king's party and the queen's party in which it was the queen's party that was expected to do all the compromising. The Ridolphi plot and Lennox's death, however, put an end to any English pretence of being an impartial adjudicator.

Curtly, Elizabeth told the king's party to elect the Earl of Mar in Lennox's place, while to Lethington and his ally Kirkcaldy, she wrote, 'I require you to leave off this discord and give your obedience to your king, whom I will support to the utmost of my power. I will negotiate with the regent and the king's party to save your lives and livings.

'But as for the queen of Scots, who has practised with the pope and other princes and also with my own subjects great and dangerous treasons against England and also the destruction of my own person, she shall never bear authority or have liberty while she lives.

'If you refuse my generous offer given above, I will presently aid the king's party with men, ammunition and all necessary things to be used against you.

'I require your answer without delay.'

7

The Duke of Norfolk was tried and found guilty of treason four months later, but Elizabeth shrank from signing the warrant for his execution until parliament met in in May 1572 and left her with no option.

It wanted Mary executed, too – that 'notorious whore', that 'monstrous dragon', that committer of 'adulteries, murders, conspiracies, treasons, blasphemies'. The Commons proposed two Bills against her, one to execute her for high treason, the other to deny her any right of succession to the throne of England.

Elizabeth rejected the first. The queen of Scots had, almost four years before, come to England for refuge. 'Can I put to death the bird that, to escape the pursuit of the hawk, has fled to my feet for protection? Honour and conscience forbid.' But she would no longer consider restoring her to her throne. Now, formally, she recognised Mary's seven-year-old son as king of Scotland.

Mary wept her heart out over the execution of 'my Norfolk', the man she had never met but with whom, if Lethington's plan had succeeded, both she and Scotland might have found some kind of peace.

Elizabeth, who rarely wept except from rage, restored herself to humour by setting out on one of the more spectacular progresses of her reign, staying at gouty Cecil's magnificent house of Theobalds, and then at Gorhambury, which was full of children, then at Warwick castle, where the fireworks went sizzling across the river and set half the town on fire, and finally at Leicester's unfinished castle of Kenilworth.

It was all very enjoyable until news came from Paris of the massacre of St Bartholomew's day.

8

Someone had shot at, and slightly wounded Admiral Coligny, who was in Paris with other leading Huguenots to attend a royal wedding. Within hours, rumour flying from mouth to mouth across the city, the incident had been inflated into the preliminary to some grand and terrible design. Panic spread among the Huguenots and they were said to be threatening to attack Catholics in revenge. Catherine de' Medici ordered them cleared out of the city. And then the Paris mob took a hand, and for the next two days Protestant blood flowed in the gutters.

No one knew how many had died, but twenty thousand was the figure quoted in England, where the massacre was believed to have been a premeditated attack, supported by Spain and the papacy, its objective to eradicate all who professed the reformed faith. In England, fear of Catholic plots and hatred of Catholic Mary redoubled.

Tragic though the affair had been, it had its political uses.

After Lennox's death in 1571, Elizabeth, who had not been able to bring herself to execute Mary, had endeavoured to persuade the Scots to do it for her. Mary was to be handed over on the understanding that they would execute her without publicity and without delay. But Mar and Morton were no more prepared than Elizabeth to take on the responsibility. They would execute their queen with pleasure, they said, but only after due parliamentary process, and only on a public scaffold, with an English force standing by to demonstrate England's participation in the deed.

Frustrated, Cecil and Elizabeth had then devoted their minds to wiping out the queen's party in Scotland, with the object of leaving Mary isolated and helpless. After more than two long years of negotiating, of offering unacceptable terms to the queen's party and having them contemptuously rejected, of fearing Lethington's bargaining with France and Spain, of pretending not to be an overlord but merely a neighbour, they had at last been forced into open involvement.

The massacre of St Bartholomew's day now made their task very much easier, and the weariness of some of Mary's supporters made it easier still.

Argyll, Cassillis, Châtelherault, Huntly, Seton and Sir James Balfour had all reached the stage of admitting to others, as they already had to themselves, that self-interest meant more to them than principle. Argyll, indeed, having been balked for years in his desire to divorce his wife – who, being of the blood royal, could not be divorced without the queen's or the regent's consent – became surprisingly amenable to the advances of the king's party when told that permission would be forthcoming.

Now, there remained in Edinburgh's besieged castle only Lethington, his brother John, Kirkcaldy of Grange, Lord Home, Robert Melville and a handful of others. They still had food supplies and were still able to pay their soldiers, but that was all. They might – perhaps – have accepted the inevitable if Mar had not died and Morton become regent. But from Morton, they knew, they could expect no mercy, and to submit to him was unthinkable.

In March 1573, Elizabeth authorised her provost marshal at Berwick, Sir William Drury, to assist Regent Morton in bringing to subjection 'certain private presumptuous persons that cannot live in peace, and that illicitly hold the king's castle of Edinburgh.'

9

The English cannon were in position by 21st May. Two days later, one of the towers of the castle fell and, not long after, the outwork connecting the castle with the town.

John Maitland, watching the English soldiers crawling around the foot of the castle rock retrieving their cannonballs for re-use, turned to Grange. 'How long?'

Grange shook his leonine head. 'Four or five days, maybe.'

'And then?'

'We'll have to parley. I don't doubt our own fate will be sealed, but there's no point in the men dying unnecessarily.'

John, who had become a hardened realist in these last years, said unemotionally, 'They're on the verge of mutiny, anyway. I'm surprised we haven't all had daggers stuck in us before now.'

'Aye.'

The sun was declining, and there was a rose-gold glow on the waters of the firth. 'Bonnie, isn't it?' Grange said.

'Yes.'

'I'll be sorry to go. But I'm fifty-three. I'm an old man, so maybe it's time.' His tone changed. 'They've done with firing for the day. We'd better get your brother up from the vaults.'

Lethington, who had thought himself inured to pain, had discovered a new and exquisite anguish in the vibration of the guns. Each day, to save his sanity, his litter had to be lowered into the cold, dank vaults of the castle, a foretaste, without the welcoming fires, of the Biblical hell to which, he supposed, he would soon be consigned. He played with the thought of meeting John Knox there – Knox, who had died a few months before, on the very day after Morton was elected regent – and continuing their unresolved theological arguments on the basis of a more intimate knowledge of what damnation was all about. But Knox had probably talked himself straight past St Peter and into Abraham's bosom. If Lethington had been Abraham, he would have despatched Knox briskly on a mission to foreign parts – the middle of the Indian Ocean, perhaps.

Aware that, as they approached death, most men came nearer to God, Lethington was distantly interested to discover that he himself was becoming further away. Greece and Rome had taught him that there were other gods than Jehovah, gods more human and more humane. It would be interesting to find out the truth of it all. If there were, indeed, any truth. If death were not, as he suspected, the end. The infinitely desirable end.

It was necessary to divert his mind with such thoughts, because otherwise he would be thinking of Mallie, and the children.

10

In the end, they surrendered – to the English, not to Morton. But they soon learned that Elizabeth, despite her oft-repeated promises of mercy, was about to wash her hands of them, and that parliament, which had already forfeited all their lands and possessions, was preparing to bring them to trial to complete the forfeitures with their lives.

In the interim, the foremost of them were held under guard at Leith, crammed into a merchant's house on the waterfront. Only Lethington was honoured with a separate chamber, for fear he should infect the others with ideas of an escape in which he himself could never take part. His guards, thinking him harmless, were not oppressive; one or two even proved to be quite kindly and, at night, were more likely to be found dicing downstairs than standing with crossed pikes outside his door.

Even so, it was a week before John and Grange, deprived of knives and daggers, discovered how to pick the lock of their own room and enable John, two hours into the darkness of the short June night, to slip up the spiral stone staircase to see how his brother fared.

Reflections from the moonlit waters of the harbour showed him a small square chamber with panelled walls and plastered ceiling, its only furniture a chair and a bed in which his brother lay awake, propped up against pillows, one hand resting on his chest. His eyes widened luminously at the sight of John, and John, his own eyes responding, did not at first see that under his hand lay a gold locket.

Lethington murmured, 'I knew you would come if you could. I have been waiting and hoping, but time, I think, is running out. I should not wait much longer.'

His throat tight, John said foolishly, 'Must you? It is so final.'

'The venom? No more final than the noose.'

'It might not come to that.'

'You don't believe that, and neither do I. Not for you, I hope and pray, but there will be no forgiveness for me or for Grange. And, you know, I find I am resistant to the idea of being hanged and disembowelled and having my head and limbs hacked off for display in the burghs.'

Despairingly, John sank into the chair. 'Why did it all go wrong?'

'Why? Because life is a gamble. If Elizabeth had left us to ourselves after James died, things would have been different. I still believe that we could have restored Mary on terms acceptable to everyone. But Elizabeth interfered, and there were outside pressures she could not control – the papal Bull, the Ridolphi affair, Norfolk's stupidity, the St Bartholomew's massacre ...'

Bitterly, John said, 'And, of course, while Moray and Lennox, Mar and Morton crawled to her, you did not.'

'That, too. But I have been lying here in my solitary confinement reflecting on the ironies of it all and thinking – not very originally, I grant you – how helpful it would be if only we could look into the future. If only we were able to picture the great oaks that were likely to grow from our little acorns. If only Cecil – and I – had succeeded in striking a better balance between persuading our queens to trust us, and doing what really needed to be done. Because if, at the beginning, I had not pushed too hard in trying to persuade Elizabeth to concede Mary's right to the succession, and if Cecil had not given in too readily to Elizabeth's opposition to it, many of the disasters of the last ten years would not have happened. A good many men who are dead would still be alive. Mary would not be in prison, Morton would not be regent.' He smiled quizzically. 'I myself might still be dying, but in more comfortable circumstances.'

John lowered his eyes, ashamed of his tears. Plucking at a loose thread in the coverlet, he said, 'How can you be so calm? But I will make you a promise. Elizabeth will never grant Mary the succession now, but if I survive I will do everything I can to ensure that she grants it to Mary's son. I see no peace for any of us unless the crowns are united.'

'Thank you.' There was silence in the room, a silence heavy with all the feelings that had never been uttered, and would not be uttered now, save in the most commonplace of terms. 'Give my love, my respect and my apologies to father, and to Mallie and the children. They have not deserved the troubles I have brought on them.'

They relapsed again into silence for a time that John Maitland was never afterwards able to estimate. But in the end his brother said, 'The dawn is coming, and you must go, but ...'

For the first time his voice faltered, his hand struggling weakly with the locket. 'Open this for me? I think I have already paid my dues in pain and humiliation and indignity. If I take my own way out, I shall at least be left with a little pride.'

Leaning forward, John took the chain and locket from round his brother's neck and slipped it into the pocket of his breeches. Then, into the pain-filled, saddened eyes, he said, 'There is a better way.'

With infinite gentleness, he slipped one of the pillows from behind his brother's back. 'You know, and I know, that there is no shame in bringing about one's own death. But others do not see things so. The venom, I think, would tell its own tale, but this' – he gestured towards the pillow – 'will not.'

The beloved grey eyes were clear and smiling again, and the light, humorous voice was murmuring something as he brought the pillow down.

'Quid est, Catulle? quid moraris emori?'
How now, Catullus? Why not be quick and die?

Chapter Eighteen

1573 – 1586

1

It was six long years since Mary had seen Lethington and almost two since she had last received a letter from him. She knew that there must have been others which had not reached her. From the sickening moment when she had first realised that she was not a guest in England, but a prisoner, she had been aware that men such as Secretary Cecil would be taking a professional interest in her correspondence. It meant that messengers ran more than ordinary risks; not even the most reliable could be expected, if caught, to withstand threats or bribes, or both.

But she did not have to rely on letters to discover that Edinburgh castle had fallen, or that Lethington was dead and Kirkcaldy of Grange, too. Her jailers told her as soon as the news arrived, pointing out with satisfaction that it meant her cause in Scotland was irrevocably lost.

A cause needed more than a castle to sustain it, and it was Lethington's death that gave her the greater pain. Except on the occasions when, convinced of the rightness of his own judgement, he had trespassed against her commands, she had always liked him – and more than liked him – for his charm and the brilliance of his mind, although she had never really understood him and never really trusted him. She knew that she would never forget those summer weeks following her marriage to Bothwell, when, because of the enmity between the two men, Lethington had so cruelly betrayed her; or so she had thought at the time, although now, given the perspective of the years, she was not so sure that it had been a betrayal after all.

George Buchanan had called him a chameleon and others Machiavellian, but she had come to recognise that, for her, it was the knowledge that he enjoyed the exercise of power not – as with the other lords – for the profit it could bring, but for the intellectual challenges it offered, that had set up the ghostly but impenetrable barrier between them. The primary loyalty of a secretary of state, she believed now as she had believed then, should be to his queen, but Lethington had been more loyal to his ideas than he was to her.

He had mystified her in life, and now in death he mystified her still. She could not understand why he, of all people, should have held out for her until the end.

There was no rational explanation of why the hurt should be so great. But although she had begun to learn fortitude and was able to bear it dry-eyed, she felt more alone than she had ever been in the whole course of her life. Now, for the first time, she found herself turning to God, not out of habit, or easy faith, but with a new depth of need.

It was to change her in the years that followed, the empty years when it seemed as if no one other than herself cared about her cause, when, save for the relatively mild restraints of her captivity, she lived very much as the widow of some country landowner might have done, ruling over her personal household of ladies, secretaries, valets, officers of the kitchen and stable grooms as once she had ruled over her royal court; complaining to her trustees in France about their handling of her financial affairs; participating in the small human dramas of those around her; even taking the waters of the spa at Buxton in the hope of a cure for the endlessly nagging pain in her side and the frequent sicknesses that her physician attributed to a weakness in her kidneys. At Buxton, she met – and charmed – Secretary Cecil, now Lord Burghley and Elizabeth's Lord HighTreasurer, who was seeking relief for his gout. At Buxton, she met – and charmed – the man Elizabeth had once mischievously offered her as a husband, Robert Dudley, Earl of Leicester. Her charm was the one thing that never failed her.

How different things might have been, if she had been able to charm them years before.

There was too much time for such reflections, too much material for melancholy dreaming when, playing with the lapdogs or the cagebirds sent by her cousins in France, she was reminded of her idyllic, carefree childhood. Or when the calendar of saints' days told her that it was so many years, exactly, since she had become queen of France, or since her mother had died, or since François, whom she still thought of as her true husband, had left her a grieving eighteen-year-old widow. Or that the beloved little son whom she had not seen for so long must be out of swaddling clothes, and into ankle-length belted and buttoned gowns, and then into the doublet and hose that, at nine, declared him a man. She sent him gifts but, although he wrote dutiful letters to her occasionally, he made no mention of having received them.

Dreaming and praying in the various castles that were her seasonally changing prisons, and writing – always writing – she was not aware of how the religious ferment in the outside world was altering the image she presented to that world. She did not know that, although in Scotland she had become merely the unregarded mother of a child-king around whom all the old, familiar plots now revolved, it was very different in England and abroad where, for restive nobles and predatory foreign powers alike, she was gradually being transformed from a human being into a Catholic martyr, a fleshless focus for the ambitions of the counter-Reformation.

2

It was in 1581 that Sir Francis Walsingham, now Elizabeth's principal secretary, returned from an embassy to Paris and summoned his own secretaries to a conference that had nothing to do with his formal business there but a good deal to do with the queen of Scots.

For Mary, Walsingham had conceived an intense and unwavering loathing. Even by passively existing, she would have been a danger to Elizabeth and a threat to the stability of England, but he saw her as the spider at the centre of an evil web. What he needed was proof of it, and then he would destroy her. Despite all his efforts over the years, however, and despite the increasing number of her confidential letters that his agents intercepted, deciphered, resealed and sent innocently on their way, nothing incriminating had come to light.

Now, looking round the table, he said, 'I believe, in the case of that woman, that we may have something at last. In France, I re-established some old intelligence contacts and set up some new ones, and I have learned that there is a plot afoot to free her. The Duke of Guise is involved, and the Jesuits, also. As soon as we hear of a Jesuit priest landing at Dover, bound for Scotland, we will have the first indication of the plot developing beyond mere talk. The closest watch must be kept on the port. Yes, Phelippes, you have something to say?'

Thomas Phelippes was his most able assistant, a weedy young Cambridge graduate whose disdain for laundries and barbers was outweighed by his fluency in five languages, soundness of judgement, talent for forgery and genius for cryptography. It was understandable, if irritating, that he should have a high opinion of himself.

He said, 'If you please. We've had no hint of anything of the sort from our day-spies at the French embassy, but there was something from the Spanish embassy that could be more than coincidence. That meddlesome fool, Mendoza, has persuaded half a dozen of our Catholic gentry to pass a Jesuit priest along from one to another, like an unwanted parcel, from Dover to the Borders. We've been keeping an eye on him and I believe he's now somewhere in the Midlands.'

'Interesting. So it may be not only the Jesuits and France, but Spain, too. Let the priest go on his way, but arrange to have the gentry arrested as soon as he has crossed the Scots border.'

'Yes,' Phelippes said. 'I've done that.'

Walsingham was not a man who often gritted his teeth, but this time he came near to it.

Phelippes said, 'What's he here for?'

'Briefly, to discover whether the king of Scots might be induced to convert to the Antichrist. If so, he will be given military assistance from the papacy to invade England, where it is anticipated that our Catholics will rise in his support.'

Phelippes, scratching himself indelicately, sighed. 'Whereupon her majesty will be deposed, the queen of Scots released, England restored to the Roman church, and the young King James set on the throne. They're not very original thinkers, are they? Ambitious, though.'

'Quite.'

'But, of course, everything would depend on the king agreeing to convert. Somers is doing most of the Scots work at the moment, so I'm a bit out of touch. What are the chances?'

With a sarcasm that passed over Phelippes' head like water off a duck's back, Walsingham said, 'I am glad you asked. The chances would be slight if it were not for the fact that our Jesuit friend is hoping to bring influence to bear through a certain Esmé Stuart, sieur d'Aubigny and the new Duke of Lennox, who is a secret papist, a friend of the Duke of Guise, the young king's cousin, his leading privy councillor – and his lover.'

3

Things had changed greatly in Scotland since the death of Lethington and the collapse of the queen's party in 1573.

The position of regent being, by definition, of limited duration, the

Earl of Morton had, from the start, chosen to make hay while the sun shone, his guiding political principles amity with England and the restoration to the country of something resembling social stability.

In theory, it was what Scotland needed, but in practice Morton had displayed an outstanding talent for making enemies and failing to make friends. His debasement of the coinage had alienated the commercial classes; his zealous 'pacifying' of cherished old feuds had enraged the nobility; his opposition to the more extreme manifestations of Protestantism had offended the church; and his personal avarice and nepotism had annoyed all of them.

He had survived for six years, expecting to have a free run for another four at the very least, and was therefore much put out when King James VI, at the age of twelve, began to throw his youthful weight around.

No royal upbringing could ever have been described as normal, but young James's had been more abnormal than most. Detached from his mother at the age of ten months, he had been largely reared and educated by George Buchanan, scholar, bachelor, disciplinarian, and one of his mother's most vicious detractors. It was from him that James had learned not only his Latin, Greek, French, Italian, theology, history and science, but most of what he knew about his parents.

On the threshold of adolescence, James showed no sign of inheriting either their beauty of feature or their physical splendour. He was, indeed, somewhat undersized and if, with his pallor, his full cheeks, high forehead and wide-set, pouched eyes, he could be said to resemble anyone at all, it was his father's younger brother Charles, the plain one of the family. But what he lacked in looks was amply made up for by his brains and a cunning that was entirely his own.

Inexperienced he might be, but he was still sufficiently mature for the earls of Argyll and Atholl to approach him directly over certain matters of dispute between themselves and the regent.

Argyll said, 'The jewels wass an outright gift, your machesty. Nothing to do with the Crown at all!'

He was not, now, the Argyll who had failed Mary so disastrously at the battle of Langside; who had died a few blissfully remarried months after the divorce with which Morton had bribed him to forsake her cause. His successor was his brother Colin, now husband to that Agnes Keith who had been wife of the Earl of Moray. To Agnes, Moray had given many of the royal jewels which Mary had entrusted to him when she was imprisoned at Lochleven, and now Regent Morton was claiming that they were the property of the Crown and he wanted them back.

James said, 'You're sure? Because if they *are* the property of the Crown ...'

'No, no. They wass your mother's own personal ornaments, and she wass giving them to Moray.' Argyll spoke with perfect sincerity, because his wife had thought it better not to confuse him with the facts.

James's acquisitive instincts were not yet fully developed, and he was, despite everything, a kindly boy. 'Well, I wouldn't want the countess to be robbed of what is rightly hers. Are they pretty? Do they suit her?'

'Inteet they do. Ferry much.'

'Well, we'll see what can be done.' The king turned to Atholl. 'And what's *your* complaint?'

'There is a lot more than one, your majesty! But the most important one is that, when my brother-in-law, William Maitland of Lethington, was declared forfeit, it left his wife and children without a home and without a penny. And his father in difficulties, too. The poor old man is blind and more than eighty years old. I have been trying for years to get some justice for him and Mallie and the wee ones. But the regent will not shift, and it is not Christian, truly it is not. If I had not given them shelter, I do not know where they would be.'

James knew all about the principles of justice. 'But traitors' families have to be penalised as a warning to others that treachery does not end with the deed.'

'Och, Lethington was no traitor. The cause of it all was that Morton was feared for his own life and possessions, and would not be hearing of compromise. It was only at the end, when Lethington was sorely sick in body and maybe a wee bit in mind, that he turned stubborn, too. It is not right that his widow and children should pay. And his brother is still in prison, after five years. It is a terrible waste of a good lawyer!'

'How old are the children?'

'The boy is about eighteen months younger than your majesty, and there is two girls after him, nine and eight.'

James had often thought it would be nice to be part of a family, with brothers and sisters who loved you, and played with you, and argued with you. He said, 'We will speak to Lord Morton. You may retire, now.'

Morton, confronted by four feet of juvenile majesty, made the mistake of sneering at Argyll's and Atholl's complaints and saying that either he had full powers to deal with such matters or he would resign. James didn't hesitate. Fixing his round, faintly mournful eyes on the regent, he said, 'All right. You'd better resign.'

But even a king wasn't allowed to have things all his own way when he was only twelve years old, and although the Countess of Argyll kept most of her jewels, although the plight of Mallie Fleming, her children and old Sir Richard was relieved by the assignment of a small part of the rents from Lethington's still forfeited estates, and although John Maitland was released from prison, Morton continued to direct the country's affairs.

It was not good enough. As the months passed, James became increasingly frustrated at being told what to do by dusty and dislikeable old men. Morton and Buchanan were sixty-three and seventy-three respectively, and by all the laws of nature ought to have been dead for years. Young kings should have young advisers about them, men who were clean, stylish and well dressed; men who were in touch with the changing modern world and would pay heed to their sovereign's views on affairs of state; men whose company was a pleasure, not a penance.

The arrival from France of Esmé Stuart, sieur d'Aubigny, could scarcely have been better timed. A cousin of Darnley's, d'Aubigny was James's nearest kinsman on his father's side. He was also handsome, charming, sophisticated and in his thirties.

James, starved of human warmth and at a highly susceptible age, fell in love.

4

In no time at all, d'Aubigny was elevated to Earl and then Duke of Lennox and had become a member of the privy council.

Morton was characteristically surly and uncooperative. He was not prepared to have his power eroded, and certainly not by a fancy French courtier who knew next to nothing about Scotland or the Scots. And in case anyone was thinking of dismissing him from the council, they'd soon discover their mistake.

He should have known better. On the last day of December 1580, he was arrested, not for his obduracy, not for his conduct of the regency, and not because the king was sick of the sight of him – but for being 'art and part' of the conspiracy to murder the king's father at Kirk o' Field almost fourteen years before.

There was irony in the fact that his accuser was one Captain James Stewart, the dashing son of the Lord Ochiltree who had been exiled with that other James Stewart, the Earl of Moray, after the Chaseabout Raid, whose return to Scotland had been achieved at the expense of Davie

Riccio's life, which had led inexorably to the murder at Kirk o' Field and everything that had followed after.

In June 1581, Morton paid on the scaffold for all the sins of a cold-hearted and grasping life. Behind him he left a wife who was said to have been mad for twenty-two years; three living children out of the ten she had borne him; and four sons by other women.

5

When Mary heard of it, she flung her arms wide with delight. 'Sweet Jesu! How many years is it since I have felt so happy! If I could dance and sing, I would.'

Seton, grateful that there was no one else present, said, 'Really, Madame! It is not right to rejoice. We must pray for the poor man's soul.'

'*Poor man*? Poor in all the human virtues, certainly. Just think what damage he has done in his day! It is because of him that I have spent all these interminable years as a prisoner. He and my brother, between them ... No. God will forgive me for being joyful at hearing the last of him.'

'The last of him,' Seton repeated with the melancholy that had increasingly taken possession of her over the years. Had it not been for her duty to her mistress, she would have withdrawn long ago to a nunnery. 'And the last of *them*, too. They have all gone now.'

'Who have?'

Surprised, Seton said, 'Your advisers. Of all the men who mattered during your years in Scotland, he was the only one who remained.'

Mary stared at her. Once she would have risen from her chair and walked about, which had always helped her to think, but this was one of the ever more frequent days when her hips ached from lack of proper exercise, and her head from lack of fresh air. Of all the penances of her imprisonment, those were the worst. So she continued to sit, arms folded, palms nervously smoothing themselves over her plain black sleeves, and recognised that what Seton said was true.

They *had* all gone. First the rumbustious Huntly, and then poor Davie Riccio. Then Darnley, whom she had married for love. And her brother James, who had betrayed her, and Lennox, and Lethington, and Kirkcaldy of Grange. Bothwell, too, who had manipulated her, and married her, and died three years before, insane and forgotten in a Danish prison. And Atholl, who had dined with Morton not so long ago and died of poison a

408

few days after. And now Morton himself.

Ten men whose destiny had been inextricably linked with hers – and not one of them had gone peacefully to meet his God.

There had been others, too. Young Sir John Gordon, and the poet Châtelard, and the Duke of Norfolk ...

She shuddered and closed her eyes – and in the whirling darkness behind her lids saw a picture of herself picking her way, tall and regal, through a nightmare landscape strewn with the bodies of the dead. It was horrible, as if she were the personification of Fate itself.

'If you had been a man,' Seton sighed, 'none of it would have happened.'

Mary, who never snapped, opened her eyes and said snappishly, 'That will do. As I recall, Argyll and Châtelherault and even John Knox died in their beds, and your brother is still alive and well.'

'Yes, Madame.'

'In any case, with that evil man gone and my son reaching years of discretion, I believe everything will take on a more hopeful complexion. I cannot expect my son to give the throne back to me, but I have thought of a scheme to allow us to rule jointly. I shall write to my cousin of Guise and ask him to open negotiations on my behalf. Please send Secretary Nau in to me.'

'Yes, Madame.'

6

Elizabeth, Cecil and Walsingham had been watching events in Scotland with their usual reluctant interest, Elizabeth less disturbed than her ministers over the advent of a French favourite until she discovered that, unlike Morton and his predecessors, d'Aubigny was not prepared to be ordered about by England.

The new Duke of Lennox was supported on the privy council by another favourite who preferred France to England – the equally newly created Earl of Arran, alias Captain James Stewart, Ochiltree's son, and there was also Lord Maxwell, a former member of the queen's party, on whom the king had bestowed the newly vacant title of Earl of Morton.

Exasperated, Elizabeth exclaimed, 'Really! This random redistribution of titles! You would think that revolting urchin was doing it just to confuse me.'

There was a blast of trumpets that drowned Cecil's reply and diverted the queen's attention. She had already been deafened and blinded by the Earl of Arundel's entry into the tiltyard, and then the Lord Windsor's, but now it was Sir Philip Sidney, for whom she had a weakness, even though he was currently in disgrace with her. His armour was partly blue, partly engraved gilt, and behind him were four pages clad in gilt-laced silver hats and hose, riding magnificent horses caparisoned in gold and silver and pearls. The thirty gentlemen and yeomen who followed were garbed in yellow velvet with silver lace. Elizabeth wondered how the notoriously purse-pinched young man was proposing to pay for it all.

She found it tedious sitting through tournaments, but recognised their value as a contribution to regal splendour and an indication of how much her courtiers were prepared to spend in her honour. It was satisfying to have their squires, after addressing her lengthily on the subject of their lords' past achievements and future hopes, mount the steps of her satin-draped gallery and present her with expensive gifts.

Jewels always met with her approval. When she had entered on her reign, she had had no choice but to rely on the handsome but ninth-hand jewels from her father's coffers, which had been worn in turn by him, his six wives, her brother and her sister. Nowadays, she had a spectacular collection of her own, including the pearls that had once belonged to her good sister Mary of Scotland. Mary, she was told, possessed no jewels now other than idolatrous crosses and rosaries.

Philip Sidney's squire addressed her, predictably, in verse, and his gift was a golden bracelet studded with rubies and diamonds and contained in a purple velvet case. Graciously, she listened. Graciously, she slipped the bracelet over her wrist and admired it. Graciously, she blew a kiss to Sir Philip. Graciously, she waved the tournament to proceed.

Turning back to Cecil, she glared at him and said, 'Well, who else is on the little brat's new council?'

'The Catholic Lord Seton, who is the same Lord Seton as of old. And Lethington's brother, John, who to avoid confusion, is generally known as Maitland of Thirlestane.'

'I do not like it. What you are saying is that the brat's council is now predominantly pro-French and probably pro-Mary. I thought we had seen the last of all that nonsense. How has it happened?'

The succinct answer would have been 'royal favouritism', but it was not an answer that could be given to a queen who was famous for it. Smoothly, Cecil said, 'The king is young and easily influenced.'

'Well, we will have to help him grow out of that, will we not. In the meantime, I wish to be kept informed of the progress of this plot

Secretary Walsingham has uncovered. It may be more dangerous than we think.'

7

If he had not had to fund most of his agents and day-spies out of his own pocket – the queen being notoriously reluctant to spend so much as a halfpenny if someone else could be induced to spend it for her – Walsingham would have enjoyed unravelling the d'Aubigny plot, with its huge cast of agents, Jesuits, French noblemen, Spanish ambassadors and papal nuncios.

The priest who had been seen on his way to Scotland by the six English gentry who were now behind bars, was a hardy soul who covered the four hundred miles back to London on foot, in the depth of winter, disguised as an itinerant tooth-puller, bringing Mendoza promising news about James's religious flexibility. Ill equipped to assess the worth of Scots gossip, the Spanish ambassador embarked on an excitable correspondence with the pope and the Guises and other equally predictable people. Soon, he – and Walsingham – had discovered that d'Aubigny wanted two thousand soldiers, preferably Italians, and he wanted them landed at Eyemouth. A month later, the figure had gone up to fifteen thousand.

Walsingham's heavy dark eyes glistened, because the figure of fifteen thousand was mentioned in a letter from d'Aubigny to the queen of Scots who, in turn, wrote to Mendoza to say she thought it a 'highly desirable' project. This time – *this time* – she might at last incriminate herself.

By the spring, in the course of some concentrated haggling, the Duke of Guise was arguing that eight thousand men ought to be enough for an invasion, while d'Aubigny was demanding twenty thousand. And not only twenty thousand soldiers but twenty thousand golden crowns – in advance.

When the project collapsed, Walsingham was not relieved but disappointed.

8

The collapse had nothing to do with agents, Jesuits, French noblemen, Spanish ambassadors or papal nuncios. It was the result of a home-based revolt against d'Aubigny's influence, his Francophile tendencies, and his suspected Catholicism, and it took the traditional Scots form of abducting the king.

The leader of the conspirators was the Earl of Gowrie.

'And who,' Elizabeth enquired sourly, 'is he?' She had been so taken up with the protracted visit to England of her 'dear little Frog', the Duc d'Alençon, who was half her age and had not yet been told that her privy council had talked her out of her inclination to marry him, that she had been neglecting Scots affairs.

Cecil said, 'He's a new creation. Just last year, in fact. Before that, he was Lord Ruthven.'

'God's death! You mean the son of the Ruthven who led the murderers of David Riccio?'

'Yes. And very like his father.'

With ill-tempered care, she replaced her spectacles in their case and said, 'What terrible people they are, the Scots. I wish the whole realm would sink into the sea, and then we could be done with them. Is that revolting brat in danger of his life?'

'I think not. The persons of kings are, in general, more useful than their corpses.'

'So what now?'

'D'Aubigny has fled to France, and most of the rest of the council is in prison.'

'What is Gowrie's policy?'

Cecil, whose physician had prescribed a potion of ground elder for his gout without mentioning that it was also likely to inspire him with the frequent need to find a pissing place, said concisely, 'Extremist Protestant. He says he is a dedicated friend to your majesty.'

Elizabeth snorted. 'And that means he will soon be asking me for money.'

9

Robert Bowes was as tireless and voluble an ambassador to Scotland as Tom Randolph had ever been, so he merely sighed resignedly when Secretary Walsingham added to his burdens by demanding that he discover and acquire the casket of the queen of Scots' letters which had not been seen since it was entered as evidence against her at the York-Westminster conference fourteen years before.

Although clerkly copies of the letters existed in London, copies were not good enough. Her majesty Queen Elizabeth, Walsingham said, was anxious to have possession of the originals to strengthen her hand in negotiations between the Scotch urchin and his mother over Mary's proposal that they might rule Scotland together. It was an explanation designed merely to forestall any ambassadorial inclination to ask questions. Walsingham felt no compulsion to say that it was he himself who wanted the letters to reinforce his case against Mary when, finally, he succeeded in trapping her.

By early November 1582, Bowes was able to report that the letters had passed in 1569 from the hands of Regent Moray to Lord Morton and, after his execution in the preceding year, to the Earl of Gowrie.

'Unfortunately, it has proved impossible to steal the casket from Gowrie, so I was forced to approach him directly, saying that the letters had previously been promised to the queen my mistress and I was sure that Lord Gowrie, in view of the affection he bore her, would wish to fulfil that promise, for which he would receive suitably princely thanks and gratuity.

'Lord Gowrie first denied all knowledge of the letters, and demanded to know who had told me he had them. I said I could not reveal that. He then said that, *if* he had the casket, which he by no means admitted, it would be necessary for him to consult not only his sovereign but those survivors of the lords responsible for deposing the queen of Scots, who would no doubt wish to retain possession of the evidence that justified their actions. He would search out the casket, *if* he had it, when he returned home, and think about it. There, for the time being, the matter rests.'

Two weeks later, Bowes tried again. He was a Protestant himself but, like his sovereign though unlike Walsingham, found the new breed of Presbyterian unsympathetic. Gowrie, who was in his early forties, struck him as a more stoutly built, smoother version of John Knox. He turned out to be just as hard to shift.

'But, my lord,' Bowes said earnestly, 'I have it on authority that the queen of Scots is declaring – without truth, of course – that the letters were counterfeited, and that she wants them stolen and delivered to her, or else defaced. As you must see, this means that, if the letters continue to be kept in Scotland, both the letters themselves *and* the keeper of them must be in constant danger, whereas they would be entirely safe in the keeping of the queen my sovereign, who would hold them ready to be produced if ever they were needed.'

Gowrie, who had not been born yesterday, surveyed the other man, well aware that he was likely to have more to fear from the English ambassador's light-fingered friends than from the imprisoned Mary's. 'Really?' he said.

It was not encouraging. Bowes went on, 'I should be happy to speak to the lords and reassure them on that score, if you have any doubts.'

'You might try, although I would take no wagers on your success.'

'And, of course, if you were to commit the papers to the good custody of the queen my sovereign, she would ever after hold a high opinion of you.'

Gowrie said, 'I wonder why?'

And so it went on until Gowrie said, 'I am ready to do everything in my power to please the queen your mistress. But I must first study the letters, which I have not yet had the opportunity to do, and then take advice, and then consult the king.'

'Would that be wise?'

Gowrie raised a furry black eyebrow. 'You are suggesting that I should *not* consult the king?'

As far as Bowes had been able to discover during his original search, the young king did not know that Gowrie had the letters in his possession and had almost certainly never seen them. Since they concerned his mother, he might have his own inconvenient views about their future.

Hastily, he said, 'Not until the papers are in her majesty's keeping, surely!'

'Why not?'

'I – er – I think it unwise that such valuable documents should be endangered by being passed from hand to hand. Surely the sooner they are in safe keeping, the better?'

Gowrie said, 'Not until I have consulted my king.'

Gloomily, Bowes reported back to Walsingham that the Earl of Gowrie was adamant.

10

Walsingham was disappointed but not altogether surprised, just as he had been over the outcome of the d'Aubigny affair. But he had learned much during the course of it all, and when he received from Gowrie, not the casket letters, unfortunately, but a copy of some evidence given under torture by one of d'Aubigny's French messengers, he further learned that Mary used the French ambassador in London to pass on correspondence that he knew nothing about. Thomas Phelippes had been saying for months that day-spies at Salisbury Court were not enough, that what they needed was a man of their own inside the embassy. It seemed that he had been right.

By mid-April of the following year, Walsingham had an agent installed whose identity was such a close secret that no one other than he and Phelippes knew the man other than by his *nom-de-guerre* of Henry Fagot. He was a highly effective gentleman. In no time at all, Walsingham was receiving a copy of every letter that passed between Mary and the ambassador, Castelnau de Mauvissière, and was in possession of a list of all those of Mary's sympathisers who frequented the place. By a piece of uncovenanted good luck, reinforced by bribery, Bowes in Edinburgh also succeeded in gaining sight of the letters that went back and forth between Mauvissière and Mainville, his colleague in Scotland.

It was all highly informative, and it soon transpired that the Jesuits, French noblemen, Spanish ambassadors and papal nuncios had by no means given up their plotting.

For the next six months, Walsingham's agents were kept busy shadowing a young man who was a regular night-time visitor to the French embassy. Walsingham had already known something about Francis Throckmorton, a nephew of the late Sir Nicholas, through one of his *agents provocateurs* who had met the young man in France and encouraged him in his Catholic sympathies. He had great hopes of the new plot that was building up.

11

He was annoyed, therefore, when he received a royal command to take himself off to Edinburgh and bring the Scots to their senses. If they had any.

The young king, who in the month of his seventeenth birthday had succeeded in escaping from Gowrie's grasp, had set up his own administration and the balance had swung yet again, though not quite as far as before. Even so, the pro-French, pro-Mary tendency was once more perceptible. Arran was back, and Maitland of Thirlestane, and Huntly, Argyll and Rothes.

As instructed by Elizabeth, Walsingham rebuked James for changing his councillors without her permission, lectured him on his inexperience, and refused to have any dealings with Arran. His contempt for the Scots was apparent, as he meant it to be.

James listened in silence, but Walsingham was unexpectedly aware of Maitland of Thirlestane, standing beside the king quiet and motionless – a man whom he had written off as merely the younger brother of the secretary he had met years before and whose reputation he had always considered grossly inflated. With some of his brother's distinction of looks, Thirlestane had none of his personal magnetism, but there was something disquieting about him.

Walsingham, failing to realise that all he had succeeded in doing was alienate both king and council, shrugged and returned to London.

12

The young King James had been inquisitive even in his infancy, and nothing that had happened to him since had diminished his need to know everything that was going on; rather the opposite.

When the Earl of Gowrie was executed, therefore, with his possessions passing into the royal hands, James insisted on going through those possessions himself and found among them a silver-gilt casket about a foot long and full of papers in handwriting he knew well.

He felt a strange, erotic thrill when he began reading them. His grey-bearded old tutor, George Buchanan, had told him about them when he was a child and what depths of depravity they had displayed. He had become quite animated about them.

James had been six when he first heard of their existence, old enough to ask what had happened to them and young enough to believe the answer. Buchanan had said they had been lost after the Earl of Moray died. And now it turned out that Gowrie had had them after all, though he had never mentioned the fact to his anointed sovereign. He had certainly deserved to be executed.

The letters were a disappointment, although there was one interminable one – which James estimated to be between three and four thousand words long – which was mainly concerned with a meeting of his estranged parents in Glasgow and gave him an insight into both their characters he had never been granted before. But James's idea of depravity was not the same as his tutor's had been. He was no more than irritated by the letters' occasional amorous outbursts, and couldn't imagine why his mother, in the middle of a perfectly rational narrative, should suddenly break off for a few sentences of sickly, swooning nonsense. Perhaps it was because he didn't understand women.

George Buchanan had gone to his Maker two years before, which had been a blessed relief for everyone, especially his erstwhile pupil. Considering the question of who else might have firsthand knowledge of the letters, James realised that the only likely man – or the only likely *honest* man – was Maitland of Thirlestane.

James said, 'I've read these carefully and they don't hang together.'

'No, sire?'

'I've looked at them through the broad glass, too. There are places where the writing doesn't match. But maybe I'm wrong.'

'I have not seen the letters myself, sire.'

'Oh, haven't you? I should have thought your brother ...'

'He was never permitted more than a sight of them, and only in haste and in company.'

James said, 'That's suggestive. Did he have views?'

'I believe there were certain doubts in his mind.'

'Will you stop being so damned careful!' said his sovereign irritably. 'Did he or didn't he think that a forger had had a hand in the business?'

John Maitland had, indeed, become a careful man since the night he had helped his brother die. He had had five years in prison with nothing to do but think, and a further six years to rise to being secretary of state, as his brother had once been. When he became lord chancellor, it would lie in his hands to achieve his brother's ends.

He smiled faintly. 'I believe he did.'

'Who was it, then?'

That dedicated turncoat, Sir James Balfour of Pittendreich, having died the year before, John Maitland saw no purpose in drawing his blameless sons into the affair. He shook his head. 'I don't know, sire.'

'You surprise me.' The king frowned. 'I *could* send them to my mother, of course, and ask if she really wrote them.'

John Maitland's head reeled. Mary would undoubtedly scream, 'Treachery!' and Elizabeth would defend herself, and the whole sorry business would start up all over again, just when things were settling down nicely, just when James was learning to display, not only to the Scots but, more importantly, to the English, that he was a remarkably promising ruler.

His sovereign grinned at him. 'I know what you're thinking. You're thinking that, if my mother could somehow prove that they were forgeries, then everyone would have to admit she was innocent. So she shouldn't have been forced to abdicate. So she shouldn't be in prison in England. So I shouldn't be king.'

He was a clever boy. John Maitland's mouth twitched. 'I doubt if your majesty's mother could prove them to be forgeries.'

'I don't know. If I can spot what's true and what's probably false, others could. Did anyone ever look at them properly at the time of the trial?'

'No one was encouraged to do so.'

He was a clever boy, but he also had a strong sense of justice. 'I think it's shocking that my mother should have been condemned on the basis of such things.'

'Yes.'

The king wiped his nose on the back of his hand. It was one of the regrettably childish habits of which he showed no sign of ridding himself. 'I don't know what to do. I'll have to think.'

Slowly, John Maitland said, 'If I may advise, sire – you should take care to think in a statesmanlike rather than in a personal way.'

'You don't have to tell me.'

13

When Walsingham at last had young Throckmorton arrested and tortured, he revealed that the new plot was very like the old, save that the Scots themselves were not involved. He listed the ports where the army of the Papal Enterprise against England might land and mentioned the probable size of such an army. He named all the leading Englishmen who had promised their support in the attempt to free the queen of Scots. He spoke of Mary's correspondence with the French and Spanish ambassadors. He said more than enough to sign his own death warrant.

But not Mary's. She had been careful about what she put on paper and Walsingham knew that, to anyone less certain of her guilt than himself, such diplomatic adjectives as 'desirable' and 'interesting' could be taken as meaning no more than 'please keep me informed'.

The plot, however, with a little judicious assistance, soon became public knowledge and hatred of Mary began to spread once more and with gratifying speed throughout England. It was increased when news came from abroad that Prince William of Orange – who was something of a Protestant icon – had been assassinated. By a papist, of course. With a little further assistance, Elizabeth's subjects were easily brought to fear that it was not only their queen's throne that was in danger from Mary, but her life, too.

The climate, therefore, could not have been more favourable when Walsingham discovered yet another plot, one which – by a curious chance – involved a spy of Cecil's who had outlived his usefulness. Dr Parry was an eccentric who had been in and out of trouble all his life, and at the end of 1584 he was reported to have proposed a plan to assassinate Elizabeth as she walked in the gardens at Westminster. Under interrogation, aided by the rack, Parry revealed that the plot had been originated by the queen of Scots' cipher clerk in Paris, Thomas Morgan, whose name had already occurred in connection with the Throckmorton affair.

This time, Walsingham thought again, *this time ...*

But still it was not enough. So Walsingham set about making sure that, next time, whatever happened *would* be enough.

Already, Elizabeth's privy council had arranged for a bond to be sent throughout the country, to be signed by every gentleman prepared to declare war on anyone who plotted against the queen. When the bond, at the demand of the Commons, was translated into a parliamentary Act for the queen's safety, it specifically declared that anyone in whose interests such a plot might be mounted, whether that person were party to it or not, was to be considered as guilty as the plotters themselves.

It was the insurance Walsingham needed. Now, all that was required was a suitable plot.

Phelippes said, 'A change of jailer would give us more scope.'

14

Sir Amyas Paulet was a man of about fifty, small and flat-cheeked, with a wide forehead above cold, angry, puritanical eyes. Mary hated him on sight. He behaved to her as John Knox might have behaved, if he had had the power.

She was already at a low ebb after a year of increasing strain; of hearing disjointed tales of plots against Elizabeth that she could not make sense of, but for which the blame seemed to be laid at her door; of losing trust in her friends in France and, worse, in her son in Scotland; of Bess of Hardwick spreading stupid rumours about an affair between herself and Shrewsbury; of being sick with nerves; of being brought back to the multi-turreted and many-chimneyed castle of Tutbury, which she hated, with its smelly middens and icy draughts and, beyond the walls, the

419

fourteen thousand acres of the great royal stud farm which she would have loved to visit but could not, because it was not permitted. She supposed they were afraid that she might leap on one of the brood mares and ride away to freedom.

And now this terrible man, who hated her for being who she was, was tearing down her cloth of state, forbidding her to go outdoors, harrying her servants, refusing to believe she was ill, seeing a snare in every helpless smile. He placed such constraints on the movements of her household that the days and the months passed without a single secret letter reaching her from outside Tutbury's walls, and she was granted a sight of even the most harmless personal letters only after Paulet had read them, as he read those she herself wished to send out. Of what was going on in the outside world, she knew only what he chose to tell her, and he told her only what he knew would frighten her.

There had been one personal letter that was not harmless, one that came from Elizabeth in March, telling her good sister of the fury of the Commons over the Parry plot and their demands that Mary should be arraigned. But Elizabeth had overridden them, as she had overridden them once before, at the time of the Norfolk affair. Now, for a second time, she had intervened to save Mary's life.

She appeared to expect gratitude, but after seventeen years of unjust imprisonment, there was no longer a place for gratitude in Mary's heart.

15

The Master of Gray said, 'Your love for your mother does you credit, sire, and if you were a private citizen her welfare would rightly be of the greatest concern to you, but ...'

'But if I were a private citizen, being a man I'd be head of the family and she'd have to do what I said. Whereas she maintains that she's still the queen, and I'm only her son.'

'Precisely.'

Fairminded as always, James said, 'And she's probably right, isn't she, Secretary?'

John Maitland said, 'It is not a case I would choose to argue in court. But she signed her abdication under duress, and appears to have rescinded it only by public proclamation – which is the debatable point – after her escape from Lochleven.'

'Well, we're not going debate it, are we! As far as I'm concerned, it's a case of *uti possidetis*. What I have, I hold, and I don't care how France and Spain feel about it.'

The Master of Gray fanned himself languidly with his gauntleted gloves, sending a waft of citron over the warm evening air. 'Bravo, sire.'

Patrick, Master of Gray, was a young man of hell-born beauty whose advent, a few months previously, had led John Maitland to some mildly embittered reflections on what a sore trial royal favourites were to royal councillors. On the whole, he thought, stupid ones were probably preferable to the intelligent, but the shrewd and clever James was bewitched only by men who had brains as well as beauty, which meant that they also had opinions which did not necessarily coincide with those of James's officers of state. After the d'Aubigny *débâcle* and the Gowrie interlude, political power had devolved on Arran, who, steering a less extreme course than d'Aubigny, was still closer to France than England. He was a man of great ability, but restricted vision.

And now had come the Master of Gray, a young man who, intimate with France and the Guises, had been sent by them to forward the throne-sharing idea that Mary had been promoting for the last three or four years. It did not seem, at first, as if Gray was going to be any improvement on Arran, as favourites went, but although nominally in Mary's employ he had soon decided that the favour of a reigning king had more to offer than that of an ageing, ailing, imprisoned queen. It had led him – if for the most selfish of reasons – to look towards the same ends as Maitland.

The king sneezed. 'I wish you'd change your perfume, Patrick. The trouble is, I haven't seen my mother since I was a baby, and I've heard little good about her, but I think she's probably paid for her sins by now. And she's prepared to make a lot of concessions over this shared rule idea. Maybe we could do a deal with Elizabeth. A formal treaty of alliance with my mother's freedom as part of it.'

It was an ingenious solution, especially since – if Mary had any sense of gratitude at all – it would leave James firmly in control. John Maitland wondered, sometimes, what the boy had done with the casket letters. Burned them, he suspected. He left Gray to answer.

The young man hesitated delicately. 'But, sire, consider the difficulties. You and your mother are of different generations, different religions. If you ruled jointly and were to disagree on some fundamental matter ... Filial duty is an admirable quality, but you have a greater duty to your subjects.'

The sun was sinking and Holyrood's knot garden buzzing with honey bees. The king and his companions turned and began to stride back the way they had come. It was exercise of a sort, although James, if it had not been for the duties of his kingship, would have preferred to be out hunting with running hounds, the sport that was his passion.

He grimaced. 'Well, Secretary, what do *you* think?'

Judicially, John Maitland said, 'The choice is your majesty's. You must decide which is more important to you – your mother's freedom, or a formal alliance with England which will give you the crown of both countries when Elizabeth dies. We can try to negotiate, but your mother's reputed involvement in Catholic plots has made her deeply unpopular in England and I do not believe that Elizabeth would dare contemplate setting her free.'

'By God, but you're a cold fish,' the king exclaimed. 'I don't understand you. You stayed with my mother's party until the castle fell and it ceased to exist, but now you're telling me to abandon her?'

Maitland was not offended. He knew he had become a cold fish. What little warmth had survived that agonised night in 1573 had been absorbed by ensuring that Lethington's loved and loving Mallie, and the children, and his father, had finally been restored to their estates; and by his own marriage to Mallie's niece, Jeanne. He was sorry, in an impersonal way, that Mary had to be sacrificed, but knew that it was for the greater good.

He said, 'Circumstances change. My object is to serve my country.'

And so, although it was to take two years to accomplish and Arran was to be overthrown in the process, the realms of Scotland and England reached an agreement that took no account of Mary. Elizabeth agreed to pay £4,000 down and give the young King James an annual subsidy in the same amount. She refused to concede his right to the succession, but that was generally held to be because, at the time, she happened to be in a thundering bad temper with Leicester and, by extension, everyone else.

It was clear that if James, nimble by nature, could with Maitland's assistance keep his political footing for the next few years, the outcome was no longer in doubt.

16

Mary had too often been reported to be at death's door for Walsingham to do other than discount reports of her ill health, and Paulet, convinced that she fell sick only to spite him, put everything down to irritation of the nerves. Otherwise, they might have saved themselves, and Elizabeth, a great deal of trouble by holding her at noisome Tutbury for an extra few months, until she died of it.

When she had been there for a year, however, it seemed to Walsingham and Phelippes that she had probably reached that level of desperation that outweighs prudence. The next stage was to offer her every assistance in being imprudent, which involved removing her a dozen miles from Tutbury to the moated manor of Chartley Hall – whose middens did not smell, even though the beds did – and providing her with opportunities to renew her clandestine contacts with the outside world.

Phelippes went to Chartley himself to set things up, and Paulet, who had had a very trying year, greeted him with modified pleasure. Phelippes was not precisely an old friend, but it had been under Paulet, during his years as ambassador in France, that he had gained his early diplomatic experience. It meant that, despite Paulet's rigid morality and Phelippes' lack of it, they took a similar view of political necessities.

'A smuggler?' Paulet repeated.

'Yes,' Phelippes said. 'For her letters. We want her to feel clever and think she's discovered how to defeat your security precautions. Tell me about the people who come in and out of the place on regular business. Are they searched when they arrive and leave?'

'Of course. Most of them are not even permitted to cross the moat.'

'Then, since everything must look normal, our man needs to have some means of carrying letters that an ordinary search won't reveal. That limits the field. Can you think of anyone?'

'Not the laundry maids,' Paulet said bitterly.

'No?'

'No. There were times last year when every shirt or chemise they carried out to the river bank seemed to have a letter rolled up in it.'

Phelippes, who had always had a regrettably frivolous streak, gave a faint hiccup of laughter. 'Never mind. If we find the right man, and she can be persuaded to trust him, everything will go through a single channel. She'll have no need for hit-or-miss tactics.'

'There's the brewer,' Paulet said thoughtfully after a moment. 'He comes every week or two, and he's a papist, which ought to commend him.'

Water and milk being dangerous drinks, most households consumed quantities of small ale. Ale came in casks. Casks could contain other things besides ale. Such as packets of letters. The problem was keeping them dry.

Phelippes, his eyes closed, conjured up a mental picture of a cask with its convex body and flat end panels. The ale was drawn by means of a small spigot in one of the end panels, but the cask was filled through a large bunghole, several inches wide, in the convex body. The bunghole had to be stoppered, either with tallow-soaked cloth or with a cork.

'A hollow cork,' he said dreamily, 'would do nicely. It might hold as many as half a dozen letters.'

'It is a possibility. But the fellow only comes from Burton. What happens from there on?'

'We use a courier. We have just the man. One of our new agents, Gilbert Gifford. He comes from a Catholic family in these parts, but he's a secret apostate. He's ingratiated himself with Mary's cipher clerk in Paris, Thomas Morgan, who's given him a letter recommending him to her.'

'Morgan? I know him. There,' said Paulet austerely, 'is a man who will never learn sense. I see. So, how is the arrangement to be handled?'

'Gifford is busy establishing relations with the French embassy in London, hoping they'll give him all the secret letters that have piled up there for the queen of Scots during the last year. When they do, he'll bring them to me to be deciphered, copied and resealed, then ride up here to Staffordshire and hand them over to the brewer to smuggle in to Mary. That should be enough to establish both men in her good graces. Once the system has settled down, we'll carry on in much the same way, with Gifford bringing me incoming letters from the embassy, and outgoing ones from here. This time, we are not going to miss any single word she writes or receives.'

Pessimistic to the end, Paulet said, 'Well, I hope it is going to be worth it.'

17

It did not look, at first, as if it was. The whole of January was taken up with cautious probing, both by Mary and the French embassy, before Gifford succeeded in laying his hands on the year's backlog of packets for her. There were twenty-one in all, whose deciphering took Phelippes several days, and they were so bulky that the brewer had to deliver them in instalments.

It was not until May that Walsingham and Phelippes began to find the queen's correspondence interesting. She knew now that the letters she had received from her son, seeming to favour her idea of sharing the throne, had been no more than palliative; that he was about to sign a treaty of alliance with England in which her own release from captivity did not feature. Deeply hurt, she wrote to Mendoza – who, having been expelled from England for his involvement in the Throckmorton plot, was now Spanish ambassador in Paris – saying that James did not deserve to rule and that she proposed to bequeath her right to the English succession to Philip II unless her son had become a good and dutiful Catholic by the time she died.

Phelippes, busily deciphering, muttered, 'Silly woman.' After four months, he had discovered how out of touch with the world she had become. He also knew that what she really wanted was to retire to France and live there peacefully like a private person. Although it would have robbed him of a good deal of spycatching fun, he thought Elizabeth and Walsingham would have been wise to agree to it, but when he said so, Walsingham had merely looked at him as if he were mad and begun talking about his boils. He was a martyr to boils.

Scribbling busily, Phelippes became aware of the secretary's massive presence at his shoulder. 'What is the situation with Ballard and Babington?' he demanded.

For some months there had been an inchoate plot wandering around looking for a sponsor, and now it seemed to have found one.

John Ballard was a priest, of sorts, who had made no secret of his wish to have Elizabeth assassinated in accordance with the papal decree that 'whoever sends her out of the world with the pious intention of doing God's service, not only does not sin but gains merit'. Walsingham's agents had been keeping a proprietary eye on him for almost two years without discovering any link with Mary.

One of Ballard's most profitable sidelines, however, was exorcising demons and it was this that had brought him into the orbit of Sir Anthony Babington, a young Catholic gentleman with a romantic turn of mind, an afflicted servant, and a great many friends. Five coaches full of them had turned up to see what the priest could do to restore the servant to sanity.

The acquaintance flourished, devotedly nurtured by three of Walsingham's agents, who had high hopes of Sir Anthony. And, in time, over lavish potations at the Three Tuns and the Castle, Babington was persuaded by Ballard's talk of assassinating Elizabeth, and Spanish invasions, and raising the Catholic north to restore England to the true religion, that it was his duty to ride to the martyred Mary's rescue. It was becoming an obsession with young Catholic gentlemen.

Phelippes said, 'Maude is tracking Ballard, and Poley has Babington. But Poley says Babington's friends aren't enthusiastic about assassinating her majesty, and Babington himself is now on the verge of backing out. He's thinking of going abroad. He'll be asking for a passport next.'

Walsingham snorted. 'We do not want his resolution faltering. You had better put Gifford on him, too, if you can spare him. We must have something in writing.'

It was a good suggestion, since Gifford was closer in age to Babington and more *sympathique* than the unctuous Poley. By early in July, he had wound Babington up to the stage of agreeing that, yes, he really ought to write to the queen of Scots to tell her what he had in mind and that he was able to promise her hope of deliverance.

'You should cipher your letter. Do you know the cipher she uses?'

'Yes. When I met Thomas Morgan in Paris, he said he would recommend me to her and gave me the key in case I needed it. But ciphering is so tedious.' The fire in Babington died as swiftly as it had flared.

Gifford exclaimed, 'How can you complain, in such a cause? Do it as soon as you may, then I will collect it and ensure it is delivered.'

Two nights later, Gifford left Babington's lodging at Hern's Rents in Holborn and made his way by Cheapside and Cornhill, stopping at every corner to glance back, vanishing into courtyards, ducking into dark alleys, to Walsingham's house near St Mary Axe, where Phelippes had his office. 'I wasn't followed,' he said with pride, and handed over not one packet but three.

'Good. You'd better stay while I work on them. I might need you.' Phelippes contemplated the packets beatifically, and even more beatifically when he had deciphered them. The plan was hackneyed enough, but whatever Mary replied – unless with an unequivocal 'no' – she was, this time, virtually bound to spring the trap.

First there was to be an invasion from abroad, while Catholic sympathisers in England rose *en masse* in support. Mary was to be delivered from her prison by Babington himself with 'ten gentlemen and a hundred of our followers'. And the 'tragical execution' of the usurper, Elizabeth of England, 'from obedience to whom we are by her excommunication set free', was to be achieved by 'six noble gentlemen, all my private friends'. Babington's final flourish was the hope that her

426

excellency's devoted servant could be assured of her excellency's generosity and bounty when the plot was brought to a satisfactory conclusion.

It was broad daylight before Phelippes said, 'Wake up, Gifford. *Six noble gentlemen?* I thought none of his friends liked the assassination project.'

'They don't, or so I was told. I can't ask them because I'm not sure which are involved. He's probably just trying to impress.'

'Possibly, but one does like to have the names and addresses of potential regicides. See what you can do. In the meantime, Walsingham's at Barn Elms, so I shall send my deciphered version to him there, and then, after Gregory has resealed the originals, I shall ride up to Staffordshire myself and deliver them to your friend the brewer. You can follow on Saturday, by which time there may be something to bring back.

'How satisfactory it all is.' He stretched his lanky length and then brought his hands down to scrub at the top of his head with vigorous fingertips. 'God, I need a haircut. I shall celebrate by going to the barber. Or should I go to the whorehouse first?'

18

Mary received Babington's packet of letters less than a week after the news that her son and Elizabeth had finally set their hands to the treaty that acknowledged neither filial duty nor good-sisterly affection. Mary, it seemed, was a woman of no importance, although James occupied the throne that was indisputably hers, and Elizabeth the throne that should have been hers.

Once, she had been able to conquer anger and despair by blocking them out with plans and visions but, after eighteen years with no such recourse, no possibility of initiative, every hurt and every slight had come to prey on her mind not for hours but for days, sometimes for weeks. She became obsessed, and she knew it, but she could not help it. When her health was so poor that even being carried outdoors to watch the duck hunting was a red letter day, she had little to do but think – and there was nothing to think about other than betrayal and injustice and the desperate desire to be free.

And so, when Babington's packet arrived, she did not dismiss his proposals as she should have done but wrote back instructing him on the tactics to be employed in her rescue, emphasising the dangers to herself if the plot should fail, and advising him that a Spanish invasion was essential to success. She did not comment on the plan for Elizabeth's assassination except by implication, as a *fait accompli* in the context of what should happen after.

Since the very existence of a plot made on her behalf was now enough to condemn her, she could see no good reason to do other than contribute towards the perfecting of its design.

19

Her letter, dictated to Nau in French, translated by him into English, and then enciphered by her other secretary, Gilbert Curle, went secretly to the brewer, who gave it secretly to Paulet, who took it secretly to Phelippes, who had been secretly installed in Chartley's third-best bedchamber.

'This is what we have been waiting for,' Paulet said.

And it was.

Mary's substitution cipher was by now as familiar to Phelippes as the alphabet itself, and his *en clair* draft took only a few hours to complete. Sealing and addressing it, he added on its cover the gallows mark that meant 'urgent' and despatched it to Walsingham in London by the hand of Gilbert Gifford.

He himself followed after a night's sleep and at a more leisurely pace, arriving back in London to find Walsingham in a state of acute irritation, convinced that the whole operation was in danger of falling apart. The priest Ballard, perhaps aware that he was being followed, had gone to ground somewhere. Tracing Babington's associates was proving troublesome. And Babington himself was offering to supply Walsingham with unspecified secret information in exchange for a passport. Even Mary's letter was a disappointment in its failure to be explicit about the assassination scheme.

Walsingham had, of course, kept Elizabeth informed about the plot; it would have been criminally negligent not to, if there had been any real danger. Since there was no real danger, it had given him an opportunity to show off. But now her majesty was becoming impatient. Herself a brilliant exponent of the art of tying Gordian knots, she had only contempt for the fumbling efforts of others.

'I cannot think,' she said, 'why you should have permitted everything to fall into such a tangle. Cut through it, Walsingham! Cut through it. If Mary has not said what we want her to say, say it for her. Add a postscript before it's delivered to Babington. Ask the names of the assassins and how they propose to go about the business. Phelippes can manage that, surely?'

Phelippes, when approached, said, 'Curle's ciphering is too neat. There isn't space to add anything.'

'Well, you will have to forge the whole letter. We need a sentence in the body of the text asking how the six gentlemen intend to proceed, and a postscript asking their names.'

Four thousand algebraic symbols, Greek characters, box lines and Roman numerals later, Phelippes was able to sit back and admire his work, which ended with the polite request, 'I would be glad to know the names and quality of the six gentlemen who are to accomplish the design, and also of others privy to it, for I may be able, knowing of them, to give you some further advice.'

Walsingham kept the original, while the forgery was delivered to Babington – who promptly vanished from his usual haunts.

It was too much even for Phelippes, whose carefully cultivated *sangfroid* gave way to an entirely human agitation. 'God! He's bolted. Where's Poley? Where's Mylles? Where's Maude? How did they lose him? How *could* they have lost him?'

'Probably too busy tripping over one another,' Lawrence Tomson remarked absently. 'The poor fellow's been seeing more of our agents over the last few weeks than he has of his friends.'

'Oh, very comical! Walsingham will skin me alive. Where's the fellow gone? Why has he gone? Both he and Ballard are as unstable as mercury. What if they've taken off for Richmond to kill the queen!'

20

It was the prelude to several days that were to appear to Phelippes, though only in retrospect, in the light of high farce.

First, Poley sauntered in, all innocence, to report that Babington had been staying with him. 'Secretary Walsingham wrote him about the passport he wanted and said something – I dunno what – that fairly addled his wits. He didn't feel safe at Hern's Rents, so we had a gage of booze at the Castle and I said he'd better come home with me. He wants an appointment with Walsingham. He's going to confess everything in hopes of a pardon.'

Sadly for Babington, the last thing Walsingham wanted was a confession. After all the expensive trouble he and his agents had gone to, he was not prepared to settle for anything less than a spectacular grand finale, complete with trumpets and hautboys.

Frustrated in his desire to see Walsingham, Babington penned a reassuring reply to what he believed to be Mary's letter – which he carefully burned – inconsiderately ignoring the request for the names of the six gentlemen who were to assassinate Elizabeth and omitting to say how they proposed setting about it. Walsingham was thrown into an uncharacteristic fever of indecision over whether to arrest him now or later.

In the meantime, Mylles, who had been deputed to find and arrest Ballard, observed his quarry entering Poley's house and marched briskly in, took him into custody, and marched out again, oblivious to the terrified Babington, still in bed upstairs. He, despite Poley's attempts to calm him, then threw on some clothes and rushed off in a panic to consult his friends about the disaster that seemed to threaten, but his friends, that morning, proved to be peculiarly elusive. From Bishopsgate to Smithfield he ran; back to Poley's; off to St Paul's churchyard; and back to Poley's again. Now it was Poley who had disappeared.

As it happened, he had disappeared into the Counter prison in Wood Street, on Phelippes' orders. It was the quickest way of allaying any suspicions that he might be the *agent provocateur* that indeed he was. In his place, Phelippes sent another agent, John Scudamore, to soothe Babington's fears. Unfortunately, when the two men were dining together, Scudamore had a note delivered to him which the keyed-up Babington saw was in Walsingham's handwriting.

He retained just sufficient presence of mind to say, 'I'll go and pay the bill', and since he had left both cloak and sword on his chair, it was some little time before it dawned on Scudamore that he was not coming back.

21

It was a beautiful August day, sunny and blue-skied, and Mary was deceived into thinking that the warmth must have melted Sir Amyas Paulet's heart, because he said there was to be a buck hunt nearby which, her health being improved, she might like to attend.

It was the rarest of treats, not only to be able and permitted to ride, but perhaps to meet some of the local gentry, to see faces other than those which had become so relentlessly familiar to her over the months of Paulet's stewardship. She dressed with great care and even succeeded in conquering the pain in her limbs as her physician, Bourgoing, helped her up from the mounting block into her side saddle. The mare, as out of training as her rider, showed a tendency to skitter, but Nau and Curle steadied her and Mary's voice had lost none of its power to soothe.

There was a soft breeze and the moors were green and kindly as the cavalcade set off to the south-west, so that, had it not been for her dismal clumsiness in the stirrups, Mary could have imagined herself restored to the time when she had ridden out every day for the simple pleasure of it, when she had been young and free, loved and obeyed. Tilting her head back, she drank in the fresh air as if it were some healing draught, a gift of serenity.

And then a group of horsemen came galloping out of a dip ahead of them, and for a heart-stopping moment she thought it was Sir Anthony Babington, with his ten gentlemen and one hundred followers, come to rescue her.

But Paulet and his soldiers drew rein, and Paulet hailed the green-clad and embroidered leader of the newcomers, and Mary knew it was not rescue they brought her, but death.

Dismounting, the gentleman in green approached her and said in a voice that might have been heard half across the shire, 'I come from her majesty, who finds it strange that you have conspired against her and against England, the proof of which she has seen with her own eyes.'

'I ... I ...' Mary stammered in disbelief, turning from him to Paulet and back again. 'I have never been anything other than a good sister and friend to her majesty. I ...'

'You are lying, and your servants are as guilty as you.' The gentleman gestured to his men. 'Take them away.'

Immediately, Nau and Curle were surrounded by a dozen soldiers and dragged from Mary's side as she gasped to them, foolishly, 'No. Don't let them take you from me.'

Then another soldier snatched the reins from her hands, and the gentleman in green, saying no more, remounted, turned his horse's head again towards the south and waved the rest of the party to follow him.

Mary exclaimed, 'No. Where are you taking me? I will not go with you,' but was ignored. 'I will not go,' she said again as rage and fear, the certainty that she was being taken to a secret death, gave her the strength to slip from her saddle and collapse on the grass. 'I will not go with you.'

A furious Paulet exclaimed, 'You will!'

'No.'

'Then we will take you by force.'

'No.'

She had, of course, no choice but to go in the end, although she knelt first and prayed to God to deliver her from her enemies. Her God was Paulet's God, too, but her language was that of Holy Catholic Church, and she could feel the tension in her jailer as he clenched the hands that would so gladly have throttled the idolatrous words even as she uttered them.

Bourgoing helped her mount again, muttering reassurances, but she knew they were false and scarcely heard them. If she were to die soon, secretly, this might be her one opportunity to speak those last public words that, when kings and queens died, were passed from mouth to mouth and remembered long after they themselves were gone.

In the hope that what she said might strike home to at least some of the men surrounding her, she cried, 'I am no longer of use to anyone in this world, and there is nothing in this world that I value – not possessions, or power, or sovereignty – only God's name and His glory, and the liberty of His church and His people.'

22

Walsingham, when her words were reported to him, smiled frostily. Mary's time had not yet come. Not quite. For the queen of Scots to 'die in her sleep' when the Babington plot had just been discovered would have convinced nobody.

His purpose in having her temporarily removed from Chartley to nearby Tixall was simply to enable Chartley to be searched for all her ciphers and papers. Her correspondence with Babington had been incriminating, but not as decisively so as it might have been if young Sir Anthony had not brought the whole delicate edifice of the plot crashing too soon about his ears. Even so, with her ciphers, letter books, and such information as he hoped to extract from her secretaries, Nau and Curle, Walsingham expected to be able to make an irrefutable case against the woman who had been a thorn in England's side for more than eighteen years.

In the meantime, after days of alerting the ports, sending proclamations throughout southern England, and searching the homes of all known Catholics, Babington and the small band of his closest associates were caught, dirty, hungry and footsore from lurking in the woods by day and plodding the roads by night. There was much cheering and bellringing in

London, and bonfires were lit to celebrate Elizabeth's deliverance from danger.

Elizabeth herself, belatedly confirming the orders for Mary's removal to Tixall, dashed off a note to Paulet in terms which might have caused a less devoted subject to wonder whether she had been indulging too freely in the sherry-sack.

'Amyas, my most faithful and careful servant, God reward thee treble fold in three double for the most troublesome charge so well discharged. Let your wicked murderess know how her vile deserts compel these orders, and bid her from me to ask God's forgiveness for her treacherous dealings toward the saviour of her life over many a year, to the intolerable peril of my own, and yet not content with being so oft forgiven must sin again so horribly, far passing what a woman might conceive.'

For the hapless plotters, what remained of their lives was a politically routine matter of torture, confession, prejudged trial and inevitable sentencing. On 20th September, Babington and Ballard led the first little group of them to the scaffold, to be half-hanged, castrated, disembowelled, and finally dismembered.

In bed with his boils, Walsingham had no more interest in them. What now possessed his mind was the exultant knowledge that, within the month, it would be Mary Stewart who was on trial for her life.

Chapter Nineteen

1586 - 1587

1

The castle of Fotheringhay lay seventy miles to the north of London, huge and ancient, towering over a wide, featureless landscape that stretched almost to the Fens. It had been one of the favourite residences of Edward IV a hundred years earlier, and one on whose enlargement and modernisation he had spent vast sums. But the work had been done before English architecture was touched by the lightness of the Renaissance, and to late sixteenth-century eyes Fotheringhay appeared as antiquated as it was forbidding. Its primary rôle now was as a state prison and everything about it – even the air, flat and enervating – seemed to have been designed to punish.

Mary was taken to it on a late September day with no kindness and little courtesy, and lodged with her chamber women – the only servants she had been permitted to bring – in a set of poor apartments surrounded by vast, empty, echoing halls. It was almost a week before Paulet saw fit to tell her that she was to be put on trial, not quite publicly, not quite privately, before twenty-four of her majesty's lords and privy councillors who had been deputed for the task.

It had not occurred to him that this news would do other than fill her with fear. Instead, what he saw in the wide amber eyes – all of the legendary beauty that still remained to her – was something closer to triumph.

He said in his thin, pursed-up voice, 'I recommend you to mitigate your sins, if that is possible, by begging the commission's pardon and confessing your faults before you are found guilty at law.'

She had the temerity to smile. 'My dear man, as a sinner I will beg pardon of God in heaven, but, as a queen and sovereign, there is no one here on earth to whom I can be held accountable.'

It was like being a child again, peering out of the nursery windows to see the well-dressed lords ride up on their beautifully caparisoned horses, to gasp over the size of their retinues and the style of their liveries, to admire the carriages bearing the elder statesmen with their gout and their armfuls of papers, to listen wistfully to the sounds of talk and laughter within the castle. It had been so long – so long – since Mary had seen even a handful of stolid country squires gathered together. Whatever her present situation might be, this was the world she had been born to.

And the world to which she intended to say farewell with every ounce of drama that was in her.

3

Nothing had been left to chance. Cecil and Walsingham had even mapped the chamber where the trial was to be held. Half of its seventy-foot length was to be partitioned off for spectators, while at the head of it were the throne and royal canopy that symbolised the presence of Elizabeth of England. Facing the throne, its back to the partition, was a crimson velvet chair for the accused, and between the two, at right angles to them, were long benches for the attendant earls and justices on one side, barons and learned counsel on the other. There was no counsel representing the accused; in treason trials there never was.

The lord chancellor, Sir Thomas Bromley, one of England's most experienced lawyers, was a cold, autocratic man in his late forties who wore gold embroidery on his black taffeta sleeves and a narrow-brimmed black felt hat that was more like a chimneypot than a sugarloaf. Opening the proceedings, he announced that her majesty of England had been informed that the queen of Scots had plotted her fall and that the purpose of the present assembly was to enquire into this. The queen of Scots, he added in the patronising tone that was peculiarly his own, would in due course be granted the opportunity of declaring her innocence.

But it seemed that the queen of Scots was not to be intimidated. Immediately, she showed her mettle by denying the right of the assembly to judge her at all.

'As an absolute ruler, I cannot submit to the laws of another land without injury to my own status, that of the king my son, and that of all other sovereign princes. I do not recognise the laws of England, nor do I know or understand them.'

Tom Phelippes, relegated to the public area behind the chest-high partition, where he was afforded a view only of the white-veiled back of Mary's head, was nevertheless sufficiently close to hear what she said. He knew enough of her from her correspondence to be unsurprised by the tenor of her words, but her voice did surprise him because it was low, musical, and youthful. She had a rather pretty Scotch accent. Previously, he had taken Paulet's word for it that her famous charm was false, but now he began to wonder. It was frustrating not to be able to see her face.

'Furthermore,' she went on, 'I came into this country trusting in my cousin's, the queen of England's, promise of assistance against my enemies and rebel subjects, but instead have been detained and imprisoned over many years. I have agreed to appear before this commission solely to prove that I am not guilty of conspiring against my good sister's life.'

The lord chancellor's tone was brusque. 'My queen made no promises to you, and, whether as sovereign or prisoner, you are resident in England and therefore subject to English law. I will now read the commission authorising this enquiry.'

When he had done so, Mary intervened again. 'As queen of a foreign country, I am in no sense one of my sister Elizabeth's subjects and cannot therefore be tried for treason against her. These proceedings cannot possibly be justified except by the Act you passed last year, an Act expressly framed to destroy me, introducing the death penalty for guilt by association even where no ill intent can be proved. I believe this to be contrary to all the tenets of international law.'

Phelippes thought, 'She's right, of course', but around him there was a dismissive muttering, and one voice said loudly, 'Keeping our good queen's life safe matters more than the laws of them addlepates in foreign parts!' A few other voices shouted 'Hear! Hear!' but, instead of silencing them as he should have done, the lord chancellor merely gestured to the blue-robed serjeant to read out the sequence of events leading to the present proceedings against the queen of Scots.

With no one to advise her, no advance knowledge of the substance of the allegations, and no one even to take notes on her behalf, Mary could not hope to make a case for herself. She had no real choice but to deny everything. She had never met or 'trafficked' with Babington, she said, and when copies of their correspondence, of the conspirators' confessions, and the depositions of her own secretaries Nau and Curle confirming the text of her letter were handed round, flatly refused to accept anything contained in any of them. 'How should I remember exactly what I wrote so many weeks ago,' she said. 'Show me the originals, and then at least I will know whether or not my ciphers have been tampered with.'

Phelippes flashed a glance at the benches to Mary's right, where a visibly irritable Sir Christopher Hatton – the handsomest man in England – was having his space encroached on by the massive figure of Secretary Walsingham. The secretary's dark-complexioned face under his skull-cap was expressionless and, not for the first time, Phelippes thought how dull life must be when one had no sense of humour. The ironic truth was that truth itself had been the first victim of this trial, because the proffered copies of Mary's letter to Babington were copies of the false and incriminating one, having been taken from Phelippes' letterbook copy of his own doctored version, while Nau and Curle had been shown Mary's undoctored original, which Walsingham still had in his possession, and had made their perfectly genuine depositions on the basis of it. Phelippes almost felt sorry for her. The evidence of her own secretaries would tell heavily against her.

Back and forth it went, with members of the commission discussing the evidence with their fellow members opposite so that, when the queen of Scots, out of their line of vision, wished to say something or argue a point, she had to attract their attention first. Cecil and Walsingham had been cleverer than they knew in arranging the layout of the room, because the attention of the spectators – from whom reports of the trial would spread far and wide – naturally focused itself on the group in the centre, their eyes passing over the featureless head and shoulders of the queen of Scots and her voice coming to their ears only in snatches. Her accusers were making an impression on them, but she was making none.

Briefly, Phelippes wondered whether she sensed how isolated she really was and how much hated; whether she knew that she had come to seem like a canker eating away at the heart of a Protestant England that had been in danger from the counter-Reformation almost from the moment she had crossed the border. Uncharacteristically tempted into political speculation, he found himself thinking that executing her – which was certainly going to happen – was more likely to precipitate a crisis than keeping her alive would do, and wondered whether Lawrence Tomson would be prepared to take a wager on it.

After a time, when Mary had denied plotting to take Elizabeth's life, saying again and again that all she wished was her own liberty, Cecil –

small, high-complexioned and silver-haired – rose to put his oar in. Phelippes smothered a grin. The old man, annoyed at not being able to take any credit for unravelling the Babington affair, had decided to remind everyone of his authority by shifting the plot into the wider perspective of which he, rather than Walsingham, was the master.

As a result, during what remained of that day and for a large part of the next, there was considerably less about the Babington affair than about Mary's long-standing desire for Elizabeth's throne, her Catholic faith, her transfer of her non-existent rights in the succession to Philip II of Spain, her correspondence with the papacy, her encouragement of plans to invade England, and her guilty involvement in the succession of plots that had preceded Babington's – those of Ridolphi, the Northern earls, Throckmorton and Parry.

No evidence was offered, nothing but accusations impossible to disprove. The sheer number of them, true or false, carried their own conviction and, although the queen of Scots protested strongly, it was without avail. With one last rejection of the validity of the trial, one last demand to be permitted to meet her good sister Elizabeth face to face, one last resignation of her cause into the hands of God, she was assisted to rise. Before leaving the chamber, she regally forgave all those present for what they had done. It was, Phelippes thought, her only bad mistake.

The court was prorogued, the trial effectively ended, but no sentence was pronounced. Elizabeth had said that, first, she herself wished to consider the report of the hearing.

The earls and barons, who had turned up for the second day's proceedings already booted and spurred, rode away from Fotheringhay with relief. Their minds had been made up before the enquiry began, and they had heard nothing to change them. If anything, the Scots queen's dignity, determination and, above all, the fluency and length of the speeches to which Cecil's intervention had opened the door, had confirmed them in their fear and dislike of her.

Phelippes, who was young and full of vigour, caught himself reflecting admiringly on the fact that, although Mary was an old woman – somewhere in her forties, he supposed – and certainly in poor health, her bearing had scarcely faltered under the strain of holding her own against the serried ranks of her enemies. She had talked a good deal about the strength she drew from her faith, but he guessed that she had drawn just as much from being the centre of public attention again for the first time in almost twenty years.

In the weeks that followed, there was peace of mind for no one entangled in the fate of Mary Queen of Scots, except Mary herself who, still at Fotheringhay, read and sewed and prayed with a tranquillity she had never known in all her life before.

It was over. No more difficulties, no more doubts, no more doomed battles of the mind and spirit. The death of a Catholic martyr would come swiftly and gratefully. She only had to wait.

5

At Richmond, Elizabeth dined in state, gowned in black velvet with sleeves so thickly embroidered with silver and pearl roses that not a scrap of the underlying fabric was to be seen. Over her shoulders was a silver shawl, gossamer-fine, and there were three long strands of pearls round her neck. Her head, its tightly curled, pearl-haloed wig a startling shade of orange, rested on her huge lace ruff much as John the Baptist's head must have rested on Salome's platter.

She sat alone, as always, under her gold canopy of state, at a table laden with forty silver-gilt dishes, each of which had been borne in separately and ceremonially, and then tasted for poison by its bearer. But she had little appetite, and when her black-clad page had served her did no more than pick up a potted wheatear and nibble at it, swallow a few spoonsful of mutton fricassée, and reject a herb fritter after poking at it long and absently with her gold-handled knife. The wine page who, dressed in green, knelt at her side while she drank, was kept busier than he ever remembered.

Her attendant ladies sat at a separate table, but the gentlemen all stood, even Cecil on his creaky legs, and old Sir Walter Mildmay, stooped and sniffling, and Sir Christopher Hatton, whom today she particularly disliked for being seven years younger than she was. She glared at them impartially, because they had that morning led the deputation from the Lords and Commons petitioning her to condemn the queen of Scots to death.

She had said – though only as a figure of speech – 'I wish my good sister and I were as two milkmaids with pails upon our arms,' and the deputation had nodded sagely. 'But we are princes set on stages, in the sight and view of all the world.' They had nodded even more sagely. She had reduced them almost to tears with a brief meditation on how she might have faced her own violent death at the dictate of that same good sister. And then she had put them off so that she might beseech God to illuminate her understanding.

She knew perfectly well that Cecil, at least, had seen through the fine phrases. It would have been odd, indeed, if after twenty-eight years as her leading adviser he had been unable to distinguish between diplomatic procrastination and a simple inability to make up her mind.

6

Twelve days later, there was another deputation, and again Elizabeth put it off. But by early December, she could put it off no longer. The death sentence was publicly proclaimed after a great deal of drafting and redrafting, and the church bells rang, and her subjects danced around their bonfires.

Proclaiming the death sentence was one thing. For Elizabeth to sign the warrant was quite another. An increasingly exasperated Cecil and Walsingham spent two months trying to talk her into it.

Executing anointed queens was a dangerous precedent, she said.

This is a special case, they said.

What about the Spanish reaction?

'With Mary gone, rescuing her will no longer offer Philip an excuse for invasion.'

'God's death!' said her majesty disgustedly. 'Can you not do better than that? He has had that excuse for almost twenty years, and amused himself with plotting much but doing nothing. Vengeance has a more stirring sound. What about France?'

'They have said as much as they are likely to,' Cecil replied, and Walsingham, who had set up another neat little plot to make sure of it, added, 'With the French ambassador under house arrest for failing to report the Stafford scheme to us, he is in no position to rouse them to action.'

Elizabeth still disliked Walsingham, but that he was effective could not be denied. Grudgingly, she muttered, 'That was well done. Which leaves us with only Scotland to worry about.'

Human nature being what it was, the Scots, who had rejected Mary Stewart almost twenty years before and barely thought about her since, had become highly excitable at the idea of a foreigner threatening to execute *their* queen.

James, indeed, wrote to Elizabeth to complain that, 'Before God, I hardly dare venture out into the streets because of the fuss they make.'

It was unexpected, and it was also inconvenient. Although James had by now learned to discount most of the tales about his mother on which he had been reared, he was still too young to understand that, although she had been a stranger to him all his life, the experience of fathering his own children would in time breed in him a curiosity about her, and a distant affection and regret. The blood tie that had for so long bedevilled Scottish politics was there in him, too, though latent.

In the meantime, he said sharply to Vice-Chancellor Thirlestane, 'Well, what do we do now?'

John Maitland said, 'It is natural for children to love their parents ...'

'Is it? I mean, do they?'

'Usually.'

'Your father has just died. Did you love him? Do you mourn him? Does the fact that you are now "Sir John" carry compensations?'

Although James was inquisitive on principle, he was seldom intrusively so, saying frankly that he preferred not to know any more than necessary about the private lives of his advisers. It was his ambition to employ only those whom he could hang if they needed hanging, without having to worry about personal considerations.

Maitland smiled faintly. 'My father was ninety years old and, yes, I loved him and, yes, I mourn him. But he was a very unusual man.'

'I see. So what you are so carefully avoiding saying is that not every son loves his parents, but if he doesn't, he should keep quiet about it?'

'More or less. The political implications may be foremost in your mind, but unless you have no interest in what your subjects think of you, you must let it be seen that you are not lacking in filial duty. You must make a convincing show of outrage.'

James wrinkled his indeterminate nose. 'Yes. No. Mind you, I think it's damned impudent of Elizabeth to talk about execution. She's no angel herself. We need to teach her a lesson. Why don't I threaten to break the treaty?'

It was the only weapon he had, but a dangerous one.

John Maitland had already considered it and been forced to conclude that peace with England and the ultimate union of the crowns mattered more than one woman's life. Mary's day was done. Briefly, he remembered his own limited acquaintance with her, and her charm, and her political ineptitude – which had not been altogether her fault – and the sweetness of nature that had been there, *au fond*. If she had been stronger, tougher, more dislikeable, many things might have been different.

He was disinclined to waste time negotiating a treaty of amity all over again after Mary had been executed, which he had little doubt that she would be, whatever James said or did. It might even be for the best, because, if she were allowed to live, the shadow of her plotting, real or imaginary, would for the English also hang over her son's head until nature at last took its course.

He said, 'It would have to be carefully done. I hear from London that the tide of opinion is running strongly against your mother and that, if you protest too much, her sins may reflect back on you. So you need to threaten vigorously to satisfy our people here at home, but not sufficiently vigorously to convince Elizabeth that you mean it.'

'We could confuse her by playing a double game,' James said thoughtfully. 'If I send Patrick Gray to do the vigorous threatening, while Alexander Stewart privately murmurs that I'm in a towering rage – and you can wipe that grin off your face, Vice-Chancellor! – but that I'll get over it ... No need to tell Gray what Stewart's up to, or vice versa.'

'What an ingenious notion, sire.'

8

Sir Alexander Stewart had already done his work when the Master of Gray arrived in the environs of London on 24th December and asked for an audience with her most gracious majesty. It was not granted until 10th January, when Elizabeth opened the proceedings by demanding bluntly, 'Well, what does your master offer?'

It was not a question that Gray had expected. Floundering slightly, he repeated, 'Offer? In what sense?'

But the question had been rhetorical, since Elizabeth promptly informed him that there was nothing James could offer in exchange for his mother's life that would interest her, and went on to wax exceedingly fluent on the subject of Mary's repetitive and unjustifiable demands for the succession.

It was what Gray had really come to talk about, but he had intended to work round to it rather more subtly. Deprived of the initiative, he landed himself in such a dialectical tangle that the queen swore she could not understand what he was talking about. Helpfully, the Earl of Leicester interpreted for her. What the Master of Gray was implying was that King James could be consoled for his mother's death by being granted the right to the English succession in her place.

'What?' snapped Elizabeth. 'Has he not been listening? I have just told him that my good sister has *no* right to the succession. God's passion! If that wily brat James were to be given a promise of my throne, I should find myself in a worse case than before.' She gestured towards Gray with a flashingly jewelled hand. 'For a mere earldom or duchy, you or such as you would not hesitate to send your knaves to cut my throat. No, by God, your master shall never be granted the succession while I live.'

The Master of Gray, who very clearly remembered Elizabeth telling him, only a few months before, that James could rely on succeeding her if he behaved himself, heard his own voice saying a little querulously, 'But, your majesty ...'

'No. No. *No.* I will not have someone worse in his mother's place. Remind your king how much I have done for him since he was born, how it is I who have so often kept the crown upon his head. Tell him I will keep the league between us. But if he breaks it, he will pay. Enough of this foolishness.'

Catching the Earl of Leicester's eye, Gray gave up. He had heard much about Elizabeth's theatrical outbursts, but had never before experienced one. There seemed nothing he could do but seek a postponement. 'Your majesty, I beg you, spare the queen of Scots' life for at least the next fifteen days, until I can communicate with my master the king.'

'No.'

'Eight days, then. It is little to ask.'

'Not for an hour.'

It was the end of the audience. Flouncing up from her chair of state, Elizabeth stalked out of the chamber in a flurry of scarlet and diamonds and rubies.

The Master of Gray rose smoothly from his knees.

Leicester, ageing now and thick around the waist, said, 'She doesn't want to sign the death warrant, you know. When she's not snapping at everyone, she's shedding tears in cataracts.' Then the famously demonic

443

eyebrows twitched and his tone changed. 'Anyway, you have done what you came to do. James has made his protest. Elizabeth has put him in his place. Honour is satisfied on both sides.'

The Master of Gray, his own elegant eyebrows groomed hourly with a damp finger, raised one of them languidly. 'Honour?' he said. 'But yes. You are perfectly right. How very perceptive you are, my lord.'

9

Cecil had made out the queen of Scots' death warrant at Christmas 1586 and given it to William Davison, the under secretary, to hold until her majesty should call for it.

But the new year came and the weeks went by and her majesty did not call for it.

And then she did. It was the first day of February and the rain was beating against the latticed windows of her privy chamber at Greenwich palace. The barge-busy Thames, under the lowering sky, was a wide, ochre-brown sea flattened and pockmarked by the downpour. On the opposite bank, a few leafless trees brooded desolately over muddy green meadows. Indoors, despite the great log fires, it was chill and dank.

The queen's back was to the window and the weather, and she was alone except for the usual little group of her ladies, who had been banished to the end of the room.

She said, 'You have documents for me to sign, Master Davison?' and pushed the big brass pricket candlestick aside to make space before her.

'Yes, your majesty.'

'Well, give them to me, man. No, no. Not one at a time. I am in no mood for reading them. Just put them all down on the table here.'

Casually, she glanced over the letter on top of the pile, a note to her godson, John Harington, whom she still addressed as 'Boy Jack' although he was well into his twenties. Then, signing it and shaking the pounce box over it, she pushed it up a careful two inches to reveal the foot of the sheet beneath. And so she went on, giving perhaps a little more attention than usual to the complex swashes with which she habitually decorated her 'Elizabeth R'.

When all were done, she gestured to Davison to gather the papers up. But she could not quite carry the game through to its end. 'There is one paper there, I believe,' she said, 'which should go to the lord chancellor for the Great Seal, and then to the commissioners. But do not omit to show it to Secretary Walsingham' – her smile was wintry – 'though I fear the grief of it may kill him.'

Davison smiled dutifully; her majesty liked her little jokes to be appreciated.

'As for the event itself, it should not take place in the courtyard at Fotheringhay, where it would be too public, but in the Great Hall.'

The quill was still in her hand. With meticulous care, she replaced it on its tray and said, without looking up. 'I wish to be troubled no more with this, to hear no more of it till all is done. Do you understand me?'

Davison, preparing to back out of her presence, bobbed his head. 'Yes, your majesty. I understand perfectly.'

'Wait.'

He waited, while she removed her spectacles and sat rubbing the bridge of her nose. 'One might have thought,' she muttered after a time, 'that some loyal subject could have taken this duty upon himself. Someone like Paulet.'

Her under secretary did not understand at first. Then he exclaimed, 'No, your majesty, you cannot ask such a thing of him.'

'Yes, I can. It would save me from great embarrassment in my dealings with France and Scotland. Send to him to say that I regret that he has not found some way to shorten his prisoner's life, considering the great peril that threatens me hourly as long as she lives. That should suffice him.'

'But, your majesty ...'

'Enough. Get out.'

10

Paulet refused in the most unequivocal terms, bemoaning 'this unhappy day on which I am required by my most gracious sovereign to make so foul a shipwreck of my conscience, to do an act which God and the law forbid.'

His most gracious sovereign, on receipt of this effusion, expressed herself pithily on the daintiness and niceness of those precise fellows who talked much of their zeal for her safety but were not prepared to do anything to ensure it.

By that time, as it happened, the event of which she had expressed the desire to hear no more was already well in train. Her signature was all her council had needed.

She had said that she did not wish to know, which meant that she could not ask.

It meant that she spent the next terrible week in the grip of nightmares. She stayed up late, watching the dancing and the masques with which her court beguiled the evening hours, playing chess, waving time to the music, teasing Leicester for having a smut on his nose, behaving as if she had no care in the world, hoping to tire herself out so that she might sleep through until the morning. But after two or three hours of the long dark winter nights, the dreams began.

She could not tell whether it was a live woman or a dead one who appeared at her bedside, an unusually tall woman in a plain black gown, with a white, heart-shaped cap on her head and round her throat a collar that might have been blood or rubies.

'I'm not dead yet,' the vision said conversationally, 'and even when I am, you won't be rid of me so easily.' She seemed to be waiting for Elizabeth to reply but after a moment went on with a charming smile, 'I am going to be a martyr, you know. I don't mind. I have had enough of life. I'm surprised you don't feel the same. After all, you're well over fifty, so you don't have many years left to you.' She peered. 'Your teeth are terrible. Do you have trouble with them? Did you know that my brother-in-law, Henri III, has false ones? They're made of bone, and they have to be wired on every day. He can't eat with them, he says, because they wobble so badly.'

'Damn your brother-in-law's teeth,' Elizabeth gasped. 'Go away! How dare you come here and trouble me with your silly, womanish bibble-babble? It's like all those letters you've written me over the years. On and on and on, as if you had nothing better to do with your time!'

The woman threw her head back and laughed. The ruby collar split, horizontally, into a yawning black chasm edged with crimson.

But then everything came together again and the vision was saying amusedly, 'Well, I didn't have anything better to do with my time. When one is wrongfully imprisoned for nineteen years, writing letters is as good a way of passing the days and the weeks and the months as any.'

'Hah! Writing and plotting, you mean!'

'Well, I had to do *something*.'

'You didn't have to plot against my life!'

'I didn't.'

'Yes, you did.'

'No, I didn't.'

'Yes, you did. Time and time again. What else can I do but execute you!'

'What else can you do? Oh, dear. How often have I heard *those* words in the course of my life! Everyone who has ever betrayed me has said, "What else could I do?" But there is always a choice, you know. Or there would be if you were not so weak and self-interested.'

'I am *not* self-interested. It is entirely my country's interests that I have at heart! Your invasion plots, your Catholic risings ...'

The woman's left hand was leaning heavily on a stick, but her right waved dismissively, a hand with long fingers that must once have been beautiful but were now stiff and distorted by rheumatism. 'Let's not go into all that. It's past. I'm told that there were indeed plots but, although you refuse to believe it, they were not mine. All I have ever wanted is for us to be good friends, *really* good sisters. But it is of no importance now.'

Elizabeth couldn't understand why everyone who had described the woman to her had been so wrong. Certainly, her body was thickened with age and her limbs crippled and clumsy. Certainly, she wore the plain black gown and white cap that she had affected throughout her years in England. Certainly, she wore no jewels other than an idolatrous cross and rosary. But her face was still young and lovely, with perfect skin, a sweet and shapely mouth that tilted up at the corners, and widely set slanting eyes touched by the most tantalising hint of laughter.

It was the face from the portrait she had sent Elizabeth almost thirty years before, the portrait that had so impressed itself on Elizabeth's mind that nothing could ever supersede it. She had always disliked beautiful women, especially enchanting ones.

She said, 'What are you doing here, anyway? I don't want you here. I never wanted you here. Go away.'

'I will, in a minute. I came only for two things. I wanted to ask you to let my servants take my body to France so that I may be buried according to the rites of Holy Church ...'

'I don't know about that. I will have to consult my advisers.'

The vision smiled delightfully. 'Yes, indeed. What else are advisers for?'

Elizabeth could taste the other woman's charm like honey on her tongue, and feared it. 'I *do* follow their advice!'

'I am sure you do. The other reason I came was to hurry you along. I know I must die, and I am tired of waiting. It has been almost four long months. Surely you must have made up your mind by now?'

'I – I ...'

'Ah, I see you have, but you don't like to admit it even to yourself. Well, if you're quite sure it's settled – you *are* sure, aren't you? – I might as well say *adieu*. You will know when they kill me, by the way. I shall scream. Oh, not publicly, not aloud. But privately – just for you, so that you will hear me and will know.'

The vision faded and Elizabeth awoke to the sound of her own voice moaning and one of her women bending over her, saying urgently, 'Your majesty! Your majesty!'

'Go away. Go. I don't need you.' She sat up, and found her stomach rising to her throat. She *never* dreamed. Thickly, she said, 'Bring me a basin. I feel sick. It must have been the fish.'

12

Walsingham had all the arrangements in hand. A wooden platform twelve feet square was ordered to be erected and draped in black velvet in the Great Hall at Fotheringhay, with stools on it for the two royal commissioners who were to witness the execution, and another for the queen of Scots while she was being disrobed. The headsman's block was also to be draped in black.

A suitable headsman was found and, having agreed £10 for his services, was escorted to Fotheringhay in disguise, with his axe hidden in a trunk.

The gates of the castle were to be locked during the execution and there were to be no holy relics. The block was to be burned afterwards, together with every item of clothing and every ornament. The body's heart and organs were to be removed and buried where they would never be found. The embalmed body itself was to be encased in a heavy lead coffin and bestowed by night on an upper shelf in the Fotheringhay church.

And since it was desirable that any initial excitement should be allowed to die down before messengers began hurrying abroad with highly coloured tales of what had taken place, all England's ports were to be closed until further notice.

There was only one other measure Walsingham could think of that might help to hasten Mary Stewart, queen of Scots, into the oblivion she deserved.

His own son-in-law and Leicester's nephew, Sir Philip Sidney, had died of wounds almost four months before at the siege of Zutphen, but although his body had been brought home, he had not yet been buried. The time, it seemed, had come. For Londoners, at least, Mary's fate was to be eclipsed by a grand and lavish funeral procession held, just a week and a day after her own death, for the beloved and widely mourned young poet, courtier and popular hero who had died fighting against the enemies of England. The Catholic enemies. The Spanish enemies. The friends of Mary Queen of Scots.

13

Mary had been preparing for death since she had been formally notified, in the middle of November, that she had been found guilty. By the end of the month, she had written letters of farewell to the pope, to her old friend Mendoza, to her cousin Henri de Guise, and many others. In all of them, she spoke more of her faith than of herself, of martyrdom and of glory.

She had few possessions now, and it was not hard to decide which of her servants should receive a miniature or a little silver box, a music book or ring, or the mementoes that were to be sent to her brother-in-law the king of France and her Guise cousins. More difficult was to arrange for pensions to be paid to those of her household who had stayed with her so loyally over the years. But even that was resolved at last.

It was fortunate that she had made all her arrangements, because the English commissioners – one of them Shrewsbury, who had been her timid and tolerant jailer for so many years – came to her after dinner on Tuesday, 7th February 1587 to tell her that she was to die at eight the next morning.

14

After she had made a few final dispositions, she laid herself on her bed to spend what remained of her last night unsleeping, the patrolling of her heavy-footed guards echoing outside her room and, from the Great Hall, the hammering of the scaffold being erected. At six, she rose and retired into her makeshift oratory alone to pray. Elizabeth's commissioners had refused her the services of her chaplain to make ready her soul.

They were late coming for her, and the February sun was well risen in a thinly blue sky when they led her towards the Great Hall. Her servants were forbidden at first to go with her because Elizabeth had decreed that she was to die alone, but in the end, when she promised that they would neither weep, nor cry out, nor try to dip their kerchiefs in her blood, the commissioners relented.

She had not thought there would be an audience, but there were two or three hundred gathered behind the ranked soldiers surrounding the scaffold and the sight of them warmed her. They should see how proudly a queen of Scotland and of France could die, a martyr for her faith. In her end was her beginning.

She did not even flinch at the sight of the great axe lying beside the block as she mounted the three steps and heard the commission for her execution being read out. And when the Protestant dean of Peterborough knelt on the scaffold steps and began to pray noisily for her, she disregarded him and herself began to read aloud in her soft, clear voice from her book of Latin prayers. When the dean had at last finished, she changed to English, and begged God to avert his wrath from England, to look on Elizabeth with mercy, and to bless her own son James, the king of Scots. Then she kissed her crucifix and crossed herself, and said, 'Even as thy arms, O Jesus, were spread here upon the cross, so receive me into thy arms of mercy, and forgive me all my sins.'

The executioners, kneeling, begged her to absolve them from guilt for her death and she smiled. 'I forgive you with all my heart, for now, I hope, you shall make an end of all my troubles.'

Then, clumsy-handed, they began to help her two women disrobe her. The pomander chain went first, and the rosary, and then the *Agnus Dei*. After that it was the peaked white headdress with its long white veil, the crisp white ruff, the black sleeves slashed with purple, and finally the black satin gown patterned with black velvet and buttons of jet and pearl. In the end she stood, still smiling, in underbodice, petticoat and sleeves of the dark blood red that was the liturgical colour of martyrdom in the Holy Catholic Church. Almost gaily she told the executioners that she had never before had such grooms and then she turned, with gentleness, to silence her servants' weeping and praying.

Jane Kennedy, who had been her favourite chamber woman for twenty years, folded a *Corpus Christi* cloth into a triangular shape, kissed it, and then covered the queen's eyes with it, bringing the three points together on the crown of her head.

It was time.

Mary knelt on the cushion before the block and, groping for it, laid her head on it, guiding her chin with her hands. She would have left them there, had not the executioner's assistant moved them out of the line of the axe.

Stretching out her arms and legs, she cried in a voice clear and passionate, '*In manus tuas, Domine, confide spiritum meum.*'

Into your hand, O Lord, I commend my spirit.

The axe fell, but the executioner was nervous over beheading an anointed queen and his aim was not true. It took a second blow to sever her head.

15

Elizabeth, at Greenwich, was having her eyebrows plucked when, suddenly, she struck away her chamber woman's hand. The girl turned pale. 'Your majesty, I did not mean to hurt you.'

But her majesty's eyes were blank.

After a moment, she said, 'No. Go on. I thought I heard a cry. But I was probably imagining it.'

16

Thomas Phelippes, who almost four months before had tempted Lawrence Tomson into a wager that executing the queen of Scots would bring about more troubles than it cured, was pleased to have his prophecy fulfilled, although he had not expected the first and most spectacular evidence of it to come from Elizabeth of England herself.

Confirmation that the deed had been done was brought to court the morning after by Henry Talbot, the Earl of Shrewsbury's son, and by the evening – although Cecil tried to keep the news from her – the queen had heard about it. She did not seem greatly disturbed. But next day was a different matter.

Next day there were mourning weeds and tears and outbursts of ungoverned emotion, fanned by the gossip that was already on every lip.

'When the executioner lifted her severed head up by the hair to display it, the head fell to the floor and he found he was holding nothing but a wig!'

'The Earl of Kent shouted out, "So end all the queen's and the gospel's enemies".'

'There was a pet dog hiding under her skirts and it would not be separated from her, but laid itself down between the head and the body

451

and soaked itself in her blood. They had to carry it away forcibly and wash it clean.'

'Her grace and dignity had old Shrewsbury in tears. She died like a queen ...'

Cecil thought, at first, that Elizabeth was – very sensibly – making a display of sorrow for the benefit of foreign ambassadors and envoys, demonstrating what a hard taskmaster political necessity could be. But he soon discovered his error.

Her majesty had no intention of taking responsibility for what had been done.

'When I signed the warrant I did so only that it might be held in reserve in case of emergency. I told Davison it was to be *kept*, not to be used! How dared he pass it to the commissioners to be carried out! How dared he disobey me!'

Within a week of Mary's death, Under-Secretary Davison found himself in the Tower. Ten days later, Elizabeth was threatening to have him hanged without a trial. Cecil was banned from her presence. She herself refused to eat and could not sleep. All that had gone before was irrelevant. What now consumed her was guilt over having put to death a divinely ordained queen.

Nothing improved.

17

Because of the closure of England's ports, it was three weeks before news of Mary's death reached France.

'I never saw anything more hated,' Elizabeth's ambassador reported back from Paris, 'whether by the little, the great, the old or the young, and those of all religions, than the queen of Scots' death and especially the manner of it.'

A requiem Mass was held at Notre Dame, and even Catherine de' Medici, now approaching seventy, listened and was moved as the Archbishop of Bourges remembered the young queen-dauphiness on the day of her first bridal, 'so covered in jewels that the sun himself shone no more brightly; more beautiful, more charming than ever woman was. This place, which then was hung with cloth of gold and precious tapestries, is today shrouded in black for her. In place of nuptial torches we have funeral tapers. In place of songs of joy, we have sighing and wailing; for clarions and hautboys, the dismal tolling of the mourning bell. Oh God, what a change is here ...'

18

In Spain, Philip II had for years been thinking of invading England. Some day. When he had settled his problems in the Netherlands. When he had managed to convince His Holiness that his purpose was zealously spiritual rather than vulgarly acquisitive.

By April 1586, however, Elizabeth's interference in the Netherlands had annoyed him into beginning to make naval preparations, and a few weeks later, the imprisoned Mary, feeling betrayed by her son, wrote to Mendoza to say that, unless King James of Scotland had become a convert to Holy Church by the time of her death, she proposed to bequeath her right of succession to the crown of England to King Philip of Spain.

By a natural logic, her execution guaranteed the ultimate launch of the great Armada against England.

19

In Scotland, James said, 'Well, if Elizabeth can stamp around, so can I. Not that I've any choice, with the Hamiltons threatening to burn Newcastle, and the Borderers wanting to take fire and sword to Carlisle, and everybody else in the country screaming for revenge. You wouldn't credit it, would you? They spat at her after Carberry, they let her be deposed, they didn't care that she spent almost twenty years illegally imprisoned, but now they're up in arms.'

He wasn't angry – he rarely was, because he prided himself on his judgement and knew that anger was likely to distort it. But he was justifiably exasperated. One of his earls had been heard to say that it was the royal duty to lead an army over the border to avenge the insult, that he should hazard his country's all and be prepared to lose all for the sake of honour.

'The battle of Flodden all over again,' James had snorted. 'Just what we need!'

He had ordered general mourning, of course, and the Earl of Sinclair had turned up at court in full armour. When James had asked, 'Did you not see the order for mourning?' the daft loon had replied, 'This *is* the proper mourning for the queen of Scots.'

John Maitland said, 'We can't afford to go to war.'

'I know we can't,' snapped his king. 'But unless I look as if I'm thinking about it, I'll find myself deposed, too.' And then his unremarkable twenty-year-old face crumpled. 'I *do* mind about her,' he said.

His vice-chancellor's expression softened just a little. 'I know.'

Elizabeth wrote to the Scotch brat about his mother's death, though not at once. It was not her fault, she said. 'I wish you to know the extreme dolour that overwhelms my mind for the miserable accident which – far contrary to my intention – has come about. Believe me when I say that it was the fault of my secretary, who is now in the Tower. If I had meant it to happen, I would never lay the blame on another's shoulders.'

James worded his barbed reply with care. 'On the one hand, remembering your rank, sex, ties of blood and long-expressed goodwill towards my mother the late queen of Scots, as well as your many and solemn attestations of innocence, I myself dare not wrong you by failing to accept your guiltlessness in the affair. On the other hand, I should express the hope that your honourable behaviour in times to come may persuade the rest of the world to see things in the same light.'

Chapter Twenty

1603

1

In February 1603, Elizabeth received the Venetian ambassador at Richmond wearing a low-necked gown of silver and white taffeta embroidered in gold, her throat encircled with pearls and rubies, her bodice covered with gold, carbuncles, balas rubies and diamonds. There were pearls strung round her forehead and an imperial crown perched on hair which, the ambassador noted, was of a colour never made by nature. Awed, he stooped to kiss the hem of her gown.

She spoke to him in the Italian she had learned in her youth, and was sweet to him, and lively of wit, and struck him as being in excellent health although she was approaching her seventieth birthday.

But within weeks everything changed.

2

She lost interest in living.

To her advisers, there seemed no compelling reason for it. But the depression that attacked her after the death of one of her oldest and closest friends, the Countess of Nottingham, failed to lift, and she began to suffer from minor ailments for which she refused to take remedies. She relapsed into a torpor, refused to be undressed, sat all day sunk among cushions.

When Secretary Cecil – the son of that Cecil who had been the other half of herself for most of her years on the throne – told her that she really must go to bed, she replied, 'Little man, little man, the word *must* is not to be used to princes.' But in the end she went. No one had any doubt that she was dying.

But still she had not named her successor and by 23rd March she was no longer able to speak.

For two years, Sir Robert Cecil had been corresponding privately with King James VI of Scotland, establishing a relationship between them which would ensure that 'when that day (so grievous to us) shall happen which is the tribute of all mortal creatures, your ships shall be steered into the right harbour without cross of wave or tide'. James had been only too happy to put himself in Cecil's hands.

Now, Sir Robert begged, 'Your majesty, we must know who your successor is to be. Show us some sign.'

She did not move.

He said, 'You majesty, who shall it be? Shall it be James of Scotland?'

Something that might have been a smile of amusement touched her face. For more than forty years she had kept them wondering, but the time had come at last.

Steepling her fingers into the shape of a crown, she raised them to her head.

In the early hours of the following morning, she slipped away, 'mildly like a lamb'.

3

James had been waiting.

Late in the evening of the second day after Elizabeth's death, Robert Carey, who had taken the precaution of setting up a chain of post horses to carry him the four hundred miles from London to the north, arrived exhausted, dusty and dishevelled in Edinburgh and demanded to see the king.

James, who had already retired, rose to receive him.

Then, kneeling before the middle-aged man in the furred bedrobe, Carey – who sixteen years before had brought him Elizabeth's disclaimer of responsibility for his mother's death – declared, weary but triumphant, 'Sire, I have the honour to be first to salute you as King James VI of Scotland and also as King James I of England. The crowns of both realms are yours.'

'Well, well,' James said.

It was the end of an old song, and the beginning of a new one whose words and melody were yet to be written.

HISTORICAL ENDNOTE

Historical Endnote

1
Fact or Fiction?

Names and dates apart, much of history as we know it borders on the fictional, in the sense of having been filtered, during its passage down the centuries, through the minds, prejudices and cultural preconceptions of succeeding generations. Which means that the more intriguing the subject, the more likely it is that truth has fallen victim to its interpreters.

Mary Queen of Scots is a classic case, a famously fascinating historical figure who has been turned, by the billions of words written about her over the last four hundred years, from a real and rational human being into a myth with an identity crisis. Whore and murderess? Pure-spirited Catholic martyr? The evidence, like statistics, can be made to prove anything, especially since the primary sources are in many cases flawed – baseless rumour, spiteful gossip, statements made under torture, letters written in calculated terms to achieve calculated ends, and everything glossed over with religio-political bigotry.

All that can be said with certainty of Mary is that she was intelligent and well-trained, gracious and kind of heart, beautiful and charismatic, but that she was also self-centred, impetuous, and unreliable in judgement. In another era – the eighteenth century, perhaps, or the icon-obsessed late twentieth – she might have been a force to be reckoned with but, as it was, lacking the mental toughness of an Elizabeth growing up in fear for her life, she was the wrong kind of personality in a situation that might well have defeated even the right kind. 'Fate, from her cradle,' wrote her late Victorian admirer Andrew Lang in his *History of Scotland*, 'lay so heavy upon her that no conceivable conduct of hers could have steered her safely through the plotting crowns and creeds, the rival dissemblers, bigots, hypocrites, and ruffians who, with jealousy, and

459

hatred, and desire, on every side surrounded her. Joyous by nature and by virtue of her youth, she was condemned to a life of tears, and destined to leave a stained and contested honour.' Despite the purple prose, Lang's point was a perfectly valid one.

In the twenty-five-and-a-half years between her return to Scotland and her death on an English scaffold, Mary was able to write her own script for only a few brief months. For the rest of the time she was at the mercy, either voluntarily or involuntarily, of others, and it is in the wider and deeply influential context of those others that the writer of historical fiction has options that are not open to the biographer or the historian. The scope of historical fiction can be as wide as the author chooses to make it; speculation, far from being forbidden, helps to power the reader's imagination; so, too, do the varied perspectives offered by matching (or trying to match) Lethington's talent for being 'subtle to draw out the secrets of every man's mind'. It helps, all of it, to give three-dimensional colour to the black and white of conventional history.

In *Fatal Majesty* I have used the same sources as I would have done had I been writing non-fiction, but with considerably more latitude and freedom in assessing them. At no point have I diverged from the overall pattern of the facts, or from the known characteristics of the personalities involved, but I have sometimes re-interpreted them on the basis of psychological probability rather than the often improbable logic of orthodoxy. One example is the murder of Darnley where, although proof is lacking, everything clearly points to a plot to dispose not only of Darnley, but of Bothwell as well.

In general, however, the reader may assume that what the characters do is historical, what they say and think is either fictional or fictionalised – though not in the case of John Knox, whose words only a genius would dare to try and paraphrase.

2

Stewart or Stuart?

Like her predecessors on the throne of Scotland – two Roberts and five Jameses – Mary Queen of Scots was born a Stewart, and I have referred to her as such throughout. Until fairly recently, because of the importance of kinship and family alliances, it was quite usual for Scotswomen to continue to be known by their maiden names after marriage.

Although the sixteenth century's approach to spelling was carefree, and although her French upbringing led Mary habitually to sign herself 'Marie Stuart', she was in fact a Stuart only during the twenty-two months between her marriage to Darnley and her marriage to Bothwell.

Her successors, however, from James VI & I onwards, *were* Stuarts, being descended from her marriage to Henry Stuart, Lord Darnley, whose surname they inherited.

3
Elizabeth of England

It is perhaps unnecessary to say that, since *Fatal Majesty* is told from the Scots point of view, Elizabeth of England does not come out of it very well. The truth is that the deviousness that worked so brilliantly in other areas was infinitely destructive where Scotland was concerned. Certainly, the Scots were an unmitigated pest, but even the hallowed old political tradition of keeping potentially dangerous neighbours in a state of disarray scarcely seems to justify the bullying, the manipulation, the lies and the endless broken promises that marked her dealings with the people to the north of the border. Her final attempt to have Mary privately murdered was entirely in keeping with what had gone before. The fact remains, however, that she was queen of *England*, with no real choice but to see everything in terms of England's interests and her own. She has to be judged accordingly.

4
United kingdom?

In the year 1320, eight Scots earls and thirty-one barons wrote to Pope John XXII – who had recently given sanction to England's claim to overlordship – to declare that 'for so long as a hundred of us remain alive, we will yield in no least way to English dominion.' There was one particular, highly emotive sentence in the letter, generally known as the Declaration of Arbroath, that has remained graven on Scots hearts ever since. 'For we fight, not for glory nor for riches nor for honour, but only and alone for freedom, which no good man surrenders but with his life.'

By the mid-sixteenth century – and, indeed, long before – such selflessness had vanished from the public scene, and it had become clear to men of intelligence that Scotland could not survive alone. But with a

Stewart (or Stuart) on the throne of a united kingdom, it seemed that all sense of independence need not be lost.

The crowns were united in 1603 and Scotland sustained its identity for another hundred years. But then, in 1707, came the Act of Union, by which both nations accepted one parliament, one flag, one sovereign, one coinage, one system of taxation and one system of trading. The negotiations leading to the passing of the Act were not edifying, and the Scots disliked the result, and in particular England's satisfaction over having got the better of them at last.

But now, after almost three hundred years, everything is once more in process of change – and the seven-hundred-year-old Declaration of Arbroath has ceased to be as politically irrelevant as, not so long ago, it seemed to have become.

5
The old Scots tongue

A Londoner in Marian/Elizabethan times would probably have had much the same difficulty with Lowland Scots as a Londoner today has with Glasgow's glottal stops. By the mid-sixteenth century, London English was beginning to be seen as standard, with northern English a provincial dialect and Lowland Scots – which had much in common with northern English, though with a more liberal admixture of early French words – as an extreme version of it. As with all unfamiliar tongues, of course, to understand Scots was easier than to speak it.

The Scots had less of a problem with standard English. When the Reformation came, Scotland had no vernacular translation of the Bible and the first one to become available was the Geneva English version of 1560. This meant that London English was introduced to Protestant – though not Catholic – Scotland under the joint imprimatur of God and John Knox. It also helps to explain why Catholic Mary actually had to *learn* English during her captivity.

For others, by a natural process, English became associated with solemnity and moral respectability, the old Scots tongue remaining the medium for the homelier realities.

6
Mary's illnesses

Although various diagnoses of Mary's recurring health problems have been advanced over the centuries, Antonia Fraser's suggestion (in *Mary Queen of Scots*, 1969) of hereditary porphyria does appear to fit the type and frequency of her breakdowns more closely than most. Macalpine and Hunter, who first identified King George III's 'madness' as being attributable to porphyria, were able to trace similar, though less acute manifestations of it back to James VI & I and Mary. The symptoms include episodes of severe abdominal pain with vomiting and agonising distress; rheumaticky aches; hysterical outbursts; and surprisingly swift recovery. Mary's post-natal depression, which lasted for a year after her son's birth and had such disastrous political consequences, may well have been exacerbated and was certainly prolonged by the attack that nearly killed her at Jedburgh in October 1566.

7
After the curtain ...

Bothwell
For the first three years of his imprisonment at Malmo, Bothwell was kept in relative comfort, but by 1571, under pressure from Regent Lennox in Scotland and Elizabeth in England, Frederick of Denmark agreed to hold his prisoner in stricter custody pending possible extradition. France, however, intervened to stop the extradition idea, after which the possession of Bothwell's person ceased to be of any great value to Denmark. By early 1573, it was reported that he was deranged and by midsummer he had been moved to Dragsholm and the rigorous confinement to which madmen were then subjected. There is a tradition that he spent the last five years of his life closely chained in a dungeon of the castle. He is believed to have died on 14th April 1578, aged about forty.

Archie Douglas
Archie Douglas, the leading suspect in the Darnley affair, led an unusually busy and interesting life as spy, traitor, forger and murderer; how he found time to carry out his duties as an ordained minister of the kirk remains something of a mystery. In 1572, as if to demonstrate his

versatility, he was simultaneously acting as an informant for the English, as lord chancellor in the 'king's government', as agent for the queen's party, and manager of a plot to kill off his cousin Morton. Ten years later, after Morton, doomed to the scaffold, had spitefully if understandably implicated Archie in the Darnley murder, he was declared forfeit and forced to flee to England, complaining bitterly at the injustice of it all. In 1586, at a rigged trial, he was cleared of involvement and in that same year became an informal ambassador in London for King James VI. He was still conscientiously plotting in 1600 when he finally disappeared from the political scene.

Mary Fleming

Very little is known about Mary Fleming after Lethington's death although, by making a personal plea to Elizabeth to intercede with Regent Morton, she succeeded in saving her husband's corpse from the dismemberment that would otherwise have been its fate and was able to have him decently buried. She remained true to his memory, never remarrying although she might have been expected to, since she was beautiful and witty and only about thirty when he died. She brought their children up as Catholics, under initially difficult circumstances, and the eldest of them, James, seems to have been a sad disappointment. Footloose, quarrelsome, driven at last into poverty and banishment, he ended his life as a melancholy exile in Antwerp writing verbose and resentful defences of his then much-maligned father's reputation.

Jean Gordon

After her divorce from Bothwell, Jean Gordon was married off again to the young Earl of Sutherland, but outlived him to be united at last – more than thirty years after the fateful days of 1566 and 1567 – with the great love of her life, Alexander Ogilvie. A woman of undoubted character and equally undoubted stamina, Jean died in 1629 at the age of eighty-three.

The Maitlands

Sir Richard Maitland of Lethington (1496–1586), father of William and John, has an enduring literary reputation based partly on his own poems but more on his rôle as compiler of an important manuscript collection of Scots poetry, mainly from the first half of the sixteenth century. It was acquired close on a hundred years after his death by Samuel Pepys, and is now in the Pepysian Library, Cambridge. His daughter Marie, in 1586, compiled an anthology of later and more varied works, also in the Pepysian.

William Maitland of Lethington's branch of the family died with his son, but his brother John (1543–95), who in 1587 became Scotland's lord chancellor – the first in the century who was neither high churchman nor nobleman – in 1590 was created Lord Maitland of Thirlestane. His son became Earl of Lauderdale in 1616, and *his* son (another John) was in due course elevated to Scottish secretary of state, Duke of Lauderdale, the L in Charles II's Cabal ministry, and effective 'King of Scotland'.

Readers who appreciate historical irony (and have successfully kept track of the family feuds in *Fatal Majesty*) may find it of interest that, in the seventeenth century, the Maitland home of Lethington tower came into the possession of the Lennoxes and was renamed Lennoxlove in honour of Frances Stewart, the Duchess of Lennox who was model for Britannia on the coinage. Subsequently, and even more ironically, Lennoxlove became the family home of the Dukes of Hamilton. It remains so today.

8
Further reading

The standard work on Mary and the world she lived in is Antonia Fraser's exhaustive *Mary Queen of Scots* (1969). Fraser is entirely on Mary's side, but not above finding her heroine exasperating, which is just as it should be. Caroline Bingham's *Darnley. A Life of Henry Stuart, Lord Darnley, Consort of Mary Queen of Scots* (1995) is a well-researched and readable work that does as much for that young man as it seems possible for any serious historian to do. The political beliefs of John Knox are better documented than his life; the essential texts may be found in *John Knox On Rebellion*, edited Roger A. Mason (1994). There is a relatively brief and well balanced background to the period in Gordon Donaldson's *Scotland James V–James VII* (1978), v.3 of *The Edinburgh History of Scotland*.

Mary herself has so much overshadowed her Scots contemporaries that in most cases there are no biographies of them now in print. The following may possibly be found in libraries. For Mary's half-brother James, there is Maurice Lee Jr's *James Stewart, Earl of Moray* (1953), a work entirely political and favourable to James, unalloyed by any trace of human interest. For Lethington there is the equally political *Maitland of*

Lethington. The Minister of Mary Stuart (1912) by E. Russell, who gives the impression of having realised halfway through that he would have done better to write about the Earl of Moray, whom he understood and approved of much more than he did Lethington. *Lord Bothwell* (1937) – in which Mary features irresistibly as 'the poor little queen' – is a spirited and entertaining defence by Robert Gore-Browne.

These are only the most basic titles. Any reader embarking on a wider study of Mary Queen of Scots and her world should refer first to the analytical bibliography in Donaldson's *Scotland* (above), or to Jenny Wormald's *Mary Queen of Scots. A Study in Failure* (1991), whose first chapter and critical bibliography are not entirely invalidated by the author's patronising approach to her subject. There are also lists of authors and titles in Fraser and Gore-Browne.